T0037783

The German Lesson

Siegfried Lenz

The German
Lesson

Translated by Ernst Kaiser and Eithne Wilkins

 A New Directions Paperbook

Copyright © 1968 Hoffman und Campe Verlag, Hamburg
English translation copyright © 1971 by Ernst Kaiser and Eithne Wilkins

All rights reserved. Except for brief passages quoted in a newspaper, magazine,
radio, television, or website review, no part of this book may be reproduced in
any form or by any means, electronic or mechanical, including photocopying
and recording, or by any information storage and retrieval system, without
permission in writing from the Publisher.

First published in Germany by Hoffman und Campe Verlag, 1968
First published in the United States by Hill and Wang,
a division of Farrar, Straus & Giroux, 1972
First published as New Directions Paperbook 618 in 1986
and reissued as NDP1493 in 2021 (ISBN 978-0-8112-2201-3)
Manufactured in the United States of America

Library of Congress Cataloging-in-Publication Data
Lenz, Siegfried, 1926–2014
The German Lesson
(A New Directions Book)
Translation of: Deutschstunde
ISBN 978-0-8112-0982-3
I. Title.
PT2623.E583D413 1986 833'.914 77-163567

10 9 8 7 6 5 4 3 2 1

New Directions Books are published for James Laughlin
by New Directions Publishing Corporation
80 Eighth Avenue, New York 10011

Contents

For L.H.L.

1 Kept In

They've kept me in to write an essay. Joswig, our favourite guard, has brought me to this room of mine, with its solid walls, has tapped the bars across my window, given my pallet the once-over, and then searched my metal cupboard and my old hiding-place behind the looking-glass. Silently, silently, with an aggrieved expression, he went on to inspect the table, the stool that's all covered with notches, turned his attention to the outlet in the hand-basin, even gave the window-sill a few inquisitorial knocks, and examined the stove to establish that it was just an ordinary stove. Then he came up to me and, leisurely, passed his hands over my body from shoulders to knees to make sure I had nothing dangerous in my pockets. Then, with a reproachful air, he laid the copybook on my table, the essay copybook – the grey label says : German Essays by Siggi Jepsen – and, without saying goodbye, moved towards the door, disappointed, suffering in his goodness. For Joswig, our favourite guard, suffers more profoundly and longer and to more purpose than we ourselves do from the punishments that are occasionally dished out to us.

Not in words, but by the way he locked me in, he demonstrated his grief : listlessly, in fumbling perplexity, his key entered the lock; he hesitated before turning it the first time, stopped again, let the bolt snap open once more, and then swiftly, as though reproving his own indecision, with two abrupt turns he locked it. No less a person than Karl Joswig, a frail, shy man, had locked me in with the essay I had been set.

Though I have now been sitting here nearly all day, I don't know how to start. I simply don't know. When I look out of the

7

window, there, softly reflected in my eyes, the Elbe flows by, a gentle image. When I shut my eyes, it still flows on, heaped with bluish glittering drift-ice. I can't help following the tug that slices out grey patterns with its encrusted bows, I have to watch the river depositing its abundance of ice on our bank, pushing it up the slope, shoving one creaking floe on the other till they reach the dry stubble of the rushes, and leaving them there, forgetting them. With disgust I observe the crows gathering at Stade. They come flapping along from Wedel, from Finkenwerder and from Hahnöfer Sand, flying singly, and then, over our island, joining to form a swarm, rise and turn in twisting angular flight, until they yield to a sudden favourable wind that sweeps them on. The knotted willow-branches, glazed and powdered with white rime, distract me, and so do the fence of white wire-netting, the workshops, the warning boards along the shore, the frozen clods in the vegetable plots where in the spring we have to work under our guards' watchful eyes. Everything distracts me, even the sun, dimly shining as through a pane of clouded glass, streaking things with long wedge-shaped shadows. Sometimes I'm just on the point of starting work, and then of course my attention is caught by the battered landing-stage that hangs out there by its chains. That's where the squat motor-launch from Hamburg, all glittering brass, lies alongside so that anything up to twelve hundred psychologists, who take a positively morbid interest in juvenile delinquents, can step ashore. I can't avert my eyes when they come along the crooked path leading up from the bank, to be ushered into the blue administration building, where they are made welcome in the usual way, probably warned to be careful, to make their inquiries unobtrusively, until their impatience is yielded to and they are let loose to swarm all over our island, harmlessly, as it were by chance, sidling up to my friends, say to Pelle Kastner, or Eddi Sillus or to hot-tempered Kurt Nickel. Perhaps they take so much interest in us because according to the management's calculations there is an eighty per cent probability that those who have been 'reformed' on our island won't relapse. And if I hadn't been locked in by Joswig to do this essay, they'd certainly be after me too, observing my whole life bit by bit as though with a magnifying-glass, trying to get a scientific picture of me.

But for me the extra German Lesson: I've got to finish this

essay for Herr Doktor Korbjuhn, the haggard German master, who is so easily scared, and Governor Himpel. Such things couldn't happen on Hahnöfer Sand, the neighbouring island, down-river towards Twielenfleth Wischhafen, where they also keep juvenile delinquents for their own good. The two islands are very much alike; both are surrounded by the same oil-tarnished water, passed by the same ships, occupied by the same gulls – but on Hahnöfer Sand they have no Dr Korbjuhn, they aren't made to write essays, these essays that cut-my-throat-and-hope-to-die make most of us downright sick. So, if we've really got to be reformed, most of us would much rather be on Hahnöfer Sand, where the ocean-going ships pass first and where the crackling, tattered flame of the refinery is an everlasting salutation to one and all.

On that sister island to ours, they wouldn't have kept me in to write this essay; the things that happen here can't happen over there. Here a haggard fellow, stinking of pomade, could simply come korbjuhning into the classroom, let his eyes roll over us, at once sarcastic and timid, wait for our 'Good morning, Dr Korbjuhn, sir' and then dish out the copybooks for essay writing, without any previous announcement, without so much as a word. Not him! You could see him savouring every bit of it as he stalked up to the blackboard, raised his mean little hand so that his sleeve slipped down to his elbow, revealing an arm so dried up and yellow you might think it was a hundred years old, and then wrote on the blackboard in that crouching, slanting script of his that falls over itself with hypocrisy : 'The Joys of Duty'. I looked around the classroom in alarm : all I saw was bent backs, bewildered faces; a faint hiss ran through the rows of benches, a scraping of feet under them, the desks were blistered by the sighs that dropped on them. Ole Plötz, next to me, moved his fleshy lips, murmuring the words, getting himself ready to produce his convulsions. Charlie Friedländer, who has quite a gift for turning pale or greenish, in any case for looking so horribly unwell that all the masters would instantly excuse him from all work, had already started his breathing technique; he hadn't discoloured yet, but by that clever dodge of his with his carotid artery he had already produced beads of sweat on his forehead and upper lip. I pulled out my pocket-mirror and, turning it towards the window, I caught a beam of sunlight, which I flashed on the blackboard, startling Dr Korbjuhn so that he turned round and, after taking two strides up to the safety of the dais, ordered us, from on high, to begin. Once more his brittle arm rose into the air and his index finger pointed stiffly, insistently, at the theme: 'The Joys of Duty'. And then, so as not to have to answer questions, he decreed : 'You may write as you wish, but the essay must be on the joys of duty.'

Being kept in like this to write this essay and not being allowed to have visitors – it's not fair. What I'm being punished for isn't that my memory and my imagination let me down. I'm in solitary confinement because, obediently searching for the joys of duty, I suddenly had too much to tell, or at least such a lot that I simply didn't know how to start, however hard I tried. And since what Korbjuhn wanted us to discover, describe and enjoy to the limit, thereby establishing its value, wasn't joy as such, but had to be the joy that duty affords, whom else could I picture but Jens Ole Jepsen – his uniform, his field-glasses, his service bicycle, his raincape, his silhouette sailing along the top of the dyke in the everlastingly westerly wind? Dr Korbjuhn's admonishing gaze instantly brought him to my mind : in spring, no, in autumn, or perhaps on a bleak wind-blown summer day he pushed his bike along the narrow brick path, and, just as always under the sign saying 'Rugbüll Police Station', raised the back wheel to get the pedal into position for mounting and with two heaves swung himself into the saddle, pedalled along, at first a bit wobbly, billowing in the westerly wind, and rode on, at first some distance in the direction of the main road to Husum, which goes on to Heide and Hamburg. Then he turned off at the peat-bog and, now blown by a side wind, rode ·along the edge of the mole-grey ditch towards the dyke, as always past the mill that had lost its sails, dismounted after passing the wooden bridge and pushed the bike slantwise up the humpy dyke. Up there, significantly outlined against the empty horizon, he swung himself into the saddle again, sailed off, a solitary sloop under his taut, billowing, almost bursting cape, along the top of the dyke to Bleekenwarf, always to Bleekenwarf, always mindful of his orders. And though the autumn wind might drive clouds big as battleships over the sky of Schleswig-Holstein, my father would be on his way. In the dappled spring, in rain, on murky Sundays, morning and evening, in war and in peace, he would swing himself on to his bike and struggle along the narrow blind-alley of his mission, which never took him anywhere but to Bleekenwarf, always to Bleekenwarf, as it was in the beginning and ever shall be, Amen.

This was the picture that sprang to my mind, this laborious journey on which the Rugbüll policeman, who manned the most northerly station in Germany, everlastingly set out. In the effort to do my best for Korbjuhn, I came still closer to it in my thoughts; I wrapped a scarf round my neck, I let myself be lifted on to the service bicycle's carrier, and as so often went along to Bleekenwarf, holding on tight to my father's uniform belt, my fingers stiff with cold, the carrier's hard iron bars pinching my sides. I travelled with him and, at the same time, watching us from the distance, I could see us both moving along the dyke against the background of the inevitable evening clouds. I could feel the buffeting wind that came head on from the desolate flats, and simultaneously saw the two of us from a long way off, swaying in that wind. And then again I heard my father groaning as he struggled on, not desperately or in anger with the wind, but an orderly groaning and, as it seemed to me, full of secret satisfaction. Along the flats, along the black, wintry sea, we rode to Bleekenwarf, which I knew the way I knew no other place except the ruined mill and our own house. There it was before me on that muddy hillock, flanked by alders, their tops currycombed by the wind and bent towards the east. I put myself down at the swinging wooden gate, opened it, and peered at the house, the stable, the sheds and the studio from which, as so often, Max Ludwig Nansen waved to me, at once slyly and affectionately warning me to be good.

They had already forbidden him to paint, and it was up to my father, the Rugbüll policeman, to keep an eye on him, day in, day out, summer and winter, and see that the ban was not broken. His duty was to stop anything that might lead to a picture, any sketch or study, any undesirable concern with the light; in short, it was his duty as a policeman to make sure that no painting was done in Bleekenwarf. My father and Max Ludwig Nansen had known each other all their lives, they had grown up together and, both hailing from Glüserup, they knew what to expect of each other, perhaps even what was in store of them, and what either of them might do to the other. Little else is as carefully preserved in the storeroom of my memory as are those encounters between those two, my father and Max Ludwig Nansen. So I opened my copybook confidently, put my pocket-mirror beside it, and tried to describe my father's trips to Bleekenwarf, and indeed not only them but all the tricks and traps he thought of in order to catch Nansen, all those ruses, simple or elaborate, those plans, stratagems and cunning manoeuvres he worked out in his slow, suspicious way. And since Dr Korbjuhn was so keen on it, I also intended to describe the joy that must surely have been gained from the execution of that duty. It wouldn't work. I couldn't bring it off. Time and again I began, sending my father cycling along the dyke, with his cape and without it, in windy weather and in calm, on Wednesdays and on Saturdays. It was all no good. There was too much restlessness, too much going on, too damned much of everything. Before he ever got to Bleekenwarf I lost sight of him, because the gulls so wheeled and whirled, because an old peat-barge capsized under its load, or a parachute came floating over the flats.

The most troublesome thing was a tiny, enterprising flame that damaged all the remembered pictures and events, making them flare up and burn brightly, twist and turn to cinders, or sometimes just hiding them behind its trembling glow.

So I tried it the other way round. In my thoughts I went to Bleekenwarf, to find my beginning there. And there was Max Ludwig Nansen, grey-eyed and cunning, offering to help me get the flux of memories moving in the right direction. He drew my gaze upon himself, and for my sake he came out of his studio, sauntered through the summery garden, up to the zinnias he had painted so often, and slowly climbed up on to the dyke, under a sky that was now a heavy bilious yellow, with slashes of dark blue here and there; he raised a field-glass and for a second looked in the direction of Rugbüll. That sufficed to make him rush back to the house and hide somewhere inside. Now I almost had a beginning, but at that very moment the window was pushed open and there was Ditte, Max Ludwig Nansen's wife, holding out to me, as so often, a piece of seed-cake. It was all simply too much. I was swamped. I heard the singing of children coming from a classroom in Bleekenwarf; again I saw a tiny flame, I heard the noise my father made as he set out on his nocturnal errand. Jutta and Jobst, the stranger children, surprised me among the reeds. Someone threw paints into a pond, and the water suddenly glowed, all orange. The Minister made a speech in Bleekenwarf. My father saluted. Large cars with unfamiliar number-plates stopped in Bleekenwarf. My father saluted. I was in the ruined mill, dreaming in the hide-out where the pictures were kept. My father came, leading a flame on a leash. He took the leash off, and gave the flame the command: 'Search!'

It all began to go criss-cross, to overlap, confuse, and then all at once I felt Korbjuhn's admonishing gaze resting on me. So in one concentrated effort I tidied up the planes of my memory, levelled out the ditches that cut it into sections, and shook off all that was unimportant, so that the whole thing should lie before me, revealed and easy to formulate, in particular my father and the joys of duty. And I did it. I had all the important people lined up on parade below the dyke, and I was just about to give the order for the march past when Ole Plötz, beside me, uttered a yell and, having brought on his convulsions, let himself fall from the bench. That yell lopped off all my memories. I could not manage to find another beginning, and when Dr Korbjuhn collected the copybooks I handed mine in empty.

Julius Korbjuhn could not see my difficulties. He did not believe what agony it had been to find the starting-point. He could not understand that the anchor of memory would not hold anywhere, would not tighten the chain, but that it would drag along, deep down at the bottom, rattling and clattering, at most throwing up mud, so that there was no peace, only turbulence, and it was impossible to cast a net over the things of the past.

So it came about that after this German master had leafed through my copybook in amazement, he called me up to the dais and regarded me with – on the one hand – a trace of disgust and – on the other – sincere perplexity. Then he demanded an explanation. But he could not see his way to accepting my explanation. He said I hadn't really been trying, he would not believe that my memory and my imagination had failed me, and denied that there was any difficulty in finding a beginning. He merely said : 'Ah now, Siggi Jepsen, you needn't think you can get round *me*', and he insisted that the empty pages were deliberate impertinence. Far from believing me, he sensed stubbornness, rebellion, and what have you, and since these are matters for the Governor to deal with, after that German lesson which had gained me nothing but the agony of reeling, blurred memories which I could not link together, try as I might, he took me to the blue building where the Governor has his room on the first floor next to the staircase.

Governor Himpel, dressed as always in a windbreaker and plus-fours, was surrounded by about thirty-two psychologists who showed a positively fanatical interest in the problems of juvenile delinquents. There was a blue coffee-pot on his desk and next to it smudged sheets of music-paper, some of them covered with his hastily scrawled pastoral compositions, short songs all about the Elbe, the wet wind from the sea, wind-blown oats growing near the shore, the radiant flight of gulls, but also fluttering kerchiefs and the urgent call of the foghorn. It is the lot of our island choir to give the world premières of these immortal works.

The psychologists fell silent when we entered the room, and listened to what Dr Korbjuhn had .to report to the Governor The report was delivered in a low voice, but I was able to catch the words 'stubborn' and 'rebellious'. As though in support of his words Korbjuhn then handed the Governor my empty copybook. The Governor exchanged worried glances with the psychologists, then came towards me, stopped, rolled up my copybook, slapped his wrist with it, then his plus-fours, and demanded an explanation. I looked into expectant faces, and heard a faint click – Korbjuhn cracking his finger joints. I felt miserable in all this tension. I gazed through the wide bay-window beyond the piano and saw the Elbe, saw two crows flying, fighting for something flabby, dangling, perhaps a piece of gut, tearing it away from each other, trying to swallow it, until it dropped on to an ice-floe and was snatched away by a watchful gull. The Governor put a hand on my shoulder, nodded to me in an almost chummy way and implored me once more – in front of all the psychologists – to explain. So I told him all my troubles, how the important things I was going to write about had come to my mind first, how it all got blurred.

how I could not find anything to hold on to so as to descend, step by step, into my memories. I told him about the many faces, the chaotic pushing and shoving, all the movements criss-crossing in my memory that had frustrated each of my attempts to start. And I didn't fail to mention that my father was still enjoying all the joys of duty well done, so that, in order to do them justice, I had to describe them in full, could not pick and choose among them.

Astonished, perhaps even with understanding, the Governor listened to me, while the psychologists drew ever nearer, whispering, nudging one another, and excitedly murmuring such phrases as 'Wartenburg perceptual defect', 'angular illusion', or even 'cognitive block', which struck me as particularly repulsive. I was being assessed and labelled, and I realized what was coming to me; in any case I refused to go on explaining in the presence of these people: I had learnt my lesson in the time I had spent on the island.

Thoughtfully the Governor withdrew his hand from my shoulder, regarded it critically, perhaps checking to see if it was still all there, and then, with his visitors' merciless attention trained on him, turned to the window and stood for a while looking out over the wintry Hamburg countryside, as though he expected some inspiration and advice from there. Then, suddenly, he turned to me and, with lowered eyes, pronounced his verdict. He said I was to be taken to my cell, where I was to remain 'in decent isolation', as he put it, not to *atone* for what I had done, but to have peace and quiet, so that I might come to understand that one had to write one's German essays. He was giving me a *chance*.

He explained that I would be spared all distractions such as visits from my sister Hilke. I would be excused all my duties – in the workshop where we made brooms and in the library – indeed, he promised to protect me from anything that might have a disturbing influence. In exchange they expected me to make good my omission and write my essay. I was to have the usual meals and all the time I needed for the task. I was patiently to track down all the joys of duty well done. I think he also said I should allow it to grow, thoughtfully, drop by drop, the way a stalactite grows. For one's memory (he said) may also be a trap, a danger, all the more because, contrary to general belief, time is by no means the great healer it is supposed to be. That made the psychologists prick up their ears, but he shook me by the hand in an almost chummy way – he has quite some experience of shaking people's hands – and then he had Joswig, our favourite guard, called in and informed him of his decision, saying something like : 'Solitude – what Siggi is in need of now, more than anything else, is time and solitude. See that he gets plenty.'

He handed Joswig my empty copybook, and both of us were dismissed. There we were, strolling across the frozen square – Joswig looking as grieved and reproachful as though my being sentenced to solitary confinement until I had accomplished my task were something of a private disappointment to him. This man, who no longer has any enthusiasm for anything except his collection of old coins and the island choir's performances, was huffy and distant while escorting me to my cell. So I took his arm and begged him not to treat me so reproachfully. But he would not yield. All he would say was 'Think of Philipp Neff.' Neff, a boy who had only one eye, had also been sentenced to write a German essay he hadn't written during the lesson. Two days and two nights, so the story goes, he had struggled to find a beginning, some basis from which to start – the theme of that Korbjuhn essay was, to the best of my knowledge, 'A person who made an impression on me' – on the third day he knocked a guard down, escaped, man-handled the Governor's dog so that it is remembered among us to this day, managed to reach the river-bank and to get himself drowned trying to swim across the Elbe in September. Philip Neff, who so tragically revealed the disastrous nature of Korbjuhn's activities, had left behind him, in his copybook, one single word : 'Wart'. So one can at least assume that some person with a wart had made a particular impression on him.

In any case, Philipp Neff was the chap who had lived in that solidly built room which I had been given when I arrived on the island for juvenile delinquents, and when Joswig reminded me of his destiny, warning me against following his example, I felt an indefinable dread mingled with an ache of impatience. I wanted to get to the table, and yet I was frightened of it. I wanted to track down my own train of thought, and I was afraid of not being able to find it. I hesitated, I demanded, I fidgeted and I yearned, I wanted to do it and I didn't want to – and the result was that I just watched indifferently, as Joswig searched my room before leaving me to my task.

And now I've been sitting here almost all the day, and perhaps I might even have started work but for the distraction of the ships coming up the wintry river, at first not seen, only heard. First of all there is the faint drone of the engines, telling one that they are on their way, then follows the crash and clatter of the ice-floes that go spinning along the iron hull until they splinter against it, and then, with the rhythmic thump of the engines becoming harder and louder, the ships glide forth from the tin-grey of the horizon, their paint faded as from too much washing: wet, vibrant, they seem more like apparitions of the air than of the water. I can't help watching them, following them until they have passed my field of vision and are gone. There they go sliding through the rigid landscape, their sterns, railings and ventilators glittering with a crust of ice, their glazed superstructures and rigging covered in hoar frost. And behind them there is a wide, jagged slash in the drifting ice, a channel meandering towards the horizon, narrowing, closing up. And the light! – the deceptive light over the wintry Elbe: tin-grey turns into snow-grey, purple doesn't stay purple, there is no complementary green behind the red, and the sky over Hamburg is mottled as though with bruises.

Over the far bank, whence a faint sound of hammering comes to me, there hovers a narrow smudgy streak of fog, like an unfurled banner of gauze. Closer to me, over the centre of the river, floats the smoke trail from the small ice-breaker *Emmy Guspel* which an hour ago went furiously ploughing through the bluish glittering drift-ice. The elongated cloud of smoke neither sinks down nor dissolves, as though the frost had called a strike and many things remained unfinished, so that even one's breath stays visible in mid-air. Twice the *Emmy Guspel* has come steaming past, for she has to keep the ice moving and prevent the piling up of floes; a clot of ice in midstream might cause a thrombosis, paralysing traffic on the river.

On the desolate strand, the warning signs hang on slanting posts. The floes have gone on chafing against them until they worked loose, and wind and high water have done the rest. Swimmers and oarsmen, whom the notices most concern, would have to hold their heads at a slant to find out that they mustn't moor their boats and that it is forbidden to go ashore and put up tents on our island. When summer comes they will of course straighten the posts again, because swimmers and oarsmen are regarded as a particular menace to the reform of juvenile delinquents. That's the Governor's opinion, and his dog takes the same point of view, as anyone can hear for himself.

Only in our workshops the eternal round is neither diminished nor interrupted. Since they've taken it into their heads to introduce us to the virtues of labour, and have indeed even detected some educational value in it, they see to it that there is never a moment's silence. So it's unceasing: the hum of dynamos in the electrical workshop, the ting-tong of hammers in the smithy, the harsh hissing of planes in the carpenter's shop, the hacking and scraping sounds from the shed where our brooms are made. It all makes one forget the winter, and it reminds me of my task. I must begin.

The table is clean, old, and scarred with notches that are darkening with age – angular initials, dates, patterns that are reminders of moments of bitterness, of hope and of stubbornness passed and gone. My copybook lies open before me, ready to receive the essay I have to write. I can't afford any more diversions – got to start, turn the key in the lock of the casket of my memory, open it up and get out of it all that is needed to fulfil Korbjuhn's demands. I've got to bear witness to the joy of doing one's duty, to trace its effects back to myself, and I have to do it in solitary confinement and go on until I've proved the case. I am ready. And since I've got to go ahead, I've got to go back, to make a selection, to find a place from which to start. Perhaps Rugbüll Police Station after all? Or, even better, the whole plain of Schleswig-Holstein, from Glüserup to the highway of Husum and along the dyke, the country that for me is crossed by one road only, the road from Rugbüll to Bleekenwarf. And even if I have to shake the past out of its sleep, I've got to start.

Here goes.

2   No Painting Permitted

In the year '43 (to get going somehow), on a Friday it was, in April, in the morning, perhaps around midday, my father, Jens Ole Jepsen, policeman, who manned Rugbüll, the northernmost police station in Schleswig-Holstein, got himself ready for a duty trip to Bleekenwarf, in order to deliver to the painter Max Ludwig Nansen, whom the people round about simply called – and always went on calling – 'The Painter', an official order from Berlin by which he was forthwith forbidden to paint. Un-hurriedly my father gathered together his rain-cape, field-glasses, uniform belt and torch; he busied himself at his desk, obviously with the intention of delaying his departure, buttoned up and unbuttoned his tunic for the second time, eyed the miserable spring day and listened to the wind, while I waited for him, muffled up and motionless. It was not merely wind one heard; this north-westerly, besieging the farms, the hedges and rows of trees, tumultuously skirmishing, testing their resistance, was what shaped the landscape, a black, windy landscape, crooked and tousled and charged with some incomprehensible meaning. It was this wind of ours, I think, that made the roofs keen of hear-ing, made the trees prophetic, caused the old mill to grow larger, swept across the ditches so that they became delirious, or attacked the peat-barges, despoiling their shapeless loads.

When our wind was out and about, one was well advised to put some ballast in one's pockets – packets of nails, or bits of lead piping or even a flat-iron – to be a match for it. Such a wind is part of our lives and we could not argue with Max Ludwig Nansen for bursting his paint-tubes, taking furious

19

violet and crude white to make the north-westerly visible, this north-westerly that belongs to us and which we know so well – the wind to which my father was listening with deep suspicion.

A veil of smoke filtered through the kitchen. A fluttering veil of peat-smoke floated through the living-room. The wind sat in the stove and puffed, filling the house with smoke, while my father walked to and fro, clearly in search of reasons for delaying his departure. Here he put something down, there he picked something up, he went into the office and buckled on his gaiters, he opened his book of regulations on the dining table in the kitchen, time and again he found something else to keep him from starting out on his mission. But in the end he was forced to realize, with irritable surprise, that he had become transformed into something new, that against his own will he had changed into a regular country policeman and that all he needed in order to carry out his duty was his service bicycle, which stood in the shed, leaning against a trestle.

So it was probably that normal, everyday sense of duty, which had become second nature to him, which in the end forced him to get going : not eagerness, not the pleasure he took in his job and certainly not the mission that had now fallen to his lot. He set himself in motion, as so often, only – it seemed – because he was now properly dressed and equipped. He said goodbye just as usual; as always he stepped into the dusky passage, listened for a moment, and finally called out to the shut doors : 'So long then.' And he was neither surprised nor disappointed when nobody answered, but behaved as if he had received an answer, nodded contentedly and, still nodding, pulled me towards the door, then turned round once more with a vague gesture of fare-well before the wind took hold of us and pulled us through the doorway.

Outside he put his shoulder to the wind, lowering his head, his dry and empty face that was so slow to become animated with a smile or a look of suspicion or agreement. It was this slowness that gave any look of his a strange importance, making it seem as though he were capable of understanding everything thoroughly, but that this understanding always came too late. Stooping forward, he crossed the yard, where the wind made pointed spinning-tops of the dust and played havoc with a newspaper, with a victory in Africa, a victory in the Atlantic, and with a more or less decisive victory on the scrap-metal front, blowing it all to shreds, crunching it up and pressing it against the wire netting of our garden fence. He walked to the open shed. With a groan he lifted me on to the carrier, and, one hand grasping the saddle, the other the handlebars, turned the bicycle round. Then he pushed it along the brick path, stopped under the arrow-shaped sign 'Rugbüll Police Station' that pointed at our red brick house, put the pedal into position, mounted and rode off in the direction of Bleekenwarf, his rain cape, fastened between his legs with a clip, blown up like a balloon.

Up to the mill and indeed almost up to Holmsenwarf with its swaying hedges, all was well, because that was the stretch where, under his billowing cape, he sailed before the wind. But when he turned towards the dyke, when he climbed up the dyke, stooping with the effort, he instantly began to look like the man on the brochure 'Cycling through Schleswig-Holstein', that stubborn traveller with his hunched shoulders and his buttocks lifted off the saddle, whose stiff and contorted posture revealed the grim effort anyone has to make who rides a bike through our country in search of its beauties. The brochure, however, not only revealed the strain, but also indicated the skill that the cyclist must possess if he is not to be knocked over by the north-westerly side wind while riding on top of the dyke. It not only gave an illustration of the posture the cyclist must adopt, but also gave a glimpse of what an experience the north German horizon is, showed the snow-white contours of the wind, and used as a homely adornment of the dyke the very same idiotic and tousled sheep who used to stare at my father and me.

Since a description of that brochure must inevitably turn into a description of my father, showing him as he used to ride along the dyke to Bleekenwarf, I should like to mention the great and the lesser black-backed gull, the black-headed gull and also the rare glaucous gull, who are decoratively distributed above the exhausted cyclist and, carelessly printed, rather smudged, looked like white dusters hung out on a line to dry.

Always along the dyke, along that narrow, compulsive path which shows brown in the low grass, parrying the gusts of wind, his blue eyes lowered, my father rode along the gentle curve of the embankment, carrying his order folded in his breast pocket. He rode without urgency, laboriously. One might have thought he was on his way to the grey shingle Wattblick Inn to have a grog and to pass the time of day with Hinnerk Timmsen, the innkeeper, perhaps even have a chat with him.

We didn't go as far as that. Before reaching the inn – which was connected with the dyke by two wooden foot-bridges and always reminded me of a dog that puts its fore-paws on a wall in order to look over it – we turned off the dyke, and, coasting gently downhill, reached the footpath leading along the foot of the dyke, from which we turned off again for the long ascent to Bleekenwarf and the house flanked by alder trees, behind its swinging gate of thick white boards. The tension increased, the suspense grew, which is only to be expected if in April, in this harsh north-westerly of ours, somebody moves towards a definite destination that he can clearly see in the distance.

Sighing, the wooden gate swung back before us, as my father slowly rode his front wheel against it. Slowly then he rode past the rust-red empty stable, past the pond and the shed – very slowly indeed, as though he wanted to be seen arriving. He rode close to the narrow windows of the house, casting a glance into the studio, which was built on to the house, before he dismounted, grabbed me like a parcel and dumped me on the ground, then pushed his bicycle towards the entrance.

Since nobody around here ever reaches anyone's doorstep without being seen, my father didn't have to knock or call out into the half-light of the hall and I don't have to describe any sound of approaching footsteps or exclamations of surprise. All he had to do was to push the door open and thrust the curtain aside, whereupon his hand would be warmly gripped and shaken. All he needed to say was: 'Hello, Ditte.' The painter's wife had doubtless been on her way to the door as we had come coasting down from the dyke.

Walking ahead of us in her long dress of some rough material that made her look like one of those severe village prophetesses with whom Holstein abounds, in the darkness of the hall she put her hand straight on the handle of the living-room door and asked my father to come in. My father first of all took off the clip that held his cape together between his thighs. He did so by straddling his legs, bending his knees and groping until he got hold of the clip. Then he would dive out from under the cape, straighten his tunic, loosen the scarf in which I was muffled, and push me ahead of him into the living-room.

They had a very large living-room at Bleekenwarf. It wasn't very high, but it was wide and had many windows and there was room for at least nine hundred wedding-guests or, if not for them, then certainly for seven school classes including teachers, despite the extravagantly large furniture that stood about everywhere, arrogantly taking up a lot of space. There were ponderous chests, and cupboards with rune-like dates carved in them, their durability implied even in the domineering and threatening way in which they loomed up in the room. The chairs too were unreasonably heavy, domineering, and one felt bound to sit still on them, hardly so much as moving a muscle in one's face. The dark, clumsy tea-set – Wittdün porcelain they said it was – was no longer in use, but was kept on a shelf on the wall. It made one itch to throw stones at it. The painter and his wife were easy-going and changed little or nothing when they bought Bleekenwarf from the daughter of old Friedriksen, who had been so careful about committing suicide that he opened his veins before hanging himself from one of the vast cupboards.

They did not replace the furniture and hardly changed anything in the kitchen, where the pots and pans, the little barrels and jugs, stood in straight rows as though on parade. They also left the venerable kitchen cupboards as they had found them, full of pretentious Wittdün plates, and giant tureens and dishes. Even the beds remained – severe, narrow bunks that made only the minutest concession to the sleeper's comfort.

But now, at long last, now that he is there, standing in the living-room, my father ought to shut the door behind him and exchange the time of day with Herr Doktor Teodor Busbeck. As always Herr Doktor Busbeck was sitting there on the sofa, that uncomfortable monstrosity which was doubtless all of thirty metres long, not reading or writing, just sitting there, carefully dressed, resignedly waiting and mysteriously prepared for that event or message which would change everything and which might arrive at any moment. Nothing of all this could be read in his pale face, from which all expression, all trace of experience, had been purposefully removed, as though washed

23

away. We did know he had been the first to exhibit Nansen's paintings, and that he had been living at Bleekenwarf since his gallery had been shut down by official order and all his pictures removed. Smiling, he got up and came towards my father, and, after the usual greeting and the exchange of a few remarks about the force of the wind, gave me a smiling nod and withdrew again.

'What will you have, Jens?' Frau Nansen asked. 'Tea or schnapps. I feel like some schnapps myself.'

My father waved off all hospitality. 'Nothing, Ditte, thank you, nothing at all today.' He didn't sit down on the chair at the window, nor did he speak, as usual, of the trouble his shoulder had been giving him since he had had a fall from his bicycle, or of any of the news of which he, as the Rugbüll policeman, was the repository – such rural events as somebody's having got a bad kick from a horse, or a case of illicit slaughter, or even of arson. Nor did he convey greetings from anyone at Rugbüll, and he omitted inquiries after the stranger children whom Nansen had taken into the house.

'Nothing, Ditte,' he said, 'nothing at all today.'

Standing stiffly, he brushed his breast pocket lightly with his fingertips. He looked through the window, across the studio. Frau Nansen and Herr Doktor Busbeck, seeing him standing there in silence, waiting, obviously unhappy, even uneasy, as far as he was capable of showing it, realized he was waiting for Nansen. In any case it was clear that whatever the duty was that had brought him here it wasn't a matter of indifference to him. His eyes were restless, as always when he was at a loss, unsure, agitated in that Frisian manner of his. Then he would look at a person and yet not straight at that person; his glance would slide off, rise, and then avoid the other's eyes. He himself was out of reach of any question he did not wish to answer. All the same, standing there in that enormous room, looking as nearly reluctant as he could manage, in his badly fitting uniform, unsure of himself and yet unwilling to state his business, he certainly did not make a menacing impression.

Speaking to his back, Frau Nansen asked: 'Is it about Max?'

And when he nodded, stiffly, without turning round, Herr Doktor Busbeck rose, came close, and, laying his hand on Ditte's arm, asked falteringly: 'A decision from Berlin?'

Surprised and hesitant, my father turned to the little man who looked as though he were apologizing for his question, or indeed apologizing for everything. But he said nothing. It was no longer necessary to give any answer. By their silence the two of them, the painter's wife and the painter's oldest friend, showed that they had understood, that they already knew what the decision was that it was his duty to announce.

Of course, now Frau Nansen could have asked him to give her the exact wording of it, and I think my father would have been much relieved and would have told her willingly. But neither of them asked him to tell them more. They just stood there for a while, side by side, and then Busbeck said as though to himself : 'They've caught up with Max. What amazes me is that it didn't happen sooner, as it did with the others.' As though they had come to some resolve, the two of them turned towards the sofa, and Frau Nansen said :

'Max is working. He's down the garden at the moat.'

She spoke with her face averted, thus at once informing and dismissing my father, who had no choice but to leave the room, which he did with a shrug, meant to convey that he himself deplored his mission and that it was none of his own doing. He snatched his cape from the coat-rack and gave me a slight push. The two of us left the house.

Slowly he walked along the bleak front of the house. He seemed to be worried, instead of confident, as he pushed open the garden gate and then, under cover of the hedges, began to move his lips, carefully trying out words and whole sentences, in his usual way when an imminent encounter seemed certain to demand more of him than his normal eloquence. Then he walked on between the hoed and weeded flower-beds, past the thatched summer-house, towards the moat surrounding Bleeken-warf, that still water, bordered by reeds, which enhanced the solitude of the place.

There the painter Max Ludwig Nansen stood. He stood on the wooden bridge that had no railings, and there, protected from the wind, he was working. Since I know his way of work-ing, I don't want to take him by surprise and disturb him by making my father tap him on the shoulder; I should prefer to delay that encounter a little, because it isn't just any encounter, and I should like to mention first that the painter is eight years older than my father, smaller and lither, less controlled and perhaps craftier and more stubborn, although both of them spent their youth in Glüserup. *Glüserup*, my God!

He wore a hat, a felt hat, which he used to pull so far forward that his grey eyes were shadowed by the narrow brim. His overcoat was old, the back of it threadbare – that grey-blue overcoat with the inexhaustible pockets, capacious enough – as he had once threateningly told us – to put children in, should they disturb him in his work. He wore that overcoat in all seasons, indoors and out, come rain, come sunshine, and very likely he slept in it. Anyway, he and his coat belonged together. Sometimes, however, when the trains of big, clumsy clouds gathered over the flats, one got the impression that it was only the overcoat, without the painter in it, walking up there on the dyke and scrutinizing the horizon.

The coat concealed everything but a few inches of crumpled trousers, and the laced boots, old-fashioned but very expensive boots, the uppers partly of black suede.

We were used to seeing him like this, but this time, I think, my father, who was still standing there behind the hedge, would have preferred not to stand there, or at least not with that document in his breast pocket, or, if it had to be, then not with his memories. My father observed the painter, but not intensely, not with professional attention.

The painter was at work. What he was concerned with was the ruined mill, motionless there, stripped of its sails in the April light. There it stood on its post, looking like a squat plant with a very short stem, some sinister growth just about to wither. Max Ludwig Nansen was doing something to that mill by transporting it into a different day, by relating it to different things in a different twilight on his paper. And, as always when he was at work, he was talking. He didn't talk to himself, he talked to someone by the name of Balthasar, who stood beside him, his Balthasar, whom only he could see and hear, with whom he chatted and argued and whom he sometimes jabbed with his elbow, so hard that even we, who couldn't see any Balthasar, would suddenly hear the invisible bystander groan or, if not groan, at least swear. The longer we stood there behind him, the more we began to believe in the existence of that Balthasar who made himself perceptible by a sharp intake of breath or a hiss of disappointment. And still the painter went on confiding in him, only to regret it a moment later. Even now, while my father watched him, he was quarrelling with Balthasar, who wore – in those pictures in which he was imprisoned – a bristling purple coat and who had slanting eyes and a crazy beard of boiling, bubbling orange from which red-hot droplets fell.

Not that Nansen often turned round to look at him. He stood his ground, resolutely keeping to the job in hand, his legs slightly apart, moving his body from the hips, forward, backward, to either side, putting his head on one side, stretching his neck to lift it higher, letting it wobble or lowering it as though to use it as a battering-ram, while his right arm seemed to be extraordinarily rigid, its movements expressing toughness and strain as though it were fighting against some incalculable subtle resistance. And yet, while this arm, on which everything depended, appeared so strangely rigid, the rest of the painter's body seemed to be actively involved.

His body's behaviour simply bore witness to and confirmed whatever he was creating. When he was painting the wind on a calm day, making it arise between blue and green, one could hear fantastic flotillas in mid-air and the flapping of sails, and the hem of his overcoat actually began to flutter. And if he held a lighted pipe in his mouth, the smoke would be pulled away horizontally. Or at least so it seems to me now as I recall it.

There was my father, watching him at work. He stood there, hesitant and oppressed, and then probably he began to feel the eyes following us from the house that we had left a short while ago, and so, still followed by those eyes, we moved slowly along the hedge, squeezed sideways through a narrow opening, and a moment later stood at the edge of the wooden bridge without a railing.

My father looked down into the moat and there, among the broken drifting rushes and tremulous duckweed, he saw his own reflection. Nansen, who had stepped to one side and was looking down into the stagnant, faintly wind-ruffled water, saw his reflection too. They saw and recognized one another in the dark mirror of the moat, and the recognition perhaps called up the flash of a memory that linked the two of them together and which would never cease to do so. That memory took them back to the shabby little harbour at Glüserup, where they used to fish from the stone mole, or do their acrobatics on the floodgates, or lie on the bleached deck of a shrimp cutter. Yet that will not have been what came to their minds as they recognized each other reflected in the moat; very likely it was only the harbour's muddy water that Saturday when my father – he must have been nine or ten years old – lost his foothold on the slippery floodgates and fell. In his memory Nansen will have dived for him again and again, just as he did then, till at last he caught him by his shirt and was forced to break one of his fingers in order to free himself from that desperate clutch and so bring him up to safety.

They walked towards each other, up on the bridge and down in the moat, shook hands by the easel and in the dark water as they always did, calling each other by their names in a tone that had the slight ring of a question: 'Jens?' 'Max?' and while Max Ludwig Nansen turned back to his work, my father fumbled for the piece of paper in his breast pocket, pulled it out, smoothed it between two fingers, hesitantly, turning over in his mind the words he should say when handing it to Nansen. He probably thought of holding out the stamped and signed order without saying anything, or perhaps of just saying: 'Here's something for you from Berlin,' and very likely he hoped that he would save himself from having to answer pointless questions if he succeeded in making Nansen read it at once for himself. Naturally he would have much preferred to leave the whole thing to Okko Brodersen, the one-armed postman; but since it was one of those documents that had to be delivered by the police themselves, it was my father's duty as Rugbüll policeman to bring it himself. Moreover – and this too he would have to make Nansen understand – it was also his duty to ensure that the order was not violated.

There he stood, the open letter in his hand, still hesitating. He looked at the mill, at the picture, again at the mill and again at the picture. Involuntarily he stepped closer, looked again at both the painting and the mill, and asked: 'What's it going to be, Max?'

Nansen took a step to one side and, pointing at the Big Friend of the Mill, he said: 'The Big Friend of the Mill'. And he went on putting clumps of shadow on to the green mound.

Now my father too must have noticed the Big Friend of the Mill, who rose, silent and brown, over the horizon, a gentle old man, bearded, a creature of amiable mindlessness and perhaps a worker of miracles, growing to gigantic stature. His brown, red-tipped fingers were tensed as though he were about to flick at one of the sails, which he had obviously just fixed to the mill. He was about to set the sails of the mill, which now lay far below him in dying grey, going again. He would make them move faster and faster until they sliced through the darkness, and until the mill ground out a clear day and a better light than could be seen from where I stood. The sails could do it, so much was certain, for even now the old man's face had a look of simple satisfaction, from which one might gather that in his sleepy old man's way he was accustomed to succeed in whatever he undertook. True, the pond near the mill expressed its purple doubts, but it would turn out to be wrong; the Big Friend's determined affection would prove the stronger.

'That's all done with,' my father said. '*She* won't shift again.'

But Nansen said : 'She'll be turning tomorrow, Jens. Just you wait and see. Tomorrow we'll be grinding poppy-seeds, we'll grind till the smoke rises.'

He stopped working, lit his pipe and looked at the picture, shaking his head. Without a glance at my father, he handed him his tobacco pouch, and without noticing whether my father had lit his pipe or not, he took it back and put it in his inexhaustible coat-pocket. He said : 'Just a little rage lacking – don't you think so, Jens? A little dark green rage, that's all, then the mill can start turning.'

My father held the letter in his hand, close to his body, instinctively hiding it, waiting for the right moment to hand it over. He did not trust himself to determine that moment. He said : 'No wind's going to move it, and no rage either, Max.'

But the painter said : 'It'll be turning long after we've gone. Just wait and see, tomorrow the sails'll start whirling round.'

Perhaps my father might have hesitated even longer but for that last assertion. Anyway, now he suddenly stretched out his arm and, holding the letter out for Nansen to take, he said : 'Here, Max, here's something from Berlin. You'd better read it at once.'

Heedlessly the painter took it and let it disappear into his coat-pocket. Then he turned round, touched my father's shoulder, poked him in the ribs, knitted his brow and said: 'Come on, Jens, let's shove off while Balthasar's inside the mill. I've got some gin that'll make your hair curl, I can tell you. Not from Holland – good God, not that stuff! From Switzerland, from one of those Swiss museum fellows – come along to the studio.'

But my father did not want to. He jabbed his forefinger in the direction of Nansen's coat-pocket and said: 'The letter.' After a pause he added: 'You've got to read it now, Max, it's from Berlin.' And as though words were not enough, he took a step towards Nansen, partly blocking the bridge and thus the way back to the house. Shrugging his shoulders, Nansen fished the letter out of his pocket, glanced at the printed name of the sender, nodded in calm contempt, and said: 'Those idiots.' Then he glanced swiftly at my father and seemed astounded by the look on my father's face. He pulled the letter out of the envelope. He read it, standing there on the wooden bridge, read for a long time, slowly and still more slowly, then he shoved it back into his pocket, stiffening, looking away from us, out over the flat country lying there in the wind, looking towards the mill, seeming to take counsel of the labyrinth of ditches and canals, the wind-blown hedges, the dyke and the self-confident farms – or perhaps he was only looking the other way so as not to have to look at my father.

'It wasn't my idea,' my father said.

And Nansen said: 'I know.'

'And I can't do anything about it either,' my father said.

And Nansen said: 'Yes, I know.' He knocked the ashes out of his pipe, tapping it on his heel and said: 'It's all quite clear, except for the signature – the signature's illegible.'

'They've got a lot to sign,' my father said.

'They don't believe it themselves, they don't even believe it themselves,' Nansen said bitterly. 'The fools! Painting prohibited, profession prohibited! Why not eating and drinking prohibited, and be done with it? Nobody can put his name legibly to that sort of stuff.'

His head lowered, he contemplated the Big Friend of the Mill, as if to make sure that he was there, brown and capable of setting the sails in motion, that he was there to do it, if not today, then tomorrow. My father broke in upon his friend's meditation, speaking in his official manner: 'Prohibition comes into force from the moment when the recipient is informed thereof. Isn't that what it says, Max?'

'Yes, that's what it says,' Nansen replied, wonderingly.

'Then I should think it's in force *now*,' my father said quietly but distinctly.

Nansen simply picked up his easel and paints. He did it alone, unaided by the Rugbüll policeman. He didn't seem to expect any help. They slipped through the hedge, one behind the other, and walked stiffly through the garden.

They went to the studio that Nansen had had built on to the house according to his own design: the ground-floor studio with a skylight and fifty-five nooks and crannies formed by old cupboards, shelves crammed with stuff, and a great number of hard, improvised beds, on which – as I sometimes believed – all Nansen's droll or menacing creatures slept, those yellow prophets and money-changers and apostles, his goblins, and those cunning green market-people. There too, no doubt, slept the Slovenes and the dancers from the beach and of course the crooked, wind-blown farm-labourers. I never counted the beds in the studio. Judging by the number of benches and deckchairs, one might have thought that at times all those phosphorescent beings that had sprung from his imagination got together here, including those slothful, fair-haired Magdalenes of his. Crates served as tables, jam-jars and ponderous jugs as vases; there were so many of those vases, one would have had to ravage a whole garden to fill them. And they were always filled; whenever I came to the studio, on every table there was a bunch of flowers flaming away in self-assertion.

In a corner opposite the door, close to the sink, there was a long trestle table: that was the ceramic workshop. Over it, on a shelf, figures and pointed heads had been put up to dry.

They came in, put down easel and the other stuff, and Nansen went to a wooden box to get the gin. My father sat down, then got up, took his cape off, and sat down again. He looked across at the small windows of the house. The windows curved slightly outwards, concealing whatever was behind them. Wood-shavings rustled inside a crate, there was a sound of tissue-paper tearing, and then a scraping on the studio floor. Nansen pulled out a bottle, held it to the light, then wiped it on his overcoat, held it up to the light again and seemed satisfied. He put the bottle down, deftly fetched down two glasses from a shelf – thick green glasses with long stems – and filled them not quite so deftly, anyway, with a hand not so steady as usual. He pushed one of the glasses towards my father and bade him drink.

'That's the stuff, Jens,' Nansen said, after they had drunk.

'It is, Max, it is,' my father agreed.

The painter re-filled the glasses and then put the bottle on a high shelf, where he could reach it only with difficulty. So they sat, facing each other, observing each other attentively but without stealth. They heard the wind roaring away over the house and coming down the chimney right into the fireplace in the room beyond. Outside in the yard it blew a swarm of sparrows up into the air, mixing it with a flock of starlings. The ridge-turrets and the weathercock didn't keep quiet for a moment. There was an indefinable smell of burning in the air. They knew the smell and had an explanation for it : the Dutch are burning peat, they said, and their minds were at rest.

In silence Nansen pointed at my father's glass and they drank again. Then my father got up, feeling how the glow of the gin permeated his body. He walked up and down, walked from the table to a corner shelf, looked up at the picture 'Pierrot Examining a Mask', scrutinized it, cast a glance at 'The Evening of the Folds' and 'The Lemon-Woman', and turned about, to come back to the table. Now at long last he knew what to say. He stretched his arm out in a vaguely all-inclusive gesture towards the pictures and said : 'And that's what Berlin wants to stop.'

Nansen shrugged his shoulders. 'There are other cities,' he said. 'There's Copenhagen and Zurich, there's London and New York, and there's Paris.'

'But Berlin is Berlin,' my father said. And then he added : 'Why, Max? why have they told you to stop? Why have you got to stop painting?'

The painter hesitated for a moment. 'Perhaps I talk too much,' he said then.

'Talk too much?' my father asked.

'It's the colour,' Nansen said. 'Colour's always got something to tell. Sometimes it even makes definitive statements. Who knows what colour is up to?'

'But there's something else in the letter,' my father said. 'There's something about poison.'

'I know,' Nansen said with a little caustic smile. After a pause he went on: 'They don't like poison. But a little poison is necessary – it clarifies things.' He pulled the stem of a flower towards him – I think it was a tulip – and he flicked his finger against the petals, the way the Big Friend flicked the sail of the mill; he flipped, or rather he shot, aiming with his accurate forefinger, until the petals were gone, and only then let the stem spring back. Then he looked up at the bottle, but he didn't fetch it down from the shelf.

My father must have felt that he owed Max Ludwig Nansen some further explanation, for he said: 'It wasn't my idea, Max. You know it wasn't. It's not me who says you're not to paint. All I've got to do is see to it that you get the word.'

'I know,' Nansen said. And after a pause: 'Lunatics! Painting forbidden – as though they didn't realize that it can't be done. There's a lot they have the power to do, I dare say, they can stop a lot of things, I don't deny it, but they can't stop a man from painting. Others have tried to do it, a long time before them. They've only got to read it up to see there's no protection from "undesirable" pictures. You can't stop it, not even if you put the painter's eyes out, or hack off his hands. One can hold one's brush in one's teeth. The fools, do they really really not know there are invisible pictures too?'

My father walked round the table at which the painter sat. He walked very close to it, encircling it, and he did not ask any more questions, he merely observed: 'They've done it though, they've forbidden you to paint, and they've told you, Max, that's a fact.'

'Yes,' said Nansen. 'In Berlin maybe.' And he gave my father an intent look, an open, searching look, he held my father's gaze with his gaze, as though to force him to speak up and say what he, Nansen, had known all along.

And he can't have overlooked that it was not at all easy for my father to say what he had got to say: 'It's me, Max, they've given me the order to see there's no painting going on. You might as well know.'

'You?' Nansen asked.

'Yes, me,' my father said. 'The nearest police station, that's me.'

They looked at each other, one sitting, the other standing, silently taking each other's measure, possibly recollecting all they knew of each other, trying to work out how they would manage to get on together in the immediate future. They both might have been thinking all sorts of things; certainly they must have asked themselves who it was they had to reckon with in future, whenever and wherever they met. The way they looked at each other with searching eyes, they looked to me like one of Nansen's pictures, one that was simply called 'Two at the Fence' and which showed two old men looking up in olive-green light, two old men who had known each other for a long time over their garden fence, but who only now, at that very moment, recognized each other, and were startled, on their guard.

I should imagine that Nansen really meant to ask something else, when in the end he asked: 'And how are you going to do it, Jens?'

Even now my father ignored the intimacy that lay in the question, and merely replied: 'Just wait and see, Max.'

Now the painter got up too, put his head a little to one side and looked at my father as though all at once it had become manifest what he was capable of. And when my father thought it time to put on his cape and fix the clip between his straddled legs, Nansen said: 'Us chaps from Glüserup, eh?'

And my father said without looking up: 'We can't help being from Glüserup, can we?'

'Well, just keep an eye on me,' Nansen said.

'That I'm going to do,' my father replied, holding out his hand to Max Ludwig Nansen, who gripped it in a long hand-shake and held it while they walked to the door together. At the door leading into the garden they both withdrew their hands. My father stood very close to the door, almost as if cornered by Nansen. He could not see the door-handle but, thinking it must be at the height of his hip, he groped a few times in vain, until finally he got hold of it and instantly pressed it down as though eager to get out of Nansen's reach.

The wind pulled him through the door. Instinctively my father raised his arms and then spread them out and, before the north-westerly really got hold of him, put his shoulder against it and trudged to his bicycle.

Nansen shut the door against the resistance of the wind. He went to a window overlooking the yard. He probably wanted to see how, or perhaps even to make sure that, my father rode off with me, labouring against the wind. For the first time he might have felt the need to be certain that my father had in fact left Bleekenwarf. So he watched our laborious departure.

I should think that Ditte and Doktor Busbeck also watched us go, watching until we reached the red-and-white occulting beacon. And then Ditte probably asked: 'That was it?' 'That was it,' Nansen may have said in answer, without turning round, adding: 'And Jens has orders to see that there is no painting done.' 'Jens?' Ditte will have asked. And Nansen will have said: 'Jens Ole Jepsen from Glüserup. The nearest police station, that's him.'

3　The Gulls

There was someone at the spy-hole in the door. I felt it instantly.
The needle-thin pain, creeping down my back, told me that
an exploring – a *coldly* exploring eye – had fastened itself to
that spy-hole, observing me as I went on writing and writing.
I had begun to feel it while my father and Max Ludwig Nansen
were drinking each other's health. From there on I couldn't
get rid of that unceasing, tormenting gaze which had fastened
itself to my back, trickling down my skin like fine drift-sand;
and into the bargain I could hear the groping footsteps outside
the door of my cell, muffled warnings, half-suppressed exclamations of delight. So I had no choice but to assume that there
were at least two hundred and twenty psychologists who had
gathered there in the draughty corridor, impatient to get first-
hand information about me and how I was getting on with my
task.

Obviously the sight I presented to them as they watched me
through the spy-hole was so exciting that some of them were
carried away into giving vent to uncontrolled exclamations :
For instance, 'Bulzer's Symptom' or 'Objective Simultaneity-
Threshold'. Who knows? – the queue might still be flooding
past the spy-hole had I not energetically put a stop to those
goings-on. Still with that uneasy feeling in my neck, still with
that pulsating pain in my back, I focused the light from the
electric bulb on my pocket-mirror and cast the beam straight
into the spy-hole. That cleared it. A garbled out-cry could be
heard, a garbled warning, and then scraping and traipsing, the
tread of a column withdrawing with a carelessness that increased

with distance – my back was again free of tension, and free of pain.

Contentedly I smoothed my copybook. Then I was just doing a few exercises beside the table to loosen my joints when a key turned in the lock and the door opened wide. It was Joswig. Still looking hurt, he came in without a word, merely holding his hand out for something. What he wanted was the essay, what he wanted was my tribute to the German Lesson, which Himpel or Korbjuhn – more likely Governor Himpel – had told him to collect. I pretended to be astonished, I pretended to be startled, I even gave him an admonishing look, but our favourite guard merely drew my attention to the fact that it was already growing light over the Elbe, and he said : 'Let's have the stuff, so that I can let you out of this place.' And at the same time he got hold of my copybook and, bending it, he let the pages flutter past his thumb, making sure I hadn't been idle.

I am sure there was eternal satisfaction in his voice when he now declared : 'There you are, Siggi, you see, what's got to be done can be done, even if it is an essay.' He laid an approving hand on my shoulder, smiled and nodded. He pointed out that I had been writing all through the night, and said he was sure the Governor would be pleased with me. He looked at me gratefully and offered to take my copybook to the Governor's office. He was on his way to the door when I called him back and asked him to give me back my copybook. Our favourite guard looked at me uncomprehendingly and suspiciously. Holding the rolled-up copybook tight in his hand, he raised it in the air and said : 'But this is all you were kept in for, Siggi.'

I shook my head. 'My punishment has just started,' I said. 'This is just a preparation for "The Joys of Duty", it's only a beginning.'

Karl Joswig leafed through my first chapter, counted the pages, and asked incredulously : 'You've been writing all night, and you haven't finished yet?'

'The beginnings,' I said, 'I've just put down the beginnings of it all. The joy is only beginning to arise.'

'But does it have to be so long?' he asked, again a little hurt.

'Well, it's a long-lasting joy,' I replied. And then I added : 'Surely one ought to take one's punishment seriously, oughtn't one?' He confirmed that. 'If the punishment is turned into success, then there is improvement and the whole thing is a success,' he said.

'Precisely,' I said.

'You know what I expect of you?' he asked me.

'Yes,' I said.

'You owe me a finished task,' he said. 'So you'll stay locked up here in this room until you have finished. You'll eat alone. You'll sleep alone. It's up to you to decide when you've finished and are prepared to return among us.'

And then he reminded me of all that Governor Himpel had ordered me to do. He repeated that there was no time-limit to my task, and all that, and in the end, before he went to get me my breakfast, he returned my copybook, asking with real sympathy : 'Have they set you something very bad?'

'Just the joys of duty,' I said.

'I'm sorry to hear it,' he said in a scarcely audible voice, 'very sorry to hear it, Siggi.' And as though against his own will, automatically, he put his hand in his pocket, pulled out two crumpled cigarettes and a book of matches, swiftly slipped it all under my pallet and said blankly : 'No smoking in the rooms.' 'Yes,' I said.

With that he left, and now after my breakfast I am standing at the barred window, gazing out into the dawn over the Elbe, the ice-bound river, where the powerful lighters and the ice-breaker *Emmy Guspel* cut their short-lived patterns into the solid surface. The buoys are aslant under the pressure of the drift-ice. Down Cuxhaven way an ochre-coloured transparent banner is unrolled in the sky, with snow-clouds forming beside it. The little tattered flame over the refinery crouches under the rising wind. The gusts of wind grow stronger and more furious and they carry the sound of the pneumatic drill right up to me.

They've been at work here near our workshops for a long time and in our library too, where Ole Plötz, handbag specialist has now taken my place. But I'm not depressed; I have no desire to be together with my friends. I don't even miss Charlie Friedländer, who can imitate all sorts of things, voices and gestures : Korbjuhn's voice for instance, Himpel's gestures. I prefer to be here, all by myself in the locked room, alone in this cell that for me is like a swinging diving-board I have had to mount by order. I've got to get off it, I've got to jump and dive, again and again, until I've brought everything to the surface: until I've got together all the little stones of memory that make up the mosaic and have put them together, one by one, here on my table.

There is yet another tanker going down river. This is the sixth one since I had my breakfast, and she's called *Kishu Maru* or *Kushi Maru*, who cares, she'll arrive all right, just like the *Claire B. Napassis* and the *Betty Oetker*. They ride high in the water, their screws beat the air, stirring about in a soup of ice and water. They'll sail past Glückstadt and Cuxhaven, and when they reach the islands they'll take the prescribed route to the West, almost on a level with us.

But I've no intention of embarking, only to find myself in Dharan or Caracas; I can't afford to be transported by a tide or even by my mood, for I too have my prescribed route, and it leads to Rugbüll, to the wharf of my memories, where everything's stacked, ready to be transported. My freight waits for me in Rugbüll. Rugbüll is my home port, and Glüserup is a port of call. So I've got to stay at home.

How eagerly it all comes along now that I've cast the moorings, offering itself up, even forcing itself upon me; how easy it has become to reconstruct it all. All I've got to do is unroll the flat country, intersect it with a few ditches and dark canals that are fitted up with Dutch sluices, set on artificial hillocks the five mills I used to see from our shed, among them the one without sails which I love best, and put the dyke like a protective arm around the mills and the farms, painted white and rust-red, and install the red-capped lighthouse in the west. Then I must let the North Sea lap against the breakwaters, just the way Nansen can see it from his wooden hut, wave upon wave rushing along with foaming crest, and breaking against the shore. And now all I've got to do is follow the narrow brick path to get to my own Rugbüll, or rather first of all to the sign 'Rugbüll Police Station', that sign which I used to stand by so often, waiting for my father, sometimes for my grandfather, and occasionally for my sister Hilke.

How motionless it all is! They are now at my disposal: the country, the sharp light, the brick path, the peat-bog, the sign nailed to the post that's bleached by wind and weather. How quietly it all emerges now, out of its submarine twilight : the faces, the crooked trees, those afternoon hours when the wind dropped. It all returns to memory – there I am again, standing barefoot under the sign, there I am, watching the painter, or rather, the painter's overcoat, flapping along obliquely on top of the dyke towards the peninsula. It is spring up there in that northern country of ours, the air is salty and a cold wind blows; and there I am again, waiting in my hide-out, in the old box-cart without wheels, its shafts sticking up into the air, waiting for my sister Hilke and her young man, who are about to walk out to the peninsula to gather gulls' eggs there. I had been pestering them for all I was worth to take me along to the peninsula with them, but Hilke didn't want to, Hilke decided against it, simply saying : 'You'll stay where you are.' So there I was, crouching on the cracked floor of the box-cart, waiting for them, in order to follow them unnoticed – as unnoticed as possible. My father was in his little office, which I was not allowed to enter, sitting at his desk, writing reports in his looped handwriting, while my mother had shut herself up in the bedroom as she did so often during that ill-begotten spring, in which Hilke began bringing her young man to the house, her 'Addi', as she always called that fellow Adalbert Skowronnek. I heard them leave the house and, through a chink in the shed, saw them walk past, towards the path. Hilke went ahead, domineering and pig-headed as ever, and he, as always, walked a step behind her with that stiff-legged gait of his. To the best of my knowledge and belief there was no holding of hands, no mute conversation by pressing of hands, no arm put leisurely around the waist in that well-known way lovers have; they just hurried towards the brick path, their raincoats making a swishing noise, then turned to the dyke without looking back. They walked like people who knew they were being watched; inhibited, with stereotyped movements, and above all eager to give the impression that all they hoped to find out there was indeed gulls' eggs. The unnatural stiffening of their backs, their heavy steps, as though they were walking on leaden soles, the way they avoided touching each other – all that seemed to be caused by the curtain at the bedroom window that would now flutter gently, now rise billowing and fall back again or even be pulled aside quickly.

I knew very well that she was standing there. I knew that she was looking down from up there, disapproving, her lips twisted haughtily, her severe, rather red face quite blank, which was her way of showing that she was exasperated. She had been aghast when she had realized that Addi Skowronnek was a musician who played the accordion in the same hotel, the 'Pacific' in Hamburg, where Hilke worked as a waitress, and all she had said to my father was, very softly, blankly: 'Gypsies.' And after she had said 'Gypsies' she had locked herself into the bedroom; that was Gudrun Jepsen, the maternal caryatid supporting my life.

I stayed quietly on the box-cart, lying flat, one temple pressed against the floor, one knee pulled up towards my chin. I watched the curtain and I listened to the voices fading in the distance, towards the dyke and the sea. I waited until there was no longer any movement at the bedroom window and I could no longer hear the voices, then I rose quickly, jumped off my cart and flitted into the ditch beside the road and, bending low behind the bank, began to follow Hilke and her young man.

Hilke carried the basket. She walked with a slight stoop as though she wanted to take a running jump, as though she wanted to get out of reach of the house in one single jump. Her white shoes, which were white with chalk, shone on the brick-red path. Her long hair, which in the house she wore hanging down loose, she had pushed under the collar of her coat, but she hadn't pushed it down deep enough, so it pushed up again and came out in thick strands. From behind, this gave her the appearance of having no neck and her head looked like a flattened ball. Her legs were too close together, her hard calves seemed to have slipped away from their natural place, so at times it seemed she was about to stumble when her calves rubbed against each other. But she didn't feel it, she had never felt it, because her way of walking expressed the same ruthless energy that was there in all she did, in all her plans and activities. An ant, that's what I'd like to call her, a red ant. She didn't look round even once to make sure she was not followed, whereas her young man Addi, the accordion-player, kept looking round quickly and sharply, walking on with a faint reluctance, a touch of indecisiveness, so that I had to reckon with his suddenly thinking of something he would rather do than collect gulls' eggs, and turning and discovering me. He kept his hands in his pockets because he was cold, and he was smoking; the wind blew the jerky little clouds over his shoulder. From time to time he jumped round and walked a few steps backwards against the wind, hunched up inside his raincoat. Then I could make out his face, a pale face, roughened as though by fever, that seemed to be capable of only one expression, that of a happy-go-lucky easy-going nature. He wore this expression when he came to the house and he did not discard it when he noticed that my mother did not ask him to sit down, nor did his face change when those neighbours into whose houses he was dragged by Hilke didn't even bother to ask him one single question. One couldn't make out whether he was hurt, or was pleased by something, or perhaps afraid, because there was always that good-natured happy-go-lucky expression on his face, the very same expression he had shown when he turned up for the first time and which had imprinted itself on our memory.

But I mustn't allow them to vanish behind the dyke and escape me, I've got to keep an eye on them, and I follow them just as I followed them that time, bending low under the bank of the ditch, then small and upright when the lock gave me cover, a bit farther on moving almost carelessly under the protection of the belt of rushes, and finally I was safe under the ridge of the dyke, where I had only to crouch down to be hidden, should they look back. They crossed the dyke at the very spot where my father pushed his bicycle on to it on his countless rides to Bleekenwarf. They did not even stop for an instant in order to cast the usual admiring glances at the sea, but instantly plunged down towards the beach, on to the path that followed the twists and turns of the dyke to the Wattblick Inn, and then to the peninsula.

There they stopped. They stood close together, and Hilke, leaning her shoulder on his breast, pointed out at the North Sea, where I couldn't perceive anything remarkable. Then with her outstretched arm she described a slow arc, evidently making him a present of the whole North Sea, including all the shoals, waves and mines and all the wrecks on the muddy bottom of it. Addi put one hand on her shoulder and then kissed her. Then he took the basket from her hand, making it possible for her to embrace him. But Hilke did not embrace him. Instead she said something, whereupon he too said something and, holding himself stiffly, pointed to the far end of the peninsula where the sun shone brightly, and now *he* made a present to my sister of some piece of the North Sea, probably one and a half square miles.

The sea lapped against the stones of the breakwater, the spray came right up to where they stood, and the water came gushing through the crevices, bubbling and foaming and then slapping back again. Out there, over the sea, rain-clouds loomed up on the horizon like dark sails moving along, billowing top-sail, top-gallant, and mainsail. Addi evidently made a remark about it and my sister said something in answer, bending backwards laughingly so that he had no choice but to grip her arm and, playfully applying a judo-hold, lead her along the patchy path.

Directly beside the path there was a tide-line of seaweed, withered sea-holly and shingle, and parallel to it there were other, older ones. Every big flood-tide had left its mark there, a memorial line that bore witness to the force and rage of the wintry sea. And every flood-tide carried in some other booty. One cast up on the beach masses of roots washed bone-white by the sea, another one pieces of cork and a battered rabbit-hutch; lumps of seaweed, shells, and torn nets were lying about, and iodine-coloured plants that looked like grotesque trains torn off dresses. My sister and the accordion-player walked past all this, out towards the peninsula. They didn't go up to the Wattblick Inn; now holding hands, they walked along the edge of the sea, their glowing faces struck by the spray. Out there, where the tip of the peninsula went flat into the sea, one could see the incoming waves, their foaming crests looking like the fleecy backs of sheep, rolling along out of the black distance and breaking on the shallow beach. Rank upon rank they came racing in, white-crested, uphill and downhill, with an unceasing muffled roar.

The peninsula stood out in the sea like the sharp-edged bows of a ship. There was a gradual rise towards a fold between the humps of the dunes, treeless, where only the tough beach-grass grew. That's where the gulls built their rough-and-ready nests every spring, there between the bird-warden's cabin and the painter's hut, which stood all by itself at the foot of the dune, with a low but very wide window overlooking the sea.

Now I was walking along the dyke, under cover of the Inn, and so I lost sight of Hilke and her Addi, the accordion-player. Presumably at my sister's bidding he had dragged his accordion along to our place, and probably he would have played it for us by now had my mother not always left the room in silent disapproval as soon as he reached for that instrument of his that was adorned with the initials A.S. in silver or silver-plate. My father would have liked him to play his favourite tune and I too should have liked to have had him play a tune for me. But since my mother obviously was not going to permit him to play, the heavy accordion just stood about in Hilke's room. I had already considered trying it out during the night, in my old box-cart.

I stopped on the wooden platform in front of the Inn and peered through one of the two windows into the tap-room. The place was empty except for one single dark man sitting alone at a table, and he put his tongue out at me and picked up the ashtray with some clean-picked mackerel bones on it, pretending that he was going to throw it at me. I flitted past underneath the windows and again out on the ridge of the dyke, and from there I could again see Hilke and her young man in the distance. They walked one behind the other on the paving-stones of the breakwater until they reached the ramp leading to the flat, bright beach of the peninsula and then, crossing the beach, they again walked hand in hand, outlined against the background of sea and sky, among driftwood and seaweed. Walking along the lonely beach and aiming for the dunes, they looked just like Timm and Tine, a couple out of Asmus Asmussen's novel *Sea-Gleams*.

No, they didn't really look like that couple; anyway, Timm certainly would not have pointed anxiously at the cloud-bank out over the sea, and above all he would not have looked as frozen as Addi did, he would not have ducked so low, with such a startled air, just because a black-backed gull came down and down at him with back-swept wings, a bright projectile whistling through the air. Addi was so frightened that he didn't really duck, but he turned away when the gull approached, and so he couldn't see how a short distance from him it braked in its flight and let itself be borne upward by the wind, to utter its alarm-cry, once it was at a safe distance, and then fly off screaming angrily and piteously. It was always the same. One gull started the attack: a black-backed gull, or a common gull, or a herring gull. No gull along our coast will let you take its eggs without putting up a fight. They'll attack. Red-eyed and yellow-beaked they fly in, making their sham attacks.

I'm pretty sure that was something the accordion-player hadn't ever experienced before. Suddenly some two million gulls rising, screaming, forming a silver-grey cloud over the peninsula, rising and falling in demented fury, with the roar of beating wings, the cloud turning and twisting and closing up again with a flapping noise, while a white shower of gulls' feathers came down, soft feathers falling like snow, filling the fold between the dunes, all loose and warm, so that my sister and her fiancé could have lain down to sleep there had they wished to do so. As for me, my heart jumped.

As soon as the gulls had risen from their wretched nests to form another sky, a noisy sky above us, I rushed down from the dyke and towards the beach and, taking cover behind a battered fish-crate, lay there breathless in the tumult filling the air above me. I clutched the stick tight in my hand, prepared, if need be, to chop off a gull's head. Or perhaps I would only smash one of its wings and take it home and teach it to talk.

By then the gulls had discovered me too, and above me too the cloud circled, their wings beating with an angry flapping sound. While the big glaucous gulls tried to gain height as though they were heavy bombers, the small and nimble common gulls descended upon me in furious, elegant curves, turning off in front of me with a hissing swish of air, to move in a steep curve far out over the sea, where they formed up again to resume their attack.

I jumped up, whirling my stick above my head, the way somebody – whoever was it? – had done with his sword, to keep the rain off, and went running inland, stabbing and slashing to ward off these lightning attacks, running, following the two sets of footprints, the only footprints in the moist sand. After only a short run among those skimpy nests, with their blueish-green, grey, and dark brown eggs, I came upon them again.

Addi was dead. He was lying on his back. A glaucous gull had killed him, or perhaps ten herring gulls or ninety of the elegant black terns. They had hacked him, riddled him with

45

holes. My sister was kneeling beside him, doing something to his clothes in that calm and efficient manner of hers that made it possible for her to plan and to decide and to bear everything except uncertainty or faltering. She put her face down close to his, she embraced him, laid herself upon him, and in the end she did bring it off: Addi's legs began to twitch and jerk, he threw his arms up, his shoulders heaved, and his body arched as though in convulsions.

I forgot everything. Swinging my stick against the diving, screaming gulls, I raced towards them and went down on my knees beside them. I saw Addi's face all purple and contorted. His jaws were clenched and he was grinding his teeth. His fists were clenched, the thumbs inside. His skin gleamed with sweat, and when he opened his mouth I saw that the tip of his tongue was covered with scars.

'Leave him alone,' my sister said, 'don't touch him.' She had no time to be surprised at my suddenly being there beside her. She buttoned up Addi's shirt and stroked his face shyly – not in agitation or anxiety, but just shyly. I saw how Addi relaxed under her caresses. After drawing some deep breaths, he got up, smiling timidly and, when he saw me using my stick to keep the gulls off him, he waved to me.

My stick went whistling through the air, now in this direction, now in that, scaring off the attacking gulls, startling them as they dived. I pretended to have no time for the reproaches my sister was bound to utter at any moment: I was fighting for Addi. Yes. I cleared a circle in the air above him. With passes and thrusts and blows I warded off the birds, while Hilke hastily filled her basket with eggs and Addi just stood there, dazed, rubbing the back of his neck – a surprisingly old neck, I noted, all wrinkled, even a bit leathery.

Suddenly the gulls changed their tactics. They had evidently realized that they were not achieving anything by feinting. Only a few Kamikaze birds, most of them common gulls, went on diving at us, their webbed feet neatly retracted, their beaks open, showing their coral-red gullets, their wings swept back Ju-87-fashion. But these were just a few unenlightened stragglers. All the others formed up in a flat cloud above us, hovering and flapping, screaming at us. Since power-diving at us was no good, we were now to be driven off by their screaming. The

46

screeching, the yelling, the clacking and general caterwauling penetrated into the brain, pierced the marrow, made one's skin crawl.

Addi stood smiling, his hand pressed over his ears. Hilke went on collecting eggs, bent low, again and again hit by swift droppings. Now I just kept on throwing my stick into the air, thereby causing tumult, feathers flying. Sometimes my stick vanished among all those bodies and wings, and once I hit a black-backed gull on its breast, but I didn't bring it down, it didn't crash at my feet. I couldn't tear any holes in that uproarious sky of hovering gulls. I could not intimidate them or stop their screeching. The gulls kept up their screaming, but we stood up to it.

Once a gull snapped at my leg and, since I missed her with my stick, I threw an egg at her, which burst on her back. The yolk gave her yellow nationality-markings: now she was flying for Brazil.

Addi gave me a nod of approval for the shot, and, coming up to me, pulled me under his raincoat, for the wind was rising, the first gusts were coming in from the sea, pressing the beach-grass flat and flicking up the sand, flinging it against my bare legs.

He called out to Hilke, who was still busily gathering eggs, and pointed at the bank of rain-clouds and the North Sea. The curved horizon was shorter, dimmed by a fluttering, whitish curtain moving towards us. Near us the water flashed and glittered, and the gale tore gleaming strips of foam from the crests of the waves.

'Better stop now!' Addi called out, but either my sister didn't hear or she did hear and was determined to get her basket full. So we followed her slowly, with me blazing a trail for us through the gulls. It was cosy under Addi's raincoat; I only kept a chink open so as to see enough to lash out at the gulls. I could feel the warmth of his body and hear his quick breathing. The slight pressure of his hand on my shoulder was soothing.

'Better stop now!' he called out again, for suddenly the wind dropped and it began to rain. Hilke seemed small and far away, seen through the dense hatching of the rain, but still she went on, rushing about, stooping among the skimpy nests, until all at once a flash of lightning came leaping or, rather, tearing across the sea. Forked roots of lightning split above the dark horizon, followed by a decent, you might say homey, thunder-clap that came rolling across the water. At that, my sister straightened up, glanced at the sea and then at us and, pointing at something with outstretched arm, began to run in the direction indicated, much impeded by her fat calves. Now there was nothing for it but to follow her.

Gulls rose in swarms, opening their beaks wide, ready to defend themselves. Their demented screaming came thundering down on us as we ran from the rain and the thunderstorm, across the sand, through the fold between the dunes and over the dunes. The wind had risen again and was blowing the rain into our faces, that Rugbüll spring rain which always shows the ditches and canals how narrow they are, which floods the meadows and washes the caked mould from the cattle's bony hindquarters.

When it rains out our way, the openness of the countryside, its defenceless depth, is lost behind a low scattered mist; everything shrinks, is foreshortened, grows black and bulbous. Then there is no sense in taking shelter anywhere, waiting for the rain to stop, for there is no end in sight, only sooner or later a morning when one wakes happily to a fine day. If it had been just rain, we shouldn't particularly have hurried home, I suppose, but the storm, with its jagged lightning over the sea, its thunder, and its great gusts of wind, forced us to run across the dunes. There was no walking in the wildness of that gale, we stumbled along on a dull, wet sand, still following Hilke, who was now running towards the painter's hut. She wrenched the door open and, instead of shutting it behind her, stopped in the dark opening aslant with rain, waving to us, calling to us, urging us on. When we were inside, she slammed the door and sighed contentedly.

'The bolt,' Nansen said. 'You must shoot the bolt.'

My sister drove the bolt home with the flat of her hand, and there we were, dripping wet, standing in the painter's hut.

I popped out from under Addi's coat, walked round the work-table to the wide window, and looked out as I had done once before – expecting – as I had done then – to see among the breaking waves some dead man, some airman whom the waves cast on the beach and then dragged back into the sea. Perhaps the painter knew what I was looking out for, because he said with a smile: 'It's only a thunderstorm today, only a thunderstorm.'

After all, I had often gone to his hut with him and sat beside him on his work-table while he watched the swell and the breaking of a wave, or the clouds, or the light lording it there over the sea; that time when the two of us had discovered the dead airman, he had held me fast on the table for a long time, while he went on observing the gently drifting, rolling body, floating limply out there with the ribbon of the swell, which turned and overturned with it and seemed to have become part of it, for ages, it seemed to me, until in the end we rushed out and pulled the dead airman up on to the beach.

'Only a thunderstorm,' he said, smiling in the twilight. Then he pulled out a big handkerchief and mopped my face, while I scanned the foamy surf and didn't keep still enough for his liking, for he remonstrated: 'Keep still, do keep still, Witt-Witt.' He was the only one who called me that – and why shouldn't he? – *witt-witt* is the quick, worried call of the sand-pipers, it's all they seem to have to say, and perhaps it's all the painter had to say about me, anyway that's what he called me and that was what I answered to; I would look round, come nearer, or keep still. Max Ludwig Nansen rubbed my hair dry and then my neck and my legs, and after that he handed his big handkerchief to Hilke, and she dried herself and then wrung out and combed her long hair, which was soaking. Raw and gusty the wind came from the sea, making uproar outside the door. There was no longer a gull to be seen, not even their look-outs were up in the air. The sea seethed and glittered, and I bent down, twisting my head as far to one side as I could, to imagine that seething and glittering to be the sky and the dark sky to be the sea. When I straightened up again and looked round, I discovered her.

Jutta was there, silent and motionless, squatting cross-legged on the floor by the cupboard, her hands in her lap, her lean thighs so far apart that her skirt was stretched tight. I could see her smiling and that she was smiling only in response to Addi's bewildered, stupefied smile. I was surprised. I looked from one to the other, from Jutta's bony, mocking face, lean as a greyhound's, to Addi, just standing there stiffly, not knowing what to do with himself, an astonished shop-window dummy, goggling with surprise at a sixteen-year-old girl with a thin neck and thin thighs and quick, adventurous eyes – Jutta, who never meant what she said and who had bewitched Bleekenwarf from the day when the painter had taken her and her violent little brother into his house after the death of their parents, who had also been painters.

Anyway, I tried to make sense of that silent game of recognition, and I was just going to say something when my sister said : 'Rub yourself down, Addi, the rain's cold.' She handed him the handkerchief and nudged him encouragingly in that way she had, whereupon he looked at her blankly and then began to dry himself, in speechless obedience. And while he was using that enormous handkerchief, Hilke said to Nansen : 'This is Addi, my fiancé, he's just here on a visit.' And Nansen, smiling, waved a hand towards the corner, and said : 'This is Jutta. She and her brother live with us.' Thereupon Hilke shook hands with Jutta, and Addi with the painter, and when I had shaken hands with Jutta, Addi did too, and then I realized I hadn't yet shaken hands with Max Ludwig Nansen, and when I shook hands with him Hilke also realized she hadn't done so and so she quickly shook hands with him too, and I was almost carried away into shaking hands with Hilke, but Nansen stepped between us to take his pipe from his shelf.

'I hope it'll soon blow over,' Hilke said.

'The thunderstorm will,' Nansen said. 'Not the rain.'

'Serves you right,' Hilke said to me. 'What did you have to come chasing after us for?' and I retorted : 'Well, I'm wet anyway,' and I saw the two men exchange a glance of surprise, a wink of amused appreciation, over my head. Addi offered the painter a cigarette, and the painter held up his pipe as a way of saying no. Lighting his pipe, Nansen went to the window and looked out into the wind, into the darkness over the sea, where presumably again something was going on that he could make out, with those patient, grey eyes of his. By then I had learned to recognize when he was absorbed in contemplation of invisible events, movements and apparitions, just as I knew from his bearing when he was discussing something with his Balthasar or quarrelling with him. I only had to observe him, I didn't need to follow his gaze, to know that his attention was focused on the fantastic people that his eye conjured up everywhere: those rain-kings, cloud-makers, wave-walkers, those helmsmen of the air, and mist-men, those big friends of the mills, of the beaches and of the gardens. Rising up, they revealed themselves to him as soon as his gaze liberated them from their hidden, furtive existence.

Pulling at his pipe, he stood at the window, his eyes narrowed, fixed on the breakers, his head lowered as though he were about to ram something, while, soundlessly, Jutta came out of the shadows, bared her strong front teeth in a smile, and again submitted to Addi's astonished, questioning gaze.

Then I heard Hilke laugh. She waved a sheet of paper that she had pulled out, without Nansen noticing, from under a folder on the work-table.

'What is it?' I asked.

'Come and see,' she said, 'just you come and see, Siggi.' She looked at the sheet and laughed again.

'What's the matter with you?' I asked.

She laid the sheet on the table, smoothed it out, and asked : 'Recognize him? Eh?'

'Gulls,' I said, 'just a lot of gulls.' For at first I couldn't see anything but gulls, one on the nest, one diving, one hovering on patrol. But then I realized that every gull wore a policeman's helmet, and on its curved chest that sovereign emblem, the German eagle. Nor was that all : each of the gulls had my father's face, the long, sleepy face of the Rugbüll policeman, and all of them had on their three-clawed feet little boots and gaiters of the sort my father wore.

'Just put it back into the folder,' the painter said, rather hesitantly, but Hilke didn't want to, she pleaded :

'Do give it to me, oh please, give it to me!'

But Nansen said again : 'Put it back in the folder, I tell you.'

And when Hilke just tried to roll it up, he took it out of her hand, shoved it into the folder and said : 'You can't have that, I still need it.' And he pulled the folder towards him and put a cardboard box full of old tubes of paint on top of it.

'What do you call it?' Hilke asked.

'That's not settled,' Nansen said. 'Perhaps I'll call it "Black-Headed Gulls On Duty", but I haven't decided yet.'

'All right then,' Hilke said suddenly, adding: 'Why don't

you make a drawing of me? You did promise. Or me with Addi. Come here, Addi.' And she seized him by the arm and pushed him towards Nansen, with an air of saying: It's much easier to make a portrait of him than of other men of his type, come on, get on with it.

'Can't be done,' the painter said.

'Why not?' my sister asked, 'Why ever not?'

'I've scalded my hand,' Nansen said.

'*Scalded*? With hot water?'

He nodded: 'Hot water – that's right. It'll be a long time healing.'

The thunderstorm was now directly over the peninsula, and the obvious thing would be to describe the various classical types of lightning and go on about squalls and all sorts of thunder-claps. I could also emphasize how remote the hut was, there at the foot of the dunes, and speak of how the timbers moaned in the gale, and the floor shook, and the putty in the window-pane crumbled. After all, thunderstorms that come from the sea are frequent occurrences out our way.

But it is not so much the thunderstorm I remember as my sister's observation that the hut could do with a thorough sweeping out and a bit of tidying up. She had ascertained this during the flashes of lightning, and she succeeded where anybody else would have failed: she found the hidden broom with the crooked, stiff bristles, and, without asking if anybody objected, she took off her coat, pushed aside the stools, and began to sweep. In her determined manner she swept the sand into one corner, urged the lot of us towards the work-table, and then started to sweep from the door. She piled the stools one on top of the other. She arranged the things on the shelves. She dusted the neglected kerosene stove. Calmly bustling to and fro in her zest for work, she made the hut too small for her, and she was reluctant to put the stools back in their places because that would mean the end of it.

And then there was Jutta – Jutta squatting on a wooden bedstead, smiling. Her strong incisors shone. Her gaze rested on Addi, who was awkwardly letting himself be pushed now this way, now that. He obviously wanted to say something, perhaps he even felt like putting his foot on the little broom and stepping on it, hard, as it moved to and fro, in short, quick strokes, at least that's what I thought, but he just said nothing and put up with whatever Hilke did to him.

I can still remember the startled way he jumped when somebody outside knocked at the door. Right in the middle of the thunderstorm there was this thumping at the door, and we all looked at each other blankly, wondering what to do, and in the end it was the painter who pushed the bolt back and opened the door, though actually Addi was standing nearest to it. Nansen had only to let go of the door-handle and the storm slammed the door against the wall of the hut. Outside there, outlined against the grey of the dunes, was my father, his cape fluttering, his face now and then lit up by flashes of lightning, standing there motionless, a stout pixie, as you might say, a sort of lumpish rain-spectre, keeping us guessing for quite some time, since he showed no inclination to enter the hut. There he stood ominously, seemingly enjoying the uneasiness his presence caused us. Then, suddenly, he said in a colourless voice : 'Siggi?'

'Here I am,' I said and snapped over to him, and he thrust an arm out from under his cape, gripped my wrist and, pulling me through the doorway after him, turned without uttering a single word and dragged me through the cloudburst, towards the dyke.

No scolding. No threatening. All I heard was that faint panting of his and all I felt was his hand like an angry vice on my wrist. So we stumbled across the dunes and up to the dyke, where he had left his bicycle. He didn't utter a single word, and I didn't dare to speak. My fear anticipated what lay in store for me, and in the depths of my fear I knew that no word I could have said would have changed the situation. So there I sat convulsed on the bar, holding on for dear life as he pushed off, mounted, and succeeded in getting under way and riding down the slope of the dyke, without so much as once dismounting despite the gusts of wind that were hitting us sideways in the thunderstorm. I knew how much it cost him in strength and skill. Close above my head I could hear him puffing and panting, heard him groan whenever he parried the thrusts of the wind with a jerky movement. If only he'd cursed and sworn! Or if he'd slapped my face when he pulled me out of the hut! It would all have been much easier to bear and I might even have come to terms with my fear. But all through

that journey my father remained silent, punishing me by keeping silent, which was his way of telling me of the punishment to
come. That was his way: he always announced what he
was going to do, always gave a warning, he was not a man to
take one by surprise, and if, say, he had to take action in the
performance of his duty, he rarely did so without first letting
it be known: Look out, I am about to take steps.

So it was in silence that we rode homeward down the slope
and then along the brick path. At the bottom of the steps he
made me jump off, with a flick of his forefinger he bade me
put the bicycle in the shed, and when I came back he took hold
of my wrist again and pulled me into the house. As he walked
he flung off his cape, and he avoided looking me in the eye –
just as if he were afraid his accumulated disappointment or
anger might discharge itself too soon. So he followed me upstairs, into my room, where the light was already on.

Since they had fetched my older brother Klaas away on
account of that self-inflicted wound, I had had the room to
myself. The walls and the window-sill were mine, and so was
the pull-out table, which was completely covered by a blue,
canvas-mounted map of the sea, on which the most daring sea-
battles took place. I even had a key and could lock my room.
The light was on. I could see the light shining through the
chinks, and so I instantly knew who was there in the room,
standing by the wardrobe, very straight, hair scraped back into
a tight bun, lips twisted: even through the closed door I could
see my mother standing there in all her overbearing rigidity,
and when my father opened the door I stopped on the warped
threshold, yet not because I was surprised.

He pushed me into the room. He turned an expectant gaze
on Gudrun Jepsen, who didn't stir, who looked at me as though
from a long way off. He waited a long time before saying:
'Here he is.' And then he walked across the room, glanced at
my mother eagerly, queryingly, got the stick out from under the
bed, again glanced queryingly at my mother, and then, coming
back to me, said: 'Down with your pants.' I knew that was
what he would say, but I did nothing to anticipate his command. Now I took my trousers off, handed them to him, and
watched him carefully smoothing the wet trousers out and laying them on the table. Nor did I bend over, I just waited for

54

the command: 'Bend over!', pressed the palms of my hands to my trembling thighs, and then straightened up again in a flash before the first blow fell.

Disapprovingly, evidently rather disconcerted, he lowered the stick and tried to catch my mother's eye, as though to apologize for my lapse; but my mother did not stir. The stick rose again, I bent over, tightening my naked behind, clenching my teeth and looking sideways at my mother – and this time too I straightened up in a flash before the blow fell. I took two steps in order to relax, massaged my behind for an instant and then stepped back and bent down under the uplifted stick. This time I was determined to take the blow. But before the stick came whistling down, the nails in the floorboards became alive, crabs nipped at the backs of my knees, an albatross slashed at the back of my neck – I couldn't help it, I fell on my knees, whimpering.

That seemed to be something my mother had not expected of me, for she started out of her trance, let her hands drop to her sides, gave me a look of weary contempt, and then walked out of the room, unheeding, no longer taking any interest in my punishment. My father turned and stared at her in bewilderment, probably wanting to prevent her from leaving, and even murmured something, but by then she was gone, she was outside in the passage, she was in the bedroom, where the key turned, the lock clicked.

My father shrugged and surveyed me with an embarrassed, listless expression. Here, I realized, was my chance: I went on whimpering, at the same time smiling at him, even trying to wink at him as though he were my accomplice and the two of us had just escaped some danger. But I probably didn't quite manage to wink, I dare say it looked as if I were pulling a face at him, for my father looked at his pocket-watch and then, listless as before, took me by the scruff of the neck and dragged me to the table. Carefully he pressed my shoulders down towards the table top. I resisted slightly. He kept the pressure up. I went on resisting. With the flat of his hand he gave me a slap on the back of the neck. That put me down on to the table, but again I pressed back. There below my face was the blue map of the sea, over which I dreamily reigned when I re-thought the great sea battles: here I had fought my Lepanto, my Trafalgar, here the battles of Skagerrak and Scapa Flow, the Orkneys and Falkland had been fought all over again. And now I drifted, floundering, in those waters of my imagined triumphs, all my sails taken in.

I hadn't expected that the very first stroke would cause such searing pain, knowing as I did that the stick was wielded by a listless hand and with some resentment, but even after that first stroke there was a red hot weal running across my behind. And when I reared up, my father's left hand held me down, dipping me into a deep, burning sea of pain and defeat, while his right hand raised the stick and brought it down quite hard, though almost absentmindedly. And when I reacted to every stroke with a dry, high-pitched, somewhat exaggerated scream, my father time and again paused, listening, waiting for my mother to reappear, since my screams were meant to offer her some sort of compensation for the disappointment she had suffered.

Since the audible proof of my punishment was bound to reach her ears over there in the cool solitude of her bedroom, she could not remain indifferent : that was obviously what he was thinking, time and again turning his head, listening, glancing towards the door. That was my father all over, eternally bent on doing his duty, the impeccable officer of the law.

My mother did not return. Even when I produced a short, choked scream that must have been something quite new to her, she did not put in an appearance. This apparently discouraged my father : the last strokes were perfunctory, and when I turned round to him, he pointed the stick at the bed.

I dropped on to the bed. But he put the point of the stick under my chin, forcing me to look up at him. Seen through the veil of tears he looked exhausted and unhappy, but, as though he wanted to counter that, raising his voice he demanded :

'Now what do you say?'

To save him the trouble of repeating the question, I answered quickly : 'I've got to be at home when there's a thunderstorm.'

He nodded, satisfied, drew the stick away from under my chin, and said : 'You've got to be at home when there's a thunderstorm. That's your mother's wish, and it's my wish too. Thunderstorm – *home*.'

Then he pulled the quilt out from under me, covered me with it, and sat down on the wooden chair in front of my map of the ocean, sat there listening, his face crooked, helpless, for he had no orders, and without orders he was only half a man. He had had plenty of practice in sitting quietly, doing nothing, and in the winter, when there was nothing else to do, he could go on staring at the stove for hours, entirely self-sufficient. But beyond all doubt he was at his best when he was given a clear, straightforward task, in the execution of which he had, for instance, to work out the questions he would have to ask later on.

I went on whimpering as convincingly as I could. I watched him out of one eye, through the crook of my arm; the weals burned, the quilt was unbearably heavy on my burst skin, and I wished he would go away. All I wanted was to be left alone. But he wouldn't, he *wouldn't* go, he didn't mind putting up with my whimpering and everything else. And suddenly he even got up, came to me, tapped my shoulder with his fingertip and said: 'All you've got to get into your head is: do what you're told. That's all anyone expects of you. Do you understand me?'

'Yes,' I said. And, just to get rid of him, I said it again: 'Yes.'

'A useful chap is a chap who toes the line,' he said, and I hastened to answer: 'Yes, father, yes.'

Monotonously, pensively he added: 'We'll make a useful chap of you yet, you'll see.'

Then suddenly he asked: 'Has he been painting?'

I wasn't quick enough on the uptake, so he asked again:

'In his hut – was he painting or drawing while you were all there?'

I looked up at him in surprise, realizing that a number of things depended on my answer and that what I knew was of some importance, and so I pretended to have trouble with my memory, or, to put it a little more precisely, I acted as if the pain he had inflicted upon me had blurred my memory.

'Gulls,' I said finally. 'He showed us gulls, and they all looked like you.'

So then my father wanted to know more about all this, but there wasn't much more I could tell him. Still, what he had learned was enough to work a change in him: gone was his irresolution, all at once he seemed alert and lithe, he pricked up his ears, his face became quite expressive. He put on a look of surprise and exasperation and cast a brief glance out of the window, a glance that held both a warning and disappointment – or at least I imagined it did – and then, I shall never forget it, he sat on my bed, gave me an urgent, probing, positively imploring look and said slowly:

'We're going to work together, Siggi. I need you. You're going to help me. There's nobody who's a match for the two of us – not even him. You're going to work for me and in return I'll make a decent chap of you. It's got to be. Now listen to me! Stop whimpering and listen!'

4 The Birthday Party

Higher, faster, steeper every time. Every time a stronger thrust. And always nearer to the tousled topmost branches of the old apple tree, planted long ago, in Frederiksen's days, when he was still young. And what a whizzing it made, the swing plunging back out of the green twilight on trembling-tight ropes, the rings creaking, and then that sharp gust of air, and for a fleeting moment the shadow-pattern of the branches was imprinted on Jutta's full-stretched, balancing body. High, high up she rose, poised for an instant motionless in mid-air, and then came diving down. And there was I, sharing in that dive by swiftly touching the seat of the flying swing or Jutta's hip or her little bottom, and pushing her forward, up towards the topmost branches of the apple tree. As though shot from a catapult she flew upwards once again, her dress flapping, her legs apart, and the air-currents kept on changing her shape, tugging her hair back, cutting out still sharper the boniness of her pert, mocking face. What she was out to do was to somersault with the swing, and I was out to give her the impetus she needed – but it was more than we could manage, even when she got up and stood with her legs braced on the seat. It was beyond us, either because the branch was too crooked or because the impetus didn't suffice – that day in the painter's garden, Herr Doktor Busbeck's sixtieth birthday. When Jutta realized I couldn't do it, she sat down again on the swing and just went on swinging to and fro, smiling, without any further ambition, at the same time looking at me in a way no one had taught her, until all at once I was caught and held fast in the fork of her thin brown legs; and then I was no longer capable of noticing anything but that she was there, and how close to me. Anyway I very well knew how close she was, and she knew that I knew, and I told myself to stay quiet and wait and see what was going to happen next, but nothing else happened. Jutta kissed me, carelessly, with dry lips, opened her legs and let go of me, slid off the swing and ran towards the house, where Ditte now was leaning out of one of the four hundred windows, holding some pieces of pale yellow shortcake on her hand, the way one holds out food to the birds.

I snatched up my stick and started to run after her. I jumped over the flower-beds and the bushes, trying to take short cuts, but all our hurrying was in vain : before Jutta and I could reach the window I saw Jobst burst out of the thatched summer-house, come rolling out of it, violent as a ball of lightning, a fat but nimble monster with stubby fingers and pouting lips, floundering unheedingly through all the great poppies and zinnias, all that great clash of colour; and of course he got to the window first, he snatched the three pieces of cake from Ditte's hand, stowed two of them in his pocket and began to devour the third, his eyes shut as he chomped. You only had to look at him to realize he wasn't going to hand over any of the cake he'd snatched – he never would let go of anything he laid his hands on – so Ditte didn't even bother to scold him, but simply beckoned us into the well-kept gigantic living-room of Bleekenwarf.

I'd have liked to catch up with Jutta there in the murky hall, but she was far ahead of me, and she didn't answer when I called out to her, and she'd opened the door while I was still groping for her among the buckets, brooms and chests that formed a lane there. She left the door open, didn't even bother to turn round. The silence made me suspicious, so I tiptoed to the threshold, supposing the sitting-room to be empty and deserted, and I was wondering where they were having their birthday party if not here. But when I had gone in, hesitantly, and looked round, I got quite a shock, as anybody might have who'd have expected, like me, to find the room empty. At the narrow, endlessly long birthday table there was a solemn con-gregation of sea-animals, all grey with age, sitting there in silence drinking coffee and gobbling madeira cake, nutcake and shortcake, sunk deep in stubborn contemplation. There were stiff-legged lobsters, prawns, and crabs crouching on the haughty, carved Bleekenwarf chairs; now and then one could hear the dry creaking of heavily armoured limbs or the clatter of a cup set down on the table by a lobster's bony pincers; some of them gave me a look out of indifferent eyes, those eyes on long stalks, imperturbable, with – if you know what I mean – the monumental indifference of certain divinities. And at the same time this silent congregation of sea-animals definitely resembled people I knew: two of them looked like the old Holmsens of Holmsenwarf, I thought I identified Pastor Treplin and Plönnies, the schoolmaster, and then I recognized my father and Hilke too and Addi, and next to the tenderest sea-trout imaginable, which looked very much like Herr Doktor Busbeck, there my mother sat, with a forbidding face, her hair done up in a severe bun, as a sea-urchin. There was of course also a lantern-fish, gesticulating, quacking and gaily dashing about, and that was the painter himself.

And it was the painter who suddenly called out: 'Put the children at the little table and give them something to eat', and Ditte was already there at my side, pulling me towards the little table, gently pushing me into an old-fashioned chair that instantly caused me to sit still and hold myself quite stiff and straight, because otherwise I should have slid off the crooked seat. Ditte took my stick, which was studded with drawing pins, out of my hand and put it on the window-sill. She told Jutta to pour out milk for me, and she turned the round dish with the cakes on it a little, perhaps the distance of a quarter of an hour.

'Go on, help yourself,' she said kindly and patted my neck. Then she returned to the table, sat down, and instantly allowed herself to be changed into a flat sole.

I forgot about the cake and about the milk too. I just went on watching Jutta, sitting there opposite me, and all at once it had become so important that she should pay attention to me that I silently ordered her to look at me. And when I didn't succeed in making her do it I kicked her under the table, time and again, until she pulled her feet back – not reproachfully, she just ignored me and her face became quite rigid and shut off. I had no idea what she was thinking about, dreaming, weighing in her mind, I just saw her dark far-away eyes and the slanting, flaming beams of the sinking sun glittering inside them; I watched her strong canines sink into the cake, biting off bits of it, while her gaze slid past me and across the living-room, which even now was filled with the silence of so many years and the solitude of winters past and gone.

Jutta's red-and-white check dress, her thin arms, her wispy hair, and those pale lips, capable of taking back every spoken word at every instant – how easily I can bring back the memory of it all – and yet how impossible it is to bring her back to that little table and ask her to sit down opposite me, even though I can still make myself re-experience my wonder that she could so quickly forget my efforts at the swing. But that's the way Jutta was: at one instant she was there with you, participating in what you did, in league with you, and the next instant she had withdrawn. That's the way she was. But I hadn't expected her suddenly to get up and, holding a piece of shortcake loosely between her teeth, walk across the room and whisper something to Addi Skowronnek – it was done so quickly and in such a way that he just had time to look surprised, but no time to protest – and then, crouching low, move to the door and disappear, without even waving to me.

I didn't bother to follow her. I put my cake on to her plate, I poured my milk into her tumbler. I moved into her chair, without even glancing through the window, although I could have easily detected her in the garden, on the unrailed wooden bridge, in front of the hedge. With the whole party there before my eyes, all of them eating, I began to eat again myself, and since there was a third plate and tumbler on the little table I took good care to eat up all the cake and drink up all the milk. No, really I must be wrong about that; I think I poured the rest of the milk into the deep cake-dish and then woke up the cat, which was asleep, its back hunched up and its paws hidden under its body, on the third chair, which was meant for Jobst. I drew the gaze of its slanting, glimmering eyes to the birthday milk and it began to lick it, rolling it up on its tongue, at first slowly, trying it, and then faster and faster. In the end it licked the dish quite clean, so that I was able to put it back on the table; then it stretched for all it was worth, licked its legs, and, gingerly, slowly, came up to me, jumped on my lap, turned round a few times on an invisible axis, and then folded up in a position it had probably worked out beforehand, put a bent forepaw into my hand and began to purr.

I looked at the silent company before me, all of whom were still guzzling, swallowing, smacking their lips and clearing their throats significantly, there at that table which was gradually blurring in an ever-deepening murk stretching away perhaps into the murk of flats and runnels. And now I also recognized my grandfather among them, Per Arne Schessel, the folklorist and greedy guzzler, the dyke-reeve Bultjohann, and Andersen, a ninety-two-year-old sea-captain from Glüserup, who had been a sea-captain in at least fifty-five documentary films on the strength of his beautifully kept, round, silvery beard and because the watery emptiness of his gaze could easily be interpreted as nostalgia for distant seas and far-flung lands. If I tried to name everyone who was there at that table, the winter would pass meanwhile and the Elbe would be free of ice again, so the last ones I shall put down here are Hilde Isenbüttel and the former warden of the bird-sanctuary, Kohlschmidt. I noticed them especially among all those snuffling, beaky-lipped birthday-party guests, and I also noticed a large phosphorescent prawn with sturdy calves that kept on beckoning to me in a way that unmistakably meant : If you want some cake, come here.

But I didn't want any cake. I was waiting for the birthday party to begin. But it didn't look as if that company would ever stop eating; not one of them sighed and groaned and capitulated in the face of those ceaselessly circling plates, heaped with all sorts of cakes, least of all my folklorist grandfather, who crouched there as a wise old lobster all covered with barnacles and slowly but steadily stuffed whole platefuls of cake into him, which the documentary-film captain obviously regarded, for his part, as a challenge to do the same. Eating in our part of the world means tucking in well and truly, and if for no other reason than for the one my grandfather used to give : time passes smoothly while you're eating. They all seemed set on seeing that time should pass smoothly, even that crustacean in uniform whom one might easily have mistaken for my father and who was hogging huge lumps of nut-cake and honeycake, obviously for no other reason than to make it possible for time to pass imperceptibly.

The women were also intent on breaking time's resistance. While drowsily getting to grips with one piece they were already eyeing the next, and when they began to choke, when their jaws began to weaken, they swilled it all down with streams of steaming coffee.

The details that strike one at a Glüserup coffee table are quite revealing : apart from the indolent greed displayed, greed that will even go to the baffling lengths of admitting that the purpose of being a guest is to harm the host, what most deserves to go on record are the nine prescribed sorts of pastry that are handed round according to a definite rule, the bowls of sugar-cubes for dipping into the coffee before being chewed, and the dishes full of clotted cream that is heaped on top of the coffee, but not before clear schnapps has been poured into it.

But I don't want to go on spinning out all these details, which certainly might form a story all in themselves, nor do I wish to interpret the silence that prevailed at that table. Admitting my impatience, I'd prefer to urge the painter to rise from his high carved chair and walk to the head of the table, straight up to Herr Doktor Busbeck, since it was he, after all, whose sixtieth birthday was being celebrated.

Busbeck seemed to become even more tender, even more embarrassed, as the painter approached him; he clammed up like a mussel that has been touched, and he became quite grey and insignificant. Only once he turned and looked behind his chair, as though he hoped to find there yet another Herr Doktor Busbeck, one for whom it would be less difficult to deal with all the attention to which he was all at once exposed. The painter bent down to him slightly and, lavishing well-deserved intimacy upon him, patted him on the back in order to fortify his courage, and said :

'My dear Teo, dear friends!'

And dear Teo crouched even lower as a result of being addressed in that manner, and the dear friends smirked and looked at him, so that the little man grew even more embarrassed, if such a thing was at all possible.

'I am not one to make long speeches,' the painter said, and for once this was true, and he proved it so, for he restricted himself to reminding Busbeck of an evening thirty years earlier in Cologne. If I understood correctly, Ditte was ill at the time.

Though not icy cold, the room where she was in bed was a seedy room in a seedy boarding-house, and perhaps there was a washing-line running right across it, and the electric bulb had been taken away by the landlady in person. The picture was completed by a hint that the rent hadn't been paid for months. Anyway, there was Ditte in bed, breathing heavily, and the painter, who had failed to get a teaching job in an art college, was just washing up the borrowed plates and cutlery, when a Herr Doktor Busbeck groped his way up the unlit stairs and with amazing diffidence asked if he might see some of the painter's work. There was no question of refusing him. If I am not mistaken, he was invited to sit down in a corner near the window, where he was given some portfolios to look through. Since he was so unobtrusive, so silent and so easy to overlook, his presence was almost forgotten and – I gathered – the last thing anyone expected was that this visitor would all at once come up to the oil-cloth-covered table, holding in his hand ten sheets he had chosen. Without a word he counted out on the table four hundred marks in gold, after which he asked with the greatest of simplicity if he might come again. Since the question was uttered as a plea, the painter did not feel (as he recounted) that he could refuse.

So such things really do happen, and the painter gaily refreshed his own and Doktor Busbeck's memory of that March day in Cologne, he even knew the exact date, and, with profuse references to 'those days', he thanked his friend for all his friendship, unfailing through all of thirty years. And now, Teo, you are with us here in Bleekenwarf. We shall never forget all that you ... in Cologne, and in Lucerne too, and in Amsterdam. ... Remembering our combined struggle against the great Schalberg. ... And so here today on your sixtieth .... Looking round this table. ... Everywhere whole-hearted agreement. ... Indeed, dear Teo ...

Startled, the cat jumped from my lap as they rose to their feet, all round that endless birthday-table and tremulously raised their glasses of clear schnapps to drink Doktor Busbeck's health, and tipped it down jerkily as if to overcome some revulsion. Then they set the glasses down with a clatter, dragged their chairs towards them and sat down again, elaborately arranging themselves, while Herr Doktor Busbeck remained standing, all

65

alone, delicate and expressive in his embarrassment, and apparently making apologies to the whole company because they had had to rise on his behalf. He stepped behind his chair. He looked down at his hands, which were stroking the carved back of his chair. And then he said the things he had probably often thought, thanking the painter and Ditte and everybody else as well, regretting that he had been a burden to them for so long. He hinted that his life here could be only a passing phase, but that the dignity of the past meant no more to him than the dignity of the present. I think he also spoke of his hopes for the future and went so far as to say that perhaps a day might come when he would be able to return to his old place and be of some use once more. Not even once, while speaking, did he cast a glance at the assembled guests, only now and then he would look at Ditte, his neck bent, his head on one side, and Ditte would always smile out at him. And again he expressed his thanks, again he said how sheltered he felt here, how wholly he was made to feel at home, and how honoured, yes, honoured, he was by the friendship of the man who outside – he simply said 'outside', perhaps without realizing the implications of the word – was regarded as one of the greatest dramatic masters of light, and so on and on. And at the end he did in fact bow to Ditte and to that whole fantastic congregation, hastily reached for his glass and tossed off the clear schnapps the painter had set before him. One could see how relieved he was. He nodded cheerfully to this one and that on the other side of the table. He pushed his starched cuffs back into the sleeves of his jacket, patiently, a number of times, and he asked for his glass to be filled again with the clear schnapps. He wiped his forehead and seemed contented.

Herr Doktor Busbeck might well be contented, seeing, as he did, how much he meant to all of us. And when Max Ludwig Nansen said : 'And now let's go and have a look at the presents,' he merely raised his pale, unlined face, without stirring, until two of the guests simply pulled him out of his chair and made him go ahead into the studio, where either the painter or Ditte or, most probably, both of them had decorated a table and arranged the birthday presents on it. I slid down from my chair the moment the whole company rose, and I was the first to enter the twilit hall and arrive at the door to the studio, but when my father beckoned to me in some irritation I slowed down, and so I wasn't the first at the table with the presents on it, but I did manage to be the fourth. And what was on that table? What had all these Rugbüllers and Glüserupers and people from in between been prepared to spend on a man who, though he did not belong here, had been driven by events they could almost understand to take refuge among them? I can remember the tiepin. I can remember the bottle of schnapps and the fruitcake and a cosy for his coffee-pot, and the socks and a book – author and publisher Per Arne Schessel – and a box of tallow candles. I also remember the tobacco-pouch (with tobacco in it). And the scarf and naturally the bottle of Cossak brand coffee-extract, since this was from us. But above all I remember the painting : 'Sails Dissolving into Light'.

The painting was at the far side of the table, leaning against the wall, with the bottles on guard at either side, the socks wriggling obsequiously before it, the cosy blowing itself up, full of self-importance, the fruitcake trying to inspire confidence, and the scarf winding itself round the tallow candles as though – softly, softly – to smother them. All of the presents were full of self-importance, clamouring for attention, but they were all put in their place and reduced to their plain usefulness by the painting.

I went closer, to where I could watch Doktor Busbeck gazing at it and being caught by its light. I saw him walk up to it, gingerly, his hand stretched out, incredulously you might even say, and I also saw him touch it lightly with his fingertips, then instantly step back again, narrowing his eyes and then briefly hunching up his shoulders as though shuddering with awe. Here sky and sea were united. Here a soft lemon-yellow talked a pale blue into self-abandonment. Floating sails evoked a feeling of great distance and of some story that was there to be understood, and then were deprived of their whiteness for the sake of the dreamlike unity that was all of it. The sails dissolved, and their dissolution meant that in the end nothing was left but light, and the light, it seemed to me, was one single chant of praise.

Once more Doktor Busbeck took a step towards the painting, his hand outstretched, and the painter said :

'As you can see, Teo, there are still a few touches missing.'

'It's finished,' Busbeck said.

But the painter said : 'That white there – it still shouts a bit.'

And Doktor Busbeck said : 'It's too much, Max, I can't take it from you.'

But the painter just winked at him and said : 'Well, you're only going to get it when it's finished.'

They all stood round the birthday table, estimating, comparing, judging the quality, calculating the value in marks and casting quick appraising glances here and there so as to find out, if they possibly could, who had given what. *That* would give them something to talk about on their way home. They picked up the presents and handled them, they proclaimed their admiration and their interest, they handed them round, commenting on them, and left nothing untouched, unexamined. Nobody dared to treat any present cursorily or slightingly. They lifted the bottles, clicking their tongues, pushed their fists into the cosy, tried the tiepin on themselves for the fun of it, and Per Arne Schessel did his best to work off that damned folkloristic stuff of his on everyone, handing around his opened book. They goggled, they expressed their admiration, they were prepared to praise everything, they nodded and whistled through their teeth, they fingered everything, explored everything. Andersen, the documentary-film captain, aimed his knotty brown stick at the painting and said : 'That'll be the English Channel, eh? We always had that sort of choppy sea in the English Channel.'

'It's Glüserup,' said Bultjohann. 'It's my own district.'

And the painter patted both of them on the shoulder, silently agreeing with both of them.

They put the presents back on the table, and now they crowded round the painting, all of them talking. I left them to their talk, for now through the window I saw Jutta running barefoot over the wooden bridge without a railing, and she was carrying something, a black something, and I saw her disappear into the summer-house with it. So I slipped through the circle that they formed, nodding thoughtfully at the picture, and left them as they stood there, fetched my stick from the living-room, and when I climbed out of the window into the garden, there was Addi following me. He too climbed out of the window and then ran across the flower-beds towards the summer-house. Perhaps he too had seen Jutta, perhaps she had

68

given him some sort of sign, anyway he rushed past me, nudging me in the ribs as he overtook me.

On the uneven black clay floor of the summer-house there lay Addi's accordion, and behind it – there Jutta stood, her legs braced, prepared for an argument, even in mocking expectation of it. But Addi said nothing, he uttered no word of protest, he just gaped at her in a baffled way and shook his head. 'Play it,' she said. Addi didn't stir. 'Come on, play it,' she said. 'It's a birthday party.' Addi shrugged his shoulders. 'You can play softly,' she said, and I said: 'Yes, softly, just for the two of us.' But Addi merely shook his head.

'I used to have an accordion myself,' Jutta said. 'Actually I had two. And I could play them, too.'

'Go on, then, *you* play,' I said.

'No, it's his, it's up to him to play,' she said, pointing at Addi.

'Your mother doesn't like it,' Addi said to me.

'But the others do,' I said, and then we all turned towards the door at the same instant as a shadow fell across the room. There was Jobst, fat and grinning as though he had caught us out. He looked at the accordion, at us, again at the accordion, came stumping in, took the accordion out of its container and undid the leather straps – and, well – why should I go on putting off what has to be told in the end? Addi slipped the straps over his shoulders and gave us an encouraging nod, and we formed up in a line behind him and then, yelling 'Alo-ahé', we marched forth from the thatched summer-house, each of us with his hands on the hips of the one in front of him.

Jutta held on to Addi's hips, I held on to Jutta's slim, bony hips, and the warm pressure on my own hips came from Jobst's fleshy fingers. Up the garden path we marched towards the studio, swaying, with little dancing steps, bending forward, and the wind blew and Addi played and the most beautiful Hawaian songs resounded in Bleekenwarf.

From inside the studio they knocked on the window-panes and waved to us, and our musical snake (though for a snake it was rather short) wriggled along past the studio and then past the four hundred windows of the living-room, and this way and that we moved, swaying along the black garden paths, urging, alluring, and I can still remember how Hilke was the first to join our winding procession and after Hilke came Pastor Treplin, and Holmsen, and Kohlschmidt, the warden of the bird-sanctuary, and Ditte herself. It was Ditte who, as she came alongside my father, seized his hand and laid it on her hip, and with that our snake all at once produced a sort of suction, an irresistible force pulling towards itself and swallowing up whatever got in its way, a merrily swinging force that nobody who came near it could resist, and thus the line of us grew longer and longer, making more and more loops as it moved along. By now the painter had joined in too, and Bultjohann the dyke-reeve, and Hilde Isenbüttel, and only my mother held aloof and I knew nothing would induce her to join us. There she was, deep inside the studio, a stern shadow, the embodiment of haughty refusal: Gudrun Jepsen, who had been one of the Schessel girls. She wouldn't even follow the example set by Captain Andersen, who for all his ninety-two years at least made an attempt to join our swaying snake on its way across the Lüeneburg Heath, over the lovely sand. The photogenic nonogenarian pushed his way in between Addi and Jutta, bending forward, creaking in every joint, and it seemed to me I could hear a rustling as though the dry poppy-heads were bursting open and the seeds trickling out of his trouser-legs. The old man actually joined in, hopping and swaying for a few yards until he had, as it were, scattered all of his autumnal poppy-seed and could only hobble to one side, gasping for breath. Addi led us on, and Jutta held him firmly by the hips, steering him, and when we had passed through the garden we pushed our way through the hedge, tripped across the wooden bridge, away across the meadow, and up on to the dam, and we might have danced along the bottom of the sea to England had Addi not decided otherwise. He made a violent turn, and so we shoved along and down the dam again, our long, billowing body producing a faithful imitation of the billowing wails from the accordion as Addi pushed it and pulled it. We wended our way onwards in the direction of Bleekenwarf, past the row of alders that were reflected in the moat and could not be satisfied with their mirror-reflection because the wind was continually stirring the surface of the water, curling it up, causing the myriad trees to sway this way and that as in an underwater gale. To prevent our train from breaking at least where I was

70

the link, I held on tight to Jutta with both hands, and Jutta did the same with Addi, and some of the others also used two hands.

I well remember that when we came to the gate, which went on swinging to and fro, there was Okko Brodersen, the one-armed postman. His bicycle was leaning against one gatepost. In his hand he had a piece of paper, and he held it up, as a sign that he had a right to be there.

'Come on, join in!' Jutta called out to him, and I echoed her: 'Come on!' We all urged and pestered him quite a bit, and in the end he was swallowed up by our snake, mail and all. Past the rust-red stables, past the pond and the shed we went, and when we turned the corner to the studio I looked back and saw that the long line had dissolved or was about to do so, everybody being exhausted and ecstatic – oh yes, ecstatic – and my mother must have been quite aware of it too. Even now, as our formation was dissolving, everybody followed Addi, who turned into the garden, still playing, now that old dance-tune 'The Air of Berlin, Berlin, Berlin', which conjured up that unmistakable electric atmosphere, so that some of the party, after carefully observing the sky and the North Sea, began carrying tables and chairs out of the house. The gleaming chinks in the banks of dark cloud encouraged us, as did the patches of blue sky among the feathery white of fast-moving clouds. We transferred the birthday party into the garden.

Now I don't want to prevent anybody from picturing that rapid transportation of furniture, the lifting and putting down of it, the turning and twisting of it through open windows, indeed the whole good-tempered rumpus of that move into the open air, which Addi accompanied with 'La Paloma' and 'Rolling Home'. But I myself have got to search for my stick, I've got to find that stick of mine which is studded with drawing-pins. I'd put it down somewhere when we formed up. But where? In the living-room? In the studio? I walked along the paths. I searched the hedges. I went into the yard and looked round the shed. My stick wasn't on any window-sill, it wasn't floating in the pond. 'Have you seen my stick anywhere?' I asked the two men at the pond. My father and Max Ludwig Nansen remained silent. They didn't answer, didn't even shake their heads, they maintained an agitated silence. So I went on searching. All at once I became suspicious and strolled down to the pond, where an old couple of white ducks were instructing four ducklings in formation-swimming. Taking cover behind the felled poplars I moved towards the two old friends from Glüserup, slid through an opening into a hollow space between the trunks, and now through a slit I saw the painter's and my father's legs up to their hips, the rest of them cut off, saw this from so close that I could make out their bulging pockets and even guess what they carried in them. The ground in my hide-out was smooth and cool, and the wind came in sharp gusts through the cracks between the trunks. According to whether I raised myself up or crouched down I could make the two of them grow short or tall, but I couldn't see their faces; their faces were outside my field of vision.

First I noticed the letter – an express letter, as one could tell from the red-pencil lines forming a cross on the envelope – that the painter held in his hand. He had obviously read it, for now he handed it to my father with a violent, exasperated gesture, tyrannically, furiously, and so I realized that my father, having had to choose – between conveying the contents of the letter in his own words and letting the letter speak for itself – had, as always, decided to do what made the least demands on him. He had got the painter to read it for himself, and now he calmly took it back, took it in those hands of his with the gingery hair on them, and folded it carefully. The painter said: 'You're crazy, Jens, the whole lot of you! You can't do that! Who do you think you are!'

I did not fail to realize that he was speaking of a number of people and simply lumping my father in with them.

'You've got no right to do it,' the painter said, and my father replied: 'I didn't write it, Max, and I don't set up to decide such things,' and he couldn't stop his hands from making a vaguely helpless gesture.

'No,' the painter said, 'of course you don't, you're just doing your best to help them get away with such damned cheek.'

'What do you expect me to do?' my father asked, his voice cool.

'Two years' work,' the painter said; 'do you realize what that means? You people have debarred me from carrying on my vocation – aren't you satisfied with that? What next? You *can't* confiscate pictures that nobody has ever set eyes on! Only Ditte knows them, and Teo, to some extent.'

'You've read the letter,' my father said.

'Yes,' Nansen said, 'I've read it.'

'So then you know the order is to confiscate all the pictures painted in the last two years. I've got to have the lot packed up and delivered to the station in Husum tomorrow.'

They fell silent. Peering sideways through the chink I saw a pair of narrow trouser-legs, round as stove-pipes, step out of the door of the house, and I heard a voice calling: 'Everybody's asking where you've got to! Aren't you coming in?'

The painter and my father called back: 'We're coming, we're just coming!'

That seemed to satisfy the stove-pipes, for they walked stiffly back into the house. After a while I heard my father say: 'Perhaps they'll return the pictures to you some day, Max? Perhaps it's just that the Board want to examine them, and then they'll send them back?'

It even sounded quite plausible, put like that: my father, the Rugbüll policeman, raising this question, mentioning this possibility. It sounded as if he himself really believed what he said. The painter seemed so disconcerted that it took him some time to reply. Then he said in a tone of mingled bitterness and indulgence: 'For God's sake, Jens, won't you ever see they're simply *afraid*? It's fear that drives them to such things: keeping a man from his work, confiscating pictures. Send them back? In an urn, perhaps! The lighted match, Jens, in the service of art criticism – that's their way of evaluating art.'

My father faced him without showing any sign of embarrassment; indeed he even succeeded in conveying impatience, insistence. I had no difficulty in recognizing his mood, and I wasn't surprised when he said: 'It's a decision from Berlin, that's good enough. You've read the letter yourself, Max. It's my duty to request you to be present when the pictures are being examined.'

'Are you going to arrest the pictures?' Nansen asked.

My father's tone was dry and severe: 'We shall establish which of the pictures have to be sequestered. I will put it all down in writing so that they can be fetched tomorrow.'

'I've got to rub my eyes,' the painter said.

'Just go on rubbing,' my father retorted. 'That won't change anything.'

'You people have reached a point where you don't know what you're doing,' the painter said, and my father couldn't stop himself from saying : 'I'm only doing my duty, Max.'

I looked at the painter's hands, strong, experienced hands, and I saw him raise them gently before him, the fingers groping in the air and then clenching in a gesture of finality. My father's hands, however, hung limp by the seam of his trousers, limp, yet ready for action; two obedient creatures, that's what I'd call them; anyway, they refrained from making themselves particularly noticeable.

'Shall we go and get on with it, Max?' he asked.

The painter didn't stir.

'Just to show them I did my duty,' my father said.

'All this won't get the lot of you anywhere!' Nansen burst out. 'Such things don't get anyone anywhere. Go on, take what you're all so frightened of! Confiscate it, cut it up, burn it! The achievement remains.'

'You can't talk to me in that tone of voice,' my father said.

'Oh, I can't, can't I?' Nansen said. 'You'll be amazed at what I can say to you! *You* – if I hadn't pulled you out that time, the fishes would have gobbled you up.'

'A time comes when people are quits,' my father said.

'Now listen to me, Jens,' the painter said, 'there are things a chap can't give up. I didn't give up that time when I jumped in after you. And I'm not going to give up now either. I want you to understand : I'm going on painting. I'll paint pictures that'll be invisible to the likes of you. There'll be so much light in them, you fellows won't see a thing. Invisible pictures.'

Slowly my father raised one hand and fumbled at his belt. Slowly he said : 'I'm warning you, Max. You know what my duty is.'

'Yes, I know,' the painter said. 'And I want you to know : it makes me puke to hear you people talk about duty. When your lot talks about duty, others can look out for trouble.'

My father took a step towards the painter. He pushed both thumbs under his belt and stiffened up. 'I'm asking no questions about the pictures of the gulls – that makes us quits. But from

74

today on, you just watch yourself, Max. That's my advice to
you : you just be careful.'
'I'm ready for you,' said Nansen.
After a while my father said : 'Shall we go, Max?'
'As you like,' Nansen said. 'Let's go then.' But before moving
he added hesitantly: 'But don't you let anybody notice anything, Jens. Least of all Teo.'
The Rugbüll policeman said nothing, which I took to
indicate agreement.

Passing by the slit through which I was looking, they walked,
one behind the other, across the empty, windswept yard. I
could have touched them or given them a fright by gripping
their trousers, but I didn't, I crouched lower and watched them
walking off until I could see them as a whole, and when they
had disappeared into the house I began to examine my hide-out,
measuring it and discovering that there was room for two, for
instance for Jutta and me. Then I slipped out into the open
and, standing alone there by the pond, treated the ducks to a
quick Battle of the Skagerrak by causing ornamental fountains
to rise behind them, in front of them, all around them. I used
various calibre stones, and the water splashed and slopped,
billowed, shot up in slim jets, forcing the ducks to change
formation time and again in order to escape from the bombard-
ment. Finally, before running back into the garden, I opened
up at them with a heavy barrage that made one of the ducklings
lose its head entirely, slip out of the formation, and run across
the water, flapping its wings, right into my line of fire. If it
had stayed with its parents, it wouldn't have suffered a direct
hit.

Anyway, I rushed back into the garden, where Addi was
still playing his accordion. He was now playing the song about
the girl who was determined to join her far-away sailor boy
despite a stormy sea that should have made her think twice,
because that was, as she went on insisting, where she belonged,
as the wind belonged with the waves, and so on and all that.
And to this tune they were dancing on the big lawn – or rather,
there were Hilde Isenbüttel and Plönnies the schoolmaster, but
also the two old Holmsens, hopping and stamping and trampling
about, waltzing and shoving each other round and round,
thoughtfully, tenaciously, in order to get up an appetite for the

dinner that lay ahead of them. I don't remember clearly who all the people were, taking their exercise on the lawn there, neither was I interested in finding out who all the others were – sitting on chairs and benches under drifting shadows – motionless but attentive creatures from the depths of the sea – for at a glance I had espied the two men over there at the far end of the studio, standing at a short distance from one another, the one with his shoulders hunched up, the other with his face lowered. I drew a bead on them through the window-panes. They were alone in the studio, standing there at Doktor Busbeck's birthday table. I put my hands to the sides of my face, very close to the glass, and now, no longer dazzled by the reflections, I saw they were standing in front of the picture on which sails dissolved in the light, and I realized that a fierce struggle for the picture was in process. Challengingly my father stabbed his forefinger at the painting, whereupon the painter put himself squarely in front of it; so it went on, a demanding and a denying, a claiming and a rejecting of the claim – all soundlessly, as though it were going on, very tensely, in the silence of a water-tank. As in an aquarium I saw them arguing, each trying to convince the other – and then all at once the painter picked up a tube of paint, squeezed a short, worm-shaped piece of paint out of it and, bending down to the picture, made an alteration, put the finishing touch to some part of it, using the tip of his finger and finally, as he so often did, the ball of his thumb. Meanwhile my father stood there stiffly, threateningly, like a sea-mark in a dangerous current. The painter straightened up and wiped his fingers clean. I recognized the look on his face – disdain mingled with caution. Now he blinked at my father, who stood there considering the matter and then nodded, apparently finding nothing to object to, at least not for the moment. The painter swiftly took advantage of this, urging my father away from the picture and into a corner that I could not see into from where I stood. I knew how that struggle had ended. I turned round and saw Doktor Busbeck walking arm in arm with Ditte in the shadow of the old apple tree, their own shadows cast upon the tree's shadow, crossing it out.

I was just considering whether I should climb into the living-room through one of the open windows and try to slip into the studio from there, when Addi stopped playing, right in the middle of a tune, and fell to the ground, just the way I had seen him fall once before, kicking and twitching, arching his back and grinding his teeth. I rushed towards him, but Hilke was there at his side before me and, kneeling down beside him, she first of all lifted off his chest the heavy instrument that was lying across him, its bag pulled out and all crooked, like a life-jacket.

'Go away,' she said, 'all of you go away,' she said, but the others came up from all sides, came closer, forming a circle of amazed, stunned and frightened faces, silent, not even nudging one another, merely exchanging glances across Addi, whose face had lost all colour, whose lips were firmly pressed together. They all stood there, craning their necks: the Holmsens, who had been dancing just a while ago, Pastor Treplin, Kohlschmidt, the warden of the bird-sanctuary, and Bultjohann, the dyke-reeve. My grandfather stood there in silence, and so did Plönnies and Captain Andersen. And tall and straight, less stricken than anyone else, in domineering indifference, my mother stood there too, and she looked not at Addi but at Hilke.

There was only one person who squeezed through the circle, softly urging everyone to let him pass, and that was Doktor Busbeck. He didn't wait. He didn't need to ask any questions. He got through, knelt down opposite Hilke, pulled out his handkerchief and mopped the sweat-drenched face. Then Addi opened his eyes and looked around almost cheerfully, obviously without any idea of what had happened.

'Give the lad a bite to eat,' the documentary-film captain exclaimed. Nobody chimed in.

'He's all right now,' Hilke said. 'It's over now.' And with Doktor Busbeck's help Addi struggled to his feet and looked in bewilderment at all the people standing round him. Hilke did the best thing she could: she took his arm and, with a smile, led him away, first of all to the swing and then along the outer, curved path to the summer-house. There was nothing the assembly could do but scatter, though a few of them, in particular Per Arne Schessel, went on staring from under their heavy eyelids at the spot where Addi had lain on the ground. And then I saw Addi picking up my stick close to the summer-house, showing it to Hilke, obviously saying: 'This is Siggi's stick, isn't it?' And I jumped up, throwing my arms into the air and shouting: 'Here, here!' And when he had seen me, Addi threw the stick through the garden, and it fell down right under the swing, and I went and got it.

I wanted to wave to him, but then I didn't because I saw my mother blocking their path, trying to stop them down by the old well, down there by the arbour of lilac trees. I sat down under the swing, unfolded my blue handkerchief, and fixed it to the stick with some of the drawing-pins, and then with my blue banner fluttering I marched back, right into the middle of the birthday celebrations, round and round the benches, tables and chairs and all the people sitting there, smoking and whispering and pensively hissing through their teeth. I let my flag flutter, I threw it high up into the air – though there was nobody in Rugbüll who could have recognized what I was doing and drawn his conclusions from it.

This is as far as I got, I got only to this point, because I have to record that in the very moment when I threw my flag high up into the air, there was a knock at the door of my cell, a very shy, very restrained knock, but still quite distinct enough to bring me right up out of my memories, make me shut my copybook and turn towards the door in irritation. Something was moving on the other side of the spy-hole. Something brown took the place of something white. A glowing button began to rotate. A few arrows of light darted into my room. Involuntarily I got up as the door opened, opened in intolerable slow motion as in a crime film, evenly, with an insistent squeaking, anyway, so very slowly that it boded no good. All that was missing was billowing curtains, and an open book with the draught turning the pages – and since I didn't want to stay away from the birthday party in Bleekenwarf for long, I said politely: 'Come on in, there's a draught.'

He entered quickly, and, taking a step to one side, he left it to Karl Joswig, whom I detected out there in the corridor, to close the door from outside. It was quite obvious he was embarrassed. The corners of his mouth twitched. If I think of the scene now, it seems to me he behaved like a young animal-keeper going into a cage for the first time. Diffidently – rather attractively, really – the young psychologist smiled, taking little dancing steps in one place. He couldn't quite bring off the slight bow he tried to make, because he was too close to the door. He was perhaps three, say five, years older than me, thin-boned, very pale. I liked the way he was dressed, a bit on the sporty side and a bit sloppy. I couldn't understand why he kept his left hand so frantically clenched – perhaps he was holding, let's say, a lump of sugar to put into my mouth, or perhaps it was a weapon. Since I hadn't asked him to pay me a visit, I contented myself with scrutinizing him in silence, that's to say, I looked him up and down with what I hoped was an expression of irritable amazement, challenging him to be brief.

'Herr Jepsen?' he asked amiably, whereupon, after momentary hesitation, I replied with much reserve : 'Granted.'

This retort didn't seem to discourage him at all. Pushing his behind off against the door, he propelled himself into the room, held out a flabby hand and introduced himself : 'Mackenroth, Wolfgang Mackenroth – it's a pleasure to meet you.' He gave me a friendly smile, took off his overcoat, laid it on the table, and, with a familiarity there was nothing to justify, put one hand on my elbow, looked at me confidently, and with a gesture towards my chair sought my permission to make use of it. I shook my head regretfully. No, he couldn't use it. 'In case you don't know,' I said, 'there's work being done here. I'm right in the middle of a punishment task.'

The young psychologist *did* know about it. He knew just what had befallen me, he professed himself full of admiration for my undertaking, went to the lengths of apologizing for disturbing me, and referred to special permission granted by Governor Himpel, for him to make this visit. 'Please, Herr Jepsen,' he said, 'you must help me, please. A lot depends on you.'

I hunched up my shoulders and murmured politely : 'Buzz off, old boy. Who's helping *me*?' And just to show him that I had no time for him, I sat down on the only chair in my cell and began to fool about with my pocket-mirror. My pocket-mirror borrowed light from the electric bulb, caused the beam of light to wander over the stove, the basin, the window, amused itself briefly with the spy-hole, behind which Joswig's eye was keeping watch, embellished the ceiling with a few fleeting garlands of light, and silently cut the cell door into small strips. Since the young psychologist still wouldn't go away, I finally used the beam of light to polish my shoes, in fact I did everything one does when one is alone. I ignored my visitor, I opened my copybook again, and began reading what I had written as a way of returning to the garden at Bleekenwarf.

Wolfgang Mackenroth stayed there. He stayed, observing me attentively and amiably, as if I were some property he'd just acquired, or perhaps rather some property he hadn't quite got the hang of yet and had to find out about. And since his chummy behaviour somehow, quite deplorably, made him seem rather attractive, I asked him if he hadn't come to the wrong door.

'Herr Jepsen,' he said, 'you and I ought to get together', and then he began to initiate me into his intentions.

This young psychologist had to write a thesis in order to get his diploma. This project, which he called his 'Voluntary Punishment Task', was to speed him on in his career. Deftly rolling cigarettes for both of us and then massaging the back of his neck, he came out with his proposal : I was to become the subject of this thesis of his. I was to form part of his thesis, as he put it; I was to be carefully worked up. I was to be given, in scientific terms, a first-class funeral. My whole case, he suggested with amiable irony, was to be elaborated in all its contours, with every climax and anti-climax lovingly delineated, and so forth. He had even hit on the perfect title : Art and Criminality, with particular reference to the case of Siggi J. But if this thesis of his was not only to be a success, but also to receive the attention it deserved – and he would like to stress : that it *deserved* – from the world of science and learning, my collaboration was indispensable. With a friendly wink, he offered me some amusing compensation for the trouble I was to take, namely : there was a very rare type of anxiety, an *anxiety* which in his opinion was the main-spring of all my past actions, which he proposed naming Jepsenophobia, which offered me the prospect of some day finding my name in the psychological dictionaries.

After having in this manner, and with Governor Himpel's special permission, candidly informed me of all his plans, the young scientist remained standing by the table, laid one hand on my shoulder, brought his face down close to mine, and produced a smile of the sort which is perhaps exchanged between accomplices but scarcely, I should have thought, between a psychologist and a juvenile delinquent. This smile flustered me and I couldn't find it in me to give him the total brush-off, particularly since he went on talking to me, murmuring away, explaining to me what he saw as the 'line' of his thesis : what he had in mind was to *defend* me, to *acquit* me, and *set me up*. My stealing of pictures was to be *justified*, he intended recognizing the founding of my private gallery in the old mill as a positive achievement; in general he promised to demonstrate that I was a *borderline case*, and to demand on my behalf that justice should be administered according to as yet non-existent laws. The quiet-voiced, righteous fanaticism with which he put it all before me made him thoroughly plausible. I must confess that among the 1,200 psychologists who at times, all behaving like animal-trainers, turned our island into an out-and-out circus, Wolfgang Mackenroth was the only one I was prepared to confide in, though of course not without reservations.

The only thing about him that I found a bit disturbing was that he knew too much about me. He had read the whole file on me; he had me taped. At first I toyed with the idea of helping him with his Punishment Task and so assuring myself of his help with *my* Punishment Task, especially if he was prepared to look after the cigarette supply, but when I gathered that he was on terms practically of friendship with Governor Himpel I decided to drop that idea. I scrutinized him with care : the pale little face, the slender neck, the delicate hands. I listened critically to the sound of his voice, but in spite of the fact that the longer he stayed, the more, instead of losing in my estimation, he gained, I told him his offer had come as too much of a surprise. Sorry, I said, I must have time to think it over.

'But I may visit you, I hope?' he asked. 'I'm sure you'll permit me to come and see you from time to time, won't you?' I agreed to that, and, to get rid of him, I also nodded to his suggestion that now and then, at irregular intervals, he might hand in to me selected, probably crucial extracts from his thesis. He actually said : 'Hand in.' He thanked me. Hastily, as though afraid I might reconsider my agreement, he put on his overcoat and said : 'I shall not disappoint you, Herr

Jepsen', held out his hand to me as if we were old friends by now, then went to the door and knocked, whereupon Karl Joswig, without exposing himself to my view, opened the door and let the young psychologist out of my cell. I listened to his footsteps as he went off; he was in a hurry.

Since then I have been sitting here at this table that's all covered with notches, trying to return to the birthday party, to grope my way back to it down along the chain of memory, to be living here and to *be* there, there in Bleekenwarf, in the painter's garden, among those solemn sea-animals who were waiting for their dinner. I could get dinner to be served, but I could also, perhaps in honour of Doktor Busbeck, design a great sunset with the reds and yellows engaged in melodramatic dialogue, and finally I dare say I could also describe the air battle that took place at a height of about eight thousand metres that arrested our attention for a few minutes, but all that can't alter the fact that I was the first one to leave the birthday party. It was not of my own free will that I left.

Where was it? Where did she catch me? Was it at the swing, in the arbour, on the wooden bridge? Anyway, I had my blue flag in my hand, and I was in search of something. The wind had dropped. Suddenly there was my mother standing before me, stern, very agitated, trying to get something out, but she couldn't speak, all she could utter was a slight groan, and she bared her yellowish teeth the way she used to do when she was beside herself, when she was hurt and disappointed. She seized my hand. She pressed my hand to her hip. With a jerky movement she turned round, throwing her head back – just as far as she could for her hair in that tight bun secured by a net and hairpins, the whole thing reminiscent of a shiny swelling – and then she pulled me away with her, out of the garden, out of the birthday. That tall, flat-breasted woman with her terrifying, frenzied stride rushed along ahead of me, pulling me after her across the lawn, past the studio, across the yard, still without uttering a single word, heedlessly past documentary-film captain Andersen, who had merely called out to us that there would soon be something to eat. With me in tow she pushed open the swinging wooden gate and went rushing along the long avenue of alders towards the dyke, which we climbed, bending low, and which we left behind us, stumbling down the other side towards the sea, without a single glance back towards Bleekenwarf.

Viewed from the middle distance, I should imagine Gudrun Jepsen must have appeared more or less like a mother who, in convincing despair, is about to walk into the North Sea together with her son. I was already wondering what I ought to do, how great my obligation was to accompany Mother through the breakers and obediently to go down with her by the buoy marking the wreck, when she once more changed direction and walked along below the dyke, now invisible to anyone who might have looked out for us from Bleekenwarf. She let go of my hand. She ordered me to walk ahead. Without turning round I asked her why we had left the birthday party so suddenly. I got no answer. Then I asked if Father had also left or was just going to leave, but she only snorted and remained silent. She remained silent until we reached the lighthouse with its red-hooded occulting light, and then she said: 'Quick, come on, quick, I've got to take a sedative, I've got to lie down.'

Then she overtook me and sped on without taking any notice of whether or not I was able to keep up with her. But I stayed close behind her, rushed up the steps side by side with her, and entered the kitchen with her. There she instantly reached out towards the shiny containers for rice, semolina, flour, sago, and barley, standing there in a painstakingly straight row and containing practically everything except what the gold-bordered lettering on them said they contained. She turned one of them upside down, and from among a heap of tubes, tins, and boxes she fished out a little paper bag, tipped its contents into a glass of water and, sitting down, drank it off, her eyes closed. I stood there beside her in the condition of frightened obedience to which she had reduced me, and watched her with interest, reproachfully: the pointed chin, the gingery eyelashes, the nostrils, the twisted lips. I didn't dare to touch her. My mother supported herself with her hands on the edge of the bench. She stretched her body. For a moment she held her breath. I asked if the sedative was making her feel better yet, and a moment later if I might go back to the birthday party in Bleekenwarf, and when she didn't answer I asked why we had had to hurry so much on our way along under the dyke. Now she looked at me with her eyes narrowed, stood up, and told me to come with her.

We went upstairs, past my room, up into the loft, and opened the door to the attic where Addi was staying. There was his cardboard suitcase. On the window-sill his razor gleamed. There was a pullover, too. Under the little stool there were new canvas shoes, waiting for fine weather. A peaked cap, a scarf, a stack of handkerchiefs, lay on the chest of drawers, and on the pillow there was a book : *We Took Narvik*.

'Pack it, all of it,' my mother said. When I didn't stir, she repeated : 'Come on, pack it all in the suitcase.' And a third time she had to tell me to put Addi's stuff into the cardboard case, and when now I did as I was told, under her watchful eye, she said quietly : 'We mustn't forget anything, he must take everything with him, everything.' She handed me a cheap camera that had evidently never been used, and said : 'Put it among the socks.' She herself folded a tie and laid it between the shirts. We folded, pushed, pressed and filled the suitcase until there wasn't anything left in the attic to remind one of Addi, except for his case. And when Gudrun Jepsen lifted the suitcase and carried it outside, nobody could have failed to see the revulsion that made her hand grow rigid. What did I make of it all? At first I thought she meant to give Addi a better room, and I began to hope he would be allowed to share my room with me. But we went down to the entrance hall and there, next to my father's office, she dropped the suitcase from knee height, pushed it against the wall, and brushed her hands.

'Is he going away?' I asked. And she said, now quite calm : 'He has no business to be here, so he is leaving. I have spoken to him.'

'Why?' I asked. 'Does he have to go away?'

'You wouldn't understand,' my mother said, and she gazed out of the window across the flat country towards Bleekenwarf. Then suddenly, without stirring or raising her voice, she said : 'We don't want any such people in this family.'

'Is Hilke going away, too?' I asked, to which my mother replied : 'That remains to be seen. We shall soon see which bonds' – she actually said 'bonds' – 'are the stronger.'

I only had to look at her stern, reddish face to know this was the end of the birthday party. Anyway, she certainly would not let me go back to Bleekenwarf. So I just nodded when she gave me a sausage sandwich and sent me to bed. I blacked out my window. I undressed and put my clothes on the chair next to my bed the way she had taught me : the trousers neat and smooth, on top of them the pullover folded into a square, on top of the pullover my shirt, carefully folded so that edge came to lie on edge, and then, likewise carefully folded, my undershirt. In the morning I would pick the clothes up in reverse order and put them on again. I strained my ears. All was quiet in the house.

5   Hiding-Places

But I must describe the morning. Even if we find a new meaning with every memory, I must produce a slow dawn now,
where an irresistible yellow has it out with greys and browns, I
must introduce a summer with an illimitable horizon, and with
canals, and peewits flying, I must streak the sky with vapour-
trails, and make audible the resounding chug of a cutter beyond
the dyke. In order to bring back that particular morning I must
distribute the trees and hedges and low-roofed farmsteads from
which no pillar of smoke rises, and with a loose wrist scatter
black-and-white speckled cattle on the pastures. It was a morning
like that when I woke, and I couldn't help waking because of a
tapping and pecking at my window; there it was, returning
again and again, increasingly impatient. For a while I went
on lying in bed, just listening to the faint beating on the glass:
wrens, I thought. Then there was a patter of rain, a rain of
sand. The tiny grains hit the window-pane hard. I sat up in
bed to watch the window; in spite of having been hit so often
the glass wasn't cracked yet. And then, after yet a few more
scattering hits, which I could only hear but couldn't see the
cause of, I saw a jet of sand that came flying, to hit the pane
with a patter and a slap, and I jumped out of bed and rushed
to the window, gazed out into the early morning, the windless
morning. Since there was nothing moving in the middle distance
or in the far distance, the brief movement in the foregound
caught the eye at once: the movement of an arm rising up,
challenging attention down there in the shade between the saw-
horse and the scored woodblock, and it took me only a moment

to recognize my brother Klaas, or perhaps I should say to recognize him as he stood there in spite of his uniform and the clumsy white bandage. After all, nobody could have expected him to turn up here at the crack of dawn without letting us know beforehand. For all we had been told after his self-inflicted wound was that he was being treated in a military prison-hospital in Hamburg, and none of us could get permission to visit him. Nobody ever mentioned him and I'm quite sure that two postcards he sent from the hospital were never answered.

Klaas came out of the shed, waved to me, and then went back in. I rushed to my bed and then to the door, listening, then again to the bed to put on my shirt and trousers. Before I went out into the passage I made a sign to him from the window. There was no sound in the passage. They were still asleep. In their long, rough nightshirts they slept, under their heavy feather quilts, on the crude, grey, home-woven sheets, and above them, out of the only two pictures on the wall, Theodor Storm and Lettow-Vorbeck eyed each other with an everlasting suspicious glare that neither the writer from Husum nor the general seemed prepared to give up. Crouching low against the wall, I tiptoed past their door and sideways down the stairs, past the Rugbüll policeman's outer shell hanging from the coat-rack in the entrance hall. The stillness of the house was incredible! How cool the key was! I turned it slowly, I felt the movement of the spring, and I was able to turn it all the way without a sound, but then the door creaked as it opened and I expected my father to appear up there on the landing and I imagined what would happen then; but all stayed quiet. I slipped out, shut the door carefully, and skidded across the yard into the shed. There indeed, squatting on the ground, was my brother Klaas, with his round face and his bright eyes and his short, fair, tangled hair. He was resting his bandaged arm on the woodblock. His uniform blouse was open at the neck. There my brother squatted in mortal fear, and that fear both made it unnecessary to ask any questions and admitted everything: how he had broken out of the military prison-hospital, the detours he had made avoiding the military police and patrols, the long, long walking by night, the long waiting under cover, and the running, bent low to the ground, until he

87

got here in the end – his fear told the whole story.

He didn't utter so much as a word of greeting, simply grabbed me by my shirt and pulled me down beside him, next to the woodblock, and from that position we watched the bedroom window, that is, he watched it all the time, while I observed his tired, blank face, the mud-covered uniform and the clumsy plaster dressing on which somebody, probably he himself, had stubbed out a cigarette. Very likely he thought they had heard me leave the house and, after discovering my empty bed, would look out of the window for me. But after a while, when no curtain moved and no shadow appeared, he held me down where I was and, sighing, sat down beside me, his legs apart, his back supported by the wall of the shed. His legs trembled and he shivered with fatigue. The gingery stubble on his chin glistened. Where's his cap? I thought, and not being able to find it, I imagined a jump, a jump from a moving goods train or over a ditch, and so he had lost it. Cautiously I shifted forward on the ground. I pulled myself up on my knees and peered into his face, until he opened his eyes and said: 'You have to hide me, Siggi.'

I told him to get up, and he clung to me, swaying, he almost crumpled up and fell to the ground, but then he got a hold on himself, he smiled hesitantly and asked: 'You've got a good hiding-place, haven't you?' 'Yes,' I said, and from that moment on he did just as I told him, he even agreed to my leaving the shed and making sure the coast was clear. And that wasn't all: he kept his eyes fixed on me, ready to do whatever I told him to do, or to follow my example in whatever I did. I ran to the old box-cart and crouched down. He ran to the old box-cart and crouched down. I jumped over the brick path and slid down the slope. He jumped over the brick path and slid down the slope. I climbed up on to the lock, he followed me up on to the lock. I said: 'We've got to cross the meadow and get into the rushes,' and he just said: 'Into the rushes, right.'

He didn't ask where we were making for, or how far it was; he followed me without curiosity or impatience, and I ploughed a way through the rushes with my arms held out straight in front of me, hands clasped, to make a wedge, keeping going in the direction of the old mill-pond and the dilapidated windmill without any sails for the wind to turn. The marshy ground was springy. Here and there the matted surface gave way under-foot and peat-brown water gurgled up into the holes. We raised some wild duck. I saw eyes everywhere. Behind us the rushes rose up again, rustling. The wild ducks flew in a loop and settled down again behind us. In the green half-light I felt as though I were walking along the bottom of the sea, through limply waving forests of seaweed, through a lowering silence. Then the belt of rushes grew thinner, before us lay the mill-pond and on the far side of it, on its rusty post, the mill.

'Here?' my brother asked. I nodded and, after looking out in all directions to see if we were safe, I climbed over the wooden fence and ran up the firm path leading to the mill.

How am I to introduce my favourite mill? There it stood on its artificial hillock, looking – despite having no sails – expectantly towards the west. Its onion-shaped top was roofed with slate, the octagonal weather-boarded tower had twice been struck by lightning. In the high-set, deep, white-framed windows all the panes were broken. The wooden structure that had once carried the sails lay broken up and rotting in the grass on the eastern side, among useless old millstones, spokeless wheels, and horseshoes. Until I had levelled the ground and repaired the hinges it had been impossible to shut the splintered door. Rain, wind, and age had caused the platform to collapse. It was draughty inside my mill, there was a ceaseless creaking, whistling and rattling, and when the wind turned from west to east a rumbling noise started up in the movable cap, and a pulley, for which there was no load, came squeaking down from on high. Broken glass splintered underfoot, bats, looking like pieces of cardboard, flittered soundlessly to and fro, and the loose metal skin clattered at the slightest touch. Dishevelled, knocked about, come-down-in-the-world, littered with heaps of dried excrement, my mill had been left to its fate, and there it stood, black and useless, in the direct line of vision between Rugbüll and Bleekenwarf, and if it still served any purpose at all, it was to arouse our amazement at its still standing there, weathering every hurricane in spring and all the autumn gales.

But we mustn't linger outside for a long time, even if a lot more could be said about the mill's outer appearance – for instance about its mirror-reflection in the pond and about the initials, the arrows and hearts carved in the door. We haven't got time for sight-seeing. Crouching low we have to get up the beaten clay path past the collapsed platform, past the entrance that's cut so deep into the artificial hillock. As for Klaas, I should imagine that at first he noticed little more about my mill than that it was there, towering black and rigid, and there was no need for him to notice more, since he relied entirely on me; he walked behind me, breathing heavily, his bandaged arm pressed to his body, his head so bowed that he can only just about have seen my bare legs.

I pulled the door open, waited for him to catch up with me, pushed him into the cool stair-well and shut the door. We stood there in silence. We listened to make sure there was no sound above. There was nothing but the chugging of the cutter, echoing away in the distance beyond the dyke. There wasn't even the faint sound of scampering mice, although at other times that could always be heard when one entered the mill. Sharp, thin rays of light filtered in through the cracks and trembled in the semi-darkness. I mustn't forget to mention the draught and the swaying of the wooden stairs. But perhaps I only imagined the stairs swayed, My brother groped for my hand and asked :

'Here?'

And I said : 'Upstairs. My room's upstairs.'

I guided him upstairs to where the grain was ground, and there I set up a ladder that I kept hidden behind the old flour-boxes. We climbed up, squeezed through a hatch, pulled the ladder up after us, set it up again, and so reached a room almost directly under the movable cap; I am going to call it – *my* room. Klaas shoved me aside and climbed in first. He instantly discovered the bed of rushes and sacks by the window, but he didn't lie down, he didn't even sit down on the orange-box, though the climbing had used up the last of his strength. There he stood, smiling, marvelling, gazing at all the pictures. He passed his hand over his matted hair, and very lightly he rubbed his eyes, but that didn't diminish the number of pictures or change them in any way.

Most of the pictures I had put up there, on all the walls of that hide-out of mine in the mill, were pictures of horsemen. Shortly after Doktor Busbeck's sixtieth birthday I had begun cutting pictures of horsemen out of calendars, magazines and books, and I had begun by gluing them over the cracks, and later I had gone on to do all the walls with them. There were Napoleon's cuirassiers cantering out of the wall, there was the Emperor Charles V riding over the battlefield of Muhlberg, Prince Youssupov in Tartar costume on a fiery Arab stallion, and on a small Andalusian grey there was Queen Isabella of Bourbon trotting into a sad sunset. There were dragoons, circus-riders, mounted chasseurs and knights in armour, and they all rode in different ways and eyed each other critically, and anyone with any imagination could have heard the beating of horses' hooves – and the whinneying and neighing.

'What's going on here?' my brother asked.

'An exhibition,' I replied. 'There's an exhibition on.'

Klaas nodded, at once amused and in misery. He dragged himself to the bed and let himself fall on to it, and I sat down by the head of the bed and looked at my pictures and then at him. His eyes were closed and he seemed to be listening to something that was pursuing him even to this place, and would not let him find rest. He could not relax, he could not stretch out comfortably. He was all the time on the alert, looking out for cover, tensing his muscles for a jump, hiding the clumsy dressing as best he could.

I put a hand on his chest, and he twitched. I wiped the sweat from his face, and he started up. It was only when I had lit a cigarette for him that he calmed down and lifted both his legs on to the bed of rushes and sacks, which was a bit too short for him.

'How do you like my hide-out?' I asked.

My brother looked at me long and hard and then said: 'If you tell anyone, I'll be done for. Nobody must know anything about it, least of all – them at home. It's a good hiding-place.'

'Nobody's ever been here,' I said.

'Good,' he said. 'Nobody must know I'm here.'

'But Father,' I said, 'surely we can tell Father. He'll help you.'

Thoughtfully, almost threateningly, he said: 'If you tell him, Siggi, I'll kill you, I'll do you in. Understand?'

He looked at me out of narrowed bright eyes, and he seemed to be expecting something of me. Suddenly he caught hold of me, pulled me down beside the bed and pressed me to the floor with all the weight of his fear, and it was only when I realized what he expected of me and promised him everything, that he let go and fell back on the bed, exhausted but satisfied. Then he told me to pull a piece of cardboard out of the frame of the broken window.

Our faces almost touched as we looked out over the flat country lying there in the morning sun, observing it together with a searching gaze, right down to the bend in the dyke and to the occulting lighthouse with its red cap. We recognized the car at the same moment. It came bowling along the Husum road, and a burst of reflected sunlight flashed on the wind-screen : a dark green car moving along slowly beside the mirroring ditches, then suddenly turning on to the brick path leading to Rugbüll, now moving slower still, but not stopping, and then disappearing behind the dishevelled hedges of Holmsenwarf. It appeared again just when I had given up expecting it, and again dazzling light was thrown back from the windscreen. Cows came ambling along to the wire fence as though to wait there for the car, but then, taking fright at the last moment, jerkily they turned their clumsy bodies aside as the car bowled soundlessly by and finally came to a halt under the sign saying 'Rugbüll Police Station', Then a window was rolled down and a head appeared, a shiny leather shoulder. If the man leaning out of the window was merely trying to make out what the rain-bleached, twice repainted notice-board said, it took him a very long time.

My brother gripped my arm, pressing it tight in uncontrollable excitement as the door of the car flew open and four men in leather coats climbed out and of one accord moved towards our house, skilfully closing in on it in that well-known manner of theirs : four men, all wearing the same coats and the same hats, all with their hands in their pockets. I should say they were all trained in raiding, in moving without drawing any attention to themselves. One of them vaulted effortlessly over the garden fence.

Today I understand why, without looking at me, without lessening the pressure on my arm, Klaas suddenly said : 'Beat it, kid ! Run home, quick !'

I also understand why he didn't give me time to ask even

one question, but pushed me towards the hatch, urgently, inexorably.

'Beat it,' was all he said. Only afterwards, when I had reached the bottom of the ladder, he called out again:

'Food! When you come back, bring something to eat!'

Since I had always been in the habit of obeying my brother Klaas, I'd gone down the ladder as he had told me to, and now I hid it behind the flour-boxes, and, doing as he had told me to, I jumped down the ramp, ploughed my way through the rushes, ran to the lock and then, crouching low, along the bank of the ditch. At the old box-cart I straightened up and behaved as though I hadn't a care in the world. Now nobody could prove I'd been any distance away from the house. I sauntered to the car, which was still there, under the sign, walked round it, and peered inquisitively at the speedometer to see what the top speed was, and then I pressed the button of the horn once. That brought a short, burly fellow in a leather coat rushing out of the house, and he seized me by the scruff of my neck. Where was I from? What was I up to out here so early in the morning? To answer all his questions at once, I told him my name and, pointing at the window of my room, I said: 'I live up there.' The burly man still wouldn't trust me, he held me by the collar of my shirt and led me into the house, into my father's office.

There they all sat. The three men in leather coats sat with the light behind them, and facing them, dressed only in his undershirt and trousers, his braces twisted on his shoulders, unshaven, unwashed, unkempt, in short, there, before the rigid silhouettes of the leather-coated men, sat an embarrassed man, the Rugbüll policeman, obviously just drummed out of his sleep and looking to me as though he were at least ninety-five years old. When he was asked if I belonged here, if I was his son, he looked at me for a long time and really seemed to find it difficult to recognize me, but, thank heaven, when the question was repeated, he nodded – faintly, but he did nod, and so the pulling at my shirt collar stopped. The short burly fellow let go of me, went up to my father and, clasping his hands behind his back and swaying to and fro on his thick rubber soles, blinked his goggling eyes at the framed proverb hanging on the wall behind my father's desk: 'Early to bed, early to rise. . . .'

Since nobody sent me away, I had a quick glance around the office, which my father never let me enter, but there was nothing of any interest to me – except perhaps a rack with four rubber stamps in it, and the sword-knot from a policeman's sabre, which shone with a dull silvery gleam. My father just sat there, sleepy and resigned, as though he had no say at all in the matter, his hands flat on his thighs, his back rigid against the back of the chair, his chin pulled in, his lips parted. He couldn't conceal the fact that he was thinking about something, at the same time observing out of the corner of his eyes the short, burly fellow, who now, with offensive slowness, was scrutinizing the photographs that covered the entire wall behind the desk.

What was it these photographs told of? They told of Glüserup and of a dark and poky shop in which a certain Peter Paul Jepsen sold fresh fish. They informed you that to the self-same fishmonger Jepsen five children were born, of whom one, a thin little boy who time and again looked at the photographer with the same look of sober suspicion, showed a striking similarity to the Rugbüll policeman. Some of the photographs gave an account of a crab-catching competition between two families, and others presented the Glüserup children's choir, as it were right in the middle of a song, their mouths wide open for all eternity. Others showed the schoolboy Jens Ole Jepsen wearing a gigantic dunce's-cap, and going to his Confirmation, and again as left full-back of the Glüserup football team. An oval photograph made it known that once there had been a young gunner Jepsen, showing him kneeling by a light howitzer as before an altar, and the same gunner, wearing a greatcoat, was shown in Galicia, together with other gunners, singing to a Christmas tree. Stretched out obliquely in front of a moustachioed team of athletes there sprawled police-cadet Jens Ole Jepsen, while in the background Hamburgian redbrick barracks rose up threateningly. And then one Gudrun Schessel entered the picture, and the photographs indicated her preference for white dresses and white stockings, at the same time bearing witness to the awe-inspiring length of her reddish-fair pigtails, dangling right down to her behind. They also announced the fact that she could read, since every photograph showed her with a book in her hand. That Jens Ole Jepsen and Gudrun Schessel were one day united in wedlock was demon-

94

strated by yet another photograph, on which a goggle-eyed wedding party was to be seen, standing to attention, or in any case stiffly, glasses in their raised hands, round the couple, clearly drinking, in a well-disciplined fashion, to their health. Some more photographs bore witness to the fact that the couple once made a journey to Berlin, and a trip from Bingen to Cologne on a Rhine steamer, and finally one picture proclaimed that three children were born to the couple. Hilke and Klaas could be clearly recognized on it, and the hairless monster in a high-wheeled pram couldn't be anyone but myself.

The burly fellow in the leather coat took his time looking at the photographs, and meanwhile my father just sat there resignedly and didn't even stir when the visitor picked up the duty-book, glancing at the last entries made in it in a copperplate hand. The three others merely sat there, motionless silhouettes; one of them smoked all the time, without taking the cigarette out of his mouth. Anything they had to say to each other they had evidently said by now. I backed into the corner, waiting for something to happen, but there all at once was my mother, slipping in soundlessly, beckoning to me briefly, and then grabbing me and pulling me out of the office, into the kitchen, where my breakfast was on the small table waiting for me : thick porridge, sugared, and a slice of bread with rhubarb-jam on it.

'Eat up,' she said dully. I ate, with her watching me, and I noticed she was listening all the time to what was going on in the office.

I said : 'They're looking for something,' and she replied : 'Be quiet, just you eat.'

'They're from Husum, I'm sure,' I said, and she replied : 'Nobody asked you.'

Then she shut the kitchen door, poured herself a cup of tea and drank it standing up. I asked :

'Are they going to take Father with them in their car?'

She shrugged her shoulders. 'I don't know,' she said slowly, put her cup down and went out into the passage.

I looked out across towards the mill, where Klaas was lying on the bed waiting for me, and then I opened the warped door to the larder : a jar full of pickled gherkins, half a loaf of bread, salted meat, onions, a bowl of unsweetened rhubarb-

95

jam, a piece of margarine, a sausage, four fresh eggs, a bag of flour and a sack of oats, that was all I could see. I licked the rhubarb off my slice of bread, broke it in half, and put it in my pocket. Now I could hear voices in the office. It was the burly fellow talking, and then the others made some remarks, only my father remaining silent. Then my mother hurried back into the kitchen, hastily picked up her cup and raised it to her mouth. The next moment the men came out of the office into the passage, and each one of them shook hands with the Rugbüll policeman, and after that they stared at us and wished us 'Good appetite' and all the rest, before leaving the house. They didn't go straight to their car, but each of them went in a different direction, surveying the landscape, checking the ditches, meadows and hedges right down to the dyke, looking at everything with a trained eye. But nothing moved, there was nothing standing, lying or crouching anywhere, that might have aroused their suspicion. One of them searched the shed, another inspected the lock. They checked the rotten old box-cart, and the burly fellow fetched a field-glass from the car and looked for a long time towards the ponds where the peat was cut. They looked disgruntled as they returned to their car. They drove away, frustrated.

My father stood on the steps, watching them drive off slowly, along the ditches; he stood there until the car went uphill towards the main road to Husum. Then he came back into the house and sat down, just as he was, at the kitchen table, putting his hands on it, one on top of the other. There he sat in his coarse undershirt, his braces twisted, sat there stiffly, his eyes watering, grinding his denture with a faint creak, ignoring the cup of tea that my mother pushed in front of him, ignoring me too – though certainly not out of absentmindedness: his face showed clearly that he'd grasped not only the reason for but also the consequences of that early morning visit. He was working it all out. He weighed and considered, he rejected it and weighed it anew. His eyebrows moved. He breathed heavily. Then suddenly he raised his right hand and, letting it drop back limply on to the table, he said to my mother :

'He may turn up on the doorstep any minute.'

'Are they searching for him already?' my mother asked, and he replied : 'The hospital for military prisoners, that's where he got away from. They're searching for him everywhere.'

'When did he get away?' my mother asked.

'Yesterday,' he said. 'Yesterday evening. He's messed it all up for himself, has Klaas. I made inquiries, he'd have got off with stockade or being put into a delinquent battalion – now he hasn't got a chance.'

'Why,' my mother asked, 'why did he do it?'

'Ask him yourself,' my father said. 'Any minute there'll be a knock at the door, and there he'll be in front of you. Then you can ask him.'

'He won't come here,' she said. 'Not after all he's brought on us. Surely he won't dare to turn up here.'

'He'll turn up all right,' my father said. 'Here it all began, and here too it'll all come to an end for him. He'll run straight into their arms.'

'You're not thinking of warning him?' she asked. 'Or even of hiding him, if he turns up here?'

'I don't know,' my father said. 'I don't know what to do.'

'I hope you know,' she said, 'what's expected of you.'

She laid the table for him, fetched the bread, the margarine and the brown bowl of rhubarb-jam, put it all in front of him and seemed satisfied when she had performed that unpleasant duty. She poured herself a cup of tea, but she didn't sit down. She rested her back against the kitchen cupboard and said: '*I* don't wish to have anything to do with him. I've finished with Klaas, and if he turns up here, I don't wish to see him.'

My father scrutinized the breakfast without touching it. 'That's not the way you used to talk about him,' he said. 'Besides, he's wounded.'

'Mutilated,' my mother said, 'not wounded, *mutilated*, and he did it himself.'

'Yes,' my father said. 'Yes – self-mutilation, but it takes something to do that.'

'Being afraid is what it takes – afraid, that's all.'

'Klaas was always a cut above the rest of us,' my father said. 'The boy had better prospects than I ever had.'

'We did our best for him,' my mother said, 'we always did our best for him. And what did he do? If he's a cut above us, he could have worked out for himself where it would lead him. Couldn't he? Now it's too late.'

My father didn't eat or drink anything. He passed his hand over his thin hair, and once he touched his left shoulder, as though the old pain had returned.

'Well, he hasn't come yet,' he said, 'and there's no knowing if he'll get through at all. And *if* he gets through I know what I've got to do,' my father said, and there was a touch of cautious reproach in his voice. He turned his unshaven face towards my mother, with a slow, appraising gaze. 'What has to be done is going to be done. You don't have to worry.'

He got up and went towards her, holding out his hand. But she didn't wait for him to touch her. Hastily she put her cup down, retreated before him, walking backwards round the table to the door and, without speaking another word, went upstairs, probably to lock herself into the bedroom.

My father shrugged his shoulders. He let his braces slip down, went to the sink, took brush and soap from a small corner-shelf, and, standing with his legs slightly apart, began to lather his face, all the time keeping his eyes fixed on me.

'I suppose you heard,' he said suddenly. 'Klaas has bolted. Quite likely he'll turn up here.'

I put rhubarb-jam on my porridge and said nothing.

'He's bound to come here,' my father said. 'All at once there he'll be, asking for all sorts of things. He'll want food, he'll need a hiding-place. Don't you go and do anything without letting me know. Anyone who helps him is liable to be punished, and that goes for you too.'

'What'll they do to him,' I asked, 'if they get him?'

My father flicked some lather from his fingers as though it were snot and simply said: 'He'll get what's coming to him.'

Then he picked up his razor, pulled a face and began to shave, from the ear down, pursing his lips as though he were about to produce a long-drawn whistling note. I went on eating my porridge rather absentmindedly, spending a lot of time spooning it up, messing around with the greyish-white mush until my father had finished shaving. Even now he would not eat or drink. He cleaned his razor, hitched up his braces, all much too slowly and thoughtfully, groped for a button that had come off a long time ago, blew his nose, spent some time gazing meditatively into his handkerchief, and then went to the window, to stand there, looking doggedly out in the direction of the main road to Husum. But there was nothing going on out there, only the sun shining, softening up the asphalt.

When, at long last, after some more delaying actions, such as polishing his shoes, cleaning his pipe and winding up the alarm clock, he left the kitchen and jogged along to his office, I drank the tea that had been meant for him, put the bread, the margarine and the bowl of stringy greenish-reddish rhubarb-jam back in the larder, everything in its place, and then listened. There didn't seem to be anyone about, so I cut a few thick slices off the loaf and pushed them inside my shirt, followed by a piece of sausage and two eggs, all of which made my shirt bulge over the belt. Gently I pushed the stuff round to my back, so that I could feel the cool eggs and the crumbly bread on my spine. The sausage I took out again and stuffed into my pocket. I also cut a slice of the pale salted meat and let it slide towards my spine. The shirt now stood out at the back above my trousers like a natural, very low-slung rucksack, but I still didn't think I had enough. Apples – I remembered the Gravenstein apples on top of the wardrobe in my room, and I decided to put a few of them into my shirt as well. I left the kitchen and climbed the stairs, the eggs, the bread and the meat dangling inside my shirt, touching me, making me sticky at every step. I walked close to the wall and got up stairs and passed the hostile bedroom without being noticed. I opened the door to my room and got a fright: there my mother was, lying in my bed, her eyes open. She hadn't gone to her bedroom as I had thought she would, to stand there behind the curtain, her lips twisted in a haughty expression, gazing out to the dyke, the horizon, or the gleaming ponds, as though they could give her some consolation. There she was, lying in my bed, doubled up, covered up to her chest, her white arms, with the freckles and moles, lying limply on the bedclothes. This sight, which in days to come practically ceased to have any effect on me, since it occurred too often, that day simply made me incapable of moving a limb. There I stood, just staring at her. I didn't even wonder what it meant, finding my mother lying there in my bed. Her hair was spread out over the pillow. Her body, which had always seemed flat, now, under the bed-clothes, seemed lumpy. Did she mean to drive me from my room? Did she mean to move in herself? The way she was lying there, she suddenly reminded me of my sister Hilke.

There was no explanation to be read in her open eyes, and she didn't apologize to me either. With an ominously damp, cool feeling up my spine, I considered how to withdraw from her field of vision. Slinking backwards, the way cats withdraw from a hostile sphere of influence, I was trying to extricate myself, groping for the door-handle, already standing on the threshold, when she said: 'Come here, come right over here to me.' I did as I was told. 'Turn round,' she said. I did so, pulling in my behind, actually believing she might overlook the bulge in the back of my shirt. But then she said: 'Unpack,' so I let the food slide forward towards my navel, put my hand into the opening of my shirt, pulled out one thing after the other and put it on the floor: the bread, the eggs, the pale slice of salted meat. I was prepared for every kind of question, and I would have told about my hiding-place, not the one in the mill but the one on the peninsula, in the bird-sanctuary warden's hut, and in my own way I would have expounded the need to store food for bad times to come. But my mother didn't want to hear anything. She merely said:

'Put it all back in the larder.'

She didn't say it threateningly or ominously, or even as if she were disappointed. Her voice sounded like that of an ill person as she ordered me to put it all back where it belonged, and I looked at her for a long time in amazement, waiting, waiting for the punishment that was bound to follow. But my fear was at fault. All at once my mother actually smiled and nodded to me encouragingly. So I pulled my shirt out of my trousers, gathered everything together and took it all down to the larder.

What had happened to her? Why didn't she punish me? Why didn't she lock me in? I put the eggs to the other eggs, the meat to the meat and the sausage to the sausages. All I kept was the broken slice of bread in my pocket, and I gave it a few blows with my flat hand, so that it no longer bulged under the material of my trousers.

From the kitchen window I watched the mill, searching and again searching the small round window for a signal, while my father in his office at the back began making telephone calls after his own fashion, shouting brief statements into the receiver and always repeating the last word a number of times. He simply wasn't capable of using the telephone without making an uproar, and I expected my mother to come downstairs, as she had done so often, and shut the office door – which by no means made his telephone conversations unintelligible but did at least make them tolerable. But upstairs all remained silent. There was nothing noticeable at the mill's small round window, behind which Klaas lay hidden, waiting for me.

'Papers from Husum to hand!' my father roared.

I imagined my brother asleep on his bed of rushes and sacks, on the alert even in his sleep, crouching in that light sleep of his, as though ready to jump.

'No unusual occurrences to report,' my father yelled. 'No incidents.'

I wondered which way to go this time, to arrive at my mill unnoticed, and in my thoughts I went along the ditches, scrutinizing the dykes and deploring the lack of a subterranean passage, and while I worked out a roundabout way, I recognized Okko Brodersen with his mail-bag, coming from the direction of Holmsenwarf. Our postman swayed on his bicycle. His scratched leather bag seemed to disturb his balance.

'Report follows forthwith,' my father roared.

Okko Brodersen came towards our house, rode clattering over the little plank bridge, tried to ram the post with the police station sign on it, missed it by a hair's breadth, approached the house, muttering to himself in a disgruntled way, and finally, with a bold swerve, came to a stop by our steps. Cursing, he dismounted, and the empty sleeve of his uniform jacket twitched and jerked as though charged with electricity. He pulled his bag to his belly, climbed the steps and, without knocking, simply came into the house and into the kitchen, wishing everybody present a disgruntled good morning. Then Okko Brodersen sat down at the kitchen table, pulled out his pocket-watch and put it down in front of him. He regarded his watch calmly, and he seemed satisfied with it, for he nodded. But when I tried to cast a glance at it, he stopped me, pushing a picture-postcard at me, saying: 'Read it, if you can read. Hilke's coming back. Your sister intends to come home for ever.'

'Shall be dealt with forthwith,' my father shouted in his office.

'You can go and meet her at the station on Sunday,' the postman said, whereupon he began to contemplate his pocket-watch again, at once excited and content – something he always did as soon as he had sat down, which sometimes made me think that perhaps his watch showed some different time and divided the day differently from the way other watches did, and that his purpose simply was to grasp that difference.

The one-armed old postman did not take any interest in my father's shouting over there in the office. Puffing, absorbed in contemplating his watch, he waited until my father put down the receiver and came into the kitchen. Then he stood up and the two men shook hands, calling each other by their first names in questioning voices.

'Jens?'

'Okko?'

The postman took the picture-postcard from me and handed it to my father, together with the newspaper. Then he sat down again. He looked round the kitchen, in search of something.

'Tea?' my father asked. 'Like a cup of tea?'

'That's it,' the postman said. 'That's what I need – a cup of tea.'

And then they drank, taking it in turn to praise the dark, strongly sweet tea, watching one another over the edge of their cups while they drank. That was all they did, and yet they did more than that, if one considers that secretly they were all the time waiting for a suitable moment for a beginning, for an unassuming beginning to what they wanted to say to each other. For there is one rule that's always observed among us : one always begins speaking about the things one wishes to say in a flat voice as if one were mentioning it just incidentally.

That's why I can't let Okko Brodersen come to the point instantly, since that wouldn't at all be like him, I've got to wait for the proper moment, I've got to mention the intro-ductory conversation the two men had with one another and the amazing courage with which they braved the long pauses there at the kitchen table, I've got to put up with their talk about diving aeroplanes and bicycle-tubes, and with their de-tailed inquiries about every member of their families, and I mustn't forget their slow but calculating gestures. Brodersen's empty sleeve swept across the table, my father bent and folded the pages of the newspaper, Brodersen gazed at his watch, while telling of the difficulties in getting hold of bicycle-tubes. In between, the Rugbüll policeman time and again raised his head as though hearing suspicious sounds somewhere in the house.

In this manner they approached each other, each preparing the other slowly and laboriously, until in the end the old postman thought himself justified in speaking openly about the matter that still detained him in our kitchen. He said :

'You ought to leave him in peace, Jens.'

My father, who seemed to have been waiting for precisely this, replied :

'Now you're at it too, talking just like old Holmsen, who looked in last night and couldn't say anything to me but leave him alone. And what in particular, I ask you, has happened up to now? The prohibition to paint was worked out in Berlin, it wasn't my idea, and the order to confiscate the pictures also comes from Berlin. I've got my instructions, and all I've done is act accordingly.'

'They say you're picking on him,' the postman said.

'Picking on him,' my father replied. 'What do they mean, picking on him? Somebody's got to make him understand what's been decided, and it so happens that's my job.'

'They say you watch him morning, noon and night, and even when it's dark,' the postman said.

'He must be kept under surveillance with respect to the ban on painting,' my father said abruptly.

'They say you're doing more than anybody's supposed to, anyway more than duty demands of you,' Okko Brodersen said, having expected that answer.

'You don't know what they expect from me, the whole lot of you,' my father said.

'True enough,' the postman said. 'Quite likely nobody knows that. But they think they know what you expect of yourself in this affair. People say you've made your mind up to see it through.'

The Rugbüll policeman shrugged his shoulders, looking calmly at the man who could be seen on a number of the photographs in the office, even on the oval one of the gunners kneeling beside their howitzer. He shut his eyes, considering the matter, and took his time before answering in more or less these words :

'I get my orders, *he's* giving his orders to himself. I've explained to him what he mustn't do, and he's explained to me that he'll go on doing it. I can't make an exception, but he'd like to be treated as an exception. You just go and tell that to the people who've got such a lot to say. You just go and tell them that the two of us, him and me, are just doing what we have to. We've had it out, him and me, and each of us knows the consequences of his actions.'

The postman nodded. He himself didn't seem to see anything wrong in that, and he also left it open what his own opinion might be.

'There are some people that are worried,' he said, 'worried about *you*. They think that times might change sooner or later. You know he's got a lot of friends.'

'I know more,' my father said. 'I know he has a lot of friends abroad who admire him greatly, and I also know there are some here who are proud of him – old Holmsen's confirmed that – proud of him because this here landscape of ours – he's invented it or created it or made it famous. I've even heard that in the west or in the south he's the one that people think of first when they think of this countryside of ours . . . no, I know plenty about it, you can believe that, all of you. But why worry? Anyone who does his duty has no call to worry – not even if the times should change sooner or later.'

'People say,' the postman said, 'that you've confiscated pictures done in the last few years.'

'I got orders from Berlin,' my father said, 'and I saw to it that the pictures were packed up properly and taken to Husum. What happened to them afterwards – that's not my business.'

'They went on to Berlin from there,' the postman said, 'and half of them was burnt and other half sold, that's what someone's found out, they say.'

'I wouldn't know,' my father said. 'I've heard nothing about that, because that's not within my competence, my competence is only Rugbüll.'

'But you know why they forbid him to paint, why they confiscate all he's done in the last years,' the postman said.

'The way it's put in the injunction is that he's become alienated from the healthy instinct of the people,' my father replied. 'Therefore he's a danger to the State and undesirable, simply degenerate, if you see what I mean.'

'Anyway,' the postman said, 'there's people worrying about you. Two of them more than the others, because they remember he pulled you out of the water that time in Glüserup harbour.'

'A time comes when people are quits,' my father said. 'Him and me – we're quits. You can take that from me and you can bring it home to the others, to them that have such a lot to say. We both come from Glüserup, him and me, and we've made a clean sweep. Now it's up to him whether the matter goes any further or not.'

'All the same,' Okko Brodersen said, 'you ought to leave him in peace, Jens.'

And while my father looked at him as if he had trouble in understanding the meaning of his words, the postman took his watch from the table, held it to his ear, listened, then wound it up quickly and put it in his pocket. He gulped down the rest of the tea, now cold, and got up noisily. He was in a great hurry – perhaps embarrassed at having talked so much. I helped him to get his mail-bag into the proper position. He nodded goodbye to my father and took himself off without waiting for the salutation to be returned, leaving behind a policeman who was neither angry nor concerned, who didn't jump up, didn't threaten anyone, who didn't even seem uneasy, but simply sat there quietly, thinking about it all in his dry manner, slow and steady.

You could always see him thinking. Though he sat there looking at the sink and the slowly dripping brass taps, grey with condensation, his gaze was, as it were, turned inward. His breathing had become inaudible, it seemed his pulse-beat had slowed down; the upper part of his body seemed to sag slightly, while his hands were tense, going on squeezing each other, and the tips of his boots went up and down at irregular intervals. It didn't disturb him in his thinking if one moved into his field of vision, or if one talked or worked; he never objected.

I gazed across at my mill, where I was expected. The bread in my pockets seemed to be getting heavier and heavier; anyway, it was very much there. My home-made bag lay on the window-sill, and I picked it up and waved it before my father's face for a moment. The draught it made, perhaps also the persistence of my signalling, made my father raise his head, and

I instantly realized that I was included in his thinking. He lit his short, stubby pipe. He fingered a sty that had begun to form on his right eyelid. Then he puffed at his pipe, making faint smacking noises with his lips, and assumed a significant pose. I hate that way of sitting, that masterful attitude of his, and I am afraid of that silence which sets out to be full of meaning; I hate that solemn taciturnity, that gaze roaming the distance and that gesture it's so hard to describe; and I am afraid, yes afraid, of our habit of listening as though to an inner voice and making do without words.

Now the Rugbüll policeman was gazing through the smoke, at the wall, steadily, with a veiled and visionary gaze, and I shouldn't have been astonished if a stain had developed there or a brick had worked loose.

I wanted to ask permission to leave the house, but I didn't dare, I didn't dare to speak and draw his gaze on me prematurely, and so I drew flying figures of eight with my flag all through the room and I nearly swept the row of rice, sago, flour, and oats containers off the shelf, when he suddenly grabbed me, pulled me towards him and said: 'Don't forget we're working together. If you see anything, you've got to report it to me.'

'I'll signal with my flag,' I said.

'Anyway you like, but you've got to report it. Against the two of us, Siggi, none of them stands a chance.'

I'd heard that one before. Quickly I asked: 'Please can I go out?'

'Go,' he said. 'If you like, you can even go over Bleekenwarf way, but keep your eyes skinned.'

He was going to say more, but the telephone rang in his office, and he jumped up, carefully laid his pipe on a saucer, placed his hand over the sharply drawn parting in his hair and, as he walked off, buttoned up his uniform blouse. 'Rugbüll Police Station, Jepsen speaking', I heard, and I was already outside on the steps.

I raced down the steps, to reach the brick path without being seen by anyone, got to the lock unnoticed or at least without being challenged, and there I crouched down and, to be on the safe side; waited quite a while, looking at the dark water passing through the lock gate, before I doubled back the way I had come and, turning once more towards the belt of rushes, ran towards the mill. I didn't touch the belt of rushes or the mill-pond, but approached the mill from the back this time, walking in the shadow of the artificial hill, and I stopped for a long time at the collapsed platform, at least long enough to be sure that the two men in the meadow outside the cemetery were really working at the drainpipes. Only then did I turn down towards the entrance and open the door leading to the stairs.

I didn't see him instantly. I stood still in the coolness and twilight, listening for sounds from up above. A creaking came from behind the old flour-boxes, from near the place where the ladder was hidden. I suddenly felt a draught and then I heard a reproachful call – no, not a call, but a sound that was like a call, and, as always, something fluttered through the lofty room, flitted through the captive twilight, and plunged downward. It wasn't gulls. Then, just as I was about to pull out the ladder and set it up, I saw Klaas. He was lying beside the flour-boxes, directly under the hatch. In his good hand he was holding a piece of rope, and above him the chain of the old pulley was swinging slowly, soundlessly, innocently to and fro. He'd tried to let himself down on it and he'd tried to lengthen it with the rope, but only the chain had stood up to his weight. I put down the ladder and knelt down at his side. I took the rope out of his hand and pulled it away entirely from under his body: it was my own rope, the one I had intended to let myself down on in an emergency; I'd kept it under my bed. The rope hadn't given, but the connection with the chain had come undone and it had slid through the last link of the chain, and the end, where it had been squeezed in and then pulled along, was blackened. But this exact explanation doesn't help to get my brother up and on to his legs again. Even after I had taken the rope out of his hand he remained lying there, doubled up or, if one looked down on him, in the crouching attitude of a runner. Anyway, he didn't stir, and when I gingerly shook or pushed him he didn't react, except with a faint moaning.

I took the bread out of my pocket and held it out to him; close to his face I held the crumbly slice, asking him to eat or at least to open his eyes. But he only moaned, raised the arm with the clumsy dressing on it and let it drop back again. I broke off some of the bread, put it to his lips, and pressed a little and then harder, until I could feel the resistance of his clenched teeth; I couldn't manage to get the bread into his mouth. I thought of moving him,. of dragging him to one of the posts and sitting him up against it. But I couldn't do that either, simply because he was too heavy for me. And since there was apparently nothing for me to do, I sat down beside Klaas and told him what had been going on at home.

Patiently I went on talking to his round face down there below me, without being able to make out if he could understand me, and, if he could, what effect it was having on him. But even that didn't alter anything, he just went on lying there before me in that doubled-up position. So there was nothing for me to do but to leave the mill from time to time, climb on to the collapsed wooden structure of the platform and watch the workmen at the drainpipes, intently watch them and also a cart coming from Glüserup, and one lonely and motionless man on the platform of the Wattblick Inn, and in between, time and again, look at Rugbüll Police Station, the house and the shed.

But how long have I to go on watching the countryside? In the end I'll have to admit that one time when I came down from my observation-post, without having seen anything that aroused my particular suspicion, my brother Klaas was no longer lying there in front of the flour-boxes, but had sat up all by himself, supporting his back against one of the posts that had been smoothed down with a hatchet. He had managed all by himself. I could hear the sharp sound of his breathing. He looked at me with a hunted expression and nodded slowly in confirmation: after I'd left him, he'd suddenly been overwhelmed by panic, by the urge to get out of that hide-out of mine, which obviously made him feel as though he'd got himself into a trap. His attempt to make the chain of the pulley longer by means of the rope, the climbing down with the help of one hand, the fall – all that was in that nod. All that he confirmed. He also indicated that he had pain in his abdomen, pressing his hand on it, tilting his head back and shutting his eyes. Even now he didn't want to eat. I held out the piece of bread to him on my flat hand, but he refused it.

'Out,' he gasped. 'Get me out of here, kid.'

'Come home, Klaas,' I said. 'Once you're there, they'll help you.'

'Pain,' he said. 'Down there, pain.'

'I'll get you home,' I said.

'No, no,' he said, 'not home. That'd be the end of me.'

'But where, then?' I asked. 'If you don't want to go home, where shall I take you?'

Klaas must have worked it out for himself, it wasn't sheer chance that he said : 'Nansen – get me to him.'

I said : 'You don't know what's happened.'

'He's the only one. He'll hide me, I know,' my brother said.

'You don't know what's happened,' I said again.

'He'll do it,' my brother said, and instantly he struggled up from the floor and, supporting himself on the wooden post, beckoned to me with his bandaged hand to come closer. It was more a threat than a command.

'Nansen,' he said. 'I should have gone straight there. I should have knocked at his door right away in the morning.'

Klaas let go of the post, supported himself on me, testing how much of his weight I could bear. It wasn't very much and it became less with every step, and when we were outside in the sunshine he withdrew his hand from my shoulder, squatted down in front of a puddle and smeared his plaster dressing with mud. He did it carefully, and I helped him and we rubbed the dressing all over with brown peat, wetting it a few times in the puddle until it looked like a shapeless and rather long piece of peat. Then we started out. Bending low, we hurried past the mill-pond, towards the ditches, and the nearer we got to Bleekenwarf, the more often I tried to persuade him to come home. He listened to me as though it didn't concern him at all and gave no answer. We didn't trust the silence around us, or the brooding heat of summer that hung over the lukewarm, black ditches : here in our parts everyone is seen as soon as he steps out of his house, and since we both knew this, we were not deceived by the emptiness of the countryside right up to the horizon. We both knew there's always someone looking with longsighted eyes across the ditches and the flat land – standing motionless at a fence, at a gate, at a window. So we ran towards Bleekenwarf, as though we'd been discovered long ago, or even as though they were already after us. With short jumps we passed the locks, crashed through the rushes at the slope, waded through the horse-pond, and slid over the swampy ground, trodden down by many hooves, where the cattle are rounded up for milking. I still remember the squeaking and trembling of the fence-wire as we pulled it apart in order to slip through, and in my mind's eye I can see us lying close to the ground, listening. I went with Klaas because I did everything he asked me to do, I would have done it even if he hadn't been as frightened as he was and hadn't had that pain which made him groan whenever we threw ourselves on the ground. I went with him on that wild rush, although I was convinced that if Max Ludwig Nansen didn't send us home, he would certainly send us back to the mill.

The last stretch we were running upright. We reached the cover of the hedgerow of Bleenkenwarf. When we had passed the wooden bridge without a railing, Klaas dropped to the ground and didn't get up again. He made one final attempt, tried to get up on his knees, but he couldn't do it. He collapsed again and stayed there, lying on his face. I ran quickly to the opening and looked into the garden towards the house, but there was no one in sight, and so I returned to my brother, pulled and tugged him to one side. I supported his head on a little mound of grass and then I asked him:

'Shall I fetch him now?'

And as my brother just looked at me and didn't seem to understand, I asked once again urgently: 'Shall I fetch him?'

'Yes,' he said in a low voice. 'Yes.'

Before going I squatted down and cleaned my brother's uniform as best I could, wiping off the grass that clung to it and wiping off the dried mud, and I also wiped his boots clean. I put his collar straight and buttoned up his blouse. 'Stay quiet on the ground,' I said; 'don't go away.' Then I left him.

From the opening in the hedgerow, standing comfortably, a branch in my left and in my right hand, I watched the garden, the house and the studio, because I wanted to make sure that I would meet neither Jutta nor Jobst, that fat little monster, whom I didn't want to take into my confidence. Over there in the flower-garden, and hens ran about freely among the beds, Hamburg Goldsprenkel and Belgian Leghorn, scratching the soil among the lupins and zinnias and pecking insects off the lilies and other flowers. Nobody was visible, the summer-house was empty. The four hundred windows would not give the slightest information. Who had given a push to the swing under the apple tree? Why were the tall poppies swaying? The studio, I thought – you must look for him in the studio. And I entered the garden, moving along the hedge all the time, keeping an eye on the flower-beds and the house. I followed the curve to the raked outer path leading to the back of the studio. Hearing voices, I stopped and listened. No, there was only one voice, asking questions in an irritable way, making sneering retorts. The door wasn't locked. Soundlessly I opened it and slipped inside, and instantly I again heard the painter's voice coming from round the corner: a pretty quarrel was going on there, I should say. Quite likely it was at that time that I heard the painter say:

'Don't talk rubbish, Balthasar, there's only one action in every painting, and that's the light.'

Barefoot, I crept closer on the firm floorboards – I can see myself even now, creeping up to him on tiptoe – I got up on one of those day-beds, pulled aside a blanket that served as a curtain, and there he was in front of me, in his old blue over-coat, his hat on his head. He was working. And he was quarrel-ling with his Balthasar, all the while working at his painting, 'Landscape with Unknown People'.

The canvas was fixed to the inside of the right door of the wardrobe, and to the left of it on open shelves there were his tools, as he called his paints. A push left and right was all that was needed to shut the wardrobe doors, causing the painting and the paints to disappear. But who can know whether he would have shut the wardrobe door at that moment, if a voice had sounded or if there had been a noise to warn him? He seemed too deeply involved in his argument with Balthasar, that partner of his in the purple fox-fur, too intent on proving to him that the landscape, in which the gigantic strangers were standing in a carefully calculated group, must show the imminence of violent acts, and of doom not in a dying light and in shading colours, but in a frightening glare – of glowing orange, for instance – and by means of white dots put in apparently in body-colours. In the greyish-black a sharp scream: yellow, brown, and white – at once the dunness, the restraint and the resignation are gone, and the drama starts. And earthy green: at the bottom he put a broad layer of earthy green, that green always needed, out of which, for him, everything grew. His Balthasar couldn't or wouldn't understand that.

I looked at him, at the strange people and again at him: there he stood, listening, imitating the expressions of his people, who evidently felt threatened, strange and exposed in a landscape such as one enters into, not by accident, when out on a walk in the country. A landscape into which one is borne by the wind, into which one is jolted: if such things happen, terror is justified. What disturbed me then – and, I must admit, disturbs me even today – is the headgear of those strangers, something half way between a fez and a turban, which seemed to belong to a period of one or the other Turkish war. But the disconcerted look, the fear and forlornness of those people were confirmed once and for all by the landscape's mood.

But now I wanted to drop the blanket that served as a curtain by the day-bed, drop it gently and creep back to the door and enter once again, as it were noisily and officially. I tiptoed to the door, knocked, opened and shut the door and called out: 'Uncle Nansen! Are you there, Uncle Nansen?'

He didn't answer at once, but only when he'd shut the wardrobe and brought the key out of the lock.

'What's that? Who is it?' Slowly he emerged out of the impenetrable depths of the studio, but he wasn't disgruntled, not reluctant, as anyone might be who had been disturbed in the middle of work. Stolidly he came shuffling along. . . . I let him get right to the door. 'Witt-Witt,' he said, when he saw me, and he said it without any sign of relief or surprise: 'Well, Witt-Witt?' and he tilted his head back towards his working-place, listening, just as if that Balthasar of his might take advantage of his not being there, and open the wardrobe and change the landscape according to his own ideas. Then he asked: 'Do you want anything special?'

Without speaking I pointed to the hedge, and only then did I say: 'Klaas.'

And since he didn't understand me immediately, but just turned his grey eyes to the garden, looking over my head in the direction in which I had pointed, I added : 'Klaas has come, he wants you to help him.'

'But your brother's away,' he said. 'He's wounded, in hospital.'

'By the bridge,' I said. 'Lying on the ground. He was trying to get to you, just to you.'

Now the painter drew his overcoat tight, dropped his lighted pipe into a pocket, strained his ears again to where Balthasar was, turned round and walked out of the studio. I shut the door and hurried after him.

'The things you people do,' he said, rushing through the garden with quick short steps.

And, speaking to his strong, slightly bent back, I said : 'They're after him. They've been to our house.'

'A downright nuisance your family is,' he growled. 'Never a moment's peace.' His long blue coat hid the movement of his legs, and so it seemed he was sailing ahead of me, driven by his mounting anger, or at least by exasperation. Again I heard his reproachful voice :

'The things you people do !'

We took a short-cut, hurrying along the hedge until we got to the opening. There we left the garden, and there we found Klaas the way I had left him, his head still resting on the little mound of grass.

The painter bent down over him, and his wide coat opened over my brother, covering him and probably making him feel cooler. I find myself compelled to remark here that the group they formed, one figure lying, the other kneeling in the un-mistakable attitude of the Good Samaritan, looked very much like one of the Leader's favourite pictures, entitled : 'After the Battle', except that in that picture the kneeling, as it were comforting figure was of the female sex. But the painter was not interested in comforting my brother, he only wanted to find out what was the matter with him, and why he was lying there behind his hedge, not even wearing a wreath of bloodstained laurels, and not getting up even now.

'Klaas,' the painter said, 'what's the matter with you, boy?' He raised Klaas's useless arm, the arm in which my brother had shot himself twice, at the shortest possible range, and put it down again. He touched his shoulder, his chest and then the lower

part of his body, and now Klaas twitched and said : 'Not there –
don't touch there.'

'Can you walk?' the painter asked, and Klaas answered :
'Oh yes. I can get up again now, I can manage.' With the
painter's help he sat upright, shook himself, and said : 'I've got
to disappear.' Then he struggled to his feet. 'Holy Mother of
God,' the painter said, 'the things you people do ! You certainly
manage to keep a man busy !'

'I can't go home,' my brother said. 'I can't show up at home.
They've been there and they'll be there again.'

'It's just one damn thing after another with your family,'
the painter said, supporting him, and Klaas said with a groan :
'If they catch me – this time I'll be done for.'

'You simply can't leave us in peace, you people,' the painter
said, pulling Klaas very tight to himself, and then he tried the
first step and pulled and dragged my brother along, all the
while grumbling, shaking his head and making his complaints
in a growling voice, dragging him to the opening in the hedge,
and then through the garden into the summer-house. There in
the dim light he put him into a broad chair made of polished
branches. He raised my brother's face, but not as if he intended
to talk to him eye to eye, but as if he wanted to re-discover
some quite definite expression, one that for some time had compelled him to put my brother into some of his paintings. Klaas's
face at times bore an expression of deep emotion that was both
unintended and of exemplary simplicity, and that was why
Max Ludwig Nansen had used him in his 'Last Supper', where
he can be seen, heavy-boned, gazing expectantly into the chalice.
He is to be found also, all doll-like unwieldiness, in the 'Still-
Life with a Red Horse', he stands at an angle to 'Doubting
Thomas', as though hoping to trip him up, and in 'Beach with
Dancers' and 'Random Summer Visitors' Klaas is there, too,
with bright eyes and a blue face, trying to make out what it is
all about.

In more than a dozen paintings Klaas displays that classical
deep emotion of his, and when, there in the summer-house, the
painter lifted my brother's face, I thought he was searching for
that expression, but it can't have been that, because all at once
he asked : 'Do you know – have you any notion – what you're
asking of me?'

Klaas just looked at him blankly.

'Well then, let's get going,' the painter said. 'Come on.'

Again he pulled my brother firmly to himself, and we left the summer-house, walking along under the windows towards the yard, and all the time we were walking the painter was grumbling and complaining, swamping us – me too – with reproaches for doing all sorts of things that only added to his worries. Not until we were in the corridor did he fall silent. He opened the door leading to the east wing of the house, where the corridor stretched away into the distance with windows on one side and about a hundred and ten doors on the other : heavy doors, painted greyish-green, and with very big, obviously hand-made keys in their locks. He shoved my brother along the corridor, past all those doors, behind which I thought not of people living but of birds : vultures with naked necks, immense condors, golden eagles with shut eyelids, perched on top of scratched bedposts – I didn't even dare to listen at the closed doors. The stone floor had dates carved in it : 1638, or 1912, and underneath them there were initials : A.J.F. : F.W.F. : the edges of the letters were worn, and some of the stone slabs had cracks running through them.

Did the painter open the right door? Was that the room he had chosen for Klaas? Anyway, he suddenly stopped, opened a door, disappeared, returned after a moment, nodded and carefully led Klaas into the room. It was a bathroom – that's to say : it was almost a bathroom; somebody, probably old Frederiksen, had decided that the room was to be a bathroom, so he had a shower fixed and a bathtub put in – an opaque white monster on griffin's feet – but neither the shower nor the tub had ever been connected up, there was no water tap, no outlet, no pipes, and one could only assume that old Frederiksen had lost interest or that the plan had gradually been forgotten, because it had been too much trouble for old Frederiksen to try to find the room again. Why there was also a stack of used mattresses in that never-finished expanse of bathroom is a question one can hardly expect to get an explanation for now, but there they were, and the painter simply pulled them about and knocked them into shape until they made a bed, and every jerk and every blow caused billows of dust to rise and move in clouds through the thin, slanting rays of sunlight that fell into the room. Then he told Klaas to lie down on it. My brother got down on his hands and knees, flopped to one side, and stretched out. He shivered. 'A blanket,' he asked, 'have you got a blanket?'

'You'll get all you need,' the painter said, and began clearing up under the high window. He put away a step-ladder and collected lead pipes, valves, metal-saws and washers and put them into a cardboard box, he kicked plaster, paper, and cigarette stubs together, took from a nail a ragged old jacket with a herring-bone pattern, went through the pockets, then folded it up to make a pillow and pushed it under my brother's head.

Klaas was breathing with difficulty. He looked up at me unhappily. If I see him lying there now, through all the dust and haze of memory, it seems to me as if he made a furtive sign to me, a secret sign asking me to stay with him. The dust fell on his face and on his eyelids. I didn't understand the sign. The painter walked up and down the room, shaking his head, working out what had to be done here, and in the end he gave up. My brother turned on his side and put his face into the crook of his arm.

'He hasn't had anything to eat,' I said, and put the piece of bread on the head of the mattress.

'Everything in its turn,' the painter said. 'If you chaps go and do some things, they've got to be put right one by one. In due course he'll get all he needs. Come along now and leave him alone. And I'll do some thinking about all this.'

6 Second Sight

First of all I make it become dark and I hand over responsibility for the first part of the evening to the projector, which is the registered property of the Glüserup Folklore Society, bought secondhand and kept, cleaned, and likewise operated by the chairman, Per Arne Schessel, whom by force of habit I call grandfather. The projector stands on a table, the table stands in the central aisle and on both sides of the aisle there are heavy, we may even say without fear of contradiction, clumsy benches, which for inexplicable reasons after a short while cause the legs of most people in the audience to go to sleep. To make the projector cast the pictures on the entire screen, it is tilted up in front with two books under it, which always lie on the table, ready for use : Storm's *The Senator's Sons* and Klopstock's *The Messiah*; the fatness of these books is a guarantee that the cone of light-rays will hit the screen squarely and make them cover the whole of it.

The screen is the back of an historical map of Schleswig-Holstein, a greyish-white rectangle, with some white spots in the top left-hand corner, and the cone of light causes the outlines of islands, coastlines and estuaries to shine through, thus proving to every doubter that this country, though not 'surrounded by water', is in fact wedged in by it on two sides. Eight people, or perhaps in fairness I should say twelve or even sixteen, sitting on the left and on the right sides of the corridor, gaze at that screen; some of them are dazzled by light escaping through a slit in the side of the projector and reflected by the glass fronts of the cupboards and showcases standing along the walls and between the blacked-out windows. Insects go buzzing around in the cone of light, and a stubby moth, which has several times paced out the distance between the lens and the screen, tumbles through it, producing a little metallic whirr whenever it bumps into anything. The people on the benches talk in low voices, here and there somebody coughs. There is no smoking. It is warm.

From the neighbouring stable a tearing sound of rattling chains can be heard from time to time, as of an animal tossing its head up; sometimes there's a thumping or a furious scraping. Gusts of wind, dogs barking. Out of the semi-darkness my grandfather's long, reddened, morose face moves before the screen; even the silhouette of his head looks morose. Per Arne Schessel's a real peasant; he doesn't laugh, he doesn't smile, he doesn't wink at anybody, he hasn't even got a wave of the hand to spare; he simply stands there, tall and brooding as a heron, and the result is that the whispering stops and there's only a sparse coughing as if to get it over in advance. I hope this gives a picture of the situation.

And now, if you don't mind, I want to make use of the silence that descends, to point out that up to this point, that's to say, up to my grandfather's appearance before the screen, all those evenings on Külkenwarf were alike, all dedicated to our homeland from Husum to Glüserup, its growth and development, its interesting geological deposits, its valuable alluvial sand, its animals, plants and ditches, above all too its character, its essential nature. If I concentrate and submerge myself in the past, I come to the conclusion that, where those meetings of our local association are concerned, what is imprinted on my memory is above all semi-darkness, the cone of light from the projector, the dazed insects, the noises from the stable next door, and the whispering, I should like to say *good-tempered* expectancy of the audience, all of whom received written invitations, in winter more frequently than in summer, to attend those meetings that took place on Külkenwarf, the place the Schessels call their ancestral home.

But I also remember that in the meeting-room between house and stable, which my grandfather had given over to antiquarian studies of our countryside, there were various objects, some locked up, some openly exhibited, pertaining to the history, the culture, and of course the natural characteristics of our land. For instance, the hooked harpoon made from reindeer antlers. Or for instance, stone scrapers, axe-heads, hammers. I should also like to mention urns and bangles of the middle Bronze Age, metal-work from sword-scabbards and richly adorned pots of the later Stone Age that I wouldn't mind using for short-stemmed flowers. There were sword-hilts, wooden jewellery and – not to be passed over – the well-known Treenbarg gold disc. Nor must I forget to mention a great number of samples of earth, sand, and minerals, the remnants of boats from the Norschlotten peat-bog, quaint, indeed impossible, garments once worn by archaic hunters and peat-bog dwellers, and finally the chief attraction, the wrinkled, shrunken, leathery corpse of a girl who had been strangled with a noose – of course made of reindeer-hide – a noose she still wore round her neck as a somewhat bizarre adornment. And last but not least the specialist library, the books Per Arne Schessel had collected. *A Geological Journey through Schleswig-Holstein, Sea-Shore Life and Pattern, A Lifetime in Schobüll, My Islands' Green Robe, The Breath of Primal Dawn,* and then, of course, the piles of his own pamphlets and books, among them *The Language of the Tumuli, Sacrificial Finds and the Bogs of Norschlotten,* and *The Great Leap-Tides and their Consequences,* and many others.

In case anyone should miss a title or some important object in the Association's possession, he can simply write it into the book; anyway, I intend to make do with the items mentioned above, because I feel I really can't leave my grandfather looking into the projector's cone of light for so long, notwithstanding the fact, well remembered by other people, too, that he had great powers of endurance for staring into either darkness or any kind of light, without suffering any injury. Besides, I feel compelled to dissipate the impression that that evening, though dedicated to the study of our countryside and having begun like other evenings, went on in the usual manner and thus might be described as just one among many such evenings.

The fact is that up to the moment when Per Arne Schessel stepped before the screen, I myself had been expecting an evening of middling quality, when nothing in particular would happen, and no doubt the majority of those present were of the same opinion. But surprise was in the air when suddenly my grandfather raised both hands and began to eye the door in a manner bound to arouse suspicion, at the same time asking us to remain quite quiet. We kept very quiet; even Captain Andersen suppressed his cough. Nothing stirred on the other side of the door. Relentlessly, his mouth slightly agape, exhibiting all his bad teeth, my grandfather kept his eyes on the door. By now everyone was looking at that door, everybody had straightened up and was holding his breath, but even so nothing special happened, no squat reindeer-hunter, no anachronistic bog-dweller and no King Sven, that early invader of England, appeared in person.

But something did begin to happen on the other side of that door as we went on looking at it : the glow of a cigarette shone through the narrow pane of frosted glass, somebody cleared his throat, and as Per Arne Schessel brought himself to make a scanty gesture nevertheless somehow indicative of invitation, at last Asmus Asmussen, the author of the book *Sea-Gleams* and honorary chairman of the Glüserup local association, entered. He was recognized instantly in spite of the fact that he was wearing naval uniform with the distinctions of a staff-lance-corporal, and he was greeted with exclamations and applause. He returned these greetings in a leisurely but nevertheless military fashion and stubbed out his cigarette. He was the creator of Timm and Tine, the two main figures in *Sea-Gleams* – who had got to know one another, if I am not mistaken, exchanging letters in bottles committed to the waves, and who found that means of communication so suitable that even when they were engaged and subsequently married they went on exchanging messages by bottle, carrying on their past-time untiringly, in their ripe old age still regarding the bottle-post as the most beautiful and certainly the thriftiest method of exchanging messages. Thus they made it possible for their creator time and again to discover such bottled-up communications on out-of-the-way beaches and go on providing his readers with posthumous news of Timm and Tine, exploiting the idea to the last.

Now, Asmus Asmussen, who was serving on a patrol-boat in the North Sea, came to Külkenwarf while on shore leave in Bremerhaven. He was a bow-legged fellow with thick, as it were blazing, hair, his neck-muscles were as strongly developed as those of a weight-lifter, and his gaze was capable of all shades of expression from audacity to kindliness. Indeed, one might not easily have imagined him to be the creator of Timm and Tine had it not been for his mouth, which gave him away: a sensitive, rounded mouth, plummy, I'd call it. That mouth betrayed him. Deftly he swept off his sailor's cap with the long ribbons and, holding it under his arm as prescribed in regulations, the cockade and eagle towards the front, he allowed himself to be welcomed by my grandfather. He nodded at almost every sentence of the speech of welcome. He seemed in agreement with Per Arne Schessel's calling him, first of all, one with an unrivalled knowledge of our district, then an armed outpost of our countryside, and he didn't object when he was hailed as the man who had given form and expression to the destiny of the people of our district, and finally even as the conscience of Glüserup. Asmus Asmussen merely nodded, and he smiled in agreement when my grandfather announced the title of the evening's talk, which was 'The Sea and our Homeland', winding up by referring to Asmus Asmussen as ideally qualified to speak on the subject. Whereupon my grandfather sat down.

The author of *Sea-Gleams* put his cap on the table, taking care that the ribbons should hang down straight and long, put his hand into the opening of his blouse, still deeper, yet without finding what he was after, then, with his shoulders hunched up and his behind tightened, groped somewhere near his left hip, paused, grinned, then slowly, very cautiously, pulled out an envelope containing slides and raised it in the cone of light from the projector. Now he was ready to start. I wanted to climb across to the first row of benches, but my father held me tight and pushed me down on to the seat and so I had no choice but to stay with him by the window and from there watch Asmus Asmussen walking down the central aisle to the projector and putting the first slide into it, but without showing it yet.

What on earth was the matter with my father? While Asmus Asmussen was expressing his gratitude for the reception he had been given, conveying greetings from those on the high seas, and working his way towards his introductory words, my father got into a state of excitement the like of which I had never before seen in him. He kept moving about restlessly on his seat. He touched his eyeballs with his fingertips. He crunched up his handkerchief, tugged it, pulled it about. At times he leaned over so far backwards that I was afraid he would fall right into the lap of Kohlschmidt, the bird-sanctuary warden. There was sweat on his upper lip. Sometimes he shook himself as if he were suffering under some intolerable pressure from within. There was a puzzled expression on his face as though he himself couldn't understand what was the matter with him. He frequently passed his hands over his forehead with a brisk, intolerant gesture.

But all that strikes me more now than it did then, when he was sitting beside me in that state of excitement which was something entirely new in him, because at the time I was of course listening to Asmus Asmussen, looking forward, above all, to the first picture he would show on the screen.

Asmussen, however, took his time, first speaking at length about the title of his talk, 'Sea and Homeland'. He pondered the title, changing it a number of times, extracting from it, or squeezing out of it, a new meaning, for instance, by replacing the 'and' by 'as' and asking his listeners to consider the possibilities that all at once opened up if one regarded the sea as one's home. He also suggested we should have no qualms about shortening the title to 'Sea-Homeland', which seemed to him, as he said, even more comprehensive, speaking more from the heart to the heart. What he dwelt on at greatest length, however, was 'The Sea our Home', a variation that gave him more ideas than anything else; here he operated extensively with the concept of the maternal, yet without omitting violence, which helps to train mankind in strength, doggedness, and defiance; then in a great sweep he came to the point of imploring us to meditate on how much would have to happen before we were justified in calling the sea 'The Sea our Home'. One thing, however, was certain, he said; one didn't fight in defence of any old sea, but only in defence of one's own, one's homeland sea.

Now Asmus Asmussen let us have the first picture. On the screen a patrol-boat floating in a sky of foaming waves, and underneath it was a dim, sliced-off horizon. We laughed, until fingers magnified to giant proportions took hold of the edge of the slide and turned it, so that the boat now floated quite satisfactorily *on* the sea. Nobody had any doubt that the armed trawler that lay there low in the water and with a heavy list, seeming to cower before the next breaker, was the patrol-boat in which Asmus Asmussen, in his 'Sea-Homeland', mounted guard. The picture was presumably taken from the crow's-nest and none of the crew was to be seen – no, that's wrong, there on the A.A. gun platform in the foc'sle were two figures dressed in grey, waving to the photographer. We abandoned ourselves to the impression made by that patrol-boat, which had no name, only a number, and which had a look of the lost, or at least forlorn. We transferred ourselves in spirit, as it were, aboard ship, we raised binoculars to our eyes, had our mess-tins filled with noodles and bacon. I knew exactly what the two white rings on the 3.7-twin-mount signified. The wind that was prevailing at the moment, however, could not be estimated.

'That's our boat,' Asmus Asmussen said in a voice as even yet urgent as the tide is in the Priel, and he added: 'A fine little craft.' 'Please bear in mind,' he said, 'that she's only one of an infinite number of boats doing deep-formation duty in our home waters. Day and night, in rain and drifting snow. Forming an unbreakable chain. Nobody succeeds in slipping through that chain, no sea-owl and certainly no Englishman. And there are countless other boats, the same as ours, that the Leader has put down out there' – he actually said 'put down'.

My father's hand twitched. He raised his arm, stretched it out, he aimed his index finger at the patrol-boat, he choked trying to utter a word, but he couldn't get it out, and slowly he let his arm sink again as Asmus Asmussen put the next slide into the projector. The picture showed an empty bit of the sea with a milky-white sun over it. The patrol-boat was nowhere to be seen, but nobody supposed it had been sunk, for there was something whitish and frothy extending across the water that had been caused only by a ship's screw: the foaming wake of the ship. The second picture just showed that wake, clearly visible, getting wider and gradually blurring towards the horizon, a luminous strip of swiftly vanishing foam-patterns.

'That'll be a ship's wake,' Captain Andersen exclaimed, whereupon Asmus Asmussen remarked in mild tones intended to evoke wonderment: 'Being on patrol out there isn't just a matter of being on duty, of course. He who fights the sea earns the sea's love; to him she reveals herself in all her moods and mysteries.'

'You mean it isn't a ship's wake?' Captain Andersen persisted. But Asmus Asmussen, who was now set a lyrical course, went on unperturbed: 'To the uninitiated, the stranger, that manifold world will not open up. The landlubber cannot read the signs of the sea. Please notice the fireworks-display in this picture – unfortunately it doesn't come out very well. It is the phosphorescence that we call sea-glitter. It glimmers and gleams, casting its green and yellow flashes across the sea. At such times the guns fall silent. The whole wake turns into one luminous track, especially at night. It is as though the sea was saluting the men on whom she has bestowed the right of domicile. It is a message to the ships sailing without lights, in which no one sleeps so long as the flashes of light illuminate bows and stern.' He fell silent, gazing unwaveringly at the picture; perhaps like me he was preoccupied with observing the stubby moth that was making attempts to cast itself into the wake, but merely hitting the screen with a dull thud every now and then. I venture to suggest that Asmus Asmussen found it difficult to give up gazing at that picture, so he was rather taken aback when the photogenic ninety-two-year-old Captain Andersen asked:

'Don't that there phosphorescence come from little bugs, name of Noctiluca or the like? Many a time we met with that.'

'Certainly, the phosphorescence has its cause,' Asmus Asmussen said. 'The flashing and sparkling is produced by microscopic inhabitants of the water, the reaction to an irritation. Flagellate they're called if you want the precise nomenclature – modest unicellular animalculae. But are they not part of the sea? Isn't it the one that shines in the other and through the other?'

He didn't answer his own question, nor did he expect anyone else to give an answer to it, he simply made a pause, dwelling among his memories, and before the pause ended my father, raising his behind slightly from his seat, exclaimed: 'V.P.-22! V.P.-22!'

Startled, several people in the audience turned round, among them my grandfather, Hilde Isenbüttel, and Ditte, and looked at us, and Asmus Asmussen observed in astonishment:

'That's the number of my patrol-boat, it really is.'

But although everybody expected to hear more from my

father, he only smiled in embarrassment, made a vague gesture of apology, and slowly settled himself again on the bench. He put one hand on my thigh and it took him some time to notice that it wasn't his own thigh, but when he did notice he removed his hand again. Even in the half-dark I could tell by looking that something was going on inside him, that he was excited, frightened and, I might even say, tormented; in any case, it was on that evening, dedicated to our native sea, that the Rugbüll policeman began to show the symptoms of a malady that – though it is something that occurs not infrequently among the inhabitants of our district – was to have a certain effect on all police activities in my father's district.

But I'll only mention the essentials, taking, as it were, one card at a time from the pack, for now Asmus Asmussen removed the phosphorescent sea from the screen in order to regale us with a new picture. What picture was it? It was some picture of evening 'atmosphere' he put into the projector: aboard ship the men were off duty and the North Sea was off duty too, and some of the crew were leaning on the railing, gazing, not into the distance, of which there was plenty in the picture, but at another sailor who was playing an accordion, and in doing so they turned their backs on the low evening cloud, which might have hidden God knows how many Blenheim bombers.

'There isn't much to be seen here, actually,' Asmus Asmussen said. 'Just an evening. The off-duty watch. The men relaxing, listening to a song – while the starboard watch – that's us – ceaselessly watches the horizon. The guns are silent, as you can see. The day's work is done. Mussels and cod, caught by the crew, are a valued addition to the menu. The sea feeds all men. Up there on the left you see our four-barrelled A.A.-gun. On the bridge, close to the yard-arm, that's our captain, not that you can see his face. There isn't much to be seen in this picture, really. This one now is perhaps a bit more interesting.' And Asmus Asmussen, the great authority on the sea, put another slide into the projector.

There the morning sun rose over the sea – a wide, clear day, a sun that made one shiver with cold. The deep swell heaved away into the distance. There was V.P.-22 visibly pitching and tossing. Some gulls had just taken to the air over the look-out on the poop. Thin smoke drifted up from the funnel, somehow evoking the memory of home in the early morning, when the fire has just been lit in the range. In the galley the cook would be just making – gloomily enough – the first coffee of the day. The crew of V.P.-22 were presumably cleaning their teeth meanwhile, which were threatened with scurvy. And presumably the radio was transmitting some early-morning sing-song to every quarter-deck and foc'sle.

'Please observe the bombs hanging in mid-air, top right,' Asmus Asmussen said. 'Four bombs falling – hardly visible against the sun, but if you look closely – they all hit the water to starboard.'

I jumped up. Around me the relaxed bodies suddenly became tense. Nobody had expected this. Nobody was prepared for such a thing. The atmosphere somehow excluded the possibility of bombs, and – here's how I should like to put it – one would have expected anything but bombs hovering in the air to starboard. Still, we saw them now. A signalman with steady nerves had coolly taken a snapshot of them, even getting two of them blackly outlined against the morning sun. They came down at different heights, and a connecting line drawn along the top of their fins would have been a diagonal through the picture. In a moment one after the other would hit the surface of the sea and explode either instantly or at the depth for which they have been set. There was some charm in it for any painter of seascapes : four middle-weight or perhaps even smallish bombs dropped by an invisible aeroplane. Air-speed, angle of inclination, the patrol-boat's course – this time mathematics were on the side of V.P.-22.

'Just one among many similar mornings,' Asmus Asmussen said. 'Still . . . one has to be prepared. The sea keeps its own counsel, come what may. Pity it wasn't possible to get a picture of the impact, the flowering fountains. In my diary I speak of a garden of fountains through which the boat keeps on her course unwaveringly.'

Suddenly Captain Andersen called out : 'Don't they bring up anything from below?' Asmus Asmussen seemed not to understand the question, and when at long last he gave an answer, one couldn't miss the note of irritation in his voice.

'The sea swiftly wipes out all traces of the bombs,' he said. 'At first, of course, algae come to the surface, red and brown algae – no green. Seaweed and dead fish litter the surface. Plaice, sole, a great many cod. Occasionally, a scorpion-shell. Rarely cartilaginous fishes like ray or dorn-hound. Never crabs or shell-fish. The sea accepts these losses with indifference. In a short while it all drifts apart and sinks and vanishes. After a while there is no way of telling that a bomb ever fell. The sea erases every trace of it.'

'No hit, eh?' Captain Andersen called out, and the speaker replied: 'If what you mean is, did we have any losses, the answer is no.'

While Asmus Asmussen now examined his slides in the light issuing sideways from the projector, shuffling them and arranging them, my father was making knots in his big, blue and white handkerchief. He knotted a hare and a hedgehog, and by putting just one knot in the middle and pulling the handkerchief tight, he instantly had in his hand a snake that had swallowed a rabbit; and he wasn't fiddling with the handkerchief in that manner because he knew the pictures and was bored. He had to distract his mind. He needed some relief. He had to reduce the pressure, for it is no exaggeration to say that what was sitting there beside me was a small dam that could hardly hold much longer against the rising flood. When would it burst? It did so when Asmus Asmussen, clicking his tongue, produced a new picture, which showed the crew of V.P.-22 holystoning. This time there were no bombs hovering to starboard, the sea was calm. There were six sailors, standing in a row amidships, at equal distances from each other, with uplifted brooms in their hands, and among them was the creator of Timm and Tine; they were obviously busy scrubbing the deck until it was white. They were all looking at the camera, all laughing. Apparently they enjoyed scrubbing the deck of their boat, they paid no attention to the bucket that had been knocked over, liquid soap pouring out of it. The sky was overcast, visibility poor. One could easily imagine that somewhere in the background or to one side there was an accordion playing, helping the men to do their scrubbing to the rhythm.

'Cleanliness,' Asmus Asmussen said. 'The sea demands cleanliness. You see the bucket that has been knocked over? We use four such buckets to get the ship clean! Even if one's homestead is afloat, it has to shine with cleanliness. Fish-scale? Pebble at the bottom of the sea? The imminence of danger is no excuse for dirt. Please observe the foam.'

'No!' my father exclaimed at that moment. 'No, Asmus!' He rose to his feet, his arm outstretched, pointing at V.P.-22. He choked, then cried out again : 'No, Asmus, not yet, not yet!'

Now almost everyone looked at us. My father wiped his forehead with his handkerchief, he swayed a little and made an attempt to turn away from the screen, as though he couldn't bear the sight of sailors rhythmically scrubbing. But Asmus Asmussen left the slide in the projector, turned towards my father, observed him with narrowed eyes and then asked :

'What do you mean by NO?'

Now everybody was looking at us, all of them tensely waiting for the answer the Rugbüll policeman was bound to give. But still he did not give it, for first of all he unbuttoned the two top buttons of his tunic and then he began rubbing his hands as though he were washing them in dry air. But still my father couldn't make up his mind to speak. He walked up to Asmus Asmussen. A streak of light, issuing sideways from the projector, fell on his cheek, a flaming scar cutting it in half. He laid his hand on Asmus Asmussen's forearm, where he wore the stripe on his sleeve, and he seemed to be pressing it. In the first rows left and right of the aisle some people stood up in order to hear what my father had to say.

'Well?' Asmus Asmussen asked, instinctively taking hold of the other slides that he hadn't yet shown.

It was very quiet in the room as the Rugbüll policeman suddenly said, in a voice that was calmer than one might have expected : 'Don't go back on duty, don't go back, all of you, not yet. I've seen you.'

'What's he saying?' Captain Andersen called out, and somebody informed him : 'He's seen something.'

'I've seen you surrounded by smoke,' my father said, 'and then a wind came and carried off the smoke and then I didn't see any of you any more.' There was no sound except for the regular humming of the projector and the muffled rattle of chains and stamping of hooves from the stable. And the six sailors were still there on the screen, grinning, their brooms raised high, intent on scrubbing their boat clean to meet its prophesied doom.

'I've seen you surrounded by smoke, and when the smoke had gone, there were just a few life-jackets and rafts drifting on the water – empty. It was your ship, V.P.-22, all wrapped in smoke.' He looked round in the semi-darkness of the room, as though in search of support and confirmation, but everyone was silent in amazement – and not only in amazement – they were all frightened and above all shocked. There was nobody who could or would confirm what one of them had seen against his own will and on a screen that existed for him alone. The way my father stood there, one might have thought he would have liked to say he was sorry for what he had said. There he stood, his shoulders sagging, looking down at the floor, and his body seemed quite strikingly relaxed. And Asmus Asmussen? Did he pat my father soothingly on the back? Did he, with his intimate knowledge of the sea, ask him to regard V.P.-22's prospects a little more optimistically? Did he reject such meddling in the ship's future? Asmus Asmussen held out his hand to my father. Silently he thanked him, holding my father's hand in his own for a long time, pressing down, even pulling down, that pair of hands which seemed to have the urge to rise into the air.

Only when Captain Andersen called out : 'Got the second sight, has he?' did Asmus Asmussen regard my father not only in amazement but with awe and say : 'I'll think about it, Jens. And I'll tell the others. We shall be on our guard.'

And then he patted my father soothingly on the shoulder and, taking hold of him round the hips, turning him, at the same time giving him a well-calculated push, propelled him back to my side. All this was done without undue haste. My father had no trouble in finding his seat again, and he sat down; the pressure had visibly decreased, and he seemed to be exhausted. He looked worn out, depressed. But the others could not see that, still staring at him out of the semi-darkness of the room, some of them quite rigid with perturbation, or perhaps afraid he might begin to compete with the projector, producing his own version of all that was being shown on the screen, and so casting a shadow on every picture and making it all questionable.

If only Asmussen would go on, I thought, and at that very moment he put a new slide into the projector, instantly attracting his audience's attention by explaining that the two men in the rubber dinghy, who were paddling towards one side of the patrol-boat, were American airmen. The photograph was taken from above, diagonally. The airmen wore inflated life-jackets, which made thick bulges round their necks, and it looked as if they were about to be strangled by them. They were keeping time with their paddle and as far as could be seen seemed quite pleased with themselves. They were paddling into captivity. They were paddling towards the side of the V.P.-22, towards a rope-ladder dangling there. There was also a rope flying through the air towards the dinghy. It wasn't difficult to imagine the rest.

'Our three-point-seven,' Asmus Asmussen said. 'We brought them down first time they attacked. One moment a smoke trail, the next they were in the drink. They fired a Verey light, and from that moment on they were regarded as shipwrecked men. They knew all about it. Americans.'

'Everything's a *job* for them, the war included,' my grandfather said.

'They have no ties,' Asmus Asmussen said. 'They have no inner call. They're at home everywhere.'

'They eat nothing but cotton candy and drink coloured lemonade,' my morose grandfather said. 'I've read all about it, their food's quite typical of them.'

'Because they're at home everywhere, they're at home no-where,' Asmus Asmussen said. 'Their songs are travellers' songs, their habitations are those of nomads, their books are the books of travelling people. American life means living provisionally, without any permanent obligation, an interim life. As it were in the covered wagon.'

'Civilians, all of them, even in uniform,' my grandfather said disdainfully.

'Precisely,' said Asmus Asmussen, and then he felicitously produced the dictum : 'Only those who are firmly rooted weather the great storms.'

This dictum was meant to conclude the discussion. Asmus had just pulled a new slide from his envelope and was about to put it into the projector when my father once more disturbed the performance – not by producing the fruit of his own think-ing as a policeman – but by stalking up to the lecturer and clutching him, his lips moving at an incredible speed, trying out words and sentences to formulate what he had seen of a future disaster and producing yet another climax to that evening by saying :

'It was you, Asmus, I saw you in the rubber dinghy. You didn't stir. Your hand was hanging over the side, into the water. There wasn't anybody with you, Asmus, and far and wide the sea was empty.'

That was all my father had to say, it was probably all he had seen, and he didn't need to say any more. Our lecturer stretched out his hands as though to ward him off, and holding him at bay he said :

'Leave off ! Have the goodness to leave off !'

'But you didn't stir in the dinghy,' my father murmured by way of apology, and Asmus retorted :

'I must really ask you not to go on interrupting the lecture.'

The Rugbüll policeman looked round in despair. He was searching for something. Was he searching for a screen? Was he looking for a bright surface on which to project the pictures he had developed in the dark-room inside his head, and so give proof of the urgency of what he had experienced?

'All right then, all right, I won't say another word,' he murmured. He was slow on the uptake, slow in thinking things out, and that was lucky for him, for it enabled him to endure quite a number of things – above all : himself. Sighing and shrugging, he pocketed the handkerchief into which he had knotted all his excitement. Without surprise he looked at Hinnerk Timmsen walking up to him – probably at the bidding of others in the audience – taking hold of his sleeve and asking :

'Shall we be going along, Jens?'

Nor was my father astonished when people rose as he walked stiff-legged down the aisle towards the door, led by Hinnerk Timmsen, the innkeeper – just as if the whole rather dreary performance had come to its official end. And when they reached the door he said :

'That's all right with me, Hinnerk. Let's go.'

He didn't notice the silent ranks through which he had to walk, and only I hesitated for quite some time, probably waiting until some of them had sat down again, before I hurried after my father and Timmsen, into the Külkenwarf yard all dotted with puddles. There I saw the two men in front of me walking arm in arm, or, to put it more precisely, saw Timmsen put his arm through my father's, guiding him through the bright summer's evening and up the dyke.

Is it worth while saying anything about Hinnerk Timmsen? He wore a scarf that was as long as the series of jobs he had resolutely tried his hand at and failed in. A flag of failure, dropping at the masthead, that's what that scarf of his was, which he wore wrapped round his neck and dangling down to his knees. Timmsen had been a sailor, a cattle-dealer, a manufacturer of grain-sacks, he'd been an agricultural labourer, a junk-dealer, and a salesman of lottery-tickets. Before he had inherited the Wattblick Inn from a sister of his we used to meet him driving his rubber-wheeled cart when he was a milkman. In keeping with his temperament he had started by trying to turn the inn into a really lively place, so to speak *the* inn round our way: he engaged a band, and he himself appeared as announcer, funny man, and magician. But his efforts availed him nothing: even while he was in the middle of his performance the bewildered guests paid their bills, left without finishing their beer, fled, leaving their plates full. His ambition wasn't given its due and he would long ago have looked for success in some other field if war hadn't broken out.

Hinnerk Timmsen, a man who delighted in making decisions, an ambitions man, led my father up on to the dyke. I walked sometimes behind and sometimes in front of them. They didn't pay any attention to me, they were preoccupied with each other. My father was feeling the worse for what he had said or, rather, revealed. He didn't seem to have any exact memory of it all, merely the feeling that he had been forced to confess something and that people had taken it amiss.

'Was it very bad, Hinnerk?' he kept on asking. 'Come on, Hinnerk, tell me, was it bad?'

And that big, heavy man, with all his experience in so many trades, merely shook his head, meanwhile continuing to scrutinize the mortified policeman out of the corner of his eye, in a rather worried way, I should venture to say, at times even with awe and admiration. He apparently thought him capable of yet a lot more than he had shown during the evening.

At any rate, his restlessness made him hurry, and he pushed

and pulled my father along the top of the dyke, all the while uttering soothing remarks, along the beach where the waves of the North Sea were slowly rolling in and retreating, as in a slow-motion film, having lost their impact on the breakwater. There was no surf, no crashing of high-foaming waves, that evening, among the boulders and concrete blocks. High above us squadrons of airplanes were flying in the direction of Kiel. The smell of iodine from the sea, the salty winds – how near everything is, how it all waits for the moment to recur, the right moment when one finds the right word! One only has to grope for it, one only has to listen, to harken to a voice that makes itself heard now and then.

But for me there must be no such relief, I mustn't trust that voice which knows no doubt : here's the dyke, here's the North Sea, here are the two men walking ahead of me.

We went down to the Wattblick Inn. We went out on to the wooden verandah that was built out over the dyke. The large picture-windows were blacked out. The small windsock hung slack on its mast. Blue shadows lay across the sea, streaked with grey ribbons. My father took his bicycle out of the bicycle-stand and turned it round, and then Hinnerk Timmsen suddenly said :

'Come inside, have a drop of something.'

'Not tonight,' my father said.

'Just a quick one,' Timmsen urged.

For a while they went on arguing about it – 'no, no', 'oh come on' – and in the end my father, still crestfallen, put his bicycle back in the stand, and in we went, one behind the other, through the side door into the taproom, which was empty, except for Johanna there knitting, and she didn't put down her needles when she recognized us. Johanna, who had once been married to Timmsen and now worked for him, returned our greeting curtly and took refuge behind her knitting, and Timmsen steered us to a table, exerting himself on behalf of the policeman who was his guest.

He made quite an effort to make us comfortable, wiping the table energetically, putting on it little mats for the glasses and then, with a knowing grin, bringing the rum bottle out of the cupboard where it was kept for special occasions, and he did not fail to indicate that he was well aware he was pouring out a generous tot : in short, doing my father proud. He had never

133

before served my father so obligingly. He also instantly broke the just-one-drink agreement by putting the bottle on the table, conveying that my father should help himself to more. There was now an expression of mad, devil-may-care gaiety on his face, the sort of gaiety that has something threatening about it and which obviously had been the very thing that had caused so many guests to take their leave as hastily as they did. I still remember it was quite some time before I dared to drink any of the lemonade he'd set before me. He thought of everything. Before sitting down at our table he shooed away Johanna by pulling a face at her and producing a long-drawn hissing sound, the kind one uses to drive hens away, with the result that the squat, carelessly dressed woman, with hairpins sticking out of the bun of brown hair perched on top of her head, rose, grumbling, rolled up her knitting, and disappeared. He sat down between us. He raised his glass, clinked glasses with my father and then, winking at me, with me too, after which, belatedly, he also produced his reason for drinking: 'Here's to you, Jens, and to this highly informative evening.'

So there we sat in the Wattblick, while at Külkenwarf it was proved beyond any doubt that our Sea-Homeland was capable of giving an answer to all questions. To all questions? Why is it only among us that everybody seems afraid of confessing there's anything he knows nothing about? The all-out narrow-mindedness into which people are lured by local patriotism probably finds its completest expression in people's notion that they're called upon to give an expert answer to all questions: arrogance born of narrowness . . .

But let us stay in the Wattblick, where the low ceiling is painted a dark green, where the door-posts are covered with shells, where navigation-lights hang on the walls and tasselled penants of the Glüserup Savings Association adorn them, to-gether with a miniature steering-wheel used as a chandelier; where empty window-boxes stand on sills from which the white paint is flaking off, where dark iron ashtrays bearing some advertisements stand on tables that are protected by oilcloth covers long mottled with age, and where a round table reserved for the regular guests stands close to the bar, on which there is a money-box in the shape of a boat, provided by the Lifeboat Association. For the rest, there's a flower-table with old newspapers on it and blurred photographs of the beach and sea-bathing during the last thousand, oh well, anyway, the last three hundred years.

We were sitting at the round table reserved for the regulars. I was the first to finish my drink. My father worked a little round pool of water next to the water-jug into the triangular shape of India and then added a few little islands to the west. He had entirely withdrawn into a brooding sense of guilt that he couldn't or wouldn't explain to himself, and he drank indifferently. After the first sip Hinnerk Timmsen didn't touch his glass. He merely watched my father, intent, eager to learn something, just the way one watches a one-armed bandit as the wheels go whizzing round. Indeed, there was yearning in his gaze : that calculating gaze, across the steaming grog that was slowly growing cold, betrayed the fact that he expected something quite definite of my father.

But no doubt the background to that scene in the Wattblick Inn is sufficiently sketched in by now – that scene which started off with the policeman saying (his eyes cast down) : 'We'll have to be getting a move on.'

Timmsen (jumping up) : 'Not yet, Jens. There's something I'd like to talk over with you. Tank up. Help yourself.'

The policeman (exhausted) : 'Not tonight. We'll finish our drink and go.'

Timmsen (standing behind my father's chair) : 'If you really wouldn't mind, Jens. Just a bit of advice, that's all. No risk so far as you're concerned.' (Quickly filling up my father's glass, taking him by surprise) : 'And no trouble either, so far as I can see.'

The policeman (slumping down in his chair) : 'Tonight you can tell me anything you like. I shan't understand a thing. I can't make out what's going on inside my head. You might just as well talk to the window.'

Timmsen (stepping to one side and scrutinizing my father's profile) : 'That doesn't matter a hoot. I do my own thinking.' (A distant explosion makes the windows rattle) : 'Land-mine, I expect. Some sort of ship out there. Spontaneous combustion, I dare say. Well, here goes.'

The policeman (trying to brush him off) : 'I'm telling you, my mind's a blank tonight. And there's the boy. He's got to go to bed, and my eyes are smarting.' (He shades his eyes with one hand.)

Timmsen (obsequiously): 'Shall I switch off the light?' (A few quick steps to the wall, switches the light off.) 'Right, we don't need any light for it, if it hurts your eyes.'

The policeman (perplexed): 'Put the light on. Else I'll fall asleep.'

Timmsen (in the dark, obsessed with his idea): 'You needn't answer at once. Just take your time.'

The policeman: 'Put the light on, I tell you!'

Timmsen (obsessed, his hand on the light-switch): 'What would you do in my place? I can get hold of eggs. I can get hold of spirit. I've worked it all out. What I want is to start a small distillery. Egg-nog! Nourishing. Keeps you warm. I could sell it to the army.'

The policeman (wearily): 'Egg-nog – mere sight of it makes me sick. Whoever dreamed up *that* stuff.'

Timmsen (stubbornly): 'Do you see any future in a distillery like that? That's what I'd like to know. No trouble getting the concession. When peace comes, one could expand.'

The policeman (laughing): 'Banking on me, Hinnerk, you'd be bankrupt.'

Timmsen (switching on the light, eagerly): 'What I'm wondering: what are the chances? Neat, shiny stillroom, tall brick chimney-stack – *you* know. Office-block and women in white smocks seen through the windows, holding test-tubes, all that. Lorries at the big main gate, getting in each other's way, honking. Every bottle with label on it: Timmsen's Egg-nog.'

The policeman (drinks, smiling): 'If you want my advice: eat eggs. And drink a schnapps when you feel like it. As for the rest, forget it.'

Timmsen (incredulous): 'That's all you can see?'

The policeman (candidly): 'What else do you expect me to see? Just take a look at one of those bottles. If you try to pour, it comes out plop, all yellow and lumpy. Is there anybody who hasn't had his fill just from looking at it?'

Timmsen (returning to the table): 'Later on we might start exporting. There are places where they *like* egg-nog. And, anyway, one might dilute the stuff a bit.'

136

The policeman (exhausted, but cheerful): 'As for me, Hinnerk, if I come to your place, I'll ask for the raw materials.'

Timmsen (drinks, looking disappointed): 'Come on, try a bit harder. Can't you do any better, if you try really hard?'

The policeman (uncomprehending): 'What do you mean, "try a bit harder"? I drank the stuff once, the day I was confirmed, and that was enough for me – down to this very day.' (He drinks and gets up, but then instantly sits down again, recognizing the man coming in out of the dark. Max Ludwig Nansen stops at the door, irresolute. He is carrying his sketching-folder.)

The painter: 'Evening all. Can a man still get a cup of tea here? With a dash of something in it?' (He sits down at a table at the window.)

Timmsen: 'You can even have some grog. The water's still hot.'

The painter (cleaning his pipe): 'Better still, Hinnerk. That's what I call striking lucky.'

The policeman leans back in his chair, watching the painter.

Timmsen (mixing the grog): 'Where've you been tonight? If you'd been at Külkenwarf, you'd have had a surprise. You wouldn't believe who came sailing in – Asmus Asmussen.'

The painter: 'Thought he was cruising somewhere out in the North Sea, in his patrol-boat?'

Timmsen: 'He's been showing us pictures. Life aboard a patrol-boat and the like. He gave us a talk.'

The painter (cutting up a cigar-butt): 'Very long-winded, I dare say. All over by now?'

Timmsen (holding out a glass towards the painter): 'If you'd come and sit down with us, I needn't carry it all the way over there.'

The painter: 'Never butt in on other people's celebrations.' (Gets up, fetches the glass, takes it back to his table. Bows cheerfully.) 'Your health, all of you over there.'

Timmsen: 'We left Külkenwarf before the end. Jens wasn't feeling too good.'

The policeman (indignant): 'What do you mean, not feeling too good?'

Timmsen: 'Right in the middle of the talk it happened. It

137

just came pouring out of him. Yes, that's how it was.'

The painter (filling his pipe, then lighting it): 'I simply can't make you out.'

Timmsen: 'Think of Heta Bantelmann, or Dietrich Gripp. What they saw came true.'

The painter (surprised): 'Are you going to tell me Jens has the second sight? This chap here? He's never shown any sign of it.'

Timmsen: 'You just ask Asmus Asmussen. He knows what to expect now. He's in the picture all right. Jens turned it on for him tonight. If you'd been there on Külkenwarf you'd have had a surprise all right.'

The policeman: 'Shut up, can't you? That's all over and done with.'

Timmsen: 'Once it's happened to you, it's bound to come back time and again. Just like malaria. My brother could never shake it off. Anyone whose got second sight has got it for keeps. Heta Bantelmann knew whose house was going to be the next to burn down.'

The painter (scarcely visible in the shadows and behind clouds of tobacco-smoke): 'Taking into account Jens's occupation, I should say it might come in handy for him – make work easier.'

Timmsen: 'He saw Asmus Asmussen drifting in a dinghy. One hand dangling in the water.'

The painter: 'There you are. He'd better stay ashore.'

The policeman (irritable, rapping on the table with his empty tobacco-tin): 'In your place, I'd keep quiet. That sort of remark won't make things easier for you.'

The painter (impenetrably): 'You can save yourself a lot of investigating, if you've got the second sight. That's all I meant to say, just that.'

Timmsen (changing the subject): 'I've heard Dietrich Gripp say it doesn't work to order. You've got to wait for it to happen, but when it does happen there's the future lying before your eyes like a valley in bright sunlight. It always left him with a headache, and he was fagged out. A stabbing pain in his temples, that's what he got from it.'

The policeman (draining his glass): 'I'd have you know I haven't got any stabbing pain in the temples. And now don't

138

start talking about it all over again, the two of you. It's happened and it's gone again.'

Timmsen: 'But what about your eyes? You said your eyes were smarting.'

The painter: 'That's a consequence of looking too deeply into certain things.'

The policeman (rises, buckles on his belt, hooks both his thumbs into it and slowly approaches the painter's table): 'May a chap ask what you've got in that there portfolio?'

The painter (unworried): 'I was out on the peninsula. In the hut. To have a go at the sunset. Red and green. A real drama. Almost pure colour, all of it. You chaps ought to have been there to see it.'

The policeman (pointing at the portfolio): 'I asked you what's in there.'

The painter (gravely): 'I've been doing the sunset. Going on with it.'

The policeman (in a tone of command): 'Open that portfolio!'

(The painter sits motionless. Hinnerk Timmsen comes over, curious about what is going on.)

The policeman (doggedly): 'I am empowered to order you to open that portfolio. I herewith order you to open it.'

The painter (calmly): 'The modulations aren't right yet. Instead of orange – purple.' (Slowly, almost solemnly, he opens the portfolio, takes out a few empty sheets and lays them carefully on the table): 'All much too decorative. Decoratively metaphorical.'

Timmsen (bewildered): 'I can't see anything at all, for the life of me, I can't see a thing.'

The painter (turning to me): 'And what about you, Witt-Witt? Surely you can recognize the sunset?'

I (shrugging my shoulders): 'I don't know. Not yet.'

The policeman (picking up all the sheets, examining them, holding them up against the light and then throwing the whole lot of them on the table): 'You can't make a fool of me.'

The painter: 'What did you expect? I've told you, I can't stop. None of us can stop. Since you all object to the visible, I've taken to doing the invisible. Just have a good look at my invisible sunset with breakers.'

139

The policeman (nonchalantly picking up an empty sheet and holding it against the light): 'You have to think of something better than that, Max.'

The painter (contemptuously): 'Just take a close look, with that expert eye of yours. With your eye that sees into the future.'

The policeman (angry after his own fashion): 'I must insist on your using a different tone of voice when you speak to me. Even if your name's Nansen three times over. You're being a bit too high-handed.'

Timmsen: 'You'd better calm down, the two of you. You aren't strangers to one another, after all.'

The policeman (still holding the empty sheet against the light): 'This sheet . . . all these sheets are confiscated herewith.'

The painter (grimly): 'That's the stuff!'

The policeman: 'If you insist, you can have a receipt.'

The painter: 'I do insist.'

The policeman: 'But I can't make it out now. The receipt-book's in the office.'

The painter: 'Then I'll just have to wait for it.'

Timmsen (in genuine bewilderment): 'I can't make head or tail of it, Jens. As far as I'm concerned, this is paper. What you're confiscating is honest-to-goodness paper.'

The policeman: 'Let that be my worry.' (He stacks the sheets carefully, puts them into the portfolio and then takes it under his arm.)

Timmsen (to the painter): 'You've got to admit you haven't yet immortalized yourself on those sheets. They're as innocent as fresh-fallen snow.'

The painter: 'There are invisible pictures among them, didn't you hear? Obviously now that's forbidden too.'

The policeman (warningly): 'You know what the game is, Max. You know what my duty is. These sheets are going to be examined.'

The painter (grimly): 'Yes, yes. Go on, have them examined, for all I care. Have them put into the mincing-machine, for all I care. You won't succeed in destroying them. Different people – different pictures.'

The policeman (quietly): 'I've got to point out to you that you'd better watch your language. It might do you no good one of these days.'

140

Timmsen: 'The way you two talk to each other!'

The painter: 'Well, no one can search a man's head. Whatever's hung there, hangs safe. You can't confiscate what's in a man's head.'

The policeman (turning to me): 'Come on.' (We walk to the door.)

The painter: 'Let me know when you've detected something. When the paper shows its true colours under your scrutiny.'

(The policeman turns round, about to say something, then decides not to. We leave.)

Although I should have liked to stay on in the Wattblick Inn, drinking another lemonade and listening to the dispute about white paper that apparently wasn't quite so innocent, without a word I followed my father into the open, held the portfolio of blank sheets while he took his bicycle out of the stand and, once I was seated on the luggage-carrier, pressed it firmly to my chest.

In silence, through the vague darkness, we rode down the dyke with only a harmless little side wind. He didn't look back at me even once, and I could easily have pulled, if not all, at least some of the sheets out of the portfolio and let them sail down the dyke. I visualized what the flat country would look like, littered with empty sheets of paper, lying there like big handkerchiefs laid out to dry. Where would old Holmsen look first when he discovered the scattered sheets? I didn't open the portfolio.

Lifeless, their roofs pulled down on their brows, the farmhouses slumped there in the dark, fenced in by hedges grown crooked in the wind. Watchdogs conversed with each other over great distances. A thumping came from the sea, as though a large ship were casting anchor there.

'Do you know that ship?' I asked, actually believing he would be able to tell me the name or number of the ship just as he had suddenly told the number of Asmussen's boat, but to my disappointment he only said:

'Don't ask questions now, do you hear, don't ask me anything at all now.'

Still, I went on believing that in that peculiar way of his he saw and recognized the ship, and I still remember to this day how during that ride home I was all at once overcome by fear lest he might see and recognize even more, a fear that warned me and made me careful and that stayed with me perhaps longer than I am now prepared to admit.

But I should like to say, I must tell, what that strange fear was warning me of. Wasn't it *that* which forced me to look past my sailless mill? Why did I avoid thinking of my hide-out at its top? Why did I not look at Bleekenwarf when we rode past it? No glance, no thought for it. Why did I struggle to rid myself of the image of the shabby, unfinished bathroom that kept on looming up in my mind? Why did I force myself not to think of one name that continuously came to my memory?

If I now give a summary of that evening with all the soberness necessary to do so, whether I like it or not, I've got to bear witness to one fact: the Rugbüll policeman, my father, the northernmost policeman in Germany, who in the war received orders to inform Max Ludwig Nansen that he must not paint and to see to it that this ban was not broken, during a lantern-slide lecture revealed himself to be possessed of the faculty of second sight. He had never before shown any signs of possessing that faculty. Hereditary predisposition there was none. Nevertheless, that faculty manifested itself in him, and from the first moment this was not without its consequences.

7   The Interruption

Joswig's footsteps, the images conjured up by the sound of his steps as he issues forth from his bare lodge: a curving iron staircase, keys dangling on his ring, flagstones with chamfers, and the systematic network of murky corridors, days strung together like dried slices of apple, a sudden silence, his watchful gaze at a spy-hole, again the lax, shuffling step approaching from a hopeless distance, the main corridor with the blackboard, and standing there in the silence, reading; the corner with dark stains from our shoulders and hips, the breakfast break, the never open window, the alarm whistle on its lanyard, the shuffling step near the broom cupboard, from where it still seems to take him the best part of half a day until at long last, exhausted and ever more frequently stopping for a rest, he reaches the wash-room; then the finish, short, desperate steps, an outstretched arm, the excited jangling of keys, something that falls, no, nothing fell, merely the sound of the key, first testing the lock, then violently persuading it to turn: how often it has been like that.

Although I'd never timed him, to establish exactly how long it took him to get from the guard's lodge to my locked room, I should venture to say that it was about the time I needed for a perfunctory wash of three pairs of socks, for rolling twenty cigarettes, or to enjoy a leisurely breakfast without being threatened by an inspection. With the same slowness with which a ship gradually rises over the horizon and draws nearer, a slowness that kindles one's expectation, he would approach from that distant lodge of his which was adorned with nothing but a calendar, he would move along over the flagstones with his time-killing shuffle. At any event, while he was drawing near, evoking these images and recalling to my mind these events, I ceased to doubt Kurtchen Nickel's assertion that in the time Karl Joswig had taken to slouch along from his lodge to Kurtchen's room he had carefully sewn together a sheet that had been cut into strips.

He kept on: coming along, coming along. I combed my hair in front of my looking-glass, I watched a tug with barges in tow worming its way through the squares into which the Elbe was divided by the iron bars across my window. I watched gulls flying down river to one of their big council-meetings. A howling siren on a ship was a demand for assistance from tugs. Joswig wasn't giving up: he kept on coming. Was he bringing along new copybooks for me? Had Governor Himpel issued ink and nibs so that I could carry on with my task? I cooled my wrists under the strong jet issuing from the water-tap over the basin. I tore open a few cigarette-butts and flushed them down the drain. I smoothed the blankets on my bunk in order not to overtax his kindness. To my surprise I saw two canoeists doggedly paddling up river. The Elbe was free of ice. Was the torch alight over the oil refinery? Yes, it was. Was Hamburg still over there, whitish-grey and brick-red as ever? Joswig was coming along, irresistibly. What did they think of my work? Did it, in Himpel's eyes, justify my demand for still more copybooks? With swift resolution I put on my clean jacket, the one I wore on parade, exchanged my gym shoes for my boots, and took a clean handkerchief out of the metal cupboard. My big mirror's judgement on me was not unfavourable: the ash-blond hair, unruly but kept under control; deep-set bright eyes, the same eyes my brother Klaas has; a nondescript nose with only a slight bridge; a square mouth, one might even say a nut-cracker mouth – Pelle Kastner was quite correct in describing it thus; a strong lower jaw; bad teeth that look as if they had been nibbled at – no doubt part of the Schessel heritage; the neck a bit too long, but not scraggy; passable cheeks; that's me. There was no sign of any ill-effects from the punishment-task at which I was slogging on, day and night. Admittedly my pocket-mirror wasn't quite of the same opinion. In contrast with the mirror on the wall it provided me with shadows under the eyes and, besides, some general retouching of the image, in that it produced a crumbled version of myself, as it were making me acquainted with a face at once fatigued and irritable. Which of the two mirrors would Joswig agree with when he saw me? All right, Joswig, come on, put on an extra turn of speed, don't stop to peer into the wash-room, there's nothing there but the showers going drip drip. Put on that great final spurt of yours, unlock the door so that I can get some certainty at long last, or at least what we're in the habit of calling 'certainty'.

Now, as always, I went as far as I could to meet him; that is, I took up a position close to the door, fixed my gaze on the bolt and the keyhole through which the blunt end of the key pushed, or rather, into which it fumbled, indicating the turning of the wards that moved the bolt : a primitive bolt-system. In contrast with it, think of my own collection of keys and locks : tumbler-locks and pin-locks, Yale locks, puzzle-locks, the Chubb lock, the Gothic key, the French key, the Baroque lock-plate. Shall I ever find them again? Anyway, the door sprang open.

Karl Joswig, our favourite guard, didn't enter, didn't show himself. I merely heard his voice : 'Come along, Siggi. Come out.'

I did as I was bidden, and I was surprised to see him lock the door of my empty cell after me. Was that just force of habit after thirty-five years on the job? Or did he want to make sure that in my absence nobody else could enter the place where I was being kept in until I finished my task?

'The Guv'nor's waiting,' he said, and then he told me to walk ahead of him – a precaution he had insisted on only during the first few weeks. I wasn't actually hurt, but I was a bit puzzled and, looking searchingly into his face, I thought I could discern a furtive look of mistrust, a sort of desperate alertness. But before there was any chance to ask him why he was so taciturn, he jerked his flattened brown thumb in a semi-circle and pointed stiffly down the corridor, so I had no choice but to walk ahead.

I walked ahead of him up to the blackboard in the main corridor, his footsteps behind me sounding like a distorted echo of my own footsteps, his elderly sighs an enlarged version of my own sighs.

But then, when we had reached the blackboard, I looked back over my shoulder and asked : 'Do I get permission?'

In a disgruntled tone he said : 'Just wait and see. Can't you wait for it?'

I walked on, feeling his gaze on the back of my neck, feeling my gait becoming stiffer and a stabbing pain working up my spine. What should I, what could I, have done? All of us doing time in that place knew one could suddenly gain Joswig's sympathy by ingeniously taking all the blame on oneself. The more one insisted that one was no bloody good at all, the more stubbornly he would stand up in one's defence, even take one to his heart. But what could I have blamed myself for in order to get a conversation going between us? What failings could I have invented? I trotted on, trying to work out what it might signify that he had come without bringing copybooks, or ink, or so much as a shred of tobacco, and that instead of expressing sympathy he had merely told me I was to appear before the Governor. Was I in trouble? Did they object to the work I'd done up to now? Perhaps they were even thinking of bringing the task they'd set me, my German essay, my punishment, to an untimely end?

The telephone began ringing in Joswig's bare lodge. I didn't hurry for that. It went on ringing, six, eight, ten times. Still I didn't hurry, I merely looked out of the corner of my eye, expecting him to catch up with me, to overtake me, in order to get to the telephone. But the stiff peaked cap didn't turn up beside me, the bunch of keys didn't pass me, jingling. Karl Joswig seemed unperturbed, he stayed behind me. But when we'd reached his lodge, he ordered me to stop and wait. I stood still as I had been told to do. I looked straight ahead, focusing my attention on the eighth step of the iron staircase. When he said : 'Wait here,' I nodded, and when he said : 'I'll be back in a moment,' I nodded again. After that I observed him out of the corner of my eye as he lifted the receiver, pushed his cap on to the back of his head, and, listening, counted the keys in his bunch, checked them, disentangled them where they'd got entangled with each other. The telephone conversation didn't bring about any change in him. Just like my father, when *he* telephoned, he gave brief answers and asked brief questions. He seemed neither amused nor irritated. When he had put the receiver down, he beckoned me into the lodge. I held my breath because the air in there was so stale, with a lingering whiff of herrings quietly rotting away.

'There's two newcomers arriving,' Karl Joswig said. 'I'll have to stay here. I can trust you to find the way to the Guv'nor's office by yourself.' I nodded, but I didn't move, although he'd given me to understand that I was to go and that he had no further use for my presence.

'Don't you remember the way to his office?' he asked me. I hung on, gave him a searching look, and finally lowered my eyes, asking what I had done to deserve getting the brush-off like this. He opened the door for me to leave. 'You and your pals, the whole lot of you!' he said. 'There a chap is, doing everything for you, taking you to his heart, sacrificing himself for the likes of you. And what does he get out of it? Clear out of here! Get moving! The Guv'nor's expecting you!' And he pushed me across the threshhold and shut the door. Since he evidently had no wish to say any more, obviously not thinking it worth his while to give me any reason for the change in his feelings, I started on my way to the Guvernor's office all by myself. Stiff-jointed, I groped my way down the iron stairs. In the draughty hall I patted the bald marble head of Senator H. W. J. W. Riebensahm, who, though he hadn't actually created our island, had dedicated it to its ultimate purpose. I also scratched his ice-cold chin. How long was it since I had last paid my respects to him? One day I had seen his ninety-eight-year-old widow caressing that marble bust, and since then I could never make myself walk past it without patting it, out of a sense of duty. I didn't encounter anybody on the way, and so I opened the door and stepped outside – for the first time since I'd started on this task of mine.

A launch's siren screamed at me. At me? Anyway, it gave me a fright, so I turned round, looking towards the jetty, where the shiny motor-launch from Hamburg, glittering with brass, was just tying up, crammed with impatient psychologists from Hamburg, all wearing brown or sand-coloured smocks. There on the pier was Doctor Alfred Thiede, Himpel's deputy, welcoming the psychologists with a grand, all-embracing gesture that he'd obviously picked up from Himpel. Involuntarily I looked around for a way of escape, say in the direction of our vegetable-garden. But there was no need for that, for Doctor Thiede, on the pier, was now gathering the psychologists around him and beginning one of his discouraging addresses. From the shore, where the warning notice-boards, which had been pushed out of alignment by the ice, were again standing straight, there came a cool breeze that made the willow-branches tremble. There was no haze over the Elbe, the air was brisk and clear, and this clear air caused the distant banks to seem nearer than they really were. The water, which is normally as muddy as river water can be, was bottle-green in some places and blue-black in others, showing where the Elbe was shallow and where it was deep. A ship flying a great many pennants was steaming downriver, probably on its way to a wharf. Out of our work-shops they were pushing carts loaded high with window-frames. Eddi Sillus was one of the party.

Not wishing to meet anybody, wanting only to find out as quickly as possible what they thought of my work and how matters stood, I ran to the back of the workshop and from there, out of sight and out of the wind, went on until I reached the winding path leading to the blue administration-building, where the Governor had his office. I took the stone steps in two leaps and pushed open the varnished oak door. After a deep breath I went up to the Governor's room. I had my answers ready to a lot of possible questions, at least I was prepared to deal with catch-questions. I was not going to take it lying down if they tried to cut short my German lesson. I was set on keeping it up. Let's say I was prepared to fight for the right to carry on with it. In that frame of mind I approached the door, I raised my hand ready to knock, and stood listening. But hardly had my fingers touched the wood, when a musical tempest broke loose in the room beyond the door. With a chord reminiscent of the demiurge's grim *fiat*, in a *forte* laid on with a trowel, Himpel seemed to be causing blocks of ice to burst asunder and glaciers to calve; in relentless cadences he liberated a number of mountain-streams from the ice that held them in thrall, and he was, all in all, hard on winter's heels, driving Old Man Winter forth into exile, and all that just in order to make the flapping wing-beats or, for all I care, the rustle of spring audible. One couldn't help hearing the stormy sky he conjured up, the battle of the unleashed forces fighting each other to the death, and he was far from making it easy for that spring of his to work its way through all the roaring turmoil and dark defiance of the elements, until at last it succeeded in hoisting its blue flag (I hope I am giving an impression of it all). But then he let spring have a prolonged triumph, with the cry of gulls and the scream of ships' sirens, with tiny waves gurgling merrily, and a kind of fanatical murmuring in the air. One could safely assume that our island choir would very soon be giving a public performance of this new spring song, even, since they had already been invited to do so, taking part in the North German Radio Harbour Concert.

Since my knocking couldn't possibly assert itself over the smashing of the glaciers behind the door, I waited until spring had finally achieved victory; then I knocked again. Now I was heard. I was told to come in. Governor Himpel, in windbreaker and plus-fours, rose from his piano-stool, bent over his smudged music-paper, said : 'Um-tata, um-tata,' nodded with great complacency and came towards me with outstretched hands.

'It still needs a few little touches,' he said, indicating the music behind him. A quick glance at his desk assured me that he had read through my copybooks. But although they were stacked up there I realized for the present he had forgotten all about me and my task and wasn't at all eager to talk to me about it at length. He was involved in his unfinished spring gales. Only after consulting his desk-calendar did he realize that he himself had made a note about me and ringed it in red, thus attaching some importance to me, and so he welcomed me a second time by raising his hands to the level of his eyes and waving them about. He asked me to sit down. He himself didn't sit down, but stood in a strenuous attitude, leafing through my copybooks. As he re-read, his smile told me things were coming back to him : he shook his head incredulously, he nodded in agreement, he indicated qualms of a grave nature by producing a repeated 'Tut-tut', and once he tried to slap his own thigh, only managing, however, to strike his more than ample plus-fours a glancing blow. After having refreshed his memory by leafing through the copybooks and reading some passages, he rushed to the door of his secretary's room, tore it open, and shouted : 'Tell them in Room 14 we're ready, will you?'

He then shut the door again and returned to his desk, ex-

149

pressly avoiding my eye. Now I realized it was not going to be a tête-à-tête.

Senator Riebensahm, who hung over the desk (painted in oils), gazing, gaunt and guileless, out of a chiaroscuro a long way after Rembrandt, seemed far more interested in ships coming up the Elbe, perhaps all the way from Cameroon, than in anything going on here in Governor Himpel's room. The Senator wasn't going to give me any assistance. So I sat there listening to the secretary's footsteps, as she left her room and, her metal-tipped high heels clicking on the floor, crossed the corridor to whisper her message of release into room 14, then instantly returning, no longer alone now, but with other footsteps in her wake. Then she opened the door and let in a few psychologists. With some relief I observed that they were five psychologists apparently taking part in an international congress in Hamburg, since each of them wore in his lapel a little card blazoning forth his name. Actually one of them wore no card, and that was Wolfgang Mackenroth, who winked at me in a chummy way. The fact that he was with them did not disperse my anxiety, but in some way that it's difficult to explain I was glad that he was there. I returned his greeting without concealing what I felt. Meanwhile the Governor was shaking hands with the psychologists, with a smirk acknowledging greetings conveyed to him from Zurich, or Cleveland, Ohio, or Stockholm, and then, in a voice that was a little too loud and too emotional, he sent his own greetings back, at the same time deftly contriving to place his visitors in such a manner that they formed a semi-circle around me. What was he up to? What did his eyes betray? What trick was that pedagogically trained circus-equestrian hoping to bring off? Tame the wild beast? Make it walk the tightrope? Psychological levitation? Was he going to send me up on to the trapeze of his ambition, where I was to do the *salto mortale* two and a half times, so that he could show off how surely he would catch me in the end?

Governor Himpel did nothing of the sort. He put his hand on my shoulder in a matey gesture. He asked my permission to outline my case briefly to the visitors and, without more ado assuming I had agreed, began to hold forth. It had all started with a German lesson, he said. The theme of a composition to be written was: 'The Joys of Duty'. After that lesson, he said,

Herr Jepsen handed in an empty copybook, giving as his reason *not* that he had too little to say, but, quite the contrary, that he had too much to say. Initial block. Korsakoff's syndrome. Disciplinary action was taken, a task being set: namely the writing of the German composition. It was arranged that Herr Jepsen would be alone and undisturbed. He then mentioned the conditions agreed upon – no visitors, exemption from normal work, and so on – and then he described to his visitors, who were by no means agog, but, if anything, rather inert, how I had set about the task. Ultimate acceptance. Euphoria. Admittedly they pricked up their ears when Governor Himpel informed them that this task of mine had already been going on for 105 days. 'Our Herr Jepsen, whom you see here before you, has spent the last three and a half months getting his composition into shape. He is certainly not lacking in perseverance,' he said, raising my copybooks on high. '*This* is ample proof of that. As you can see, the composition is growing downright alarmingly. Names compulsion. Place compulsion. Psychoid Mnemism.' Finally he asked me to correct him should I feel he had misrepresented the situation in any way. I shrugged my shoulders.

The visitor from Cleveland, Ohio, Mr Boris Zwettkoff, asked Himpel to let him have a look at my copybooks, flicked the pages over, and was in the picture. The gentleman from Zurich, one Carl Fouchard Junior, and the gentleman from Stockholm, Lars Peter Larsen, likewise revealed hitherto unheard-of ability to seize hold of and assimilate a subject merely by opening the copybooks at various places, but chiefly by weighing them in their hands, thus arriving at a judgement that summed up the case. Only Wolfgang Mackenroth, the last one to handle my copybooks, did nothing of the sort. He took hold of them in a gingerly way, went to the trouble of smoothing them out, and then laid them back on the desk.

I heaved a sigh of relief, thinking the performance was over and done with, and was just transferring my weight to my other leg when Governor Himpel issued forth from the background and came over to me.

After a glance at the psychologists that urged them to be particularly alert and take note of what happened now, he turned to me, remarking that the work I had done was not merely adequate, but had far surpassed his expectations. He offered to call off the German lesson. I had convinced him, and Herr Dr Korbjuhn as well. He suggested I should now return to the bosom of the island community and take up my job in the library again.

'You have now realized,' he said – these were his very words – 'that German compositions have to be written, and what concerned us was that you should come to see that – not the punishment.' And as though he were giving me a present out of his own private funds, he added: 'Meanwhile spring has arrived.'

He might just as well have skipped that final remark, especially since he really ought to have known that none of us here cared a damn about spring. Anyway, I looked at him in amazement, not having expected that suggestion.

'Well?' he asked. 'Well? Wouldn't it be a pleasant prospect – to have done with your task? Be reunited with your chums? Well?'

'I haven't finished my work,' I said.

'That doesn't matter,' he said. 'What you have got done is quite satisfactory, and we can waive the rest.'

'Without the rest the work isn't worth anything,' I said, and I meant what I said.

Himpel was flabbergasted. He asked me to explain to him and his visitors why I was so intent on finishing the task, continuing a punishment, going to the lengths of renouncing the community life of our island, the spring sunlight, and my job in the library. I gazed out of the wide window in the corner of the room, on to the Elbe, and at first I couldn't detect anything to fix my gaze on. I let my eyes roam along our beach, and then I discovered two canoe-men in a silver-grey canoe drifting out from under the willow-thicket, out of control, not being paddled, simply drifting obliquely across the river, and I saw it drifting further and further because the man in the rear was holding the one in front in a tight grip, pushing him down on his back and pressing his own face against the other's face or doing something of the sort, despite the fact that it must have been very uncomfortable, while the paddles were being drawn along through the water, dipping in, but not getting lost.

'But why?' Governor Himpel asked. 'Why?'

'Because,' I said, 'of the joys of duty. I should like to understand it the unabridged, from the beginning to the end.'

'And supposing joys never came to an end?' he asked,
making sure that the psychologists were paying proper attention. 'Supposing those joys went on for ever?'

'That'd be just too bad,' I answered. 'Just too bad.'

I felt they were after something, they wanted to get something out of me, drag it out into the light of day, but I didn't
know what it was. The men in the canoe were still drifting
down river, clutching at each other, lying on top of each other
in an exaggerated position, mouth upon mouth, but unfortunately no ship turned up to cut them apart with its bows.
They didn't even lose a paddle.

Then suddenly Carl Fouchard Junior asked: 'To whom are
you telling the whole thing?'

'Myself,' I said.

'Does it make you feel easier in your mind?' he asked.

'Yes,' I said, 'it does make me feel easier in my mind.'

The Swede remained silent, only now and then giving me a
hostile look as though he'd have liked to knock me down. Boris
Zwettkoff, the American, was thoroughly pleased when, in reply
to the question whether, while working on the task, I sometimes
felt as if I were standing in water, wading through water or
swimming in clear water, I was able to produce a definite no.
One big, brawny chap whose name I couldn't decipher because
he wore his little name card upside down in his buttonhole,
but whose accent revealed him to be a Dutchman, surprised me
by wanting to know: first of all, my age, and secondly, what
size shoes I wore, and after I had told him both, he wanted to
know whether I frequently broke into a sweat and suffered
from states of anxiety while engaged on my task. Since I didn't
want to disappoint him completely, I admitted to states of
anxiety. The fact that Mackenroth didn't ask any questions,
indeed even gave me an encouraging smile now and then, made
me like him better than ever. I gathered they realized I hadn't
the makings of the sort of case on which to work up a scientific
controversy, for that international group delegation thereupon
left me in peace, not troubling to investigate any further.

Governor Himpel clearly hadn't expected that. He would
obviously have preferred a longer interrogation, a more search-

153

ing investigation, and discussion that would be, if not heated, at least lively. But since nothing of the sort happened, it was left to him to go on dealing with my case. I shot a glance at the spot where the two men in the canoe ought to have been, but they had capsized and got drowned, and the Elbe was flowing on, empty and innocent.

'Well, Siggi,' Himpel said, 'now the two of us must try to work this thing out. This can't go on. Being set a composition to write,' he said, 'is nothing extraordinary. It is done everywhere. Here on our island it has been of the greatest use educationally. But even a punishment must be within reason – and 105 days is *enough*. So from today your punishment is over.'

He held out his hand to me, that hand which was so experienced in bestowing salutations. He wished to shake hands on our agreement to bring the German lesson to an end. But I refused to shake hands on it. I protested. I asked for an extension. I promised never again to be a source of annoyance to anyone if only he'd let me return to taking my punishment. I think I also appealed to his generosity. But all those protests, appeals, and promises seemed to be of no avail. How did I manage to get away with it in the end? I simply reminded him of his promise that it was to be me who should decide when the task was finished.

'Didn't you yourself say it could be as long as seemed necessary?' By quoting his own words to him I succeeded – not in making him change his mind entirely – but in getting him to agree that for the time being I should go on with my task.

'All right,' he said in gentle resignation, 'all right, all right. For the present you may go on.'

He went to his desk and handed me the copybooks filled with my work. He looked inquiringly into the psychologists' faces and, since he didn't detect any qualms there, released me with the words: 'You can find your way back alone, I'm sure. You may have a new copybook and more ink.'

Relieved, though with my mind not entirely at rest, I edged through the semi-circle of the visitors, manoeuvring in such a manner that I had to pass close to Mackenroth. He winked at me. I should think his glance expressed respect. But while *above* he merely winked at me harmlessly, *below* he was less harmlessly occupied. His quick, nimble, delicate fingers opened the pocket of my jacket, put something in, pushed and pulled at it for a second and then smoothed the pocket as well as possible, and in the next second had withdrawn again. I remained almost unaware of it, but that's how it must have happened. I am not exaggerating when I say that Ole Plötz, who is a specialist in ladies' handbags, is the only one among us who could have done it as well.

At the door I turned round for the last time, for a fleeting bow to the group delegation, at the same time casting a long and searching look at Mackenroth's face. His face didn't admit anything of what had happened; he had meanwhile masked himself again in indifference. Standing there he could successfully have refuted any suspicion uttered, and, what's more, without having to speak a single word.

Outside in the corridor I put my hand in my pocket to identify what the young psychologist had secretly slipped into it. It wasn't much. My fingers felt a few sheets of paper clipped together, and also, to my delight, a smooth packet of twelve cigarettes.

I went straight to the wash-room. There I hid the packet of cigarettes in my right sock and made the sheets of paper into a sort of shin-pad, which I put round my left shin and calf, then I pulled the sock up and let the elastic top snap back into place. I pulled my trouser-legs down carefully, washed my hands, drank some water, moistened my forehead. All the windows were open, and the spring air, presumably entering by permission of Governor Himpel, took the sting out of the smell of ammonia that permeated the place. Down in the yard somebody was whistling 'Rock Around the Clock', much too slow. I didn't want to hear it whistled wrongly, so I pulled the chains in all three lavatories, causing the 'Rock' to vanish under roaring cascades of water. Then I went out into the corridor and for a brief moment listened at Himpel's door. But I could hear nothing except a sound as though somebody were moaning with pleasure – just as if someone were being massaged there – and so I went to the stairs and down to the stationery department.

The stationery department is on the ground floor of the administration building, next to the library. The two rooms have a connecting door, and the two jobs – issuing stationery and handing out books – are the responsibility of one and the same chap. I knew who it was who would appear when I knocked, would welcome me with a sly smile, and, chewing something as usual, would ask : 'Went off all right, did it?' He's the eldest of us all. We all have to be friends with him and stay that way by paying him regular little attentions. Because he's been here on the island for five and a half years he simply insists on his special rights, and there's not a single one among us who wouldn't make him over his pudding if he's so bidden in, let's say, these words : 'Your pudding wants to come over to me, Siggi, be a good chap and help it on its way.' That fellow, with his lustreless hair and his fleshy lips, if he comes up to you, or if you watch him during a German lesson, while he is preparing for one of those fits that will make him shake all over and collapse, you'd think him capable of quite a number of things. It's doubtful, however, whether the mere sight of a handbag on a woman's arm will really inspire him to such an extent that he'll be able to say, just by looking at the outside of it, what's inside. I also regard it as an exaggeration to assert that he's capable of opening any type of handbag just by stroking it gently, but there are two among us who insist they've watched him doing it.

Anyway, Ole Plötz was my successor in the library, and it was his job, as it had been mine before him, to hand out the stationery. When I knocked, it brought him along. He opened the upper part of the door, grinned, pulled out a board that turns the lower part into a counter, leaned his elbows on it, raised his face to me, and asked :

'Went off all right, did it?'

I said yes, it did, listened, and then, still listening, got out the packet of cigarettes, took out three and put them into Ole's open hand. I was about to cause the packet to disappear, but I hadn't reckoned with Ole's delicate sense of justice : with an elegant movement he caught hold of the packet, swiftly counted the cigarettes, establishing the fact that he had been given three less than was his due, silently adjusted that matter, handed me back what was left, and then raised a finger to his forehead in an expression of thanks.

'What can I do for you?' he asked. And now I was able to make out that what he was chewing was a button, a genuine

156

horn button, if I'm not mistaken, the sort that's used on great-coats. I asked him for a copybook with unlined pages, and a bottle of ink, and then I changed my mind and asked for two copybooks. Ole said :

'You'd better work out exactly what you need. We're in a generous mood today. For all I care you can have five copy-books, for all I care you can cart off the whole of this rubbish here. We've given up racking our brains about you.'

'They've set me this task,' I said by way of apology. 'You all know that.'

'Yes,' he said, 'we know that, but we've never before had a chap among us who seemed to relish his punishment the way you do.'

'I haven't been mucking things up for you,' I said.

'You haven't,' he answered, 'exactly endeared yourself to those inside here. But today we'll forgive you. Today we are prepared to forgive everyone.'

'Is something special on?' I asked.

'Nothing special,' he said, grinning. 'It's just that a few of us are going to move : change of locality, change of air. Man has come of age, or so I happened to read in a book, and when someone of age leaves a place of his own free will, that implies some criticism, and so forth.'

'Do you mean to blow?' I asked.

'We hope you'll come along,' he said softly. He listened to make sure there was no one in the corridor and then he grabbed me by my shirt and pulled me across the counter towards him.

'Eleven o'clock tonight,' he whispered. 'It's all fixed. Six of us.'

I inquired how they'd organized the boat, and his contemp-tuous answer was that only chaps who couldn't swim needed a boat. I asked if he was familiar with the currents of the Elbe, and he drew my attention to the advantage the incoming tide was to swimmers. He couldn't and wouldn't regard Karl Joswig as an obstacle, since Eddi Sillus had volunteered to deal with our favourite guard singlehanded – Eddi, who at a very early age had earned a Black Belt in north-west German Judo. I wanted to know what arrangements they'd made for the event of a favourable current taking us to the other bank, to some-where near Blankenese. Now he let go of me, looked me up and down with a malicious glare, said something that sounded very much like 'yellow bastard' and then calmly lit a cigarette. He took only a few puffs, then put the cigarette out again. He went up to the shelves, took three copybooks from the stack, and slammed them down on the counter in front of me. Then he dug into a cardboard box, brought out a small angular bottle of ink, slammed that down in front of me too, and finally pointed his sensitive forefinger at the place where I had to sign. I couldn't possibly miss the point : he had finished with me.

I couldn't afford a mute, hostile farewell, I had to smooth it out somehow, since one can't ever be sure a chap won't come back. So I said :

'Have you any plan what you'll do over there?'

He moistened his fleshy lips, lifted up the counter and opened the lower part of the door. 'My sister,' he said. 'We're going to ground there, the lot of us. Her husband's at sea.'

'You'll be able to weather the first storm there, I bet,' I said.

Quick on the uptake he retorted : 'I thought you were coming along? I always thought : one doesn't leave one's friends in the lurch?' He glanced down the corridor. 'Well?' he asked. 'Eleven? You don't even have to open the door. We'll come for you.'

What sort of impression must I have made on him as I stood there, painfully undecided, wanting to do the one thing and obliged to do the other, knowing that the one thing was my duty, while the other was an obligation? On the one hand I imagined our collective escape, Joswig tied up and gagged, all of us running, bent low, down the corridor, stopping under the cover of the workshops, then one after the other taking short jumps down to the willows on the bank. Perhaps there'd be the barking of a dog, just the way Philipp Neff must have heard it suddenly, having no choice but simply to choke it to death, then wading and shoving along until we reached deep water and sank into it, and then six faces all lit up by the moon, six faces on trembling silver, as it were six small, drifting, ball-shaped buoys, of a kind that's unknown on the Elbe, moving aslant against the current, cleverly using the current, drifting in the direction of Blankenese. The prickling cold, a sudden scream, arms flung up into the air, no, no scream, but lights, the

158

near, welcome lights of Blankenese, now for once so dear to us, the shimmering strand that Philipp Neff must have seen ahead of him but could never reach, and then six figures moving in single file towards the bank, gradually emerging from the water, walking along as though they'd been walking all across the bottom of the Elbe.

That's what I imagined on the one hand, and I entirely saw its very promising possibilities. On the other hand, there were those copybooks of mine, all filled up with what I had written, and I weighed them in my hand just as the psychologists had done, and while Ole was looking at me with a sly expression, I thought of the composition that Korbjuhn had set, perhaps even with me expressly in mind. I thought of the joys and of the duty I'd begun to describe, of all I'd tried to communicate and to confess to – was I to leave it all unfinished? The northern-most police station in Germany, the painter, my brother Klaas, Asmus Asmussen, Jutta – was I to deny them the right to state their case and to defend themselves? Was I to pull down the curtain and thus of my own free will cause darkness to fall on my field of action? Was I not bound to take it all further than the mere pre-history? Did I have the right to decide on with-drawing from all that had come to me, and this by no means as a result of my own free will? Wasn't it my duty, now, after having summoned up memories from so many sides, to wait for the echoes of my own voice?

'No, Ole,' I said, 'it's impossible. No. I'm sorry, but I can't do it. I can't run away with you chaps. I can't get away from the punishment I've been given, not yet.'

He shut the lower part of the door. 'I see *the joys of duty* have got a hold of you,' he said. 'Go ahead, burrow into it, and for all I care choke to death.'

'I want you to understand,' I said.

'Take your copybooks and get out,' he said.

'I want you to see my point, Ole,' I said.

He grinned with disgust and retorted: 'See your point? What is there to be seen if someone insists on stirring around in all that shit? Take your copybook, boy, and get lost!'

'I wish you'd wait for me,' I said. 'I'd like to join you later on.'

'We're off tonight, and that's that,' Ole said.

'That's too soon for me,' I said, and I added : 'Watch out, I've got a feeling Joswig smells a rat. He was rather suspicious.'

'Let that be our worry,' he said and gave me to understand I was to step back so that he could close the upper part of the door.

To conciliate him, to change the subject, I asked a few questions about the library, but Ole Plötz wouldn't listen to me. Ole slammed the door in my face, so I uttered my last words to the sign : Stationery Issue.

The battle was over. But who had won the victory?

'Good luck,' I said to the sign on the door, 'and all the best for tonight.'

I went back to where I'd come from, I had to go back, the copybooks under my arm, carrying the ink bottle, new but dusty, the things that were my guarantee that I could go on with my task. Nobody could talk me into giving up; not even the invitation to join the chaps meaning to escape from this place tonight was sufficiently alluring to make me give up my task. I simply had to return to my locked room. I pushed the swing door open with my shoulder and walked through the violent rustling and blowing of the spring-time winds, obviously produced by dear old Himpel in the privacy of his office. Apparently he was just about to cause some migrating birds to return on those keen winds, starlings, swallows, storks, admittedly only a few of the last, and he even permitted those swarms of birds to rush, flapping and fluttering, through the entire administration building, but for all that he couldn't prevent his spring song from approximating pretty closely to a spring song already well established and very often sung.

Outside on the sandy square, in clear air and mild sunshine, a different sort of Hamburg spring was noticeable. The cabbages needed watering. The willows, continuously tugged at by the river currents, were not hanging down stiff and dead. The sky was a watery blue. Lettuces and radishes were already coming up. The swarming psychologists wore their dustcoats hanging open. In the workshops and in the vegetable beds my fellow inmates were obliged to discover the blessings of work : smoking, worn out from merely looking on, our guards stood there beside them.

No, it was not a Himpel spring that extended in all directions here and left me stone cold as I walked across the square and towards my room, I should say, anyway without the slightest urge to watch it pushing itself into the foreground everywhere. And then all at once I started to run. I ran with my copybooks held tight under my arm and the bottle of ink in my hand. Of course some of the guards gave me a suspicious look across the yard. But since I wasn't running towards the river-bank, but towards the living quarters, they didn't stir. And if they had followed me they'd soon have been sorry they'd exerted themselves, merely in order to see a chap in the uniform worn by juvenile delinquents rushing up the stone stairs, only to stand outside the guard's empty lodge, listening, looking down all the corridors, then finally calling out for a guard to come along and shut him in. And after that they would have seen the boy, whose reformation everyone had decided to undertake, entering the guard's lodge and quite harmlessly looking for a key and, when he couldn't find one, sitting down on the spotty revolving chair in order to wait.

I was waiting for Karl Joswig. I tried to while away the time by examining the contents of the desk, but found nothing beyond an old fifty-billion marks banknote left over from the inflation, an item in our favourite guard's collection, for he collected all kinds of worthless paper money. I also found a cheese sandwich, twisted and petrified in years of oblivion. In order to pass the time I read the table of telephone extensions : West Wing, East Wing, Governor Himpel, Reception, Office, Alarm. Would the alarm bell ring this coming night? Workshops I to IV, Nursery, Storeroom, Infirmary, Kitchen, I read.

Karl Joswig didn't come. I put the table of telephone numbers back in its place and took the calendar off the wall to read the sayings on it, just to kill time. I leafed through it from back to front, from autumn to summer and from summer to spring, and there, rather taken aback, I discovered the first drawing : it was a giant man standing in the water up to his calves, passing water from an enormous penis and spraying an island. Turning the page, I discovered another rather rude picture, one that might even offend some people's sense of beauty : from a large behind a string of musical notes were rising into the air, making an ailing, somehow rachitic impression, and under the drawing was the caption in block letters : Himpel's gala concert No. 1.

Somewhat disconcerted, I turned another page. Here was a chimney-stack, smoking and bowing to the moss-grown door of a shed. I turned page after page : there was a drawing on each of them, and each of them had been given a scathing caption, a bitter remark. The whole month had been spoilt, marred by disfiguring drawings that offended one's sense of propriety - shameless doodles. It all betrayed the hand of Ole Plötz, and I didn't have to make any effort to recognize him as the originator of it all. I could well imagine that he intended leaving these masterpieces of his to the guards as a souvenir. Karl Joswig also got what was coming to him.

I must admit I was shocked when I saw the spoilt calendar, even though it was a talented hand that had spoilt it, and I glanced up to make sure no one was watching me as I looked through it, and then I put it back on the wall. Was Ole going to see it through? Were the others going to see it through? Would they manage the crossing of the Elbe? In all the stories of attempted escapes that I can recall – that I can recall without any particular wish to do so – these things start badly and come to a bad end too.

Karl Joswig failed to turn up. I pulled out my cigarettes but instantly put them away again because there was no chimney in that glass lodge for the smoke to escape through. From my other stocking I then took out Mackenroth's folded sheets of paper, smoothed them out and searched for a personal message, rather curious to discover how he would address me. Dear Herr Jepsen? My dear Siggi? or, pretending we were on somewhat intimate terms, but nevertheless keeping his distance : Dear Siggi Jepsen? But there was no such message. What he had put into my pocket was merely part of the article he had mentioned being about to write, a draft, as was expressly stated at the beginning. The title, however, seemed to be definitive : Art and Criminality, a Study of the Case of Siggi J. The whole title was underlined. Should I read it? Should I not read it? I felt like a butterfly on a pin. A. Positive Influences. I. The painter Lugwig Nansen, an outline. Was it worth reading on?

Since the influence [Wolfgang Mackenroth wrote], both active and passive, of the painter Max Ludwig Nansen on the subject undoubtedly outweighs that of school and home, it seems desirable to begin by providing some data on the life and work of this artist, in order to clarify the relationship. These data are derived in the main from his autobiography *The Greedy Eye* (Zurich, 1952), from *The Book of Friends* (Hamburg, 1955) and from Teo Busbeck, *The Language of Colour* (Hamburg, 1951). These works contribute, albeit indirectly, to an understanding of the relationship between our subject and the painter.

I raised my head, listened, and then hastily lit a cigarette. I felt a faint restiveness, a hot pressure in my temples, a twitching in my right leg. 'The subject,' eh? Oh well, all right. . . . Was he the wave, was I the boat? *The Language of Colour* was published in 1952, he ought to have got that right.

Max Ludwig Nansen [Wolfgang Mackenroth wrote], the son of Frisian peasants, was born in Glüserup, in the landscape that he later immortalized in his paintings. He began to draw, paint and model while still a boy at the village school. He was then apprenticed to a wood-carver in a furniture factory in Itzehoe, where he also took a course in draughtsmanship at the College for Further Education. He subsequently worked in various south and. west German furniture factories, continuing to attend evening classes, studying and copying works of art in museums and going on walking-tours alone in the mountains, where he did landscape drawings and water-colours. In winter he applied himself to life-drawing and portraiture. His forceful character and his unwavering faith in his gifts carried him successfully through periods of frustration, as when galleries rejected his first paintings and later when he was not admitted to the Academy. According to Busbeck it was, indeed, the unremitting rejection of his work that decided him to give up his job as a teacher at a technical school and devote himself to full-time painting. He travelled to Florence, Vienna, Paris and Copenhagen, returning afterwards, disappointed, to his parents' farm. His solitary nature and his deep, positively mediumistic, feeling for nature caused him to feel, as he has himself written, 'like an outcast in the gay centres of artistic life'. He has confessed his need to be always in close touch with nature, because for him nature has absolute symbolic value. At once embittered and stubborn, impelled by an almost obsessively high opinion of himself, he took in his stride the continued rejection of paintings that Busbeck was later to call 'epic colour-reports on landscape' and which from an early period embodied all those legendary and imaginative elements that he discovered in nature.

163

During one of his tours along the Baltic Flats he met the singer Ditte Gosebruch, later to become his wife, and it was she who helped him to carry on through years of poverty and neglect.

Nansen and his wife lived for some time in Dresden, Berlin, and Cologne. But the obstinacy with which he resisted any compromise of his artistic integrity time and again reduced him to penury, forcing him to return to Glüserup.

In 1914 the journal *Wir* published a number of woodcuts entitled 'Grotesque and Legendary Motifs of the North Country'. The 'My Sea' series was exhibited in the Busbeck Gallery. On the outbreak of war Nansen volunteered and, disappointed at being rejected on medical grounds, for a whole year shut himself up in his studio on his parents' farm. It was during this period that he painted the cycle 'Doubting Thomas'.

After Nansen's work was included in an exhibition in Hanover, Ludwig von der Goltz wrote an article on Nansen's lithographs, and shortly afterwards published a volume of his coloured lithographs, with the title 'The Crashing Waves'. In Berlin Nansen's work continued to meet with rejection. A group of painters in Jena, the 'Tomorrow' group, invited Nansen to become a member. Having accepted, he subsequently withdrew when, during a short stay in Jena, he learned that the group's leader was a notorious pacifist and a follower of the French Impressionists. The 'Northern Harvest' series was hung in a winter exhibition in Munich, and the 'Autumn in the Marshes' series was exhibited in Karlsruhe. Nansen spent a number of summers alone on the Halligen Islands, where he painted a series of water-colours, the theme of which is spectres and fabulous monsters, the dark spirits of earth, the mysterious forces of nature. Together with his wife he joined a nationalist movement, only to leave it in disgust on discovering that the innermost circle of the movement had homosexual affiliations. During an exhibition in the Kunsthalle in Basle, Nansen destroyed his painting 'Peat-Barges', slashing it to pieces. He has never offered any explanation of his action. In 1928 he was awarded an honorary doctorate by the University of Göttingen, and the same year the Museum of Modern Art, New York, bought his painting 'The Revolt of the Sunflowers'. In Berlin Max Ludwig Nansen became the talk of the town as a result of a number of small ads he put in the papers, pleading with a young burglar to come and see him : the boy, whom Nansen had surprised burgling his house, had stabbed him in the lung, and Nansen wished to adopt him. After they had bought Bleekenwarf the Nansens rarely left their country home. According to Ludwig von der Goltz 'Nansen held cities and towns in contempt', regarding them as accumulations of 'yellow corruption and unedifying intellect'. In Bleekenwarf he painted the cycle entitled 'Stories told by an Old Mill on the Sea Coast'. For this cycle the influential art-dealer Malthesius offered Nansen the highest price he had ever been offered, but Nansen refused to sell. Just as once in the past Malthesius had kept the young painter waiting outside his office for four hours, only to reject his work, so now Nansen kept Malthesius waiting for four hours before telling him he would not sell. Although Nansen at first welcomed the events of the year 1933, a year later–in a telegram subsequently much quoted in artistic circles – he declined the directorship of the State Academy of Arts (Gratefully acknowledge honour. Suffering from colour allergy. Brown diagnosed as source of trouble. Regrets. Yours faithfully Nansen painter). Not long afterwards he was ejected from the Prussian Academy of Arts, and soon also from the National Chamber of Visual Arts. Shocked by the confiscation of more than eight hundred of his pictures, the property of German museums, Max Ludwig Nansen cancelled his membership of the National Socialist Party, which he had joined only two years later than Adolf Hitler. In collaboration with Teo Busbeck he published *Colour and Opposition* (Zurich, 1938). He declined an invitation to Berlin for the purpose of discussion, his declared reason being that he was indispensable where he was because he had to paint a part of his confiscated pictures all over again. Rugbüll police station received orders to keep as complete a record as possible of all foreign visitors to Bleekenwarf. According to Ludwig von der Goltz, during the last months of the war Nansen produced some paintings 'in which the painter proves once and for all that great art also takes its revenge on the world by immortalizing the things the world despises'.

That was the point I had reached in reading through Wolfgang Mackenroth's outline – without, I should like to add, finding anything to which I violently objected – when I sensed somebody's gaze resting on me, in fact piercing me – a gaze from outside in the corridor. I didn't look up instantly. First of all I folded up Mackenroth's draft, put it inside a copybook, and then opened another copybook, just as if I intended to go on reading. Only then did I look up, and I saw it was Joswig. To be on the safe side, I smiled. He didn't come in. There he stood, his shoulders sagging, his arms dangling at his sides : a sad chimpanzee in uniform, silently showing his grief by the way he looked and the way he let his head droop. I pushed my copybooks under my arm and went out to meet him, saying: 'I got permission to carry on! They've shown some understanding, so I can go on with my task. I'm afraid I wasn't able to lock myself in all by myself.'

'Judas,' he said softly. 'Little Judas.'

Holding up the new copybooks and the ink bottle I said: 'This will see me through the next few weeks.' He looked at me in silence. Then suddenly he pointed at my trouser-leg and snapped: 'Those cigarettes – come on, hand them over', and when I had done so he added: 'Get moving! Nobody's going to disturb you from now on!'

8 The Portrait

Man in the red cloak, now I must speak about you. At long last the time has come for you to perform your handstands on the desolate beach, or even to dance on your head before my brother Klaas, who happens – though it's not entirely chance, either – to be standing next to you. Now you can make us ask, yet once again, why it is not gaiety that pervades the picture, but greenish-white flaming fear. You, with your ancient face, with your ancient cunning, now advance to make your contribution; for it was, I surmise, on your account that the studio wasn't blacked out according to regulations. Because Max Ludwig Nansen wasn't satisfied with you, because he had to go on changing you, with embittered slashes of his brush, because he was helping you, sometimes rashly, wildly, to look like yourself – in the morning as well as in the evening – he did not find the time to walk round the house and make sure there were no chinks in the black-out! Anyway, he was busy with you, improving you and correcting you, and hence failed to notice that one of the blinds had got stuck, the way a sail gets stuck, letting a ray of light – his working light – out of the window.

So all at once there was a trembling light hovering over the dark plain between Rugbüll and Glüserup. It didn't move away from Bleekenwarf, it didn't go out at calculated intervals, didn't travel, didn't swing to and fro; it merely pierced the wind-blown autumn evening, making the gently rising curve of the dunes look like a ship lying at anchor in the plain, under great lumpy clouds, in the lee of the dyke. So far as I know it was the first light that had appeared in the plain for years. It stretched out thin as a finger across the ditches and canals, and anyone seeing it could only wonder: 'Who's going to see it first? Who within an angle of a hundred and seventy degrees will discover it first, work out its position and draw his conclusions? Blacked-out ships on the North Sea? Secret agents? Or the Blenheims?'

Long before any ship, agent, or Blenheim bomber, the Rugbüll policeman had observed the illicit light, he whose duty it was to see that after darkness fell everything *stayed* dark round our way. He rode along the dyke, his cape fluttering about him. A well-known apparition leaning heavily against the side wind, he plunged down the slope, coasted headlong down to the alder path, dismounted, and went into the garden to check, at close quarters, the source of the light. The light came from the studio. All the big house's windows were blacked out according to regulations; only from the studio a sharp beam of light fell into the garden. The Rugbüll policeman went up to the offending window. He paid no attention to where he walked, simply stamped right through a bed of asters, past the summerhouse, pushed through dripping shrubs and bushes and finally got so close that he could dip his hand into the beam of light. He noted that a blind had got stuck, saw the displaced cords and the dangling china ring. He listened. There was no hum of engines in the air, but only a short distance from him he could hear a desultory, querulous argument. Now he might have called out, or he might have knocked, yet, as far as I know, he didn't do either, but, since the opening in the black-out was at the top of the window, dragged a garden table along, climbed on to it and pressed his face to the window-pane. Never before had he had such a view of what went on at Bleekenwarf.

The wind played with his cape, the cape hit the window, making a faint slapping noise, and he cautiously eased himself away and tucked the corners of the cape under his belt. To complete the picture we ought to make him remove his cap and shade his eyes with one hand, and perhaps before that he ought to look round to make sure there was nobody in the garden watching *him*.

That will serve as a sketch of my father acting resolutely, dutifully and patiently – my father, who, if need be, would hold out longer on that garden table than the officers of other police stations would have. Putting all this together, I might proceed in the following manner : he raised his eyes.

There was a man in a red cloak and there was Klaas – or, anyway, a chap who instantly reminded one of Klaas – and facing them, partly blocking my father's view of them, there was the painter, his hat on his head.

The painter was working. With short, slashing strokes of his brush, talking, scolding, he was working at the man in the red cloak. He foreshortened the coboldish feet that stuck out from under the cloak. He made the blue background stronger, to contrast with the red of the cloak. And the red cloak shone out over the desolate shore of a black, wintry North Sea, glowing and floating, denying the force of gravity, for although the man who wore it was walking, even dancing, on his hands, the open bell-shaped cloak didn't drop down over him. It didn't drop down and cover his face, that ancient face in which, as he poised there on his hands, an ancient cunning was very perceptible indeed. How thin his wrists were! How delicate the curving, poised body! He was obviously laughing and giggling, trying to infect Klaas with his laughter, he was eager to please my brother, he wanted to get round him and cheer him up, and he was trying to do it by – of all things – walking or dancing on his hands, which he did, it must be admitted, with the greatest of ease.

But, however easily he was able to stand on his hands, he couldn't win Klaas over, he couldn't even persuade him to stay. The fear he had unintentionally aroused in my brother, a greenish-white flaming fear, made Klaas try to work his way out of the scene. Klaas had his fingers spread out, his head thrown back, and the drooping shadows under his open mouth made one think of a choked-off scream. Just two or three more hesitant steps, one could see even now, and Klaas would be running, driven across the beach by his fear, running towards the indifferent skyline, anywhere – just to get away from the man standing on his head in the red cloak. The picture was called 'Suddenly on the Shore'. Or at least that was what the painter had called it, but in his diary he had also given it the title 'Fear' – a fear that wore my brother's face. Anyway, if I look back at it all from here, I can't describe it in any other way.

Did the Rugbüll policeman perceive all this, one thing after the other? Or did he merely, from where he stood on the garden table, watch the painter doggedly, cantankerously, working away? And why didn't he act at once, seeing that two offences were being flagrantly committed? Why did he go on standing there outside, that windy autumn evening, screening his eyes with his hand, full of curiosity, just as if he expected a lot more to happen and was intent on getting the evidence? Wasn't what he had already seen enough to satisfy him?

Although the beam of light from the studio shone far out across the countryside, a treacherous signal to ships, secret agents and Blenheims, my father remained standing on the garden table, watching the painter at work.

He followed the argument between the painter and that invisible know-all, the painter's friend Balthasar. He noted the resistance the painter's right arm had to overcome. And then the repetitions: he observed how with his own body the painter re-enacted and confirmed all that went on between Klaas and the man in the red cloak: the incitement to gaiety, the unexpected fear, and all the rest of it.

What kept him there, of course, was incredulity, was intolerable amazement that this man who had been born in the same village as himself, and who therefore ought to be the same sort of man as himself, refused to recognize any authority, would not submit to prohibitions and orders from above. After all, he had been warned often enough. Was his contempt greater than his anxiety? Surely he had sufficient imagination to realize what his carelessness was bound to lead to one of these days. Or was he so self-confident that he didn't so much as give a thought to the possible consequences? Might some other police-man – one from Husum, say – have been more successful in making him toe the line?

He didn't seem to get any *pleasure* out of his work, nor did he show any sign of gloating over this defiance of the ban. He was completely wrapped up in Balthasar and in coming to terms with the paint. It all seemed to amount to just what he himself had foretold: that a painter can't stop painting. Or was he going on working just to spite the Rugbüll policeman?

Perverse satisfaction must have been what my father felt, there at his observation-post, where he remained longer than he ought to have in view of the fact that the beam of light could be seen from far out on the dark plain – probably even in Gatwik or thereabouts. The offence against prevailing regulations that he was here contemplating afforded him a complex sort of pleasure, and who knows how long he might have stayed out there if he hadn't thought, all of a sudden, that he heard Ditte's voice. He scrambled down from the table. Then he put it back in its place, pulled the pointed ends of his cape out from under his belt, and then – at least, this is how I imagine it – cast a final glance at the lighted window before knocking at the studio door.

He knocked again. Probably he was turning over in his mind what to say when Ditte – with her haughty expression of suffering, her grey bobbed hair – opened the door, but the door flew open and there the painter stood, showing no sign of fright or even surprise, simply asking :

'Well, what is it?'

The policeman explained his presence by silently beckoning the painter out into the garden, pointing briefly at the light and then silently returning to the door. Then he said :

'I'll have to bring a charge against you, Max.'

'Do as you think you must,' the painter said, and then added : 'I'll have it right in a moment – in a moment you'll have all the darkness everyone's so keen on.'

'I've still got to make the charge,' my father said. He followed the painter in, shut the door after him, and then watched as the painter stood on a chair and tried – first with a ruler and then with a broomstick – to free the blind that had got stuck, pulling it up and pushing at it, until at last it came down, covering the whole window. Satisfied, he stepped down from the chair, threw the broomstick in a corner, and took his pipe out of his coat pocket, but before lighting it he tossed off a glassful of some whitish, oily liquid.

'How much is it going to set me back?' he asked. He got no answer. Turning round, he saw my father standing before the picture, which was not fastened to the inside of the wardrobe-door the way the 'Landscape with Unknown People' had been, but quite openly there on an easel. My father looked at the picture from points of view that seemed to him important; he neither shifted his weight nor changed his distance, nor did he move his head, merely clasped his hands behind his back : I should imagine his way of standing there must have been impressive. The man in the red cloak performed a handstand, if it wasn't indeed a dance on his hands, my brother Klaas watched him doing it, was frightened and seemed about to run away. These facts, however, my father apparently did not notice.

'As you see,' the painter said, 'it's an old thing I've dug out. I'd almost forgotten it. It can hardly be of interest to you people.' My father said nothing, but he turned his face towards the painter, who went on: 'You don't mean to lay your hands on these old things, do you – or do you? Surely you chaps aren't interested in *these* pictures?'

'You've been working, Max,' the policeman said quietly. 'Don't let's pretend. I've been watching you. You've been following your profession, Max, in spite of the ban. Why?'

'This is just old stuff,' the painter said.

The policeman retorted: 'No, Max. No, this isn't old stuff. The way Klaas is standing there, frightened – it's only now he can stand like that and be frightened like that. Anyone can see – that boy there, that's not old stuff.'

'Do you know when I did the man in the red cloak?' the painter asked. 'In September thirty-nine.'

'That's not the point,' my father said. 'This time I've got to report the matter.'

'Do you know what you're doing?' the painter asked.

'My duty,' my father said, and that was all he needed to say to bring about a change in Max Ludwig Nansen, who up to that moment had been talking casually and calmly enough to his belated visitor, and who might even have been thinking of offering him a glass of gin. He took the pipe out of his mouth and shut his eyes. He leaned against the cabinet, holding himself very straight, and he made no attempt to hide the expression of bitterness and contempt that slowly came over his face.

'All right,' he said softly. 'You believe one's got to do one's duty, but I'll tell you the opposite. One's got to do something to defy duty. Duty is nothing but blind arrogance, so far as I am concerned. One inevitably does things that are not dictated by it.'

'What are you getting at?' my father asked suspiciously.

The painter opened his eyes and pushed himself away from

the cupboard. He laid his pipe on the window-sill. He listened to the sounds from outside, where the wind was knocking the branches of the walnut tree against the gutter, and then, without showing any trace of excitement, he went to the easel, took the picture off, held it for a moment far away from himself, then very quickly brought it close to his body. His strong, experienced fingers were close together at the edge of the picture, they hesitated, they wanted to do it and they didn't want to, and then with a jerk they flew apart and in that movement the picture tore in two. The tear separated Klaas from the man in the red cloak and thus removed the cause of his fear. Max Ludwig Nansen put the two halves on top of each other – no, that's not correct, he first tore the man in the red cloak to shreds and dropped the glowing shreds on the floor, then he dealt with my brother, tearing up the portrait of fear, tearing it into pieces the size of a packet of cigarettes, put the shreds together, went up to my father and held them out to him, saying: 'Here's something for you to take along. I've saved you people the trouble of having to come and get it.'

My father didn't protest, he didn't stop the painter from talking and, as far as I know, he didn't caution him either. Attentively, but no more than attentively, he watched the destruction, and when the painter had handed him the shreds, he opened the leather pouch at his belt and, with a matter-of-fact expression on his face, he crammed them into it; then he carefully collected the bits on the floor, and what he couldn't get into the pouch he put into the big pocket of his blouse.

'Satisfied?' the painter asked. 'Are you satisfied now?' and instantly, as though he were sorry about what he had done, added: 'No, one ought to leave it to you people, one shouldn't do any destroying on your behalf. No, I shouldn't have done it.'

'You could have saved yourself all this trouble,' my father said.

'Well, that's what I'm like: I'm not given to saving myself trouble. I've always got to probe until I know where it hurts. That's the way we are, down Glüserup way.'

'That's the way *you* are,' my father said, 'just you. There are plenty of others that are law-abiding – but you want to be a law unto yourself.'

'And it's one that'll prevail,' the painter said, 'even when there's no trace left of the lot of you.'

'There you go talking, that's just like you. But just you wait. You'll see. There are many who've been changed, and you'll change one of these days, too.'

They stared at each other. They heard the door open and the sound of nailed boots, and even before they could see her, Jutta called out: 'Uncle Max? Are you there, Uncle Max?'

The painter remained silent. He waited till she came in, dragging her feet in the heavy military boots, and when she was standing before him, shivering in her thin dress, her skin roughened by the cold, but smiling, he gave her an intent look and shook his head reproachfully. Those thin legs, those lean arms with gingery down on them. The bony, derisive face. The strong incisors. Jutta gathered up the stuff of her dress and wedged it between her thighs, to show how big the boots were for her. Then she said:

'I've come to fetch you. We're all waiting for you.'

The painter put both his hands into his coat-pockets, just as if he were trying to prevent one of them from making a rash gesture. He also avoided looking at Jutta as she linked one arm with his, pulling him, pressing his arm against her small hard breast. He freed his arm with a jerk.

'I'll be with you later,' he said. 'Tell them I've got a visitor.'

'We've finished,' my father said. 'As far as I'm concerned, it's all quite clear.'

'But I've still got something to say,' the painter said, and he made a sign to Jutta to take herself off. It was rather brusque, and he took a few quick steps in her direction, as if intending to drive her out of the room. When at last she moved, slouching, her feet wide apart, her thin arms flailing, he followed her, and after she had disappeared he locked the door. Slowly, his shoulders sagging, he came back, sat down on a crate and stayed there for a while like that, his face lowered. My father stood in front of the empty easel, directly under the work-lamp, which cast sharp shadows over him. He was ready to leave.

'Jens,' the painter said, 'listen to me, just listen to me for the last time. We *must* still be able to talk to each other. We've known each other long enough, haven't we? I realize you can't be neutral. I'm not neutral either. Each of us is under orders.

But we can foresee – we've always been able to foresee where a thing was leading. Even if we've both changed, we can still see what the end of it all is going to be. Let's forget all that has happened. Let's think what the situation is going to be in two or three years – perhaps even sooner. If we're under any obligation, it can only be the obligation to look ahead. I know, anyone who has pledged himself is particularly touchy, and we've both pledged ourselves. But can't we put it aside for a while? Who's forcing us to pronounce final judgements? Sit down. I'd like to make a suggestion to you.'

Max Lugwig Nansen now raised his face and got up from the crate. But when one glance showed him that the policeman was not prepared to agree to any suggestion of his, whatever it might be, he sat down again. Rejection was all that the policeman's attitude expressed – and the wish to go, now that he had done what he had come to do. The policeman looked at the painter with that empty gaze of this which seemed to come from far away and pass through everything, that second-sight gaze which seemed to. know everything, or at least to know better; he looked at him and he shrugged his shoulders.

The painter clasped his hands in resignation. He wagged his head. His grey eyes became narrow and cold. He cleared his throat and said :

'Well, now we certainly know where we stand. Now there's no hope left, Jens. I ought to have known what to expect of you and the like of you.'

'So much the better,' my father said. 'There are things one doesn't forget.'

'I dare say that's true,' the painter said. 'Here we don't forget what people have done to us. We only forget the things we can't bear.'

'They're waiting for you,' my father said.

And the painter retorted : 'Yes, and you were just going.'

In silence they walked to the door, past the cupboards and niches, past the huge mass of autumn flowers in vases and buckets on the floor. At one point Nansen said : 'There's no such thing as a neutral colour.'

They walked past the long table for doing ceramic work, past the scratched potter's wheel on which a naked couple, skinnily yearning upward, was just emerging from the clay. They didn't shake hands when they parted. The painter unlocked the door, and my father left the studio without saying goodbye. He merely turned round briefly before the door shut on him, and said :

'You'll be hearing from me.'

'I've heard enough,' the painter replied.

Then he stood there outside with his booty, in that restless autumn evening, in the regulation darkness, the maintenance of which was not the least of his duties. Stiff-legged, his cape fluttering, he crossed the Bleekenwarf yard, walked past the pond and the empty stable and shed, and I dare say, while he did so, he developed, inside the dark-room of his head, a different picture of Bleekenwarf.

Did it show him what had remained hidden from him outside? I believe him to be quite capable of making for himself a picture in which he depicted more than alders, apple trees, hawthorn hedges and the rambling, brooding buildings that seemed withdrawn from the outer world. While he was looking at the silent, forbidding place, a quite different image of Bleekenwarf arose in him : it lay there before him, its roofs and walls sliced open, a model, as it were, that he could gaze into at his ease. I should say that, while he was crossing the yard, he could see himself crossing the yard and he could perhaps even look into the rooms that lay cut open before him and see Ditte and Teo Busbeck, see them raise their heads because they thought they could hear his steps, could perhaps see Jutta in those cast-off military boots, and perhaps even Jobst, who was up in the loft, trying to catch an owl that lived there among the rafters. And at the same time, as it were apart from all that, he kept seeing himself, walking stiff-legged past those countless windows. Which was the true image? Which the imaginary one? How can it be explained that he suddenly stopped, pulled out his torch, switched it on and off to test it and then, instead of proceeding towards the wooden gate, turned towards the east wing of the house? What picture in his mind forced him to do that? Would he find in the Bleekenwarf that lay there before him whatever the picture in his mind had evidently revealed to him?

The wind swirled the leaves around in circles and whipped the mirror of the pond. It whistled through the cracks between the felled and stacked tree-trunks. My father walked to the pump, and there he turned aside and approached the corner window. He raised the torch, the glass eye of which was covered with black insulation-tape, leaving only a narrow slit for a thin beam of light to penetrate. The light fell on a lowered blind. On then to the next window. The narrow beam peered through the window, lighting up the door opposite and, moving along the wall, showed an old-fashioned three-legged washstand, a blackened mirror, a pile of cardboard boxes, an armchair with gaping holes in the upholstery, a brown monster of a chest-of-drawers, and a calendar that insisted it was the first of August nineteen four.

The next room was empty. So was the one after that. In places the plaster had fallen off the walls, revealing the rush matting of the insulation-wall. Then the beam of light passed on, exposing a dusty bedroom, went over a bunk, over faded clothes and damp, mildewed nightshirts hanging on wire coathangers. As always, a nightcap lay on a stool beside the bunk, there were worn-out slippers and a bulgy chamberpot with a glittering metallic blue pattern, as if the thing had been shot at and hit by a catapult. Further, all along the windows. What was that? Right in the middle of the room there was a table and on it sat a great crested grebe, which seemed to be having a conversation with a clothes-brush. Who could it have been that had the bird stuffed? And who had wanted to give it a brush and had then walked off and never returned to do the job? I imagine the haggard man with his narrow face, who had himself at times reminded me of a water-bird, turning the beam of his torch on the grebe so that the glass eyes sparkled in the light, before walking on inexorably from window to window, taking room after room, examining walls and furniture and nooks in the beam of his torch, driven on by those intimations that visited him, until finally he came upon that unfinished bathroom. There were the spotty mattresses on the floor, the stepladder, a pile of plaster, nails, cigarette-butts and bits of old lead-tubing. A shabby jacket with a herringbone pattern. A naked electric bulb. Did he hope to discover something more? Or did he know more than we credited him with?

Shifting his narrow beam of light here and there, my father examined the abandoned bathroom. Now it wouldn't have mattered to him any more if Ditte or the painter had surprised him at it; the time when he would have apologized for his action was definitely past. He inspected the bathroom with – as I should like to put it – dogged endurance, in a painstaking way that clearly showed he believed himself near his goal. He observed that the electric bulb was gently swaying to and fro. He saw a plate with left-overs of food on it, and, as I was told later, a sweat-band belonging to a uniform-blouse. The beam of light rested on the sweat-band and then slid over the plate and towards the swaying light-bulb. Then the policeman switched his torch off, listened, pressed himself against the wall, and heard more than he cared to hear.

In our parts, anyone who stands listening in the autumn, in the evening, in the wind, is bound to hear more than he bargained for or has any use for : there is always talk going on in the hedges, fantastic structures spring up in mid-air, and anyone who is intent on hearing voices gets what he has asked for.

Standing beside the window, straining his ears, what my father heard was too many footsteps, too many voices. Time and again he shone his torch into the bathroom, and time and again he realized that he was deceived. In the end he fixed his torch to his chest and walked to where he had left his bicycle.

We may tacitly assume that as he returned to his bicycle he felt relieved, not satisfied but relieved, and so he made a point, as he rode off, of not keeping an eye on the heavy raft that was Bleekenwarf anchored there in the darkness. After all, in his pouch he had sufficient stuff, red on white and green on white, he had seen to it that darkness prevailed, and he also had confirmation of what he had known or suspected. So we can let him ride briskly down the dyke, through the salty drizzle, with all he had gained by the exercise of his professional suspicion. Perhaps, as he was riding along, he was considering how he would formulate his report, but it is more likely that he was just thinking of his favourite dish, fried herring with potato salad, which was meanwhile being prepared in the kitchen by Hilke. Anyway, we were all in the smoky kitchen when he entered the house, put his hat and cape in the cloakroom and then came in, rubbing his hands.

'Well? Dinner ready?'

'Yes.'

I was the first to sit down at the table while my mother was laying the places and Hilke was standing at the range, her eyes streaming, the melting lard sizzling and crackling in the pan. It spluttered fiercely, exploded, foamed and formed twenty thousand bubbles, as Hilke put in the headless herrings wrapped in batter.

My father said good evening to us all as he entered the room, and he didn't seem to mind that nobody responded.

'Evening everybody,' he said, patting me on the shoulder, and went over to the range, where he stood, nodding his approval as he watched my sister taking the swiftly fried herrings out of the pan, putting them on a platter, wiping her eyes with the back of her hand and then again putting herrings, white with flour, into the pan, causing the boiling fat to hiss and splutter.

My father winked at me, rubbing his stomach in exaggerated anticipation of the delights to come, then unbuckled his belt with the pistol-holster and the pouch attached to it, put it all in the kitchen cupboard and sat down next to me. Yellow and brown and glistening with fat, there the fried herrings lay on the platter, their scales brittle and curly, and if I remember them here in my well-aired cell, I can again smell that fierce odour, I instantly choke with that irritation in my throat which has always made me cough.

Whenever Hilke did any frying, she wore her high-necked apron over her peasant jacket, which had coins instead of buttons on it; her long, thick hair was tied up with a ribbon at the back of her neck. She wore knee-high woollen stockings, and round her wrist dangled a silver-plated bracelet that Addi had sent her one day, out of the blue, from Rotterdam, where he had been sent by Army Welfare. Each time after she had successfully fished some herrings out of the boiling fat, she pushed out her lower lip and blew a strand of hair out of her face, turned round to look at us, and gave us a sourish smile from the midst of the acrid smoke.

At long last my mother put the herrings, and the bowl of rather glassy-looking potato salad with apple slices in it, on the table, and after we'd all taken each other by the hands and in a monotonously rhythmical way wished each other 'good ap-pe-tite', which we only did when Hilke was at home, we began to eat.

One after the other, we dug large helpings out of the potato-salad bowl and speared some of the herrings on the platter. Some pressure from one's fork was all that was needed to loosen the fillet forming the back, and with the prongs of one's fork one could lift out the backbone; I didn't have to make any great effort to consolidate my advantage over Hilke, being two herrings ahead of her, and to get still farther ahead. But I couldn't catch up with my father. The Rugbüll policeman had his own special method of removing the backbone, and after that he put half a fish on his fork at one go and shoved it straight into his mouth without blowing on it. So all I could do was to look on excitedly as the pile of fish-bones on his plate grew ever bigger. Whenever we had fried herrings he was a match for Per Arne Schessel, who was the greediest eater I've ever watched, though I must say in my father's favour that he showed more appreciation of the blessings of hot food, more enjoyment interspersed with sighs, than that old sourpuss of a folklorist. I simply couldn't manage to heap as many fish-bones on my plate as my father did on his, but I had no trouble at all in beating Hilke and my mother.

As the chewing and munching and gulping down went on at our table, the mound of herrings on the platter became lower, and craters, grottoes, and cliffs developed in the potato salad, and I was beginning to feel fatigue, all tired and warm, when Hilke discovered the shiny red piece of paper peeping out of my father's pocket. She pulled it out, and with a question-ing look held it over the table on her flat hand. When none of us uttered a word, she put it down beside her plate and said :

'The things you carry about in your pockets!'

Without a word my father reached across the table, pulled the scrap of red paper towards himself, and put it back in his pocket.

'Oh, so it's confidential,' Hilke said.

And my father, speaking to the plate before him, said :

'If only one could get enough herrings these days – if only one could get them!'

'How is Max?' my mother suddenly asked.

'He seemed all right to me,' my father said. With one move-ment of his fork he slit open a herring and added : 'Now we've reached the point where I can't be generous to him any longer. It's the way he wanted it.'

'That Doktor Busbeck,' my mother said. 'Perhaps Max would be different if it weren't for that Doktor Busbeck, he has such an influence on him. Nobody knows the slightest thing about him. He doesn't belong anywhere. Rootless – that's what he is, a slightly superior sort of gypsy. Doesn't think much of work.'

'No,' my father said. 'We've got nothing against Busbeck, and as for Max, whatever he does he does of his own accord. Max thinks he owes nothing to anyone. Laws, he thinks, orders – they apply to the rest of us, but not to him. Now we've reached the point where I can't go on turning a blind eye to it all. Friendship's all very well, but it doesn't give him the right to do just as he likes.'

My mother stopped eating. She put her elbows on the table, looked at the straight parting on my father's head, and then she actually said :

'Sometimes I think Max ought to be glad about the ban. I mean, if you just look and see the sort of people he paints – those green faces, those mongol eyes, those lumpy bodies. There's something strange about it all – there must be something ill about that kind of painting. Now you don't see a German face in any of his pictures. In the old days – oh yes, you did then. But not now. You can't help thinking it's a kind of fever, it's all done in some fever.'

'But abroad they buy his pictures,' my father said. 'He counts for something abroad.'

'Because they're ill themselves,' my mother said, 'that's why they surround themselves with sick pictures. Just look at the sort of mouths his people have. Black and crooked, and they're always shrieking or stammering, those mouths never produced a sensible word, anyway, no *German* word. I sometimes wonder what language those people speak – those people in his pictures.'

'Not German, anyway,' my father said. 'You're right there.'

'It must be Busbeck,' my mother said. 'He got Max where he is now. He got him to paint all those strange and sick things, to please those people abroad – those green faces, those gaping mouths, those queer bodies. Max ought to be glad about the ban, because it's going to bring him back to himself. And to our own ways.'

My father pushed his plate back and wiped his mouth. Hilke got up, took the plates away, and brought little bowls of stewed apple, which she put down in front of us.

'He's got to be taught a lesson this time,' my father said.

And my mother added: 'If you think how Ditte dislikes parting with her money, there's nothing would hit her as hard as a fine would.'

'I reported to Husum, not to Berlin,' my father said. 'It's up to the chaps in Husum to do something about it.' He ate some of the stewed apple, praised it, and left some for me. Then he said: 'Offence against black-out regulations and violation of the ban on painting. He won't be let off lightly.'

He pushed his bowl towards me. Then he leaned back, passed his tongue over his lips, sucked his teeth noisily, clicked his tongue, cleared his throat. Another bowl of brownish stewed apple slid towards me from my mother's side.

'He couldn't hoodwink me this time,' my father said, pulling some red, green and white scraps of paper out of his pocket. He laid the scraps on the table before him, and tried fitting them together in the right order, but the pieces didn't fit each other, they didn't form a unity.

'Did you do that?' my mother asked anxiously.

But the policeman shook his head loftily, and there was a trace of approval in his voice as he said: 'Did it himself. I'd cornered him and he couldn't get out of it. So he tore up his own picture. But that won't help him.'

'His own picture?' my mother asked.

'What was it of?' Hilke asked.

'Can I have the bits?' I asked.

My father waved his hand, waving off all three questions, got up, stretched, then fetched his pouch from the cupboard, opened it, and simply poured out its contents as though he were Dame Holle creating a flurry of red, green, white and blue flakes, a storm of irregular but radiant flakes that came down on the table, on my stewed apples, on the floor, even drifting as far as the door. Then he also emptied his pocket, slamming batch after batch of shreds on the table, and saying: 'It all goes with the report, it's evidence.'

'I'll sort it out,' I said. 'I'll sort it out and arrange it.'

'There's no need for that,' my father said. 'You can save

yourself the trouble. These scraps are all we need.'

'But I'd like to sort it out,' I said.

Wham, wham! We listened. Somebody was outside, banging at the door. My father quickly signalled to me to remove the scraps of the painting from the table and put them somewhere and get the table cleared. He obviously had a definite idea about who it was outside, hammering at the door, so one could see the disappointment on his face when it turned out to be Hinnerk Timmsen whom he had to let in. They stayed outside in the hall, talking, while we sat still and listened. The light from the kitchen only shone on my father, not on Timmsen.

'Suddenly startled by the drone of engines in the air . . . on the Wattblick verandah . . . and all at once a four-engined plane came diving down, lower and lower . . . flames from one of the engines . . . and the plane . . . and then, over there, over the sea . . . the explosion would have woken anyone up . . . definitely a parachute coming down on the flats . . . no, couldn't see anything . . . but there was a parachute all right . . .'

Out of the darkness, where Hinnerk Timmsen was invisible, his account of what had happened came to us. And then he said : 'Americans – I'd definitely say Americans.'

From my father's serious face one could see what an impression the story had made on him and that he was resolved to get to the bottom of it all, to find out whatever he could, and confirm it all. Nodding ponderously, he went and fetched his cap and cape from the cloakroom, and he called out to us to bring his belt. Hilke brought him the belt with the pistol-holster on it, and he buckled it on, adjusted the holster, and in two strides was at the door. But then he turned round and again with two strides came back, just to say to us: 'Well, so long then – good night.' Then he went out, following the innkeeper, who was waiting for him outside to show him the way.

I didn't follow them, though this time I should have liked to. In my lap lay the shreds of the painting, and I pushed them carefully under my pullover, wedging them in between my pullover and my shirt. Then I slipped under the table, and since nobody stopped me, I gathered up all the pieces of paper that had fallen on to the floor. I collected them from under Hilke's feet, from under the window-seat, from under my mother's chair and the kitchen cupboard, and in the end I had the whole picture, or at least the bits and pieces of it, safely hidden under my pullover, which by now made a large, sagging bulge. With my hands folded over my belly I stood there in front of the cupboard. Hilke and my mother sat facing each other in silence, perhaps trying to hear whatever was going on outside. In the air outside there was a far-off, singing hum of engines, but it was suddenly drowned by the ringing of the alarm-clock that stood next to the bread-bin, and which now began to dance about on its short steel legs, turning around one hundred and eighty degrees, telling the time to the soft, well-gnawed herring-bones on top of the range.

What had become of the heartburn? I was waiting for my mother to get her heartburn, because then she would go to the sink, turn on the tap, and let the water run, while she fetched herself a glass and a little paper bag containing her powder. Then she would fill the glass, tear open the little bag and empty it into the glass, and, sitting down again at the table, would drink the stuff off. Never before had I waited so impatiently for that heartburn to come on. I meant to make use of the moment when she was attending to it to disappear without being questioned, admonished, and given a warning. But something seemed to be holding up the heartburn, or perhaps the fried herrings did not cause it. So I tried a new and determined approach, I simply walked up to them and said :

'There's something I've got to do in a hurry.'

Hilke laughed, and my mother turned towards me with an amused expression, but before they could say anything I had left the kitchen, was on the stairs, and in my own room.

Would they call me back? They did not. I went over to the table, which was covered with blue maps of the ocean, with all my fleets of grey model warships laid out there. I think what was going on there was yet another battle of the Skagerrak, with Hipper in his tactical wisdom disengaging himself from the superior Jellicoe. But I had no time now to think about that sort of thing, I simply put the battle aside and removed it from the agenda, emptying my pullover on to the peaceful oceans. The bits and pieces fell and floated on the sea. Red brought out blue, white caused green riot, brown asserted itself against grey. Here was a crooked brown toe, a triangular eye, the speckled crest of a wave. Was it the battle of the Skagerrak going on after all? The scraps of paper were in considerable disorder, as I found out pretty quickly. Listening to what was going on in the kitchen down below, I could hear water running and the clatter of dishes. Hilke was energetically engaged in removing all traces of our dinner. They were leaving me in peace. So I got going.

It was you, man in the red cloak, who helped me to get started on reconstructing the picture that had been destroyed, reassembling it from the irregularly shaped bits and snippets, and I still remember the tense excitement and the pleasure that the task caused me. I didn't start at the edge, nor in the centre either, I let myself be guided by colour, putting red together with red, and green with green; I didn't at first try to fit the pieces together, I simply distributed them according to colour, dividing the whole thing into sections or, as one might perhaps say, into chapters, which had to be arranged afterwards.

I must admit it was by no means easy to decide, for instance, to put every brown into the brown section, and some of the green I had to look at three times before putting it with greens. In other words, determining the colours was what took longest.

What illuminating results can come from the tearing up of paper! I should have to make use of a great many comparisons in order to describe this wealth of forms. There was the island of Crete, the tip of a lance, the roof of a house, a lampshade, a cabbage, a clock, the boot of Italy, a mackerel, a vase – of all this and more was I reminded by the bits of coloured paper with their jagged edges, which I was now putting together, changing them around, and moving them to and fro.

With my forefinger, I pressed the pieces of paper to the table and briskly manoeuvred them about to wherever there was a possible join, guiding a black yacht into a harbour and closing it with the triangle of India; by adding some bits that matched I transformed a ball-shaped red tree into a rearing horse, then into a flying dragon, and finally, by adding more bits and pieces, into a red bell, into the red, bell-shaped cloak. How many possibilities there were in one picture! How many times, at the beginning, I had to stop and think!

What was the man in the red cloak doing? Why did he carry the beach, balancing it on his hands, while his cobold feet were pointing into the air? Could he go on giggling while he carried that grey load? I went on fiddling with parts of feet, with outspread fingers, with a heavy green-and-white body. I searched for and found a mouth enlarged by shadows. Experimenting again and again, I got something that suggested Klaas to me, and by adding triangles and rhomboids I managed to make my brother look more and more like himself, until in the end there he was, poised for flight, yet not a portrait of Klaas, but a portrait of fear.

In this way I reconstructed my brother and the man in the red cloak, freeing them from all disturbing elements; I put them together from scraps of paper by mere guesswork. There they were, but still they wouldn't form a unity. The man in the red cloak went on pushing the sand-grey beach into the air, the same beach over which my brother was trying to escape. Should there be two pieces of beach? Had a connecting piece got lost? Had I made a mistake in assembling the picture after all? Circling the table, toying with a scrap of paper here and there, I worked out the relationship between the two men and, since the foreground would not yield any information, I worked on the background, the black wintry North Sea. Out of the black of the sea a bluish-green wave was rushing towards the beach, which could be seen in the space between the two figures. It was a broad but rather limp wave, and I now used it as a guiding line and completed it, letting it take its course regardless of the two figures, and in doing so I had to turn the man in the red cloak round and force him to stand on his head. Now the beach across which my brother was trying to escape and the beach which the old fellow had previously been pushing up into the air fitted together. Now the horizon became the horizon behind both of them, one steady line, and now it turned out that my brother's fear and his wish to escape from the scene had their immediate cause in the thin, twisted man in the red cloak who was getting the better of the force of gravity. There was no shred of paper left over.

Instead of calling Hilke or my mother to show them what had been hidden in the bits of paper that my father had confiscated, I went to the door and locked it. Then I looked for a suitable backing-sheet, but all I could find was an old, torn black-out blind that had been put under my bed. I pulled it out and unrolled it on the floor, stopping it from rolling up

186

again by putting a chair on each end and putting on each chair a load consisting mainly of superannuated books of fairy-tales. Then out of my 'Little Carpenter' tool-kit I took the tube of all-purpose glue, I knelt down in front of the blind, squeezed a honey-coloured worm out of the tube, and used the top to spread the glue on to the blind. I put the stuff on in spirals and garlands, and it seemed to dry quite quickly. When I had prepared the black-out paper, which had been black once but had become whitish with age, I took the bits and pieces of the reconstructed painting from the table and systematically glued them on, row upon row, putting them together carefully; but I could not prevent their tattered edges from becoming rather dark, so that the picture that came into existence was overlaid by a vein-like pattern, a web that would for ever bear witness to the destruction that had been wrought. Starting in the top right-hand corner I fitted together the sky, the North Sea and Klaas, and finally it was your turn, man in the red cloak – you with your ancient cunning and your fixed smile.

I picked up one of the chairs, whereupon the blind snapped back and rolled up all by itself. The painting disappeared in the rolled-up blind. Carefully I pushed it back under the bed.

Now for the paint-box, I thought, and my sketching-pad. The window-seat is large enough if I push the cushions to one side. Now I've got to be quick, because I should have done this first, actually, and not the other way round. I can still see myself kneeling before the window-seat with the paint-box and the sketching pad, armed with my oldest brush, slapping red paint on in jagged patterns, and I can still hear the sound that a sheet of paper makes when it's ripped off the pad. I can see myself putting on a sombre brown, and in my memory I again make green and white run into each other. I put all the picture's colours on to paper, covering three or four sheets of my pad. I waved the sheets to and fro. I breathed on them. I took my reading-lamp and passed it over the sheets, going round in small circles, watching the paint dry, sinking into the paper. Then I cleared away the sketch-pad and the paint-box and put all those coloured, those merely coloured sheets, on the table, and then I tore them up. Carefully I tore the paper up, dividing it first of all into almost regular rectangles, then taking the rectangles one by one, and some of them I tore so that they had jagged edges, others I rounded off, or I gave them beautiful saw-tooth patterns. Then I mixed the variously shaped shreds together and showered them down on the table, on the maps of the oceans, seeing to it that they became satisfactorily mixed up.

There was the sound of footsteps. One rectangle after another turned into coloured snow, the flakes of it heaped up before me. Carefully, so as not to give any impression of completeness, I stuffed some of the flakes into my pocket. Crooking my fingers, I swept the heaps together once again, shuffled them once again, and then produced yet another well-calculated snowstorm, throwing the bits and pieces into the air, taking care not to throw them too high. Again, footsteps. A voice called : 'Siggi!'

I flitted to the door, unlocked it, and back to the table, and there I shoved the bits of paper round and round, fitting together pieces that didn't think much of each other, sighing convincingly as Hilke came in and asked me: 'Have you got somewhere with it?'

She stood behind my chair, looking down at the bits of paper, and instantly she had an inspiration. She actually took the whole thing out of my hands. She said : 'You don't know anything about it – come on, let me have a go.'

'I can't see anything but red and green,' I said, 'fire and water.'

'Just leave it to Hilke,' she said.

She couldn't ever stop treating me as her baby brother. Confidently she collected the bits and pieces, piled them up on a book, and said : 'It'd be much easier to do it on the kitchen table,' and, holding the book tightly to her belly, she went straight downstairs again. First of all she turned on the wireless in order to listen to some gentleman who, undaunted by atmospheric disturbances, was singing away about what girls meant to him. I sat quietly, imagining her sorting out the scraps of paper : red together with red, brown with brown. 'How I loved to kiss the girls!' Where does this white bit belong? What is this piece of grey good for? I imagined her trying to fit together the reds I had so skilfully torn, critically examining the result and then rejecting it and then starting all over again, without solving the puzzle. 'And never asked, was it the thing to do.' And just like Hilke – I went on imagining – others would sit bent over those scraps, trying to discover how to put the picture

188

together again. In Husum, perhaps even in Berlin, they would sort out those exhibits despatched by my father, they would spread them out on a table and, in the attempt to put them together properly, they would treat them as if they were a jigsaw puzzle, all the time becoming more and more exasperated. And finally, somebody would point out that there must be pieces missing, and then, comforted by the thought of those missing pieces, they would simply file the whole of my handiwork away.

But for the moment it was Hilke who was busy with it. She went on arranging the stuff, at the same time softly whistling the tune that issued from the wireless, now and then even singing the words. I pulled the blind with the picture in it out from under the bed again and went out into the passage – 'never asked, was it the thing to do' – and, keeping close to the wall, I tiptoed downstairs. At that moment the singing lady-killer had to give away to fanfares introducing a special announcement. With the aid of these fanfares I was able to open the front door and shut it again after me. Carrying the loosely rolled-up black-out blind as if it were a bazooka, I rushed towards the old box-cart, took cover, and made sure there was nobody about to see me; then I jumped across the brick path, slid down the slope and, crouching low, ran all the way to the lock-gate, where I once again looked round to make sure I was unobserved. Now I was hampered by the wind, which pressed the bulky blind against my hip. There, beyond the belt of rushes, darker than the skyline, was my sailless mill. I put the blind on my shoulder, but if anything it was still harder to carry it that way, and so I went back to carrying it in both arms. Later, as I was working my way through the rushes, I held it perpendicular, pressing it to my chest, and to anyone watching it must have looked like the periscope of a submarine sliding through the rushes, getting into position to torpedo the mill.

Something had worked loose in the cap of the mill and was making a clattering noise, but I had no time to pay any attention to that. What I meant to do was to hide the blind, with the picture glued on to it, and I ran past the mill-pond and up the concrete path. I meant to hide it in one of the flour-boxes, just for that one night, and afterwards to take it up into my hide-out and hang it on the wall next to the pictures of the horsemen. With this picture 'Suddenly on the Beach' I meant to begin an exhibition that – I don't hesitate to say this – I would dedicate to our countryside.

The far-off dyke, the Wattblick Inn, and my father, who was out on the flats in search of a parachute, were all invisible from here. I wrenched open the door of the mill and listened. There was a sound of something flitting away, a rustling and whistling, something invisible threatening me, watching me on all sides, and from high up in the top of the mill something came swooping down, hissed away over my head and soared steeply out of reach. As always, glass splinters crunched underfoot, and now and then one could hear the screech of an invisible pulley. I didn't need any light. I groped my way to the stairs to the room where the flour was ground. Keeping well to the left, I touched the smooth pillar with the notches in it, made by a hatchet, and all around me there was that creaking and mouse-like scampering. I took the blind in one hand, stretching out the other hand towards the flour-boxes. There was a clatter and a screech as I touched the cool lid of one of the boxes – but I don't want to rush things.

As I said, I touched some flour-box, and suddenly an arm came round my neck, choking me. It was not violent, it was not determined, but still, it had strength enough in it to make me drop the blind, as I took hold of the arm. Perhaps I screamed, or perhaps I tried to bite the arm that held me. I can still remember the feeling of my face, the touch of the scratchy material. I lashed out behind me and tried to wriggle out of that grip, but I couldn't free myself. We both remained more or less on the same spot, and the pressure didn't increase. Then suddenly it stopped, and the arm let go of me. I heard Klaas' voice:

'What do you want here?'

'Klaas?' I asked, speaking into the darkness: 'Klaas?'

'Beat it,' he said, 'run off home, and don't let me catch you here again.'

For a while all I could hear was his breathing. 'Who told you I was here?' he asked. 'Who was it?'

'Nobody,' I said. 'Nobody told me anything, really and truly, Klaas. I only came to hide the picture.'

'Did he send you?' he asked.

'No, he didn't, truly he didn't,' I answered. 'He isn't even at home. He was called out – to the Wattblick.'

'He's looking for me, isn't he?' Klaas said. 'He knows I'm around. He's after me all the time.'

'I promised you, didn't I?' I said. 'They won't get anything out of me.'

'It nearly happened today,' Klaas said. 'Take it from me, he's got wind of it somehow. Somebody's put him on my track. I had to get out of Bleekenwarf. He was there, right outside my room.'

'Did he see you?' I asked.

'I don't know,' Klaas said. 'I hid under the window-seat when he shone his torch through the window. I've no idea what he was aiming to see, but somebody's put him on my track, he knows I'm about.'

My brother moved in the dark, silently coming towards me in the canvas shoes the painter had given him. I could hear him step on the blind. He stopped, slowly lifted his foot, and the blind made a rustling sound. He bent down. He touched the paper, pulled it apart some distance and then let it snap back.

'Come here!' he demanded.

I obeyed. I held the blind as he told me to, while he pulled it open and put a plank on it. He struck a match. The flickering light from the match lit up his face from below, sending shifting shadows across it. He lowered the match towards the painting and moved it that way and this across it, in slow circles, and then he struck a second match when the first one went out. 'What is it?' he asked.

'Don't you recognize him?' I asked.

'Who?' he asked.

'The man on the right – you mean you don't recognize him?'

9   Homecoming

Jobst couldn't stand me. I couldn't stand him. But he got more out of it. No sooner had our teacher Plönnies handed me back my drawing of the trawler, no sooner had I carefully put that drawing away, that drawing which was meant to serve the whole gang of dullards as an example of how to see a trawler, and no sooner had schoolmaster Plönnies – a taciturn man who had been shell-shocked twice in the war – sent us home, than they started on me, kicking me in the back of the knee, bombarding me with well-aimed balls of paper, jostling me and cuffing me.

I didn't need to turn round to know that the one nearest me was Jobst, that fat, sly chap with ears as big as sails and probably adjustable at that, with rolls of fat on his neck and his wrists, with thick lips and an empty, contented look in his brown eyes. Jobst with his corduroy trousers reaching to his knees and with his wrist-watch that didn't go, the hands always pointing to twenty to five. Jobst was always after me the instant we had break or school was over. Sometimes I think his only reason for coming to school at all was to have a go at me. When he sat down, he seemed to consist of nothing but rolls of fat right from his neck down to his fat knees. When he edged that round, broad arse of his – that was always threatening to burst his trouser seams – off the seat of his desk and totteringly straightened up, he reminded me of a rather wobbly rubber pig blown up to full size, which would shrivel to nothingness at a single pin-prick. When he came after me, perhaps with a ruler in his hand, or an elastic band and the paper-clips to be catapulted from it, all that one could hear was his eager, panting breath and a sort of high-pitched breathless laughter, which is, however, not to say that he lacked endurance.

No sooner had our schoolmaster Plönnies sent us off than Jobst would be after me, spurring me on by swiftly kicking me in the backs of my knees, through the door, down the two stone steps, into the treeless, gravelled school-yard. There he would give me a taste of his ruler, and whenever I turned round he turned round too with a flabbergasted expression, pretending to look for whoever it might have been. He would follow me when I crossed the Husum road, and when we turned on to the brick path he would incite Heini Bunje to join in the game. Jobst and Heini would try to push me off the path into the swampy ditch that looked as though it were covered with a film of oil.

Without using their hands at all, they would drive me sideways, forcing me right to the edge of the ditch, and when I went on walking, leaning towards the slope, they would come down and try to push me into the ditch. Having expected to get a push, I would dodge out of the way, with the result that they pushed into empty air. Then Jobst, who was always full of bright ideas, would collect pebbles or, more precisely, loose bits of brick from the path and throw them into the ditch, making the peach-brown water splash up on my legs, my satchel, my trousers, and my shirt. Heini Bunje also enjoyed making muddy fountains arise in the ditch. I would hear bits of brick whizzing past, see them hit the dark surface of the water, and instantly feel the cold splashes on my skin. Whenever they had to pause to collect more lumps of brick, I would get a little ahead, perhaps gaining as much as fifteen or twenty yards, but, as I instantly realized, that was really no advantage to me because at that distance their throwing lost in precision. Now the projectiles came whizzing past my head or my hips, and when one of them hit my satchel, I was no longer inclined to serve as a target for them. I climbed up again on to the brick path and, balancing my satchel on my head, proceeded in the direction of Rugbüll, walking upright though admittedly a bit stiffly. Almost instantly then they caught up with me. Their shadows gesticulated, their shadows silently communicated with each other on the brick path.

I braced myself for an attack, without knowing what they were up to, but this time they got the better of me. At a word from Jobst, they closed in on me from both sides and, telling me to get out of their way, they pushed me to the other side of the road. Then, without actually pushing me, they forced me steadily down the slope so that in the end I had to jump into the ditch. They had it all very well worked out, I should say, for although I didn't fall into the water, but stepped upright into it, there I was in the middle of the ditch, gradually sinking deeper into the cool mud with the iridescent bubbles rising all round me and popping. The peat-brown water reached right up to my hips, giving off a smell of mould and things rotting, and right there in front of me was a frog hurriedly and skilfully swimming towards the weedy bank.

Jobst and Heini Bunje were delighted to see me standing there before them in the swampy ditch and slowly sinking in deeper, but it didn't satisfy them long. While Heini Bunje was collecting more lumps of brick, Jobst got his elastic band ready to flick a paper-clip and, aiming at my arm, let fly. As the shots whizzed past me, crickets chirped, mosquitoes whined, hornets buzzed, and wasps, bumble-bees, and wild bees started up their little sewing-machines. When Jobst began firing his paper-clips at me, I protected my head with my satchel and, twisting my hips from side to side, I waded laboriously towards the other bank of the ditch, pulled myself up, slid back, again pulled myself up, the paper-clips all the time whizzing and chirping around me. I could hear them laughing at my mud-caked, chocolate-coloured legs, which were dripping with brownish water. I was lying on the slope when the first paper-clip hit me on the neck. It made a stinging, burning pain, a sharp bite, and I yelled and pulled myself up to the top of the bank, no longer thinking of taking cover. I was hit again while I was slipping through the barbed-wire fence to which shreds of sheep's wool stuck, and then I was running zig-zag towards the peat-bogs. Were they giving up? No, they weren't. They saw through my plan at once and started running ahead of me in the direction of Rugbüll, now and again stooping to pick up suitable bits of brick. They ran to the first lock-gate and there they sat down on the wooden wall, because they knew very well that they had cut off my way home.

I still remember running on and on. And I also remember the burning pain in my neck and my right thigh. I remember my fear, which wouldn't subside, wouldn't permit me to rest, but made me go racing on with great leaps across the meadow where the sheep were grazing. I told myself that if only I could keep on running and get further ahead of them, they might lose heart and give up pursuing me. But they were certain to catch me.

From the way they sat there on the wall of the lock-gate, their legs dangling, turning their lumps of brick around in their hands and inspecting them, they seemed very sure of getting the better of me; they seemed to enjoy it hugely. I could see that, and I knew they were right. That's why I kept on running north-west, actually north, and whenever there was a fence in my way, I threw my satchel over and then climbed after it. Just let them wait there for me!

Was the sun shining? There was no wind, and the plain was warm in the sunlight and all sorts of things would have been growing had it been not autumn but spring, the normal time for things to grow. Were there any wild duck in the peat-ponds? Walking over the springy grass alongside the large pond, kneeling down to wash the mud off my legs – the mud that had meanwhile dried and now looked slightly blueish – I couldn't hear them rushing over the water nor could I hear the flapping of their wings as they rose into the air. Was the peat-barge still there? Where the ditch opened out into the pond I found the old barge, its stern under water, its sides tarred black, its bleached deck covered with the droppings of gulls. I climbed into that old barge, lashing out with a stick at the sleepy water-spiders and watching the dorsal fins of carp and the slow wake near the rushes where one of them was moving past.

There I sat all by myself on the old barge, and from there I couldn't see the wall of the lock-gate, not even if I stood up. At home they must have had their midday meal long ago, and Hilke would be sure to have put my portion on the range to keep hot. There was no need for me to hurry, nobody was after me, nobody was chasing me. The burning pain in my neck and in my thigh was slowly wearing off. I pushed the peat-barge out into the water and got it afloat, and then I began to bail it out with a rusty old tin I'd found inside it. And what did I do when I heard the voices? Suddenly I heard voices, there was a man calling out something and a woman laughing. They were coming from the place where the turf was cut, from those exemplary straight rows of piles of peat, where the cut peat was stacked and left to dry. There was nobody to be seen, only the sound of the man calling out again and the woman laughing again. With my stick I pushed the barge to one side and managed to get it across the ditch and so form a bridge between the two banks. I waded across and stood still, listening out for the voices. But now there was silence. In the ditch there was no current and the barge lay there safely, it would be there for me to get aboard again if need be.

I walked up the gentle slope towards the place where the peat was cut, and even before I got there I saw a glittering wet spade describing a semi-circular movement in the air and vanishing out of sight again. It appeared close to the ground and moved like the hand of a clock, moving across the face of a clock of which only the upper half was visible. I went to the edge of the pit and looked down. There was a wheelbarrow, a duckboard, and the angular shadows of the dark terraces of peat.

Hilde Isenbüttel and her Belgian were there, cutting peat. Léon, the Belgian, stripped to the waist, was standing there on the terrace, driving his spade into the moist shimmering ground, lifting out the square pieces of turf, which were about the size of a brick, and skilfully throwing them to Hilde Isenbüttel, pulling his spade back with one and the same movement and pushing it back again into the juicy ground. That was how the glittering blade time and again became visible over the edge of the pit. Hilde Isenbüttel watched the flying lumps of peat and caught them, bending at the knees. She then stacked them on the wheelbarrow, which was black with sticky bits of peat and moisture. Both the man and the woman were wearing trousers, the Belgian black breeches and she grey cloth trousers with wide cuffs. Presumably both pairs of trousers belonged to Albrecht Isenbüttel, who had been away for a number of years now, besieging Leningrad. Both of them wore clogs, but presumably only Léon, the prisoner of war, wore those belonging to Albrecht Isenbüttel. I have already mentioned that the Belgian was stripped to the waist. The woman wore a washed-out blouse loosely stuffed into the waist of the trousers. She also wore a kerchief on her head, with a printed pattern of a globe, a compass and a slide-rule on it. Is there anything I have forgotten to mention? Yes, I ought to mention the basket, which was covered with newspaper, a shirt, and a faded Belgian uniform-blouse that lay beside the basket.

Whenever one saw Hilde Isenbüttel, from whatever side one looked at her, even if she was not actually laughing she seemed to be on the point of laughing. What gave one this impression was not her stumpy teeth with the wide gaps between them or her wide shoulders which needed no padding, nor was it something about her eyes, which focused in such a way that what the one asserted the other denied. It was her general appearance that created that impression : the sturdy, somewhat bandy legs, the protruding belly that was kept under control by a belt severely tightened, the heavy and cosy breasts, and her freckles, of which there were some even behind her ears. Everything about Hilde Isenbüttel contributed to the impression that she was laughing. With what sureness she caught the turves! And how deftly she stacked them on the black wheelbarrow! Not one single one of them got broken. The Belgian went on cutting until the barrow was full; then he drove the spade into the ground, jumped down from the terrace, picked up Hilde Isenbüttel in his arms, set her down on the wheelbarrow and began to push it along the broad, springy duckboard, past the holes in the ground that were filled with dark water. Making his way up a slight incline, with a well-directed shove he pushed the barrow on to a second duckboard and then allowed it to roll until it came to a halt just in front of the rows of peat-stacks. These stacks, which were set up there in ranks of six in order to dry, were about a yard high, narrowing towards the top, and they were suggestive of one thing only, particularly from the distance and in mist or at dusk : they made one think of soldiers.

Hilde Isenbüttel got off the barrow, and the two of them first of all made a circle of turves and then, leaving spaces between the lumps of peat to let air get through, they built their stack, which, because of its distance from the other and in the conditions described, also reminded one of a soldier. Bending low, in silence, they went about their work, taking the turves from the wheelbarrow with both hands and patting them firmly into place with their hands. When Léon had laid the last turf on top of the stack, he put a feather in it, I suppose a duck's feather that he had found lying beside his clogs. He saluted the newly made stack in a military way, but broke off the gesture abruptly in order to scratch his back and pull a face. Perhaps an insect had stung him right in the middle of his saluting. Then he sat down in the empty wheelbarrow, folded his arms across his chest and just sat there, waiting for Hilde Isenbüttel to pick up the wheelbarrow and push it. And while the barrow went rolling backwards towards the pit, he acted the part of someone out for a pleasant drive: silently gesticulating, he pointed out to some invisible companion the special sights on each side, and bowed to left and to right in greeting and in response to imaginary greetings received.

Looking up towards the edge of the pit, he saw me and waved to me, but Hilde Isenbüttel didn't stop to find out whom he was waving to, believing, as she did, that his waving was meant for his companion or one of his imaginary passers-by. Only when she had got to the basket at the bottom of the pit did she stop. When he had pointed me out to her, she looked up. Recognizing me, she called out: 'Come on, Siggi, lend us a hand!'

I jumped down from terrace to terrace, making the loose walls of peat tremble. The two of them saw my damp trousers and the dried mud on them, but neither the man nor the woman said anything about it nor did they ask me why I had my satchel with me. They shook hands with me. The Belgian picked up the basket and Hilde Isenbüttel rummaged around in it until she found a ham sandwich and a piece of Madeira cake. She held them both out to me, for me to choose. Since I found it very hard to make up my mind in such circumstances I decided to have both, and I didn't mind their nodding to each other in ironical resignation of this fact.

They gave me time to eat and afterwards they told me what they wanted me to do. I was to clean up and prepare a plot where the Belgian would then cut the peat. I worked ahead of them, first of all taking off the layer of grass. Then I took off a second layer of dried vegetable matter that hadn't rotted away yet. For the peat we cut for burning must be entirely decomposed. Generations of plants have to get pulped by the pressure of their own weight and to produce gases, dissolving and de-composing through the action of carbonic acid to produce good peat that doesn't burn away too quickly in the stove. I pulled up shoots of alders and willows and roots of trees that looked like toys for the children of the Spectre King. There were bits of root, smooth and shiny as though made of wax, and mouldering rushes. There was fibrous matter of unknown origin, bits of wood from a plank, presumably from some old boat. I pulled and tore everything up, but what I secretly hoped to find and would have loved to take back to my mill, a neat, portable bog-mummy, flattened out to a piece of parchment, that I did not find. There wasn't even the skeleton of a bird, to say nothing of any archaic weapon. There was just a smell of sulphur, ammonia, and gas.

The Belgian cut more slabs of peat and the woman carried on with the stacking of them. Now and then, when they went up to the stacks, they would talk to each other, but I couldn't understand what he said. Léon spoke our dialect, but he spoke it with a French accent, and the result was that only Hilde Isenbüttel could understand him. He had been in the artillery, and the winged grenades that he had worn on his epaulettes I had hung up a long time ago in my mill, fixed on a piece of cardboard.

In this voluntary return of mine behind the bars of my past life I again see Léon there in the pit, and I also see the woman who was always laughing or at least was always ready to laugh, with her printed kerchief, and I recall her heavy, rhythmical breathing as she caught the slabs of peat in her hands. Now and then I glanced across the mounds in the direction of Rugbüll, but there was nobody approaching us from over that way. Only cows and sheep were moving in the meadows. Cows and sheep – these are simply words one puts on paper – yet I've got to put them into the background there, black and white, speckled, grey, with tangled wool, merging with each other, so that it becomes hard to decide where one sheep ends and another be-gins. For I don't want my plain to be mistaken for any other plain. I am not speaking of *some* landscape, just any land-scape, but of my own landscape, and I am not trying to re-discover some unspecified misfortune, but my own particular misfortune – in short, I am not telling just *somebody's* story, some story that doesn't commit me personally. And because this is so, I must insist on an oppressive sky, hazy air and weak sunshine, because this is so, I have us working with the sound of not very heavy breakers around us, and the rustle of rushes, while above us birds are flying over in formation and around us the bog is throwing up bubbles like boiling soup. The moor, the mud, the primeval mud – wasn't it Per Arne Schessel, my grandfather, who in his writings asserted that not all life, it is true, but whatever is strongest, toughest and most resistant, originates in primeval mud? Wasn't it part of his doctrine that all life begins with the tadpole, the tadpole using his whip-like tail to fight his way up out of primeval mud towards the light? Per Arne Schessel – that sourpuss of a naturalist.

I sat down for a break. I listened to the singing hum of engines drawing nearer from away out over the North Sea. It is possible that neither the man nor the woman down in the pit could hear that sound. Or perhaps they did hear it and were only paying no attention to it, since airplanes did frequently pass over our heads on their way to Kiel, Lübeck or Swinemünde. The sound came nearer so quickly that I looked towards the dyke and, shutting one eye, subdivided the skyline into sections with the aid of four telephone wires running along over the dyke. In this way, I should have the airplane in my sights the moment it loomed up over the greenish-brown protuberance. I swivelled my A.A. gun around, my secret gun, on its twin-carriage, towards the dyke. Now let them come on! They must be flying very low over the water, approaching under cover of the dyke, and then suddenly there they were with the circles of their airscrews glittering, swooping over the telephone wires and instantly diving at us: two airplanes, two of those stubby Mustangs.

They came closer and closer, and I was able to make out a shaggy buffalo's head in front of the first machine's cockpit, attacking in blind fury, simply relying on its tempestuous strength, and I thought I could also make out the pilot's face under the transparent hood. Calmly he steered his buffalo's head towards us, aiming it at us, dipping even lower. Behind the first machine came the second, swooping down in exactly the same way, repeating every movement that the first one made, just as if they were firmly connected to each other and both flying to the orders given by one and the same mind.

My arms went up and I fired my gun. At the same moment they fired back. Flames shot forth and a shower of sparks, glowing threads, came flashing down to the ground, there was a smacking, slapping noise where the bullets hit the soft ground. And the stacks! Léon's and Hilde Isenbüttel's brown peat-stacks went spraying and splashing in all directions, they simply exploded, falling down left and right, collapsing. The turves burst apart and disintegrated. A snake of fire came rushing through the dry grass. A shower of crumbling peat came down on us, and then all at once I was lying on the moist ground of the pit and all I could feel was the weight of Léon's body, his breathing close to my ears and the grip of his hands, firm but not hurting me. Léon covered me with his body while I could still see fiery wheels and glaring sheaves of light moving across before my eyes and some bullets were still hitting the peat-wall opposite us, rather ineffectively, I should say, since they merely made some unimpressive holes in the peat, which was light brown on top and increasingly dark towards the bottom.

It seemed to me that Léon went on lying on top of me much too long, for after zooming over us very low and disappearing, the airplanes had turned and, diving steeply, almost standing on one wing, came down at us, or rather at the ranks of peat-stacks, which, though thinned out, were still holding their ground with excellent discipline. The stacks seemed to annoy them, obviously because they maintained such discipline and did not take cover, indeed did not even take any notice of their casualties. It was the peat-stacks, their numbers amounting to perhaps the strength of a battalion, parading in stupid rigidity, that had to bear the brunt.

When the two machines had turned and disappeared in the direction of Husum, where they would find whole divisions of peat-stacks petrified in well-disciplined ranks, we climbed out of the pit. What the Belgian did was to shake his fist in the direction in which the airplanes had disappeared, and laugh. He called something out after them, something that sounded like 'pennshittair' but which was meant to mean 'penny-shitter'. He pointed at the devastated parade-ground and then, pulling Hilde Isenbüttel towards him by a corner of her kerchief, kissed her, still laughing, and with a disparaging gesture towards the peat-stacks, some of which were totally and some of which were more or less severely damaged, he said : 'We'll set them up again, we've got plenty of time,' and slapping me on the back, he added : 'We'll do it, won't we, mon petit, n'est pas?' And then he instantly began clearing up the mess and creating order out of chaos among the stacks, by collecting the undamaged turves and starting to build new stacks with them. We helped him. Hilde Isenbüttel and I collected the undamaged turves and brought them to Léon, the Belgian prisoner-of-war, who didn't seem to miss anything, neither his shoemaker's last, with which he used to earn his living, nor his fiancée.

He whistled while he worked, and it might have been that whistling of his that made it impossible for him to hear the whimpering that we all suddenly heard, there among the peat-banks. For some time I didn't hear it either; it was the woman who was the first to become aware of it. At first, she paid no attention to it and simply went on working, but then she signalled to us to be quiet, and as we looked at her questioningly we suddenly heard the whimpering and a monotonous feeble groaning down there in the pit among the collapsed peat-stacks. Léon called out, but there was no answer. He called out again, then we all went down to where the débris lay scattered about. I don't know what we expected to find, what we were prepared for. Now the sounds had ceased, and we moved slowly through the shot-up, broken peat, this way and that, and then, where the banks came to an end, we found Klaas. He was lying on his back. He didn't stir. He didn't look at us. His face was peaceful, his hands were limp and open. There was a dry slab of peat under his head like a pillow. He was wounded, with a shot in the belly. He was wearing his belt, or rather, he was not. Where the buckle of his belt would normally have been, there the bullet had hit him. The patch of blood was larger than a large zinnia.

What I must put on record before all else, in recalling all that happened, what strikes me in particular, is how calmly we took it, standing there around him : no exclamation of horror and dismay, no dramatic 'No, no, this cannot be !', none of us dropping to his knees, touching him, trying to find out how badly he was wounded or whether he was alive at all – what I see in my mind's eye is the three of us standing there as though it were too late to do anything.

It was Léon who was the first to bend over Klaas, Léon who with his hands removed bits and pieces of broken peat from my brother's body. He cleaned him up. Then I followed his example, and after some time I began calling out to Klaas. But he didn't hear me. Hilde Isenbüttel pulled me up from the ground and pulled me to herself. And then she whispered to the Belgian, at once instructing him and seeking his advice. The Belgian went down into the pit, put on his shirt and returned with the wheelbarrow. He wheeled it level with Klaas, cleaned it up, and then laid his jacket in it like a lining. Very carefully he lifted my brother into the barrow, in such a manner that his head was supported by the slanting back.

'We must get him to Bleekenwarf, to Uncle Nansen,' I said. 'That's what he wants.'

Hilde Isenbüttel shook her head. 'Of all things to happen!' she said. 'We must get him home, child, there's nothing else for it. Never you mind, child, we must get him home.'

'But Klaas,' I said, 'Klaas wants us to take him to Bleekenwarf, to Uncle Nansen.'

'He's got to go to hospital,' Hilde said. 'First we must get him home and then he must be got to hospital. Oh Lord, of all things to happen!'

She pointed in the direction of Rugbüll. The Belgian nodded and gripped the handles of the wheelbarrow. I was allowed to carry the basket. So we moved off from the pit. Time and again the wheelbarrow got stuck, the large wooden wheel with its iron rim sinking into the ground, rumbling and stumbling along over tufts of grass, grinding its way through the soft turf. My brother's body was shaken to and fro, sagging in the barrow, his head sliding to one side or hanging down, dangling over the slanting back; his hands also hung down over the sides, dragging and scraping over the ground. Blood oozed from the corners of his mouth, and on one of his temples there was dried blood in the shape of a cross.

The Belgian lifted and pushed, he shoved with the whole of his body until the veins on his neck stood out. His back grew stiff with the effort, and all the time he gazed down on Klaas.

It seemed that he himself suffered pain whenever Klaas's body was jerked up and down on the rough ground.

We took the path towards the dyke, then we went along below the dyke. Now and then the Belgian set the barrow down. Hilde Isenbüttel tried to make Klaas more comfortable, or she would straighten the jacket beneath him. She and Léon talked in a whisper whenever we stopped. They asked me if I wouldn't like to run on ahead. No. Wouldn't I like to tell them at home what had happened? No. Wouldn't I like to tell my father to come and meet the slow-moving barrow? No. What I wanted was the strap, the strap fixed to the front of the barrow, by which one could pull it. They looked at me in approval and put the leather strap over my shoulder. And I leaned as far forward as I could, to pull with all my weight, at the same time thinking of the lock-gate and of Jobst and Heini Bunje, before whom I had fled.

Klaas didn't stir. How easily he lay there! His mutilated hand, which was now covered only with a dressing, time and again slid over the edge and dragged along the ground, and time and again Hilde Isenbüttel picked it up and laid it on his chest. I can still see that and also the Belgian's dark eyes and his face contorted with the effort he was·making.

How am I to remember that homecoming of ours if I am forced to say more than the mere truth, or to say less? I can still hear the squeaking of the barrow's wheels and feel the strap cutting into my shoulder. I can see Rugbüll coming closer, the red brick house, the shed, the box-cart with its shaft pointing up into the air. My own Rugbüll. But there's nothing for it – we're getting closer and closer in spite of the fact that there were a number of things I feel I ought to mention that were slowing us down, for instance the fact that the Belgian was beginning to become exhausted, and my fear, which made me imagine all sorts of things. Still, we're rolling over the wooden bridge, and from there the lock-gate can be seen and its wall, on which there is nobody sitting waiting for me, ready to shoot at me with his catapult.

They had gone and we were rolling on, past the lock, past the signpost, past the box-cart. Now, I thought, now Klaas will sit up, now he'll realize where he is, where he's being taken to. I expected him to roll off the barrow, jump up and run – back to the peat-bog where he'd been hiding during the day, since he had disappeared from Bleekenwarf. But my brother didn't sit up, he didn't even blink one eye when he stopped at the steps to the house.

Hilde Isenbüttel went into the house. The Belgian sat down on the stone steps and began to rummage in his pockets for a half-smoked cigarette, poking his outstretched forefinger inside the pocket. Not finding anything and then, remembering, he pointed to his jacket, which he'd put into the barrow for Klaas to lie on : the half-smoked cigarette was there in one of the pockets. He made a gesture of renunciation. He'd smoke it later. Looking grave, he pointed at Klaas and then spread out his hands in a querying gesture. He didn't speak a word, he merely conversed with me in silence. What he meant to say was that if he could have helped in any way he would have done so, but there was little to be done. He had brought Klaas here, but that was all that he, considering his position, could be expected to do. He turned his head towards the house, listening, and it was obvious that all he wanted was to get away from here as fast as possible. Perhaps he would have liked to raise my brother's hand from the ground and lay it on his chest, but he didn't dare to touch him there under the windows of our house. I kept my eyes fixed on Klaas. I hadn't given up hope that at a suitable moment he would get up and run away. Hadn't he stirred? Wasn't he moving one leg, preparing to jump up? But only a shudder went through his body. Klaas was cold.

Now my father appeared at the top of the stone steps, coming out of the door of our house, his uniform blouse unbuttoned. He ignored the Belgian prisoner-of-war's salute, he just stood there. Slowly his face took on an expression that it is hard to find words for : perhaps it was reproach mingled with despair. He didn't rush towards the barrow, he just stood there, appearing taller than he was from where I looked at him. He gazed down at Klaas just as if inside his head he had long known of this homecoming and had been through it all in his thoughts. He hesitated, he seemed to be taking stock of the situation. Then slowly he came down the steps, much too slowly, he walked round the barrow before coming to a halt at its head and aimlessly touching Klaas's shoulder. There he stood in his defenceless silence, neither speaking to him nor calling out to him.

But he did lift up Klaas's arm and lay it on his chest. Hilde Isenbüttel, who had followed him down the steps, took off her kerchief and shook out her hair, saying over and over again: 'Of all things to happen, of all things to happen . . .'

The Belgian stood there, ready to be of help if asked. And now my father asked him to take hold of Klaas's legs while he himself grasped him under the shoulders, to lift him up. So they carried him into the house and, swaying from side to side, they entered the sitting-room and laid him on the grey divan.

My father didn't see the glance that Hilde and Léon exchanged, he didn't notice them tiptoeing out of the house without a word. He stood there upright in front of Klaas, as though straining to hear him breathing in answer to his own standing there with a questioning expression. It was as though he felt himself alone with Klaas and wanted to tell him something, something that might be important. Klaas didn't open his eyes. Cautiously my father groped for a chair, placed it beside my brother's head, sat down and bent over him. After a while he took Klaas's hand, his mutilated and bandaged hand, in his own and studied it with great attention. He did not let it go. His lips moved. He simply could not bear to remain silent. All at once he said:

'It's a long road for everyone, but this isn't the end.'

He spoke softly and hastily, lowering his head towards Klaas, not caring whether or no his words were understood. He spoke as though in this way he were fulfilling an ancient duty, a duty that ought to have been fulfilled long ago, one that he had been conscious of since the day when Klaas had come back. He hadn't finished what he had to say when the door opened, but he stopped, without either turning his head or letting go of Klaas's hand.

He listened to my mother's dragging footsteps coming from the door. He sat bent over, holding his breath, while she moved across the sitting-room that was scarcely ever used, her lips compressed, her face not showing – at least not yet – what she felt, except perhaps for an expression of grief controlled. Now my father rose and tried to make her sit down on the chair. She resisted in silence. She came so close that her knees touched the sofa. When she did sit down, she raised her hands, and it seemed that she was about to lay them on Klaas's face, but then she pulled them back and laid them on his shoulders. I am not mistaken about all this, because at such moments I become very alert, I listen with redoubled attention, not allowing myself to be distracted by anything, because those are the moments in which something is communicated, or something has to be accepted, for which every spoken sentence is too long. My mother was incapable of screaming, she didn't throw herself on Klaas, she didn't stroke him, call him by his name or kiss him, she just held him firmly by his shoulders. Only once did her hand move along his right arm, and then it stopped as though frightened, as though that movement were too much, and as though she felt guilty – or almost guilty – she moved her hand back to his shoulder. She didn't pay any attention to his wound. For a while she just sat there, motionless, and then her body began to twitch, she sobbed and cried without a sound, without tears. My father put his hand on her shoulder, but she didn't seem to notice it. Perhaps my father pressed her shoulder more strongly now, because she stood up and turned towards the window where the house-plants stood, still sobbing without a sound and without tears. And then, as though speaking to the window, she asked what was to happen now. And my father said that first of all he was going to telephone for Doctor Gripp and that there was no point in talking about anything else yet.

My mother, supporting herself on the window-sill, asked how ever it had happened, and my father answered that he hadn't been there, but it happened out there, in the peat-bog, during an attack by low-flying planes, which had occurred quite suddenly right where Hilde Isenbüttel and her prisoner of war – that Léon, you know him – were working. Hilde and Léon, my father went on, had brought Klaas to Rugbüll in the wheelbarrow.

My mother said nothing at all to all that, for that was what she knew already, having seen it herself. Was he going to telephone to Husum? Yes. Was he going to telephone the hospital in Hamburg? No, that was a matter for the station in Husum. Would he call her when Doctor Gripp had been? Yes, he would call her, and he would discuss with her whatever was to be done. She turned round, casting a sharp glance at Klaas, who was still lying there just as he'd been laid down. There was a look in her eye as if she were trying to find something out, and I wondered what she was up to when she went from the window to the sofa or – I'd rather put it this way – worked her way laboriously towards it as though she had to overcome some invisible resistance. I was amazed when all she did, after making that difficult approach, was to pick up a folded blanket, open it up, stretching her arms wide, and, with limp fingers, spread it over Klaas. Then she left the room.

What is there to be told next? What detail impresses itself on my mind? The telephone call. My father can't help leaving the door open whenever he has to make a telephone call. I heard him ask for the doctor and then tell him twice, roaring at the top of his voice, what had happened and what he was needed for. In my mind's eye I can still see him coming back, bent over and murmuring to himself, holding in one hand the desk-calendar with the movable cards for the days. He walked round the dining-table at which we never had our meals. The homely-looking brown sideboard shook under his footsteps. He walked round close to the lamp, close to the cast-iron flowerpot stand, with its three shelves, he went on doing his round just so as not to have to listen, not to have to understand, and he didn't even tie up his boot-lace, but allowed it to drag along behind his right foot. I didn't dare to speak to him. During the telephone conversation he had buttoned up his uniform-blouse, and now he unbuttoned it again so that his everlastingly twisted braces could be seen. Suddenly he stopped in front of the sideboard, raising the hand in which he held the desk-calendar, glanced at it briefly and then threw it on to the floor. The little pack of cards, the white cards for all the days, fell, scattering, opening out like a burst of shrapnel. Some of them landed among the branches of a fuchsia. Then he resumed his rounds, but after circling the table twice he found it impossible to go on with that, left the room and walked down the hall and into his office. I could hear the tinkle of the telephone as he lifted the receiver and then, almost instantly, another tinkle as he put it down again without having made a call.

Klaas stirred under the blanket. I rushed over to him, whispering his name, imploring him to open his eyes at long last, to listen to me, to realize that this was the moment he'd been waiting for. He bunched up the blanket on his chest. There was nothing to stop him, I said, nothing in the way either at the window or at the front door or at the cellar door. He opened his trembling lips and clutched the blanket, tugging it up to make an elongated mountain-range of folds. There's nobody here, I said, and I added: 'If you can do it, this is the moment.' But I simply couldn't get through to him, he didn't pay any attention to me at all even when I ran to the window, opened it and stretched out my hand to show him. He didn't turn his face towards me. I went back to him, put my hands under the blanket in search of his mutilated hand, wanting to make him understand that I was there, to give him some sign of my presence and my readiness to help him. He let his hand stay in mine, but that was all.

I gave up, I shut the window, gathered together the calendar-cards, returned them to their little box and put the calendar on the table. I pulled out the card for 22 September 1944 and put it in front of the rest. Klaas whimpered, perhaps he wanted something, but I couldn't make out what it was. My father, who had now come back into the room, couldn't understand him either. My father stood there, stooping over Klaas, listening, his back bent, helpless, doing nothing. Then he straightened up, shrugged his shoulders, came over to the dining-table, sat down next to me, and gazed at the calendar. He no longer seemed agitated, he was not mumbling to himself now and he didn't look embittered either. He seemed resigned, he looked blank and resigned. He laid one hand on top of the other and just sat there, his shoulders sagging, his head low, waiting. Or rather, this is what he did after, to my surprise, he had opened a drawer and taken out the framed photograph of Klaas and put it on the sideboard – the photograph of Klaas in uniform standing in front of a sentry-box, the photograph that had been banished into that drawer shortly after his self-mutilation. My father put it in its old place between a twig of honesty that shone like mother-of-pearl and a painted china money-box, and then he paid no further attention to it.

We sat there waiting, each of us locked away within himself. We waited – and what I mean by that is: there wasn't anything else for us to do. We had simply accepted what had happened. And, by waiting the way we did, we made it clear that we had accepted it. It was something that had added itself to the prevailing uncertainty. At best we hoped something might happen which it was beyond our power to make happen. What mattered had obviously happened already and now we were merely waiting for the rest to happen. We were waiting, as it were, for the whole thing to be cleared up. Remembering him now, the way he sat there beside me, I must confess to myself that his frightening calm and resignation were simply the declaration that now everything was decided. It seemed that my father, the Rugbüll policeman, knew what was expected of him. What then, if that was the case, did he expect of Doctor Gripp? What did he expect from him and his visit?

As soon as we heard Doctor Gripp arriving, my father made a sign to me, and I went to the door to let the doctor in. Our doctor was a heavy old man who walked rather lame, a red-haired wheezing giant whom experience had taught to keep his head down because otherwise he knocked it against the beams of low ceilings. He would never diagnose one single illness; being chronically suspicious he would always offer at least two or three possible illnesses. He would let people take their choice. I took his bag from him and walked ahead of him, very slowly, setting one foot before the other, as I had the feeling that I had to lure him into our sitting-room. Even on the short way from our front door to the sitting-room Doctor Gripp rested twice, leaning against the wall, bending his already curved, massive neck even lower and snapping his fingers, while he took deep breaths. Despite the fact that I drew his attention to the step at the threshold of the sitting-room he nearly stumbled and was just saved by my father, who seized him under the arms and supported him, afterwards guiding the huge man to the chair next to the sofa, pressing him down on to it and only then saying good day to him. My father sent me out of the room, then called me back and ordered me to put the bag down beside the doctor's feet. Then with an absentminded gesture he sent me out again, telling me to wait in Hilke's room, which opened off the sitting-room. He ordered me to wait there, and himself shut the door after me.

The first thing I did was to say hello to a film-actor who not only smiled at me from where he was fixed to the wall but even raised his glass of champagne to me, toasting me. He seemed to feel at home there, in the midst of many women and girls in white gym-dresses, all swinging their hoops and clubs and gyro-wheels in the service of 'Belief and Beauty', forming a loose frame around him. All these pictures had been cut out of an illustrated journal, and in one of them there was Hilke, clearly recognizable by her calves, which fit so tightly together, Hilke swinging two clubs, whirling them round, standing on tiptoe, her breasts expanded. The actual clubs were there in the room, in a corner next to the wardrobe, and I picked them up and kicked them against each other and then, not being really interested in them, put them down again. The back of the only chair was being kept warm by Hilke's peasant jacket, and on the seat lay a black skirt and a black patent-leather belt. There was a field postcard stuck into the frame of the looking-glass, and on a glass shelf below it I discovered nail-scissors, hair-pins, four combs, a tube of cream against itching skin, cotton-wool, elastic bands, a tube of tablets, and still more cotton-wool. On the bed there reposed a large hen with a hurt expression on its face, a hen made of some yellow stuff. Under the bed there were Hilke's shoes. Where was the puzzle? The puzzle lay on the night-table, and all three mice were in the three traps.

I tiptoed to the door and peered through the keyhole. Doctor Gripp was sitting on the sofa, my father standing beside him. The blanket was on the floor. I could see my father's face, contorted in an expression of mingled pain and curiosity. His lips were parted. Klaas was hidden from me by Doctor Gripp's back. My father asked a question to which Doctor Gripp shook his head. My father spoke so loudly that I could hear what it was :

'Why can't it be done?'

Looking down at Klaas, the huge old doctor answered :

'It can only be done in hospital, we've got to get him into hospital as quickly as possible.' And he waved his hand at Klaas as though indicating the proof of what he had said. Again my father asked a question, whereupon Doctor Gripp raised his opened hand, which had been sliding downward, and, raising it to about shoulder height, let it speak for him. His bag was still there on the floor, unheeded. He hadn't even opened it. Now my father went up to him. I could only see their backs. The doctor was presumably explaining something to him, trying to make him understand something which my father seemed to have difficulty in grasping. Even now, Doctor Gripp didn't bother to open his bag – that cracked leather bag with the old-fashioned locks. The doctor whispered something to my father without turning his face towards him, and it seemed to me that he was destroying, one by one, all the hopes my father had still clung to. This could be made out from the way my father turned his face aside, looked out of the window, and gradually stopped asking questions.

The front door slammed. I rushed to the window to see who had come, but, of course, I was too late and so I quickly went back to the keyhole. My father didn't stir, he didn't even look towards the door of the room. The doctor was just buttoning up Klaas's jacket. And then there he was, in the open door of the sitting-room, at first small, and then growing, as it seemed to me, in jerks, holding his pipe in one hand and his hat in the other, wearing his shabby blue overcoat, breathless. He stopped halfway from the door, not really because he was hesitating, afraid that he had come at the wrong time, but because he was fighting for air, hunching up his shoulders. And my father? He didn't even turn round, he obviously didn't care who had come into the room. My father had no more questions to ask. What had to be done now was to do whatever was necessary. The painter came right in and went over to the sofa, and he turned not only to the doctor but to both the men facing him as he asked :

'Is he dead? They say he's dead.'

Then he took two swift steps closer to the sofa, and his eyes darted from Klaas to the doctor and back. I heard the doctor say :

'Hospital. We've got to get him into hospital. May I use the telephone, Jens?'

'It's over there in the office,' my father said.

The painter helped the doctor to rise. 'Is there any hope?' he asked. 'Will he pull through?'

'Let's hope so,' Doctor Gripp said. 'It could be a lot worse.'

Dragging his feet, his arms stretched out before him, he left the room, this time getting across the threshold without trouble. The painter bent over Klaas. For a long time he gazed at him searchingly, as though looking for something special. He seemed calm and composed. He seemed to be searching for something, or if it wasn't that, to be trying to imprint something on his mind. His lips moved, he swallowed and his jaws moved as if he were chewing. There was anger – yes, there was anger too in his face as he now shook his head gently, as though disappointed, above all incredulous. Suddenly he turned towards my father, about to ask a question, then stopped short and, as though by way of apology for his presence, said :

'They told me he was dead. That's why I came.'

The policeman nodded. His nod did not convey any understanding, but merely that he had taken notice of the statement.

Nansen wanted to know how it had happened. The answer came with a shrug of the shoulders :

'It happened, that's all there is to it.'

'Out there in the peat-bog?'

'Yes, out there in the peat-bog.'

'There was a lot in him, wasn't there?'

'Yes, a lot. We all hope he'll pull through.'

'But pulling through isn't all that matters. It doesn't look as if that were all. The madness of it all, Jens – the damn bloody madness.'

'What do you mean?'

'They'll come and fetch him, they'll get him all right, just so that he can hear the verdict. They'll make him well again just for the firing-squad! Don't you know that? Or don't you?'

'Me? I don't know anything.'

'Are they already on their way to fetch him?'

'Nobody's on his way.'

'So it's all up to you now.'

'Yes, it is, and you'd better leave it that way.'

'I only came because of the lad.'

'Yes, all right.'

'You know, I've got a soft spot for Klaas, I'm fond of him.'

'I know all about it.'

'Can I speak to Gudrun?'

'I don't think so, she's upstairs.'

'Is there anything I can do?'

'I don't think so, we must see it through alone.'

'Well then – good luck.'

Nansen went to the sofa, he touched Klaas's hand slightly, and then he touched him a second time, on the shoulder. Then he left the room, his eyes unseeing, and while I was still waiting to hear the front door slam, there he was already on the outside steps and then at the signpost at his bicycle; through the window I watched him fixing his hat to the luggage-carrier, saw him licking his thumbs and then pushing his bicycle along instead of getting on it.

For a long time I gazed after him, watching him until he vanished behind the shaggy scrub of Holmsenwarf. Then I left the window, but now I didn't peer through the keyhole, I just went into the sitting-room. As soon as I had done it I got a bit of a fright and stopped, the doorknob still in my hand, waiting. But when I wasn't told off, and wasn't sent out of the room, I shut the door after me. There were Doctor Gripp and my father standing in the passage, and Klaas was lying under his blanket, quite still. The doctor was just saying that he was prepared to do something or other, and he went on :

'I'll see to it, leave it to me, just you let that be my worry.' He patted my father's arm as though he wanted to cheer him up. He gripped my father's shoulder, turned him round and pushed him back into the room where I was, and then, all by himself, found his way to the stairs and with a heavy stomp – I can't call it anything but that – went upstairs, stomp, stomp, stomp. My father and I just stood there, heads raised, doing nothing, just listening to that heavy-footed climbing of the stairs.

'Thank God for that,' my father murmured and all at once he no longer seemed so tense. Then he noticed me. He stretched out one hand towards me and pulled me to him and with his body urged me towards the sofa, but not too close.

'This is what it has come to. After all we hoped for and looked forward to, in spite of all I've taught him, it had to come to this. He knew what he owed us and yet he brought it to this.'

He fell silent and I asked :

'Is he going to get better?'

And my father, beside me, said : 'And he knew, he knew what I had to do. He knew very well what my duty was. Now it's happened. There it is and we can't undo it. We asked all the questions, all the questions that mattered, and we answered them as best we could. Not just today. Ever since the day he came back. All the questions. Come along.'

He pulled me along with him, his face ashen. Side by side we walked across the hall into his office. He picked up the receiver and waited and then he asked for the police station at Husum. He didn't shout the way he usually did, but his voice didn't shake either.

10 Zero Hour

If I know a thing, I've got to put it down. Even if what I know will be washed away the next time it rains. I've got to put down here what I know about the rust-red stable at Bleekenwarf that hadn't been used for so long, about a misty morning with the haze forming flat expanses over the countryside, I've got to open the stable-door and show the injured animal and assemble once again all the people in sufficient light to make them clearly visible – the people who were present that day, either to take part in a forced slaughter or just to watch it. I'd like to go about it by first setting the scene : there is the draughty and, as I've said before, unused stable at Bleekenwarf, with its bays for the pigs, the rusty rings for tying up the cattle, and a slanting chicken-ladder covered with droppings; there's old Holmsen, sitting on a wobbly pile of boards, his wife, Jutta, the painter and myself. Leaning against the whitewashed stable wall, on sagging forelegs, breathing hard, and foaming at the mouth, there's the injured animal slowly bleeding from wounds in its neck and its back.

If I say that the bomber that released those two bombs over Rugbüll jettisoned them, somebody may, of course, ask how I know. Well, apart from the point that I can't imagine any pilot, least of all one flying above the clouds, considering Rugbüll worthy of a bomb, I regard the question 'How does he know?' as beside the point. Anyway, the bomber did release those two bombs, jettisoning them, and one of them fell into the sea, the other went deep into the swampy pasture near Bleekenwarf and made a crater there. Some of the fragments hit the cow in the neck and back. It was Holmsen's cow.

There we were in the stable, sitting on the pile of boards and watching the animal, which could no longer get up, but which also didn't seem to be dying of its wounds. On a potato-sack that had been spread out there were an axe, knives and a saw, not a bone-saw but a greased pad-saw. There were also some bowls, a wooden tub, a dented milking-pail, and there was a huge leather apron, in fact everything was prepared for the slaughter. We watched the animal. Now it was almost squatting on its hind parts. Its dirty udder with the inflamed teats was spread on the mud floor, there was a pulsating inside it, a throbbing and twitching. The animal's tail, with its tangled tassel, swished the floor and sometimes the wall. The cow stretched out its neck the way they do when they drink, it snorted and licked its mouth and nostrils, spluttered and blew out bubbly foam. Now and then it scratched the floor with one of its fore-hooves, trying to push itself up along the wall, but it couldn't do it and dropped back again, making a scraping noise. All the time the blood was oozing out of the wounds, trickling over the black-and-white speckled coat, dripping on to the ground. A fragment of the bomb had smashed its right hind leg, torn the skin and flesh and laid bare the bone.

Twice already old Holmsen had tried to begin the slaughtering, urged on by his wife, a bow-legged, cranky person in a grey hairnet, who was bound to make him feel at times that he was married to a dachshund. He had taken the axe, gone up to the animal, accompanied and urged on by the old woman's exclamations. We had watched him aim at a certain point on the animal's curly haired forehead, placing his feet firmly on the ground, but in spite of the fact that the old woman had gone on urging him in an increasingly angry voice, he had been incapable of bringing himself to swing the axe. Shrugging his shoulders, each time he had returned to the pile of boards and sat down again.

The old woman went on clamouring and vituperating, she wouldn't shut up for a moment, and now she even threatened him that she would go to Glüserup and fetch Sven Pfrüm, who had for a long time been the itinerant slaughterer in our district and whom Holmsen would have to pay for doing the job if he, Holmsen, couldn't bring himself to kill the cow. While the painter sat there, staring at the animal, she went on :

'Come on, Holmsen, get going, man, or else the beast will perish before our eyes. And then we shall have nothing out of the misfortune!'

And to make him get on with the job she got up, snatched up the emptied milking-pail and went up to the cow, saying that she herself was ready to catch the blood and in general to give a hand.

But that didn't help, it didn't give old Holmsen either strength or confidence. He scrounged some tobacco from the painter and, turning to one side, began to puff away at his pipe. She reminded him that he had killed ducks and pigeons and fowl. She even took up the axe and pressed the handle into his hand, and she asked him to remember that they might be able to save the cost of paying Sven Pfrüm. He could understand that. He nodded and sighed and got up from the pile of boards, but one long glance at the injured animal sufficed, he realized that it was more than he was a match for, and he let the axe slide to the floor. Perhaps, he said, if it had been some other cow, but not Thea, no, he couldn't kill Thea. She was my second-best milk cow and she understood every word I said.

'But now,' the old woman said, 'now she doesn't understand anything any more because she's half dead. All anyone can do now is put her out of her misery by killing her.'

And now Jutta actually asked if it was not possible to dress the cow's wounds and hope she might get better. And the old Holmsen woman answered irritably :

'It's you who need a dressing – you!'

Perhaps Jutta realized how silly her question had been.

When the animal began to scrape its feet on the ground, and its forelegs finally gave out and it lay there, its neck stretched out flat on the ground, the old woman again picked up the axe, but this time she didn't hand it to her husband, she merely held it in her hand as a reminder of what had to be done now. Axe in hand she went up to the animal, which took no notice of her, only moved its head from one side to the other. It tried to reach a wound on its back, and when it couldn't do that, it snorted so violently, towards the floor, that chaff and dried leaves blew about. Now the animal tried to rise, supporting itself against the wall, but after a moment, in which it seemed to be gathering its strength together, it collapsed again. Panting, it no longer tried to lick the foam away with its tongue. The tension that had been there in the body up to now seemed to be slackening. The tail no longer swished across the floor. The old woman pointed at the cow with her open hand. The gesture, which conveyed an accusation that couldn't be overlooked, was meant not only for old Holmsen but for everybody present. Gaunt, with ice-grey hair, Holmsen went on smoking, his head turned to one side, and one could see the effort he was making to get his thoughts clear. He sat there, bowed, his eyes averted from the injured animal.

All at once the painter slid off the pile of boards, pushed his hat to the back of his neck, knocked out his pipe on the doorpost and, without speaking, without hesitation, went up to the woman. He waved one hand casually towards Jutta and me, indicating that we should take ourselves off, but he didn't wait for us to obey his command, he seized the handle of the axe and took it out of the old woman's hand. He shoved her away, right back on to the pile of boards, and again went up to the animal, which took no notice of him, its neck stretched out and moving over the floor as it made a laborious effort to lift its head.

The painter weighed the axe in his hand. He took one short step, scraping the floor with the soles of his shoes, and planting his feet firmly. There was no trace of emotion in his face as he looked down at the animal, at the hard, heavy skull with the dark, indifferent eyes, the skull that was trying to rise towards him. The sticky hairs formed black and white circlets on the animal's forehead, and from the mouth a long thread of mucus hung down; the hairy ears were turned towards the man as though listening. Now the painter seemed to be measuring the distance between the animal's eyes, to find the spot where he would hit it with the axe. Then he glanced back across his shoulder and raised the axe in a big sweep, while we sat there motionless. I can still see him standing there in his own stable, the axe raised in his hands, his head tilted slightly backward, looking down at the animal, which even now didn't take any interest in him. He had stretched up so high that his long coat was lifted up to the hollows of his knees.

When the axe struck home, the painter groaned. Making use of the impetus of his blow he pulled the axe back, raised it over his shoulder, took one step backwards and let it come down again, this time with the blunt side. He followed the movement through with the weight of his body to give more force to it and, in doing so, he lost his hat. After the second blow he wiped his mouth with a quick gesture, murmured something that none of us could understand, and looked towards us – at Jutta and myself. I had the feeling that he didn't really see us, at least he did not seem to be surprised that we were still there. Holding the handle of the axe vertically in front of him, he let it slide to the ground between his feet. The third go, which he decided after a moment was necessary, he struck faster and with less force, even a little hesitancy. After that he handed the axe to old Holmsen, sat down on the pile of boards, and massaged his fingers.

But this isn't all I recollect of that morning there in the stable: I can still hear the blunt side of the axe hit the skull, see the skull being thrown to the ground by the force of the blow, and I can feel Jutta's fingers pressing painfully into my arm. The axe had hit the animal between the eyes, and it sounded like a blow against a hollow tree-trunk. The axe had smashed the forehead. The animal's body seemed to flatten out, but then the forelegs began to scrape the ground as though in search of support, of some resistance. The neck twitched, the back grew rigid, the hind legs jerked and stuck out. The blow seemed to bring some memory back into the unwieldy body, perhaps of resistance or perhaps of flight, for one moment it set the injured animal's sense in motion: but there was no longer sufficient strength for any such thing, its strength just sufficed to produce some scraping and twitching that showed what it hoped to do. A few times the head rose from the ground in a clumsy rhythm, and each time it dropped back again, each time producing a dull thud. The flanks trembled, and after the second blow they twitched violently, the way they used to twitch in order to drive away stinging flies.

And now, I think, it is high time to let the animal perish, let it lie there by the whitewashed wall motionless, stretched out, relaxed except for some scarcely perceptible reflex-movements. Now that it was dead, it seemed to me much larger than before, and I had the impression that it was growing all the time, bulging out as though it were being blown up to gigantic dimensions. And another thing I know is that I hated that woman who couldn't wait until the animal lay quite still, who snatched up the huge leather apron, and held it out to her husband and then handed him the knife, at the same time irritably pointing at the bulging mass there against the wall. The milk-pail was dangling from her arm. I hated her – I didn't hate old Holmsen, nor the painter, either – and that hatred of mine heightened my attentiveness to all she did, as she now squatted by the dead animal's neck and, pushing the pail on the ground, held it at a slant and, without asking her husband again to begin his work, crouched there, all the time staring into the pail just as if the blood had already begun to gush forth. Old Holmsen saw it. He touched the edge of his knife, tried the point on his thumb and then he felt the animal's neck and, holding the head between his legs, slowly bent down, but now no longer reluctantly. He set the knife to the neck and drove it in, thrusting it several times, and he looked at the woman before he pulled it out again. It seemed that he directed the jet of blood so that it spurted forth exactly into the middle of the pail.

At that moment, somebody seized me by the neck. I tried to turn round but the pressure round my neck proved stronger. And then I felt myself being pushed towards the door. At my side was Jutta, moving the same way as I did, just as if we were tied together, she imitating each of my movements with an amazed expression on her face. In this manner we were moved towards the door by Nansen and shoved out into the yard side by side. He shut the door on us but opened it again immediately, having seen Ditte, who had just come out of the house and was walking towards us and who made a sign to us all, or rather, to the painter.

'Get going,' Nansen said. 'Away with the two of you. This is not the sort of thing for the two of you to look at.' And he drove us away from the stable where the slaughter was going on, made us move up to the black tree-trunks that lay there on top of each other.

'Yes, Ditte, what is it?' He sounded impatient and then, as if to justify his impatience, he added : 'We're right in the middle of it.'

She whispered something to him. He looked at his hands and then first in the direction of Rugbüll, and then at his hands again and at his coat, which was spotted with blood. 'They find out everything,' he said. 'Nothing goes on around here that they don't know. Let them come for all I care. Holmsen can't let the animal just die, he's got to kill it. And it would have been dead long before he got a permit.'

Ditte whispered again and Nansen said : 'But why? Just leave them in the stable to get on with it. Nothing can happen to them if they can prove the animal was hit all over by bits of shrapnel. And they can prove it. When the car arrives, we're all in the stable. And will you make tea for us, please, Ditte? We shall all need it.'

Then he turned and, walking off, already stretching out one hand for the stable door, he glanced in the direction of Rugbüll. We must all have seen the car at the same time, as it came along slowly through the ground-mist, sometimes disappearing in it and then turning up again where we had expected it, all the time moving at the same speed until it reached the avenue of alders. There it stopped. But nobody got out. The silhouettes of the men inside didn't stir and the engine wasn't turned off.

The painter let his outstretched hand sink and, taking short steps, he walked towards the car or, more precisely, towards the wooden gate. Perhaps it was only because nobody got out of the car that he went there, opened the gate slowly and with a brusque gesture invited them in. Now the car moved again, coming towards us. The painter simply let the gate fall to after the car had passed through it. Slowly the car drove across the yard, turned by the pond, and, instead of coming towards us, went to the house, where it stopped at the door.

Two leathercoats got out first. They walked slowly, unhurriedly, so that it almost looked like a time-exposure, round the car and met in front of the radiator, where they stopped without exchanging a word and stood looking across at us. The leather-coats had patch pockets, and one could guess their weight by the way they hung down, long and straight, and I should say there was an air of toughness and somewhat exaggerated gestures matched by the heavy mountain-boots and the wide-brimmed slouch-hats that kept the faces shaded. While they were standing, their legs apart, in front of the bonnet, the Rugbüll policeman stiffly got out of the car, cursing his cape, which had got caught somewhere. My father struggled to free his cape, which had got involved with some hook or door-handle or window-handle that wouldn't let go of it. At last he succeeded, with an energetic jerk tore himself loose, then walked up to the leathercoats in front of the radiator. They didn't make any attempt to move towards us, they simply stood there waiting, and they didn't move even when the painter waved to them and pointed to the stable door.

Now he went halfway to meet them, jerking his thumb over his shoulder, said : 'It's in there, come over here.'

But the leathercoats didn't seem interested in what he said. They stood just where they were and thus forced him to come across to them. I heard him say once again that they were in the stable, but my father shook his head and waved that aside; he clearly wasn't interested in what was going on in the stable or at least it didn't strike him as being as important as the errand on which he had come. The wave of his hand seemed to mean : later, later, now we're concerned with something else.

The Rugbüll policeman took a short step back behind the two leathercoats and from there looked intently at Nansen – just intently. Jutta made use of the opportunity to slip back into the stable, shutting the door from inside. I stood beside Max Ludwig Nansen, who now hesitated, hunching up his shoulders and murmuring to himself : 'What are they up to?' Then, walking up to that motionless group of men, he asked outright : 'What's the purpose of your visit, Jens?'

Suddenly one of the leathercoats spoke : 'Get ready.'

The painter asked : 'Why? What have you got against me?'

Instead of answering, the second leathercoat said : 'We'll give you half an hour.'

The painter looked at them, shrugged his shoulders, and asked : 'So you've come for me?'

Nobody thought it necessary to give him a direct answer.

Finally my father said : 'You've got half an hour.'

I wasn't at all amazed to see him pull out his watch and, looking down at it, repeat quietly : 'Half an hour.'

Stretching out one hand, he made a brief gesture as though by way of explanation, nodded, and put his watch back into his pocket.

How little, how little they had to say and to learn on that day, to understand one another, and how quickly they grasped what was expected of them : I don't recall Max Ludwig Nansen making any effort to find out more when they had given him just half an hour to pack his things and to prepare to leave. He gave up asking why they'd come and merely asked :

'How long will it all take?'

And when one of the leathercoats shrugged his shoulders and my father lowered his head, the painter walked slowly past them, simply saying :

'I'll go and get ready. I shan't take more than half an hour.'

They didn't go into the stable. One foot on the bumper or on the running-board, they stood there smoking, slouching idly and obviously relaxed, confident in themselves and certain of having got their man. They waited in silence, probably without a thought in their heads, and without taking the slightest interest in what was going on in the stable, unworried because they had no doubt, knowing that somebody like Max Ludwig Nansen would use the time that was given him but would not misuse it. They didn't even glance at the stable. They just stood there waiting, while the painter went into the house and had by now presumably wasted some of the allotted time standing, as one can easily imagine, very straight, there in the hall, his back against the door, listening.

If I set down all that is essential and leave out what is of no importance, if I go back in time, I can only give this account of it all: while my father, the Rugbüll policeman, and the two leathercoats were calmly waiting for him, the painter went into the house. Stopping inside the door, he leaned against it and probably stayed there in the dark hall until Ditte opened the door of the sitting-room and saw him standing there. Then he pushed himself away from the door and walked towards her. He didn't want to talk out there in the hall, so he took Ditte's arm, pulled her towards him and with her walked into the sitting-room. From the way he had taken hold of her, she must have guessed that something had happened or was about to happen. She let him lead her past the threatening row of sixty-two grandfather-clocks, all of which showed a quarter past. Herr Doktor Busbeck got up from the sofa and came over to them.

'They've come for me,' the painter said after a moment's silence. 'They're taking me with them.'

'It's not about the slaughtering of the cow?' Busbeck asked.

In a low voice the painter said: 'They've given me half an hour to get ready.'

'It's Jens,' Ditte said. 'You can thank him for this, he's sure to have reported everything to Husum.'

'They're going to interrogate you,' Busbeck said. 'I know that sort of thing.'

'I'm not back yet,' the painter said.

'But how long are they going to keep you?' Ditte asked.

'Usually it takes a day and a night,' Busbeck said.

'I'm not back yet,' the painter said, and began carefully filling his pipe.

Without looking at Ditte he said: 'I'll take the small brown suitcase, two pipes, my shaving stuff, letter-paper. You know what I need.'

'You'll see,' Doktor Busbeck said. 'They'll interrogate you and give you a warning. They've got to do it, as they've received a report from Rugbüll. They won't dare to do anything to you.'

'People like us, people with imagination – we think they won't dare. But just look around you. All the things we thought impossible are being done. They do dare. It's their utter ruth-lessness, after all, that's their strength.'

He said goodbye to Teo Busbeck, he nodded towards the clocks and said: 'I've got half an hour, you know, I must get a move on.'

Then he went into the bedroom, sat down on one of the narrow beds and took off his shoes. He took off his overcoat, his jacket and his shirt, jerked open the drawers of the chest-of-drawers and pulled out socks, shoe-laces, handkerchiefs and threw it all on the bed. Last of all he put a flannel shirt with the rest of the stuff. He lifted the water-jug and poured water into the washing-bowl, he bent over it and, by no means hurriedly, washed his face and neck and rubbed his chest with a damp cloth. He cleaned his hands with pumice-stone and combed his thin hair twice.

After he had poured the dirty water into the bucket, he wiped the bowl clean with great sweeping movements and put the jug back into it. Then he cleaned the wash-stand by rubbing it over with a damp cloth. He put the cloth over the rim of the bowl to dry. And now we must imagine him discovering that his braces had spots on them and had lost their elasticity, and so he had to get out new braces. He searched through drawer after drawer for them and found them at last. They were still wrapped up as they had come from the shop. He buttoned them on, tested them by pulling them over his shoulders, and was satisfied with their elasticity.

What now? One mustn't cut the film at such a moment, and so it simply has to be mentioned that he put new laces into his shoes, carefully slipping them through each eyelet, holding the shoe in his lap. He took a few steps to try out the shoes, flexed his foot, was satisfied. Then he took the shirt and pulled it over his head; he raised his arms as though about to drown in the shirt. Finally he put on his jacket, the blue overcoat, his hat. He walked up and down the room and tidied up, he put together in one heap all the clothes he had cast off. And then he even smoothed the counterpane. He didn't go to the window. He didn't look out. Before leaving the bedroom, he fished out of a blue china box his pocket-watch, which he wound up and put in his pocket. He would set it later.

When he returned to the sitting-room he could see that Ditte and Busbeck had been waiting for him. Ditte came towards him, holding out the little brown suitcase to him. He said :

'Later, in a moment. I've got to sign some papers first.'

Standing at a table in a corner he signed two sheets of paper that he had taken from a sealed envelope and which he then put into another envelope and put in a drawer. I can well imagine that his fastidious calm and his conscientious use of the allotted time stopped Herr Doktor Busbeck from producing any more of his soothing reminiscences of his own experiences. The painter set his pocket-watch, taking the time from a tall grandfather-clock. He made a gesture that meant ' in a moment, just one moment and I'll be with you', walked to the mouse-grey clock and opened it. Out of it he took a cigar-box and went back to the table. Out of the box he took a handful of cigars and with what I take to have been a used razor-blade he cut them up into pieces just the right size for his pipe. Then he put the pieces into a tin with the lettering scrubbed off it. He put the cigar-box back into the clock and the tin into the pocket of his overcoat.

What about the hip-flask? Ditte remembered that he had filled the flat canvas-covered hip-flask with corn-brandy and had put it in the back pocket of his trousers. Then he went over to the window, where Ditte and Herr Doktor Busbeck were standing waiting for him. He put one hand on the suitcase but he didn't open it. He merely asked: 'Everything packed?'

'It's just because Jens reported you,' Ditte said. 'They haven't got much that could incriminate you.'

'That's true,' the painter said and smiled resignedly when all the clocks now began stubbornly chiming the half hour, each one in its own way. There was a clanging and booming and groaning, creakings and clickings in the works, brass chains jerking along, weights coming groaning down. When the Bleekenwarf clocks told the time there was nothing one could do but wait in silence for it to be over. And when the clocks had quietened down the painter said: 'Wait here for me, I'll be back in a moment.' Leaving his suitcase on the window-sill, he went to the studio.

From the garden I saw him go into the studio, that is, I saw his shadow and afterwards I saw him letting down one of the blinds. The leathercoats stood by the car, smoking. My father was walking about and seemed to be searching for something he had just lost, perhaps a button, perhaps the badge off his cap. On previous occasions when the badge had got lost I had succeeded in finding it. Nobody noticed me slipping into the studio – or did one of them, after all, see the door shutting from inside? Anyway, I tiptoed into the studio and crouched down near the jugs and jars that served as vases for flowers during the summer and were now gathered together in a corner, exuding a brackish smell. I looked up at the pictures and got a fright: the prophets, money-changers and cobolds, the cunning market-people and gnarled agricultural labourers – they were all bathed in a green light, gleaming and smouldering, a green fire seemed to be burning in the room, lighting up all the

227

pictures. I can still remember wanting to call out, to call for help, but when I stepped closer the gleaming ceased and the green light disappeared.

The painter was walking to and fro. He dragged a crate along the floor, opened it and shut it again. He turned on the water tap. He threw an empty tin on to the pottery table. Making use of all the nooks and crannies and keeping hidden behind the makeshift bunk, I worked my way as close to him as I could so that in the end there was only a narrow passageway separating us. I pushed aside a blanket that had been hung up as a curtain, and there he was, standing right in front of me. Cautiously he pulled open a wide cupboard, listened for a moment, and then bent down. And out of that cupboard – I shall never forget what came rolling out of it : an irresistible, relentless brown, a brown occupying the whole of the horizon, a brown that was streaked and bordered with grey, unrolled and went on growing and growing over a countryside sinking into dusk. The picture was called 'The Cloudmaker'. The painter looked at it, he tilted his head, he stepped back, he came so close to me that I could have touched him with my hand. He was not convinced by what he saw. Thoughtfully he shook his head, walked up to the picture and put the flat of his hand on the place out of which the brown grew.

'Here,' he said. 'Here's where the action starts.'

He let his hand sink and hunched up his shoulders as though suddenly chilly.

'Stop jabbering, Balthasar,' he said. 'I can see for myself what's missing. There's no foreboding, no foreboding of the storm. And so the colour has simply got to say more about flight, what it takes is watchfulness, alertness, somebody there revealing how frightened he is.'

Somebody opened the door of the studio, but Nansen didn't hear. I felt the draught and I waited for the sound of the door shutting again. But there was no sound and so I lifted the blanket, came out of my hiding-place and, pressing my forefinger to my lips, walked up to him and touched him. He started, and turned round in a fright, his mouth fell open. He was about to say something, but then he realized what my outstretched arm meant, pointing towards the door. He seemed to have been prepared for it and, quickly grasping the situation, he hastily took the picture from the wardrobe door, rolled it up and pushed it under the wardrobe. But he instantly pulled it out again. He looked round. There were a hundred hiding-places and yet none that was suitable for 'The Cloudmaker'. There were dark corners, nooks and crannies, cracks in the wall and in the floor, the gaping mouths of jugs, all of them offering their services, and yet there was no suitable place. In that moment they all seemed useless to him. He had discovered me. He pulled me towards the cupboard and looked at me closely and with an urgency he'd never shown before. I smelled the scent of the soap and the tobacco on his breath. I felt the cold-ness in his grey eyes.

'Witt-Witt,' he suddenly whispered. For a moment he strained his ears in the direction of the door, and then he whispered again : 'Can I trust you? We're friends, aren't we? Will you do something for me?'

'Yes,' I said, nodding. 'Yes, yes, yes.'

And then I realized what he wanted me to do, and I pulled out my patched green pullover, right up to my armpits, and the painter put the painting around me, pulled the pullover down, and pushed it inside my trousers. The pullover was too tight all round and so I pulled it out a little to make it appear natural. I tried to move, to find out if it would work.

'Take it out of the place and keep it safe somewhere,' he whispered. 'And bring it back later to Aunt Ditte. I shall be needing it.'

He held out his hand to me. I got quite a shock when he gave me his hand, gravely, without his usual wink at me. Nor did he stroke my hair the way he usually did or jab me in the ribs or take me by the scruff of my neck.

'I'll do what you want me to do,' I said. And he nodded, listened again for a moment in the direction of the door, and then whispered once more :

'Thank you, Witt-Witt. I shan't forget it.'

He shut the cupboard and made a sign to me to take myself off, more precisely he raised the blanket and waited until I had slipped through. Then he called out :

'Teo? Is that you, Teo?'

There was no answer, there was only a slow footstep coming closer and closer, a footstep I instantly recognized.

'I'm just coming, Teo,' the painter called. 'I've just finished.'
With a wave of his hand he ordered me to squat beside the
bunk. Then he took a sip from the flask he carried in his hip-
pocket. The stiff paper wrapped round me rustled as I squatted
down directly in front of a shadow that passed by me as I
raised my head. The footsteps ceased. A foot pushed the jug
and tins on the floor as though examining them, and a file on
the table was pushed to one side. Although the painter must
have realized by now that it was not Doktor Busbeck who had
entered the studio, he called out :
'Why don't you come in, Teo?'
He must have opened and shut the cupboard again, pretending that he was doing something there, and in this way
caused the feet to move again. The footsteps now approached
him.
I had, of course, instantly recognized my father's footsteps,
and Nansen also must have recognized them by now, because he
didn't seem surprised. He merely stepped to one side and made
it clear by his whole attitude that he was ready to go. My father
raised his face, his dry, pointed, taut face, to the skylight while
he calculated. A faint look of superiority, perhaps even of
satisfaction, lay on his face. He pocketed his watch and informed
Nansen that the time wasn't yet up, that there were still a few
minutes left that he might use in any way he liked, implying
that a man ought to make good use of the time allotted to him.
The way the painter stood there, very straight, his feet apart,
his hands behind his back, it was obvious that he was determined
not to let himself in for anything. He gave no answer when my
father asked if he might take a pile of faded, yellowing drawings
from an easel. He watched in silence while my father got on to
a footstool and inspected the top of cupboards and wardrobes,
and he neither said nor did anything when my father opened
that cupboard and dived into it, not even when he bent down,
picked up from the cupboard floor some small blank sheets that
he held up, one by one, towards the skylight, twisting and turning them in his hand, and then laying them carefully on the
table.
He was up to something with those blank sheets; he arranged
them in two rows on the table, then he once more dived into
the cupboard, rummaged about in it stubbornly, peered and

probed, and finally gave up and went back to the table. With a satisfied expression he collected the blank sheets and stacked them carefully, all the time looking at the painter. It seemed that he was waiting for Nansen to smile, simply because he had prepared an answer in case the painter should smile at him. But Nansen did not smile. My father asked permission to take the blank sheets with him, but Nansen remained silent.

'Up to now,' my father said, 'you've been lucky, Max, in spite of everything, and what's happening now is something you've only got yourself to blame for. But I wouldn't lay any money on your luck if I were you, you won't always slip through the meshes. One day you'll get caught and then nothing's going to help you. Invisible pictures or visible ones – I'm going to find them. We've found quite different things before this – things that have tried to remain invisible.'

He tapped the small blank sheets with his forefinger and then walked up to Nansen, who was still standing there very straight, looking at the policeman contemptuously, betraying neither hostility nor anxiety, just looking at him with contempt. I can understand why my father was so eager, that day, to break through that wall of silence, to get some answer, but Max Ludwig Nansen wouldn't let himself be drawn, he just stood there, showing neither amazement nor fear nor anger. And so there was nothing my father could do but repeat that all that had happened to Nansen and all that was going to happen to him any day now was all his own doing and nobody else's fault at all.

'You wanted it this way, just you,' he said. 'You're one of those big shots, a cut above everyone else. The things that go for anyone else don't go for you and your sort.'

He looked rather startled when the painter, speaking more to himself than to my father, suddenly declared : 'Time's up, we've got to go,' and then, without waiting for the policeman, walked through the door and out into the yard. My father, who clearly had been eager to be the one to determine the time of departure, followed him irritably.

The leathercoats were still there, standing in front of the car, smoking. At the front door, the brown suitcase on the ground between them, were Ditte and Herr Doktor Busbeck. The two couples stood there in silence, each with a different expectation of what was going to happen now. Nobody spoke. I would have loved to run and catch up with the painter and walk at his side as he went towards the car, but I was afraid my father might discover the picture hidden under my pullover. So I slunk away towards the stable, and from there I watched the two men approaching the car.

I must confess I was amazed that Nansen made no attempt to escape. He'd had plenty of time to get safely to the peat-bog, perhaps even to the peninsula. It wouldn't have been difficult to climb out of a window and get through the garden unnoticed. But he hadn't shown any intention of doing that, he didn't want to, probably the idea had never struck him. As though intending to be punctual, he picked up the suitcase without a moment's hesitation. He shook hands with Ditte and then with Doktor Busbeck. Then he went to the car and offered himself up – I can't describe it in any other way, only that he offered himself up to the leathercoats, saying gruffly:

'Here I am. What are we waiting for? Let's get it over and done with.'

The one leathercoat opened the door of the car, holding out his hand for the suitcase, indeed he had already taken hold of it and was about to give the painter a shove, as he climbed into the car, and sat down, his shoulders hunched up and his legs pulled in, when Herr Doktor Busbeck, who had been looking on in silence, suddenly raised his arm.

'Wait! Just one minute, wait!' he called out, taking a few strides towards the car, lowering his arm and excitedly repeating: 'Please wait, just one moment.'

The leathercoat straightened up and looked at the small man in his way. He clearly had not the slightest interest in finding out the reason for this interference and so he beckoned to the Rugbüll policeman, who instantly approached, ready to intervene.

'What's the matter?' my father asked, as he pulled Busbeck away from the car. 'What do you want?' he asked.

'Please listen to me,' Busbeck said, speaking not to my father but to the leathercoat, who just stood there in stolid silence. 'It was my fault, I alone am responsible for the fact that the studio was not blacked out that night, I am to blame for it. It was not Herr Nansen's fault.'

My father stretched out his hand, gripped the little man by his sleeve and looked at him reproachfully, but he didn't say anything, for he had obviously made up his mind to leave the talking to the leathercoats.

'Take me along,' Herr Doktor Busbeck said, 'take me with you and leave him here. It was my fault.'

Again he took a step towards the car, but my father pulled him back. The leathercoats gave each other a sign, and then the one behind the wheel started the engine. The other pointed at Doktor Busbeck and asked my father: 'Who's he? What's he up to?'

My father gave a disparaging wave of his hand and said :

'This is Herr Doktor Busbeck, a friend, he lives here.'

'Please do understand,' Busbeck called out, 'Herr Nansen didn't know that the black-out—'

'Shut up,' the leathercoat said, 'get out of the way and don't waste our time. For your own good, pipe down and scram.'

He got into the car beside the painter and slammed the door. My father let go of Busbeck, looked at Ditte, who was standing on the doorstep, looked briefly at me, then walked round the car and got in next to the driver. The car began to move and I rushed to Busbeck, and while the car was moving slowly towards the gate I looked at it and through the rear window I saw the painter's head. I nudged Busbeck in the ribs and waited, just like him, for Max Ludwig Nansen to look back at us. But he didn't turn his head.

I gazed after the car as it disappeared into the distance and then I looked towards the stable, where they were still busy with the slaughtered cow, and so I didn't hear the key turning in the lock or Joswig's footsteps, and indeed I even missed his first words of greeting as he entered.

Only when our favourite guard laid his hand shyly on my shoulder and thoughtfully whispered : 'Don't get a fright, Siggi, don't get a fright, it's only me,' did I get a fright. Jumping up, I instantly retreated to the window. Joswig stopped at the table, and there he stood, looking like a mournful spaniel. He picked up my pocket-mirror and presumably tried to look at his own reflection, but all he got was a flash of reflected light from my naked electric bulb. He put the mirror back on the table next to my copybook and sat down on the much-gashed stool, without saying a word.

Had he come, as he had done before, in order to tell me to switch off the light in accordance with regulations? Was he going to work out in front of me how much light I was wasting? Or was it the insomnia that plagued him during the summer months which had temped him to burst in on me, hoping that I would read him a 'good solid chapter', as he used to call it? He bent over my work and began to read, shaking his head all the time, and as he read he was pulling two crumpled cigarettes out of the breast-pocket of his jacket, American cigarettes that had probably been given him by an American psychologist. He laid them in my copybook as a marker and then forgot about them. I didn't hold that against him.

None of us ever managed to be angry with Joswig, that shy, kind-hearted man to whom everything that had happened to us seemed also to have happened, who suffered with us when we suffered and who regarded himself as being punished when we were punished. He went on reading, and I looked out on the Elbe, where nothing in particular was going on. Only one sturdy lighter, belching out dense smoke, was moving past, very slowly, very tiredly. The cloud of smoke from its funnel covered the moon, bulged, and disintegrated, and from it there issued a herd of black Shetland ponies standing silently around the moon as by a horse-pond. No gulls. No cloud-formation worth mentioning in the direction of Cuxhaven. The moon, however, was doing its best. In the distance there was the dark river-bank, and a chain of cars' headlights.

As a reader, I should like to point out, Joswig was exactly like other readers. Scarcely had he glanced over the last page and learned that Max Ludwig Nansen had been taken away in a police car, when he wanted to know whether, and if so, when and in what condition, he would return. Why did he have to ask that typical question? I shrugged my shoulders, pretending it was a problem I myself couldn't solve so easily. Joswig gave me a perplexed look, but he stopped asking questions. He came up to me and, standing beside me, looked out into the dark and at the Elbe, which was now tricked out in silver in various places, for instance behind the large buoy marking the navigable water. The arc-lamps in front of our workshops were lit, drenching the courtyard in a shadowless glare. Willow branches hung down into the river, marking the direction and the force of the current. The Governor's dog roamed our beach in search of trespassers trying to use it for swimming or canoeing. What was that howling? Far up-river in the harbour a warship's siren was howling signals for assistance from a tug.

Joswig gave me plenty of time to observe all this and a number of other things as well. He stood there beside me, humming and ha-ing, and by now it was clear to me that he intended neither to turn off my light nor to send me to bed. Was he unhappy? Obviously he was unhappy, but not very unhappy. Was he in search of something? He seemed in search of some way of confiding in me. Joswig wanted something from me, but he hadn't yet quite made up his mind. He made a beginning, but his doubts wouldn't let him go on, so he started again and stopped again. He clearly wanted to confide in me, but he had no confidence. Showing that extreme irresolution of his, which was precisely what many of us liked about him, he gazed out of the window at the Elbe flowing on so busily and silently. What he wanted of me was that I should take on some of his burden, support him.

I turned away from the window and went to the table. And then suddenly I knew how I could help him to make a start: I picked up one of the cigarettes he'd put into my copybook as markers and lit it. The tiny explosion of the match made him swivel round – to see me standing there at my table, smoking. Instantly his arm went up in a gesture of protest, and he came towards me, waving his open hand to and fro. In a voice that sounded not so much indignant as surprised he said: 'No smoking in rooms – good heavens, don't you know yet there's no smoking in rooms!'

I killed the cigarette before he asked me to hand it over to him.

'You, Siggi, you of all people,' he said, 'do such things, and precisely now when I need you!'

He heaved a sigh, and I begged him to sit down on my bed. Shaking his head he sat down, watching me scrape the charred bits off the cigarette, not minding my putting my cigarette back into the copybook as a marker. Any moment now, I thought, he is going to ask you not actually for help but for your collaboration. And indeed I wasn't mistaken. Joswig had come to ask for my advice.

Naturally he started telling me about his difficulties, in his characteristic manner, starting a long way back and beating around all the bushes along the way.

'You as the oldest – or rather, as one of the oldest boys,' he said, 'surely you know what's allowed on the island and what is not.'

He went off at a tangent and then, aiming for the rules laid down in writing, went on harping on the paragraph about smoking in public rooms and bedrooms and, sliding down two paragraphs, reminded me of the consequences of breaking the rules. Now, as it were, running his finger up those invisible but ever-present rules, he stopped at paragraph 2 : the person of the guard is sacrosanct and his orders must always be obeyed. I still didn't know what precisely he was aiming at when, with affected indifference, he mentioned Ole Plötz and the recent attempt to escape. He kept saying more often than was necessary :

'You remember? You remember that rainy evening?'

Like a dripping tap he kept on about how they had prepared everything and thought of everything. In the end they decided to use keys they'd made in the workshop. And you remember the fog coming up from the sea, so dense that the ships anchored in mid-stream? How one could hear the rumble and clatter of the trains? The others wanted to give up, but Ole was determined to see it through and so they went through with it as planned. You realize now, I dare say, that you can consider yourself lucky. You'd have been nearly drowned, just like the rest of them, pitifully yelling for help. Swimming across the Elbe in fog with no visibility at all – it simply can't be done. And do you remember them standing outside, in the early morning light, shivering in their wet clothes, with all of us standing around them?

I didn't want to hear the whole story all over again, so I said :

'Yes, yes, I remember the night and I remember the fog and I also remember how hard the guards took it, particularly one of them. I remember it all. It's quite a long time ago, but not so *very* long.'

Joswig nodded, he ground his teeth and spread out his arms in a – I can't put it any other way – in a gesture of pained incomprehension.

'What is experience for, Siggi? Do you know why people learn nothing from experience – well, almost nothing? What else would be the meaning of experience?'

Now I pricked up my ears and looked at him queryingly for some time. In the end he couldn't stand it any longer.

'Can you understand it, Siggi? After all that?' He added: 'They don't suspect that I know all about it. They talked about their plan in the lavatory – for anyone to hear. What am I to do? Next Friday Ole, your old friend Ole, is going to scrape the jam off his bread and take it with him wrapped up in paper. The idea is that in the evening during the final inspection he's going to deceive me with the aid of the jam and then they'll break out again, they'll try it once again.'

'I don't know anything about it,' I said, 'really nothing at all.'

He went on ratLer sadly: 'Ole's going to lie on the floor with the jam smeared all over his face to make me think he's been beaten up or has fallen and hurt himself. I'm supposed to get a fright, open the door, rush in and bend over him. And when I bend over him to lift him off the floor, he's going to finish me off. He won't have to ask me twice for the keys. Then they'll be off again. I ask you, Siggi, if you learn of such a plan, aren't you bound to ask yourself: does experience really count for nothing at all?'

'Who else is in it?' I asked. He didn't want to tell me but I thought they'd probably be the same chaps as before. So I asked:

'And Friday's the day?'

'Yes, Friday,' Joswig said. 'And now I keep thinking all the time what to do about it, knowing their whole plan. There are a number of possibilities.'

And now he asked me for my opinion: for instance, if he didn't go inside at all, or if he did and simply finished him off instead of bending over him. That, after all, would be self-defence. Or, of course, he could simply blazon it forth – he only had to say a word to the Governor, who would instantly make an example of the chaps.

Joswig lowered his eyes and fell silent. And then I suddenly realized that he expected me to mention yet another, a fourth way of dealing with the whole matter. I'd scarcely begun to speak when he raised his head hopefully.

'I could have a go and speak to Ole,' I said. 'I could tell him it wouldn't work, that it would come to the same unhappy ending as before. I could try to make him see that, if he is prepared to listen to me, if he is prepared to listen to me at all.'

'He'll listen to you,' Joswig said.

'But I can't do it,' I said. 'I can't go and warn him. If I do that, he's bound to think I'm collaborating with the guards. Nobody here can afford to do that.'

'But what *am* I to do?' Joswig asked, genuinely worried. 'What am I to do, Siggi? It'll soon be Friday. If you won't warn him, what's going to happen?'

'Jam,' I said. 'Have a whole jar of jam put on the table with a label on it : help yourself and make sure the bruises look convincingly red and gory.'

Joswig looked at me incredulously. At first he seemed inclined to reject the idea. Then he began to consider it, seemed to like it better and even to be amused by it. He seemed to like it better the more he thought about it, and in the end he seemed to regard it as the only possible solution. He got off my bed and, holding out his hand to me, said :

'I knew it, Siggi. I knew I shouldn't come to you in vain.'

11 Invisible Pictures

Well, so it's here, where Hilke and I caught our plaice, that it's supposed to have started : life and all the rest of it. Did you ever hear such a thing? In these flats, here in this expanse of mud – grey wilderness, hollowed and dotted by shallow puddles, here the emergence of life is supposed to have begun. One fine day everything that could breathe arose from the bottom of the sea, moved across the amphibious belt of the beach, washed off the original slime, lit a fire and made coffee. Or at least that's what's supposed to have happened, according to Per Arne Schessel, the writer and explorer of this homeland of ours, that's what he wrote, my grandfather, that old hermit-crab.

Be that as it may, there we were, on those flats, out to catch our plaice, walking on the slippery bottom of the sea, a fair distance out from the peninsula. The sea-birds went fishing with us. Hilke had her dress hitched up and gathered in front of her belly, her legs were caked with mud up to her knees, the hem of her petticoat was black with moisture. The way the sea-birds fish is by pulling their open beaks through the water of the pools, plucking and gulping. The sharply incised runnels in the sand branch out towards the open sea; at low tide this is good fishing-ground. Mostly we walked hand in hand right into one of those grey pools or to the edge of a flat runnel and simply let our feet sink into the mud, fumbling, groping with our toes. Supporting each other, we pulled our legs up, dragging our feet systematically through the mud and the slime, always alert, waiting for something to move under our soles. Whenever we stepped on some kind of flat fish, a flounder or turbot or, much more rarely, a sole, the creature began to jerk and twitch and wriggle, and Hilke would yell and squeak whenever it was she who had found the fish by stepping on it. I know of no one as untiring in catching flat fish by treading them down into the mud as my sister Hilke. Although she was very ticklish and jumped for fright every time it happened, it was very rare for a fish to escape from under her foot. She would keep her foot firmly on it until I got hold of it and pulled it out.

Sometimes she would sink into the mud right up to her thighs and then she would pull her dress up to her chest. And then again she would slide over a layer of smooth clay as over ice. The gurgling and gulping in the cool mud, when bubbles burst and when she sank in softly and irresistibly, gave her a lot of pleasure. She never forgot to observe the current in the runnels. Where the wavy, rippling ground of the flats grew harder she would hop on one foot, every time alighting on the threadlike droppings of the sand worms. She caught hermit-crabs and fan-worms, watched them for a while on the flat of her hand and then put them back into the water. She collected wentletrap-shells and put them into her pants; the elastic around the legs prevented them from falling out. All this is part of the scene.

And there is the murky sadness of the flats, low clouds in the west, gusts of wind curling the water in the runnels and pools, and causing the sea-birds' feathers to bristle; in the distance there is the faint hum of a lonely airplane. The shimmering sand of the peninsula and the height of the dyke – looking even safer, more impregnable from the flats – and far behind it all, on the dunes, the painter's hut.

I carried the basket of fish. I walked behind Hilke across the flats, now and then taking a pot-shot at the fishing sea-birds, trying to hop on one leg the way she did. I stepped on yellowish ribs of foam that the wind had blown into a heap. The fishes twitched in the basket, gasping. A number of times Hilke ordered me to wash her mud-caked legs in the swift water of a runnel, and while I did so she would support herself on my back. The shells inside her pants made a clattering sound like a rattle. I set my feet on tiny mounds, pressing down until the mud rose up between my toes. The reddish-blue rings on Hilke's thighs were caused by the elastic; they looked like a rash or

rings of insect-bites. The wind blew her hair to and fro, and
sometimes it covered her face entirely.

I should say we were well on our way to the peninsula when
Hilke, who was hopping along in front of me, suddenly uttered
a faint scream, sat down on the wet ground, gripped her left
foot in both hands and twisted it until she could see the sole.
In a flash I was there beside her, going down on my knees. The
jagged end of a piece of mussel shell was sticking out of the
sole of her foot.

'Careful, don't break it,' she said, and then she herself took
hold of it with two fingers and swiftly pulled it out. She had no
handkerchief, so she took the hem of her dress, but then she
changed her mind, pulled the tail end of my shirt out of my
trousers and wiped the wound clean with that. There was a
sickle-shaped wound which looked as if it were about to stop
bleeding.

'It's going to stop,' I said.

'It mustn't stop yet,' Hilke said, 'the wound has got
to bleed until it's clean.' After a moment she asked: 'Can
you do it, Siggi? Do you think you can suck the wound
clean?'

'How?' I asked.

Hilke shook her head impatiently. 'How? With your mouth,
of course. Suck it and spit it out.' She supported herself on one
elbow, stretched her leg out and raised her foot towards me.
'Come on, have a go!'

I took hold of her ankle and shut my eyes. Her foot exuded a
faint smell of mud and iodine, and I pulled it towards my face
and looked at it once again before I touched it with my lips.
At first, all I tasted was mud. I spat. Then I sucked again,
pressing slightly with my tongue, and gradually all that taste
disappeared. Then I opened my eyes and saw Hilke lying there
in front of me, nodding at me appreciatively.

Hilke pulled her foot away, looked at the wound and then
stretched out both her arms towards me. I helped her to get up.
She supported herself on my shoulder and I put my arm round
her waist. In this way we moved towards the peninsula and
the beach, where we'd left our stockings and shoes. Hilke was
cursing under her breath and it seemed she had planned to do
something for which she needed her feet, because she kept on

murmuring: 'Today of all days it's got to happen – damn it, why couldn't it happen tomorrow?'

Her hand began to twitch restlessly and she kept looking at her wrist-watch, the way people do. She was limping, using only her heel, walking with a short twisting movement of her knee.

'Today of all days it's got to happen.'

'What's so special about today?' I asked.

Literally all she said was: 'If you carry on the way you're doing, you'll dislocate my hip joint.'

We avoided the deeper runnels and skirted pools whose depths we didn't know, but even so we couldn't help getting into a mud-hole time and again, sinking in right up to our knees. Wild geese flew low over our heads in the direction of the peat-bog, and the gulls were busy on the flats, together with all the sand-pipers and oyster-catchers. And still there was no rain. On reaching the beach of the peninsula I let myself fall on to the fine sand and took hold of Hilke's ankle in order to clean the wound, to suck it out again, but Hilke didn't want me to do it again. She put one finger into the elastic of her pants, and let the shells drop out on to the sand. Then she crouched down and counted them, while I went to fetch her shoes and stockings.

'I haven't got enough of them,' Hilke said suddenly. 'I need another ten or fifteen. Would you go and get them for me, Siggi?'

'Will you wait for me?'

'No,' she said. 'I'll go ahead.'

It was her way of getting rid of me.

She collected the shells and dropped them into the basket on top of the fishes. She wiped the wound on her foot clean with one stocking and then shook out the stocking before putting it on again. Then she brushed the sand off her dress and turned into the wind to do her hair up at the back of her head. Then, after a casual goodbye, she hobbled off homeward along the beach.

I stayed where I was, lying on the sand, supporting myself on my elbows. I watched her disappearing in the distance, becoming smaller and smaller and less distinct, first blue and green, then blue on brown sand, just the way everybody seems to shrink when he or she approaches the dyke. Somehow the dyke seemed to make people appear less significant, its bulky mass seemed to reduce everybody, at least while one was still below at the bottom of it and moving towards it. When Hilke had reached the top, she looked back in search of me, and when she had seen where I was she stretched out one arm, pointing to the flats in a gesture of exhortation : go and find those shells for me.

I stayed there lying on the sand, waiting until she had disappeared, and even then I didn't go back to the flats, because in the very moment when Hilke disappeared on the other side of the dyke a man rose out of the sea-grass in front of the dune, a small man – Busbeck. He had been lying there until she passed, and he was carrying something. Herr Doktor Busbeck was carrying something that he held pressed tight to his body, and he turned round a number of times as if he were afraid that Hilke might come back. He leaned forward into the wind, moving his free arm to and fro frantically as he climbed up the dune. Now it was obvious why he was crossing the peninsula and where he was going. He seemed to have a handkerchief in his hand and now and then it looked as if he were wiping his neck and his forehead with it, and he had the look of someone afraid of being pursued, for he didn't stop even when he looked back over his shoulder or scanned the beach in front of him. All his movements conveyed the feeling that he was both angry and stubbornly determined, he couldn't cope with the sliding sand of the dune, he couldn't get a proper foothold. True, he had chosen the shortest way to the painter's hut, but it was also the most difficult one. Bent very low, he was moving on towards it, and now and then, with a very quick gesture, he rubbed his eyes, actually every time he entered into one of those eddies of drifting sand that the wind carried up on to the dunes and whirled around up there furiously before carrying them further inshore. Going down the dune was easier, and all at once it seemed that Herr Doktor Busbeck enjoyed a little dance; he jumped and hopped and slid down the slope and then ran towards the hut, where he pushed the bolt back with the edge of his hand. Twice he glanced around him, the first time hastily, the second time for longer, suspiciously scrutinizing the peninsula, the beach, and the narrow strip of land below the dyke, before dashing into the hut and pulling the door shut after him.

Now I no longer had any thought of getting those shells and, as for Busbeck, well, the long and short of it is that anyone who moves so blatantly and conspicuously across somebody else's field of vision need not be surprised if that other person develops an interest in what he is doing and, suspecting all sorts of things, goes in pursuit of him.

No sooner had he pulled the door shut behind him than I jumped up and, making a detour, rushed for the windowless side of the hut, bent low and ready at any moment to throw myself flat on the ground. But there was no need for me to do that.

Slowly, ever more slowly, on tiptoe, under the cover of the hut, one ear pressed to the stained wooden wall, straining my ears, then on all fours round the corner to the window, waiting: now there was a knocking, a creaking, as of a rusty nail creaking as it is pulled out, then getting up carefully, with my back to the wall, now closer to the window, not touching it – what was he doing in there, working away at the floorboards, don't cast any shadow into the room, he seems to be taking up the floorboards with a chisel. There I was, bending forward to gaze through the window.

There was a flash of recognition. He seemed to have reckoned with the possibility of my turning up there, because as I bent forward towards the window, shading my eyes with one hand, Herr Doktor Busbeck looked up at me, seeming less surprised than annoyed. He was kneeling on the wooden floor, holding in front of him a chisel with which he had loosened and raised up about a square yard of boards. I was startled by the fact that he had instantly recognized me and even more seeing that he, with his delicate hands and wrists, had succeeded in using the chisel and getting the boards up. There we were, looking at each other. He had stopped working, and there I stood, cautiously spying through the window just as if I hadn't been caught in the act. We looked at each other as though transfixed, and the longer we looked at each other, the less I considered running away and the less he seemed to consider proceeding with his job. He didn't drop the chisel, and I didn't lower the hand with which I was shading my eyes.

Then at long last he beckoned. Beckoned to me with an abstracted expression on his face – I was to come in. He no longer looked annoyed. When I had pushed open the door and gone in, he was waiting for me, standing in front of the work-table. The chisel lay on the floor, and next to it was a folder, tied up with a piece of string. I must have made a guilty impression, because he instantly began to question me in an accusing tone:

'You followed me so stealthily that I didn't notice you. Why did you do it? Who sent you after me? What are you following me for?'

Obviously he would have been satisfied if I had told him that my father had ordered me to do what I had done. He simply couldn't bring himself to believe that I had done it of my own accord.

'What were you expecting?' he asked. 'What were you wanting to find out?'

I just looked at the folder and shrugged my shoulders. Following my gaze, he was silent for a while.

'Well, why?' he asked again.

'I don't know,' I said, 'honestly I don't know.'

Now all at once he lost his assurance and seemed as helpless and embarrassed as he usually did. It almost seemed to me that he was in need of help. He clasped his hands and then wedged them into his starched cuffs, looking out of the side window with a frightened expression. Then he went to the door and looked out at the dunes.

'Do you want to hide this?' I asked, picking up the folder. He pulled the folder out of my hands as roughly as a man like him could, and then instantly made a conciliatory gesture as though to apologize for his violence.

' "The Cloudmaker",' I said. But he waved that aside. He knew that Nansen had entrusted the picture to me and that I had handed it over to Ditte, a short time after the police car had disappeared. He knew all about us and there were some things he knew even before we did. The long and the short of it was that he was in search of a hiding-place for the folder. Perhaps Max Ludwig Nansen himself had sent him on that errand almost instantly after he had come back from Husum. No, that was not quite the way it was: when Nansen had come back that morning – he had been pretty exhausted and distracted and had refused to talk to anyone – after a silent nod to Ditte he had locked himself into his room for several hours. Even when he came out of his room he had said nothing about what had happened in Husum, simply shaking his head in reply to all their questions, probably because he had been told not to say anything about it. Then he had gone and fetched the folder, he had kept it hidden somewhere at Bleekenwarf up to then, and handed it to Teo Busbeck, asking him to take it somewhere where it would be safe, or at least safer than at Bleekenwarf. Perhaps here in the hut. That was what I learnt from Busbeck, and I also learnt that the folder contained what Nansen thought his best and most valuable work. At least he himself had said something to that effect. The only question was where and how it could be hidden here in this hut.

Herr Doktor Busbeck began to search for the oiled paper that was supposed to be in the cupboard or under the cupboard or behind it. We searched for the paper together, and while we were searching I noticed he hadn't stopped scrutinizing me and at a certain point he was only going on searching because he didn't know what to do about me. We didn't find the oiled paper. Perhaps someone had taken it away, perhaps it was drifting somewhere on the sea, perhaps Nansen himself had used it up. Anyway, that paper, which was supposed to be used to protect the folder and its contents, wasn't there any more – and Busbeck stated the fact rather more with relief than with disappointment.

'Gone,' he said. 'Nothing we can do about it. Without oiled paper we can't hide the folder here under the floorboards. Besides,' he added, 'who knows if this is a good place anyway?'

And as though in answer to his own question he stepped on the floorboards he had raised, treading them down again. In the end we both stepped on those boards, jumping on them and knocking them in with our heels, and finally Herr Doktor Busbeck hammered the nails back into position with his chisel. The dark opening at the bottom of which moist sand glittered had been shut up again.

'Are you going to take the folder back again?' I asked.

'Yes, I'll take it back,' he answered. 'There's no oiled paper here, and anyway it's not a good place.'

I begged him to show me the pictures in the folder, but he didn't want to. He refused, stretching out his hand in a forbidding gesture when I attempted to untie the string round the folder.

'Are they new pictures?' I asked.

'Invisible pictures,' he replied.

Now I begged him to let me see, I offered to carry the folder back to Bleekenwarf for him if he would show me just one single picture, only for a brief instant, but he didn't want to, he said it was impossible.

'You don't get anything out of it, do you? They are invisible pictures,' he said.

'But you can hold them in your hands?' I asked.

'Certainly one can hold them in one's hands.'

'One can carry them?'

'Yes, one can.'

'And hang them up on the wall?'

'Yes, one can hang them up.'

'But if one can do all that, why do you call them invisible?'

Herr Doktor Busbeck glanced about the room, made sure that everything was in order, then took the folder under his arm.

'But why?' I asked. 'If they're invisible, then nobody can find them, then you don't have to hide them. You don't have to wrap them in oiled paper and put them under the floorboards. If they're invisible, nobody can find them. Anything that's invisible is safe.'

'If you look at it like that,' those were the actual words he used, 'if you look at it like that, you're right, of course.' He spoke with his face averted, casually, already on his way to the door. But then he stopped, turned round and added: 'You must realize that these pictures are not entirely invisible. They are small hints, pointers, allusions – like arrow-heads – that's something one can see, of course. But what is most important, the things that matter, that's invisible. It's all there but invisible, if you understand what I mean. Some day, I don't know when, at some other period, it will all be visible. Now don't go on asking me questions, don't go on talking, just go home.'

'And what are you going to do?'

'I'm going home, too.'

He smiled goodbye at me and then, pressing the folder to his body, left the hut. I followed him with my eyes for a short while, watching him walk towards the point where the dune changed direction, walking at first hesitantly and then rapidly, the upper part of his body bent a long way forward.

The rushing noise out there in the flats was the incoming tide. It came foaming shorewards, across the sand, filling up the runnels and moving in bubbling tongues across the flats, filling all the pools and water-holes, bringing with it grass and shells and bits of wood, covering up the traces that the sea-birds had left, and our own tracks. It came in northward right up the shore, quickly covering an expanse of grey clay and moving farther towards the peninsula.

Now it was too late to collect shells for Hilke. By the time I left the hut Herr Doktor Busbeck had disappeared. Crossing the peninsula, I walked across the shore, walking in a curve, always at an angle to the advancing waves, then turning away from them as they came in towards me in earnest, over the firm sandy ground. The beach. The sea. First I walked up to the red beacon, then up and over the dyke and on to the brick path, past the lock and the bleached signpost saying 'Rugbüll Police Station'.

The old box-cart that had no wheels, my hiding-place of earlier years, seemed to have sunk even deeper into the ground; the shaft, pointing upwards, was rotten; there were long cracks in it, a board in the splintery floor was broken. Now past the box-cart and past the shed. But at the foot of the stone steps I stopped. I had to stop there, because above me, looming gigantically – just like that time when we had brought Klaas home in the wheelbarrow – there was my father blocking my way. There was no getting past him. As he stood there, motionless, looking down at me, not stepping aside, not stretching out his hand, not moving a muscle in his leathery face, he seemed to be growing even taller, and so threatening did he seem to me that I didn't even attempt to look him in the eye, but kept my eyes lowered, staring at his shoes, which were whitened from having got wet, and at his gaiters, crusted with dry clay. I was thinking that he not only wore such gaiters but positively enjoyed wearing them, and I noticed that the laces of his boots were tied in neat loops of even length. He liked having his laces tied in neat loops of even length. And he also liked to have people facing him, feeling ill at ease and tormented by uncertainty, simply because of that eagerness of his, that almost greedy way of expecting something of them. It was enough to stop anyone thinking well of himself.

What's he found out now? What am I expected to confess to now? I kept on staring at his boots and enduring that silence by means of which he caused me to dwindle. At long last, when he had made me dwindle to the size of sixpence, his boots shifted in the doorway, now displaying to me their ridiculous, buckled-up profile. Having made a turn of forty-five degrees, my father showed me his own profile, too, and, with his back against the right doorpost, he not only allowed me to pass, his posture was now definitely a demand that I should go inside the house. I walked in past him and, stopping in the hall, I heard him turn round.

'Go on – into the office,' he ordered, and so I walked ahead of him into the little office. So we were going to have a talk, were we?

He began by searching my face, holding me fast with that ancient face of his. But whatever he read in my face clearly didn't satisfy him. He sat down with his back to the window and said at random : 'Come on, tell me!'

What is one supposed to say when one is given an order like that?

'Speak up,' he said, 'come on, let's have it, I haven't heard a word from you yet.'

It was obvious to me that he was after something in particular. But what was it?

'Don't be so sanctimonious – speak up!'

So he wanted me to confess. What he meant by speaking up was the same as confessing.

'You know more than you've told me. Didn't we agree to collaborate? What's the matter with you?'

He got up. Slowly, with his hands behind his back, he came up to me. It was not difficult to foresee what was going to happen now, but he refrained from hitting me – more with the intention of spurring me on than of punishing me – he refrained for so long that the slap, when in the end it came, was after all a surprise to me. My father really believed that the slap had stimulated my memory, had refreshed it, and with his mind at rest he returned to the chair.

'You spend all your time there,' he said. 'You hang about Bleekenwarf all day long. Nothing escapes you. So come on, tell!'

Since he was so insistent, I began:

'Yesterday we had seed-cake at Bleekenwarf. Herr Doktor Busbeck was sitting outside in the sun, reading. Jutta and I climbed into the carriage, that old carriage, you know, in the shed, and Jobst got so furious that he broke a whip.' I told him all the stupid things I could remember, for instance that they always gave a cup of tea to Brodersen, the one-armed postman, that Ditte always had a nap after lunch, that the ducks had flown from the pool to the bog. My father forced himself to listen patiently to all that pointless stuff, but then all of a sudden he asked:

'Are you sure you're not forgetting anything?'

'You mean the rain?' I asked.

'That fellow Busbeck, who left the house carrying something that looked like a folder. He left the house carrying it with him, and he went to the peninsula, where you've been. Unless you're blind, you must have seen him.'

'Oh, him,' I said. 'Yes, I saw him. He came over the dunes and he was in a bit of a hurry. He went to the hut and vanished inside – perhaps he's hidden something in there.'

'You think so?' he asked.

'He stayed in the hut for quite some time, perhaps he hid something under the floorboards.'

'Under the floorboards?'

'After all, it's the only place there where you could hide anything.'

My father was silent for a while. But at last he said:

'He's not observing the ban. He's gone on working all the time in secret. But I'll catch him or I'll find the stuff. And this time I shan't let him off. Nobody's going to be able to help him. I'll show him that he's no exception and that the law applies to him just as much as to anyone else. It's my duty to catch him. Under the floorboards in the hut, you think?'

'It's possible,' I said. 'It's the only hiding-place there.'

My father got up and, walking past me, went to the window. I could more or less tell from the scraping sound he made that he was scraping the dry mud off his boots. But I didn't dare to turn round. I was standing there listening to the noise he was making behind me, when another, louder noise began in the kitchen : my mother had turned on the radio.

At first it sounded as though swarms of grasshoppers were hopping over a sheet of corrugated iron, then it began to howl and whistle until somebody switched on an electric drill. Finally there was a voice that was all fluffy until my mother moved the knob for changing the stations. Now the voice became clear, self-assured and almost cheerful. It could be heard all over the house. It informed us that Italy had declared war on us because her royal nonentity by the name of Victor Emmanuel and a bogus, windy brasshat by the name of Badoglio had considered it necessary to do so. But that needn't worry us, the voice went on, we shouldn't even feel let down because our former brothers-in-arms, and so on and so forth, because only now, being quite on our own, was it possible for us to show the whole world what we were made of, because only now, no longer hampered by consideration for an unreliable ally, could we display all our virtues. That was the way the voice talked. It sounded relieved, it indicated optimism, it sounded self-assured.

'There's Italy for you,' my father said. I turned round and saw him standing at the window looking out at the peat-bog. 'They did it in the First World War and now they've done it again. That's the Italians all over – tarantella and brilliantine, that's all.'

He straightened up, stood very straight, clenching his fists, tensing his behind. Then all at once he turned round, walked past me without a glance at me, and buttoning up his tunic and buckling on his belt, complete with service pistol, he turned himself into a policeman equipped according to regulations. He shouted to the kitchen :

'Well, so long !'

And since my mother asked what time he would like to have his dinner, he added : 'Later – all that's got to wait,' then opened the door, got his bicycle out of the shed, pushed it to the brick path and rode off in the direction of the dyke. Have a nice ride, I thought, you just have a nice ride.

I wasn't hungry either, I'd have liked to eat later too, because I'd planned to get a few things done in the old mill first.

But I'd hardly got into the passage when I was called back: 'Dinner's ready, Siggi, come along!'

Lest anyone should fear we were going to have fish again – by no means, we were having stew: beans and pears and potatoes, no meat in it, only bacon rind. We sat facing one another in silence, my mother and I. Hilke hadn't got home yet. My mother gazed away over my head, thoughtfully, while sinking her teeth into a potato or a pear, she didn't even have to blow on it, no food was ever too hot for her. She ate listlessly, staring into empty space, swallowing slowly. She was capable of spearing a green bean and glaring at it for so long that one couldn't help surmising the worst. The least one expected was that she would put it at the edge of her plate, or down the sink, after that suspicious inspection. But then she would pull it off the fork with her long teeth and, without chewing it, squash it with her tongue and swallow the stuff, her face remaining expressionless. If ever during a meal I tried to tell her anything, she would point at my plate with a domineering gesture: 'That's what you're here to do! Eat, don't talk!' If I ate too fast, she would scold me. If sometimes I had no appetite, she would threaten me. There was nothing I enjoyed less than having a meal alone with Gudrun Jepsen.

I had finished long before she did, but for all that she wouldn't let me go. She insisted on my staying there, she ordered me to clear the table, to put the used dishes into the sink and the half-full pots into the hay box, and I even had to wipe the table while she just went on sitting there, indifferent, only sometimes grinding her teeth. But I don't want to go on spelling out how furious I was, and I'm even less inclined to describe that back view of her – the tight bun of her hair, her long neck dotted with moles, her stiff back, her over-bearing hips – I prefer to let the dyke-reeve Bultjohann make his appearance instantly, the old gurnard, who, as I have seen with my own eyes, wore as many as three Party badges, one on his shirt, one on his jacket, one on his overcoat. He was one of those fellows who knock at the door only after they have come into the room. Since he could never tell the difference between his own nine children, it's only natural that he called me by some other name every time he saw me. He would call me Hinrich or Berthold or Hermann and sometimes even Little Asmus. But that didn't worry me. All I cared about was his sending his regards to my money-box. By way of a greeting he'd give me a penny and say : 'Give my regards to your money-box.'

Today he called me Joseph, waved his penny, and even uttered some words of praise in recognition of my work in the kitchen. He didn't *sit* down, he rolled on to a chair that was much too small for him, supporting only half of his behind. He patted my mother's hand, breathing hard all the time as if he'd got to get rid of the wind that had got into his lungs. He winked at me in recognition of my work, which forced me to move about busily between sink, table, and larder.

It strikes me now that my mother would never ask anybody the reason for their visit : anyone who came was simply there. The fact that Bultjohann hadn't come to see her was obvious to me from the way he strained his ears to hear anything that was going on inside the house. At long last he asked : 'Is Jens at home?'

My mother shook her head. Leaning his bulky torso across the table, the dyke-reeve whispered : 'He's got to take action.'

Or rather he did what he himself would have called whispering, but even in the larder I could make out every word. He had noticed something and he considered it his duty to make a statement, that was why he had come along. He wanted to report what he had discovered at midday in the Wattblick Inn, the whole place empty, you know, Gudrun, and so I went on sitting there for a while, at the window, waiting, you know how it is. Not thinking about anything in particular, just waiting for Hinnerk to come along – but he doesn't turn up, so I get up and stroll around a bit, call out a few times, for somebody to come, after all, you don't want to help yourself to a drink, you know what I mean, Gudrun. Well, what I was thinking was, were they perhaps—? Makes you feel a bit awkward, you think they're waiting for you to ... and perhaps they *are* waiting for you to.... Well, the long and the short of it is they have their radio next to the bar, I dare say you know where, Gudrun. So I switched it on, takes a bit to warm up ... and all at once there's Radio London. They'd left it at the last station they'd been listening to ... London, you know.

Bultjohann, the duke-reeve, looked intently at my mother, doubtless hoping to read approval in her face, or at least confirmation of the fact that he had done the right thing in coming here and telling the whole story. But whatever he might have been expecting didn't happen. My mother said nothing. She didn't even look at him. She just sat there at the kitchen table, staring out of the window at the colourful autumn outside, while Bultjohann was obviously thinking hard how to arouse her interest. It was quite something to watch that old gurnard sitting there, puffing and blowing, again patting my mother's hand and forearm, positively massaging it, and meanwhile treating her to a rehash of his story: 'Just think of it, Gudrun, my dear, how Jens is going to prick up his ears, over there they're listening to enemy broadcasts, Hinnerk is, I can testify to it.'

My mother didn't stir, she was just waiting for him to finish. Then she roused herself from her brooding. She touched her head, fingering her bun, and all at once she turned towards me and snapped: 'Off you go, Siggi, to your room. It's time for you!' Resentfully I came out of the larder, whining, trying to get to the sink in order to wring out the rag, but she wouldn't let me, she said impatiently: 'Get a move on, you've finished your work!'

So, still protesting, quite reproachfully, I put the greasy, sticky, dripping washing-up rag over the tap. Silently I took my leave, shaking hands with my mother and with the dyke-reeve. And in order to show them that I didn't care if they preferred to be left alone, I shut the kitchen door and, taking my father's field glasses, which he'd either forgotten or deliberately left behind, I went up to my room. Meanwhile not much had happened on my private oceans on the extendable table; all that was going on there was the doom of the *Graf Spee*; I put her up together with three British cruisers at the end of **La Plata** estuary, and the *Graf Spee* did, in fact, have no chance whatsoever, she simply had to scuttle herself, my playing it over again established that beyond any doubt. I went to the window and sat on the sill. Dusk had scarcely fallen.

How long the autumn lingers here in our part of the world, and how quickly the spring goes by! I took the field-glasses out of the warped leather case and brought the autumn closer in round, starkly clear discs. Let them go on talking down there in the kitchen! The scraggy copse to the right of Glüserup, deformed and cankered by the wind, was already brown. The meadows and the boundary-hedges running towards Husum were still pretending to be green, but there was already a brownish-yellow shimmer on them. The shadowy ditches were the colour of lead. Everywhere there was brick-red entering one's field of vision. We have no mountains, no river, no banks, just the plain: green, yellow, with brown streaks. Rows of alders with black berries that the wind blows into the ditches. Everything – the land, the trees, the small garden – is browned, streaked, streaked almost as if it were mildewed, like things that have been put away for a long time. The cattle standing quite still in the evening, breathing regularly, some of them already covered with tarpaulins to protect them from the coolness of the night. I moved the field-glasses this way and that, searching the horizon. In his apple orchard there was old Holmsen picking apples. He was standing on a stepladder, shaky, rather shaky, visible only from the hips downwards. The other part of his body had disappeared into the still leafy top of the tree. On the flagpole outside the Wattblick Inn a pennant was fluttering in the wind. Hinnerk Timmsen's private pennant, white with two crossed blue keys. 'He's got the keys,' my grandfather used to say sometimes, 'but he hasn't yet got the door to unlock with them.' On the peat-ponds the moorhens were swimming about like pieces of cork, fat after the bountiful summer, incapable now of rising into the air. There was my mill. The glasses enable me to see my hide-out, the dome-shaped top covered with slates, the octagonal tower, the window-frames still showing some white paint, from which the last bits of glass had fallen out, swept away by the wind. I recognized the sheet of cardboard behind which Klaas and I had lain and watched the arrival of the leathercoats. Were they having a quarrel downstairs in the kitchen? It's the radio, mother's turned on the radio. I raised the field-glasses to my eyes again and focused on the mill, and I saw them coming out of the door.

I must admit that the first thing I thought was the painter must have discovered my hiding-place: the bed, the pictures of horsemen, the collections of locks and keys, and of course also 'The Man in the Red Cloak'. He must have discovered it by chance and now he'd been up there with my sister to have a good look at his discovery, to check what was there – perhaps, if it had to be, somewhat grudgingly admiring it all. And

255

I was afraid too, I well remember how afraid I was, that he might simply have taken the black-out blind with 'The Man in the Red Cloak' off the wall, to take it away. But he was not carrying anything under his arm nor anything in his hand. He took my sister lightly by the arm and pushed her gently ahead of him. What had they been doing in the mill? Hilke was still limping a bit as they walked towards the peat pond; at the crossing they parted. They walked slower and slower and came closer to each other, and when they came to a halt, their shoulders touched for an instant. It was probably just by chance that Nansen grazed Hilke's shoulder when he walked past her and then abruptly turned round to face her, just as if he intended to block her path. But he didn't spread out his arms, he took both her hands, put them together in front of his stomach and pumped them to the rhythm of his words – I should say encouraging words, anyway, short sentences such as : 'You must remember,' or : 'That's what we'll do,' or something like that. Hilke's face was lowered and she didn't say anything; she gave the impression of being entirely passive, the way she allowed her hands to be pumped up and down.

And then all at once, to my surprise, the painter let go of her hands, indeed threw them away, turned round and trotted off, or, more correctly, sailed forth in the direction of Bleekenwarf, leaning forward, his big coat billowing behind him. And Hilke? She went along at a great pace in spite of the wound in her foot, she took enormous strides and sometimes she would turn round with a jump and wave to Nansen, without avail I must add, because the painter didn't look back even once. Suddenly Hilke stopped and stood there, thinking – it was just as clearly recognizable as it is when the Rugbüll policeman is engaged in thought – and then she turned round and began limping back, all of a sudden limping, towards the mill. For an instant she disappeared inside and then she returned with the basket over her arm, and instantly again, and clearly enjoying it, running and leaping, she proceeded in the direction of Rugbüll, not forgetting, however, to wave in Nansen's direction. When she'd reached the lock, she waved for the last time, quite mechanically now, and then she leaped on to the brick path. And there she promptly remembered the cut in her foot that forced her to walk with a limp.

256

She discovered me at the window and made a threatening gesture in my direction. I made a sign to her, indicating that there was a visitor in the kitchen, but she didn't seem interested, she came up the steps, smiling all the time, throwing her hair back before she entered the house. I was already at my listening-post by the door. Hilke gave a shrill laugh, which indicated that Bultjohann had indeed pinched her behind, which is a local custom. Hilke didn't take a plate out of the kitchen cupboard, so she wasn't hungry. She went into the larder, which meant that she was leaving it to my father to clean and sort the fishes. She was in a great hurry to get out of the kitchen, but she didn't say good night yet.

When I heard her on the stairs, coming towards my room, I darted to the table, bending over the sinking of the *Graf Spee*, waiting for her to come into the room. 'Who won?' she asked, still in the doorway.

'Her hash is settled,' I answered. In spite of her injured foot she came up soundlessly and, bending over what was going on at the La Plata estuary, she rubbed my neck with her out-stretched forefinger. What does he know? she was probably thinking. And what doesn't he know? Or perhaps she was thinking, 'Better treat him nicely, just to be on the safe side. It can't do any harm.' She didn't ask about the shells, but she went on fiddling about with my neck, stroking the back of my head, and she also laid her chin on my shoulder, intending to make a dreamy impression, which, however, wasn't successful, because in the mirror I could see her eyes looking sideways at me, which gave the whole operation a different slant, as you might say.

'You won't guess what I'd like to do now,' she said.

'What?'

'I want a smoke!'

'A smoke!'

'Yes, I want a cigarette,' she said. 'We can air the room straight afterwards so Mother won't notice.'

My sister produced – I don't remember where from – one of those little packets of four cigarettes, and laid them on the map of the ocean, somewhere north of the Azores. I shook my head, pushing the cigarettes towards her, but Hilke raised her hands in protest, forcing me to keep them. So I took the packet and lit one of them. She lit one too, after going to the door and listening.

We sat down on my bed and smoked. At first, we puffed hastily, paying more attention to the cigarettes than to the whitish-blue clouds of smoke. But then we began blowing the smoke into each other's faces, and, doing that, we began to see a variety of things in the smoke: for instance, sea-cows, and woolly sheep and the tops of trees; the rolling, fluttering smoke coming out of our mouths dissolved rather slowly and the two clouds were wafted into each other and mingled with each other, and between Hilke and me there rose whitish-blue stags and flying buoys and more and more sheep. Even a face arose there, a strange and dreamy, incalculable face all made of smoke, and I groped in vain, trying to remember whom it resembled.

We blew trees and barges, and once, by making our clouds of smoke glide, I succeeded in creating a three-master under full sail. There was quite a lot going on there as we sat on my bed, smoking.

We didn't even cough, but when I had opened the window and was driving out the smoke with a stocking that I whirled round over my head like an electric fan, Hilke disappeared to the lavatory and was sick. She soon came back again, sat down, wiped her mouth with the back of her hand, and carefully pulled out a thread of spittle, slowly extending it until it broke. I got rid of the butts, shut the window and, looking at my sister, was quite amazed to see her grinning at me.

'What are you grinning about?' I asked.

'Just think, Siggi, if they found out what we've been doing – what do you think they'd do to us?'

'Make black pudding?' I asked.

'Minced meat,' she said, adding: 'You haven't been doing anything, d'you understand, nothing special has been going on, d'you hear me? You can't remember anything.'

She stretched out on my bed, turned over on her front and relaxed her lazy bones. I gave her a chance to breath deeply, and stretched out a bit on my bunk, but when it seemed to me that she was about to fall asleep, I asked: 'And the mill? What have the two of you been doing in the mill?'

She didn't seem to understand the question, and I was just

going to make my meaning a bit clearer to her, when she gave a jerk, jumped up and went for me, her face livid with fear and fury.

'You just shut up and forget it,' she said. 'Watching me through the field-glasses! Nothing – we weren't doing anything in the mill, you understand?' But she said it a bit too vehemently. 'We just happened to meet.'

'Up at the top?' I asked, but when she looked at me blankly I was satisfied and calmed her down: 'For all I care – I haven't seen a thing.'

Visibly relieved, my sister collapsed again on to my bed, burrowing her face into the pillows and making a funny attempt to get her arms round the mattress. I imagined her being dead, and I looked at her more closely: the heavy necklace of polished cubes of natural wood, the strange salt-cellars above her collar bone, the reddened, rough and wrinkled skin above her elbows. There was nothing wrong with her hands, they seemed quite normal to me, but where her ears grew out of her head the skin made a rather creased impression, and her spine struck me as being a bit too long. I touched her once where her brassière made the flesh on her back bulge, but I left it at that, although I should have liked to count how many vertebrae there were and to have tapped them with my fingers to find out if they would all sound different; and now I remembered Addi, the good-natured accordion-player.

Cautiously I pushed my sister to one side, and she gave way, grumbling, rolling the warm mass of her body to one side to make room for me. But she did it too slowly and drowsily for my liking. After all, it was my bed.

'If you don't want to make room for me, then shove off,' I said, stretching out beside her, and I was quite unexpectedly overcome by increasing dizziness. There were flying sea-cows and buoys and sheep spinning around me, endlessly repeating the same counting-out rhyme. I clutched Hilke and lashed out at the woolly sheep, and then I heard someone calling my name. Faintly, from very far off, somebody was calling me. There it was again: 'Siggi, come downstairs, Siggi!'

Hilke sat up, she looked benumbed, and sitting there the way she did, with her hair hanging down and covering her face, she looked like a mop.

'It's Father,' she said. 'He's back.'

And at the same moment I heard his voice from downstairs : 'Get a move on, Siggi!'

He'd been rather irritable recently and so I didn't think it advisable to irritate him more by not instantly obeying his orders, and therefore I got up, helped by Hilke in my attempts to regain my balance. She guided me to the door and even to the stairs. He called out again :

'Do you want me to come up and fetch you?'

There was a note of urgency in his voice, but it didn't sound angry, and I called back :

'I'm just coming,' and hurried down the stairs towards him. There he stood, waiting for me, a slight look of displeasure round the corners of his mouth. He had one hand stretched out towards me, he pulled me down the last step in his well-known way and dragged me along the passage to that office of his that was no bigger than a bath-towel. So it was something official again. By now my dizziness had become bearable, there was nothing whirling or flying around me any more, and I felt capable of walking along one of the straight gaps between the floorboards if anybody should have asked me to do that. What did he want of me?

My father dragged me to his desk, and to my amazement bestowed on me a long approving gaze, even considered it right and proper to slap me on the back in token of recognition, all of which alarmed me extremely. He even went to the lengths of saying : 'Well done, Siggi – very observant of you.' At that I really got into a state and began twitching in order to get rid of the suddenly awakened suspicion that went creepy-crawly over my back. I couldn't manage to stand there quietly in front of him, I turned to one side, bending forward in order to look through the triangle formed by his arm and see what was on the desk.

'Well done, indeed,' my father said. And quickly and no doubt anxiously I asked :

'What is it? What's well done?'

He took a step towards the window, thus letting me have a clear sight of the desk, and quite superfluously he even pointed to it.

'You see what I mean?'

260

Of course I saw it, and there was no need for him to tell me what was hidden under the brownish-green, greasy oiled paper. As far as I was concerned, there was no longer any need to speak a single word.

'In the hut,' he said, 'on the peninsula, just where you thought it might be hidden, under the floorboards.'

I went to the desk and touched the oiled paper, which was cool and smooth, and as though jokingly I took the folder in both hands, weighing it.

'I took the floorboards up with a chisel, there was one just lying about,' my father said.

'Wasn't anybody at all there?' I asked.

'Not a soul to be seen.'

'Not even Herr Doktor Busbeck?'

'Not even Busbeck.'

'And the hiding-place – was the stuff put there just recently?'

'What do you mean by recently?' he asked. 'The bird was in its nest, I dare say that's the main thing.'

He took the folder out of my hands, laid it on the desk, and, pointing his forefinger at it, ordered me to open it.

I stalled. I didn't want to, didn't want to at all.

'Get a move on,' he said. 'You've been a great help to me in this matter, so you're entitled to the privilege of being present and opening it yourself.'

He was holding out to me his black horn pocket-knife, with the blade open, slowly lowering it towards the string. I didn't even try to undo the knots in order to get hold of a good long piece of string, I pressed the blade against it, and when I moved it the string split with a cracking sound.

'Now take the paper off,' he said. 'It's a good sheet of oiled paper.'

Fussily I undid and folded the oiled paper, thus exposing the folio, and then I read the heading, done in elaborate lettering : 'Invisible Pictures'.

'Get a move on,' my father said. 'Let's have a look, let's see what he's up to now.'

He lit his pipe, put one foot on the desk chair, rested one elbow on his knee, and in that comfortable position our policeman was ready for the picture show. My thoughts went back to Herr Doktor Busbeck, to our meeting in the hut, and his explanation of the invisible pictures, an explanation that had seemed a bit unsatisfactory to me. The things that matter are invisible. But what are the things that matter?'

'Get going,' my father said.

But how am I to describe those invisible paintings? Those paintings of which Max Ludwig Nansen once said that they contained all he had to say about this age in which we lived, a sort of confession including everything he had experienced in the course of his life. What had he got out of it all and how had he expressed it all once he had ceased to paint? In what light did his sorrows become visible now? And how is one to give an account of them, indeed what is the way to see and contemplate those invisible pictures of his? Even when it is a matter of visible pictures one's good will alone is not enough. His eyes tested all there was to be tested, and his hand left out all that had to be left out. And yet I can't help thinking he must have been trying to convey a meaning.

My father tapped his foot. He gave me an encouraging prod, he clicked his tongue and said : 'Get on with it!'

So I lifted sheet after sheet, rhythmically doing his bidding, turning over then putting down each of them as he gave a short sign with his hand. I don't know why some sheets took longer than others. After all, only what was most essential was there to be recognized – or so one was told – for all I cared, perhaps a seventh of it all; the rest – and one could see without difficulty that the rest was a very considerable amount – remained invisible. Did he perhaps allow his imagination to run away with him? Was there sufficient to be seen for him to make out what Herr Doktor Busbeck had called the little hints, the pointers and allusions, to run to earth and get hold of what was concealed? Was it perhaps his second sight that helped him to fill in the empty spaces? Was even what had been left out safe from him? I could see only what there was to be seen, and I had no intention of seeing anything else.

I saw a paddle-wheel, saw it swirling the water around and turning it with a rushing sound, the water of a black river without end and without any sky above it : anybody can take his chance and try to find out what can't be seen. Or on another sheet : just the eyes of an old man, no pondering, friendly expression, no readiness to yield an answer. Those eyes gave one a sense of some exasperating presence confronting them, something with which no agreement was possible. Something was expected of that invisible presence, but certainly not any willingness to meet you halfway. Or a sunflower, half done, drooping, the stamens earth-coloured, on the leafless, bent stem the yellow, tattered corolla still luminous with sunlight – it would be easy enough to connect it with 'Autumn' or 'In the Gloaming' but for the fact that the painter had left five-sixths of the sheet blank. Or that tree, no, not a tree but just the place where the bark bulges after grafting, with an alarming beam of light falling on the spot; I remember the different shades of brown, and it might in fact have been quite easy to tell a story about it, a story about all that had been suppressed there.

My father showed no impatience; he didn't rush me. He didn't speak, nor did any gesture or any look on his face betray whatever those invisible pictures suggested to him. Well, here's the next sheet: the carved back of a North German chair – more crosses than stars on it, crudely shaped roses and pierced semi-circles, garlands everywhere, secretly suggesting that perhaps even the North German bottom that might sit on the chair was garlanded. Or that jacket – perhaps a uniform-blouse worn to shreds – hung up on a nail: one could see holes and specks and triangular rents; or perhaps it was the other way round: the holes and triangular rents looked at the beholder, the blouse revealed itself as a witness, was some man's memory – this hole was from a bullet during the escape, this rent made by an ordinary piece of barbed wire. Was leaving out the thing that mattered even more important than anything else? Or that flying fish, beautifully curved like a whiplash; or that trigonometrical point, a triangular wooden scaffolding at loggerheads with the plain on which it stood; or those old-fashioned anchors, nailed to the sky, their rusty chains dangling down to earth, swaying in the wind; or that dive of swallows, two burning darts searching for their aim, sure of their aim; or the exploding haycock set in motion by a storm that carried it along towards some farmstead left to the imagination; or those tracks in the snow, black, coming from nowhere, that would make anyone stop short; or the cracked water-jugs tied together with a piece of rope; or that woman's head, thrown back, the mouth opening in a cry that nobody would ever hear; or those crooked shadows cast by the shrouds of a derelict cutter that one imagined to have run ashore; or the ropes hanging from the disc of a sun, which might be tied into so many patterns. Nor can I ever forget those blue boards from a fence, perhaps five of them, perhaps only three, with their cross-beams, there's nothing behind them and nothing in front, no people, just a touch of olive-coloured background, and on that background a tiny red gleam. I had just lifted up the sheet with the blue boards from a fence, a sheet like the others, about which only very little can be said, when my father suddenly caught me by the wrist, pulled me towards him and asked : 'Why are you trembling like that? At your age there's no cause to tremble.'

'I didn't even know I was trembling,' I said, 'I didn't notice it.'

'Might be brought on by these pictures,' my father said. He took his foot off the chair and turned towards the window. 'Pictures! You call this stuff pictures – to be hung on the wall and looked at all day. Invisible pictures – enough to make a cat laugh.'

Sceptically, reproachfully, not at all triumphantly, but rather with growing disappointment, he gazed at the folio on the desk. And then a look of mistrust came into his face; he was beginning to suspect something; he walked up and down his office, growing more and more suspicious. For a long time he looked at the photographs on the wall as though seeking advice from them and getting confirmation of his own thoughts from them, and finally his lips curled in a thin, scornful smile. He beckoned me over to him and, waving his omniscient forefinger in front of my face, said : 'We aren't going to be fooled by that stuff, Siggi.'

I pretended to be surprised, but I also kept my eyes on his forefinger.

'He's trying to get the better of me with these things, that's what he's doing. As though I didn't know his pictures! He wants me to swallow this, hook, line and sinker, to distract my attention. It's all quite obvious. Just bait.'

Energetically, he took the folder and wrapped it up again in the oiled paper, pulled out a drawer and popped the parcel into it.

'If he thinks I'm going to leave him alone now, he's making

a bad mistake,' my father said. 'He's got my monkey up now, trying to make a fool of me. He ought to know how much you can get away with, with a chap from Glüserup, and what you can't, oughtn't he? This stuff isn't even good enough for me to pass it on to Husum – they'd only shake their heads there.'

'Shall I take it back?' I asked.

'It doesn't eat anything,' he replied. 'We'll just leave it there in the desk. What's the matter with you? You're trembling again. Why don't you stop? Is something wrong?'

12   Under the Burning-Glass

Just consider: forty cigarettes and the situation I'm in, left alone with my memories, which are supposed to flourish as a result of my labours – how can a chap refuse? And apart from that, Wolfgang Mackenroth didn't look at all well when he came tiptoeing into my cell; to say the least of it, he looked a bit weak and like somebody running a slight temperature, and he swayed a bit when I patted him on the back to get the whitewash off his jacket, which he had brushed against the wall of our big communal lavatory. The paint comes off almost all our walls. We shook hands in silence. He made a gesture of appreciation when he saw how my work had grown, and then he turned his head, that delicate psychologist's head, towards the window, looking out into the open where once again the winter was doing its stuff to the Elbe. He seemed to be going to remark upon the view, but then he decided not to and instead conveyed to me best wishes from Governor Himpel, with whom he was on fairly intimate terms. Himpel had received my letter – he, Wolfgang Mackenroth, had been present when Himpel opened it, scanned it, and then sat down and read it once again. And then – all this according to Mackenroth – instead of blowing up or letting off steam by composing a song, he had just said: 'Compulsion, a didactic compulsion', and had walked round the room in ever smaller circles, which seemed to clear his mind. And when he had finally found his way back to his desk, he had added that compulsion had sometimes produced good results. He didn't say what was in my letter, anyway what Mackenroth had told me was enough for me to realize that he had given his consent and that I had permission to carry on with my task even after Twelfth Night.

All I could offer Wolfgang Mackenroth was a seat on the edge of my bunk, but he declined, he didn't want to sit down, because he didn't want to stay, he wanted to get back home, away from our island, back to Altona and to his furnished room where, as he told me, the eight bottles of beer were waiting for him that he needed if he was to sleep deeply and soundly for fifteen hours. He had been overworking and he was exhausted, all empty inside, he informed me, at the same time tapping his spine lightly with his hand.

I asked him if he still assisted his landlady, who was the North German champion on the trapeze, with her training at home by correcting her posture. Yes, he did, but that wasn't what he had come to talk about. And did her husband, who was a crane-operator, still ask him on Friday to take charge of a 20 mark note that he had to return on Sunday morning? Yes, he did, Mackenroth said, but he didn't want to talk about that, either. That led me to ask why he had come at all, if he was so exhausted that he didn't want to talk about anything. But Wolfgang Mackenroth, delicate as he was, answered the question before it was even uttered, gingerly putting his hand into his inside breast-pocket, pulling out a folded manuscript, putting that manuscript on my pillow and weighing it down with two packets of cigarettes.

Then he made a gesture of impatience in the direction of the cigarettes and the manuscript, conveying something like : Help yourself. Anyway, he didn't make any effort to hide his gifts under the grey rough blanket that made one itch all over during the night, and to me that carelessness of his was a sign that he really was all worn out. He gave no further explanation, he just bestowed a tired smile upon me, he patted my upper arm by way of farewell. That's what Mackenroth could be like, though he wasn't always like that.

And even if you should have guessed it by now, I must mention that the manuscript he had placed on my pillow was part of his thesis – Art and Criminality, The Case of Siggi J. – an unnumbered chapter with the illuminating, or at least informative, title, 'B. Youth and the Influence of Environment'. So once again he wanted an opinion from me, he wanted me to say whether I was satisfied with him or not. He had held his scientific burning-glass over a chap by the name of Siggi J.: now he wanted me to use the burning-glass – and this was to go on until one of us began to smoke and catch fire under the beam of collective light-rays. What was I supposed to do? And in what way? Did he expect suggestions for improvement? Agreement? Rejection? I pulled the manuscript towards me and lit a cigarette. Reading, I learned the following about myself:

...born the third and youngest child of the country police-officer Ole Jepsen. His home is in Rugbüll, a hamlet near Glüserup in the extreme north of Germany, not far from the Danish border. Siggi – his full Christian names are Siegfried Kai Johannes – comes on his mother's side from an old peasant family, proud of having been independent peasants working their own ground for centuries, whilst his father's family was mainly [mainly!] composed of small tradespeople, artisans and minor officials. At home, where everything followed a normal, well-regulated course, the child grew up without experiencing any tensions, passing through the normal stages of apperception. His affection for his father was equalled by his love for his mother, which might be described as shy. Since his brother and sister – Klaas and Hilke – were considerably older than the subject of our study, they did not qualify as playmates, which caused the boy to create his own realm of play for himself, one animated in a variety of ways and dominated, according to his mother, by two characters named Kaes and Püch. They were sources of both joy and anxiety.

So Wolfgang Mackenroth had been to see my people at Rugbüll and he had managed to make them talk.

Despite the intense experiences afforded by the sphere of play, the child's ego-relationship to the external world remained undisturbed; even the long intervals during which the child was left to his own resources do not seem to have had any damaging effect, so far as can be observed from our subject's reactions. According to the parents and a number of neighbours, the subject gave the impression of being a modest, quietly contented and unassuming child, liked by all. What some witnesses particularly recall is the child's 'abnormal' sense of cleanliness and the fact that he never tired of asking questions, questions that are said often to have caused embarrassment to adults; they also stressed his early developed sense of justice, which manifested itself for example when food was being served. Over against this one elderly neighbour is of the opinion that he detected traces of malice and downright greed and also an inclination towards unbridled exaggeration; but this opinion seems to be mistaken. It is generally agreed that from the day Siggi J. entered school he was always top of his class. It is notable that for a long time he enjoyed school. The boy could frequently be found in the classroom an hour before school began. His parents state that there was never any need to wake him in the morning. He found the summer holidays too long. His teachers called him 'precocious', partly because Siggi J. not only never joined his schoolmates in their pranks, but frequently even persuaded them not to play such pranks or found some ingenious way of preventing them. On a number of occasions when school inspections took place, he not only earned praise but also came in for ungrudging admiration. Former classmates of his have spoken appreciatively of his sense of solidarity, which manifested itself for instance by his finishing his written homework very quickly simply because he wanted to pass his copybook on to his friends.

Through the mediation of his form master the subject of our study repeatedly appeared in Radio Hamburg's Children's Hour, and according to the editor of that programme he made an extraordinary impression in 'Children Look at the World' and 'The Children Reply'. As a participant in the children's quiz, Siggi J. won a number of prizes. He did equally well in all school subjects with the exception of religious instruction. His form master has spoken of his particular gift for drawing and for the writing of German essays,, and mentioned that some of his essays were read in public on prize-day. His speciality was the description of pictures; the description of a ship-wreck painted by Paul Flehinghus was so successful that the essay was sent to the Ministry in Kiel. The fact that later, at the secondary school in Glüserup, Siggi J. did not always succeed in being top of his class, was due to the many interests he had outside school, about which more will be said later. Here too, however, everyone has spoken of the sureness of his judgement, his determination and his markedly artistic turn of mind.

All in all, the picture resulting from the information that has been gathered seems to justify the conclusion that the reason for Siggi J.'s becoming an outsider at an early age lies in his talents. Since the community always regards the outsider as a source of irritation, being made to feel inferior, possibly even threatened, by his existence, it turns its whole attention to him, regards him with suspicion, and ultimately pursues him with its hatred.

The subject of our study had that experience from the moment when he was held up to his classmates as a shining example; the more often this happened, the more isolated he became, and the fact that his help was expected in class did not stop his schoolmates from showing him their contempt, even physically assaulting him. Those at home remember the boy occasionally running away from his schoolmates to hide somewhere, returning home only after dark. Just as he was an outsider at school, so he had a peculiar position in the family: his brother and sister being grown up and his parents' responsibilities continually increasing, it frequently happened that he was treated as though he were an adult. He was allowed to be present when police inquiries were being made and decisions taken and also during discussions and other procedures. He took part in police operations, which naturally helped to develop his cognitive faculties. Taken into confidence by his father in official matters, Siggi showed his independence by not doing what was expected of him or by quietly doing the opposite, if he thought he was justified in so doing. If he was of the opinion that he deserved a beating, he not only put no difficulties in the way of the person who was to punish him, he collaborated by volunteering for his castigation.

The child's early independence cannot be explained entirely by the fact that owing to the war his father was so taken up by his official duties that he no longer had time to fulfil all his parental duties. There is no doubt that the child had a tendency to become a lone wolf. On the other hand, his relationship with his brother and sister was one of deep affection, as was confirmed in many quarters, a relationship of absolute trust and readiness to help in any way. Perhaps it was this relationship with his adult siblings that made it possible for the boy to feel on equal terms also with other adults and thus to form a close relationship with them.

But all this casts no light on the relationship between the painter Max Ludwig Nansen and Siggi J., which appeared inexplicable to the boy's parents, a relationship of which they showed no understanding even in retrospect. Exhaustive inquiries have led to the establishment of the fact that the friendship between these two began during the period when Nansen painted his famous picture 'Foals and Thunderstorm'; in the beginning the boy assisted the man in small matters and for the rest just sat there in silence, watching the creation of a work of art. Neighbours have referred to their astonishment at the fact that the painter, who up to that time had almost always resented the presence of other people while he was working and who at times would behave quite offensively to onlookers, not only tolerated the boy's presence but after a while even asked for him to be there. They were quite frequently seen walking about hand in hand. Our subject's father had no objection to this relationship, since both he and Nansen were Glüserup men and they had been on terms of friendship since their boyhood.

Like his brother Klaas and later his sister Hilke, Siggi J. served the painter as a model. Siggi J. was used only twice : for 'Little Nis' and for 'The Hay Devil's Son'. In both paintings the friendly, indeed affable character of the spectral figures is due to him. It has been said that Nansen made up a cycle of fairy-tales for Siggi J., fairy-tales in which every colour tells the story of its origin. The essay 'Learning to See', never completed, was also intended for Siggi. From time to time, the painter would give the boy paper and paint and, after discussing the subject, would invite him to compete with him. Neighbours occasionally saw them together, both hard at work, painting.

When the child had to run away from his classmates, he often hid in the painter's studio, and once he was locked in there for a whole night. For some time he was forbidden to enter the studio; this was after he had interfered with the painting 'Nina O. of H.'. He intensely disliked the violet dress and therefore painted it over green.

[Not green, Wolfgang Mackenroth, *yellow*. At least colours are something we want to get right. As for all the rest of it, you can work it up as wildly as you like, to serve you as a thesis.]

Nothing definite can be established about the origins of the boy's passion for collecting. Perhaps it was an expression of unconscious rivalry with the painter.

He collected, and kept in a hiding-place, reproductions of equestrian paintings; he also showed some expertise in collecting keys and locks. When word of this got out, some people thought they had found the explanation of the otherwise inexplicable disappearance of various keys, and in the local museum at Glüserup they thought they were on the track of a thief who had taken nothing but locks and keys. The assumption that Siggi J. had committed some thefts of this kind seems justified.

During the last years of the war, the painter Max Ludwig Nansen was placed under an interdict against continuing his profession. It fell to Police-Officer Jepsen to deliver the written order of interdiction, and he was likewise responsible for seeing that the

interdict was not violated. The subject of our study inevitably became a prey to inner conflict. Urged by his father to act as a spy on his behalf, and entrusted by the painter with tasks that occasionally included the salvaging of pictures, the boy instinctively showed real understanding of the problems of the time.
[Well, this might be expressed quite differently.]
An event subsequently occurred that caused a rift in the family's harmonious mode of life and which was therefore also a traumatic experience for the boy: his brother Klaas escaped from the Military Hospital where he was being treated for a self-inflicted wound, and when he was brought home, severely wounded, he was rejected by his mother and handed over to the authorities by his father. The inevitable consequence was the child's estrangement from both parents. It was probably at that time that Siggi J. realized that he was in want of parental love.
[And what comes now is the old bromide about extenuating circumstances.]
Lonely, deprived of affection, growing up in an age in which there could no longer be any trust in human values [Well, well] the boy went through experiences that no child can undergo unscathed. Although the boy had no direct experience of the whole impact of the war, he did experience its aftermath much more intensely than many others of his age could. This from the temporary food-shortage and lack of other commodities to the awareness of death. Sensitive and observant as he was, what preoccupied him more than anything else and – we may reasonably assume – caused him suffering was the changed relationship between his father and the painter Max Ludwig Nansen.

That's enough, that's quite enough. I've more than earned those forty cigarettes. What Wolfgang Mackenroth writes about me is in its way correct. I don't want to say any more about it, it isn't for me to say more than that it's correct in its way. For all I care, let him carry on along his chosen line, it won't do anyone any harm, as nobody's feelings are going to be hurt. But if there should be anyone who wants to find out more about the places and the people mentioned in this study, anyone who wants to go to those places and look up those people, perhaps even hoping to get along well with them, I should advise him to provide himself with some other sources as well, to listen to other voices, to read other descriptions of it all. Let him read, for instance, about cloud-formations, about the migration of storks, about our memories and our hatred, about our weddings and our winters. As for Mackenroth, let him take me under his burning-glass, let him travel to Rugbüll and question them all for all he's worth; let him assemble his information, classify it, stick it all on his scientific pins, let him boil my past up until it jellifies, let him pass his examinations with the aid of this concoction : both he and this stuff of his are not of the slightest use to me.

Of course I know what he's after. But it's no use at all to me. I can't even recognize it, it's all words, yarn-spinning, and all of a sudden it's finished. All I know is that nothing's ever finished, nothing ever comes to an end, and I should like to tell this story of mine all over again, differently. But with Himpel already being difficult and allotting me time for my punishment-task only from month to month, I've got to get on with it, down the years as you might say, because there's still so much to be said. It means going back as light does : only then can one see all that's still there, waiting. For instance, there's the moment when peace came. But before the outbreak of peace there's still a winter to come, one of those North German winters with their thin cover of snow bursting open, with overflowing ditches and wet winds, those winds that loosen the bricks in the wall and make the wallpaper blister and come unstuck, those winters.

It went on and on snowing and raining. The unmetalled roads turned to mud and finally were flooded. The lock could no longer be opened, so great was the pressure of dammed-up black water. The water in the ditches ran faster than ever, swinging with it the dead grass on the banks. The paddocks were deserted and drops of water ran along the wires and finally flew off. Tracks in the snow disappeared in less than half a day. The crooked trees gleamed black, the beach was deserted, and the North Sea was veiled in fog. Nobody left the house who didn't have to. Inside every front door were the wet, patched rubber boots, and anyone who had to go outside had first of all to pass through a barrage of trickles coming down from the overflowing gully. The paint on the outside of the houses – wine-red or whitish-grey – ran down along the wall in streaks, and the window-panes were misted up all day. That was the winter when Ditte fell ill.

Here and there people talked about it, dropped hints, whispered, but all I could make of it was that the painter's wife was suffering from unquenchable thirst. It wasn't clear to me whether that was because of her illness or if it was the illness itself. Anyway, she kept on swilling down elderberry juice and tea all during that winter; she drank water, malt-coffee, milk, and the broth in which the fish had been boiled. She groped greedily for every vessel with some liquid in it, and if anyone tried to stop her she would moan: 'I'm burning, I'm burning.' No liquid was safe from her. In her long, coarse-woven dress, her head thrown back, she walked about Bleekenwarf in search of something to drink. She even drank the water from the rain-butt. It was as if that unbridled, that blind thirst had made its mark on her face: her beautiful, lean face, framed in grey hair, seemed to glow and to be puffed up.

They had called in Doctor Gripp, and he came, bearing his big bag with the old-fashioned locks on it. First he saw Ditte alone, then the painter was allowed to come in too. Jutta and I walked across the swampy meadows to the chemist in Glüserup to fetch drops and tablets that the doctor had prescribed, but they only made her thirstier than ever. After she had taken the drops, she shut her eyes and said: 'More to drink!' And she took the tumbler she had used when taking the tablets, filled it with water from the jug on the wash-stand, and emptied it at one gulp. The painter didn't say much; he hardly ever stopped her from drinking. He looked at her almost all the time, and the pupils of his eyes seemed to become smaller, round and sharp. He now spent almost all his time alone with Ditte, and if ever he had to leave her would give a sign to Teo Busbeck to take over. Jobst, who had repaired an old gramophone, wasn't allowed to use it; Jutta, who had grown a bit plumper – which happened to her every winter – was forbidden to try out her dance-steps in the room adjoining the sick-room.

I discovered that what worried Doctor Gripp most was that the incredible thirst didn't even cease at night. Ditte would get out of bed a number of times, and if the jug on the wash-stand was empty she would grope her way into the kitchen or the larder to find something to drink. She was give a few injections, but these too, it seemed, increased her thirst. When her temperature began to rise, Doctor Gripp ordered her to stay in bed. She sat in bed, not at all relaxed, stiffly leaning back against her pillows, her grey eyes fixed on the door, listening for something, not to anything that went on in her room, but for something far off in some past or future.

Sometimes, when visitors came to see her, to hold her thin hand and nod to her, I thought I could hear a rustling, fainter than rain, softer than snow; it was as if the light were trickling past the window.

Teo Busbeck was there, sitting almost all the time at the head of her bed; carefully dressed, devoted, he would sit there all day, shaking up the pillows whenever it was necessary, fetching cool drinks whenever she demanded; whenever she asked for anything, he seemed to be the only one who could understand her whispering. Not even the painter understood what she wanted as quickly as Teo Busbeck, who, if one looked at him long enough, seemed to be absentminded and not really concerned about what was going on; but he probably adopted that attitude simply in order to be able to dedicate himself exclusively to Ditte's every movement and wish. Once I saw the painter put his arm round Busbeck's shoulder and pat it gently, not out of gratitude, rather more as if he were comforting him, and it seemed to me that Busbeck was more in need of consolation than the painter himself.

One evening Doctor Gripp, who up to now in his generous way had suggested a choice of maladies from which Ditte was to choose, came to the conclusion that she had pneumonia. Of course, he didn't deny that she also had some other illness, but he was now quite certain that her emaciated body was ravaged by pneumonia. He could even provide an explanation of how she had got it. She must have got it from going barefoot through the house, on the stone floor, in search of something to drink. So he treated her for pneumonia, forbidding her to get out of bed. Ditte obeyed his orders except on one point: once she got up and took out of a chest of drawers the shroud that she had made herself and an embroidered belt and a simple silver bracelet that the painter had made for her when they first became engaged. All these things she laid neatly on a stool, clearly visible for everyone to see, and she insisted on having them there beside her. I don't know, but I think the story that went around may be true: the painter, they say, went into his wife's room one night, looked at her for a long time, then went out for a moment and returned with his sketchbook and charcoal. Anyway, it's a fact that he made two portraits of Ditte during that winter. Whether he made them from memory or at the sick-bed, nobody knows. Both portraits are reproduced in the volume entitled 'Two', which is dedicated to Teo Busbeck. There she is, lying stiffly and severely, her face half in shadow, her mouth open as though she were uttering some demand, as though she were asking for something to drink – which was the only thing she was still able to think of and to ask for. Her body is so thin that the blanket looks quite flat. Her arms lie stiffly at her sides.

Ditte died alone. Since Doctor Gripp had diagnosed pneumonia himself, he had no trouble in writing the death certificate. It was snowing, but the snow soon melted. The death agony must have been brief, or at least very quiet. Sitting on his chair at the head of the bed, Teo Busbeck hadn't noticed anything. They washed her body and dressed her in the shroud and the embroidered belt and put the bracelet on her arm, and then the people came to pay their last respects. Nobody was left alone with the dead woman. In the background, under a shrouded looking-glass, sat the painter, and Busbeck stayed on his chair at the head of the bed.

So they came marching in and played their part as best they could. Hilde Isenbüttel came along in leaking galoshes, undid her wet kerchief, blew her nose, gave a cry that was certainly not premeditated, rushed back to the door, and that was the end of her visit. Old Holmsen of Holmsenwarf murmured a quick prayer, standing on the threshold, but not clasping his hands, just holding his wet hat by the brim and twisting it round a number of times, clockwise, roughly at breast-height, and when he had finished he walked up to the dead woman, took her hand in his, raised it a bit and then put it carefully back. Then, shaking his head, he went up to the painter, exchanged a glance with him, but didn't shake hands with him.

Schoolmaster Plönnies, on the other hand, first of all walked up to the painter and clasped his hand; then he walked, in a well calculated curve, I must say, and with an excellent sense of space, towards the foot of the bier: there this man who had twice been buried alive during the war, and so had been face to face with death himself, turned to Ditte and made a short, stiff bow to her. The warden of the bird-sanctuary, Kohlschmidt only gazed, as it were, round the corner and then willingly stepped aside to let Frau Holmsen of Holmsenwarf pass, who, even before she reached the bier, got down on her knees – she'd obviously misjudged the distance – and had to cover the last bit on her knees; then she got hold of the dead woman's arm and broke out into well-timed spasms of crying and sobbing.

Her lamentations nevertheless sounded convincing and there was nothing wrong with her high-pitched sobbing. When she withdrew, she did so shaking her head, just as her husband had done. And now Captain Andersen could be heard, whom the dyke-reeve, Bultjohann, had brought along in his carriage; he was grumbling and muttering about the beastly weather Ditte had chosen for her death.

'Couldn't the lass wait for spring?'

Since he had to be kept from falling down, indeed wouldn't have been able to get up again unaided, Bultjohann supported him, leading him to the house, desperately trying to get the photogenic old fellow with his silvery beard and the silky locks at his temples to put on an expression befitting a mourner. But the old chap was past mourning. Hobbling along, leaving small puddles of rain-water on the floor behind him, he entered the silent room, blinked his eyes, and asked :

'Where is she, where's our lass?'

Then he saw the body, struggled up to the bier, and stroked her cheeks with an uncertain hand, at the same time mumbling :

'Couldn't you have waited for the spring?'

When they drew his attention to the painter's presence, he said to him :

'Take it easy, lad.'

I should also like to mention my grandfather, Per Arne Schessel, the peasant and folklorist, who came in bearing that dried-up, sourpuss face of his as carefully as if he were balancing it on a long stick. He stopped right in the middle of the room, raised his head, and shut his eyes. He mimed emotion and displayed a sort of paltry mourning, putting his hands together slowly in front of his groin. What he managed better than any-thing else was an expression of morosity, which he produced simply by turning down the corners of his mouth. Before leaving, he raised his arms in an exaggerated gesture of helplessness and let them fall again, taking good care that everybody should hear the sound. And Gudrun Schessel? And the Rugbüll policeman? There's nothing to be said about the Rugbüllers, because they didn't put in an appearance at Bleekenwarf.

At first they intended to go there, then they changed their minds. They promised Okko Brodersen they would go there, but while they were in the middle of their preparations some visitor from Husum came in. They talked at length about the matter during breakfast, but when the time came to set out my father cancelled the whole thing. They had put out feelers to discover what the neighbours would think if they were to turn up there, but although they were given to understand that the neighbours wouldn't think about it at all, they finally refrained, after much rumination, careful consideration, and even after having decided that they would go. So they were never again to see Ditte's face, from which meanwhile the swelling had disappeared, so that, now that she was released from that fateful thirst of hers, besides its usual severity it bore even a ghost of a smile. It's hard to say whether they, or more precisely, all of us Rugbüllers, would have gone to the funeral but for Per Arne Schessel, who had been nagging them about it during an endless supper. It goes without saying that my grandfather had taken care to arrange his visit to Bleekenwarf in such a manner that he could drop in on us for supper or, as one might say, collect his dues.

So we were having sauerkraut and shoulder of bacon and two bowls of potatoes, and our folklorist insisted on having hot bacon-fat poured over the kraut. While we watched him gorging himself, munching noisily, putting chunks of bread on his plate and shovelling his food, he held forth, giving us the reasons why we must not be absent from the funeral: 'At the graveside nothing else counts ... in the face of death we have to ... when somebody's left this world we must ... beyond the grave there's no ... it always pays to make it up ...' He also mentioned the 'last lesson' and said that 'the last farewell' was something one had to take, and that 'the duty of the living consists in' ... and finally he added that: 'Anyone who shirks the last duty, even if he happens to be a policeman, will be ...' and so on and so forth.

He ate with great gusto and spoke at great length, and on

that occasion he also succeeded in producing an unforgettable remark: 'A person's kinsfolk aren't necessarily responsible for what he does.' When he left, it was settled that we were to go to Ditte's funeral.

The funeral was held at midday on a Saturday. It was the first funeral I was allowed to go to. I was so worked-up that I dreamed of Ditte the night before: the two of us were building a hill, a great mountain of sand-cake – working hard at it, but in quite a jolly way. We were carrying sacks of icing-sugar and emptying them down an incline. Then we dragged a sledge up to the top and rode down at a great speed; whenever we fell off, I licked the ground, and it tasted sweet. Ditte held on tightly to me, almost always succeeding in steering us safely past alder trees, their trunks glazed with ice. Our scarves flew in the wind.

One the morning of the funeral I was the first to be ready, and I waited impatiently for my father, who didn't seem to be able to come to terms with his clothes. First of all he put on his everyday uniform, then he irritably took it off again and got into his old-fashioned black suit, which had been tight in the arms even at his wedding and now was even tighter; and in the end he chucked this civilian stuff on the bed and, obviously feeling rather relieved, donned his walking-out uniform. He now looked, as Klaas once said, like a bobberjohn that's been given permission to wear his keeper's uniform on a Sunday. He didn't look dressed, he looked disguised, somehow put together and artificially arranged, and although even his everyday trousers were of a peculiar fit, the sagging seat of his walking-out trousers was something that had to be seen to be believed. But the tunic fitted, because it had been cut to allow for changes in weight and size.

My father stretched his arms energetically towards the floor and then went up to my mother to be inspected:

'Can I wear it, Gudrun, can I wear it at all? Can I show myself like this?'

Indifferently, Gudrun Jepsen looked him up and down, while taking her sedative dissolved in water, and let her silence be understood as consent. Then she went to the looking-glass inside the wardrobe door to tug at her black silk dress, which was at loggerheads with a woollen underskirt and her enormous woollen undershirt. They might easily have spent the whole day dressing up for the funeral, but fortunately they discovered something that turned their minds away from their worries about their own clothes : they discovered me.

'Why isn't the boy wearing his black stockings? What, no cap? We can't let him go in rubber boots, not even in this slush. If he wears a scarf, it mustn't show. And what about under-pants? What pants is he wearing? Let me look at your nails. He needs a hair-cut. You really ought to have sent him to the barber.'

They fell upon me, tugging and pulling me about, making me change things, turning me out according to their own ideas, and at about eleven o'clock they realized that they ought to have done something about me much earlier.

'Leave the boy the way he is, Gudrun, or we'll be late,' my father said irritably. So they got into their coats, put their rain-capes on, and stomped downstairs, where Hilke – I must men-tion this – was waiting for us in a state of excitement. Her excitement didn't go with her black stockings, black galoshes, and her black cloth coat. She was lashing the air with her leather gloves, which she had been given for Christmas, she was beating her own wrists with them, and hitting out at imaginary flies in the wardrobe.

'Something wrong?' I asked, whereupon she slapped me in the neck with her gloves by way of answer and drove me before her through the door, out into the snow and rain. From over the North Sea more snow and more rain were driving inland, a dark bank of cloud with whitish shreds hanging down. The wind instantly began to test our steadfastness, attacking us from the side. It tried to get under our coats, but since they were firmly buttoned up, it worked on our rain-capes.

It wasn't easy to keep one's direction, I'd like to point out, in that wind, and with the ground being so slippery; standing there, waiting for my father, who of course had forgotten some-thing, didn't exactly give one a break, either.

At last we marched off, Hilke and I in front, Herr and Frau Jepsen about five yards behind us, silent, arm in arm – a family convoy that one could take in at a glance, moving along the brick path towards the flooded muddy road, crossing a wooden bridge, and then across the fields towards the Riepen cemetery, which doesn't belong to a village called Riepen – there is no village of that name – but to Glüserup.

If an airplane had flown over our district that Saturday the pilot would have had the following aerial view : a smallish square, cut into two rectangles by a brick path and surrounded by a hedge with gaps in it here and there, and people converging on it from all sides, forming a star-shaped pattern, some of them leaning back into a following wind, sailing before the wind, others crossing against the wind or bent low, struggling against a head-wind, all of them moving over a darkening plain of dirty snow, meeting on footpaths and wooden bridges across ditches, now jammed together, waving and bowing to each other briefly, and then, in a new, larger formation, moving on towards a regular-shaped and doubtless artificial elevation of the ground with one single tall, long, red brick building on top of it. The pilot would also have been struck by the uniformity of those people's movements : they were all hurrying, but they all moved with amazing discipline, none of them breaking into a run, all moving towards an open gate by which two cars were parked, while the third one was just driving up towards it. Outside the gate a larger number of people were jammed together, and there they greeted each other at greater length; some of them set down objects they had been carrying in their hands – many of them were carrying something in their hands; they formed groups, talking, gesticulating, holding umbrellas over each other. From the air a great number of things might have been observed, but not enough.

When we met the Holmsens, Hinnerk Timmsen, Hilde Isenbüttel and Okko Brodersen – who was wearing his postman's uniform – my father whispered to us :

'Stay together, and God help you if I get any complaints about you.'

After that, he allowed himself to be monopolized by the landlord of the Wattblick Inn, who talked to him as urgently and seductively as though offering him a partnership in some enterprise he was about to start – as he so frequently did.

'After the war, of course, Jens,' he said.

Hilke was wearing her gloves, but she had pulled her fingers back inside them and I was holding on to the empty, cool glove-fingers. I stayed beside her, and I would have done so even

281

without any admonition from my father, because my sister had never before seemed so beautiful to me. Black suited her. The closer we came to the cemetery the more excited she became, looking around her as though she were looking out for somebody or wanting to be seen by somebody. Doing this, she sometimes stepped into a puddle, splashing her legs all over; she got splashed right up to the hollows of her knees, which were a bit too fat, and she covered herself with mud. But it was not only Hilke's legs that looked like that, everyone I saw was mottled with mud, and on Okko Brodersen the splashes even reached up to his hips; in that respect my father had come off best of all, which was probably the result of the way he walked.

More and more people joined us, there were more and more people we had to exchange greetings with; there was Karl Wilhelm Bühning, there was Jens Lampe, Hedwig Struwe, whom everyone simply called Mother Struwe, there were Anker Bülk and Detlev Hegewisch, there were Bultjohann the dyke-reeve, and Plönnies the schoolmaster; there was also Frau Söllring of the Söllring estate, mounted on her ticklish gelding, and Jap Leuchsenborn and Paul Flehinghus, Nansen's two painter friends from Glüserup, one of whom specialized in people moving along the road, the other in dramatic seascapes; there was also Frau Studienrat Booysien and Carpenter Heck, all crooked with gout, who had made Ditte's coffin.

Nobody would have believed we had such a vast population. It all thronged and shoved uphill towards the cemetery, a glaring contrast to the bleak landscape. Fancy if they had asked an entrance-fee! There they were, standing on the main path, standing in black groups next to the sagging mounds of the graves, standing in front of and behind the melancholy-looking chapel, under dripping alder trees and besides the wind-blown hedge. Captain Andersen could neither be seen nor heard, but Jutta was there, pale and attentive, and not far from her the fat monster, now squeezed into a dark knitted suit made (I fervently hoped) of some scratchy material. We had found a good place in front of the chapel, but gradually we were pushed on to a side path and came to a halt near a few desolate-looking graves with bleached wooden crosses sticking in the grey ground, with foreign names on them. A few crows flew towards the cemetery, but turned away before reaching it; that was all of our bird population that turned up. No red-throated thrushes. No magpies, no finches, not even great-tits. Hilke pulled me along a row of graves, past a young juniper hedge, and we slipped through the hedge and, though we were wedged in, now we came out again in front of the chapel, which had a tin weathercock on top of it, which had been pushed into a horizontal position by the wind and seemed to be strenuously looking down, as though searching for worms. The painter? The painter wasn't anywhere to be seen; nor was Teo Busbeck. Very likely the two of them were already inside the chapel; the door hadn't been unlocked yet. I don't know why they didn't unlock it, but a woman in front of me who looked, from behind, like a charred square loaf of bread, said to a knock-kneed, thin giant: 'If we go on standing here much longer, it'll be my turn next.' Everyone who could hear her words agreed with her more or less openly, only the knock-kneed giant, who could see everything from his great height, and who was clearly enjoying himself, didn't seem to have taken in those words of protest. Actually, his name was Fedder Magnussen, and if I recall rightly he was the boatbuilder at Glüserup.

Since I don't intend to make the square woman – and, together with her, that whole assembly of mourners – die of consumption, I now simply make Sexton Fenne, a chap whose bad breath could be smelt a yard off, open the door of the chapel, which was painted rust-red, and at the same time incline his head in a manner that made everyone feel they were being invited to step inside. So we shuffled inside, squeezing ourselves into the pews, which were too narrow, with seats that were too high.

Now I discovered the painter and Herr Doktor Busbeck, who were sitting in the first row next to the aisle. They both had their eyes fixed on a mountain of flowers under which here and there a bit of polished brown wood gleamed. Lighted candles were flickering in the draught. Pastor Bandix was standing at the altar, apparently contemplating his fingernails. There was a smell of fungus, mushrooms, chanterelles. Hilke had pulled off her gloves, she was clutching them, rolling them round in her hands, clearly no longer capable of raising her eyes, which before had glanced about so enterprisingly. I had got pins-and-needles in my legs, the way I used to get them on the benches at my grandfather's place in Külkenwarf. Why couldn't they shut the door?

A lot of people turned round, and so did I, looking at the door, which Sexton Fenne would have liked to shut but had to leave open, because he didn't want to lock out those mourners who couldn't get into the chapel and who were noisily making it evident that they didn't wish to be locked out. So the door stayed open. So Fenne gave a sign to Pastor Bandix, who now raised his face with the glinting spectacles, as though gazing at something on the ceiling, at the same time spreading out his arms. We rose for prayer, sat down, and instantly rose again in order to sing :

'O God, our help in ages past.'

Hilke sang eagerly, in a high-pitched voice, without looking at the words even once. The painter also sang, and so did my father, who was standing three rows behind him. The only person who didn't sing was my mother.

'I will trust in the mercy of God for ever,' Pastor Bandix announced, and when we had all sat down again he gave us his reasons for doing so.

He described a general, powerful, of course, cunning, of course, a man successful in his wars and therefore also wealthy, as it were half the earth already belonging to him – in Pastor Bandix's words : half the round world. Well, earth or round world, this general we were confronted with, whose identity was never established, he grew ever more sad with his every victory, with every conquest, and it even happened that he would fall into a state of melancholy in the presence of a messenger who had just informed him of some new triumph he'd achieved, simply, as you will by now have realized, because with every conquest the chances for new conquests became smaller.

Everybody now realizes that this general is very slow in subduing the last as yet unconquered countries, but although he cunningly spins out his last victories, he can't help one day having the whole earth or, as Pastor Bandix says, the whole round world, belonging to him. This general, when his spirits are at a very low ebb, consults his astronomers, and they are in a position to offer him new delights : they suggest he should devote himself to conquering the vast spaces of the heavens. The general is delighted, he is so attracted by this plan, so certain of his victory, that he informs the Almighty he is going to dispute his claim on the firmament. But it never comes to that because the Almighty, for his part, holds the opinion that the general has by now done enough conquering and it is time for him to prepare himself to die. But the general isn't at all pleased with this announcement, he has all sorts of objections to it. In Pastor Bandix's words : In his blindness he remonstrates with the Almighty, informing him that his own innumerable guards are quite capable of keeping Death out. And so the general is rather taken aback when, the very next evening, without much ado, Death enters his tent and has a conversation with him. He begs to be given another last chance. His request is granted. He has the fastest horse in the world saddled, and sets out for his remotest territories, which are in the Lebanon, with gardens extending down to the sea. But who is there, waiting for him in those gardens? Precisely – it's Death, and he apologizes for his premature arrival, then bids the general walk ahead. The general obeys and on this last walk even shrugs his shoulders, filled with superior serenity. In Pastor Bandix's words : a serene gaiety – because now at last, in the nick of time, he realizes how little all his conquests meant, and so he submits to the will of the Almighty.

Now Pastor Bandix paused, looked briskly and boldly at the assembled mourners, from left to right, from the front to the back, and when he flung up his arms and his forefinger pointed away past me, I couldn't help turning round, whereupon I recognized behind me the two dully gleaming leathercoats, sitting there side by side in perfect amity, their sleeves bent in exactly the same way, as if they had been posed by a producer.

'But love,' Pastor Bandix exclaimed, 'love never ceases !'

After this he lowered his forefinger towards the mountain of flowers under which Ditte lay, waited for a while, and then, when nothing happened, pulled his forefinger back again, nodded to the painter, and then addressed Ditte with the words :

'Now thy journey is ended.'

He made a pause. Now sobbing and whimpering could be heard, and a dark howling sound that reminded me of a fog-horn – which seemed to be produced by Mother Struwe. With a mildness that he never displayed during Religious Instruction,

Paster Bandix now reviewed all the stages of Ditte's life.

He turned her into a girl again, a girl in white dress and white buckled shoes. He conjured up the quiet, spacious house in Flensburg. 'Don't stay out in the garden too long, don't go down to the beach, you must take care of your voice, my child,' mother and grandmother exclaimed. Soon Professor Ziegel, the smiling, pompous singing-master, would arrive in his morning-coat, to accompany you on the piano that is tuned too high, and he has every reason to be satisfied with you, considering the handsome fee he receives for his lessons. And he is certainly included in the emotion that overcomes everybody who belongs to society in that poor provincial town whenever the little girl sings her little songs, on winter evenings, after dinner – why must Pastor Bandix make her grow, why must he send her to the Academy of Music, why must he give her the leading part in 'The Bartered Bride'? But he swung himself up higher and higher on the rungs of that career, mentioning small theatres and her friendship with the composer Friedrich Drewes, who wrote nocturnes and arias for her, mentioned the unceasing care she took of her paralysed brother, and then at last he brought in Max Ludwig Nansen and their first meeting in the Post Office, where both of them were asking whether money had arrived for them and both of them – as they had probably expected – received nothing but a shake of the head from the man behind the grille. Nansen could just about manage to pay for some coffee, and a week later they sent out home-made cards informing everyone of their engagement. He spoke of their wedding, from which both their families stayed away; how Ditte had given up her career, and about the long period of poverty stolidly borne, and the lack of recognition. Illness, too, was an inevitable part of such circumstances. The young woman wore grey clothes and aged prematurely – one does seem to have heard it all before – no doubt they also coughed in unison during those nights, though that wasn't mentioned, anyway, she bore their moves from place to place and their miserable lodgings with the same equanimity with which she later accepted the days of honour and reward, all of which for Pastor Bandix came under the heading of 'the heights and depths of an artist's life fulfilled'. 'To him you were what we all need and what so few of us find,' he said to Ditte, 'his companion in the days

286

when he was starting on his way, his comforter in the days of error and blindness, his helpmeet in the years of solitude.'

The whimpering now increased, and from outside a real fog-horn began to answer to Mother Struwe's laments with a snorting, mournful sound, while Pastor Bandix clambered to the highest point of that life-story, now speaking of happiness, of the 'happiness of a life that is shared', which needs must leave traces in this world of ours, even though dark spirits – he actually said : dark spirits – were bent on extinguishing those traces. With a : 'behold, you too have not lived in vain' he came to the end of his account of her life and suggested that we should now pray and then sing one more hymn.

And when we had prayed and sung a hymn, Sexton Fenne came in, followed by six coffin-bearers, all of them old men with chilblained hands and great black cracks on their necks, and we watched them remove the wreaths and flowers. The painter and Teo Busbeck led the procession behind the coffin, then came Jutta and Jobst, with Pastor Bandix and then some women I didn't know, from Flensburg. After that everyone joined the procession as best he could, wherever he found a gap in it or when, like Hilde Isenbüttel and Frau Holmsen, they managed to twist round and step out of their pew. My father deliberately held back, walking at the tail end of the procession, and as though that weren't enough, he lowered his face in order not to be noticed or at least not to be noticed at once. The two leathercoats tried to be even more inconspicuous by modestly walking right at the back. As the painter walked past us, his face was pale but alert; he was badly shaved and his skin was roughened by the cold.

I left Hilke and, overtaking the whole procession on its left, arrived at the open grave almost at the same instant as the men carrying the coffin. The head end of the hole was covered with some planks and it wasn't as deep as I had expected it to be; there was a little water in it, not ground-water, but melted snow. At the edges one could see some thin, whitish roots that had been severed by the spade; from the formation of the ground one could see the whole cemetery had been built up artificially, for the top layers of sand and clay went down only about two feet, and after that there came blackish-brown earth; one might in fact have dug deep there. The painter looked at me and I said hello to him, but he didn't say hello back to me. He was now supporting Herr Doktor Busbeck, who seemed to be dragged down by the weight of his wet coat and who could not get a firm foothold on the slippery ground in his galoshes, which were too big for him. At a signal from Sexton Fenne the coffin-bearers put the coffin down and passed ropes under it, keeping the ends in their hands, as it were, ready to lower it into the grave. But before that was done, Pastor Bandix raised his hand over the grave and let it flutter to and fro like a leaf in the wind : he was blessing the coffin, and his hand lingered up there in the restless air, only dropping down when he began to pray.

After the prayer the bearers supported themselves on the clay at the edge of the grave, raised the coffin and then slowly lowered it, and while that was being done the painter put an arm round Teo Busbeck's shoulders, pulling him close to himself so that their bodies formed a triangle.

Was there any incident? Any outcry? Any picturesque collapse at the open grave? However much that sort of thing may come to one's mind, I have got to make do without it, and I must also deny myself the pleasure of repeating vows, obituary speeches, any wild exclamation of longing, the sort of things that can so often be heard at open graves, especially if the weather is favourable to such utterances. For when Ditte's coffin had disappeared into the ground, the painter and Teo Busbeck cast a handful of sand on to it and then took up their stand at a corner of the hedge in such a way that everybody who had followed their example and thrown a handful of sand on to the coffin had to pass by them. And many people bent down, gathering up sand in their crooked fingers – although there was a small trowel waiting there to be used – let it drizzle down, or, if the sand formed a clod, let it thump on to the coffin and then they held out their hands to the painter and Herr Doktor Busbeck, some of them speaking a few words, and some in silence.

I waited for Hilke to take her turn, and then I followed through, dropping two handfuls of sand on Ditte and afterwards shaking hands with the two men. My father was also there in the queue, between Brodersen and Bultjohann, edging up to the grave. He too cast two handfuls of sand on the coffin and

288

after that – I shall never forget the expression of sweetish-sour impartiality on his dried-up face – he walked up to the painter, who faced him with the same tranquil attentiveness with which he had looked at all the others. There didn't seem to be anything in the air. It didn't look as if anything was going to happen. All there seemed to be in it was a brief handshake, at most they'd call each other by their first names in that faintly questioning tone : 'Max?' 'Jens?'

But as soon as the painter took the policeman's hand and held it longer than the others, one could see that some idea had come into his mind and that he was trying to put it into words – now, at this very moment, when everyone was coming up to him to express their sympathy.

'Are you coming over for a bit, Jens?' he asked in a low voice. And when my father, who seemed to have been expecting precisely this question, very hastily said no, he added : 'I have something to show you, Jens.'

My father hunched his shoulders in order to express moderate interest. 'What might that be?'

'The last portraits I made of Ditte,' the painter said without hostility, rather more with an expression of intimate contempt. 'If you'll come, Jens, I'll show them to you.'

After that the Rugbüll policeman no longer considered it necessary to shake hands with Herr Doktor Busbeck. He turned away, his lips tightly compressed, and with long strides he made for the main path, where my mother was waiting all by herself. Taking her arm, he dragged her along. Then, however, he suddenly remembered us; it happened so suddenly that when he turned round, with a jerk, he jerked my mother almost off her feet and she had to jump twice to save herself. Yes, yes, we were coming, we were following them; obediently I hurried along at Hilke's side, holding on to the empty fingers of her glove. This time it was my parents who walked ahead, walking in silence, now and then nodding hurriedly and absentmindedly to somebody, and the speed at which they moved was the Rugbüll policeman's admission of how he resented the incident. He didn't stop to talk to anybody, either at the chapel or at the cemetery gate, and when Captain Andersen, whom they'd just brought along in a carriage and were peeling out of a rug, called out to him : 'Is it all over, now?' he merely nodded in passing and didn't stop to exchange a few words with the old chap.

At a jog-trot we went across bridges and stiles, always across country, through hollows filled with water, and over fences. Once again the wind veered, the way it so often does in our parts, and came right at us. There on its snow-covered earthen socket Bleekenwarf lay before us, where the big coffee-table was prepared. True, there weren't any dishes heaped with Ditte's sand-cake, but there were biscuits, treacle-cake, walnut-cream cake, and many other things on all those tables down the middle and along the sides of the room. Those women from Flensburg had got it all ready, expecting many guests, among them, I dare say, us as well. But my father didn't cast so much as a glance at the place as we passed it. Hunching up one shoulder as a protection against the wind, he stormed ahead until he reached the lock, and only there did he pause for a moment and glance back, and we too glanced back, for an instant thinking he might have changed his mind and that he would take us back to Bleekenwarf to join the scattered procession that we now saw moving, singly and in small groups, towards the farmstead.

But he had only turned round to wipe away the tears that the wind had brought to his eyes; then he walked on towards the brick path and home. There was, of course, a lot we all had to ask and to tell the others when we had got into the house and shut the door, but he began to busy himself with the stove, furiously rattling it through, blowing at the embers and piling on fresh peat, making it quite clear to us that he was not in the mood for any exchange of opinions. When Hilke and my mother had disappeared upstairs, he ordered me to go up and fetch his everyday uniform, and while the stove was puffing out smoke and filling the house with fumes, he began to change. What a relief, what a blessing! His temper now began to improve, and he seemed to unfreeze more and more with each piece of clothing he took off and flung on the kitchen bench, until at last he was in such a good mood that, when somebody knocked at the kitchen door, he didn't merely call out 'Come in', but 'Come in, come in, whoever it is.' I well remember him standing there in his underwear as Okko Brodersen came in, waving a greeting to him and instantly going to the table, pulling out his pocket-watch and putting it down in front of him so as to make us realize that he had allotted a definite period of time to his visit, though without informing us exactly how much time he did intend to spend with us. After that the postman sat down. One empty sleeve was pinned to the pocket of his coat. He glanced at his watch, and at my father, then again at his watch. He must have walked across the fields just like us.

'You can't have brought us anything today,' my father said, now standing on a footstool and undoing the waistband of his trousers.

'No, not today,' the postman said. 'Today I've come to fetch something.'

'And what might that be?'

'You!'

My father staggered a bit in putting his right leg into his trousers, lowered them and aimed his left leg at the dark opening, paused and finally, trying again, succeeded in getting his foot through the left trouser-leg. He tugged at the trousers, smoothing out the wrinkles around his calves, got them over his thighs and his behind, and in this way the battle of the trousers was decided in his favour.

'And at what address do you want to deliver me?' he asked, speaking to Brodersen from where he stood on the footstool.

'We're all at Bleekenwarf,' the postman said. 'Nobody's told me to get you, but I daresay everyone'll miss you. Come along, Jens.'

My father made some adjustments to his garters and to the elastic bands around his shirt-sleeves, pulling them and letting them snap back into place.

'Better one too few than one too many,' he said.

'The two of you could have a talk,' Brodersen said.

'We've just had a talk,' my father replied. 'We've said all there is to be said.'

He stepped down from the footstool, went over to the mirror at the sink and, standing there, his legs apart, knotted his tie.

'The way things go,' Brodersen said, addressing his back, 'who knows how long it'll last, all of it? And on a day like this – you ought to ask yourselves, the two of you, what's to be done now. After all, it can't go on much longer.'

'Okko,' my father said, 'I'd rather not have heard what you

have just said. And if you really want to know what I think, let me tell you : I don't ask what good it does a man to do his duty, nor whether it's good for him or not. Where would it get us all if every time we did something we asked ourselves what it was going to lead to? You can't do your duty just according to your mood or by letting yourself be guided by caution – if you get my meaning.'

He put on his tunic, buttoned it up, and then went up to the table, to where Brodersen sat.

'There's been many a one,' the old postman said, 'who's saved himself just by not doing his duty at the right time.'

'Then he's never done his duty at all,' my father said curtly.

Okko Brodersen got up and put his watch back in his pocket, went over to the door, and there turned round once more, asking :

'Well, so it's no, is it?'

I could see that my father was weighing something up in his mind. He didn't answer, and even when the postman repeated his question it still took him a while to think it all out. Finally he said : 'Wait for me, we'll go together,' and he disappeared into his office.

'You grow taller every day,' the postman said, and I said something like : 'And you grow older every day.'

When Hilke came into the kitchen, to put the potatoes on, he said to her :

'I'll be bringing you a nice letter again soon. If it doesn't come from Holland, it'll be from Bremen.'

All Hilke said in reply to that offer of his was : 'I'm not expecting any letter.'

'The ones you don't expect are the best ones,' Brodersen said, and it was obvious this wasn't the first time he had said it.

My father came back with his rain-cape all ready on, still shining with wetness. He had put his cap on and squeezed his trousers into his high rubber boots. He was ready. 'Well, Okko,' he said, 'let's get a move on.'

'Do you have to go out again?' Hilke exclaimed.

'To Bleekenwarf,' my father said. 'I've got to go to Bleeken-warf for a short while.'

'I've put the potatoes on,' my sister said, and as always it sounded like a threat.

'I'm just going there to deliver something,' the policeman said. 'It won't take me a minute.'

'And if Mother asks where you are?'

'Tell her I've taken the summons to Bleekenwarf. I'll be back for dinner.'

13 Biology

Tetjus Prugel was quicker to resort to beating us than any other master, and he did it more effectively. Since those he would beat most ferociously were those who didn't pay attention – not the lazy ones, the stupid ones, or those who were slow on the uptake – nobody in the classroom dared even to glance at the windows, which all that morning had been shaken by the distant detonations, and nobody dared to follow with his eyes the airplanes that came roaring along from the sea, flying low – so low that one could recognize the British markings – over the dyke towards the metalled highway and there making a sharp turn in the direction of Husum. When the roar of the engines drowned his words, Prugel would look up to the ceiling with a sneering expression, waiting for the noise to subside, in order to carry on, effortlessly taking up his sentence again where he had broken off, never becoming confused about the construction. That squat, bald-headed man who went bathing in the river even when there was still ice floating in it and who could turn so red that it became quite cosily warm – if not throughout the school, at least in one classroom – this man saw no reason to cancel the last lesson; he insisted on giving his biology lesson, even though he had to start again and again because of the explosions and the airplanes roaring past all the time.

There we sat in our desks, our backs straight, our hands side by side on the slanting tops of our desks, our faces turned towards him, our eyes fixed on his lips, in awe and trembling, while we absorbed the wisdom offered to us. The natural history of the fish, or perhaps rather the reproductive system of the

294

fish, but that's not quite correct either; let's say: the mysteries and marvels of the fish's reproductive system. That's what he was going to show us in this biology lesson, on this hot day at the end of April, or was it the beginning of May, with the aid of his own private microscope, which he had brought to school. There the microscope was, all assembled and ready for use, and beside it there were the two thin boxes with their mysterious contents that were to bear witness to those mysteries and marvels. Heini Bunje and Peter Paulsen had been chosen to represent the whole class, to be admonished and to get three well-aimed blows of the ruler over the knuckles, blows that were almost imperceptibly administered. By these means an atmosphere of collective attentiveness had been created and was guaranteed to prevail for some time.

It would certainly be profitable to dwell on Prugel for a while, to describe his old war-wounds, or, better still, to let him tell the story of each individual wound – when in a good mood he would show us the bulge made by a pistol-bullet wandering across his ribs – it would also be instructive to pay a visit to his family, which hailed from Mecklenburg and whom he persuaded to come for outings on the flats in every possible kind of weather, wearing their track-suits, of course. But since I have no intention of making him unrecognizable by describing him too much, I'll confine myself to establishing the fact that he was our biology master and that today he was going to initiate us into the mysteries and marvels of the fish's reproductive system.

So he went on talking, while in the distance, so far away that it didn't concern us, an 8.8 gun and, more frequently, the 2 cm four-barrelled A.A. gun put a few words in. We had learnt to distinguish them by their reports and the blast they produced. Steadfastly he stood in front of the blackboard and would undoubtedly have made a good partner for a knife-thrower, taming us with his eyes and in a quiet voice insisting that we should dive down into the world of fishes. 'All these species,' he said, 'all these names, big and small. Just try for once, you blockheads, try to imagine that swarming life at the bottom of the sea: sharks, don't you know, garfish, mackerels, the eels and the lump-fish, the cod and, last but not least, the herring, that sparrow of the seas. What would happen,' he demanded, 'if the fishes did not go on and on multiplying? One by one,' he answered his own question, 'the species would die out. And what,' he asked then, 'would a sea without fish amount to? A dead sea, of course.' He then hobby-horsed around for a while on Nature's masterly plan, in which apparently everything, literally everything, had been designed and organized. He dragged in the example of the steam-engine in order to convince us that combustion is essential to life, he gave natural selection its due, and then he took a header back down among the fishes.

'Well now, these dumb fish – not that they're all that dumb – have sexual characteristics, sexual differentiations, sexual orifices. In the spawning season both sexes gather in fairly large shoals, in search of shallow spawning-grounds, near river-banks or along the sea-shore. They sometimes travel great distances, even, as you boys will certainly have heard, going up-river, at times – think of the salmon, for instance – overcoming remarkable obstacles. The eggs are then laid in some sheltered place where food is plentiful. They are often laid in clusters, and the male fish fertilizes the eggs with its sperm. Actually, the vertebrate fish' – Prugel stopped short, waiting, with ostentatious self-control intended to convey contempt, until the hurtling shadow of an airplane had raced across our playing-field and the noise had subsided – and then went on : 'and a great many of the sharks give birth to their young – but that's only a marginal remark, you blockheads won't remember that anyway. The egg : life is in the egg. It is strange that only very few fish take care of the eggs they have laid, much less look after the young when they are hatched. There *is* the little stickleback which does build a nest, keep watch over its eggs and even protect its young for a while, and there are species that swallow their eggs or carry them about under their gills until the young are hatched. But most fish leave the egg to its own resources, taking no interest in either the development or the care of their young. And the baby fish? You blockheads needn't think it grows inside the egg. It lies flat on top of it and gradually detaches itself from it.

'But this is something,' Prugel said, 'that you can see for yourselves in a moment. Today I have brought you the stuff' – he actually said : the precious stuff – 'out of which life evolves, and we shall now take a close look at this matter through the microscope.'

In the distance the four-barrelled A.A. guns started up, and their 8.8 big brother rattled the already cracked putty out of our windows. But Prugel was set on not noticing it. He went up to the dais, opened first his pocket-knife, then the two tin boxes, sniffed at the contents, lifted out some of the grey-green mass on the point of his knife, dabbed it on to little glass slides and then spread it out with his fingertip, that is to say, with gentle dabs he distributed it over the slide. Then he pushed the slide under the microscope and bent over the eyepiece, closing one eye and twisting his face up into a ferocious grin. He fumbled for the black screw, missing it several times, then turned it until he had the specimen in focus, and straightened up with a jerk that made his bones crack. He surveyed the class trium-phantly, exultingly. Indeed, he surveyed us sceptically, too, just as if what he now intended to show us was far too good for us, wasted on us. 'Stand up!' he commanded. 'Sit down! Stand up!' He made us line up – 'in line, you blockheads!' – pushing us and buffeting us around until we stood there in formation, straight as ramrods, in perfect order, in preparation for casting a fruitful glance upon the marvel, the egg, the spawn.

Thank heaven Jobst was the first, so he would be the first to have to say what he could see. Tensely we watched him crouch, timidly turn round to look up at Prugel and then, standing on tiptoe, from high above, bend over the microscope. 'Lower!' Prugel ordered. 'Closer!' And the fat monster now gummed his eye to the eyepiece, staring for all he was worth. His trouser-seat tightened over his huge behind, the round corduroy slicing in between his buttocks while he stared and stared, and sud-denly he said in a strangled voice: 'Roe, perhaps herring-roe.' 'What else can you see?' Prugel asked. And after intensive observation, Jobst replied: 'Roe – quite a lot of it.'

Since he thereupon received permission to go and sit down again, at least we knew what we had to say in order to get our-selves sent back to our places. After Jobst, Heini Bunje grasped the microscope with bruised and swollen fingers, undoubtedly still buzzing with pain, and while he was peering in, Prugel said: 'For once don't think of fried roe, smoked roe, or pickled roe. For once, you blockheads, try not to think about eating. Think of the marvel hidden in each of these little eggs. In every single tiny egg – an independent life. Many of these lives come to an early end, serving as food for other lives, and so on. Only the strongest, the best, the fittest, survive, perpetuating the species. It's the same everywhere, always excepting you lot, of course. Valueless life has to perish so that valuable life can survive and be maintained. That is the purpose in Nature's plan, and it is a plan which we must admire.'

'A tadpole!' Heini Bunje exclaimed. 'A teeny weeny tadpole!'

'Well, that's something,' Prugel said and corrected him: 'A baby fish, just about to detach itself – look at it carefully.'

'It's dead!' Heini Bunje exclaimed.

'Waste,' Prugel said. 'There you have the wastefulness of Nature. Hundreds – thousands, indeed hundreds of thousands of little eggs, all of it in the hope that some few will be spared to provide for the continuation of life. Selection, don't you know. And always the fight for survival. The weak perish in the struggle, the strong survive. That is the way it is with the fish, and that is the way it is with us. Get this into your heads: all that is strong lives on all that is weak. In the beginning all things have the same chance, each single egg, however small, holds and feeds a life. But then, when the trouble begins, the trash' – he actually said: the trash – 'falls by the wayside.'

After he had spawned this and similar great thoughts, he beckoned me up to the microscope, told me to take a look, and said: 'Now let's hear what our friend Jepsen can discover', at the same time stepping up beside me, the ruler in his hand.

No sooner had I bent over the microscope than he asked: 'Well?'

Hastily I surveyed the random pattern of little grey-green balls, some of them a bit squashed, which looked as though they were made of gelatine. I was just trying to think something up when the ruler came tickling the back of my knees and slid over the skin, painlessly, coolly up my thigh. But I did not withdraw my eye, I endured the ruler's explorations and searched for some sign of the promised marvel. Tiny staring fish-eyes, a tiny, transparent fish-body, the intestinal cord linking egg and fish: so much I seemed to have made out, but it did not seem enough to me. I wanted – well, I can't remember now what I wanted, perhaps the only reason I couldn't get a word out was that I was disappointed by what the microscope revealed.

'Nowt?' Prugel demanded. 'Nowt, eh?'

'Haddock,' I said at random. 'It might be haddock spawn.'

At this he withdrew the ruler and confirmed my surmise : 'Right, haddock it is.'

But his words received scant attention, for at the shout : 'The English! It's the English!', we all rushed to the window.

There in fact in the schoolyard was a dusty scout-car, the long aerial quivering, the somewhat unimpressive gun trained on one of the white goal-posts, and two men who looked as if they were English were getting out of the turret, having machine-pistols handed up to them. They shouted something back to their vehicle and came towards the school building, at the ready, keeping a look-out in all directions. They wore khaki and laced boots. They were very young. Both of them had their sleeves rolled up.

They walked side by side to the entrance, in the sun, past the flagpole, and I was just thinking : 'When are they going to look up and see us?' when they looked up and stopped. They drew each other's attention to the schoolboys up there with their noses to the window-panes. They consulted. Then they made up their minds to go on and vanished, diagonally under us, into the building.

We should have stayed at the vibrating windows if Prugel had not commanded : 'Fall in!' and, since we didn't move fast enough for his liking, wielded his ruler on our backs, slapping here, poking there, driving us away from the window and making us form a line from the dais down the middle aisle. Jobst, Heine Bunje and I were allowed to sit down.

The schoolmaster didn't ask anything like : 'Where were we?' but – despite the fact that there was an armoured scout-car in our schoolyard and Englishmen in the school – said : 'It *is* haddock's roe. Jepsen got it right. The spawn of the fish on which many other fishes feed. But what else can be seen in the egg? Bertram!' and Kalle Bertram pushed his ash-blond hair off his forehead and bent over the microscope, while all the rest of the class – except Prugel – were listening, open-mouthed, our eyes always shifting back to the door-handle.

Weren't those footsteps? English voices? It was Kalle on the dais, shuffling his feet as he strained to see through the microscope. Wasn't the door-handle moving? It *was* moving. Before Kalle Bertram had worked himself up to some utterance about the marvel in the egg, the door opened and stayed open, at first without anyone appearing, and just as it seemed it had opened by itself and Prugel was presumably on the point of saying: 'Jepsen, shut the door,' the two of them came in, both fair, both pale-eyed, both ruddy-faced.

They came as far as the middle of the side aisle, turned to face us, and surveyed us, as though out to identify someone out of the past. One of them said: 'Nix war, war finished, you go home.' I think we simply goggled at them. As for them, they scrutinized us, though not for long. Then their attention was distracted by the blackboard. One of them took the sponge in his hand, squeezed it out and then flung it back into its container. The other one made his way round the desks and, without speaking, with a wave of his hand, indicated to Schoolmaster Prugel that he was to sit down. Schoolmaster Prugel didn't sit down, and the Englishman didn't insist that he should do so, probably because he had now discovered the microscope. He went to the microscope, cast a suspicious glance at us, lowered his face to the eyepiece, then straightened up and, I must say with an expression of consternation, beckoned to his friend. In two strides the other reached his side, glanced at him questioningly and was referred to the microscope. The second Englishman also looked into the microscope and then all at once, as though he had discovered a mermaid that had slipped out of one of the eggs, or some extinct species of cephalopod, in short, as though he had discovered something that all of us, even the biologist Prugel, had overlooked, he pressed his eye to the eye-piece and stared into it. What was he observing? What was he discovering in the haddock spawn?

He did not let go of the microscope until his friend tapped him on the back of the neck, and now the two of them nodded to each other: they had seen all that mattered to them. One after the other they walked past the windows to the rear of the classroom, to our zoological cupboard: a cupboard with two glass doors, which was kept permanently locked – one of the keys having become a valuable item in my collection a long time ago. In order to get rid of the mirror-reflection in the glass, they brought their faces up quite close to it : the entire dead contents of the cupboard grinned – the stuffed crested grebe grinned, the stuffed coot grinned, so did the pole-cat that was running up a varnished tree-trunk, the stuffed hare grinned, the raven, the mounted head of a pike that lay there shimmering like parchment, and even the slow-worm in its round glass container – they all grinned, the latter despite the incredible contortions into which its body was forced. In silence the two Englishmen pointed out their discoveries to each other, even crouching down in order to look at a seal's skeleton. One of them tried to open the cupboard. Finally they nodded to each other and went to the door, and we all thought they wouldn't say anything or that they had nothing to say before leaving us, but they stopped again, looked round the classroom, and one of them said again : 'War finished.' Only then did they shove off.

And how about Prugel? Had he forgotten about us? Had he forgotten about the microscope and the marvel in the spawn? Why did his ruler not get to work to re-establish discipline in our ranks? Why did he put up with it when some of us stayed glued to the windows? I can still remember his hand crumbling a piece of chalk to dust. And I remember how he twisted his lips and put his head back, with his eyes shut, and how spasmodically his breathing came, and I also remember how rigid and pale his face was, so that he looked like an athlete in a condition of utter exhaustion. He seemed disappointed, flabbergasted, and furious. A slow, ebbing movement went through his body. He panted. And I can also remember him staggering towards his desk, pulling himself up on to the dais and letting himself drop into his chair, just about managing not to miss it. The whole class saw him hide his face in his hands, and he sat like that for some time. Then he sighed and began to rub his face with his hands, gently and as though he were rubbing off peeling skin. I can also clearly remember the moment when he straightened up as though he was doing it against some immense force that he could scarcely overcome, I can remember how he shut his tin boxes, shrugged his shoulders and then gazed at the class. He obviously wanted to say something, but he couldn't. At last he succeeded in saying :

'Go home, the whole lot of you.'

301

While we hurriedly packed up our stuff, he himself showed no sign of leaving the classroom; he just stood there beside his microscope, undecided, very much at a loss, letting us leave before him and not replying to our goodbyes. That was the way I saw Schoolmaster Prugel for the last time.

Now that he had set us free the corridor and the staircase turned into an apple-chute and we simply went hopping, rolling, sliding out of the building. But the schoolyard was empty now, the armoured scout-car was already on the tarred road, where it turned and moved off northward. They all rushed out into the road to watch the vehicle disappearing into the distance, and they were still there on the road hanging about in clusters, by the time I was well on the brick path, by now out of reach of Jobst and Heini Bunje, who perhaps didn't even miss me that day. So I got farther and farther away from them, and I didn't even want to throw myself flat on the bank of the ditch when some light aircraft came roaring along over the dyke, whizzing away over me, their propellers glittering like circular saws, cutting their way through the clear day. Only in spring do we have such days: clear, with just a few clouds hanging motionless in the air, days with a harsh light, when the north-easterly wind burns on the skin.

The front door of our house was open. Hinnerk Timmsen's bicycle was leaning against the wall next to the stairs. My father was in his office telephoning, shouting so loudly that I could hear him by the time I'd reached the shed.

'Arms to hand, yes, sir, all correct and in order, sir, the men have their instructions. We shall secure the road, yes sir!' After a pause he added: 'Order received and understood.'

I took the stone steps in two leaps and rushed into the hall.

'We've got the armlets, yes sir!' my father shouted, and he undoubtedly meant the pile of armlets I could see lying on top of our kitchen cupboard when I looked into the kitchen from the passage. There was Hinnerk Timmsen standing at the kitchen table, and he greeted me with the words:

'Now it's starting.' And in order to save himself all further explanation he just pointed at the weapons on the table. There were hand-grenades in brand-new boxes, a few anti-tank grenades, carbines and ammunition. I asked him who'd brought all this stuff into our kitchen, and he said:

'Nobody, Siggi, nobody thought we should have to jump into the breach.'

'From Husum?' 'I asked, but he didn't answer, he took an anti-tank grenade off the table, pulled out the sights and aimed it at our alarm-clock; then he aimed at the hostile jars of rice, semolina and sago, and soundlessly finished them off. He examined the carbines, read the trade-marks on them and said they were captured Italian stuff. He didn't sound very confident. He put the hand-grenades under the table and counted the ammunition until my father came into the kitchen.

'Just about six hundred rounds, Jens.'

'They're all on their way,' my father said. 'The positions have been assigned. Our job is to secure the road.'

'The two of us?'

'Kohlschmidt and Nansen are going to join us.'

'Nansen?'

'Yes. And now you'd better put on an armlet. The whole Volkssturm of the district's being activated.'

So Hinnerk Timmsen put one of the armlets on the sleeve of his saffron-yellow jacket, and he didn't do it casually, he did it with painstaking devotion, now thinking that he'd put it too high, and then again too low, and when at long last he was satisfied, I fixed it for him with two safety-pins. The thing was simply meant to identify him as a soldier. Once again that bulky man, who was at home in so many professions, cast a glance into the mirror to check the position of his armlet, and then he helped my father to make four piles of the weapons, meanwhile taking little sips of the tea that Hilke had made for him. But he didn't seem to enjoy his tea. When I mentioned the English scout-car that had strayed into our schoolyard, Hinnerk Timmsen at once gripped an anti-tank grenade and went outside to have a look round, but he returned after a short time, making reassuring gestures in all directions and telling us that all was quiet. Then he sat down beside my father on the kitchen bench. The two men waited. They were silent. After all, there was not much to be said now, for everything had been decided. Bultjohann, the dyke-reeve, had withdrawn his denunciation of Timmsen of his own accord – this was after a discussion at which the Rugbüll policeman had also been present.

I was standing at the window watching the meadows for

them. Who would be the first to arrive? So now our Volkssturm was going into action.

The painter was the first to come. I saw him coming across the meadows in his long, blue overcoat, his hat on his head, both hands buried deep in his pockets.

'Here comes Uncle Nansen,' I announced.

'Just about time,' my father said.

'Why,' Timmsen asked in a low voice, 'why do you want him here at all, Jens? Now when probably everything is going to be decided one way or the other?'

'Precisely for that reason,' my father said. 'Now that everything's probably going to be decided one way or the other, I should like to be able to keep an eye on him. It's better that way, take my word for it, Hinnerk.'

'Don't tell me you trust him.'

'That's just the point,' my father said, 'if I thought I could trust him there'd be no need for me to have him by me.'

With these words he got up and looked out of the window to watch the painter, who wasn't the first, after all, and hadn't come all by himself, either; he had stopped under the signpost saying Rugbüll Police Station, waving in the direction of the Söllring estate. There he waited, waved again, only more perfunctorily, and then walked towards Kohlschmidt, the warden of the bird-sanctuary, who was approaching. They shook hands. They exchanged some hasty questions. Kohlschmidt talked eagerly to Nansen, his hands spread out, trying to convince him of something or at least to make him agree with what he, Kohlschmidt, was saying. The painter seemed unable to make up his mind; listening to Kohlschmidt, he took his arm, at the same time steering him towards our house and up the steps. Even before their shuffling footsteps could be heard outside in the passage the Rugbüll policeman had prepared himself for their appearance, that is to say, he had taken up his position. Very erect, his legs slightly apart, firmly planted but also comfortably, though not too comfortably, he had placed himself in the middle of the kitchen, thus insisting on the authority due to him as an instructor of the Volkssturm, one who had spent many evenings training the men in their duties and who was now the warrant-officer in charge of the detachment. To

Timmsen, who was making an attempt to roll himself a cigarette, he said brusquely :

'No smoking in here.'

So he received the men in the attitude that seemed to him appropriate to the occasion, and the way in which he responded to their greetings left no doubt about who had to greet whom first here. He pointed to the bench, saying : 'Just sit down over there, next to Hinnerk.'

When they had sat down, he too relaxed, went over to the table and put one hand on the butt of one of the captured Italian rifles. He stroked the butt. So he succeeded in getting all the men to fix their eyes on him, in silence, tensely. Yet he was not the first to speak. The first one was the anaemic bird-sanctuary warden, Kohlschmidt, who all at once shook off the oppressive atmosphere, straightened up, and said :

'It's rubbish – what we're doing here is all rubbish. They're on the Elbe, they've taken Lauenburg and even Rendsburg, by now their spearheads may even be here. Everyone's giving up, only we're trying to start all over again. We're trying to stop them with a few nutcrackers and tin-shears. If there were any sense in it – but there's no sense in it, it's simply rubbish !'

He slumped down again and, still agitated, got out his short pipe, which was mended with a piece of black insulation-tape, and put it in his mouth.

'You can't smoke in here,' my father said, and he prepared to deal with what Kohlschmidt had said. But Hinnerk Timmsen was quicker. The landlord of the Wattblick Inn, who had never been successful despite his many enthusiastic stunts, didn't regard resistance as useless; now when everything had come to an end, he wanted to carry on. 'We owe it to ourselves, because it's easy to be reliable as long as all's well,' he said. What he was asking of himself was reliability, precisely when there was no clear chance of success. Besides, he himself had never given up anything without first having made a stand. And who was to say that it was all over? After all, one might set an example and one might make the enemy think twice by putting up some unexpected and tough resistance. It needn't go on for ever, but one ought to have a try. One definitely ought to.

Since they had started talking without having been asked, my father said nothing after Hinnerk's speech, merely gazing at

305

Max Ludwig Nansen in a way that was supposed to make him feel it was now his turn to utter his opinions. The painter did not hesitate. He said :

'Why should we stay at home? We can just as easily wait for it outside in the road.'

He said no more, not even when my father asked him to be a bit more explicit. He renounced the chance to clarify his position.

And the Rugbüll policeman? Naturally, he couldn't refrain from uttering his own opinion, since the decision as to what was to be done depended, if not completely, certainly to a great extent, on him. But he took his time, he was probably separating the pluses from the minuses in the personal declarations that the others had made, weighing them against each other, adding it all up. After turning it all over in his mind, slowly and doggedly, he declared that he had been given his orders and that orders were not given for nothing, they were simply to be obeyed, and they were to be obeyed literally. In the present case, this meant holding the road. 'Therefore,' my father said, 'we are going to hold the road and we'll start doing it now. Anyone who isn't yet wearing an armlet is to put one on now, and after that we'll take up our positions.'

After that palaver our Volkssturm took up position. Since my father and the painter were now about to secure our road, an admittedly out-of-the-way road, by no means one of great importance, but all the same one along which traffic could move, the inevitable picture entered into my mind : a dank hole in the ground just big enough for four men up to their chests in it, at its southern edge an earth-wall to be bespattered by bullets; that wall was hit by those bullets only at first, for meanwhile, after many futile attacks, yet another wall formed in front of it, a wall of motionless bodies, rigid hands stretching out towards the sky, and far behind it, scattered on the meadows, many tanks with torn caterpillars and turrets, some of them still belching out thick clouds of smoke into the peaceful evening. And hidden behind such smoke there was the amazingly unimpressive wreckage of airplanes that had penetrated into the soft, peaty earth, right up to the cockpit, after having been shot down. And I also saw myself carrying ammunition, rations and water, and like the men I too was wearing a fresh bandage round my head, probably one that Hilke had put on for us. Fantasies! Fantasies about another, different game of Indians and Cowboys!

Nor did they disappear when everyone had put on one of the stamped armlets, the arms had been distributed, and it had been decided where the English tanks and scout-cars were, as it were, to be held up. Below the mill – my mill – that was the place. From the artificial hillock there, where they intended to dig themselves in, one had a clear view of our road, right down to the main road to Husum, and from there it was also possible to defend the old lock, and the Holmsen's pastures offered sufficient space for destroyed armoured vehicles and airplanes. They slung their carbines, shouldered the anti-tank grenades, picked up the ammunition boxes and hand-grenades and set out at a trot, which was the only way they could move, considering the weight of the arms they were carrying. They left the kitchen and moved down towards the brick path, their knees already sagging. I trotted after them, while Hilke looked out of the window of her room and my mother looked out of the bedroom window, watching our departure, watching it with sympathy. Since the others, being so heavily loaded with all that stuff, couldn't wave back to them, I waved to the women on their behalf, and Hilke responded with a threatening gesture, my mother, however, not at all. That was how our Volkssturm went into action.

They began digging their trench close to the mill, after I had brought two spades along. They dug a hole in the ground deep enough to cover them up to their chest, without striking ground-water – which in our parts is quite something – and from the main hole a number of horizontal shafts extended, into which the hand-grenades, the ammunition, and some anti-tank grenades were put. It was instructive to watch the four men digging the trench. Hinnerk Timmsen was whistling silently to himself all the time, keeping an encouraging smile in readiness for all the others. Bird-sanctuary warden Kohlschmidt showed his exasperation quite openly and managed to go on cursing all through the digging, and succeeded in producing interesting variants of some of the curses he used. Max Ludwig Nansen, who did everything my father ordered him to do with a cold expression on his face and with ruthless attention to the job in hand, seemed determined to restrict himself to sign-language. Finally, any observer would instantly have identified the Rugbüll policeman as the man in charge by his thoughtful, judicious, and corrective activities, both while the parapet was being built and when it came to examining the field of fire. Indeed my father was totally absorbed in his concern for the defence-position at the foot of the mill and in his job of constructing and camouflaging it.

In three, or at the most four, hours, the four of them, for all their different temperaments, had succeeded in building a well-concealed defence-position that dominated the road and could be easily defended on three sides, only being endangered towards the North Sea, which seemed to be permissible, since nobody expected a sea-borne attack. And from the air? By the time they had covered the flat parapets with slabs of peat, from the air the whole thing probably looked like a fairly large but peaceful mound of cow-dung, lying there in the shadow of the mill. When all the necessary reconnoitring and all the inspections from outside had been satisfactorily completed, the men finally helped each other back into the trench, set up carbines and three anti-tank grenades on the parapet, and then, crouching alertly, began to keep a conscientious watch on the road in the direction of the main road to Husum.

Twice they had sent me away and twice I had come back again, but after the third warning my father gave me, speaking with a calm deliberation that struck me as pretty ominous, I knew what I had to expect if I returned again, and so I took myself off, decapitating buttercups on my way, made a detour and, unseen by our Volkssturm, tiptoed back to the mill and climbed up into my hiding-place under the dome, pulling up the ladder so that nobody could follow me.

Was there yet anything to be seen? Had I missed anything? I pulled the pieces of cardboard out of the window, threw myself on my bed, put out my aerials, and first of all looked down at the defence-position – the whole garrison was still there. Then I looked along the glittering tarred ribbon of the main road to Husum. Something was moving there, something was being pulled along there, it was a handcart loaded high, and around it, as if they were protecting the cart, half a dozen men. No armoured scout-car. No tank. In the direction of Glüserup there was nothing to be seen either, and the North Sea, which I scanned just to be on the safe side, was clear right away to the horizon. No enemy aircraft had mistaken the schoolyard for a landing-ground. Nothing stirred in Riepen cemetery. So there was just a handcart, no target worthy of the four men on guard down below, no reason to work up any excitement.

Even then and there I was amazed that they hadn't put a man up in the mill as a look-out, but since they had omitted to do that, I regarded myself as their personal advanced observation post, although I hadn't been appointed, had indeed not even been given permission to be here. I was acting as it were on my own initiative. After all, one can make oneself useful even without permission. I would have faced any danger and would have called out to them, informing them as best I could about the approach of a tank or an armoured scout-car, but nothing appeared, nothing either in the foreground, or in the background, so far as I could observe for a long distance. It was hard to understand why this was so, but nothing turned out worthy to be shot at. The skyline yielded nothing. The men down below me seemed to have come to the same conclusion, because after half an hour of conscientious but futile guarding of the road they took counsel together and clearly decided it wasn't necessary for all of them to watch the empty horizon all the time. So they agreed to split their small group into two smaller groups. Now only two men faced the skyline, while the other two – let's call them the guard off duty – sat down in the trench to doze, to gather new strength and so on. It was clear to me that my father and the painter formed one guard, while the other consisted of Timmsen and the bird-sanctuary warden. They were waiting. They waited behind their carbines and anti-tank grenades. If the round bushes over Söllring way had suddenly advanced upon us, I should have been able to raise the alarm, but the bushes did not stir. Or if the hawthorn hedge at Riepen had lain down flat on the ground . . . or if some unknown species of animal adorned with branches of birch had come rolling towards us. . . . There was nothing for us to do but wait. I had nothing particular in mind – all I wanted was to while away the time – when I began collecting curved bits of hardened putty and little pieces of broken glass. Having got together a small heap of this stuff, I

309

made the experiment of dropping a piece of putty from up where I was down into the Volkssturm position, and it struck Hinnerk Timmsen on the back of his neck. It wasn't that he thought he had been hit by a bullet, but he did think Kohlschmidt had pinched him, and he gave his startled partner such a push in the ribs that he almost fell over. Even from up where I was I could hear the brief altercation that ensued and which my father had to put an end to, probably by reminding them of the situation. And so now they again offered each other some of their tobacco.

I put one arm out, opened my hand, instantly withdrew my arm and watched the bit of glass falling, obeying the law of gravity, sometimes flashing in the light, and landing not in the trench but – as I had not in the least intended – in Timmsen's tobacco-tin, which Kohlschmidt was just reaching towards in order to fill his pipe from it. The amazed bird-sanctuary warden picked out the piece of glass, stared at it as if it were, say, a splinter of some meteorite that had just come down, then held it up to one eye like a monocle, surveying the almost motionless cumulus clouds, and finally handed it over to Hinnerk Timmsen who, with much head-shaking, flung it out of the trench.

I resolved to send a whole handful of putty and glass showering down on our Volkssturm, this time aiming at my father. But I had no time to carry out this intention, for at that moment I saw something moving in the landscape.

Someone hopped past the lock, walked along the ditch, turned sharply aside and came running towards the position, obviously without an inkling of its being there. It was Hilke. Without an inkling? Hilke was carrying a basket and a can, letting the basket swing in her right hand, the can in her left, so that their pendulum movement bore her forward, up the overgrown path to the mill, on up the lushly green mound and to just in front of the trench. If I had had anything to say in the matter I should have given the men something to eat earlier, but Hilke did not come earlier, it was only now that she handed the basket and the can into the trench. Then she wanted to slip down into the trench herself, but my father would not let her, so she sat down on the decaying cross-beam and waited while the Volkssturm ate and drank. They ate sandwiches and drank tea, and the Rugbüll policeman, wanting to know what was in his sandwiches and how much of it there was, opened his up – he was the only one who did so – investigated what was inside and then joylessly ate whatever it was. Hinnerk Timmsen considered it appropriate to make furtive but generally comprehensive signs to my sister, indicating that she should get down into the trench and join them, but she waved that off, smiling, evidently aware of what he was up to. The painter ate nothing, he merely drank some tea and smoked, standing, leaning against the earthen wall of the trench, all by himself. Kohlschmidt sat, munching away and at intervals giving vent to his resentment about having to be there at all. During the meal there was only one of them who kept an eye on the horizon, and that was my father.

I couldn't stand watching them all eating, I simply had to go down, so down I scrambled, popping up in the midst of them so suddenly that Hilke jumped and spat three times for luck, and Timmsen, the innkeeper, said : 'What a lad, as soon as there's some grub, he's on the spot. And where have you sprung from?'

'Up there,' I said, jerking my head vaguely in the direction of the dyke.

'Flew, eh?'

'Yes,' I said.

So they gave me some tea, which I drank out of the lid of the can, and I ate the sandwiches that the painter didn't want, and I also gobbled up what the bird-sanctuary warden had left over, because his sandwiches were made with home-made liversausage. My father made no objection to my eating with them and listening to their talk for a while. They were talking in the character of Volkssturm men, about a type of tank that one had to let come quite close, to get at the soft under-belly by the exhaust; they talked about the prospects for the coming night, about mist and spring frosts, and also about electric torches and how to save the batteries.

Only the painter took no part in the talk. He had of his own accord taken over sentry-duty. The other three men sat down on the ground in the trench, discussing what things they lacked. They wanted playing-cards. Had anyone any cards with him? Timmsen had an old pack in his jacket pocket : they had formed part of his 'equipment' in the days when he still had the big place and used to frighten off the customers with his card-tricks. All right then, who'll deal? The painter kept his gaze on the horizon, and behind him, at first abstractedly, now and then stopping to listen, but then becoming more and more absorbed and relaxed, they began to kill time with endless games of skat. They reproached each other and checked their scores and held post mortems: If you hadn't. . . . I should have. . . . So the last two tricks were actually. . . . You know how it goes.

Twice running my father played diamonds and twice running he lost. Kohlschmidt, on the other hand, twice made all the tricks, positively without wanting to, in fact he seemed to be furious about having won. I've never seen anyone win at cards with as much gloom as Kohlschmidt, whose resentment could only feed on losing; but he just happened to be lucky.

'Another rotten hand,' he said and simply laid his winning cards face-upward on the ground.

Despite all the tricks that he claimed to be able to perform in his sleep, Hinnerk Timmsen turned out to be a mediocre card-player. Anyway, they became so taken up with their card-playing that they forgot all about me, if not the enemy as well. None of them told me to buzz off. So I had no chance to observe the effect that a handful of dried putty and glass-splinters, thrown from the top of the mill, would have had on them.

At last, late in the afternoon, airplanes came over, some Spitfires and Mustangs flying over from the direction of Flensburg or Schleswig, swooping low over us and disappearing again over the North Sea. Even before they were visible, Timmsen opened fire with his carbine (taken from the Italians) – a protective barrage, as he later asserted in order to justify himself. Skimming the tree-tops, almost hedge-hopping, the planes came right at us, the roar of their engines becoming harsher, louder, more and more challenging, and then they were already sweeping over our school building, dipping, diving down into the wind-blown hedge of Holmsenwarf – hitting it? no, not hitting it – pulling up a bit but then, then all coming in as if to land, their shadows growing bigger and slower – they were definitely going to land – then all at once they gave up that idea, probably because all the men in the trench opened fire, Kohlschmidt included, in fact Kohlschmidt firing even more rapidly than the others – firing, cocking, firing again, without being able to take proper aim at their fast-moving targets.

The painter too? Yes, the painter Max Ludwig Nansen also fired, sometimes at the planes, but sometimes too, because he cocked his carbine too jerkily, into the mill-pond, sending up a few thin fountains and startling some wild duck, which rose out of the belt of rushes, wildly flapping their wings and flying off over the trench, their necks stiffly stretched out. The planes did not fire back at us, presumably having dropped their bombs and emptied their magazines, or perhaps – I shouldn't care to be dogmatic about this – they didn't notice our barrage, although Timmsen was prepared to swear that he had several times hit one of them, 'doing considerable damage', as he said. Was their intention to hit the dyke and breach it towards the sea? No, they skimmed over it and flew out to sea, dark streaks rushing towards the horizon, dwindling to mere dots, then vanishing. The Volkssturm could put on their safety-catches.

While they were gradually beginning to talk about what they had just experienced, I collected the empty cartridge-cases, counted them, and observed with surprise how many there were: I had not heard so many shots. The Volkssturm men agreed on one point: 'We should have concentrated our fire, one machine at a time, get *one* machine in your sights, that's what we must do next time . . .' And after this easily achieved unanimity and after some minutes during which all four of them kept a look-out, their attention again began to falter, they picked up the scattered cards, brushed them off, smoothed out the dents and, when Timmsen said: 'I was just going to play, and this time I'd have made mincemeat of you,' they were quite willing to let him have a try, and they squatted down on the well-trodden ground in the trench and cut.

'You want to go on standing?' my father asked.

The painter's only reply was a gesture that meant: Stay where you are.

I sat down beside the painter on the turf-covered parapet, not daring to speak to him, just following his gaze out over the countryside which he had painted so often: the heavy green, the glowing red of the farmsteads. Together we inspected the lanes and the main road lined with wild fruit-trees and at the same instant detected a horseman in the distance – he nodded when I pointed – nor did we fail to notice the lorry throwing up a cloud of dust as it travelled along the sandy track to the Söllring estate. I followed his gaze as best I could, our bodies turning this way and that in accord with each other, and sometimes he drew my attention to something that I had seen at the same instant that he had, and then I was the one who nodded. But I was the first to see Hilke. She came from the Wattblick Inn, going along the top of the dyke towards our house, and now and then she swung the empty can on her arm. At Bleekenwarf nothing stirred; but at Holmsenwarf old Holmsen was ceaselessly dragging coils of wire, obviously barbed wire, out of a shed into the yard, probably in order to fence himself in on his farm and so be safe from his old wife. Only rarely did the painter raise the policeman's binoculars to his eyes.

We waited; we waited until dusk fell, and still nothing appeared, nothing happened. The sun went down behind the dyke, just the way the painter had taught it to, on firm non-absorbent paper, in streaks of red, yellow, and sulphurous light; it sank, or rather, dropped into the North Sea, the crests of the waves began to flourish darkly, and in the opposite quarter of the sky shades of ochre and vermilion spread, not with distinct outlines, but merging with each other, indeed even sloshed on a bit clumsily; but that was the way he wanted it. Skill, he had once said, skill and deftness are no concern of mine. So it was a long, clumsy sunset, now and then with a touch of the heroic, at first localized and with its definite place in the sky, then painted wet on wet; that was what was going on in the sky behind the trench, stylistically quite impeccable.

The skat-players had now each of them had their good hand, and the post mortems became shorter and more casual. Hinnerk Timmsen asked at intervals if that 'body' was yet in sight; he meant his former wife, who was supposed to bring us food and drink from the Wattblick Inn. The painter and I told him we would let him know in good time. The mist, which usually rises at dusk on such evenings, didn't come, but as usual at that hour the cattle began to low. It began with a dark moo from an invisible animal far off beyond the skyline. It sounded like a question. Then over here, below our position, the cattle, speckled black and white, turned in the direction from which the sound

314

came, moved, twitching their hairy ears, but did not yet respond. Only when the distant lowing came again, one of the animals twisted its body and, laboriously jerking up its head and blowing white vapour through its nostrils, called back. There was no answer from far off, but now another beast fell in, with a loud bellowing note that started off somewhere near Riepen, producing an incredibly deep growling bass note, perhaps in answer to the far-off bellowing, because now that first animal started off again, and before the growling bass could answer, the cow next to us again began to low.

I didn't mind listening to the animals on evenings when their lowing could be heard from horizon to horizon, and so this evening too I listened to them and didn't notice that the painter had suddenly made up his mind to act. There beside me in the half-light all at once he supported himself on the parapet, scrambled out of the trench, dusted his coat, turned to the other men and said:

'Soon none of you'll be able to see a thing either – well, see you tomorrow.' And then he moved off towards the path.

My father threw his cards on the ground and called out:

'Hold on, Max, just a moment!'

But the painter walked on. The policeman, with a hoist up from Hinnerk Timmsen, got out of the trench. Clutching his cap, he started running in an oblique direction towards the pond, to cut the painter off. He needn't have done that, because the painter walked slowly. He caught up with him, put his hand on the other's shoulder and said:

'What's the matter with you? You can't just take yourself off like that.'

'It's getting dark,' the painter said, 'it's the hour when a man wants to be at home.'

My father went up quite close to him, facing up to his contemptuous gaze and bearing, and said slowly: 'You seem to have forgotten that you're wearing an armlet. Don't you know what it stands for?'

Without speaking a word, the painter pulled the armlet off and held it out to the policeman, who made no move to take it. In the end he handed it to me, saying:

'Keep it till tomorrow.'

'Take that armlet back,' my father ordered him. 'You're

on duty, you can't simply knock off when you feel like it, you can't go home when you like.'

'You can go on playing,' the painter said. 'I'm not interfering with your game,' but the carefully calculated note of contempt in his words didn't achieve its aim, because my father was so agitated that he didn't hear it. Or if he did, then perhaps he didn't see his chance, at that moment, to take in the meaning and give the right answer, because what he was concerned with now was preventing what was about to happen and keep the situation in hand by means of applying the prevailing regulations. For there were regulations for dealing with such a situation. He obviously knew these regulations and was considering them at that moment. He now used the following words :

'I am giving you the order now for the second time.'

In saying this he had made inevitable what was to follow. Timmsen and Kohlschmidt, who had up to now been observing what was happening from the trench, seemed to realize at this point that the tension was growing, and they moved towards us. And they were instantly rewarded, for now my father said :

'Everyone's got to stay at his post.'

'Precisely,' the painter said, 'at his post. And my post now is at home.'

Having said this, he was about to walk off, just like any man who has given his reasons for leaving. The Rugbüll policeman was of a different mind. He jerked open his holster, pulled out his service-pistol and aimed it at Max Ludwig Nansen – aiming roughly at his waist – and did not repeat his order. There he stood. It was twilight. There was nothing to be seen far and wide. How steadily his hand held the heavy-calibre service-pistol that had hardly ever been fired ! How little it seemed to matter to him, standing there armed like that ! He had used that pistol twice in the execution of his duty : once, when that rabid fox had got its teeth into the calf and wouldn't let go, and once later on, when Holmsen's cow got into Glüserup station and tried to wreck the time-table.

Kohlschmidt suddenly said : 'Be reasonable, man.' But it wasn't clear whom he meant. How long they kept it up, standing there silently, facing each other, not even very watchful, perhaps not even intent on finding out how far they could go, but calm and controlled, just as if they knew in advance what

316

the outcome would be, knew it because they had faced each other like that a number of times before. The service-pistol was there to repeat according to regulations, time and time again, the one sentence: 'I am ordering you for the last time . . .'

I held out the armlet to the painter in my outstretched hand, but he ignored it. He couldn't avert his eyes from my father, and now at last his body abandoned that strenuous attitude of composure and bent slightly forward as though under the pressure exerted on it by the weapon he was facing. The way I knew the two of them, I had no doubt that the painter would go, since he had made up his mind to go, and I had just as little doubt that my father would then shoot. After all, they were both Glüserup men. And the painter confirmed what I was thinking. He said:

'I'm going, Jens. Nobody's going to force me to stay, not even you.' When the Rugbüll policeman remained silent, he added: 'Nothing, not even the impending end, will ever change the like of you. One's simply got to wait until you've all died out.'

My father didn't answer. He simply went on insisting on having his order obeyed. He had given the order and he was waiting for the other to comply with it.

'If you're going, Max,' now Kohlschmidt said, 'then I'll come with you.'

He buttoned up his jacket.

'All right,' the painter said, 'let's go together.'

'You must see the point, Jens,' Kohlschmidt said to my father. 'We're doing no good to anyone by staying here all night. As though we could stop anything from happening! It's just a lot of rubbish going on like this.'

The Rugbüll policeman didn't seem to take any notice of the fact that now a second man had announced his intention of leaving his post. He merely kept his eyes on the painter; he was intent on having it out only with him.

'Come on, Jens,' Kohlschmidt said, 'don't go on like that, put away that thing in your hand.'

And with these words he made a movement as though he wanted to pat the policeman on the back, but then suddenly he seemed to take fright: he stopped, and then slowly, very slowly, withdrew his outstretched arm.

My father's lips moved, he was preparing to speak, and then he turned to Kohlschmidt: 'Deserters – you probably don't realize what happens to deserters.'

'Easy does it,' the warden of the bird-sanctuary said. He walked round my father and then took up his stand close to the painter, thus making common cause with him, common cause in rejecting what was demanded of them. Very quietly he said: 'Strong words, Jens. Perhaps you should rub your eyes and look around. We're going now. We'll be back tomorrow morning.'

'If everybody's taking himself off,' Hinnerk Timmsen said, 'then I'll be taking myself off, too. There's no sense in spending the night here, particularly if we're alone.' He stepped forward and joined the painter and the bird-sanctuary warden, thus making it clear that he too had made up his mind. But although they were all of one mind, had indeed said so, none of them was prepared to take the first step, actually less because they were afraid of the service-pistol in my father's steady hand, still there in front of them, than because they were still hoping that through being all of the same opinion they might succeed in persuading the policeman to join them and leave the defence-position together with them.

My father's eyes were still unwaveringly fixed on the painter, who now had the opportunity to say something, but who apparently didn't want to say any more. Even when Timmsen nudged him encouragingly, he refrained from speech – perhaps because he alone realized that my father had given up arguing when he saw that the others had also decided to go home. So he simply left him to his own resources. He just stood there with a blank face, and so the others also had to wait; in a moment the one party would turn its back on the other.

Of course, I could keep our Volkssturm together out there in the growing dusk, below the mill that had no sails. But anyone who remembers it all has to go about it just like a grocer who, when he weighs his goods, has to allow for a certain amount of loss. So that's what I'm doing; so I let my father cast one brief, alienated glance at the whole group and then extricate himself from the spell by ceasing to stare at them and walking past them with even tread, up the hill to the trench, which he believed is the place where he has been ordered to stay.

So I had no choice but to follow my father, who, without speaking a single word, helped me into the trench and pulled up a crate for me to stand on. I got up on the crate, and there was a carbine lying in front of me, but I didn't touch it. We both looked across at the men who still hadn't made up their minds to leave, standing there very close together, whispering. Perhaps they were now again of different opinions about the whole thing. But then they did walk off, and from time to time their footsteps could be heard in the distance as they walked together to the lock. Though only the bird-sanctuary warden had to go that way, they all went, because even now they didn't seem to be able to part for quite some time. No, they didn't find it at all easy to separate, and when in the end they did so, walking off in their different directions, now invisible to us, I counted on at least one of them, perhaps Hinnerk Timmsen, turning up in the trench and taking up his post again behind his rifle as though nothing had happened. But none of them came back.

So there I was, alone in the trench with the Rugbüll policeman, who now lit his pipe behind one hand, which he held protectively round the bowl, and then in his dry, imperturbable manner began to scan the roads and meadows and the rest of the countryside, which was gradually sinking under darkness and the mist that had risen as though to be of aid to the enemy. The cattle were silent now. They had lain down, and just beyond the mill-pond one could make out their elongated shapes. The mist rose, forming flat isolated banks that then merged with each other, rising higher and gradually, gently, making the farmsteads seem to rise, gently, the way boats rise off the ground on the returning tide. From far off, only now and then, explosions that sounded more like demolition-charges going off than like the reports of guns, sent their blast-waves towards us.

'Go home,' my father said.

'And what about you?' I asked.

'Go to bed,' he said. I looked at him incredulously, but he meant what he said, he even gave a slight jerk of his head in the direction of Rugbüll. So I climbed out of the trench and left the defence-position to him alone.

'What about you?' I asked again.

'I'll think of a name for it all,' he said.

319

'A name?'

'For all the misery. Yes, for this misery of ours and all the rest of it – I'll try to find a name for it.'

'And what about supper?' I asked.

He made a deprecating gesture, then seemed to change his mind, shrugged his shoulders and said: 'If there's a bit of the pickled herring left, you could put out a bit of it for me. I shall be busy here for a while.'

I didn't feel like going off, circling back and stealthily coming back again as I had done once before. With his eyes on me, I walked back home, without turning round, and even from the yard I could hear the short bursts of the telephone-bell. The telephone went on and on. Why didn't they lift the receiver? There was a light in the kitchen, Hilke and my mother had just been having supper there, and now they were upstairs in the bedroom. They must hear the telephone. All right, then, say they were pretending not to be at home. Let it ring. Perhaps Mother was sitting on her bed and Hilke was combing her gingery hair for her, then twisting it up and squeezing it into a shiny bun. That's what I thought to myself. Or she was dissolving a sedative in a glass of water, swinging the water around clockwise in the glass. Or she was massaging her, with those strong, deft fingers of hers. I wasn't allowed to enter my father's office by myself, so the telephone was no concern of mine. So I wasn't at home either. In the larder I found the dish of pickled herring. I took it out and put it on the kitchen table. I ate one of the ash-coloured herrings that were floating around among onion-rings and cloves, ate the shrivelled skin off another one, and covered the remaining two with a newspaper from which a man by the name of Dönitz looked up at me with an urgent, empty stare. I took a scrap of paper and wrote: 'Not to be eaten!' and laid a fork on top of it. Bread? He could cut bread for himself. I took the fish-bones outside and threw them into the dark yard, went upstairs and listened, vainly, at the bedroom door before going to my own room. I didn't even bother to let down the black-out blind, I just lay down on my bed as I was, in my clothes, and waited for him to come back.

I remember how I stared into the darkness, straining my ears, and suddenly there was Hilke playing the piano. She had never learnt to play, and yet there she was painstakingly playing the piano somewhere out in the open air, near the lock, and there were gulls drifting past overhead while she played and it was as though icicles, very small ones, small ones, bigger ones, were melting from a roof-gutter and dropping on to a sheet of glass, splintering, and, as they splintered, there was a feeling that they were coloured, mostly red and yellow, and then a shadow fell across Hilke, it was the shadow of an airplane flying nearer without any sound of engines, a rather large, grey airplane that tried to land near my father's defence-position, and after circling several times, causing an icy draught, it succeeded, coming down gently on one wing, and then the oval door was pushed open and men and women jumped out, all of them people I knew, first of all Captain Andersen, and then, following him, old Holmsen and Schoolmaster Plönnies and Bultjohann and Hilde Isenbüttel, and Hilke accompanied their jumping with bouncing chords on the piano which was reflected in the rising water in the lock, and it was her playing that made them all join hands and encircle my father's defence-position, a dancing ring, circling closer and closer, chokingly tight, their coats fluttering, but not in the wind, and in the end they were beside him and on top of him, they trussed him up, they lifted him out of the trench and carried him, with a sort of dancing step, up the green hillock to the mill, which now had sails, sails of dirty canvas, which were trembling with impatience, and they tied him to the sails and clapped their hands rhythmically as the sails began slowly turning, jerking my father up off the ground till he hung down, his feet pointing to the earth, and then the turning went faster and faster, there was a rushing sound, the centrifugal force intensified and his body flew out horizontally, and the shadows of the sails whirled over our faces, and there was a shadow-mill in the pond doing the same thing, and it all went on until the smoke rose from the onion-shaped cap of the mill, there was smoke coming out of the mill, there was a smell of burning in the air.

Then I jumped up and ran to the window. There was a thin column of smoke rising out there. Down in the yard, in the early-morning sunlight, my father was standing by a fire. He was slowly feeding the fire with sheets of paper, records he was removing one by one from box-files, and he was taking care that the draught from the flames didn't bear any half-

321

burnt paper away. He kept on gathering up scattered bits and putting on only as much as the fire could consume. As soon as the flames grew too high, he would wait, leafing through the papers, reading.

I stood there, watching, till he noticed me. Since he neither made any threatening gesture nor shouted at me, I went down to the yard and helped him, of my own accord, fetching back sheets of paper the draught of the fire had blown away. He seemed to realize that I was continually looking at him out of the corner of my eye, but for a long time he didn't react. At last, however, he asked; 'What's the matter? Never seen me before?' I didn't tell him about the mill and the airplane that had landed while Hilke was playing the piano, I merely asked : 'When are we going over?'

'That's all done with,' he said. 'All done with.' And he tore several sheets out of a file, crumpled them up, and threw them on the fire. He was grey in the face, unshaven, his cap was askew on his head, and on his shoes there were still some wet clay from the trench. I remember his sagging shoulders, his dogged movements, his hoarse voice. Anyone seeing a man like that instantly thinks : He's chucked his hand in, there's no future for him. One is shy of saying anything to him, because one knows all one needs to know. One leaves him there sitting on a chopping-block he has dragged along. One just looks at the back of his neck.

He left it to me to watch the bonfire. All he did now, sitting on the notched block, was to feed it with old, presumably obsolete papers, now and then reading aloud, indifferent, as if they had never meant anything to him. After he had burnt the first stack of files, he went into his office and came out with a new lot – these things mount up with the years, and he had never been able to throw anything away, he had always collected everything and filed it and kept it, as if it were all a record of his life, keeping it for the time when he would have to render an account of it.

He was pleased with me, with the way I watched the bonfire, keeping it low. The last time he went into the house, he came out with some books as well as two box-files, and a notebook and a small package done up in oil-paper and loosely tied with string. So that was to go too – the invisible pictures.

'All this too?' I asked.

Dully he answered: 'All of it. It's all got to go.' He began tearing up the notebook.

Now Hilke appeared on the steps. She came right out of the house, calling us in to have some tea, that's to say, she called out:

'The tea'll be stone-cold if you don't come in soon.' And after a while she came out again, this time coming across to where we were by the fire, and there she repeated her summons, without conviction, she just looked at me and suddenly said: 'I say, Siggi, your face has gone quite grown up, you look as if you were all of twenty-eight.' That's my sister for you: sometimes she talks about a person as if he were a horse. 'Shove off,' I said to her.

Then when she picked up a half-burned sheet of paper that lay at the edge of the fire, I took it away from her and threw it back into the fire.

'Run away and play by yourself,' I said.

'Play,' she said uncomprehendingly. 'What am I supposed to play?'

'The piano,' I said.

She turned to the brooding policeman and said: 'He's cracked – this chap with the grown-up face.'

By now I had realized that I wouldn't get rid of her unless I said something really offensive, and I was wondering what would be worst, when Hilke exclaimed: 'Over there, look! Look! Both of you – over there!'

We turned round and looked towards the brick path, and there was a green, an olive-green, armoured scout-car. There it was, its engine running, its gun lowered, and, looking out of its turret, there was a soldier's head with a black beret on it.

The angular, slanting front of the armoured car came pushing slowly past the signpost saying Rugbüll Police Station, turned in our direction, brushing against the post but not knocking it over, steering very close past the old box-cart and moving towards the fire.

My father got up from the chopping-block. Involuntarily he pulled his uniform jacket straight. Standing there tensely, not really uneasy, just tense, he looked towards the armoured car. When it stopped right in front of the bonfire, my father said under his breath, so quietly that I could only just make out what he was saying :

'Get rid of that stuff. Burn it all.'

How was I to do it?

I pushed one of the box files nearer to the packet wrapped up in oil-paper, doing it gradually, inch by inch, with the toe of my shoe; there was a little scraping sound, and a flat track remained in the sand, just as if an animal, perhaps a tortoise, had dragged itself along.

A shoulder appeared out of the turret, arms, a soldier beckoned to my father to come closer. The soldier asked him questions, to which my father replied merely with a brief nod. Now the box-file was touching the packet, and while the soldier was climbing out of the turret, while he jumped to the ground, I picked them both up and, walking backwards towards the shed, I let the packet drop, simply drop to the ground, and, keeping the box-file in my hands, I again moved forward, walked slowly round the fire and towards my father, who was now talking to the soldier.

The soldier had curly gingery hair and two gingery stars, if you see what I mean, on his epaulettes, and he wore a bleached canvas belt, with a bleached pistol-pouch on it in which there was a pistol of the same calibre as my father's. Was he going to stamp out the fire? Was he going to confiscate any papers that were still legible and take them somewhere to be deciphered? Was Rugbüll Police Station so important?

The English soldier took no notice of the fire. He paid no attention to either the unburnt or the charred records. Haltingly, but in German, glancing down at a slip of paper that he had taken out of his breast-pocket, he asked my father if he was Police Sergeant-Major Jepsen. My father nodded. Was this Rugbüll? My father nodded. If that was so, the English soldier said, then he must arrest Police Sergeant-Major Jepsen of Rugbüll. Forthwith. He folded the slip of paper and put it back into his breast-pocket. He made a sign to the armoured scout-car, well, not to the scout-car, but to the bright, shiny eyes behind the observation-slit which were watching us; then he gestured to my father to hop in.

The policeman hesitated. A few things, he said. He supposed he was allowed to take a few things along. The soldier thought it over for a moment, said something to the bright eyes beyond the observation-slit, turned back to my father, and pointed to the house. My father went ahead, followed by the soldier and myself.

The dread, the suspense, as we went into the house – I believed anything possible except this : that my father would pack and hop in and let himself be driven off without making the slightest attempt to escape, without putting up any resistance, packing his things without a word, all just as he was ordered to do. We went into the kitchen. There was the breakfast on the table, the teapot an invitation to sit down. My father went to the sink and collected his shaving-things from the window-sill. We went into the office, all the shelves now empty, the drawers of the desk open, as if they had sicked up their contents. The policeman picked up his dispatch-case, took out a tin box with nothing in it except a spare key to it, and packed the shaving-things in that. In procession we went up to the bed-room and knocked a number of times until finally my mother opened the door a crack; she was in her dressing-gown with her hair hanging down her back. Without a word she handed out two pairs of socks, a towel and a shirt. She didn't see either the soldier or me. We went into my room, my father leading the way, and I wondered what he wanted from here, but he only walked round the table, tapped the map of the ocean on it, tapped the bedstead, and then led the way out again and back downstairs into the kitchen. The soldier kept several paces behind my father, his fingers hooked into his washed-out canvas belt, and he didn't seem to be at all in a hurry. He watched my father pour out some tea for himself and, after a vague movement of his arm, implying what he was doing, drink the tea out of the thick stoneware cup. As he drank he observed the soldier over the rim of the cup, taking his measure, with concealed animosity. While my father was drinking his tea, I held his dispatch-case. Fancy being able to drink so doggedly and in such a leisurely way! Fancy being capable of pouring out a second cup, although the soldier had now set one foot on a chair and begun to tap his foot. When my father had finished the second cup of tea, he took the dispatch-case from me and shook hands with me. He called Hilke out of the larder and shook hands with her too. Then he went out into the hall and listened for some sound from upstairs, seemed to be in two minds about something, smiled rather wryly at the soldier, who did not smile back, and finally called upstairs: 'Well, so long.' He pulled his shoulders back; he was ready.

We accompanied him outside and stood there at the top of the stone steps, on a level with the turret of the olive-green scout-car, which had a picture on it of a rat sitting up and begging.

'I'll be back soon,' my father called out. 'Soon.'

Hilke was crying quietly, I knew that without looking at her, for the way she cried was like other people having hiccups. Now they were standing by the scout-car. The soldier took the dispatch-case from my father and jerked his thumb upwards. At that moment Hilke and I were thrust to one side, pushed back against the wall of the house by two freckled bare arms.

She had come. My mother passed between us, her hair hanging down her back, wearing her short-sleeved brown smock, her steps unsteady, but her flabby, yet strong body held very straight, her head thrown back. The way she walked, she reminded me of some proud, wicked queen – what story was it in? – anyway, her appearance had the effect of making the soldier prod my father and say something to him. The bonfire had almost quite burnt out. My mother stopped at the fire, waiting for my father to approach her, waiting until he had come quite close. She held out her arms, the way people indicate the size of the fish they have caught. She hugged him hastily, clumsily. Then she put her hand into the pocket of her smock and handed him something, something small and glittering, I think it was a pocket-knife. He took it, he made a curt movement with his hand, a sort of wave, as if he were answering a signal.

'Ready?' the soldier asked.

The Rugbüll policeman scrambled up in to the armoured scout-car, all the time looking only at us as they drove round the bonfire. And as the massive olive-green vehicle ground by, quite close to us, my father jerked himself up straight, straight as a ramrod – even at that last minute conveying to me that I was to hold myself straight.

14　Seeing

The entrance-fee was half a loaf. So with two loaves under our arms we were sure of getting four tickets, and we set out from Bleekenwarf, along under the dyke, cutting across the meadows in the direction of Glüserup, but then veering to the east, towards the scruffy copse that was already part of the camp, and right to the prohibited area, as they now called the whole countryside between Klinkby and Timmenstedt. They couldn't very well call it a camp, for there was none of the barbed wire that every schoolboy knows of, none of the hutments, watch-towers, searchlights, and none of the guards that go with them, who would have been able to command a view of the whole barred zone and thus control it.

In order to keep together something like six hundred thousand captured soldiers, many of who probably hadn't even cottoned on to the idea that they were prisoners of war, they had created a prohibited area. You can imagine them bending over a map : Here's the road from Klinkby to Glüserup, then we'll take in a bit of the main road to Husum and turn southeast towards Faltmoor, continuing the border-line as far as Timmenstedt, so the whole prohibited area will be surrounded by a continuous road, which we shall patrol with armoured scout-cars.

The war, which had gone so well at the beginning, was finished. Everyone coming from the north, everyone who had fled from the east, everyone who had made a successful retreat from the south, was picked up by the patrolling scout-cars and herded into the prohibited area. In this zone one was not merely able to move about freely, the soldiers were allowed to choose their camp-sites, lectures could be given, for instance about divorce-law, you didn't have to get a permit to pick your sorrel and the nettles that are so good for you, nor was their any ban on sing-songs, literary evenings, and theatrical performances. There was no lack of artists. The population of adjacent farmsteads was allowed to enter the prohibited area in order to see the plays. They insisted, however, on getting half a loaf of bread as an entrance-fee, as a contribution to the artists' keep.

Don't let's ask what Wolfgang Mackenroth's psychological evaluation of this will be – the fact that I had to pay for my very first experience of the theatre with half a loaf of bread, which, incidentally, was Army issue bread that some paymaster had helped out of the prohibited area and which we were now bringing back in again. Anyway, there we were marching towards the scruffy copse : me, Hilke, Busbeck, and the painter, who was carrying the two loaves in a cardboard box. Weather-conditions? Traditional cirro-cumulus. Wind : west-nor'-west, decreasing. Overcast, with occasional bright intervals. Perfect theatre-weather – not that I knew that then, but I want to put it on record now. We handed our loaves over to a paymaster, were counted and allowed to pass. Long-haired Marines who were playing ushers led us down to the front, quite close to the flat stage, which had been built in to the copse – firs, beeches, alders – and roofed over with tarpaulins tied together. Sitting cross-legged on the dry meadow, laughing, here and there eating out of mess-tins, there were something like twelve thousand people in the audience, many asleep, amazingly many of them with bare feet, cleaning between their toes. Again and again a pair of magpies flew towards the thin copse to find cover, but couldn't make up their minds to land, and turned away again. Curlews had long ago deserted the prohibited area, and the pheasants had also moved on, as had the rabbits – rabbits like peace and quiet.

Before the show started a man in shiny boots, with a puckered-up baby face, came out of the copse on to the stage, called for silence, and gave us one more of his talks. I dare say he was a paymaster, too. He really let go, talking about emotion. Round about me there were little slapping noises and muttered curses :

328

the midges and horse-flies had got going. Still, they couldn't hold up the performance.

Well, there was this man with a great fuzzy beard and an iron hand – having sacrificed his own, according to the play, in the service of his Emperor. There was a lot about how brave and noble he was, and all that, and about how he mowed down enemy knights like hay, and about how he was naturally proud of his wounds. It wasn't the Emperor he had anything against, the Emperor was his friend, but he couldn't stand the Bishop and the Princes, they were a pretty awful lot, and because he was a nuisance to them, it goes without saying they wanted him out of the way. His friends and all sorts of brave knights were able to prevent that for a while, but in the end he was had up for arson and murder and thrown into jail in Heilbronn, where the guard allowed him to sit in the garden in the sunshine. But it was too late. He died, even as he died lashing out at the horse-flies, just as the Princes and the ladies kept lashing out at them. Such things do happen at the theatre.

I was pretty surprised to discover how boring it was being at the theatre. I mean, the way they talked : Zounds, and Gadzooks, and Begone! Or : Unto Death. Or : Tell thy captain : I owe as ever His Imperial Majesty my faithful devotion. After a while I was paying more attention to the frantic slapping and cursing by the audience and the actors, directed against our bloodthirsty insects, than to what they were holding forth about up there on the stage. I can't help it, I couldn't join in the laughter, to say nothing of joining in the applause, when the chap with the iron hand at a certain point exclaimed : 'But as for him, tell him from me he can kiss my arse.'

The only one who interested me was a certain Brother Martin, an actor who came on in a monk's habit : he reminded me at once of Klaas – his voice, his movements, his way of standing there silently bent, it all reminded me so much of my brother Klaas that I nudged the painter and drew his attention to this Brother Martin. The painter nodded, as if he knew more than I did. Brother Martin didn't get much applause, whereas all the others could hardly get off the stage for all the clapping there was, and that went particularly for the women with the deep voices : they only had to come on or to pull the petals off a flower or wipe away a tear, and instantly there was a burst of clapping. And when – it was in the farewell scene at Jaxthausen – the magnificent hair-do of one of them slipped askew, revealing the neat parting in the short hair, the whole twelve thousand spectators went wild with delight.

Hilke, of course, cried as though it meant something to her, and afterwards the painter gave her a testimonial for being the only one who had understood what was going on. The theatre brings out such things in people. At first I thought it would be fun to creep round behind the stage into the copse. I thought it might be interesting. But the longer the play went on, the less I cared about what was going on in the shade of the beeches and firs. I counted the civilians, working out how many loaves they would have piled up to keep the ever-hungry artists going. Thirty loaves? Or thirty-five? Doubtless only the paymaster knew the exact figure. The Ah-me-ing and alas-ing that at long last – by now it was beginning to get dark – began on the stage sounded fairly plausible : for a certain Weislingen, a pretty bad lot, by now had a fairly swollen face, from all the insect-bites, but mainly the increasing lamentation was an indication that we were getting to the end of it. Yes, the end was in sight, for the chap with the iron hand made it clear that he was dying either of grief or of vexation, or perhaps it was an unfortunate combination of grief and vexation. I couldn't manage to work up much interest in it, and I didn't contribute to the applause supplied by the captive audience. I was just too disappointed by my first experience of the theatre.

I was in a hurry to get home, but the painter still had something to do. He kept us waiting, while he vanished into the copse behind the stage. The audience got up and began to disperse. Some of them winked or whistled at Hilke, some even asked her to come with them. And now it turned out that a lot of people in the audience had gone to sleep. So everyone just left them lying there; people just stepped over them. A lot of people were eating out of their mess-tins as they went along, talking to other people to left and to right of of them. A lot of people were barefoot, carrying their socks in one hand, their boots, the laces tied together, over one shoulder. There were even some people in the audience who were quite inconspicuous, going away without tempting anyone to follow them with his eyes.

Hilke said hello to a certain Laura Lauritzen, who, I happened to know, had diabetes. Herr Doktor Busbeck had a chat with Frau Söllring from the Söllring Estate; that's to say, he listened patiently while she told him what he had just been seeing on the stage. She claimed to know someone exactly like Weislingen, she considered the type not at all overdone. 'I assure you, Herr Doktor Busbeck,' she said, 'the world swarms with Weislingens,' and Busbeck made no attempt to disagree, for she could talk the hind leg off a donkey. What she said to me was : 'Well, Siggi dear, did you enjoy the play our soldiers put on?' and without waiting to hear my opinion, she explained to me not only what I had enjoyed, but the reason why I had enjoyed it. Thank heaven she soon caught sight of the Magnussen family, who likewise still needed to be enlightened about what they had seen on the stage. So we got rid of her.

Where was the painter?

When at long last he came back, his way of walking and the look on his face made it quite clear that he had learnt something he was in a hurry to tell us about. With his arms stretching in the air, his lips pursed up, clicking his tongue, he worked his way through the talking groups of people towards us and said :

'It's really him! Klaas! He'll come home tomorrow.'

We all wanted to hear more about it, and Hilke even thought of running behind the stage into the copse, but the painter pulled her away, repeating over and over again : 'No, not now.'

And he pushed and pulled us away and across the border of the prohibited area, past an armoured scout-car and over a foot-bridge made of tree-trunks.

'It is Klaas,' he said, adding : 'The boy's alive. Just think of it, he's here among us.'

'Was he the one in the monk's habit?' Hilke asked.

'I couldn't believe my eyes,' the painter said. 'But I wasn't mistaken. How did he get into the prohibited area? Quite simple, they picked him up. He'd twice tried to make his way home, and they picked him up twice, and then they brought him here. He was in hospital for a long time, I gather. His papers, his file, the file about his desertion, it was all burnt in an air-raid. Probably somebody slowed the case up afterwards when he'd been moved to the military prison, and after the liberation he walked from Altona, he'd have come all the way on foot but for the scout-car – and now he's waiting to be released. Since there's priority for the release of agricultural workers and artists, he's become an artist, which is quite a change for him.' The painter told us he had put in a word for Klaas and they had promised that Klaas would be released as quickly as possible – certainly tomorrow. Just imagine that. Klaas was home again.

On the way home the painter did all the talking, now and then interrupted by brief questions from us. We wanted him to tell us everything that had struck him during his meeting with Klaas, and if I wasn't amazed then, I am amazed now at all the things he had seen and told us about. The old man's joy was such that he couldn't stop himself from exclaiming over and over again. There was only one moment when he fell silent and became gloomy. That was when Hilke said she would move out of her room and let Klaas have it, because he deserved it.

'I'll begin getting it ready tomorrow morning, and when he comes at noon, he can move in.'

'You'd better wait a bit,' the painter said. 'You oughtn't to start organizing yet.'

'But he's coming tomorrow, isn't he?'

'Yes, he's coming, but first of all perhaps he'll stay a few days with us at Bleekenwarf.'

'Did he say that's what he wants to do?'

'He asked me to have him. He only wants to leave the prohibited area if he can stay with us. I'm sure it won't be for long. Just a few days. After all, he's got to get his bearings.'

What could he mean: get his bearings? How was one to explain that? Everyone I asked either thought about it for a while and then asked me how indeed one was to explain it, or they said: Just wait and see. So I could scarcely wait for Klaas to come home.

My questions didn't get me an answer from anyone, either in the beginning or later on. Nor did I get any answer out of Klaas. When I saw him again, after such a long time, I couldn't get anything out of him, because he was asleep. He slept in the morning and at midday, in sunlight and in rain. They had given him the unfinished bathroom at Bleekenwarf, and there

332

he slept on a bed made up on the floor. It's true they had removed the stepladder and the heap of plaster, the nails, bits of lead-tubing and cigarette-butts. There he was, lying on a wide mattress under the green-and-black striped rug that the painter had bought in from the studio. At times one could only see his lustreless hair, or one foot, or his wounded hand over which he had pulled a woollen sock. Since I wasn't allowed to go into his room, I often stood outside the window, standing there for long spells, my hands close to my face, and I envied Jutta, who had permission to sit beside his mattress, watching him, apparently having been told to watch over him while he slept. She brought his meals to him and sat there looking at him while he ate – half reclining, supported on his elbow – and sometimes she covered him up when he lay down flat again. She paid no attention to me, not even when I appeared at the window while she was busying herself more than necessary with my brother's clothes, for instance holding his trousers and his jacket against her own body before folding them up carefully. And even when Klaas slept outside in the garden or in the apple-orchard, or protected from the wind by the hedge, she would crouch there beside him, bony and alert, and wouldn't let me come near him. Klaas was there, and yet he wasn't there, he could be seen, but he was out of reach under her protection.

'Hello, Siggi,' he said to me on one occasion. That was all.

So there was nothing for it but to get used to his always being so tired; I used to go over to Bleekenwarf expecting to find him asleep, and I would find him asleep, and after watching him for a while, which didn't get me anywhere, I would realize it was no use at all and would take myself off in search of the painter, who couldn't tell me how long Klaas would go on sleeping, but who seemed to understand why he didn't want to do anything but sleep.

But even if I didn't get anywhere with Klaas, even if at best he would only blink at me or twist his lips in a brief and troubled smile, I used to go over to Bleekenwarf as often as I could manage – perhaps because I wanted to be there when he woke up at long last, but probably more because in those days the painter was just finishing his self-portrait, which he had started

333

a short time after he went off, leaving the defence-position under the mill.

First I would go to Klaas, who was always in the same state, and then I'd walk through the garden to the studio, to the painter, who would recognize me by my way of opening the door and would call out to me from the far side of the studio : 'Hurry up, Witt-Witt, come over here!' More difficulties, then. Differences of opinion between him and the colours. Dissatisfied glances. He was working on his last self-portrait. He had made himself his own interlocutor, and he was coming to realize that there was no agreement between the two. 'I simply can't see myself,' he would say. 'Nothing stays put, it keeps on changing too fast, I can't resolve the contradictions in paint.' All at once colour ceased to be 'amicable' and became a transitory state, with an accursed tendency to emancipate itself, he said. It kept turning into involuntary energy. 'Now just look at this, Siggi, try to describe this, that'll show you how you can't get anywhere with description, if colour turns into energy. Into movement. Into movement in space.'

I was sitting behind him on a crate covered with cloth, and I was following his attempt to 'get himself on to canvas' in a particular place, under a given sky, in a landscape through which Balthasar walked in his fiery-red fox-skin coat, rather subdued, in fact rendered pretty harmless by means of perspective. The Japan paper, saturated with paint, suggested fabric, and the face, divided up by various kinds of light, was reminiscent of a very thin transparent mask with the world showing through. The left half of the face was a strengthless reddish-grey, the right half greenish-yellow, the ground reddish, patchy. That was how he'd confronted himself. A face with two different halves, and the grey eyes, gazing from far off, through blueish veils, betrayed something of the effort of concentration. If now I say : the mouth was slightly open, as if about to speak, at once the gleaming white brow contradicts. If I say : the shadowy blue over the bridge of the nose mediates between the two separate halves of the face, then I must also admit that it can accentuate that separation. Nothing was unequivocal : neither the mouth nor the eyes, not even the ears, which struck me as artificial-looking, as though made of metal.

'What do you get out of it?' he asked impatiently. 'Well,

334

what do you get out of the picture? You must be able to say. If you reflect : not without speech. If you see : not without words. Well, then, what?'

I didn't know what he wanted of me. I didn't understand why he could not or would not come to terms with two different halves of the face, the reddish-grey and the greyish-yellow.

'Content,' he said, 'content isn't what you should get out of a picture. But then, what? No, Balthasar, the colour can't become texture. Think of the winter when the water-colours were suddenly frozen on the paper, when the snow bled them, when, in the thaw, they ran together. What happened? Did colour turn into energy? The same energy that produced crystals and algae? Moss? What do you think, Witt-Witt? Why can't we find colour for anything? Is it that we can't submit? Or is it that we can't see? Balthasar thinks we have to start learning to see again, right from scratch. Seeing – my God, as if everything didn't always depend on that!'

He laid two studies for his self-portrait on the easel, placing them side by side. He stepped back, and the tense, slanting way he held himself from the waist up was an expression of dissatisfaction and fault-finding.

'You can see it even here, Siggi,' he said. 'Too poor, too immaculate. This gleaming blue that seems to come from within, covering the whole face, doesn't leave any room for movement. Do you know what seeing means? Enhancing. Seeing means penetrating and enhancing. Or inventing. In order to get your own likeness, you have to invent yourself, over and over again, with every glance. Whatever is invented turns into reality. Here in this blue in which nothing wavers, which has no unrest in it, nothing has become reality. Nothing has been enhanced. When you see, you yourself are also seen. Your gaze comes back at you. Seeing – heavens! it can also mean investing or waiting for something to change. You have everything spread out before you, the things, the old man, all that – but they weren't what did it, unless you yourself did something about it. Seeing doesn't mean putting something on record. After all, one has to be prepared to recant. You go away and come back, and something has been transformed. Don't talk to me about registering things. The form must waver, everything must waver. Light isn't such a good boy.

335

'Or look at this, Witt-Witt, this little picture all warm and
sunny : Balthasar holding out a tiny mill to me on his outstretched hand. And I'm taking no notice of him. There you
can see : wherever there's someone else, wherever there's something else, there has to be a movement leading towards it.
Seeing's a sort of mutual swapping. What that produces is
mutual transformation. Take the rivulets in the flats, take
the skyline, the moat, the larkspur : the moment you get hold
of them, they get hold of you. There's mutual recognition.
Another thing that seeing means is coming closer, diminishing
the distance between. What else? Balthasar thinks all that's
not enough. He insists that seeing is also exposure. Something
gets laid bare in such a way that nobody in the whole world
can pretend he doesn't understand. I don't know, I have something against this strip-tease act. You can strip all the skins off
an onion until nothing is left. I tell you : one begins to see
where one stops playing the beholder and simply invents what
one needs : this tree, this wave, this beach.

'And now here : do you get anything out of this picture?
I had to divide the face, here reddish-grey, there greenish-
yellow. I don't know how else I could say it, but the whole
thing doesn't clinch. Looking at this self-portrait I could easily
say it doesn't concern me. There's too much missing. It lacks
its potentialities. That's the point : when you make something
– a face, a thing – you have to provide its inherent potentiality
as well. Some have done it in their self-portraits. You look at
the man's face and recognize the illnesses he's had, perhaps
even the financial situation he's in. Here there's simply too
much missing. It hasn't been *seen*, and so it hasn't been mastered.
And that's something else that seeing can mean : mastery, taking
possession. I shall have another go at it, doing it differently.
What do you think?'

Yes, Max Ludwig Nansen could talk like that too, at given
times, at moments when he was in search of something, thinking aloud. At such times there was no need to answer his
questions, for they were addressed more to himself than to
anyone else present, that's to say, me. The fact that he was so
talkative was perhaps attributable to the schnaps he drank,
diluted either with mineral water or with marrow-juice. 'Oil
thy speech,' he would say, 'and put down a dram.' The bottles

336

and the jug of marrow-juice were not in, but on, a cupboard, as in the old days the gin had been. Probably this was his way of making it not too easy to refill his glass. Or he wanted to have to earn each glass by making some effort. Or it was a way of preventing himself from drinking too much. For every time he got the jug and the bottle down from on top of the cupboard, there was a risk of spilling at least the marrow-juice all over his head; and the more he had drunk, the greater that risk became. The moment he had poured himself out a fresh glassful, he adopted a grieved expression, always making the same gestures in my direction, indicating regret that he could not offer me a drink as well. Anyone who came to see him had to start by clinking glasses with him : Teo Busbeck, Okko Brodersen, two British officers, visitors who arrived in cars with foreign number-plates. Oil thy speech. The only person he never offered anything to was Bernt Maltzahn.

I was sitting on the cloth-covered crate when Maltzahn came into the studio, a very tall man with sunken cheeks, his threadbare suit hanging loose on his bony frame. The painter was just thinning down the blues that divided his face into two halves. Maltzahn claimed to have had to go to Hamburg on business, so he had thought he might as well drop in. Under his arm he had a copy of the book entitled *Colour and Opposition*.

'I see,' the painter said, not stopping work, nor inviting his visitor to sit down.

Maltzahn said he had been turning this trip over in his mind for a long time, and he had been meaning to write, for years. There was something to be cleared up, to be discussed, things to be seen in the right light.

He was standing behind the painter's back, rubbing his chin with one forefinger, sometimes taking a few long-legged steps to one side. First of all he had a request. Had Nansen heard of the new periodical appearing in Munich?

'*Art and the People?*' the painter asked coldly.

Without showing the slightest embarrassment, his visitor answered : 'No, *Abiding Things*. It's called *Abiding Things*.'

Although he wasn't on the staff, he said, he had a sort of prospect of getting a free-lance contract. The periodical was a monthly.

'Never heard of it,' the painter said, just working away.

Maltzahn glanced towards the door, obviously thinking he would have done better not to come. But the difficulty was how to get out of it once one was there, especially having started on such a rigmarole. One thing led to another, and the most one could do was to try to get it over quickly. So here goes. The periodical would appear monthly, and it would be a first-class job. Maltzahn didn't merely know what he was talking about : he knew a thing or two more. The fact was he had heard of a series, a cycle, with the remarkable title *Invisible Pictures*. Couldn't he – he would really be very grateful – have a look at it? Might the paper – in principle, he meant – reproduce a sheet, or perhaps several? It would of course be a great privilege, blah, blah, blah.

He gazed at the painter out of restless, narrow eyes. A good deal would depend on the painter's first reaction. Nansen shook his head. The cycle was not complete. It has been confiscated, passing through a number of hands, and some sheets – actually the most important ones – had been lost. Although he had got it back now, it was impossible to show it to anyone, incomplete as it was.

This answer was evidently more favourable than Maltzahn had expected. He took some steps forward in order to draw the painter's gaze to himself, and at that moment Nansen began to talk again, addressing his self-portrait.

Was the editor of *Art and the People* not making a mistake in paying so much attention to him, of all people? Was there not some misunderstanding?

Falling back with a pained smile, Maltzahn said he was talking about a new periodical entitled *Abiding Things*. He mumbled something about its including all shades of opinion ... policy of catching up on all that had been missed during the deluded years ... that was the most pressing task. The painter nodded. He didn't seem to have anything against all that in general, but he had his doubts where he himself was concerned. The corner in which 'abiding things' were to be found was not one that he found habitable; there was too much light there for his liking; so he would prefer to remain in the 'chamber of horrors' into which *Art and the People* had once banished him. He felt quite at home there in the chamber of horrors, with no lack of friends. Besides, that was the place he had always wanted for himself and his pictures. Horror was not the least of the things in this world deserving to be expressed, and since he had so often tried to reproduce horror in his own way, he was a fitting inmate of the relevant chamber. If Maltzahn would be so indulgent as to let him speak a word on his own behalf : he was grateful to him for having granted him that place. He had been pleased about that all during these years. He asked merely to be left in the chamber of horrors.

Maltzahn heaved a sigh, twisted himself round like a screw and, nodding dolefully but not hopelessly, said : 'Yes indeed, I know, something of the kind did occur. It is difficult to understand now.' But it was quite right, he added, to bring it up, indeed he, Maltzahn, had been hoping that the subject would come up, this being another reason for his visit. He wanted to clarify the situation, he wanted to contribute to 'getting things seen in the right light'.

'Seen in the right light?' the painter inquired.

Eagerly, Maltzahn said : 'Yes, it's a matter of the way of looking at things.' Very few people, he said, had seen things in the right light.

He was about to go on, obviously having worked it all out in advance, but the painter was already talking again, in the same tone as before. He couldn't help it, he said, he saw himself just the way Maltzahn had seen him : a witches' sabbath in paint, an essay in the degenerate. That, after all, had been Maltzahn's view, that was the way he had put it – and what would be the result of trying now to 'see that in the right light'? For him this world was really and truly haunted, and if a man who painted pictures tried to extend his frontiers, he would inevitably cease to be himself. Adolf Ziegler, of the House of German Art, had never been able to grasp that, and that was why he had remained a painter of Germanic pubic hair, a truly national painter, of course. No, he would beg Maltzahn to go on calling him what he had once in the past called him : he had seen him 'in the right light' from the beginning.

Maltzahn produced a thin smile. Apparently he had been prepared for this. He professed himself delighted that the painter

339

had mentioned that ambiguous formulation, for it could be used to demonstrate what unfortunately very few people had understood : a witches' sabbath in paint – yes, indeed, he had said that, he had written that about Max Ludwig Nansen's paintings, he certainly would not deny that. But had it not been obvious what he had meant by it? Whom had he been attacking? The sentence as a whole read : 'We are surrounded by a witches' sabbath in paint.' 'We are surrounded' – surely that was clear enough. What he had meant by a witches' sabbath was what was going on around one. Nansen had found his own way of depicting that political witches' sabbath. And what he, Maltzahn, had set out to do was to indicate the relationship between the external world and the world of paint – by implication, of course, in discreet ambiguity. He still found it astonishing that this had escaped most people.

Maltzahn went on talking, talking faster, seeking to prove that there were, perhaps contrary to what one would expect, various ways of seeing things. He was obviously annoyed when the door opened right in the middle of his argument.

'That you, Teo?' the painter called out.

Busbeck did not answer. He came slowly nearer, noticed the visitor with a fleeting look of surprise, was on the point of going away again, and said apologetically: 'I've finished packing, Max. I just wanted to let you know I'm ready.'

'We have a visitor,' Nansen said, turning round. Now Busbeck scrutinized the tall man in the threadbare suit. He evidently had difficulty in recognizing him. Finally he asked: 'Bernt Maltzahn?' Maltzahn replied with a stiff little bow. 'That Maltzahn of *Art and the People*?' Busbeck asked incredulously.

'Quite so,' the painter said. 'My patron and anonymous defender, in case you didn't know that. He risked a lot, and none of us noticed, it now appears. We simply didn't see things in the right light.'

Maltzahn bared his teeth, raising one hand as though asking leave to speak, then shook his head and cleared his throat. He glanced from one man to the other. He spread out his arms, conveying : Do let me finish saying what I have to say. But the painter had no intention of listening to any more from him. Calmly he went up to Maltzahn, his face set, showing neither anger nor contempt, then indicated the door and, without raising his voice, said : 'Get out !' When Maltzahn looked at him blankly, he repeated : 'Get out !'

I shouldn't like to commit myself as to how I should retreat after being so curtly told what to do. Anyway, Maltzahn swayed, straightened up with a jerk, uttered the words 'Good day' in as staccato a fashion as possible, and left.

'Maltzahn – would you believe it !' Busbeck said.

'The rats are boarding the new ship,' Nansen said. 'You'd think they'd stay in their holes for a while, you'd think they'd keep quiet, play possum, alone in the dark with their shame. But you've scarcely heaved a sigh of relief, and there they are again. I knew they'd be back one of these days, but I never dreamt they'd be as quick as this. You can only wonder which is greater, their ability to forget or their utter shamelessness.'

He put one arm round Busbeck's shoulders and drew him over to his self-portrait. I joined them. The way they contemplated the unfinished painting was different from their usual way: they stood quite still, showing no inclination to talk. When their silence seemed to have lasted too long, the painter said : 'Well, you'll still have your room here. I'll see that nobody else uses it. It'll be kept just the way it is.'

'I'm leaving a cardboard box here with you, Max,' Busbeck said. 'I hope it won't be in the way.' He did not shift his gaze from the painting, did not even turn his face to the painter.

In an affectionate tone Nansen reminded him of an old agreement between them, saying : 'That's permanent, whenever you want to spend some time here – you don't have to write, you just come. Not that I can make out why you're going away at all.'

'It's all over now,' Busbeck said. 'You don't need me any more, and I want to try to make a fresh start. But you know that.'

'Well, of course. That's the way we are. All right, Teo. But you will come and visit me regularly?'

'Every summer, Max. You can count on that.'

'And what about this picture? What do you say to it? What does this self-portrait amount to?'

'I can't say yet, Max. I've got to get used to it.'

'So it's no good.'

'That's not what I meant. I've got to get to the bottom of what you're saying here. But I'd better go now.'

'We'll come with you, Teo. We'll see you to Glüserup – no arguing. Siggi and I'll see you on your train, we'll see you off, won't we, Witt-Witt? We're not going to be done out of that. Now where are we going to get a pole? We'll sling your cases on it and off we'll go to Glüserup station with it on our shoulders, without stopping once, if Siggi will carry that midwife's case of yours.'

I carried the leather bag with the snap-lock, which the painter called a midwife's case, the two men lifted the pole on to their shoulders, the luggage first sliding, then swinging, then hanging steady as the balance was established, and we set off along the winding track to the dyke, along marshy ditches all blanketed in duckweed. Maltzahn was nowhere to be seen. It was a good day for haying, warm, dry, as you might say flagged with blue. Over Timmenstedt way there were, in fact, some people out fetching in the hay : their torsos bending, straightening up, long-tined forks glittering as they plunged. We clambered up the dyke with all the luggage. One last time the painter asked : 'Won't you change your mind and stay, Teo?' and Busbeck, his face turned towards the sea, said : 'I'll be back, Max, but at the moment it's better this way. Believe me.'

I ran ahead. It was a real swallows' day, a day of diving, swept-back wings, of arrowy flight over the hot sand, of thin screeching whenever some birds' track converged on another, to slice away only at the last moment. They came shooting over the meadows, again and again almost grazing the dyke, again and again borne up swiftly by sudden bursts of wind from the sea, steeply into the sky, hissingly down again.

'We'll do it nicely,' the painter said. 'You needn't keep on looking at your watch, Teo.'

All at once they halted and set the luggage down. They turned to each other, turned to the peninsula.

'Can you see what I see?'

'Over to the left in the dip down by the water?'

'Don't you see?'

'You mean Jutta?'

'Yes, Jutta – and who's that lying beside her?'

'Klaas?'

342

'Klaas – as large as life.'

So Klaas had woken up at last; at long last he had pulled himself together and left the shelter of Bleekenwarf. He was lying on his face in the sand, Jutta kneeling beside him in her tight, scruffy bathing suit, which was darned under the arms and over her hard little bottom. Klaas had taken off his shirt and rolled up his trousers and underpants, so high that it looked as if he had dirty-white turn-ups round his calves. His dull, furry hair stuck up over the edge of the dip in the sand, and his half-boots stood there, their uppers drooping sideways like two tired creatures of some alien order. Jutta was massaging his back, rubbing him with something, swinging forwards and then backwards, forwards and then backwards, now and then slapping his shoulder-blades. Whenever he raised one leg she forced it down into the sand, and whenever he tried to lift his head, she seized him by the back of his neck, pretending to strangle him.

'Shall I call out to them?' I asked. 'Shall I go and get them?'

'No,' Busbeck said. 'I said goodbye to them in the garden. Let them be.'

Now Jutta threw herself face down in the sand and deftly slipped her shoulder-straps off her shoulders. Klaas sat up, obviously rather dazed, and it was a moment before he found the bottle of oil. He splashed it all over her back, wiped his hands and was about to begin massaging her back, when he suddenly stopped and glanced down at Jutta, his head on one side. Lying there, all relaxed, she probably asked: 'Well, why don't you get on with it?' So he began rubbing the oil into her skin, rather mechanically, you might say, not taking any interest in what he was doing: for while he rubbed away, he was gazing out over the North Sea and along the hot beach. He could not fail to see us.

He waved, prodded her, pointed towards us. Both of them waved. We waved back. We all stayed where we were. Then we picked up the luggage and now I let the two men go ahead. From time to time they had to change step in order to steady the dangling luggage, which now and then seemed to come alive, lashing out to left and right.

'Thank God the boy has come through.'

'Yes, thank God.'

By now Glüserup was in sight, in fact doubly so on this

343

shimmering day: the second Glüserup seemed to hang upside down in the air as in a mirror, complete with the dusty white sheds of the cement-factory, the water-tower, and the rusty gas-meters.

'There's no fun, Max.'

'What do you mean?'

'This countryside of yours doesn't know what fun is, not even on a day like this. It's always so solemn, even when the sun is shining. There's this austerity hanging over everything.'

'Have you found it hard to bear?'

'One always feels one's under some obligation.'

'Obligation? What do you mean?'

'I don't know. Perhaps it's a matter of seriousness, seriousness and taciturnity. Even at noon it's all uncanny. Sometimes I haven't been able to help thinking that this countryside here has no surface, only . . .'

'Only what?'

'I don't know how to put it: the depth of it – it's got nothing but this baleful depth, and everything that's down there is a threat to you.'

'So you regard it as something baleful, Teo?'

'What I mean is simply there's so much that's human in surfaces.'

'I know what you mean, Teo, but if it's really like that, oughtn't we to try to make it habitable – this countryside, I mean?'

'I know there's this uneasiness, but what makes everything so uneasy is moods – perhaps this whole countryside consists of nothing but moods, and anyone who knows and understands it all is perhaps less disconcerted by it.'

'Perhaps we have to learn to see it.'

They went on talking like this while we walked along the top of the dyke. It was their way of saying goodbye to each other. One had the impression that they didn't want to leave anything unsaid. They went on talking, and very likely they hadn't yet noticed Hinnerk Timmsen standing there outside the Wattblick Inn, his hands on his hips, looking at them. All the windows of the inn were open and hooked back to the wall; on the white flagpole Timmsen's private pennant was fluttering in the breeze, the two crossed keys to which there was allegedly no lock. The wooden ladder on the pavement looked scrubbed and lay there bleaching in the sun. Does anybody think the inn-keeper bothered to take even a single step towards us? There he stood, grinning, waiting for us to come towards him, and then he stopped our procession; more precisely, he didn't just stop us, he tried to divert us from our road and make us walk into the Wattblick. But Nansen and Busbeck just put the luggage down. They stopped, and Busbeck, pulling out his watch, said:

'We mustn't miss the train, Hinnerk.. There's only one non-stop train to Hamburg.'

'Just a drop, just one for the road, after all these years,' Timmsen said. 'It's all ready, just waiting for us.'

He put his head inside through the window, clapped his hands, and there was Johanna in a white apron, carrying a tray of tall glasses filled to the brim, a slice of lemon floating in each of them.

'What's this?'

'You just try it.'

'Nothing for Siggi?'

'You're quite right. Johanna, a lemonade for the boy.'

We clinked glasses, drank to a good journey and a happy return, and Nansen and Busbeck liked the stuff they had been given, obviously. They asked:

'Where do you get this gin, Hinnerk?'

'What do you think we're going on airing the place for like mad? We're having lots of victory-celebrations here, they come from Glüserup in their cars to celebrate. All we have to provide are the premises, that's why we air the place. You should have been here just once,' Timmsen said, and drank as if wanting to enjoy the drink on behalf of us all. 'You just wait and see, I'll soon be having something even better, you must come and try it. And, Max, there were some fellows here this morning wanting to know where you live. They came in a jeep. They didn't know enough German, and I don't know enough English, but I could make out they wanted you to draw their portraits, or something. Just like that major, you know. What could I do? So I gave some directions how to get to Glüserup.'

'I am sure they'll find the way there,' the painter said and put his glass on the bench under the window, looking at us in a manner that implied we were to put our glasses down there, too. Then he thanked Timmsen, patting him a few times on the shoulder, and while Busbeck and Timmsen were shaking hands he said: 'Come on, you two, hurry up. After all, it's not for ever.'

'So you're sure you won't come in for a while?' the innkeeper asked, and Busbeck said:

'I'm afraid if we do, we'll miss the train.'

There was yet another leave-taking and all the usual things were said.

'Come back soon,' and 'Keep smiling,' and 'I hope you won't stay away very long.'

We picked up the luggage and went on our way. Standing there on his footpath Timmsen waved to us, and Johanna waved from the terrace.

'A few more leave-takings like that,' the painter said, 'and you'll have to stay, Teo.'

'We'll still make it,' Busbeck said.

I suggested they should take a short cut across to the railway embankment, along the embankment and over the iron bridge. They agreed. So we went down the dyke, swaying, and walked across the sun-warmed meadows.

'Don't forget the flowers,' Busbeck said. 'On her birthday, on the 8th of September.'

'Do you expect me to forget when Ditte's birthday is?'

'No, of course not, I just wanted to mention it.'

We climbed up the embankment and walked that well-trodden path which isn't used only by the railway-men, but by almost everyone who has to catch a train.

I threw gravel into the dark, wide ditch that lay there in the brooding heat. I banged a stick along the railing of the iron bridge. By now I could make out the face of the station clock, criss-crossed with sticking-plaster because the glass was cracked.

'There you are, we'll do it quite comfortably. We'll even manage to get you your ticket,' the painter said.

'I should hope so,' Busbeck said.

Here now is Glüserup station: four tracks, two platforms, a sooty repair-shop, the box-shaped main building built of red brick, a few sidings, a number of more or less burnt-out or damaged trucks and wagons. On some of them it said : Transport For Victory. In the main building there's the ticket-office, other offices, left-luggage office, lavatories and a waiting-room. If you removed the tables, chairs and benches out of the waiting-room it would make a good-sized gym-hall; since its height, up to the whitewashed ceiling, is over thirty feet, it follows that one could even play ball-games in there.

The barrier is closed by means of a chain hanging down to the level of one's knees, and only people in uniform are allowed to climb over it. Crossing the lines is forbidden, and in order to get from one platform to the other one has to use a boarded-up wooden footbridge, the inner walls of which are scribbled over with obscene drawings and initials of travellers resentful about unduly long delays. Behind the window-pane of the ticket-office one can see some uniformed officials sitting at desks and very busy with something; it's quite useless to knock at the window if the cardboard notice saying 'Closed' is hanging behind it. The enamelled plate 'Please use the spittoons' has lost its justification because there aren't any spittoons any more – presumably they were withdrawn because there was no longer any demand for them. The floor of the building is made of fluted floor-tiles, one of which records the year in which the place was built : one thousand nine hundred and four.

When we reached the station, the ticket-office was already open and passengers were being let on to the platforms. We had to cross over to platform two, and there we stood in the sun, dumbfounded, together with what seemed to be the entire population of Glüserup, who had, it seemed, all decided to leave the town. There they all sat on baskets and rucksacks, on cardboard boxes, suitcases and crates, or they were busy dragging along sacks, pendulum clocks, bedding, and antlers, doggedly and imperceptibly making their way towards the edge of the platform in order to be in place for the rush on the train that was to follow.

'As you can see for yourself, Teo, you aren't going to have a solitary journey,' the painter said.

'So it seems,' Busbeck said.

How patiently the people managed to sit there! Some of them seemed to have fallen asleep on top of their shapeless luggage. I was struck by the presence of a great number of ex-soldiers, whose weapons were elaborately carved sticks; most of them had no luggage except for a very full haversack. I also noticed a bearded old man who for many minutes had been clinging to the drinking-water tap, contorting his neck under it and hissing and casting vicious glances at a group of children who were also wanting to get some water. Then there was a woman in a tight tailor-made, who pushed her way through the throngs of waiting people, here and there getting hold of a man who stood with his back turned towards her, and turning him round roughly, and, every time disappointed, she pushed him back again in a positively offensive manner, because he wasn't the one she was looking for. Of course I also noticed the woman with the white bird-cage in which, however, there was no bird, but a clock with old-fashioned alarm bells. And then there was Hilde Isenbüttel. Naturally I didn't fail to see her when she stopped on the steps of the footbridge, from where she could see over the whole platform and, of course, could also be seen instantly herself.

'There's Hilde Isenbüttel,' I said.

And the painter, after casting a brief glance at her, said to Teo Busbeck :

'Just look, Teo, only a pregnant woman can stand like that : it's effortless superiority.'

'She's sure to get a seat,' Busbeck said.

A uniformed official came out of one of the offices, holding a trowel in his hand, and walked along our platform, right at the edge, inexorably forcing the waiting people back for the sake of their own safety. He walked right along the edge, showing everybody how close he could get to the edge without being in danger of being hit by the incoming train. With the routine of someone who has uttered these requests many times he turned to the travellers, appealing to their reason :

'Move aside, please! Step back please!'

'Now the time seems to have come, Max.'

'Yes, I can hear the train.'

'How can I ever thank you, Max?'

'Don't talk about it.'

'All these years . . .'

'For God's sake, stop it, Teo!'

348

'I feel I'm leaving home.'

'I should hope so. And do write and say what things are like in Cologne. Here's the train.'

Grinding and jerking, slowing down, the train was coming in, ahead of it a wall of shimmering heat, then a sharp draught that almost singed one's skin; it moved on a little further and then stopped, clanking and vibrating as iron struck iron and hot vapour escaped with a hissing sound, the knocking of the valves changing with the diminishing pressure. On the bumpers, the roofs of the coaches and the running-boards, cramped limbs loosened up, hands let go not only of what they had been desperately holding on to, but – at least so it seemed to me – let go of the whole train that they had been covering with their bodies the way seaweed gradually conquers a ship's hull, clinging to it, steadily diminishing its speed. The train actually seemed so overwhelmed and occupied by all these people that one couldn't help thinking they were dominating it simply with the number of their bodies and their united will to travel. And since they had got so far along their way, they were unwilling to make room, to yield any of their space to the new travellers now surging from the platform towards them : but in the end they couldn't do anything about it, they had to yield to the accumulated pressure exerted from the platform, they had to make room for the newcomers, who instantly began to settle down in space where previously others had been. And remarkably enough, despite the turmoil, the noisy conquests, disputes and quarrels, one could quite distinctly hear the voice of the man with the trowel calling out :

'Glü-se-rup! Glü-se-rup!'

And how did we get Busbeck on to the train? The painter held us back.

'Keep calm, just keep calm, let them go on struggling and fighting.'

Standing back, he let his eyes roam along the whole length of the train, then he suddenly made up his mind.

'Over there – that brakeman's cabin!'

Now we attacked, and the three nurses who were already in the cabin sulked, trying to be difficult as we started to get Busbeck's luggage inside, and then, when we pushed Busbeck himself inside, a grey-haired nurse, protecting her unjustifiably large breasts with her hands, turned quite pale and started faintly calling for help.

'This gentleman,' the painter said, putting his face to the open window and addressing those inside the cabin, 'this gentleman will provide you with refreshment on the way, ladies, so be good to him.'

And then he secured the door by tying a piece of string from the door-handle to the bar you hold on to when getting out. And after a short while, standing out there on the platform, we could hear them all laughing inside the cabin, which made us quite sure that they were getting on good terms with each other. When, after repeated signalling, the train belatedly moved off, covered with bodies lying flat on the roofs or hanging on to the bumpers and being jolted by the rhythmical knocking of the rails, Teo Busbeck couldn't get to the window to wave goodbye to us and one of the nurses had to do it on his behalf. I still remember small bunches of people simply dropping off the train or jumping off as it started to move, and how some people began running after it for a while, shouting and waving, running right to the end of the platform, where a large beam blocked the way and from where, leaning over the beam, they went on waving and shouting their farewells after the departing train, farewells to which nobody responded.

The platform didn't empty even now when the train had disappeared round the glittering curve of the tracks. The people occupied benches that had emptied, they sat down on their luggage, thus proving that people are prepared to go on waiting even if there is hardly more than the merest ghost of a chance for another train to come.

Exhausted by the heat of the morning, they were all trying to find positions in which to relax. We were just about to leave the station when we saw Hilde Isenbüttel running along the platform to the place where the luggage-van of the train had been. What was going on there? What was she up to? That was what we wondered, following her with our eyes, but noticing at the same time that other people were watching her too as she ran along, that woman who was always so gay, so ready to laugh, with her batique kerchief on her head, now making a final spurt round the mountain of luggage and the people lying on the platform and, as she ran, briefly and skittishly waving.

And there was a man in uniform sitting on the ground, and she was running towards him. The man was sitting beside a small flat cart with wheels that had once belonged to a pram, Obviously the whole thing home-made. He was sitting up straight. He had no legs. The man was bare-headed, his face was still young, with a hard expression. He looked at her carefully as she knelt down in front of him, taking care of her belly, and then he grasped her firmly by the upper arms. Their faces, now roughly at the same height, didn't draw any closer to each other the way one might have expected.

'That's Albrecht,' the painter said, 'Albrecht Isenbüttel. So he did get back from Leningrad alive.'

The woman freed her arm from the man's grip and suddenly embraced him, so that they both swayed a little. Then she got up and lifted him, first tentatively, then more vigorously, and got him on to the flat cart. She surveyed the stumps of his legs, working out what to do, then she folded the field-grey trouser-ends under the stumps. She picked up the rope of the cart, put it over her head and slantwise across her body, and started pulling.

Hilde Isenbüttel pulled the cart along the platform all by herself, and the man sat stiffly upright on the square wooden cart, holding on to the sides with both hands, and he seemed to be nodding all the time as the cart jerked along. He didn't look to either side of him, he paid no attention to anyone calling out, and even when we stopped them, offering our help, he took no notice of us, not so much because he was entirely indifferent as simply because for the present he was leaving everything to the woman, he was prepared to agree to whatever she accepted or rejected on his behalf. The woman thanked us, saying :

'No, thank you, Max, don't bother. I can manage alone all right – well, just up the stairs perhaps . . .'

Nansen and the woman carried the legless man up the stairs, and I walked behind them, pulling the cart. When we reached the top, they put him back in the cart.

'At last,' she said, 'at last I've got him home.'

Outside in the bumpy station square, in the shade of the lime trees, we offered them our help again, and Hilde Isenbüttel declined. The painter jerked his thumb at her big belly, but she just threw back her head, saying :

'I'll manage, I've got to manage.'

She took off her kerchief, wiped the sweat from her face with it, and then pushed it under the stumps of his legs.

'But thanks very much, all the same.'

We let her get ahead a bit and then we followed, making for the harbour, and then on the mud road along the coast, where the hard rubber wheels of the cart were whirling up fine dust. We saw the woman stopping from time to time to wipe the sweat from her face, and to relieve the pressure of the rope for a moment, and since she wouldn't let us help her, we held back, walking more slowly.

'They still haven't spoken a word to each other,' the painter said.

'Why don't they?'

'They can see enough,' he said.

There on the road along the seashore the wheels of the cart went squeaking and wobbling, but Hilde Isenbüttel paid no attention to that, she followed the winding little road up to the dyke, and we kept some distance behind her. There was a smell of dust and hay in the air. The man in the cart continued to look straight ahead of him, not once did he turn his face towards the sea, nor did he glance across the country towards the farmstead, which was still some distance away, the place that he must, after all, have missed during the years of his absence. Only once, when the woman went down on her knees to brake the cart and he himself pushed his hands on to the ground to help brake it, did he glance towards us as though expecting help from us, but he did not call out. However, they managed to get down the steep incline without any help from us, and now we stopped, because the woman hauled away with unexpected energy along the peat-brown path, moving towards the poplars ahead of her with the masses of starlings that had alighted on them. It is rewarding – it is always rewarding here in our countryside – to watch somebody moving into the distance under our sky: one simply stands still of one's own accord and turns all one's attention to the interplay of space and movement, and one always marvels at the oppressive dominance of the horizon.

We stood there on the dyke for a long time, turning our backs to the sea, watching those two people becoming smaller and smaller, watching them turn into one single body which then also became smaller and smaller, until there was nothing left but a far-off, scarcely recognizable movement on the ground.

'Do you think we ought to be getting along?' the painter asked.

'Why not?' I replied, and the painter put his hand on my neck, exerting a tolerably strong pressure, and so pushed me along down the dyke, not in the direction of the Wattblick Inn, but eastward towards the main road to Husum. Presumably he felt no inclination to meet Hinnerk Timmsen again. Even when he was silent and shut up in himself I enjoyed walking along with him; not matching the rhythm of his steps, but simply being there, partaking of his kindly and incalculable presence, which always made one expect that something was going to happen: perhaps a question was coming, or just as likely a glance. Walking at his side like that always meant one was fully occupied, in a state of tense expectation, and don't let's say anything about joy.

15   The Continuation

Today, 25 September 1954, I have become twenty-one years old. Hilke contributed to the occasion by sending me a little packet of sweets, my mother sent a scratchy pullover, Herr Direktor Himpel the usual swiftly dripping candle that the institution presents on such occasions, and Karl Joswig, our favourite guard, gave me twelve cigarettes and spent about two hours trying to console me. Those were the things by means of which they made tolerable the day on which I came of age. But for my task, but for having to go on spinning this yarn of mine, I'd be together with all the others and not in this cosy little cell; I'd find my place in the dining hall adorned with flowers – short-stemmed asters in a jampot – the whole crowd would have to sing a sort of canon in my honour, a birthday song of Himpel's composition, I'd get an extra piece of meat and an extra slice of cake, of course I'd have the day off, and in the evening I'd have permission to keep my light on an hour longer than the others. But it wasn't meant to be like that.

From today on I've got to put up with being regarded as an adult, of being reproached with being of age. While shaving at the hand-basin, I couldn't as yet register any change in my appearance. Reading the parts of my task that are finished, I nibbled some of the sweets and contemplated the dripping candle without, so to speak, getting much illumination from it. I smoked a whole cigarette from the store with which Wolfgang Mackenroth had provided me. At last that damned candle did the trick, it got me to the point of asking myself the questions I had found so unbearable when I used to be with my grand-

354

father, the folklorist and interpreter of life: Who are you? Where do you want to go? What is your aim? and so on and so forth. And some other memories rose up: the submarine coffee-table on Busbeck's sixtieth birthday . . . Jutta on the swing, dotted with patterns of light . . . my sea-battles . . . the moment when we had found Klaas in the peat . . . and Ditte's funeral.

I thought about all this and it didn't get me anywhere. So I wasn't disturbed when Joswig came in, shy but genial, wishing me a very good morning and a hearty welcome, a welcome, Siggi, to man's estate.

Smilingly he shook the cigarettes out of his sleeve, letting them drop on to my copybooks. He sat down on the edge of the bed. He looked at me sympathetically for a long time, without speaking, while outside on the autumnal Elbe the chain of a dredge that was anchored out there went rattling round and round, just as it had been doing for days, the tooth-edged buckets thundering down to the bottom of the fairway and coming up again, shaking and dripping and then plunging again, after vomiting the bluish mud into a barge.

Mightn't it speed up my work if he told me that all the boys missed me? Including Eddi?

No, it wouldn't speed it up.

Was it perhaps because of the subject that Korbjuhn had set me, 'The Joys of Duty', that I looked so haggard, so vulnerable, so impatient?

It might be because of the subject.

Couldn't I simply make short shrift of it and simply bang it on Himpel's desk, he wanted to know. Since the joys of duty hadn't yet come to an end, I simply couldn't finish it off by making some audacious twist, not without missing the point of the whole thing.

Now Karl Joswig rested his face in his hands, lowered his eyes and nodded in agreement. And not only did he do that, he also and explicitly bore witness to my stubbornness, he praised my obstinacy. His question had been made solely in order to test my steadfastness.

'A punishment is a punishment, Siggi,' he added. 'The joys of doing one's duty are so varied,' he went on, 'are so varied that it always pays to put them in the proper light.'

'Varied?' I asked.

355

'Well, yes,' Joswig said. 'That is, if you get my meaning.'
I didn't get it. So he said :
'Just listen to this,' and he produced a story, telling me I
was free to make use of it if I wanted to.

'If it helps you along,' he added, 'for it is also to do with the
joys of doing one's duty, and it happened to a nephew of mine,
over yonder in Hamburg, in a rowing club on the Alster. Well,
here goes.

'Once upon a time there was a good rowing eight belonging
to the Hamburg Rowing Association Zero Two, and one of the
crew, his name was Pfaff, but he was called Fiete, was pretty
much of a local hero. There was lots of photographs showing
him taking off his oarsman's vest to give it to somebody as a
present, and he was a fair sportsman, only there was just one
thing he couldn't help : when he came into contact with money
it seemed to feel so at home with him that it simply stuck to his
fingers as though glued on. Unfortunately, that went for other
people's money, too, and so a number of things happened that
couldn't be kept dark. Once there was a big seeding race for
the championship being held on the Alster, and as so often
before Fiete was Hamburg's white hope. All round the Alster
the prevailing mood was the kind you expect at a minor
public festival, the river-police were seeing to it that the stretch
where the race was to take place was free of traffic, and even in
police circles Fiete was well known. The light boats went all
out, but the public watched them without much interest. As
always, the main interest was focused on the eights, and that
race was still to come. Well, once upon a time there was a big-
boned, fair-haired oarsman by the name of Fiete Pfaff, who
had a discussion with a polite but resolute gentleman; the gentleman showed himself well informed about Fiete's tastes and
habits, and when he took his leave Fiete had promised that he
would suffer from an untimely attack of giddiness during the
race, a thing for which an unknown oarsman would never be
forgiven, but an ace oarsman could be sure of everyone's
sympathy.

'Now we can let the boats line up for the start. It's the usual
picture : the helpers lying flat on their bellies, holding the boats
until the starting shot is fired, and then the slight, slim boats
with their highly varnished hulls shot ahead down the course,

which was scarcely wrinkled by even the tiniest wave, propelled by the mighty forty-six stroke in accord with the cox's commands, and egged on by the roar of many voices. For some time they surged on neck and neck, but then when the rival boat – there I go, even I'm saying rival boat – changed its stroke, Fiete Pfaff and his crew put on such a furious spurt that they gained half a length. It was obvious they were determined to win the race. The slightly built coxes shouted at the oarsmen, who jerked to and fro on their sliding seats, whipping the water with their long oars, you know the way oarsmen move on their seats is said to be very important, and no other man moved so supply and surely as Fiete Pfaff, and with him that wasn't just the result of training.

'Eight hundred yards, twelve hundred yards – now it's time for our oarsman to have his attack of dizziness, and that should decide the race. But what's this? Instead of breaking the rhythm and bringing confusion on his crew and then letting his oar slide over the water, doubling up and sinking forward, Fiete seemed to gain in strength. It was as though bitterness drove his stroke, and also some inscrutable joy; anyway, he'd forgotten all about his promise to that polite but relentless gentleman. He was, as he had so often been before, a shining example to his crew. Well, if you ask me what urged him, despite his promise, to work so wildly and so joyfully for his own boat's victory, you have to admit in the end that it was the joys of doing one's duty. There you are. Nothing else counted, nothing else was of any value. As soon as he sat on the sliding seat, the oar in his hand, in his ears the gasping of his fellow-oarsmen, he no longer had any choice. We might say he simply had to do what duty demanded of him.

'Once upon a time there was an oarsman called Fiete Pfaff, a sensitive giant, who, a victim of blackmail, agreed to feign an attack of dizziness during a seeding race, only the net of duty caught him and dragged him along to within a very short distance of the goal, to be precise, to within exactly two hundred yards of it. And then something happened that sent a moan through the ranks of the spectators and made the officials jump up from the benches where they sat. Fiete had a genuine fit of dizziness, he slumped forward, the other oarsmen became confused and broke the rhythm of their stroke, and the rival boat won the race. Did people believe it was genuine? Most of the management of his Club believed it was, even after they'd learned of Fiete's conversation with the polite gentleman. They didn't entirely lose confidence in him. They even wanted to let him keep his place in the crew. But Fiete himself didn't want to, he couldn't bring himself to remain in the crew: he considered it his duty to resign, and resign he did.'

Joswig sat there waiting to hear what I would have to say. He expected a snap judgement from me, but I remained silent, because I was trying to imagine what his story would be like if turned into a film. The only way I could see it was in terms of a film.

'Do you see,' he asked, 'do you recognize what the joys of duty may compel a man to do? What it may turn you into?'

And he waved his hand in an inviting gesture that meant as much as: Help yourself if you like.

'All this,' I said, 'is the sort of joy in duty that Korbjuhn wants us to see. As for the victims, that's a different matter. One doesn't wish to speak about them.'

He got up from where he was sitting on the edge of my bed, put one hand on my shoulder and patted it with indulgent respect.

'What you say shows that you have come of age.'

He gave me official permission to smoke as much as I liked for the rest of the day, and in farewell he touched me lightly on the back of my head.

'Aren't you going to give yourself a day off today?' he asked, standing in the doorway.

'What for?'

'Well, one's twenty-first birthday,' he said. 'That's when one begins to commit oneself, when one begins asking oneself questions. That's the time when one starts going for walks. When I was twenty-one I was working to become an inspector. It's also the right age for emigrating. When one's twenty-one, one chooses something out of one's stock of ideas, one makes up one's mind to become one thing or another – for all I care, a guard in a museum. You get me? One begins to owe something to oneself when one becomes twenty-one: one's going to be asked to the cash-desk. As soon as the candles on the birthday-cake have burnt out, they have you pinned down as an adult.'

358

I wouldn't have expected that sort of maxim from Joswig, but I knew how he meant it, and so I didn't wish to irritate him by asking him about his own life.

I nodded in a resigned way, pretending to be in a reflective mood and willing to undergo a change of heart. I gazed persistently at the quick-dripping candle, which made the smoke of my cigarette rise to the ceiling, and I refrained from disturbing him while he unloaded his admonitions and his advice, expecting it all to fall on fruitful ground, and then once again circled around the chair and the table before taking himself off.

I wonder what it was Joswig smelled of. I can't help it, but every time he's been in my room, he leaves behind a sharp smell that may be of some disinfectant. Could it have been that he dusted or sprayed himself secretly every time before entering a cell? Be that as it may, it forced me to open the window every time and air the room.

The Elbe! How dully and sluggishly its waters run past in the autumn. Over there on the other bank the haze comes down, veiling the countryside until it becomes invisible. The tops of the trees rise out of the haze as though out of a flooded forest; the thudding of the diesel engines turns into a soft pulse-beat, the clanking from the wharves no longer produces an echo, and the rattling of the dredger's chain now hardly reaches me. The lights, the dim lights moving slowly past, seem to express the laboriousness of all motion. The superstructures of the ships glide past very close; it seems as if they had no contact at all with the water. For me these are perhaps not the most exciting, but certainly the most thrilling moments of life on the Elbe: the time of nightfall when the whitish haze sinks down and everything along the river becomes strange and uncertain.

I now become aware that a birthday-mood is trying to push to the front of my mind, a sort of intently summarizing contemplation of one's navel, but I've got to go back into the past, to go down to where this very personal Atlantis of mine lies, which has to be brought to the surface chunk after chunk. Time presses, duty presses; what after all do twenty-one years mean if one thinks of Captain Andersen who last spring celebrated his hundred-and-second birthday, and who, the very next day, that is in his hundred-and-third year of life, being slightly drunk, played a part in a documentary film that is now

359

being shown in the cinemas and is entitled *The People and the Forces of Nature along the Sea Coast?* How does the Elbe concern me, with all the hardware on it and the haze over it? The rowing and sailing chaps have long ago tied up their boats under the branches of trees that by now give them but scanty shelter. The last motor-launch has slunk away, grinding its way up river against the current. It doesn't interest me. Nor does it interest me who's going to make what discoveries from the oceanographic ship that's just putting out to sea. All I need is the soil and water tests for Rugbüll. Here I cast my plankton net over my dark plain. Here I gather in whatever I catch.

As always when I open the net, the first thing to appear is my father, the Rugbüll policeman, who on his release from internment once again became what he had been before and what everyone between Glüserup and the Husum highroad would have expected him to become. For no more than three months there had been no policeman in Rugbüll. But then there he was again with his desiccated face and his ill-fitting trousers, taking up his duties again as matter-of-factly as though he had been away, not on enforced, but on voluntary leave. He just had to blow up the bicycle tyres again, because they had gone flat in the interval.

After my mother had unstitched that precious emblem, the eagle, from his jacket, he himself removed the cockade from his cap, but, instead of throwing them away, put them both into a tin and put the tin away in his desk. And that same day, even before he was officially reinstated, he mounted his bicycle and went pedalling off down the dyke, readily letting himself be stopped by one and all, always referring to his period of absence in the same words, always with the same disparaging gestures: 'Yes, in Neuengamme. Not all that bad. Food? No complaints. On the whole the treatment was. . . . All perfectly correct . . .' And so on.

Not once did he go to the trouble of trying to put it any differently – every time he talked about his experiences, people got full value; he always managed to repeat it word for word. Coming back, he simply took things up where he had had to drop them, all in his own way and in the same order in which he always did things. He made his entry in his day-book, chopped firewood, rode into Glüserup to hand in his pistol, dug over a corner of the garden where he meant to grow tobacco, which in the course of time he did, dragged Hilke home from a party at the Wattblick Inn, dislocating her arm in the process, made several trips to Husum, returning from one of them with a copy of *New Directives for the Police*, which he immediately locked up in a drawer, unread; and went out on duty-trips on his bike. And then one morning, after breakfast, it was the turn of 'the matter of Klaas'.

There is really no need this time to give an account of what we were having for breakfast – presumably it was porridge, bread and plum jam, and *ersatz* coffee – and there we were munching away, each at his own pace, each of us counting the slices of bread the others took, all in silence, thinking of nothing, or at most thinking things we had thought plenty of times before, and then all of a sudden my father said to Hilke : 'Go and get the photograph.'

My sister, who never put a spoon in her mouth without chomping at it, making a clattering and banging, bit her spoon harder than ever when my father repeated what he had said. And she kept the spoon in her mouth, gulping, goggling, staring at him like a great cow, apparently not understanding what he wanted of her.

'Klaas,' my father said. 'Photograph. Bring it here.'

My sister let go of the handle of the spoon, but with the bowl of the spoon still in her mouth, and like that she got up, all in a tizzy, asking with her eyes – she couldn't do it in words, what with the spoon in her mouth – what it was all about, finally left the room and after a while came back with the framed photograph of my brother, which had been lying in the darkness of a drawer ever since the day when it was banished from sight.

My father took the photograph from Hilke's hand and laid it, picture-side down, beside the alarm-clock on the dresser. He then finished his breakfast, possessed himself in patience until we had all finished ours as well, and then asked to have the table cleared. The table was thereupon cleared. I remember counting the spoons : four of them there were. We put the plates in the sink, and I wiped the table. The policeman moved his lips, apparently trying out phrases, occasionally casting a worried look at my mother, who, however, did not look at him but just

361

sat there busily sucking her hollow teeth. At a sign from him Hilke and I sat down again, and my father stood up, placed the photograph on the windowsill, and gazed at it penetratingly, not so much reproachfully as in exhortation, just as though trying to make Klaas step out of the frame and stand there in the flesh.

'I want him to listen,' he said. 'I want him to be here too, one way or another.'

I gazed intently at the photograph.

Now my father gripped the back of his chair, jerked, flung his head back, looked Klaas straight in the eye, and addressed the photograph as follows :

'A clean sweep – got to make a clean sweep with you as well. We can't go around for ever not saying what we think. We've got to get it out. We are gathered here together in order to get things straight. We all know what you did. The times may have changed, but what you did – there's no changing that.'

He paused and put the thumb and middle finger of one hand over his eyes. My mother seized the opportunity to shift her chair closer to the table and sit up even straighter. Hilke quietly scratched at the fat backs of her knees. The policeman made a hissing sound as he dropped his hand, looked hard at the photograph, shook his head, and said :

'We must clear the whole matter up – clear it up and arrive at a verdict. Where I've been I've spent all my time thinking of what he brought on us. I kept on thinking of how he came back and never once set foot in this house. He never said a word about being sorry. First the disgrace and then not even being sorry. Over there in Bleekenwarf, that's where he lived, with that chap, before he went off to Hamburg without so much as a word. What's got to be said must be said now. We've got to make a clean sweep.'

In this manner he went on, confronting Klaas with all the disgrace he was supposed to have brought on us. He did not mention any mitigating circumstances, since he obviously saw none. He addressed the photograph, pointing out to it that even a family could constitute a tribunal, could pronounce a verdict. At that point I pricked up my ears. I tried to anticipate and imagine that verdict. Was he going to lock Klaas in the cellar for several years? Or was he going to order him to drink weed-killer in our presence? It also occurred to me that he might make him jump off the mill as a punishment for all he had done, or make him go and hang himself from the sign saying Rugbüll Police Station. Or didn't he mean to go as far as that? Would he let him off with a life sentence of kitchen-duty? Or five summers in the peat-bogs?

Nobody will be surprised to hear that he took his time before passing sentence, though one could see that he was not enjoying talking about it, that he was having to overcome an inhibition when he reminded us – and himself – in great detail of Klaas's self-inflicted wound, his escape, how he was handed over to the authorities, and finally his refusal to return home. But at long last he got down to brass tacks, made Hilke hand him the photograph, removed it from the frame, placed it on the table, and uttered his sentence.

I was amazed. At the time it seemed to me that the sentence was after all rather feeble: Klaas was forbidden the house.

'Now listen to me, all of you! As long as I live he will not enter this house again.'

We were forbidden to utter Klaas's name or even to think it.

'You will simply blot him out of your memory.'

Then my father tore up the photograph and threw the pieces into the fire.

My mother got up. I suppose she had known just what was coming, in fact she had probably discussed it with him. She brushed the crumbs from her skirt and actually went into the larder, where she bustled about, covering the jampot with some crackly paper, opening a bottle of fruit-juice. Hilke and I went on sitting there, carefully not looking at each other, and of course not daring to utter a word. And how about the policeman? He had just wound up the alarm-clock, or rather he was just winding up that old-fashioned but reliable monstrosity with its loathsome alarm when suddenly he began to turn the screw slower and slower, as if he were listening to something, yes, he seemed to sense something, to catch a sound of something somewhere, with the same strange agitation that he had shown that first time, that evening in Külkenwarf, at the lecture about our homeland or the sea, well, anyway, our sea-girt homeland.

He was listening. He had discovered something. His hands were shaking. He put the alarm-clock back on the dresser, hooked his thumbs into his braces and twitched them. What was he listening to? His head was tilted as if it were something upstairs in my room. But there was no one up there. Pressure ... the pressure on him was making him unsteady, and he had to support himself. What else? Sweat, of course. . . . Parted lips. . . . Eyes bulging, yet veiled ... Visionary, if you know what I mean. He was trying to ward something off, and he was losing; there was no help for him. Then his lips began to move, he began to talk to himself, in fits and starts, he nodded vigorously as though in general confirmation of something, then he staggered into the passage, where he hastily pulled on his uniform jacket, buckled on his belt and put his cap on. Sitting round the kitchen-table, we were amazed to hear him rush out of the house, to the shed, to get his bicycle, which he then swung round and mounted.

This time he rode off without a word to us. You needn't think that when my mother came out of the larder she noticed my father's disappearance. And when Hilke said, without being asked : 'I suppose he's having one of his visions again, or something,' she merely looked up for an instant and then calmly turned on the wireless, and as it began blaring out 'Little Glow-worm, little glow-worm' she started on the washing up in the sink. It was as simple as that. Although I expected something further, that was all that happened, and I slunk out of the kitchen and went upstairs to my room, which I would hence-forth have all to myself, now that Klaas had been forbidden the house.

There were the corner shelves with his things on them. I yanked back the thin curtain, and there on the bottom shelf was the cardboard box tied up with string, which I had promised him I would never open. I had kept my word all during his absence. There had been three or four times when I had been on the brink, but then I hadn't done it, and now all at once I was 'hot', the box came out all by itself, the string undid itself, and I didn't have to do anything, well, hardly anything, and the lid came off, and there on my bed, handy for getting the box out of sight again in a flash, I unpacked what my brother had collected and entrusted to me. Down in the kitchen they were fully occupied. My father was out of the house.

Wouldn't Klaas expect me to open the box and find a safe place to keep the things that mattered to him, now that they had forbidden him the house? Surely he would expect it. So I unpacked the things, inspected them, surveyed them. I remember a glass jar full of carefully selected, bleached shells, a catapult, a book entitled *The Little Gardener*, a dirty, bood-stained handkerchief, some copybooks with essays in them, some string, more and more string. I remember a paper bag full of 'thunderbolts', a box of tin soldiers – all in perfect condition – and a short hand-made candlestick that the painter must have given him; a photograph of Klaas at school – eighteen old men with boys' faces and five old women with long plaits; one of the painter's sketches for 'The Apple-Picker', which I instantly hid under my pillow; a knife with a mother-of-pearl casing. And I remember the packet of letters tied up with string, which I would not have opened if they had been from a stranger, but they were in my brother's own handwriting and all addressed to Hilke. Each of these letters was at once a complaint and a threat : he complained because yet once again she had not come – to the peat-bog, to the beach, to the lighthouse – and he threatened that 'all' would be 'over' if she stayed away the next time. Sometimes he alluded to a memory they had in common, some experience they had had on the beach during a summer, I don't remember it exactly, what it was all about, they had watched something, a man and a woman in the dunes out on the peninsula, strangers whom they simply watched and later followed.

I unpacked the whole contents of the cardboard box, appropriating several items for myself, in particular the sketch for 'The Apple-Picker'. Downstairs the telephone began to ring. Hilke went and answered, saying, as she always did : 'This is Hilke Jepsen speaking. Who is that?' Then I heard nothing but 'No' and 'Yes' and 'Yes' and 'No', and by the time she hurried back into the kitchen, I knew that someone had been trying to get my father. I barely had time to shut up the cardboard box, tie the string and hide it again when they started on me from downstairs :

'Siggi! Siggi! Come down! Hurry up, Siggi!'

So there was just nothing for it, I had to go down again,

where Hilke was waiting for me. Was there something in the way I looked at her, a sort of challenging curiosity, that made her shrink back and, instead of giving me the message, start off by saying: 'What are you staring at me like that for? Stop staring at me as if I'd done something to you.'

'I'll stare at you any way I like,' I said.

'Not like that,' she said, 'not with icy eyes like that.'

'Come on, spit it out,' I said.

Well, there was quite a balloon going up at Bleekenwarf: any time now, in about two hours, they were expecting a very important visitor, apparently very important indeed, the *Landeskommissar* or something of the sort – anyway, a big shot who wanted to see Nansen about something, and the policeman had to be there. 'Get a move on, Siggi, go and tell Father there's been a telephone message for him to go straight to Bleekenwarf. And stop staring like that, I tell you! I don't like it.' Suddenly my gaze made her so unsure of herself that she went up to the mirror in the wardrobe in the passage, peered at her face, tried to see herself sideways, examined her blouse and skirt suspiciously and finally, when she had failed to discover anything, turned on me in a fury: 'Get along out, get on with it, it's urgent.'

To the dyke – first of all I had to go to the dyke. It was a dark but windless day in early autumn. There was a ground swell on the smooth sea. Two mackerel-fishers were out in a boat. There wasn't a gull anywhere; to make up for that there were crowds of them on the water, a slight current bearing them along parallel to the shore. There was no cyclist in sight, either in the Wattblick direction or in the direction of the lighthouse. Far out towards the horizon two minesweepers were clearing the water. Under the dyke a jeep was moving along towards Glüserup. I decided to go in the Wattblick direction, because at the inn they sometimes had information; anyway one could ask. I don't know what it was about me that made the tousled sheep crowd round me as soon as I came on the scene: they came trotting along, they pursued me and I had to kick them out of my way. Their matted wool stank.

If it hadn't been for that stench I should have noticed the smell of burning sooner and so should have discovered my father, and what he was up to, sooner. But as it was, pursued and prodded by the sheep, I ran past the peninsula, and it was only by chance, when I glanced back, that I saw the bicycle leaning against the painter's hut, there at the bottom of the dune, and thought it might be my father's bike. Only that it *might* be. I made the most of the situation, raced down the side of the dyke, escaping from the sheep, who glared after me, their jaws moving – escaping from their stench and their bleating. There was someone in the painter's hut. There was a smell of burning in the air. There was no sign of the fire, no column of smoke, but the smell of burning grew stronger as I trudged up the dune and then stood at the top of it. And then I did see the faint column of smoke rising from behind the hut, and I simply can't describe the terror that suddenly made me run and run. It was a throbbing terror I had never known before. That's all, at least for now.

It *was* my father's bicycle that was leaning against the side of the hut. The door was open. But he was not in the hut, he was standing outside, at the back, smoking, gazing at a fire, the remains of a fire that he kept carefully poking with one foot, stirring about some charred stuff that was still smouldering. Was he furious or amazed when he saw me coming? He scarcely seemed to recognize me. He just stood there, exhausted, absent-looking, staring into the fire. He did not try to stop me from poking a stick into the remains of the fire, hastily pulling it apart, there at his feet. It was all over. There was no longer any sense in interfering. That bit of paper – that tiny bit of pale blue paper that had escaped the flames – was from the cover of a sketchbook. My father had burnt the painter's sketchbook for his series 'Heads Along the Coast'.

I straightened up and looked at him in horror. There was an expression of gloating satisfaction on his face. Now that he had done it, he could stand there calmly, smoking, as though he had carried out an official duty. There on the peninsula, by the remains of the fire, I began to be afraid of him, not of his strength or his cunning, or his obstinacy, but of his unflinching way of pursuing his aims. This fear was stronger than the hate that suddenly welled up in me and bade me hurl myself at him and thump his thighs and hips with my fist. That gloating! That horrible smugness! I couldn't bear to go on looking at him. I squatted down and threw sand on the place where the fire had been, letting the fine sand shower down on the charred remains until it was all covered and there was nothing left to show that there had been a fire there at all.

All this seemed not to concern him, the Rugbüll policeman. He watched me in silence, several times drawing a deep breath as though about to wake up, but he did not really wake up, he sank back into his gloating satisfaction. No, I was not surprised then when for the first time I suddenly felt a drawing pain in my temples, accompanied by a faint numbness and a hammering sense of fear that made me realize that nothing, nothing at all was safe from him in his official capacity. In that terrifyingly unerring way of his he could find every hiding-place, I realized, and I instantly thought of my collection in the mill and of how I would have to hide it from him – but where?

'What are you trembling like that for?' he asked. 'There's nothing to tremble about at your age – you're too young.'

Tomorrow, I thought, I'll clear the things out tomorrow, or better still, this evening.

'Well,' he asked, 'what's the matter?'

Perhaps I'll take them to Bleekenwarf, I thought. Perhaps the painter would help me to find a new hiding-place at Bleekenwarf.

'Speak up!' he ordered.

'You mustn't do that,' I said, 'you mustn't confiscate anything any more, you mustn't make fires, you mustn't burn anything.'

'Who told you that?'

'Everyone. Everyone says there's no more ban on painting and it's none of your business any more, and if I tell them what you've done here, the painter won't put up with it. Things aren't the way they used to be, that's all over now. Everyone says the same. And I've heard and seen what you used to do, and you mustn't do it any more. You can't give Uncle Nansen any orders now, he can do whatever he likes now. I know.'

He lashed out. I fell down on the sand, on my knees, and remained there like that. He had hit me on the lower jaw. The second blow only grazed my cheek.

'Get up,' he said.

I stayed lying where I was. He grabbed me by the collar of my shirt and hauled me up, pulled my face quite close to his, so that I was standing on tiptoe, my whole body touching his.

Then there was a long peering into eyes, that way he was so good at, a serious examination of my retina. This time I did not avoid his eye, I kept it up, gazing back into his contracted pupils. I didn't often get a chance of seeing him at such close quarters. How wrinkled he was, and how sullen! That sullenness of his suited him very well, making it clear to everyone that the policeman was not on good terms with the world.

'Oh, so you know a thing or two, do you?' he said. 'Just fancy! So you know what I can do and what I can't. You're the expert on where my powers begin and where they end. And so you've discovered, too, that things are different now from what they used to be.'

His grip loosened and he pushed me away from him, not very hard, not hard enough to make me stumble and fall over.

'You've heard a lot,' he said, 'but not this: that a man has to keep faith with himself. That he's got to carry out his duty even when circumstances alter. I mean a duty that he knows he has. And so you think you're going round telling people that your father does something he knows it's his duty to do – all right, you just go and tell people, you can go and tell him over there at Bleekenwarf, you spend enough time there anyway. All right, just you work against me. I've settled with Klaas, and I can settle with you any day.'

He raised his face: lips colourless, compressed, teeth grinding. A considering gaze – not amused, just considering me. Vague, floating gestures, as if talking to himself.

'Any more to say?'

To my own surprise, although I was on the point of shaking my head, I found that I had. I repeated that there was no longer anyone he had to keep under surveillance, no longer anything for him to confiscate and destroy. I told him there was no longer any ban on Nansen's painting and that it was not his duty to take any action. However, I did not threaten him, nor did I say how much I hated him. But he must have sensed this, just as he sensed my fear, for he came up to me, saying:

'If you keep out of all this, we shall get on together the way we used to – so long as you just keep out of it.'

Then he contemplated the place in the sand where the fire had been. He nodded, went to his bicycle, lifted it, turned it towards the dyke, paying no attention to whatever I might do, but probably assuming that I would follow him, for I heard him muttering to himself and saying my name. I followed him as far as the water and there, addressing his back, I gave him the message they had given me for him at home. You needn't think that Jens Ole Jepsen stopped when he learnt that he was wanted at Bleekenwarf because the *Landeskommissar* and some big-wigs . . . He listened to my message in silence, went round the dune and then off along under the dyke on the seaward side until he only had to cross it in order to strike the alderedged track leading to Bleekenwarf. He coasted down to the gate and into the yard and then, after dismounting, gazed towards the Husum high road just as I did, so that we both saw the two olive-green cars at the same instant, as they turned off and came our way.

My father first of all leaned his bike against the side of the house, then, farther along, against a pile of wood. He did not go into the house, but opened the gate and stood there waiting. There I joined him, and there we stood with our backs against the gate, keeping it open, a miserable little guard of honour for the cars, momentarily hidden behind Holmsen's hedge, which must be slowly approaching. Since his return from the internment-camp, my father had not once been to Bleekenwarf, had neither seen nor spoken to the painter, had not even inquired whether everything at Bleekenwarf was still the way it had been. Since he could not bear change, he did not ask about things that might have changed, or at least took his time about taking note of them. He did not stand at attention there beside me at the gate. He was relaxed, though not indifferent. He told me to inspect his uniform back and front, and to clean his boots at least a bit with a handful of grass.

I didn't know what I was standing at the gate for, but he raised his hand to his cap, saluting, even before any of their faces could be made out. Saluting, we stood there as the cars drove in, the second close behind the first, and drew up in the yard.

Well, and now here are four men getting out, men of different shapes and sizes, variously dressed and with various expressions on their faces. First of all, they look around, taking in the pond, stables, studio, and garden, and also a slice of the countryside that can be seen from here. One can see on their faces the almost compulsive unanimity of the thought that strikes them : So this is where he lives, this is his world.

The men nodded to each other. Each of them knew what the others meant. The drivers drove the heavy olive-green cars round the pond and parked them side by side. Well, how are these four men to be described? The grinning one is quickly dealt with, for he was the only one in uniform : bare-headed, with a curved pipe in the corner of his mouth, a pepper-and-salt moustache, freckled face and hands, a paint-box round his neck, a crown and several stars on his epaulettes, and all in all resembling a slightly lame, persistently grinning seal. The *Landeskommissar*, by contrast – that's to say, the man who subsequently turned out to be the *Landeskommissar* – did not cut much of a figure, in fact he was pretty unimpressive : a head shorter than the seal, slender, with a marked stoop, both hands in his pockets as though he were cold in his threadbare suit : Mr Gaines. The youngest of them was remarkable not so much for the bony angularity of his face or the everlasting cigarette in his mouth and the (as it seemed to me) excessively large chamois gloves he wore, as for his voice. The moment he spoke – and since he was the interpreter, he talked twice as much as the others – it sounded as if someone had started up all the rattles and gongs in the Söllring cherry-orchard to scare off the starlings. And the fourth? He wore a slouch-hat and steel-rimmed spectacles and carried a bulgy briefcase.

It can be taken as read not only that this visit was by appointment, but that it had for some time been noticed by those inside the house. Nevertheless, the door did not open. Nobody appeared to welcome the men who were now standing at the edge of the painter's flower-garden with all its autumn colours, in silence, perhaps trying to recall the proper names of the flowers. They looked inquisitive, in the know, and admiring. They took some steps into the garden, walked round the studio, came back into the yard, drew each other's attention to the ducks nervously paddling around in the middle of the pond, and then came towards us. My father and I were standing to one side, near the front door, still, as you might say, forming a miserable guard of honour, he farther away, I nearer the door. We did not take our eyes off the men. I should say the persistence of our standing there forced them finally to pay attention to us, and this they did by noticeably quickening their pace from a leisurely, almost indolent step to a purposeful stride that rapidly brought them nearer.

My father saluted. Hands were shaken. A few kindly, condescending inquiries were made. A few brief, non-committal replies came from the policeman. The grinning one and the interpreter also shook hands with me, though with model nonchalance, not bestowing so much as a glance on me. The interpreter asked me, in his grating voice: 'And how are you?' I make a point of never answering such questions. Less out of eagerness to be of service than out of a sense of duty, my father asked if he should not knock at the door, as it were on behalf of the visitors. The *Landeskommissar* smiled and himself knocked twice, with loosely bent knuckles. He was beginning to turn round to face his companions, with an expectant look, when the door was flung open, obviously taking him by surprise.

Of course the field-mouse should have let a little more time pass, should have counted, say, up to twelve, before flinging the door open, but I dare say that, having been waiting there for quite some time, she couldn't stand the nervous strain any longer. Anyway, the painter's housekeeper, who came from Flensburg and was distantly related to Ditte – her name was Katrine and the painter called her Trinchen – appeared in the doorway, rather hastily bade us all welcome, and stepped to one side to let us in. The four men disappeared into the obscurity of the hall. We remained outside and were just wondering how best to pass the time, when the *Landeskommissar* reappeared, not merely beckoning us in, but actually making us go ahead and shutting the door after us.

Daylight fell into the hall through the doorway to the enormous sitting-room. One after the other, we went in. I squeezed in sideways, right in front. There the painter lay. He was lying rather than sitting on that long, long sofa on which Teo Busbeck had spent so many years sitting, and under his blue overcoat he was wearing a rough linen nightshirt, and on his bare feet, with the protruding veins, he wore slippers. On his head, of course, he had that hat of his. His pipe and tobacco and a pile of unopened letters were on a table beside him. There was a grey woollen blanket on the floor, which the field-mouse fished up, with reproachful haste, folded once, and laid upon the painter's legs.

'He's only just up after the 'flu,' she said.

As if to get rid of her, the painter said :

'Go and make coffee, for everyone, and make it strong. But bring us some chairs first.'

The woman looked at him furiously. He laughed, holding out his hand to the *Landeskommissar,* who shook it vigorously. Then he shook hands with everyone, the grinning one, the interpreter, the slouch-hat, then me, and finally the Rugbüll policeman, who actually tried to avoid it, but, when it came to his turn, couldn't help giving the painter his hand.

'Jens?'

'Max?'

There was nothing about it to arouse anyone's suspicions.

We pulled up chairs, seated ourselves in a half-circle round the sofa, and gazed into the painter's face as he reclined there, his brow moist with feverish sweat, himself scrutinizing us with his cunning grey eyes – boldly enough.

Now how does one begin a conversation that, at a given point, has to become official, when the person chiefly concerned is sprawling there before one in a nightshirt and overcoat, just getting over influenza? The first subject to touch on was obviously his illness, so everyone talked about influenza, the time of year when it was going round and the time of year when one didn't expect to get it, and the various ways it was treated in Schleswig-Holstein and in England. The *Landeskommissar,* for instance, had never had 'flu in his life, whereas his wife got it every spring. And so on. The painter said :

'Well, it's not the sort of thing you die of. It hits you, and then it passes off. Drink lots of coffee with something strong in it, that's the thing for it. What's taking Katrine so long with the coffee?' They talked about the painter's garden, about flower-gardens in the autumn, and about autumn colours, and it was the man in uniform who had the most to say. He also talked to the painter about various types of flowers, labiate and papilionaceous in particular. Then the field-mouse came in with the coffee, and no one could fail to notice the reproachful glances she kept casting at the painter all the time she was setting out the cups and pouring out the coffee. Finally, with obvious resentment, she put a bottle of schnapps on the table. The painter instantly seized it and drew the cork. 'In these parts,' he said, 'we drink coffee laced with something.'

Everyone but me drank coffee laced with schnapps. The interpreter said : 'Cheers !' as he raised his cup, and the painter said : 'That's it, when we drink coffee, we've every right to say Cheers !' The *Landeskommissar*, who could speak German perfectly well when he wanted to, not only had that translated for him, but even explained, and after he had the briefcase handed to him, he stood up, opened the snap-locks, pulled something out, something large, blue, and stiff, what you might call official-looking, then he held it in both hands, sort of weighing it, as he went up to the sofa. It was, as I now realized, a stiff, linen-covered folder. He held it out to the painter, not exactly with reverence, but certainly with a kind of twinkling solemnity, slightly withdrawing it just as the painter began to reach out for it : for there was something to be said first, he had something to say, and he was collecting himself. We all rose to our feet.

What followed was the quietest speech I have ever heard. Well, there was a Royal Academy in London, which ... in recognition of the extraordinary services to European painting ... unanimously resolved. ... Since the painter had done the Academy the great honour of accepting membership, it was the *Landeskommissar*'s privilege to. . . . Once again the painter stretched out his hand for the diploma, and once again the *Landeskommissar* gently withdrew it, for he still had something to say, he now wanted to say something on his own behalf, he said it was not exactly part of his official duties to act on behalf of the Royal Academy, but in this case it had been a great pleasure and privilege ... and since he happened to have been visiting his friend, General Tate, in the district, the General had insisted on accompanying him. They were therefore gathered together solely in order to present the Diploma of Honorary Membership of the Academy to Herr Nansen, they also wished to convey by their presence their profound esteem for him as a distinguished representative of the artistic world and champion of its liberties. Or words to that effect.

After these words had been uttered, the painter received the diploma and the *Landeskommissar* raised his coffee-cup, saying :

'So we may drink to your very good health' and we all raised our cups to the painter, even my father. With his little finger quirked, his cup held level with his chest, one eye on the important visitors, he too congratulated the painter. And the painter, casting a casual glance at the diploma, laid it on the table beside the letters and pointed at the bottle, indicating that his guests were to help themselves. So they helped themselves. Everyone was smoking except my father.

At home, in Nottingham, the man in uniform said with an amiable grin, he had a number of Nansens on his walls, and he gave their titles, together with their dates. The painter raised his head, looking amazed. But those paintings – 'Girl Picking Poppies' for instance – had been in Dresden and in Heidelberg, surely, and had later been sequestered from the museums and taken to Berlin, where they had been destroyed? No, the General had just recently bought these very paintings in Switzerland. So then the rumours that the painter had occasionally heard, and which he had refused to believe, had been based on fact : those madmen in Berlin, being in need of foreign currency, had used intermediaries to sell the sequestered paintings abroad. Since the General had bought them in Switzerland, they had obviously not been destroyed. The General knew that many modern paintings had not been destroyed, but had been sold abroad. And there the painter had been, believing that all eight hundred of them were lost. No, the General said, he could reassure him on that score, if 'reassure' was the word to use. There were actually approximate figures of these sales, and no doubt one of these days exact figures would be available.

Conversation . . . subjects picked up and dropped again . . . questions raised and then somehow turned aside. . . . And how, the *Landeskommissar* asked, had he managed during the period when he was forbidden to paint? How did anyone manage in such circumstances? He, the *Landeskommissar*, simply couldn't imagine. He had heard of worse things, the painter said. One simply had to get used to such a situation, one had to adapt oneself, one had to take precautions for all sorts of eventualities. For the rest, he didn't know of a single painter who had complied with such a ban and really stopped painting. After all, a painter wasn't just a man who dabbed paint on canvas, one was a painter always or not at all. How could anyone stop a man from doing what he did in his dreams?

That was not exactly what he had meant, the *Landeskommissar* said. What he had meant was how the ban had been enforced. Had there been inspections? Searches? If so, who had carried them out?

Was my father going to answer? He shifted on his high-backed chair, pressing his shoulders against the carved back, turning his cap round and round in his hands and then scraping his twitching cheek with his thumb.

Yes, the painter said calmly, the surveillance had been in the hands of the local police. That had cut both ways, seeing that they had known each other for a long time. Still, all in all it had worked out not too badly.

And had he lost much work?

Yes, he had lost some things. That had been inevitable.

But he had also done some?

Oh yes, there was some work dating from the period of the ban.

And what had happened to the pictures that had been confiscated?

The painter shrugged his shoulders, then suddenly said:

'What is open to a man who only wants to do his duty and makes no other demands on himself? That's not exactly an enviable position either. He has his own difficulties to contend with.'

Conversation. . . . They followed a certain line for a while, they got a hold of something floating on the current and then lost it again. People sitting round, talking . . . the turns that talk takes, the things people think of . . .

Was there any chance of there being a Turner exhibition anywhere soon? the painter asked. He would be prepared to make quite a long journey, even with lingering 'flu. . . . If he ever came to Nottingham, the General said, they had some Turners in the gallery there . . . but why precisely Turner? Because, the painter said, he left everything in the air. Yes, well, there were other painters who did that too, in fact most painters did, but Turner did it all with light, and he, Nansen, wanted to see a lot of his work together some time. Why not in Nottingham? the General suggested.

376

Had he ever been in London? the *Landeskommissar* asked. No, the painter said, he had never been in London, and he rather doubted whether he would ever go there. In the old days he had enjoyed travelling, but now . . . anyway, he had no liking for big cities. He never had had. Besides, there was still a lot for him to explore here, between Glüserup and the main road to Husum. He realized that he would never discover everything about this countryside and the people who lived here. All the same, he still wanted to learn a bit more about it.

Now the General wanted to know whether there wasn't anything about a big city that was essential to Nansen's work. I shall never forget the painter's answer:

'The big cities we need are within ourselves. My own metropolis is here. I have everything I need, indeed even more: the few years that are left to me won't suffice for me to say all that's worth saying about this countryside. One has only to think of the hidden population, of those who dwell underground or in the air, of those who meet in the bog at night or on the beach, and of people's acute sense of hearing here, their fears, their visions, their slow way of thinking, or their way of coming into conflict with the law. Don't you agree with me, Jens?'

My father started and looked uncomprehendingly at the painter.

'What I mean is,' the painter said to my father, 'if you, for instance, were to talk about people here, speaking from your own experience about the people here, I'm sure nobody could tell more about any big city. Here you can find everything that happens in the world. Or would you say I'm wrong?'

There was a pause. Everybody expected my father to answer, perhaps to confirm what the painter had said. But the Rugbüll policeman didn't utter a single word. He just nodded, that was all.

The painter suggested that they should all fill up their glasses again, but nobody accepted the invitation. As for the General, he would of course have liked to have a look round the studio, but he realized that it couldn't be done. The painter, pretending to be grieved about this, made a gesture in the direction of the kitchen, where the field-mouse was rummaging about, regarding this as adequate apology. Perhaps it could be seen some other time? Oh yes, certainly some other time, with pleasure. Just today it was impossible; if the mistress of the kitchen had had her way he wouldn't even have been allowed to get up. She was very strict with him and he didn't think it would be sensible for him to try rebel against her rules. So it was agreed that they would all come again. Perhaps it could be arranged during the following month. Everybody said how delighted he was. Once again everybody conveyed his heartfelt congratulations, and this time I, too, joined in. The painter thanked them for coming, but they insisted on being the ones who had to thank him for the privilege. And above all they wished him a speedy and complete recovery from 'flu.

Four men of different occupations, all of whom had joined in the conversation to some extent, took their leave, pushing their hands out of their sleeves, showing their teeth, the skin of their faces twitching and tensing, advancing towards the sofa, stepping back again and walking sideways towards the door without taking their eyes off the patient. My father was the last to leave, after several times wondering (as I could tell from his face) whether just to slip away under cover of the general leave-taking, without saying goodbye. He now went up to the painter, stiff, very solemn, though not inimicable, just pulling the longest face he could. He stretched out his hand, with the pale hairs on the back, and limply let the painter shake it.

'There's still time for a well-laced coffee,' the painter said.

'I've got too much work waiting for me,' my father replied.

'Oh well . . . sorry about that.'

My father left the room without keeping his eyes on the painter as the others had done. And what did he do outside? He fetched his bike, posted himself at the gate, and waited until the heavy vehicles came towards him, whereupon he saluted prematurely, keeping his hand to his cap till the second car had passed, letting it fall only when, with two brief rolls as of thunder, the cars had crossed the wooden bridge.

16 Fear

On the one hand, the Theodor Storm Grammar School in Glüserup was a school that was well thought of. On the other hand it now took me three times as long to get to school. On the one hand I no longer had to run away from any Jobst or Heini Bunje; on the other hand, they messed up one's whole afternoon with piles of homework. On the one hand, the masters were not allowed to hit us; on the other hand, I missed School-master Plönnies, even if he did dole out painful slaps and buffetings. On the one hand, I had to admit my mother was right when she said, as she did everlastingly, that knowledge was power and that a grammar school gave one a better 'start in life'; on the other hand, I wondered why I should have to learn Greek verbs, when I had no intention of ever going to Greece. On the one hand, I realized that it wasn't everyone who could get a free place in a grammar school; on the other hand, I certainly didn't appreciate the way in which my father went round telling everyone I had got into the grammar school.

Having a split mind about the Storm Grammar School, both then and later, didn't get me anywhere. They made me accept the scholarship, they gave me a new satchel, bought me an almost brand-new bike, did their best to arouse some possibly latent enthusiasm in me, gave me two sandwiches more than in the old days, inspected my shirts, socks, and finger-nails before I left the house, and sometimes waved to me – even my mother did – while I mounted the bike, bending over the handlebars. Up the dyke : on the left the sea, on the right the plain. Down the dyke: on the right the sea, on the left the plain. That was the same route that the Rugbüll policeman had covered so often and which he occasionally travelled over now at the same time that I did. 'Come on, I'll pace you, you keep behind me,' and I'd agree to every damn thing they thought up, taking out my reward in sweets, sandwiches, extra pocket-money and – what mattered most to me – uninterrupted hours in my room. It may very well be that my father treated me to all these extras because he had discovered, from his reading of the Police Handbook, that a secondary education could lead to a career in the higher echelons of the police force. And so with the idea that I might end up as Commissioner of Police, or at least as a Superintendent, Hilke wasn't allowed to sing or switch on the wireless in the afternoon. She bore me a grudge for that, of course. You know what people are like.

Even if it was a route I knew like the back of my hand, even if I could have taken every twist and turn of it blindfold, the trip to and from school in Glüserup never bored me, not even though it was strenuous and tiring against a head wind. Everything was always in its place, but everything looked different every day, in an altered light, under a different sky. How many surprises the North Sea alone could produce! On the way out it would lie there wide and sleepy, licking the shore, and on the way back it would be flinging tumbling waves of greenish-blue ink against the breakwater. Or the farmsteads: sometimes they would be modest little places as though bewitched and under long veils of rain, lost in greyness. And then again, when a milky light fell on them or when the meadows around them suddenly shone, they would look portly and smug, with the midday smoke rising from their chimneys. Or the wind: sometimes it whistled through the spokes, mirthful, ready to burst with laughter when one swayed, and then it would furiously hurl one's rain-cape into one's face, or make it flutter and flap, or blow one off the dyke. How often everything here changes, daily, hourly, how often one can think about these differences, one can even get worked up about these differences if one feels like it.

Well, this is a time when I am on my way home. It's autumn. About two in the afternoon. Sea-birds, deserted sea-shore.

The wind was blowing from the north-west, diagonally, a

380

following wind, it ballooned out my cape, which flapped like a wet sail. There were footprints in the sand, down there on the beach – who had been walking along there? The wind was full of moisture. Salt. Iodine. My satchel, squeezed into the luggage-carrier, was sprinkled all over, sparkling with wetness. There was a wisp of smoke on the horizon, but no ship to be seen. Sandpipers calling : Witt-Witt. The cattle over in the meadows were again in their tarpaulin covers against the coolness of the nights, against the cool rain. Someone was out working at the drainage again. Ahead of me I could already make out the silhouette of the Wattblick Inn, with the paint peeling off it and Hinnerk Timmsen – electrified by the prospect of a new enter-prise, wholesale fuel-merchant, having read some statistics about the winters becoming steadily colder – had sold it to the Govern-ment, which at minimum cost had transformed it into a home for mentally deficient children. The flagpole had broken, and nobody had replaced it. Where now was the pennant with the crossed keys? Four – no, five nurses were standing in the wind, out on the platform, all talking, all talking at my father, who stood there among them, his head lowered, taking note of some-thing in his characteristic way. Bird-sanctuary-warden Kohl-schmidt, dyke-reeve Bultjohann, who now wore a miniature bronze version of the German Sports Badge in the buttonholes of his overcoat and his jacket lapels. . . . I raised my behind from the saddle and pressed down hard on the pedals, but still I couldn't manage it : by the time I reached the platform, the nurses and the men had gone down the narrow steps on the seaward side, and they were now scattering, forming a chain, turning towards the peninsula, keeping in touch by means of signs. A wide-meshed net : they moved diagonally towards the peninsula – then one flank fell back, and, keeping the same distance from each other, they moved on, down into hollows, up over hillocks, along the shore and over the dunes towards the tip of the peninsula – where two cross-currents met, churn-ing the water, making the flotsam bounce.

They were looking for something. They were out to catch something. Who wouldn't want to join in! I was off. I pushed my bike on to the platform and ran after them, first after the search-party, then just following the tracks left by bird-sanctuary warden Kohlschmidt and on the hills where the wind was tousling the newly planted lyme-grass. I caught up with him, smiled at him, tried to fall into step with him. I didn't want to ask what they were looking for, nor did I need to ask, for after a while he couldn't help saying out loud what he feared, so I learned the reason for their search.

Two of the children had disappeared, evidently in the very early hours of the morning, well before breakfast: a boy and a girl. At first the nurses had searched for them only in the house – wasting time, Kohlschmidt remarked. The tide was out when they disappeared, so there should have been a search out on the flats as well. He was afraid they had run out on to the flats; he feared the worst. He kept on stopping, gazing down from the hillocks on to the beach, out beyond the breakwater, and out to sea. He seemed to expect to catch sight of the children there rather than on the peninsula. We came to some scruffy osiers, which we investigated: there was no sign, no trace. One of the nurses, a tall bony woman in a tweed coat, called my father to her side and showed him something in the sand. My father scratched round a bit there with his foot. So it couldn't be tracks. Then they separated and went on. We climbed up the dunes. There were no tracks here either, and none by the painter's hut, which we went all round without entering. I buried a charred bit of paper that was sticking up out of the sand. The long chain of our search-party – it was only at the beginning that each of us could see all the others: the longer we went on searching, going further and further into the dunes, the more uncertain it became who would catch sight of whom, say, just emerging from one of the hollows between the dunes. Sometimes the left flank was out of sight, sometimes the right flank, and then again the centre of the search-party would vanish, or individual members would become invisible, and occasionally it happened that I could see nobody but the two extreme outsiders, dyke-reeve Bultjohann and the matron.

Why did the Rugbüll policeman suddenly drop out? Why did he fall behind? Kohlschmidt noticed it and sent me to fill up the gap. I looked for my father's tracks and went ahead in his place, but not for long. Suddenly the matron stopped, waved, called, waved again, beckoned everyone, and everyone retraced their steps, making towards her. The matron went on pointing at the tracks side by side, leading up from the sea

382

and towards the tip of the peninsula, keeping her hand outstretched until we were all gathered around her, and everyone
had seen that the footprints in the sand were those of children,
light footprints, very close together – perhaps they had been
holding hands when they came through the flats and then up
here.

'It's them all right,' the matron decided, and since she set
off, following the footprints, without another word, we followed
her. By the little, almost submerged, wreck the sea flung up
fountains of water that leaped so high that the spray came over
us. The wavy marks in the sand, which seemed to be a continuation of the waves of the sea, ran slantwise over the tip of the
peninsula, as far as the bird-sanctuary warden's cabin, right
through the poles and the seine-nets. Faster – everyone was moving faster now. There was nothing in the cabin, nothing under
the bench or the table, nothing on the beach either, although
the tracks led across it . . . but there in the nets . . .

So there in the long net with the weir-basket at the end of
it – the basket was loosely slung, the lines fastened to pegs –
squatting on the ground, amid a whirr of birds, caught also
in the shallow pattern of the meshes, we found the children.
There was nothing timorous in the way they looked at us, and
nothing joyful either. They merely glanced up indifferently.
They were squatting back to back on the sand inside the weir-
basket, the girl twisting the neck of a greasy rag doll, the boy
breathing on a dead bird. The girl had an old, apathetic face
and short plaits like rats' tails, which stood out stiffly from her
head. She wore a check dress. The boy was barefoot, and his
heavy head looked to weigh him down, bowing his shoulders.
His head waggled as he blew on the bird, pressing it to his
lips, and I could hear him grunting, perhaps with impatience,
perhaps contentedly. The girl pressed the rag doll's face into
the sand, twisting it round, suffocating it, doing it to death
between her outstretched brown legs.

Birds whirred and flitted over her, past her, but she took
no notice of them. She did not try to beat them off. The boy
stuffed the dead bird into the open neck of his drill shirt, and
he laughed and flung himself to and fro, spittle dripping from
his lips. He clawed at the meshes of the net, trying to pull it up,
but he couldn't. The girl sang in a harsh, ear-splitting voice,

turning her face to us. Now the matron had found the seaward way into the nets, and was groping her way along the sides, then she crept into the weir-basket, seized the girl and hauled her out. The bony woman with the stern eyes held the girl to her, pressing her to her, while the girl struck out at her head with the rag doll, until the matron's cap fell to the ground, followed by a shower of hairpins. The girl went on and on hitting her, even after the matron had kissed her. Blankfaced, she went on beating her with the doll.

Then, with Kohlschmidt's help, two nurses dragged the boy out of the weir-basket. He made no attempt to fight them off, just as he obviously didn't understand, either, what they wanted of him. With his head lowered, like a battering-ram, lethargically, uncomprehendingly, imperturbably shut away in himself, he let them shove him out. There he stood then, breathing heavily, with us all round him.

'It's all right, Jochen,' one of the nurses said. 'We're going home now, and you shall have some hot cocoa if you give me the bird.'

The boy wiped his hands on his pants, mechanically.

'Give me the bird,' the nurse said quietly, reaching into the boy's shirt, reaching down further, and the boy grunted as her hand fumbled over his belly, then stopped and pulled the dead bird out by its tail-feathers. The boy made a grab for the bird, missing it. 'All right, now we're going along home, now you're going to have a nice hot drink, and then you'll go to sleep, won't you?'

The boy cupped his hand to his ear, presumably hearing something that only he could hear. He did not resist. He went along with her, only now and then coming to a halt in order to listen again in that complicated way.

So we were on our way back to the Wattblick. Nurses, children, the housekeeper, and even the two cooks, were outside on the platform, waiting for us. There were exclamations, embraces, swift caresses, sighs of relief. 'So there you are!' 'Yes, here they are.' I peered through the open door. My father was nowhere to be seen, but suddenly I saw the girl who waved to me so clumsily every morning, when I cycled past, and who was sometimes sitting in the window in the afternoon, in her blue smock, and waved to me then too. I had thought about a name for her. I had decided to call her Nina. She came through the open door. With unsteady movements she came out on to the platform.

I made a sign to her, but she didn't understand. I said hello to her, and she noticed that, but she did not answer. As inconspicuously as possible I edged my way nearer to her, smiled at her, nodded to her, and tried, by imitating her clumsy way of waving, to make her recognize me. But she didn't look at me, or if she did she didn't remember anything about me. And then, when I had got so close to her that I could have touched her, she uttered a frightened sound and clutched at one of the nurses, seeking her protection. So there was nothing for it but to slip away again in silence, and I edged through the shifting bunch of children and adults, pursued by the astonished nurse's gaze as she absently petted the girl, comforting her.

There was my bicycle. I pushed it up on to the dyke, broke into a run, just as my father did, jumped on and went energetically pedalling off in the direction of Rugbüll.

'Well, are you *coming*? What do you think you've been doing?' Hilke called out from the steps. 'I can't go on keeping the rice hot for you.'

So there was rice pudding, with sugar and cinnamon, and perhaps even stewed plums as well. 'You needn't get all worked up like that,' I said, and she calmed down and said in a more reasonable tone: 'Well, I've warmed it up for you twice, Siggi. Where on earth have you been?'

Being instructed to treat me with some consideration, if not actual respect, she felt compelled to carry my satchel for me, winked at me, and passed her hands down the back of my head. She would have taken me by the hand, but I didn't fancy that, and I just trotted into the kitchen after her.

'Father in?' – 'No, he's out. He was called to the Wattblick. Perhaps something's happened there again. Two children have run away, perhaps they've been drowned.'

'Give me something to eat, instead of talking about things you know nothing about.'

It *was* rice pudding with stewed plums. The plate came floating towards me and was shoved in front of me: she was offended. 'Two of them got lost, that's all. As it happens, I was

385

there, I joined the search-party. Imagine: they had got themselves inside Kohlschmidt's net.'

'So that's what kept you. We were beginning to think something had happened to you.'

'How did school go today?'

'Middling,' I said. The last question came not from Hilke, but from my mother, who had come in unnoticed by both of us. She had her hair down and a towel over her shoulders, all set to wash her hair. I didn't need to turn round to know what she looked like and what she was doing. I just knew she was wearing the pale green petticoat and the shapeless old leather slippers with the dried splashes of foam on them. Now she got her shampoo out of the cupboard, now she rinsed out the washing-up bowl, now she slipped the thin shoulder-straps of her petticoat off her shoulders, over her fleshy, freckled arms with all the moles on them. Now she was pouring warm water into the bowl.

'I don't want you going inside that Wattblick place, Siggi. Understand?'

'Well, I never have been inside.'

The water seemed to be too hot. She cooled it by dipping both hands in and swirling it around.

'It's bad enough sending those children here. At least I won't have you going there.'

'Two of them got lost,' I said. 'I just helped to look for them.'

She moved her feet apart, bent her neck, threw her hair forward into the bowl, and said in a muffled voice: 'There'll always be something going on over there now. There's no saying what they'll do. Worthless creatures! They'll be nothing but trouble, you mark my words. Pity they ever came.'

'But where are they to go?'

No answer. She scooped up water, wet her hair, and then dipped it right into the bowl, panting with the effort. 'If they were really ill – but they're just useless, they're a dead weight on all of us. You can't feel anything for them, because they don't feel anything. Do you hear me, Siggi? I won't have you going there and looking at them, perhaps playing with them.'

The water trickled and dripped out of her hair. Now she dabbed some of the viscous, honey-coloured shampoo on to the back of her head and began rubbing it in, producing a lather that gradually became stiffer. Foam lay trembling on the back of her neck, flicks of it slipping into her ears, into her face and – as a gasp from her revealed – also into her eyes. Now Hilke had to lend a hand.

'The mere sight of them, Siggi, is enough to do you harm. You don't notice anything till it's too late. Impressions, you know, can stick – make you see things wrong.'

There I sat, spooning up my rice and listening. I sat there quite still for a moment longer, while Hilke rinsed my mother's gingery hair and squeezed it and rubbed it with the towel. I asked if I could go upstairs now and do my homework. Yes, I might go.

'But remember what I've told you, Siggi.'

'Yes.'

'And what have you got today?'

'Today? Math, history, essay.'

'What's the essay?'

'A Shining Example.'

'Well, that shouldn't be so hard.'

'No.'

'I'm looking forward to reading it.'

The pale green petticoat was tight over her broad beam. The back of her neck was reddened. She puffed and gasped into the bowl. There was a dark brew slopping about in the washbowl, with some streaks of lather still on it. You could see the foam getting flatter, deflating, dissolving. I was thankful to get out of the kitchen and into my room, to my homework.

Since history always left me cold, I started with the essay, and the same thing happened that always happened. At the start the subject seemed promising, something you could really write about, in fact just the thing for me; I had never yet thought an essay too difficult, when they set it, whatever it was; say, 'The Best Day of the Holidays' or 'A Visit to the Local Museum', or 'A Shining Example'; at the start I felt the same confidence about any subject. But all these quite attractive subjects turned out to be not at all up my street as soon as I began to do what we had to do, 'organizing the material'. Essays had to be 'organized'. Introduction, exposition, argument, evaluation : that was the moving staircase that the whole thing had to run on, and if you didn't construct your essay on that pattern, it was no good. Although I almost always managed to come to terms with the subject, I always went wrong, for the simple reason that I couldn't make up my mind. I could never manage to decide what the main problem was, and what the subsidiary problems. I couldn't bring myself to treat some people as main characters and others as minor characters. Politeness or pity or suspicion prevented me. But the worst thing was that I was incapable of evaluating, and that was the very thing that Herr Doktor Treplin, our German master in Glüserup, was so set on. He wanted everything evaluated: Odysseus's wiles and Wallenstein's character, the Good-For-Nothing's dreams, and the behaviour of the citizens during the Great Fire of Magdeburg. Anything that wasn't evaluated was not worth talking about. Evaluation! To this day I get the same pressure in my head, the same choking sensation, whenever I think of it.

Well, so this time the subject was 'A Shining Example'. Who could serve as one? My father, the Rugbüll policeman? The painter, Max Ludwig Nansen? Herr Doktor Busbeck perhaps, that embodiment of patience? Or my brother Klaas, whose name we were not allowed to utter, or even think, at home? Whom did I want to resemble, to emulate, to hold a candle to? If not my father, then why not? And if the painter, then why him? I already sensed the way everything in this essay was going to clamour for evaluation, to culminate in evaluation. And because I couldn't manage, never would manage, to evaluate people I knew in the way Treplin wanted, I had to seek my shining example in some other place, some other time. It would be easiest, I thought, to deal with an imaginary exemplar, one that I had concocted, a home-made one, not a living one. But what was it to be like, to make me want to be like it? I can still remember first of all choosing a surname, Martens it was, then a first name, which was Heinz, and then I made this Heinz Martens have one arm, I presented him with an extra-long scarf, fitted him out with sea-boots, and set him down on the desolate Kaage sandbank, which for some inexplicable reason was not only the breeding-ground of the barnacle geese, but also, since the end of the war, a much-favoured target for R.A.F. trainee bomber-pilots.

Heinz Martens was supplied with a short-handled spade with which to dig himself a dug-out. He was supplied with provisions and a change of shirts. I also equipped him with plug-

388

tobacco and a flare-pistol, for warning both the sitting geese and the pilots. He survived the first bombardments without anyone noticing him; then it was realized that somebody was there on Kaage, intent on protecting the brent-geese's breeding grounds. The word went round, the story became known in Hamburg, then in London, and above all it spread among the members of British societies for the protection of birds and animals – not so much among R.A.F. pilots, towards whom Heinz Martens sent up red flares without being able to prevent the necessity of collecting innumerable more or less edible roast geese after each attack.

As soon as the singing sound of the engines became audible he would rush out of the dug-out, first of all fire some flares horizontally across the breeding-ground, whereupon clouds of geese arose, at first in panic, then swiftly forming into circling formation. Then he fired the pistol straight up at the approaching planes, right to the moment when the first bombs fell. The flapping, the whistling sound of the wing-beats. The singing sound of the high-flying airplanes engines. The trembling lights of the descending flares.

The reddish glow was reflected in my window, covered my hands, my copybook, flickered over the wall of my room, and suddenly there were shouts and footsteps, a great many footsteps here in our house, downstairs. Doors were flung open. And there was Hilke calling out :

'Fire, quick, Siggi, fire !'

'Where?'

'Over there ! Come down !'

My hiding-place was on fire ! My lair was burning. My exhibition, my collection of keys and locks was burning. The pictures of the horsemen and 'The Man in the Red Cloak' were burning. There on its earthen platform above the pond my old sail-less mill, my favourite mill, was on fire. Was that the fire-engine's bell? I could hear bells ringing, but there was no sign of the fire-engine, and probably it wasn't even on the way. It was the cap of the mill that was burning. Flames were licking out of the upper windows, through the broken panes, shooting up high, waving about. And there in the mill-pond was the fire all over again, only quieter. Above and below a shower of sparks went up, a garland of yellow and red flares, which the wind, the draught of the fire itself, sent floating over the plain towards Holmsenwarf. They were all burning : Prince Yussapov, Queen Isabella of Bourbon, and the Emperor Charles V riding over the battlefield of Mühlberg. Two invisible pictures were burning, and 'The Apple-Pickers', which belonged to Klaas. The flames joined together over the cap of the mill and were pressed out sideways. There was a crackling flurry of sparks. A whirling shower of ashes against a white-grey sky. And still the cap didn't fall in.

I ran. I saw others running. From the farmsteads, across the meadows and below the dyke, they were running towards the fire. Everyone wanted to get there in time. What an effort they were making! How hurriedly they pushed through wire fences, jumped over ditches, overtook each other, all just in order to get a good sight of the fire.

I jumped down the steps. Hilke called out to me to come back. My mother called out to me to come back. I ran across the yard, along the brick path, past the lock. The ditch, along which I flitted, was lit up by the flames. I took a short cut through the rushes at the edge of the mill-pond and had just reached the path, when the cap fell in. The blazing cap fell into the tower and broke apart on the floor, sending up a flurry of sparks. The next moment the draught drew the fire up as though out of an unwieldy chimney-stack. I stood still, watching the fire do its work, the flames probing, parting, leaping, all of it with a harsh, flapping sound like, one might say, canvas in the wind. A lump of blazing embers flew out of the broken door, landing with a hiss in the wet grass in front of me. I didn't stamp it out. I stood there under the whirling rain of ashes. I watched the fire. Two men were trying to shut the door and buttress it with a beam, but they couldn't do it. All that happened was that under the blows the door rose out of its hinges and hung askew in the doorway. Nobody brought up any water, though everybody was shouting for it. Now the flames were bursting out of the lower windows and licking up the outside of the tower.

What was the last time I had watched a fire? It must have been at the beginning of the war, when Holmsen's stables burned down and the men on the farm did nothing beyond preventing the animals they had rescued from running back into

390

the flames. I didn't notice the ring of onlookers falling back from the heat.

All at once I was alone. I shut my eyes, feeling nothing but a throbbing pain that quickened, a thrusting and pushing, a stabbing, something hot and cold beating at me. But I wouldn't give in – not yet. I was resisting the compulsion, which was increasing; everything was swaying, the burning mill, and the onlookers' shadows, and I saw my hiding-place revolve, spinning round together with my bunk, the boxes full of locks, the walls covered with pictures, spinning round me faster and faster, the pictures running into each other, turning into a single strip. I stretched out my hands and ran towards the door, towards the wall of flame, that flickering curtain. Dodging under the slanting door, I dashed up the huge, worn, wooden stairs to where the flour-boxes were burning, and the ladder, and the roughly hewn beams.

There was too much light, there was simply too much light to make anything out. I had to hold my arm across my face to protect it, I couldn't breath any more, and I was thinking of the hoist when I was grabbed and hauled down the stairs into the open. Two men did it, I don't know who. I got nowhere by struggling, twisting and turning, dropping to the ground – they didn't let go of me. One of them said : 'Look out, or he'll be off in there again.' Then they both clutched me so tight that I was on tiptoe, my mouth wide open. Pushing through the ring of onlookers, who grudgingly made way, they dragged me down the path to the mill-pond, where they let me go. I collapsed, and then did what they told me : cooled my face, neck, and arms with water.

Once, when I raised my face, they laughed, and one of them said : 'Nicely scorched the lad is, ain't he?' Then they turned their backs on me and looked at the fire.

I watched the fire too, or rather, I watched its torn reflection in the pond. But not for long. When the fire-brigade arrived from Glüserup, when they unrolled the hose and dragged the pump down to the pond, I stood up and went away, without turning round. I left the mill to them, and the fire that kept away the twilight from the plain.

As I walked along, past the pond, past the willows, past the cattle standing there quite still, the stabbing went on and on : it went up my spine, jumped into my temples, penetrated me with hot and with cold. Once I stopped, hearing my father's voice. So he was there. He shouted an order, that was all. The fence, the cattle, myself – everything had its flickering shadow. I was walking in the direction of Bleekenwarf, as though it were a matter of course, as though I were expected there. The wind was rising. There was some shouting behind me, at the fire. Something must have happened. I didn't glance back. There was a trail of smoke over my head, fairly low, held down by the wind, which stretched out long and flat, twining itself into the Bleekenwarf hedges. They must have begun putting the fire out. Now the ground rose slightly. Here was the wooden bridge.

I stopped. The painter must have recognized me some time earlier. He was standing quite still at the end of the bridge, his curved pipe slanting over his chin, his hands deep in the pockets of his overcoat, which fluttered slightly round his legs. As he stood there, one might have taken him for part of the hedge.

'Come along,' he said, 'just come along.'

And I went to him, and he put one hand on my shoulder, and together we stood looking across at the burning mill. Was the tower already swaying? I thought of 'The Big Friend of the Mill', the old man with the brown fingers that had a reddish glow in them, the old man rising up, gigantic, out of the picture. Was it not a twilight like this in which he tried to set the old mill in motion with a flick of those fingers? One side of the tower broke apart and fell, and as it fell a burst of sparks flew out. Of what avail was his kindliness, his simple-minded trust?

'Do stand still, Witt-Witt,' the painter said. 'Or is something the matter? Have you got something to tell me? Do stop wriggling, boy.'

He could stand there, motionless, watching the sail-less mill burn down, the mill that was, after all, not a thing of indifference to him. He could bear it, here on the wooden bridge. Perhaps he had even been nearer and then had come back here. I don't know. I can imagine it.

The trail of smoke passed over us like smoke from a steamship. The painter's eyes were narrowed, his gaze did not waver. He stood firm on the plank. Now the whole mill collapsed, breaking in two halfway up, leaning over, falling towards the path, then, as it struck the ground, splitting asunder, sending up rotating fireballs and bouncing lumps of blazing embers. Glowing chunks of timber rolled down the hillocks, some plunging into the pond, going out with a hiss, others, each time they bounced, throwing up a shower of sparks. The trail of smoke changed colour, turning sulphur-yellow, changed its smell, becoming acrid, suffocating. The wind was now driving it into our faces, and after a while the painter said :

'It's over now, Witt-Witt. Come on, let's go inside.'

And he instantly pushed me through the hedge, through the garden, into the studio.

He turned the light on, put on his spectacles, and raised my face.

'Were you in the fire? Your eyebrows, your hair – they're all singed, just as if you'd been in the fire. Are you feverish?'

I shrugged my shoulders.

Still peering down into my face with a worried expression, he said :

'Lie down for a bit, Siggi. Just for a while. I'll fetch you something to drink. A glass of buttermilk wouldn't hurt you.' Tenderly he led me to one of the fifty-five divans in the studio, which I had for a long time thought were reserved for all the people in his pictures to sleep on : the Slovenes, the dancers on the beach, the yellow prophets, the labourers in the fields, crooked as though bent under the everlasting wind, and the crafty-eyed, green market-people. I had once amused the painter by telling him what I believed, and he had agreed that the whole phosphorescent riff-raff that he had put in these pictures did sleep there. He was taken aback if someone looked incredulous. He insisted on one's believing what he said.

So the cover was pulled back from one of these sleeping-places. There was a washed-out tarpaulin, and under it nothing but straw. I sat down on this bunk. Gently Max Ludwig Nansen lifted my legs on to it, covered me up, and gazed down at me with mock severity.

'Now you just lie there, even if you don't feel like it. Right? And you just stay quiet and wait till I come back. Right? I shan't be long.'

'But the light – you'll leave the light on?'

He nodded. 'I'll leave the light on so that you don't run away.'

Thus hedged in by his care for me and by his words, I lay back, after he had shaken up the canvas-covered pillow for me. He looked grave as he went out. I listened to his footsteps hesitantly approaching the door. Then there was a sudden draught, which fluttered the loosely stacked scraps of paper on the work-table, and some of them skimmed to the floor. I couldn't see him, but I could feel him stopping outside the window and taking another look at me before he went across to the house.

I must collect my thoughts, recall what happened then, because it was the first time. All I meant to do was wait. I was shivering under the blanket. Up to that point I could explain most things to myself by means of comparisons. The brightness of the light sufficed, the room was familiar, the time that I was to spend there was limited, at least it would not be long before the painter came back with a glass of buttermilk. I didn't feel as if I were a visitor. So far, so good. From where I stand today I can view myself there on that bunk, the brown blanket drawn up to my chest, surrounded by paintings that I knew. It's the transition – what I need to find is the transition. Or wasn't there one for me?

Perhaps it began like this : I noticed that I was being looked at and not only looked at, but recognized. There were the Slovenes, sitting at a round table, their eyes goggling contentedly from all the schnapps they'd drunk. The market-people were interested solely in an old woman going by without taking any notice of them, and the wind-blown, crooked labourers in the fields had plenty to do before the thunderstorm broke. The dancers on the beach? The prophets? They talked only to themselves.

It must have been the two money-changers, the ones with the faintly greenish-gold hands and the mask-like faces : they were looking at me. They were no longer communicating out of the corners of their eyes over the man sitting bowed before them, whose despair didn't concern them, whose sorrow suited them very well. It seemed to me they had raised their eyes, ice-grey eyes in which there was now no trace of that superiority. I couldn't explain it, nor did I want it explained. The picture contracted. There was a pretty identifiable pain, there was a vice round my temples, something bright was moving towards

394

the picture, swaying, emerging from the depths of the background; the money-changers seemed to be holding their breath. I clutched the blanket with both hands, for now it was plain that it was a little naked flame that was moving up out of the background, steadily, irrevocably. What predominated over my fear? Astonishment? Weakness? Shock? My fear kept me quite still, just watching, at least for a while. All I know is: there the picture was. There was the little naked flame. There was the fear. That was almost all. And I wasn't thinking much when I threw back the blanket and got up. I simply had to take down the picture, had to turn it round, remove the cardboard from the back and lift the money-changers out of the frame. Where would they be safe? Under the pillow? In the cupboard?

I pulled my shirt out of my trousers and laid the picture against my body – just the way I had done that time with 'The Cloudmaker' – pulled my shirt down again, lay down on the bunk and resolved not to tell anyone, not even the painter. All I wanted was to save the picture. I wanted to get it away, somewhere, I didn't yet know where, but away from here, where at any moment it might burst into flames. How cool it was against my skin! How safe it was there! I thought, shutting my eyes, in order not to have to see the other pictures. Should I tell him? Would he believe what I told him? Or should I run away? It wasn't that I wanted to keep the picture – any more than, later on, I wanted to keep other pictures that I carried off to safety because they were in danger. I only wanted to have them under my protection for a while. After all that had happened I simply couldn't let it come to the point where they went up in flames at some moment when they were unguarded. I just had to do something. I just had to do as my fear bade me. My only mistake lay in realizing too soon when a picture was in danger and in taking measures for its safety too soon.

I didn't run away. I lay, waiting, until the painter came back. He had some trouble shutting the door. He sat down on the edge of the bunk. 'Here, drink this.' I drank, scrutinizing him over the rim of the glass. Was he changed? Had he done more than just fetching the milk? 'You look terrible, Siggi,' he said. 'But there's nothing to be frightened of now you're here. Are you feverish? You just rest for a bit, and then I'll see you home.'

He took a bottle down from a cupboard, pulled the cork out

with his strong, yellowish teeth, poured out a glassful for himself, knocked it back, poured himself a second glassful, and then lit his pipe. Looking out of the window, he said: 'The fire's almost out now, Witt-Witt. They've got it under control. We'll be missing our old mill tomorrow morning. You must have been inside it pretty often, eh? Quite a few times I've seen you coming out. Why did you run away from the fire?'

I had to go to the lavatory. I lay there rigid, not daring to stir, for the picture was beginning to weigh on me, and a new fear kept me from moving: when he noticed the picture was missing, when he found it on me – what would he do? That was what I wondered, glancing stealthily at the empty frame that I had hung back in its place. Would he forbid me ever to enter his studio again? Was everything over between us? The frame hung crooked. I had put it back on its hook too hastily, and the rough brown blanket was lashed round me as tight as if it were trying to betray me. This sudden heat, these hot waves running through my body ... suddenly I simply couldn't breathe regularly and I'd got to go to the lavatory.

'Two hoses,' he said from the window. 'They've got two hoses trained on it now, as if there were anything left to save. It'll rain tonight – they might as well leave the rest to the rain. What do you think?'

'Yes.'

He turned away from the window and came over to me, with those short steps of his, while I gazed up at the ceiling. What a distance he had to cover! How long it took him! At last he was beside me. He set the glass on the floor and sat down on the bunk, puffing slightly. Out with it now, I thought, tell me what you've discovered.

He pulled out that enormous handkerchief which always smelled of tobacco, and mopped my forehead and temples with it.

'Now you just quieten down, Witt-Witt,' he said. 'One of these days you'll see: all we've done, all we've got together, doesn't cease to exist just like that. We leave traces behind us that will last longer than we think. Things don't vanish as easily as all that. Just think: I don't know much about old Frederiksen, who used to live here, but every six months he used to measure his son's height against one of the door posts, and mark it with a notch. Even if it's no more than that – something remains.' He patted me on the thigh. 'You don't have to see a thing again to make it remain. There are some things you have to lose before you can possess them in peace. You know, when I think . . . there may be seven hundred pictures, perhaps even eight hundred. They won't cease to belong to me, even if I never set eyes on them again. And what about you? Oh yes, I know – there were quite a lot.'

'What do you mean?' I said.

Without taking my question amiss, he said : 'It was a good hiding-place, and you had some good things up there. Sometimes I was quite amazed. And somethimes I was so pleased that I'd have liked to add something to your collection.'

'You've been up there? You knew?'

'Of course I knew, of course I was up there, and not just once, either.'

' "The Man in the Red Cloak".'

'Yes, I saw "The Man in the Red Cloak" up there too, and all sorts of other things.'

'How did you find out?'

'You just lie quiet. There you are, you see : I left it all to you, including the two invisible pictures that you organized for yourself, and I'd been thinking that one of these fine days I'd slip in and put something on the wall for you.'

'He did it,' I said. 'It was him, and he'll keep on doing it, he thinks of nothing else, he's always looking for a chance.'

'Steady, you don't know what you're saying.'

'He did it outside the shed and on the beach and now this time. I know he finds everything, nothing is safe from him, there'll be no end to it.'

'We'll look for a new hiding-place for you.'

'He'll find it. Definitely.'

'Then we'll look for several hiding-places and keep on changing them. Only you just be quiet now, and let go of my arm.'

'You must do something, Uncle Nansen,' I said. 'You're the only one who can do anything. Something's stopped functioning in him, or perhaps there's something he can't realize. He frightens me when he stands there like that, listening to something nobody else can hear.'

'I've known your father longer than you have,' the painter said. 'It was certainly not he who set fire to the mill. You mustn't have ideas like that. Do you want some more to drink?'

'I'm telling you we must hide everything from him.'

The painter pressed my shoulders back on to the bunk, and now his eyes admitted that he knew more than I had supposed. In his voice there was no disappointment, no sorrow, and least of all any indignation, as he slowly said: 'I'll take care of "The Money-Changers" myself. Come on, let me have them back.' Thinking the picture was under the bunk, he bent down for a moment. Then he gave me a worried look and said: 'Come on, they're safe with me.'

'There was a flame,' I said. 'There was a tiny flame moving towards the picture.'

'All right, all right.'

'It was quite clear. I saw it.'

'Yes, I quite believe it. But now let me have the picture back.'

With both hands he stripped the blanket off me, felt the picture on my body and pulled my shirt out of my trousers, not letting me help him, just calmly ordering me: 'Hands off, I'll do it myself.' No disappointment, no anger – as I said.

His wrists were surprisingly thin and pale, coming out of his very wide sleeves, as he took the frame from the wall. Without a word he put the picture back into it and hung it back in its place. 'Hungry?'

'No.'

'Then there must be really something the matter with you,' he said, smiling, and after a while he went on: 'You'll have to get used to the fact that in this life things get lost, Witt-Witt. Perhaps it's just as well. After all, one mustn't get stuck with what one has. One must always keep on making a fresh start. As long as we do that, there's always hope for us. I've never yet been satisfied, Siggi, and my advice to you is: do your best never to let yourself be satisfied.'

He gave me a startled look and covered me up.

'My God, what a sight you are. Come on, I'll take you home.'

'I want to stay here,' I said.

'Well, you can't.'

'But I want to.'

'You can have supper with us, and then I'll take you home.'

17   Illness

It wasn't worth trying to stop Okko Brodersen, to stop him in
order to ask him if he happened to have a letter in his bag, and,
if so, whether one might take it oneself and save him the trouble
of delivering it, and all that. It wasn't worth trying, for the one-
armed postman, sitting stiffly, bolt upright, on his bike, insisted
on delivering mail himself, in the house or at least on the doorstep, always with accompanying remarks, of course, sometimes
with admonitions, anyway in a manner suggesting that he knew
more about the contents of the letter than the recipient. One
didn't exactly get the feeling that he had written it himself, but
certainly that he had been there when it was written. That
was the impression one got, watching him hand over mail. How
he could tap at a letter! How admonishingly he could wave
it to and fro! No, anyone who knew him would not stop him
to ask if there was a letter. One simply let him ride past or ran
after him as I did, into the yard, up to the door.
   'Anything for us?'
   He put his bag on the saddle, opened it and flipped his thumb
along the tightly packed letters, bending them back so that the
addresses showed.
   'Nothing for us?'
   Well, only one, a large brown envelope, block capitals, no
sender's name.
   'No sender,' Okko Brodersen said, wagging his head dubiously,
possibly contemplating keeping the letter back. Finally he
pushed it towards me and pointed to the house. 'Off you go,
take it in and tell your old man in future to accept

only letters with the sender's name and address on them.'

'Right you are.'

He didn't say goodbye, but just rode off down the brick path towards Holmsenwarf.

'Here's a letter for you.'

My father was cleaning shoes. Once a week he cleaned all the shoes in the house he could lay hands on. He hauled them all in to the kitchen, set them in a fairly straight line, and treated them to three processes: brushing, applying polish, shining up. I had to lay the letter on the table. Polishing away at the top of a boot with a woollen rag, the policeman glanced at the letter, shrugged, turned away, glanced at it again as though something had just struck him, and this time looked at it longer. He was about to turn away again, but the mounting curiosity that was always so instructive to watch in my father was by now too much for him. Now he looked to see who the sender was, then he put down the boot and the rag, ripped the envelope open, read, still standing, seemed at a loss, sat down on the bench and went on reading, went back over something he had just read, held the letter to the light, and still seemed unable to grasp what it was all about. He looked at me blankly and shouted: 'Get Mother! Get her to come down! Look sharp!'

So I got Gudrun Jepsen out of her bedroom, let her go first, then overtook her on the stairs and was able to watch as she came into the kitchen, to watch the disgruntled but long-suffering look on her face as she stopped by the table, shivering in her dressing-gown. My father didn't notice her. Or perhaps he did notice her and was just reading the letter over again to make quite sure before he handed it to her. She waited. He went on reading. She seemed to realize that he was having difficulty in understanding something. He turned the letter over on the table, reading it now with his head on one side. Suddenly he pushed both the letter and the envelope towards her, jumped up, took her by the shoulders and gently but firmly made her sit on the bench. He remained standing behind her while she began to read.

Was he calm? One couldn't say he was. 'Just read that,' he said, or: 'Just have a look at that,' or: 'Do you get it?' or: 'Makes you goggle, doesn't it?' She paid no attention to him.

She wouldn't let herself be rushed. She too turned the letter over on the table. Then she raised her head and stared fixedly in the direction of the range. She made an attempt to say something, but didn't succeed.

I should like to leave the two of them to themselves in that dumbfounded or disconcerted state for a while, gasping for air, for words, and at long last recount what it was that the mail had brought into the house. As I have said, there was no sender's name on the envelope. Inside, there was a single page torn out of a magazine. One side was almost taken up by the reproduction of a painting entitled 'The Dancer on the Waves'. Written in block capitals in the margin were the words: 'Note the interesting resemblance.' It was a painting by Max Ludwig Nansen. It was Hilke dancing. She was dancing among little rippling waves only a short way out from a dazzling beach, under a red sky. She was dancing with her hair down, wearing nothing but a short, striped skirt, and her breasts seemed to be a nuisance to her as she danced, for she was already lowering one arm in order to press it on them. Her head was flung back, and on her face was a look of resentment and exhaustion. She was dancing with the waves, against the waves, the rhythm of the waves determined the rhythm of her dancing, which, it was quite easy to see, was taking her farther and farther away from the beach, out to sea, where her dance would end. So the Dancer on the Waves was my sister Hilke. A signature? Naturally there was no signature. Just as there was no sender's name on the envelope. Postmark? The letter had been posted in Glüserup.

'What do you say to that?' my father exclaimed, thumping the picture with his fist. 'It's her all right. Nobody can tell me it isn't. It's Hilke, and it's pretty obvious what that means.'

'I can see it's her,' my mother said.

'Anyone can see it's her,' my father said.

'She showed herself to him,' my mother said.

'She offered herself to him,' my father said.

'No self-respect,' my mother said.

'No shame,' my father said.

Gazing down at the picture they had still more to say, still more denunciations to utter. The gravest offence was evidently that which Hilke had committed against them. For they couldn't get over pitying themselves, grieving for themselves, and the bitterness they felt about Hilke was equalled by the pity they felt for themselves.

'To think she could do that to us! To think she could bring such shame on us! And where is she, anyway?'

My father went out into the passage, shouted for Hilke, listened and shouted again. When the door of Hilke's room opened he came swiftly back into the kitchen, looked round for the best place to take up an impressive stand, preferably on some sort of pedestal, and, since there was no such thing available, placed himself at the long side of the kitchen table. Drawn up to his full height, legs apart, his dry face strenuously raised, he stood there waiting for her.

'Anything the matter?' Hilke asked and then, when she saw our faces, in a quieter voice: 'What on earth's happened?'

Hesitantly she came farther into the kitchen, unsure of herself, rather frightened. She looked anxiously into our eyes, without becoming any the wiser. She laid the palms of her hands together and rubbed them. 'What's the matter with you all? What have I done to you?' She gathered her hair together at the back of her neck and tied it with a ribbon. She moistened her lips. The Rugbüll policeman kept her on tenterhooks, the way he always liked to keep people on tenterhooks. As always, he took his time before broaching the subject, relishing the uncertainty that his calculated silence aroused in others. Indeed, sometimes I thought – or at least, it's what I think now – that his calculated silence was meant to constitute part of the penalty, simply because he would hold back the charge, leaving one no opportunity to defend oneself.

Hilke went up to him, spreading out her arms in a pleading gesture. He remained silent. 'Say something – someone!' Finally she looked at me and followed my gaze, by which means I drew her attention to the kitchen table, to the page. Standing behind my mother, she looked down at the picture, gazing for a long time, much too long as it seemed to me. She did not dare to pick up the page.

'So that's it. Now I understand.' She made a gesture with one hand, smiling bitter-sweetly, trying to make light of the matter. 'Oh well, if that's all you mean.' She gave a sigh of relief, turned away from the table and said: 'That was ages ago, that was at least last spring, some time like that,' and she positively seemed to expect that everyone would now brighten up, or at least that it would reduce the tension.

My mother was staring, as if transfixed, at the blue pattern of the oilcloth on the kitchen table. As if from a long way off my father was gazing down at the page. 'Well, if that's all,' Hilke said, and she went on : ' "The Dancer on the Waves" – my God, what can you have against that? He needed a model, and he thought I would do. That's all there was to it. Just once. One single time. "The Dancer on the Waves." Fancy getting all worked up like this – I mean, it's just like going to the doctor,' she said, evidently feeling quite exculpated, her way of moving already more relaxed.

'So it's true,' my father said dully. 'What's insinuated here is true. You showed yourself to him. You posed for him. And this is proof enough of how much self-respect you have.'

Hilke turned round and looked at him in amazement. 'Self-respect? What do you mean, self-respect?'

'You live with us, don't you?' my father said, his eyes narrowed. 'You've known very well how things stood between him and me in recent years.'

'But that's all over and done with,' Hilke said. 'Those times are over.'

His mouth twisted with contempt, my father retorted : 'Once anything's gone as far as that, there can't ever be an end to it. But that's another matter. We're talking about you, about you in this picture. Can't you realize what's happened?'

'She's like me,' Hilke said. 'The Dancer on the Waves is like me, that's true.'

'Anyone can recognize you,' my father said, 'it's not only us who can. There! Someone's sent it to us anonymously. And there may be plenty of other people who'll react in the same way when they see that picture. You don't need to wonder what anyone'll think when they recognize you. If at least it had been painted by someone else. But him! Him, a law unto himself! With that arrogance of his! With that scorn of his for people who are only doing their duty. You can't tell me you've never heard the way they talk about him and me.'

Slowly Hilke went over to the window and stood there, head bent. It was clear that she would not find anything more to say now. My father did not look at her, he went on addressing his remarks to the place where she had been standing. 'Just try to realize what you've done to us, what this means to us.' I couldn't help glancing at my mother, who suddenly stirred, awakening out of her apathetic brooding, pulling herself up and murmuring: 'Terrible', then again: 'It's terrible what he's made of you: the foreign thing, the alien thing that peers out of it. Possessed. Intoxicated. And what he's made of your body. The gleaming hip. The crooked thigh. And your face. Oh, you can't tell me you like the face he's given you.'

'It's an insult,' my father said.

'He's always insulted everyone he's ever painted,' my mother went on. 'And he's done the same thing for you. A gypsy might dance like that.'

'Yes,' my father said, 'a gypsy. He's turned you into a gypsy.'

'It's an outrage,' my mother said.

And the policeman said: 'I suppose you know what you have to do now.'

'There's only one thing for it,' my mother said. 'This picture – a picture like this must not be allowed to exist. For your sake and for our sake.'

'You helped with the making of it,' my father said. 'Now you can help to rid us of it. It can't be so hard for you.'

Hilke pulled a stool towards her and sat down clumsily, as though she didn't belong. She gazed down at the upturned palms of her hands, and then suddenly put her hands to her face, moaned and gulped. Anyone who didn't know her would really have thought at this moment that she was just having hiccups; but we knew she was crying.

'Have you got that clear?' my father asked. 'Have you got that clear? That picture has got to go.'

Hilke gave no sign of having understood him. The upper part of her body was now swinging to and fro as though in search of some resistance or as though she were trying to find something to lean against.

'You can insist on it,' my mother said. 'You have a right. This picture mustn't be there for everyone to gape at.'

'He has given you a bad name,' my father said, 'and you, you yourself, will put that right.'

404

How swiftly and naturally they took their cues from each other, each of them reinforcing or elucidating the other's words, just as if they had rehearsed it. And the fact that they did not speak the rest of it to Hilke but uttered their statements, their accusations, their demands, talking away over her head, disregarding her, made it seem that they had worked the whole thing out in advance and were far less concerned with Hilke's part in it than in what it all meant to them. They complemented each other. Each took up where the other left off. They worked each other up, while my sister worked herself, as you might say, into her crying, got going with a feeble, steady howling only occasionally broken by a sob. Nobody told her to stop. Nobody tried to make sure that she had understood what was expected of her. They went on at her, belabouring her ceaselessly, until the telephone summoned the policeman to his office. Now my mother also got up and left the kitchen. Or rather, before she went upstairs, she went over to Hilke, laid one hand flat on her shoulder, pressing lightly, and then left the kitchen. How was I to calm Hilke down? I followed my mother's example, laying one hand flat on my sister's shoulder and massaging it for a moment, then I patted her shoulder, casually drumming out the rhythm of 'You're my popsy' on her collarbone, not, I must confess, taking much interest in what I was doing, for my attention was, of course, directed to my father's telephoning. He was roaring away that, yes, this was Rugbüll Police Station, yes, this was number two-o-two, yes, it was himself speaking – so he trumpeted on.

A road accident! So it was a road accident, was it. . . . A road accident on the Husum road. . . . A milk-van and a bicycle. . . . Oh, a Mercedes and a cart, thirty-eight dead. . . . Oh, I see, a thirty-eight model. . . . Couldn't Glüserup Station. . . ? Oh, *two* injured, that was a rather different matter. . . . At the turning for the Söllring Estate, right. . . . All quite clear, right.

He replaced the receiver, went into the hall and put his uniform jacket on, buckled on his belt. In the mirror I watched him grab his pale leather dispatch-case, put his cap on, button up the pockets of his jacket. He stopped in the doorway, gazing at us without reproach or chiding, cocked his ear towards upstairs, then called out : 'Well, so long,' and walked out. Not a word more, no final gesture.

What was I to do with Hilke? I tried to pull her to her feet, but I couldn't manage it. I tried to pull her hands away from her face, but I couldn't manage it. 'Come on,' I said, 'come on, I'll take you into your room, so you can lie down, you can think it all over in peace and quiet.'

She shook her head. She whispered: 'Don't go away. Stay with me a bit.'

So I said: 'But only if you come along, if you come to your room.'

And after a while she got up with a jerk and gave me one hand. I led her, still crying, her other hand still pressed to her face, into the hall and into her little room. I could feel the gentle heavings of her body as she wept, and I said: 'Do stop, Hilke, really, do stop howling now, there's no sense in it.' She sat down on the bed, and I sat down beside her, and gradually I succeeded in getting her hand away from her face, which was flushed and sticky with tears.

And then she asked me if I too had always wanted to get away from home, and I said: 'Yes.' And then she said that she had several times been on the point of clearing out, but she had stuck it simply for my sake. And she said: 'I'd really like to put an end to it all,' and so I said: 'Right, I'll bring flowers to your funeral, red poppies.' And then she asked me why our house was so alien and so hostile and whether I felt anyone at home understood me. And I said: 'No.' And then I asked her who had invented them, and she asked: 'Invented who?' And I said: 'The Rugbüll policeman and his wife.' And then she asked couldn't we go away together, perhaps to Hamburg, where she knew her way about and where there would be various chances for me too, and I said: 'Why not?' And then she said: 'How on earth am I to stop that picture from being seen?' And I said: 'You can't.' And then she asked: 'What does it matter anyway if he looks at you?' And I said it didn't matter at all. And then she asked what she was to do now, and I said: 'I don't know.' And then I asked if she had heard the story too, and she asked: 'What story?' And I said: 'About Klaas getting a prize for photography,' and she said: 'No.'

Suddenly she let herself drop on to the bed, turned on one shoulder and pulled her legs up and seemed to be breathlessly listening to something. I undid the ribbon that she had tied her hair with. And then she said: 'Addi's back in Hamburg,' and I said: 'Yes.' And then she asked me, if I were her, would I marry Addi, and I said: 'If it had to be.' And she said: 'Everything would be different if it weren't for them,' and I said: 'We ought to exchange them.' And then she asked: 'Who?' and I said: 'The Rugbüll policeman and his wife.' And then she said: 'You mustn't say a thing like that,' and I asked her: 'You mean you wouldn't like to?' and then she said: 'Yes, I would.'

So it went, this way and that, in her room. Gradually she calmed down, also getting into a somewhat more comfortable, anyway more relaxed, position, and I slipped off her shoes and pulled the quilt over her as best I could. But Hilke didn't want to stay lying on the bed, least of all under the quilt, what she wanted was a piece of bread, with plum-jam, and as I thought this was a good sign, I promised to go over to the larder and fetch it for her.

I didn't get as far as the larder, for there in the hall, wearing his wide-brimmed hat, his hands deep in his pockets, looking at me with a sternly, urgently questioning face, was Max Ludwig Nansen, pretty agitated, so that it was clear at a glance how hard it had been for him to make his way to our house. He didn't smile as he usually did, he didn't give me the usual affectionate cuff on the ear. Tight-lipped, his chin thrust out, his shoulders tense – he looked ominous. The first thing was to meet his gaze and his challenging attitude. Then he said: 'Where's the picture? Bring it here, I'm taking it with me.'

'Picture?' I asked. 'What picture do you mean?'

'Don't talk, don't pretend, bring it here, and there'll be no more said. You know very well the one I mean: "The Dancer on the Waves".'

'You mean it's gone?'

'Yes, it's disappeared, and I've come here to get it. Let's get that clear. Well?'

'I didn't take it.'

'You want me to search?'

'You can search everywhere, it isn't here.'

'Listen to me, Siggi, If you don't hand over that picture you won't set foot in Bleekenwarf again. I know the reason why you took it, but I've got to have that picture back. That's what I've come here for.'

'It's not here, honest.'

'We shall soon see,' the painter said, seizing my wrist and pulling me upstairs to my room. 'This room, isn't it?'

'Yes.'

'Well, open the door.'

How he took possession of my room, turning everything upside down! How purposefully he walked into the middle of the room, bent down and first of all turned right round, looking everywhere for possible hiding-places! I went to the window and watched him searching the shelves, lifting the ocean-maps off the table, suspiciously investigating the bed; I watched his attempts to discover in the harmless crate what it couldn't possible contain because it wasn't big enough. Finally he knelt down and even peered under the rag carpet. He wasn't satisfied. He was so sure he was right that after he had searched the whole room he came over to me and shook me, asking in time to the shaking: 'Where – where – where is the picture?' And I answered, likewise in time to the shaking: 'I don't know – I don't know.' 'You've got it!' 'No, I haven't got it.' 'You thought it was in danger and you wanted to get it to safety.' 'No, not that picture, not "The Dancer on the Waves".' 'Then one of you has. If it wasn't you, then it was one of the others who took it.' He seized me by the front of my shirt, bunching the stuff up in his hand and twisting it, his hard, broad hand pulling me off the floor, and with his eyes quite close to mine he repeated his accusation. He got nothing from me but: 'No.' I was able to bear both his grip and his gaze, in fact I was even able to think in his grip and under his gaze: who's that chopping wood down there? For while we were arguing there was a sound of axe-blows coming up from the yard, from the shed. My father, of course! He had reached the scene of the accident too late, the people involved had already gone their ways, so to speak, and since the pile of wood had been a reproach to him for some weeks, he was now chopping firewood – waste wood as a matter of fact, from the saw-mill in Glüserup.

Over my head the painter looked down at my father. Slowly he let go of me, then he thrust me aside and went to the door. He went downstairs, paused in the passage to light his pipe before going outside, went down the stone steps rather too imposingly and then, taking short puffs, made for the shed. My father hadn't yet seen him, or at any rate he was pretending not to have seen him. He was chopping wood, very attentively, very grimly. Carefully he put logs on the chopping-block, stepped back, measuring the distance as he raised the axe and then, without putting all his strength behind the blow, indeed rather more as if he were just guiding the axe, brought it down on the piece of wood, calculating it so well that the pieces into which the wood had split stayed on the block, whereupon he pushed them to one side with the back of his hand. Go on, look up! He must have known for ages that the painter, who had stopped beside the pile of chopped wood, was there, he must have seen his shoes, the hem of his overcoat, every time he bent down to pick up another log, but he was still behaving as if he were alone in the yard. I thought: Let's see how long he'll keep him waiting. And I thought: Let's see how long Nansen will put up with it. They aren't half good at ignoring each other in our part of the country, when it suits them, and they're quick to say 'He's lost' when one gives in, gives up, or throws in the sponge. My father was wielding the axe, letting it bite into the wood – the old axe with the dark stains of pigeons' blood. The painter was standing there, puffing, watching him, with narrowed eyes. Was there no change? Yes, my father was working faster, even more grimly, scarcely leaving himself time to measure the distance before letting the axe fall – that in itself was an admission.

I could leave the two of them standing there like that for a week : that would make a story that would be entirely justifiable. But in the end I have to admit after all that it was the painter who picked up a log that had flown off the block, threw it back on the pile, and said : 'You needn't rush. I'll wait till you've finished.' My father said nothing. As if embarrassed, he tested the sharpness of the axe, running his moistened thumb along the blade, and then continued his work, driving the axe into a log that was full of knots and would not fall apart at the first blow, but actually came up with the axe, twice, sticking to the blade, so that the policeman had to exert all his strength in order to split it. Once again a chip flew to the ground in front of the painter, once again he picked it up and threw it on to the pile. 'Everything in its place,' he said. He got no answer, and there he stood, persistent, but pretty hopeless all the same, and as though superfluous, in the way. This he realized, and finally he seemed to see that it was up to him to make a new onslaught in order to get where he wanted, and so he went closer to my father, his thumbs hooked into the pockets of his overcoat. He simply went up beside him and said disparagingly : 'I suppose one can still get such a thing as an answer to a question here – or can't one?' The policeman split a log so dry that it was all splintery, rammed the axe into the block, pulled it out again and used it as a support : leaning on the handle of the axe, his face averted, he waited to hear the question.

The painter did not trouble to lead up to what he had to say; he simply demanded the return of his painting. The policeman, after for a time staring as though lost in thought, shrugged his shoulders and said scornfully that he didn't know what the painter meant – so far as he was concerned, a receipt was given for anything that was confiscated. Could he have a look at the receipt? Now for the first time he looked at the painter, who repeated, patiently and insistently, that a painting of his was missing, a painting called 'The Dancer on the Waves', and that he had come in the firm belief that it was from here, from Rugbüll, that he would get it back.

My father thought it over. Then he asked whether the painter realized what a charge he was making, and so forth : it sounded as though he were suggesting that he, the policeman, had stolen the painting. The painter thereupon urged the policeman to remember that it was not so long since he had been under orders to confiscate all work produced in defiance of the ban, and that he certainly had confiscated things, and even that after the originators of the ban had bolted he had continued to act in accordance with their will, had taken, destroyed, burnt, had blindly and mulishly carried out the orders he had been given – didn't he remember? Had he forgotten how often in the execution of his duty he had loitered around Bleekenwarf? And had he, the painter, after all that had happened, no right to ask questions? My father listened, then raised the axe in one hand, holding it close to the blade, and pointed calmly towards the brick path. His arm didn't tremble. If he had quite finished, my father said, would he now kindly take himself off. All there had been for them to say to each other had been said in past years – and that was the way out of the yard. The painter said he could understand that the policeman preferred not to remember all sorts of things, and he was quite ready to go, but first of all there was just one thing he would like to draw his attention to : the time when a man could be forbidden to paint was well and truly over and what might then have seemed to the policeman to be his duty would now doubtless be given another name.

He just wanted to point that out, and above all he wanted it to be clear – completely and finally – that something had changed since those days : he didn't need to possess himself in patience and stay quiet, and he was no longer *going* to possess himself in patience and stay quiet.

My father dropped the axe on to the block and inquired, with laborious mockery, if that was a threat and whether the painter perhaps intended, given the opportunity, to finish him off. He actually said : shoot him down. All he wanted, the painter said, was to get down to brass tacks. The time of beating round the bush was over. That time was certainly over as far as he was concerned, my father said. He was gradually realizing, he said, that he had sometimes shown too much consideration, contrary to his orders, at any rate so much that now they could both be here talking to each other. For if he had carried out his orders to the letter, without taking thought, doubtless the two of them would not now be standing here together. Perhaps the painter had never yet realized that.

He had realized quite enough, the painter said. Certainly he had come to learn what a disease 'duty' was, and whatever he could do against it, he would do. That was what the victims expected – the victims of that duty. Had he now finished what he had to say? my father asked. He had work to get on with. His mouth twisted in an expression of scorn that the painter could not fail to notice. He bent down for a log, painstakingly placed it on the block, raised the axe and then let it sink again. He had not got the painting, he said. But even if he had had it, he would have thought twice before giving it back, since after all it concerned him too. Then he raised the axe in both hands and struck : the log split and flew apart, and the axe bit grindingly into the wood. Now the painter seemed to have learned what he had wanted to learn, but he still did not go, he still wanted to make sure whether they had completely understood each other. What sort of situation did he, the Rugbüll policeman, think he would be in, supposing . . . ? Might he once again stress the fact that there was no longer . . . ?

Even if he did not mean it, each of his utterances sounded like a threat. I could not go on listening to him talking like that to the policeman, who was now again grimly working away. Walking backwards, I moved towards the house, and saw my father once more raise the axe and point to the brick path. Still going backwards, I went up the steps, and I felt myself turning hot and cold : there was that drawing sensation again, that tension, that pressure round my temples. When I was back in my room I had to massage my stomach. Were they still down there by the shed? Yes, they were still there, the painter now half turned away, on the point of going. But having started this discussion, he obviously wanted to get everything off his chest : all his disappointment, his accumulated rage, his condemnation, his warnings. Now and then my father gave some answer, or himself asked a question, or simply looked at his interlocutor in slow astonishment and what I should like to call a kind of controlled contempt. Superior? I could not have said who was superior to whom that time by the shed.

Finally Max Ludwig Nansen took himself off. I couldn't have borne any more of it, either. I would have made him go faster if I had been able to, and when he stopped, irresolute, by the brick path, I thought : Get on with it – oh, do go on! On the landing there was no sound to be heard. Hilke didn't stir; she had probably been and fetched herself her slice of bread with plum-jam on it. From the other side of the bedroom door I could now hear a monotonous wailing that was not only familiar but positively reassuring : my mother was capable of keeping it up for hours on end. I untied the rope to the loft trap-door and jogged it once; the trap-door opened. I pulled again, and the special ladder that Hinnerk Timmsen had got for us came sliding down. Once I was up there, I pulled the ladder up after me, as I used to do in the mill, and then shut the trap-door. Easy does it, I said to myself. Just take it easy. How many ways of taking cover there are! How many hiding-places for a human being! Nobody would find me here!

412

They never came up here more than twice a year, and that was to put away all the things they couldn't bear to throw away – and the Jepsens never could bear to throw anything away. Old mattresses, sofas with broken springs, laundry-baskets, rickety kitchen chairs and tables, bundles of dressmaker's patterns, books too, and suitcases with broken locks : all this they would drag up here and leave to the twilight and the soundless process of decay. Nothing was arranged, nothing was stacked, everything was simply chucked in or dropped with a sigh of relief. There was the tiled stove with the brownish smudges of putty. Over there was the wardrobe with the door hanging open. And over there was the little skylight that nobody had ever opened.

I took off my shoes and climbed cautiously over to the sky-light. From the yard I could hear the blows of the axe and the splintering of the wood. Here was my crate, covered with paper and old rags, surrounded by bits of old chairs. I cleared away the camouflage, the bottom layer of which was several sheets of oil-paper. I removed the lid and sat down. When I saw my new collection all intact, the tension and the drawing sensation ceased, and the pressure on my temples diminished.

I took out 'The Dancer on the Waves', propped it up against the side of the crate and, with the thin light falling slantwise on it, gazed at Hilke dancing for me among little tumbling waves. And all at once she was a personal concern of mine, there under the red sky, her hair loose. All at once it was important for me to understand her, there in that short striped skirt, with those pointed breasts, this Hilke who did not cease dancing despite her exhaustion, alone there by the dazzling beach. Nobody, nobody would ever see this picture again, that was settled, and the other pictures, too, were there only for me now. I had learned something, I had found out something about myself and what I needed in order to live with myself.

There was a knocking.

There had been a knocking before that, and I had thought to myself : That can only be the Rugbüll policeman knocking the handle of his axe vertically against the chopping-block to fix the axe-head more firmly into place. But the knocking was here, at the door of my cell. It was not a timid knock such as Joswig gave, but hard and desperate – a knocking that heralded not only Wolfgang Mackenroth but likewise some more dismal news about his situation. The only person who knocks like that, in my view, is someone who believes he has a right to come and bemoan his lot to you.

I turned slowly to the door and there he was, already coming in, his trench-coat open. He didn't even wait till whoever was outside had shut the door, but rushed straight up to me without pausing to think : What is the correct approach to a juvenile delinquent who is, moreover, the subject of my thesis?

'Misery!' he exclaimed. 'Of all the miserable rotten luck! You've never seen the like of it, Siggi. Can I sit down?' The young psychologist slapped me absentmindedly on the back, sat down on my bed, and for a while presented the sight of a man not merely unfortunate but drowning in his misfortune.

'Well, what's happened now?'

'First of all, here are the cigarettes – five packets today, two of them from your sister.' He threw a packet over to me, pushed the others under the bedclothes and waved his hands in a gesture of resignation that might have meant : 'It's all up, the whole thing's done for', or possibly : 'The world will never be the way we try to make it.' Deftly he tipped two yellowish tablets out of a little tin box on to the back of his hand, caught them up with his tongue and swallowed them without more ado.

'The work?' I asked.

'My landlady,' he said. He jumped up and strode swiftly from the window to the door, clasping his hands above his head, then lashed out with long swinging movements of his arms, movements obviously meant to help him to relax. Then, with a great sigh, he flung himself back against the door, so violently that I expected Joswig to put his eye to the spy-hole at any moment, then he crossed to my table and stood there. Well, so it was his landlady, the North German female champion on the trapeze. Wolfgang Mackenroth gave a bitter laugh. Well, his landlady was expecting a child, which could just as easily be his as her husband's, the crane-driver's – an uncertainty that oppressed her less than it did him. All she wanted was a child, but he insisted that it had got to be *his* child. 'Just think of it!' He had forced her to try to remember. She had remembered and then had shaken her head. He had told her she must reckon it up. So she had reckoned it up and then she had shrugged her shoulders doubtfully. 'Understand me, Siggi! Think of be-

ing only a bit of a father, at best half a father!' I agreed it was
too bad and suggested he should go on living with the family
until the child was big enough to choose its father for itself from
the supply on offer. 'Oh, you don't mean that seriously!' He
writhed, twisting his head nearly off his neck, then blew on his
left wrist as if it needed cooling down. 'You just try to do
your writing in a situation like that, Siggi. Here!' He laid some
sheets of writing on the table: it was a new chapter of his
thesis, covered with frenzied corrections – you could see that
at a glance. 'Of course this is only a draft, but all the same I'd
be glad if you'd ...' He smoothed out the folded, bespattered,
slightly torn pages, saying: 'I don't know, but to write a thing
like this one has to be free, anyway not worried. How are you
getting on?'

'It's different with me,' I said. 'The more worries I have,
the better. Just don't go wishing to be well and free and having
no worries – it only leads to disappointments.'

He took the manuscript from the table again. Could he read
some of it to me? No. Just a few pages? No. Well, could he ask
me to think of his rotten situation while I was reading it? No.
Well, why not?

'There's no excuse for bad work,' I said, and for a moment
I hoped he would take his draft chapter away again. But there
was never any knowing what this psychologist would do next,
and now he pushed the manuscript back to me, repeating something he had read somewhere:

'It's only failure that one learns from,' or words to that effect.

I dare say he had expected more from me, more sympathy,
comfort, encouragement. But I couldn't work myself up to it.
And I never shall work myself up to it as long as he wears that
thin gold chain round his neck, which may very well have a
locket on the end of it, and the locket may very well contain
a photograph of his landlady swinging from the trapeze. I loathe
men who wear thin gold chains round their necks. All I could
do for him was to say that I was prepared to read his manuscript. And since, after this declaration, I took up my pen again,
he had no choice but to take his leave – with a great show of
dejection, at that.

I didn't want to start reading, at any rate not before supper.
I felt drawn back to Rugbüll, to the loft, to my crate, to the

415

collection I had begun to make in those strange circumstances. But the farther away I pushed those sheets of his writing, the more they bothered me, positively blocking my way back, over-shadowing my memory. So I reluctantly pulled them towards me, lit a cigarette, and began to read.

How far had he got with me, chopping me up small and boiling me up for stew? Where had he got me skewered? What sort of sight did I present, as it were, in a state of being stuffed and dried, a piece of taxidermist's delight?

So here goes – art and criminality and all that, we've been through it all – what's this chapter about? Chapter Four – and the heading? 'D. Forms and Functions of a Limited Obsession', with a pencilled note: 'provisional title'. And then Wolfgang Mackenroth wrote:

Siggi J.'s early sufferings and his disturbed relationship with the external world must be regarded in the context of the development of relations between the painter Max Ludwig Nansen and the subject's father, the country police officer Jens Ole Jepsen. What for the policeman had originally been a routine assignment, albeit one of an extraordinary nature, namely surveillance of the painter to ensure that he did not violate the ban on pursuing his pro-fession, gradually, as a result of specific events and undoubtedly also owing to his characterological peculiarity, became transformed into a compulsive fantasy. In his mind surveillance of the painter became a personal matter that he continued to believe he must pursue even when the period of the ban, in the course of events, came to an end.

Well, you really couldn't put it any more harmlessly than that.

The compulsive fantasy of the father, who, moreover, had the faculty of second sight – known locally as 'foreglimpsing' – had its correspondence in the boy's obsession, which was initially caused by fear, the origin of which can be dated. The boy's unusual passion for collecting, which was not inhibited by any moral taboos and which will later be discussed in more detail, has already been mentioned above. He subsequently developed an additional obses-sion. This manifested itself for the first time on the day when a dilapidated mill, in which Siggi J. had hidden his collection, burnt to the ground. The boy's distress at the loss, exacerbated by the conviction that the fire had been started by his father and that his father, in pursuit of his obsessive fantasy, would cause more such fires, triggered off hallucinatory sense-perceptions in connection with certain pictures in the painter's studio. He saw flames moving forward out of the background of the paintings. He believed the paintings to be in danger, and in order to protect them he yielded to the compulsion to take them to a place of safety. This was not yet associated with the desire to appropriate them. It is, rather, a case of anxiety pure and simple, one so rare and so exclusively associated with one person that I shall, where convenient, speak of Jepsenophobia. It must be borne in mind that the subject's father once employed him as a go-between, whereas the painter occasionally entrusted him with the task of taking paintings to a place of safety. The negative results of the dilemma arising out of these divided sympathies could never be overcome. Originally arising in a loose, indeterminate sequence, these obsessive ideas later manifested themselves ever more frequently and more or less predictably. They automatically appeared whenever a relationship arose between Siggi J. and a painting. The distress associated with these conditions justifies our referring to them as an 'affliction'.

However, the boy's obsessive idea that he must move paintings to a place of safety did not arise only when he was in the painter's house. It might manifest itself anywhere : at school, in a savings bank, in a museum. Indeed, in the course of time the subject yielded to the demands of his obsession in various localities, first of all in Glüserup, but then also in the towns of Husum, Schleswig, and Kiel, and finally in Hamburg. The fact that the intention was always to save the paintings from some imaginary danger is implicit in the fact that they were at no time offered for sale. Carefully packed up, they were intended to remain in selected hiding-places until such time as the danger should be over.

The records of the criminal investigation departments in Schleswig and Hamburg offer valuable material for the assessment of these obsessive acts. After Siggi J. had been caught there *in flagrante delicto*, his defence was that he had to save endangered paintings, and the records explicitly state that he did so in a manner indicating the presence of a delusion.

So that's the way Mackenroth means to twist it.

In most cases the records use the terms 'amateurish' and 'fanatical', stress the fact that the acts did not constitute theft in the ordinary sense of the word, and state that during interrogation the subject gave the impression of being a decent, intelligent boy.

417

It was not least owing to this impression that no formal charge was preferred at that time.

The point must now be made, however, that fear for the paintings was not the sole cause of this obsessive behaviour. Equal importance must be attached to the subject's passion for collecting, which dates back to his early years, increasing with the passage of time and becoming steadily more compulsive. According to Bengsch-Giese's investigations (*The Forecourts of Crime,* Darmstadt, 1924) collecting is one of the activities that tend to enhance instinctual force : the pleasure-factor may become so strong that legal forms are no longer acknowledged. As has been mentioned above, Siggi J. committed thefts in order to enlarge his collection of locks and keys; when asked whether he thought his behaviour morally defensible, he admitted that he had committed inexcusable offences against private property.

There is, however, no clear consciousness of having done wrong in respect of the stolen paintings. Indeed, Siggi J. went so far as to claim that he was 'predestined' to collect certain 'endangered objects'. This was likewise his explanation of his passion for collecting : he rejects the view that collecting is a specific, in some cases artistic, mode of creating order over against the disorder of the world. His notion that he was predestined was to play a decisive part in arriving at a verdict on his case. The outsider can claim exceptional rights. It is nevertheless remarkable that the boy's obsessive ideas and behaviour were diagnosed as pathological too late.

After Siggi J.'s offences had become known to his parents, it was decided that corporal punishment was the only suitable correction. The subject was then locked in his room for days on end, nobody spoke to him, and, as a further punishment, he was often made to go without meals. He was forbidden to go to any of the neighbouring towns. During this period there was marked deterioration in the quality of his school work. But this improved as soon as the various punishments were reduced and Siggi J. was again able to 'collect endangered objects'. It must be regarded as merely coincidental that there were valuable items among the paintings he regarded as endangered.

A noteworthy change took place in the relationship between father and son after the Rugbüll policeman had been assigned the task of recovering a water-colour by Max Ludwig Nansen that had disappeared from the Savings Bank in Glüserup. Since all the evidence pointed to Siggi J. as the culprit, Police Officer Jepsen set several traps for his son. When these failed to be effective, a violent altercation took place between them one night, as the result of which the subject was solemnly cast out of the family.

Cast out – that's pretty good! He wanted to run me to earth. What he said was : I shan't give up till I've run you to earth.

In this way, the Rugbüll police officer's official endeavours from a certain point onward were concentrated on Siggi J. The only person to recognize the boy's condition as pathological was the painter Max Ludwig Nansen. Although he found himself compelled to make his studio out of bounds for Siggi J., his deep affection for the boy remained unchanged – a circumstance that provoked the police officer to the most ruthless persecution.

No, Wolfgang Mackenroth! It was like that and yet it was not like that at all.

I couldn't go on reading, there was too much he had hushed up; too much of the antagonism had been prettified. Wherever he found me guilty, he did it in such a way as to invoke mitigating circumstances – and whatever I need, it certainly isn't mitigating circumstances. I decided to hand him the chapter back with the advice that he should rewrite it – and in a manner in keeping with my ideas. What I expected was a description of a pathological condition, not a laboured justification. After all, we had discussed it often enough. I promised to help him. I shall help him.

18 Visiting

Once again I had arrived early. I've never succeeded in turning up anywhere at the agreed or appointed time: not at school,
not for meals, not at Bleekenwarf, and not at railway-stations
– I'm always early. So I wasn't surprised to find the doors of
the Schondorff Gallery in Hamburg still locked and the grey-
clad, gloved chimpanzees who would be directing and super-
vising the stream of visitors did not so much as glance at me,
but merely continued their desultory chats, standing at some
distance from each other in the glittering foyer. Even when I
shook the middle one of the glass doors, politely, you might say,
experimentally, they paid no attention to me. Much too early,
as usual. Just let Wolfgang Mackenroth work that one out.
    I peered through the glass doors. I walked ostentatiously up
and down outside in the drizzle, from time to time trying the
door-handle. For the nth time I read the poster announcing the
opening and closing dates of the great Nansen Exhibition. The
attendants either didn't or wouldn't see me. When the runners
in the Alster relay-race, which started this Sunday, came pounding along the tramlines, drenched, their running-shorts splashed
with mud, the attendants came up to the glass doors and surveyed the athletes not without sympathy as they ran, open-
mouthed, elbows working, with flagging footsteps, in the direction of the Goose Market. I signalled to the attendants, but they
didn't notice. Slowly, infinitely slowly, their hands clasped behind their backs, they returned to the middle of the foyer,
posting themselves under the big chandelier as though they
themselves were objects on view. Whatever they said to each

other was purely between themselves. Perhaps they were evaluating each other's appearance, assessing the degree of severity, alertness, and authority that emanated from them or was meant to emanate from them to the highest possible degree. How many people would have to gather outside to make them open the doors before the time?

The second person to arrive was a bent old man who tapped his way up the wet marble steps with his walking-stick, tried to push the glass door open with one shoulder and, having failed, glared at the attendants from under bristling eyebrows and struck the glass with the knob of his stick. He knocked to no avail. He went over to the poster, jerked his head up and gazed reproachfully at Max Ludwig Nansen's self-portrait with the two different halves of the face, as though about to make a complaint to him. He put the metal ferrule of his stick on to the blue ridge of Nansen's nose and read aloud to himself the opening and closing dates of the great Nansen Exhibition and the hours when it was open, strained his eyes at the electric clock at the tram stop – it was no more than a quarter to eleven, a fact he had to make his peace with – and after darting a glance at me he drew in his head and settled down to wait, a large, morose bird unworried by the duration of time.

Who next? The next to come was a couple, a fat, sulky fellow in patched rubber boots, bare-headed, unshaven, in a vast polo-neck pullover made of natural wool, a garment that came down round his thighs and in which he obviously also slept. His thin ash-blond hair flopped across his forehead, and between his lips, permanently curled in mockery, an unlit cigarette-stub dangled. His expression made it apparent that he had come here reluctantly, against his will, perhaps talked into it by the long-legged, long-haired girl in the shiny black plastic mac. She had one arm round his shapeless hips, and in the other she clutched a home-made rag doll that was rather like herself and not only because of its little plastic mac. The girl wore sandals on her bare feet. She had very bright eyes, red-rimmed from crying, and her face was broad, with regular features. Her affection was evenly distributed between the fat fellow and the rag doll. She was shivering with cold.

The two of them made their way to the poster and surveyed it for longer than one usually surveys a poster. The fat fellow shrugged his shoulders, asking if she still thought it a good thing to wake him so early on a perfectly harmless Sunday morning. Since she had no answer to that, merely tightened her hold on his shapeless hips, he jerked his head in the direction of Nansen's self-portrait and said something about a house-painter . . . dauber of clouds and wind . . . cosmic stage-designer . . . all right, let's see it through. Seeing we've got up. Just look at that self-portrait, there you have the whole thing: the master-dyer. That was the way he talked, and the girl hummed 'Lullaby of Birdland', rocking the rag doll.

The middle one of the glass doors was opened and we instantly made for it, but two carefully groomed attendants stopped us, letting in only the television and radio chaps, who seemed used to getting preferential treatment, shoving in with their metal boxes, cameras and other equipment. Nor was that all: the moment they were inside the foyer they had ten or twelve attendants working for them, hauling cables about, looking for outlets, setting up arc-lights, and all that sort of thing. We pressed our faces to the glass doors, watching the preparations in the foyer and, now and then, stepping back, I saw in the glass the dim reflections of new arrivals coming up the steps in ones and twos and, if they didn't press their faces to the glass doors as we were doing, casting glances at the electric clock or talking or simply standing there, possessing themselves in patience.

The nearer it got to eleven, the larger the crowd became, people arriving in taxis, by tram, in their own cars, or on foot, coming up the marble steps, greeting each other in every manner from a hardly perceptible nod to elaborate exchanges of kisses and tremendous, lingering embraces. Anyone would have thought these were all people who, if they didn't exactly belong to one family, at least knew each other very well indeed from somewhere or other. There was lots of shaking of hands, plenty of slapping on the back. Kissing of hands. Alertly casual glances. They seemed positively to revel in hailing each other. Faces adopted smiles ranging from the bitter-sweet to the jovial. Lots of waving. And again and again gestures meaning: later, we'll see each other later, we must get together afterwards. Smoke went up from cigarettes and pipes. Exclamations up the steps and down the steps. And while talk went on to left and to right, swift glances were checking who was there, who was just coming, who was missing.

I too discovered faces I knew : Bernd Maltzahn in his raincoat, and the Hamburg art-critic Hans-Dieter Hübscher, who had twice visited the painter at Bleekenwarf : wavy, silky hair, horn-rims, sallow skin – a grub with pin-point eyes.

Each of these people on the Schondorff Gallery steps was worthy of notice in his or her own way : the horse-faced woman in black with the broad-brimmed black hat and the earrings on each of which at least three spider-monkeys could have swung; the man with the slit trouser-leg and the astonished baby-face; the red-faced man with the stubby pipe, all the time watching the shapes of the clouds of smoke which he puffed out, a man I thought capable of portraying his interlocutor in smoke; the elderly couple in camel-hair coats, both of them with the same mauve hair-rinse; the man with the shaving-rash and the little ivory-handled stick; the girl in the leather skirt and the sea-green pullover, patiently massaging the back of a short-legged male companion; the flat-chested, red-haired woman with the spotty legs . . . each of them deserved to be noticed, each of them gave one an inkling of, shall we say, the multitude of human possibilities.

You need not believe that the attendants recognized this or joyfully acknowledged it by letting us in before the appointed time. They actually waited until the hands of the electric clock pointed exactly to eleven. Only then did they open the doors, and they stood about by the cloakroom, grinning, as if waiting to be thanked for having opened the doors. But they were probably grinning because the television people were filming the opening of the exhibition and they had realized that both the cameras were trained on them more than on anyone else. Anyway, we all pushed, shoved, thrust our way past them – I hadn't managed to be first inside – into the depths of the Schondorff Gallery, into the brightly lit, blank room with all those cardboard partition-walls that subdivided it into passages, so that from above it must have looked like a maze, a miniature maze. Into these passages and bays the stream of visitors flowed, but not to stay there; through the well-constructed ways they were automatically brought back into the large foyer, where they stood along the walls, their backs to the high windows, their faces turned to the entrance. How naturally they could stand there, whispering and watching each other! How easily they suppressed a wish to contemplate the paintings, arranged according to periods in the artist's life, before the inaugural speech! For the fact that somebody was going to make a speech was obvious from the way the visitors had taken up their stand.

There was talking and subdued laughter, and time and again exclamations of greeting. Well, what a place to run into you again, we *must* get together more often, I'll ring you next week. . . . Yes, the old man is going to be here in person, it was in the papers. . . . Not at the Thalia Theatre, the Kammerspiele . . . you can be thankful you weren't at the first night . . . there are times when he looks like a monument to himself . . . the way he contrives to delimit the crescendo of colour . . . theatrical, don't you know, the vision's excessively theatrical. . . . What *ever* did Schondorff think up to lure the old man into town. . . . The colour-metaphor, darling, is what he evolves his symbolism from. . . . I still think his work merely decorative. . . . Balduin's gone over to television completely, the theatre simply doesn't give any more scope for dealing with contemporary problems. . . . My dear, it's a *visual* age we're living in, all the other senses have lost out. . . . For him colour hasn't merely poetic significance, it's metaphorical. . . . But he's German to the bone, more German than six Pomeranian grenadiers put together. . . . And as soon as we can get away, we'll go and have lunch somewhere. . . . There's nobody to touch him for evocative power of colour. . . . Isn't that Thomas Stackelberg over there? That's Stackelberg, isn't it? Stackelberg. Tossing his long mane, with his frozen, helpless, close-up grin, got up like Edward the Peacemaker, there as large as life the singer and actor, Stackelberg, was, bestowing fleeting nods on everyone as though everyone had hailed him, pacing – accustomed as he was to an audience, to inquisitive stares – with accomplished casualness through the open circle and inserting himself, together with his dainty, large-mouthed female companion, into a group of friends. . . . Just like his father. . . . Isn't he the very spitting image of his old man? And what are we going to see him in next? . . . Well, what a surprise, meeting you here at Nansen's show. . . . Surprise? Stackelberg said. Every time Gabriele produces another one, she pines for a Nansen water-colour – and she always gets one – don't you, darling?

Two men in open trench-coats were looking across the foyer at me, inspecting me – a young man and an old one. Nobody said hello to them, and they didn't say hello to anyone. Nor did they speak to each other. They didn't belong to the family. When the television camera veered towards them, in silent accord they turned away; but they didn't go away. They did not cease to watch me. It even seemed to me that they were more interested in me than in Rudolf Schondorff, who now swept through the crowds, his face smooth and arrogant, and stopped at the foot of the stairs, indeed not only stopped but took up a position there, dignified and dictatorial.

Everyone was looking at Rudolf Schondorff. He seemed to sense the collective gaze on him; holding his hands before his chest, he massaged his fingers as though to make them suitably supple for some special handshake. He turned round and made a sign to one of the attendants. Talk had almost ceased, the laughter quietened down, people were now standing still. The gallery-owner drew himself up, his arms hanging loosely at his sides, one foot slightly in advance of the other as though trying out a fencing-position. And here came Max Ludwig Nansen.

He came accompanied by Teo Busbeck. I had never seen the painter got up as he was for the opening of the great Nansen Exhibition in Hamburg: buttoned half-boots, striped stovepipe trousers, a morning-coat shiny with age, silk stock and tie-pin, high stand-up collar, and, on his huge, heavy head, an old-fashioned bowler. He could have put himself on view in the Arts and Crafts Museum in Altona, as a figure in the recon-structed eighteenth-century Frisian house. His expression was at once domineering and reserved, his lips curling in vague con-tempt. And the way he walked was in keeping with his attire : a solemn, conquering stride that assumed the way was clear for him – that was how he came up the stairs, arm in arm with his friend, Teo Busbeck. He did not smile, he showed no sign of pleasure, as Schondorff came forward to welcome him. He acknowledged his reception distantly, with an almost imper-ceptible nod, and when the crowd began to clap, he again nodded faintly. While the applause was dying down, he joined the circle, still holding on to Busbeck, who had made an attempt to slink away. Now he raised his head and gazed with hostility at the arc-lights and the humming camera – a stiff-necked, haughty apparition. When Schondorff held out his hand to him for the second time, he ignored it, and when the television producer went up to him and asked him to shake hands with the gallery-owner once more, slowly, for the camera, he waved him aside. Then he bent his head, indicating that he was ready to listen to the inaugural speech. 'Get on with it,' he seemed to be saying.

Well, Schondorff, the host, started off, speaking mildly, with the aid of notes on a slip of paper that he twisted into a roll between his fingers, while the painter listened, at once sunk in thought and critically alert, just as if he were waiting for a chance to protest or at least to correct something the speaker said. So here all over again respectful welcome was uttered. The honour of having him there . . . years of hardship and struggle . . . Max Ludwig Nansen the greatest living representative of . . . celebrated telegram to the Reichskammer of the Visual Arts in Berlin, now reproduced in all art-histories . . . priceless works irrevocably lost . . . then, turning to the painter : for nevertheless accepting our invitation . . . assurance of deep gratitude of all concerned. . . . Handshake. Applause.

Then Hans-Dieter Hübscher spoke. The Hamburg critic did not cling to a slip of paper. He spoke with his eyes shut, in short, clipped sentences, frequently licking his lips and smiling in a feeble, worried way as if the words he was using did not entirely meet with his approval, as if they were merely a stop-gap. He went on and on, extending himself over the full range from 'panic natural force as the nucleus of the painter's experience' down to 'mighty sweep of artistic expressiveness in Nansen's work'.

The painter himself gave the critic an astonished but approving look, nodded when he spoke of hieroglyphs of expressiveness and new conception of planes, and seemed likewise in agreement when he talked of his, the painter's, quest for the primal human condition.

The painter whispered something to Teo Busbeck, but immediately turned back to the critic when the latter began to speak of the enduring pictorial elements, plane, colour, light and pattern. Once again Max Ludwig Nansen nodded, and I

426

realized that what chiefly surprised him was his own approval of what the critic was saying. As if involuntarily he moved closer to Hans-Dieter Hübscher, who was now talking of colour-schemes that Nansen was always experimenting with in the attempt to unify them in a 'universal chord', a general tonal tension comprehending everything, and so on. To this too the painter had no objections, nor did he protest when the attempt to achieve this universal chord was declared to be the essential problem that he shared with Rembrandt. He looked rather taken aback, in my opinion. Hübscher wound up by saying: 'This work bears testimony to the fact that the sonority of colour can transform an intuitively glimpsed meaning into pure paint.'

He thereupon opened his eyes, bowed slightly to the painter and then to the assembled company, and was about to retire when Max Ludwig Nansen touched his sleeve. To the accompaniment of a crescendo of applause, Nansen gripped the critic's hand, drew it towards him and gazed for quite some time at the man who had wrung such unqualified agreement from him. He also said something, but it was inaudible. In a way, the exhibition could now be considered open, and, moving backwards and sideways, the crowd dispersed from the foyer, the circle dissolved, everyone again began to talk and laugh, not least those who had gathered round Stackelberg. The public strolled through the passages formed by the partitions, scattering, or rather pushing their way alone or in groups past the pictures, and occupying the seats disposed here and there for the convenience of those who wished to indulge in prolonged contemplation.

The little group of the elite – for of course there was such a group headed by Schondorff, the painter, Busbeck, and Hans-Dieter Hübscher – had no time to waste. Schondorff occasionally uttered some explanation in passing and sometimes he obviously wanted to stop and comment, but nobody was prepared to listen, least of all the painter, who set the pace, pulling the group along after him. Now and then he made a sign to the critic, urging him not to get separated from the group; it seemed he wanted to keep in touch with him, perhaps he wanted to hear more about himself – I don't know, but it seemed to have been quite a revelation to him, hearing someone talk about him and he himself standing there, amazed, taken aback, perhaps even quite shocked at being able to agree with it all.

Who knows how he might have come up to me if he had seen me there, but I kept in the background, always covered by other people, always on the look-out. The last time he had sent me away from Bleekenwarf with a warning, saying he couldn't have me any more. 'You can't be relied on any more,' he had said. 'You can't be trusted any more, Witt-Witt.' And then he had gazed suggestively in the direction of Rugbüll. It was enough for me to watch him, following him around as best I could. As for Busbeck, he did once seem to have recognized me, at least he hesitated for a moment when he set eyes on me, but since I didn't return his gaze he must have become unsure – no wonder after all those years.

And Teo Busbeck, too, was the only person to notice the sniggering provoked by the painter's garb, the head-shaking, the smirking, the smiles. He noticed it all right, and each time he quickly turned away. Someone said : 'It's too good to be true – he's straight out of one of his own paintings.'

I don't want to repeat it all, especially because it's high time to get to the painting that I hadn't seen before and which was hanging on a wall all by itself.

So there, all of a sudden, was the painting 'Garden Masks', and I simply couldn't tear myself away from it. The garden glowed like a workshop full of colours, a frantic blossoming, an extravaganza of forms and apparitions, but everything distinct from everything else, all of it in its own right. And dangling from a tree, from a long branch that had to be imagined, hanging on green strings, were these masks, two of them men's faces, the other one a woman's. Sunlight struck these masks from the side, lighting up one half of them. There was a terrible certainty emanating from them, some enigmatic authority. The eye-slits were earth-brown, the sky behind them was bright and cloudless. Were these masks a menace to the garden?

I conjured up a breath of wind, first a gentle breeze that set the masks swaying slightly, then the wind rising, throwing them against each other, making them spin round. Whom did these masks resemble? They struck me as familiar, they seemed to be taken from faces I had met somewhere before, but I couldn't

428

put a name to any of them. I imagined them multiplying by night, hanging from all the branches, from all the bushes, rising on dried stalks out of the flower-beds, and I went closer to the painting, to the garden full of masks, and I can still remember wishing I had a thin, hard stick to strike the masks off the stalks, off the bushes and branches, I wanted to behead everything the way one beheads flowers and afterwards, for all I care, cart them off to the compost-heap.

Then they took up their stand beside me. Then they lifted me up, taking me under the arms with their arms. I kept on looking at the garden, at the masks, and yet at the same time I recognized the pale waterproof stuff of the trench-coats. The garden camouflaged itself. It was only now I realized how many things tried to camouflage themselves when confronted by those dangling masks. Without using force, jerkily, but with constant pressure, they were shifting me to one side, pushing me away from the painting. The presence of the masks in the garden seemed to be all that was needed to make every-thing pretend to be something else : either bursting into blossom or hiding it, enhancing the glow of the colours or toning them down. To left and right of me I was aware of two vaguely familiar faces. Even at this moment they wore the stamp of reliability and professional suspiciousness.

An elbow and a gentle fist introduced themselves to my ribs, still only in such a way as not to hurt. Twisting to one side, I saw, hidden among the flowers, two eyes gazing spellbound at the dangling masks. Why should I turn round, raise my voice, and protest, when I knew perfectly well who had closed in on me like pincers, and why? They let go of me, but the rustling that their trench-coats produced at every movement didn't stop, it was still right beside me. We didn't need to come to any agreement that everything had to be done without causing a stir. No fuss, nothing of that sort, no arguing. I reacted the way I had seen other people react in similar circumstances at the cinema : passive, calm, resigned. That kept them happy.

Slowly I moved towards the exit, casually, now and then pausing to look at a painting for a moment, my hands hanging loose at my sides. Only once, a short distance from the stairs, did I stop, waiting until the trench-coats caught up with me, and asked, in such a way that both could regard themselves as

429

being addressed: 'Is this a tip-off from Rugbüll?' One of them said: 'Shut your trap!' and the other said: 'Get a move on!'

I understood all right, there was no need for them to start shoving me, and there was no need for them to shove me again, harder, after I had gone down the stairs and only stopped because I didn't know which door they wanted me to leave through.

Anyway, I lost my balance, only saved myself from falling by taking two swift steps, and all at once I was running, leaping down the big flight of steps outside, and I kept on running after being started off in that uncivil way, and I found myself enjoying running more and more. I paid no attention to warnings, to shouts telling me to stop. All I heard was the sound of my own footsteps, the thump, the echo, carrying me onward, whipping me on towards the bridge, diagonally across the street, almost grazing the side of a tram-car that forced the two men to stop, those two trench-coats that had also broken into a run – and the longer the pursuit lasted, the fewer the shouts became, telling me to stop, and still they came after me, doggedly pounding along after me, across a building-site, between sheds and lorries and the parked yellow cranes and bulldozers, following each other across bounding duckboards over which I had run, on down the street to the traffic-lights, which were still green for me, and then through the arcades full of shop-windows, where for the first time they lost sight of me, but other people, Sunday window-shoppers, drew each other's attention to me, turning round in wonder and amazement, but I was already farther on, running towards the railway-bridge. I caught sight of the sign with the warning: Smoke!, thought of smoke, wished for smoke, longed for smoke, a dense cloud of smoke to rise and hide me, but the petrol-station on the other side remained plainly visible, the arm holding money out of the car-window, the attendant putting the hose back in its place – they didn't vanish. So I went on into the crowded parking-lot in front of the Central Station, ducked between the cars, saw that the hotels were no use to me, nor the Deutsches Schauspiel-haus either, even though a well-known actor was, as I had read that morning, giving a recital of poems by Hölderlin and Storm and Goethe, and there they were, already across the bridge, the man at the petrol-pump was already joining in,

430

nodding, pointing in the direction where I had gone, and the only chance I had now was the station, with all its waiting-rooms, lavatories, ticket-offices, kiosks, all the people standing about, moving up, walking this way and that, and I dashed into the cool, draughty hall, saw and considered all the possibilities, but made use of none of them; instead I crossed the hall, ran to the tram-stop and jumped on to a tram that was just moving off – there actually was one just starting – and for as long as I could still see the station, there was no sign of the two trench-coats.

Were they eyeing me? Was there suspicion in their faces? Were they wondering why I was panting like that? None of the passengers took any notice of me. The passengers all focused their attention, in various degrees, on the ticket-inspector, who was examining the ticket of a fairly old woman. The inspector said : 'This ticket's not valid – do you understand me now?' The old woman took off her wet kerchief and said : 'Nobody's never talked to me like that,' and then she lifted a heavy shopping-bag, with a bunch of flowers sticking out of it, off the floor and placed it demonstratively on the seat beside her. The inspector rubbed the ticket between his fingers, then raised it to the light. 'It's no good,' he said, 'this isn't a transfer ticket.' The woman turned away with an embittered expression and murmured to her shopping-bag : 'Four children I've brought up, and nobody never talked to me like that.' The inspector, in that excessively long coat which the Hamburg tramticket-inspectors wear, bent over the woman, propped himself on her shoulder as the tram went round a curve, and then held the ticket up in front of her eyes. 'Anyone using public transport,' he said, 'must be in possession of a valid ticket.' The woman wiped the misty window-pane with her wet kerchief and said : 'You just take your great paws off of me, if you please, when speaking to me, and how should I know if my ticket isn't valid?' The inspector said : 'You changed trams without having taken a transfer ticket. It's laid down in the public transport by-laws that if you want to change trams you have to ask for a transfer ticket.' The woman shrugged her shoulders : 'Nobody's never talked to me like that, not with by-laws they haven't.'

So they went on, to-ing and fro-ing, without getting any

nearer to a point of mutual understanding, and I don't know what happened in the end: whether the inspector put the woman off the tram or the woman hit the inspector over the head with her bag. For suddenly I recognized the vinegar factory and had to get out.

I crossed the deserted yards, passing the stacks of barrels, over to the old office building. The door was always open, day and night, the stone steps were cracked, there was a lamp hanging from the ceiling, but someone had removed the bulb, and the walls were covered with scratches, stains, and scribbles. Here, on the second floor, was where Klaas lived. Although he didn't live alone there, there was only his name on the door, on a visiting-card, fastened with drawing-pins: K. Jepsen, Photographer. There was no bell, so I knocked. I kept on knocking, and after a while my brother appeared, in crumpled pyjama-trousers, barefoot. He gave me a bad-tempered stare and then said: 'Come in!' The long passage was his portrait-gallery, with his series 'Dead Hamburgers', photographs of the people who had been drowned, battered to death, stabbed, strangled, shot, or run over in the street, and also some who had died peacefully in their beds.

He pushed open a door that was standing ajar. The turn-table of a record-player was spinning round without a record on it. On the table there were bottles of red wine and five glasses. On the wide divan were the bedclothes, on a cane-bottomed chair a jumble of male and female clothing. 'Jutta!' Klaas shouted in the direction of another door, and then again: 'Jutta – don't you hear?'

A moment later Jutta appeared, in washed-out jeans stretched tight over her little bottom, and a thin pullover that was too short, so that the skin showed beween it and the top of the jeans. They exchanged a glance before she greeted me. She kissed me. Klaas threw the clothes on to the divan and pushed the chair towards me. 'Sit down. Jutta'll make you some coffee and a sandwich.' Both of them lit cigarettes, and Klaas gulped down some red wine.

'And how's Siggi?' Jutta asked.

'They've got something on me in Hamburg,' I said. 'I only just managed to give them the slip. There were two of those trench-coats after me. I shook them off at the Central Station.'

While I was talking, my brother raised his glass, full of red wine, and closed one eye, aiming over the rim of the glass at imaginary targets on the wall and the ceiling, seemingly not listening with much interest. He did not interrupt me once. Only when I had finished did he say: 'A pretty lousy outlook, boy.' After a pause he added: 'You can stay here till tomorrow, but then you'll have to think up something else.'

'He can sleep in the dark-room, can't he?' Jutta said. 'On the deckchair.'

'Siggi can sleep here on anything he likes,' Klaas said, 'only tomorrow we'll have to think up something else. They don't give up just because they've lost track of someone.'

Jutta brought me coffee and a ham sandwich. She put on an L.P. disc, the Andrews Sisters I think it was, and, softly humming the tune in between puffs at a cigarette, with the aid of a safety-pin she threaded a new piece of elastic through the top of an old pair of briefs. Klaas went to the window and looked down into the yard, then, raising his eyes, into the street, and there too he aimed over the rim of a glass of red wine at all sorts of targets, windows, roofs, and presumably also the green lettering of the vinegar advertisement.

'What are they after you for?' he asked. 'Why, all of a sudden?'

'I don't know,' I said.

'Made trouble for you, has he? Our old man in Rugbüll.'

'Could be,' I said. 'Yes, it must have been him. He's probably found something.'

'Your hide-out?'

'Yes.'

'You can get away from here easily enough,' my brother said. 'If they come, you skip into Hansi's room and up the back stairs. I'll show you.'

'Well, for the moment I'm here.'

'Yes, for the moment you're here.'

My brother pressed his glass of red wine into my hand, urged me to drink, and went into the kitchen, leaving the door open. I could hear him washing, with the tap full on.

'Can you dance?' Jutta asked.

I shook my head.

'Then drink,' she said. And I drank, and she filled up my

glass again. Then she began tidying up the room, humming, a lighted cigarette in one hand, tapping the ash off wherever she happened to be.

And then . . . we both jumped, and even Klaas seemed to be startled, over there in the kitchen, when two deep, resounding roars came from out in the passage. It was a demanding and triumphant roar, heralding something, of course, and footsteps were approaching, footsteps that stopped outside our door. We stood motionless, just looking at each other, and just as Klaas beckoned me into the kitchen, the door flew open and the fat fellow in the natural wool pullover and the patched rubber boots appeared in the doorway, clutching half a dozen bottles of red wine to his chest. He roared again, but more briefly, not quite so loud, then growled and jerked his head in the direction of Hansi's room.

So this was Hansi. Without uttering another word, he moved towards his room, and in the open doorway the long-haired girl in the shiny plastic mac appeared, holding her rag doll high above her head. She waved to us, laughing, as she followed him.

'We're coming,' Klaas shouted.

How shall I describe Hansi's room? It was a gloomy cavern with two doors – one of them leading straight on to the landing – and, high up, three windows over the old factory-yard, now used only for stacking rotten barrels in. Along the walls were ranged a number of sea-chests, painted bright blue and draped in sour-smelling skins, to serve as chairs and beds. There were some old tins used as ashtrays, an easel, a narrow shelf with a collection of rag dolls sitting, squatting, standing, or lying jumbled together on it, and, under the window, fixed to a sheet of pale-grey cardboard, Hansi's declaration of faith, his cycle 'The Rebellion of the Dolls', done in charcoal, in silverpoint, and also in water-colour. Behind the curtain there was a gas cooker, a sink, some crockery, and an array of variously shaped tins. Behind the easel, in a corner, there was a deckchair, in which a bald-headed young man was asleep, his leather jacket hanging open. It looked as if he had always been asleep, and as if he would go on sleeping for days, if not weeks. And I must not forget to mention the tables, two round garden tables with the legs cut down, and a cardboard box full of bicycle-pumps – Hansi collected bicycle pumps, which he re-painted and numbered.

Now Hansi started drinking. Doris – that was the name of the girl in the plastic mac – opened bottles, poured out, kissed everyone she handed a glass to, kissing Jutta with particular affection and with a faint smacking sound, whereupon Hansi, who was lying on his back with his legs drawn up, called out to them : 'Put on a disc, my popsies !' So we had a disc – guitar. The record-player was beside the deckchair in which the bald-headed young man was asleep. Klaas sat on the floor, resting one elbow on one of the sea-chests and balancing his glass on his right knee. Doris pulled one of the evil-smelling skins to the floor and lay down on it. A man sang to guitar accompaniment, singing about a black sun and a black river in which someone or other had drowned, a child I think. Hansi smoked and nodded, then suddenly leapt to his feet, scratched the hollows of his knees, and pressed his glass into my hand. What now?

'Jesus !' he said, 'my teeth are all on edge ! I've got a taste of glue in my mouth, I've been wondering all the time what it was from, and now I know. It's from that cosmic razzamatazz, that exhibition. We encountered the dauber in person, I'd have you know. The greatest of cloud-cuckoo-painters was there in the flesh.'

He went to the easel, fixed a sheet, looked around for something, found the box of crayons in a crate behind the sleeper. Doris laughed and slammed her feet together. 'Now look at this. Now we're all going off together on a quest for man's primal condition, all very Germanic, with bags of emotion, if you please. Keep your pins quiet, Doris, and stop laughing, all of you.' He drew a ribbon of yellow and white across the paper, then added jagged golden edges. 'Right, there now, to start with, we have this beach, a bit of beach along the North Sea – right? – the waves of our German Ocean nagging at it. In-articulate grandeur of Nature, or what-have-you. You shit some-where and the next day something grows there.' Then he took black and white, and a black ankle appeared on the beach, no, an angular black-clad man, in stove-pipe trousers and morning-coat, holding a book in his hand, reading, or having just stopped reading, walking along the beach, and obviously one had to see it as an important book. 'Working like this,' Hansi said, 'the chalk must groan, of course, it must be talked into intensifying the colour, just as Nature talks plants into intensifying their growth – if you know what I mean. It's colour, after all, that must give the answer to man's emotions when confronted with the world. What is to spring forth from it is a view of the primal condition.'

He worked violently, his lips compressed, making exaggerated sweeping, dictatorial gestures, flashing blue through yellow, making white explode in shimmering green, until colour became a visual motif and what arose spontaneously – I must admit it – was *fear*. That's to say, the green face of a man, who was walking along the beach with a book open in his hands, expressed fear and surprise. As yet one could not tell what caused the fear. Now came brown, a dark brown with dramatic black stripes in it; it expanded, arched itself over the beach, was drawn out thin in one place, cut off short in another. 'Right, so here we have the great cosmic bird – obvious, isn't it? These two recognize each other. The North German prophet is frightened : for here, goddammit, is the primal condition. But now we have to get the planes to cooperate as well, we need some clouds, otherwise the encounter isn't mythical enough – right, so we organize some wafting and weaving in the sky, nightfall isn't far off. All that's missing is the cries of startled animals – and how are we to paint *them*?'

While Hansi was outlining, distributing, dividing clouds some people came in without knocking : two chaps and a stumpy girl with black hair. They calmly took off their coats, poured themselves out some wine and, without a word, sat down wherever they found room, and began to watch Hansi. He, having got the clouds to join in, was now pondering on the title for the picture : 'Prophet on Beach Meeting Overlifesize Bird'. 'And now let us join together in elucidating the primal condition in man, as demonstrated by the cosmic window-dresser Nansen.'

He was about to launch into another speech, but he had reckoned without me, in fact I dare say I'd reckoned without myself, for suddenly I heard myself saying aloud : 'That's all very well, that's all quite amusing, only you haven't got the perspective right.' And when Hansi gaped at me in amazement, I was already on my feet and at the easel, showing him where

436

the perspective had gone wrong. Hansi kept quiet, his eyes narrowed; he abandoned the idea of saying whatever he had been going to say, stretched out his hand for a glass of red wine and gulped some down. 'The point is,' I said, 'in the window-dresser's works the perspective's always right. Always.'

'Anything else?'

'The bird,' I said, 'that bird hasn't been *seen* the way everything's *seen* in the dauber's work. I mean, if fantastic creatures really exist, they're there in their own right. But anyone can see that bird will never hatch an egg.'

'Anything else strike you?'

'In the stage-designer's work nothing's left to chance in the colour-scheme. Everything is logical, everything justifies the rest. What's missing here is inevitability.'

'Well, and what are you getting at with all this? Speak up.'

I looked round for Klaas. Klaas was gazing at the floor. I looked across at Jutta, and she avoided my eyes.

'I happen to know him.'

'Who?'

'Nansen, that great landscape-window-dresser. I know almost everything he's ever done. I've watched him doing some of them. He'd never have brought off anything like your Dolls series, but he's done his own things, and he's quite in harmony with them.'

'Don't beat around the bush,' Hansi said, emptying his glass.

'Of course you're so much better than he is,' I said, 'only if you're going to slay him, I should have thought you ought to get it right.'

'Oh, isn't he quaint!' Doris exclaimed, circling her pins in the air.

'I suppose you think you're terrific,' Hansi said. 'Bought you a lollipop, did he, or let you carry his sketch-book for him . . . just his type. Of course I saw you at the show this morning, and you know what I thought the moment I set eyes on you? I thought: There's a born model for Nansen – for certain pictures, of course – say "Young Man Bringing in the Hay".'

Now Klaas spoke up. 'Come here, Siggi,' he said. 'Sit down.'

But I couldn't simply turn away without answering. 'Believe it or not,' I said, 'I have been his model, and that's how I know his technique. And if you're going to take him apart like that in his own technique, then you've got to get it right. 'That's how I see it.'

'I can't stand people who repeat themselves,' Hansi said, and Doris exclaimed cheerfully: 'I think he's quaint. He's the sort you could look at pictures in the dark with.'

I said nothing. In silence I walked past Hansi, and they all watched as I squatted down in front of the series 'The Rebellion of the Dolls' and with infinite leisureliness looked at the pictures one by one. Well, here were the rag-doll people: triangular faces, flattened spherical faces, pin-man faces. Arms that could be bent in any direction. Legs that could have two knots tied in them. Floppy, patchy, but above all imperishable bodies. Dolls climbing up a factory chimney and occupying it. Blowing up a water-tower, destroying a bridge, derailing a train, hauling the flag down from the top of a building. Dolls digging a grave for K.A. Dolls leaning into a head wind. Dolls on the Munsterlager rifle-range. Dolls tying up a sleeping girl, Doris of course. Dolls escaping from a humming-top, riding on a cock, slashing an upholstered chair with twelve pairs of scissors.

All the time I was looking at the pictures, they were watching me without uttering a word. I could hear their breathing and the faint sucking sound when they drew on their cigarettes. Then I stood up, turned round slowly to Hansi, who was pushing his thin hair back off his forehead, just waiting to make fun of me. 'Oh, do sit down, Siggi,' Klaas exclaimed.

'Well, what now?'

'Very distinguished,' I said. 'All this is really very distinguished.'

'Not the way I look at it.'

'What I don't understand,' I said, 'is why a pat on the back, condescension or contempt, is all that you people are capable of where an old man is concerned. You all think you're very superior: "Fancy, he actually knew that, he saw it too, he could do it." '

'Don't you go telling me what Nansen was.'

'But it seems to me you don't yet know everything.'

'Now you just listen to me,' Hansi said. 'Your friend Nansen is the very type I regard as a disaster: back-to-the-land and all that, visionary, and political.'

'He wasn't allowed to paint,' I said. 'You probably don't

438

know he was under police surveillance, to make sure he didn't paint. Hundreds of his paintings were destroyed.'

'Yes, that's just what's puzzling about Nansen,' Hansi said.

'Isn't that in his favour?' I said. 'But I suppose you can understand everything.'

'Certainly,' Hansi said, 'I understand what matters. For instance, I know exactly what it is about you I don't like.'

'Same here,' I said, 'but what I can't make out is how the likes of you can be so frivolous. You run things down without even trying to understand them.'

I had more to say, and I was just going to say it, but I didn't get a chance. Quicker than I should have thought him capable of, Hansi raised one knee and kicked me in the groin, and the sudden pain doubled me up like his prophet on the beach. And when he had me there in front of him, bent over, distracted with pain, he dealt me two not moderate, not shattering, but very well-aimed blows, an upper-cut on the chin and a hammer-blow on the back of the neck, which sent me sprawling.

I still remember the red dots dancing before my eyes, and they were the bits of red bicycle-tubing that Hansi's rubber boots were patched with: they seemed to have detached themselves from the dark background and to be rotating around me. As I fell I heard a cry, without being able to tell whose voice it was. Anyway, the discussion was finished for the time being, the film had torn, and Hansi's hospitality likewise turned out to be at an end; for when I opened my eyes, I did not see the faded wallpaper in Hansi's room, the paper with the pattern of sporting scenes, the ducks brought down into the rushes, but I was in darkness, and there was a smell of chlorine, at least I think it was chlorine.

I was lying in a deckchair, my legs wrapped in a blanket. I heard Klaas saying: 'He's asleep' and heard Jutta say: 'Then leave him asleep, let's go back to the others.' They tried to slip away without a sound, and to shut the door without a sound, but I heard them, and I lay there quite quiet in the dark-room and considered walking out without saying goodbye to anyone. Was it afternoon? Was it evening? Where was I to go? Back to Rugbüll? Join the crew of a fishing-trawler setting out for Greenland? Go to Strasbourg and sign up with the Foreign

Legion? Or should I go and look for the two trench-coats and give myself up, if for nothing else, to find out what I was in for?

I lay there thinking it over, reckoning up my chances. I hatched an elaborate plan to stow away on a ship to America, and there I would change my name, to Sig O'Jepsen, say, and make enough money to open an art gallery, where I would gather the young American painters around me, organize, with their assistance, National Art Weeks which would be opened by the President, after whom I would make a speech ... thank heaven nothing came of *those* dreams of glory.

I went on considering and discarding one plan after another for quite some time. I didn't get up, I didn't leave the dark-room, much less Klaas's home. Instead, I tried to ignore the sound of a dripping tap, the dripping going on through my plans, inside my head, turning into a relentless counting, and by the time it was somewhere in the eighties I must have dozed off again – sleeping uneasily, very lightly, all the time prepared to be shaken awake by Klaas or Jutta or perhaps even Hansi.

And I can't forget the dream I had when I was lying there in the dark-room. I was in a broad-bottomed wooden boat, alone, and the boat was taking me across to one of the sand-banks far out beyond the peninsula. I was sitting in the shadow of the lugsail, and the boat glided towards the flat blue rise of the sand-bank. That was where my new hide-out was. I had built it out of the ruins of a stone church – the only thing I had found on the uninhabited sand-bank. The hiding-place was cool and spacious. I had stopped up all the chinks. I landed, pulled the boat up on to the beach, drove the little anchor into the sand, just to be on the safe side, and then glanced over at my hide-out. It was besieged by seals. The seals were lying in the sunshine in a semi-circle, their skins gleaming, and they had raised their heads and were surveying me. There were some baby seals there too. I must lie down – I lay down on the sand and began wriggling towards the seals, and they didn't stir. I moved along between them, crept into my hide-out, and was just relaxing when I heard the first shot. It was fired somewhere out at sea, and the bullet struck a piece of debris and ricocheted with a chirping noise.

And then two boats came, little boats without sails or engines or oars, as though hauled along on a pulley, bearing straight down on the sand-bank, as if they were running on rails. Standing very straight in the boats, strangely stiff, aiming their rifles, were two men: in one boat my father, the Rugbüll policeman, in the other Max Ludwig Nansen, the painter. In my dream they were both out hunting seals. They fired from the moving boats, and little pale clouds of smoke curled up prettily from the muzzles of their rifles. At the sound of the first shot the seals began to lollop awkwardly towards the water. The herd divided, then re-formed, in agitation, and veered away to the southern tip of the sand-bank. Right by the entrance to my hide-out they laboured along on their fins, slapping the sand, the leaders barking and growling their warnings. I rushed outside, but a shot forced me to drop to the ground, and I wriggled along to the southern tip together with the fleeing herd. They were faster than I was, even the baby seals were faster, overtaking me, but I didn't give up, I followed them over the sand, through the wild lyme-grass, away over wounded ones, and then I saw that the first of them had reached the water, were plunging in, diving.

My attempt to escape to the southern tip together with the herd was too slow and too clumsy; I got left farther and farther behind. My strength was failing, I could no longer get to my feet. Even when the men's boats reached the shore I couldn't manage to stand up. They both leapt from their boats at the same time, with a nod to each other they unrolled a net and came towards me, holding the net wide, dragging it along the ground. Both of them were wearing pale trench-coats.

I wriggled like a seal, I crept and crawled over the sand, my traces scarcely distinguishable from the traces left by the seals. They had only to make a slight effort, to run a few paces, and they had encircled me with their net. Laughing and laughing, they drew the net tighter, walking in a circle round me – always in such a way as to keep the opening of the weir-basket in front of my face. Urgently, persuasively, the thin wooden hoop kept on bidding me capitulate: Come on, do come on. . . . The hoop rolled and bounced ahead of me, and now they were bending over me, tapping me on the shoulder, without hostility – pointing, like patient animal-tamers, to the net, which became gradually narrower towards the further end. 'Allez, allez *hop*!'

I didn't actually jump, but finally I squeezed through the hoop and crept towards the knotted end of the net. Instantly I felt them lifting me up, the meshes cutting into my skin, and the sand heaved and swayed before my eyes.

'Siggi Jepsen?'

'Yes,' I said.

'You're coming with us.'

The sun came toppling down, blinding me. 'Switch on the light.' A small blue light came on, a curtain was jerked to one side, a voice said: 'Hasn't come round yet after his beauty-sleep.' Somebody lifted me up. Somebody unwrapped the blanket from my legs. Stretching out one hand, I touched a trench-coat. 'It really is a dark-room,' a voice said. And another voice said: 'Well, mind the little bastard doesn't get over-exposed.'

19 The Island

On rising ground, facing the blue administration building, what we call the Rookie House still stands. Think of a flat-roofed one-storey timber house, hang window-boxes outside the windows, make cottagy red-and-white check curtains flutter, have the door open – the floor in the bright passage is newly scrubbed, and there is no warder's lodge. What else? Imagine all eight rooms occupied by 'rookies', the new arrivals who have been brought by the motor-launch from Hamburg. I am in room 7, together with Kurtchen Nickel, who only the previous day smashed up all the furniture in one of his tantrums. He has black hair and wears a black shirt, open right down to the waist – the former circus-artiste – strong-man act. At the moment he is lying on his bed, motionless as a log. Is he listening to the voices? Is he, like me, listening to the voice of Governor Himpel showing a party of foreign psychologists round, going through the Rookie House, room by room, expounding the pros and cons of a new rehabilitation scheme? I am standing by my bed, close to the wooden wall, smoking. Outside, a squad of juvenile delinquents trudges sullenly past, in denims, shouldering forks and spades – off to work in the fields. Some of them glance across at our house, exchange remarks, and laugh.

'A sluice,' Governor Himpel is saying, 'if I may put it so : this house for new arrivals is intended to function as a *sluice*.'

A psychologist (sceptically) : 'That means, if I understand aright, that the young prisoner is here prepared for the period of his sentence?'

Himpel (ad-libbing like the practised speaker that he is) :

'One might, alternatively, call it the pressurized cabin, or the slipway. To obviate the shock of the new milieu, the young prisoner is, as it were, slid gradually into prison conditions. The transition is made easier for him. As I was saying: although he will not here enjoy the liberties that he enjoyed in the world outside, he will still be entitled to some – minor liberties, that is. For instance, he may smoke, listen to the wireless, spend half his day as he himself wishes, and also go anywhere he likes on the island.'

Psychologist: 'And how long does he stay here?'

Direktor: 'Three months. Boys who come to us with a court sentence spend three months in the New Arrivals' House. Experience hitherto has proved this gradual acclimatization extremely valuable.'

Kurtchen suddenly comes alive, leaps off his bed, and stares at me with loathing: 'Where are they? Where are the swine?'

Me: 'You can hear for yourself – Number Five.'

Coming up to me, Kurtchen whispers: 'You can think yourself lucky!'

Me: 'Why?'

Kurtchen (going to the window, spinning round, and then leaning back, holding on to the window-sill with both hands): 'You'll have a ringside seat, boy-o, you'll be my audience when I do one of them in. Acts of violence – that's what they hauled me in here for. Acts of violence against the person. Twenty-seven cases. Now they're going to see for themselves what I'm like when I get violent.'

Governor Himpel (in the next room): 'Quite so – the boys don't all spend the same period in the New Arrivals' House. We have worked out a specially graded system for deciding how long any particular boy remains here.'

Kurtchen unbuttons his trousers, puts his hand down the inside of his left thigh, pulls at something, and produces a little knife in a leather sheath.

Me: 'Chuck it.'

Kurtchen (with loathing): 'If I can't do the Prosecutor in, I'll do one of them in. They hate us. They're jealous because we're young.'

Me (trying to calm him down): 'Put the knife away. You never know what you may need it for another time.'

444

Kurtchen (as though to motivate his hatred): 'We scare the pants off them. They can't understand us.'

Governor Himpel (in the next room): 'With less serious cases a fortnight's stay here in the sluice may suffice. As I said, the length of the stay is adjusted according to the degree of psychological sensitivity, with the result that there is rarely anything in the way of disturbed behaviour after removal to the prison proper. We seek to avoid trouble, but if there is any, this is where it occurs.'

Kurtchen (continuing to motivate his hatred): 'None of these buggers has even tried to understand me. It's the way I am. Anyone who doesn't keep his eyes on my girl too long, anyone who keeps his paws off her, doesn't need to be afraid of me. But if anyone keeps on staring at her, or anyone touches her, I go wild. I won't have that, see? I just go up to him and tell him – speaking very civil – if he doesn't want his teeth bashed in, he'd better keep his distance from my girl. Some of them see sense, some don't. And if they don't, it's self-defence – but these swine call it violence against the person.'

Governor Himpel: 'I suggest that we now move on to Room Six, where I can show you a special case: a young thief specializing in works of art, and one, moreover, who knows something about painting.'

Joswig's voice (expressionlessly): 'Room Seven, sir.'

Himpel: 'Ah yes, the room after the next, then. Who's in Six at the moment?'

Joswig: 'The attempted homicide case and Rossbach.'

Me (to Kurtchen, going slowly up to him): 'Put that knife away.'

Kurtchen (menacingly): 'Stay where you are.'

Me (staying where I am): 'If you do that, you'll never get out of here again.'

Kurtchen (laughing): 'I don't want to get out, see? All I want is to show them. After that I don't care.'

Me: 'Supposing you get the wrong one?'

Kurtchen: 'There isn't a wrong one, they're all the same. Instead of leaving us in peace, just locking us up, they turn the island into a circus-ring, they make performing horses of us. They're making a performing horse of you too.' (Suspiciously): 'How long are you in for?'

445

Me (going a bit closer to him) : 'Three years' reformatory.'

Kurtchen : 'Stealing cars?'

Me : 'How did you get that idea?'

Kurtchen (with a disparaging gesture) : 'Didn't you have your picture in the papers?'

Me : 'I took some paintings, I took them to keep them safe, that's all.'

Kurtchen (blankly) : 'Paintings?'

Governor Himpel (as the party emerges into the passage) : 'Of course there are gradations within the prison itself as well. In grade one, for instance, conditions are very similar to those here in this house for new arrivals.'

A psychologist : 'That means, if I am not mistaken, that the whole rehabilitation scheme here is of the nature of a sluice?'

Governor Himpel (delighted at being so well understood) : 'Yes indeed, we see everything here as a sort of transit-camp. From the very beginning the young prisoner is given the feeling that this state of affairs is merely temporary.'

Kurtchen tiptoes past me to the door, bends down, listens, watching me out of the corner of his eye. Light falls on his hair, light is reflected from the short blade of the knife; the black stuff of his trousers tightens over his buttocks, the ornamental studs on his high heels throw off a silvery gleam, and his free hand opens and shuts convulsively. 'They're going into Number Six.'

Me : 'Put that knife away!'

Kurtchen : 'You keep out of this! Why don't you go and have a piss until it's over? Now's your chance.'

Me : 'They'll finish you. I tell you, they'll finish you. Have some sense.'

Kurtchen (with loathing) : 'They've done it already, the swine. They've broken up my girl and me. She wouldn't even shake hands with me after the sentence.'

Governor Himpel and his party disappear into Room Six, becoming inaudible.

Me (switching on the radio) : 'How about a bit of music to welcome them?'

Kurtchen (sharply) : 'Turn it off.'

Me (switching the radio off) : 'You'll get yourself in a hell of a mess if you do it.'

446

Kurtchen: 'You don't seem to have noticed, boy. They've *got* us all in a hell of a mess. You should have heard the Prosecutor. Talking about protecting society from me. Saying society has a right to be protected from me. So what I'm here for is to give your Auntie Glad and your Uncle Charlie a break.'

He plays about with the knife, throwing it up into the air and catching it deftly. He sends it spinning almost to the ceiling, then steps back and watches it diving to the floor.

Me: 'Don't you ever think what your old woman'd say?'

Kurtchen: 'If you happen to mean my mum, she's at sea, no joking, she's the second woman ever to be sparks on a German ship.'

Me: 'What about your father?'

Kurtchen: 'I'm not asking you any personal questions, so cut it out, will you?' He goes to the open window, where there are geraniums flowering in the window-box, and with a few short slashes of his knife he strips several plants of their flowers and leaves. Without turning his head, he asks: 'What sort of paintings, anyway? Like out of museums? Or photos of girls?'

Me: 'What some of those paintings would fetch, you could live on the money for a year. I only took them somewhere where they were safe.'

Kurtchen (leaping to the door, and crouching down): 'Here they come.'

Me: 'Don't be a fool.'

Governor Himpel, out in the passage: 'Thanks to this New Arrivals' House, there has been a considerable drop in attempts to escape – there are now only about eight a year. It is usually the same prisoners who make repeated attempts.'

Slow footsteps approach our door. Kurtchen steps back, lowering the hand with the knife in it, and gathers himself together with a warning side-glance at me.

Me (at the open window): 'Don't do it. You're crazy.'

Kurtchen (furiously): 'Shut your trap.'

The door opens, hesitantly, and Kurtchen slowly retreats, crouching as for a leap. Joswig comes in, an admonishing finger to his lips, obviously meaning to prepare us, warn us, get us ready. He sees me first, and like a flash I direct his gaze to where Kurtchen is ready to pounce, perhaps I also shout, I don't know, anyway a faint warning shout that cannot be heard

447

out in the passage causes Joswig to react, he ducks and raises his long arms as in judo, ready to ward off the attack. As Kurtchen leaps at him, brandishing the knife, I take two long strides towards him, no, I stay at the window, resolving to help Joswig if Kurtchen gets the upper hand – I *could* reach him in two long strides.

There is no scream, no groan. Kurtchen has to attack silently, just as Joswig defends himself in silence. Kurtchen's body stretches in a leap. Joswig is all alert. Now the camera zooms in on a chopping blow struck upwards on Kurtchen's forearm, hitting the arm as it comes down, knocking it upwards so that the fingers open and the knife flies up to the ceiling. When Joswig strikes and Kurtchen's arm flies up, it sends Kurtchen spinning. The knife clatters to the floor, at Joswig's feet. Crouching, with a glare of hatred, Kurtchen watches Joswig and is about to snatch at the knife when Joswig stamps his foot on it.

Joswig (mournfully): 'Want some more? Slow on the uptake, aren't you?'

Kurtchen (between his teeth, nursing his nerveless forearm): 'You wait, I'll get you another time.'

Joswig (taking his foot off the knife): 'Come and get it. Come on, try now.' He steps back, invitingly. Kurtchen falls for it, bends down, stretches out his hand for the knife and, just before he can touch it, Joswig brings his foot down hard on his hand. Kurtchen rears back, Joswig picks up the knife and puts it in his pocket. Kurtchen staggers to his bed and drops on to it. He breathes on his hand and rubs it.

Joswig: 'Had all you can take, eh?'

Kurtchen (snarling): 'You wait, you bastard.'

Enter seven psychologists from five different countries, followed by Governor Himpel in windbreaker and plus-fours, exuding rude health and pedagogic breeziness. The visitors look round the room, surveying us as though we were pieces of furniture.

Joswig (good-naturedly, to Kurtchen): 'Aren't you going to get up?'

Kurtchen: 'You can kiss my arse.'

Joswig: 'The Governor is here.'

Kurtchen: 'He can kiss my arse twice over.'

448

Governor Himpel and a psychologist exchange glances of faint professional excitement. Instead of looking taken aback, their faces express sudden interest.

Himpel to Joswig: 'Has anything happened here – anything special?'

Joswig: 'Not really.' Jerking his head at Kurtchen: 'Shall I get him on his feet, sir? Do you wish me to teach him some manners?'

Himpel (waving that aside): 'Thank you, Joswig – we'll deal with him ourselves.' He goes over to Kurtchen's bed, and the pyschologists form a semi-circle around him. 'Yes, yes, Herr Nickel, we understand. We all get into a bad humour now and then. But we've all got to get on with each other here; I'd almost say: we've got to *help* each other.'

Kurtchen (nursing his hand): 'You shove off. I don't want any squares sucking up to me.'

A psychologist: 'Jussupov's hate-factor, I think.'

Himpel (with unabated friendliness): 'Of course we shan't bother you for long. But won't you first do me a favour? These gentlemen, who have come from abroad, would like to know why you are here.'

Kurtchen: 'Don't tell me you don't know. Read them the bloody record.'

Himpel: 'But they would like to hear it in your own words, Herr Nickel – or rather, Kurt – I call all the boys here by their first names.'

Kurtchen: 'I don't give a damn what you call me.'

Himpel (insistently): 'Well, then, why do you think you are here – why?'

Kurtchen (throws himself on his back and stares up at the ceiling, continuing to nurse his hand): 'Because I eat little children, and I had one for breakfast.'

Himpel (far from being annoyed, apparently regarding this answer as satisfactory): 'And what else? That isn't the only reason, is it?'

Kurtchen (calmly): 'Because squares make me puke. And because I founded a club.'

Himpel: 'What sort of club?'

Kurtchen: 'For the abolition of squares.'

A psychologist: 'Abnormal aggression co-efficient.'

Second psychologist, bending over Kurtchen: 'Tough lad, eh? Scares the pants off everyone, eh? If you're as strong as all that, why don't you come over to the gym sometime tomorrow and let's have a work-out with the gloves? Then we'll see who knocks the other one out.'

Kurtchen: 'Bugger off, grandad, and mind the sawdust doesn't trickle out of your pants.'

Himpel: 'My dear Kurt Nickel, we are not your enemies, you know. We are trying to help you. But if we are to help you, we have to understand you.'

Joswig: 'Do you want him on his feet, sir?'

Himpel: 'No, just let him relax.'

Kurtchen: 'That's all you're going to get out of me. I'm not going to talk to you. Why don't you pick on *him*?' (jerking his thumb in my direction).

Himpel: 'Well, well, we have plenty of time ahead of us.' He turns to me, while the psychologists whisper to each other in English: they do not seem to be in agreement about Kurtchen Nickel's case and would really like to ask some more questions, but since Governor Himpel holds out his hand to me in a quite chummy way, they too turn to me and focus their attention on me.

Himpel (to me): 'And this is our art-expert.'

Joswig (intervening): 'Siggi Jepsen, sir.'

Himpel: 'Oh yes, I know – I know Herr Jepsen and his history. But perhaps he would like to tell these gentlemen himself why he is here with us.'

Joswig (in a low voice): 'If you don't speak up, I've finished with you.'

Me (shrugging my shoulders): 'What do you want me to tell you?'

Himpel: 'Just what I said – why you are here. We should like to hear it in your own words.'

Me: 'I took some paintings, I took them to keep them safe, because my old man was after them. That's all.'

All the psychologists prick up their ears and nod to each other. Some of them get out notebooks and pencils.

Himpel (patiently): 'Why was your father "after" these paintings, do you think?'

Me (glancing at Kurtchen, who is lying on his bed, taking

450

no notice of anyone) : 'At first, in the execution of his duty. In Berlin they issued a ban, they wouldn't allow the painter Nansen to go on painting, and it was my father's duty to notify him and then to keep him under surveillance. He was the local police officer at Rugbüll. Afterwards, he just couldn't stop. You know all the rest.'

One of the pyschologists (checking up) : 'Max Ludwig Nansen?'

Another pyschologist : 'The Expressionist?'

Himpel : 'So it was your father's duty as a policeman, Siggi, to make sure Nansen did no painting. And when the times changed and there was no longer any ban, your father, you say, continued to keep the painter under surveillance.'

Me : 'In the end it was a fixed idea – the way people always develop it if they're just set on doing their duty and nothing else. It turned into a sort of disease, or perhaps even worse.'

A psychologist : 'Worse?'

Himpel : 'Did your father confiscate paintings?'

Me : 'He confiscated them, burnt them, destroyed them – however you like to put it. Nothing was safe from him.'

Himpel : 'Well, now I think we must come to your part in it. So you took paintings away to keep them safe from your father. How did it come to that? Tell us about it.'

Me : 'It began when the mill burnt down. My hide-out was in the mill, and when it burnt down, everything was gone. My collections. The paintings, the locks and keys. That's when it started. I don't know : I'd be looking at one of the paintings, and suddenly something would begin to move, a little flame would start coming out of the background, all by itself. So I just had to do something.'

First pyschologist : 'A determining obsession, don't you think?'

Second pyschologist : 'Hallucinatory defence-reaction.'

Me : 'It was just like that. I could see when a picture was in danger, and I took it away to save it from him. You'd have done the same, I dare say. After the mill burnt down, I had a new hide-out, in our loft. That's where I took the paintings. But he found out. He kept on watching me until one day he found the pictures. Then he'd got me.'

Kurtchen (from his bed) : 'You should've eaten them, you drip.'

Himpel (soothingly): 'But your father was only doing his duty.'

Me: 'He wanted to run me to earth, that's what he said himself. And he did. So if you want to know why I'm here . . .'

Governor Himpel (eagerly): 'That's just what we've asked you to tell us.'

Me (going slowly across to Kurtchen's bed and sitting down on it): 'I can tell you that. I can tell you that exactly. I'm here in place of my old man, the Rugbüll policeman. And I have a feeling that Kurtchen's here in place of someone else, too, in place of some Auntie Glad or Uncle Charlie. Perhaps all the boys here are here in place of someone else. Juvenile delinquents – that's the tag they hung on us in court, and here it's brought up against us every day. Perhaps some of us here really are delinquent – I shouldn't like to say. But what I'd like to ask is this: Why isn't there an island and a building like this for elderly delinquents? Don't older people just as much need to be reformed?'

Kurtchen (grimly): 'There isn't an island big enough.'

Me: 'When can people be regarded as no longer needing to be reformed? That's what I want to know. When they're eighteen? Or twenty-five?'

Himpel (eagerly agreeing): 'A very good question. A really excellent question.'

Me: 'I mean, something's being put over on us here. Perhaps everybody's putting something over on themselves. I shouldn't like to guess how many bad consciences are going around in this place.'

A psychologist: 'Deflected aggression, don't you think?'

Me: 'Because they don't want to condemn themselves, they send other people here – boys. That's a bit of a relief to them. It takes a load off their minds. Simple – you put your bad conscience on a motor-launch, bring it over, and dump it here, and then you can enjoy your breakfast again and drink your hot punch in peace of an evening.'

Himpel (eagerly but with some scepticism): 'Now you are generalizing, Siggi.'

Me: 'All right, then I'll tell you why I'm on this island. Because no one had the nerve to make the Rugbüll police officer undergo treatment for his addiction. It's all right for him to go on being an addict to his damned duty. And I'm here because he's reached a certain age and so he's no longer eligible for rehabilitation. Yes, I'm here in place of him, if you ask me. But perhaps it'll work, perhaps some day he'll be able to get the benefit of the progress I shall make here. Let's hope so. But that's all we can hope for. I can't see it happening, myself.' (Pause.)

Himpel (clearing his throat): 'What you have to say is pretty harsh, but I can understand that. Oh yes, I can understand your being disillusioned. It's really splendid the way you speak up, so frankly.'

Kurtchen: 'He can understand it all. I've always fancied people who can understand everything and don't do a damn thing.'

Joswig (to Kurtchen): 'You're speaking to the Governor.'

Kurtchen: 'So what? I'm my own governor. If I start telling you all I'm responsible for and have to see to.'

Joswig (slightly menacing): 'We shall be meeting each other again.'

Kurtchen (addressing the ceiling): 'Once, for sure.'

Himpel (to Joswig): 'Let it pass. We don't want to start by having any friction.' (To the psychologists): 'Would anyone like to put any further questions?'

They would all like to put questions, so they glance at each other politely, each prepared to give way to the others, all of them gesturing invitingly towards the bed on which Kurtchen is lying and I am sitting.

First psychologist (to Kurtchen): 'If I may, I should like to ask you whether you were a lonely child or had other children to play with.'

Kurtchen (after a moment's silence, grimly): 'If you're set on knowing, I grew up next door to an old people's home. The only people I had to play with were the inmates, the youngest was seventy-six, and I bashed his brains in with my little spade.'

First psychologist (smirking uneasily): 'The question is by no means irrelevant.'

Kurtchen: 'I'm sure it is. But I'm tired now. And I've run out of ideas.'

A psychologist turns to me, notebook in hand: 'There's still something not clear to me. You said you took the paintings to a

453

place of safety when they were endangered by a flame. Does that mean that you do not regard those acts as theft?'

Me (to Kurtchen): 'I wonder why I suddenly feel tired too? Do you think it's the air?'

Kurtchen (propping himself up and addressing the psychologist with the notebook): 'Haven't you heard enough? Can't you see the boy's tired? What do you think you're getting at, anyway? Come on, Siggi, make yourself comfortable.' (He draws me down on to the bed.) 'I'll stroke you till you go to sleep.'

Me: 'There are people standing round our bed, Kurtchen.'

Kurtchen (sardonically): 'Never you mind, boy-o, they don't know any better.'

Himpel (summing up the situation): 'I think, gentlemen, we have now got a general impression and you are now familiar with the essential points. With your agreement, we shall proceed, in conclusion, to Room Eight.' (Exeunt, with more or less friendly nods of farewell, Governor Himpel and the psychologists.)

Joswig (grieved): 'I thought better of you two. That wasn't much of a show you put up. But we'll make different boys of you before we've finished with you, you'll see.'

Kurtchen: 'Shut your trap – your guts are getting cold, and there's a draught.'

(Exit Joswig, closing the door. Kurtchen jumps off the bed, goes to the door, and strains his ears to hear what the party is talking about.)

Kurtchen: 'They've got us by the short hairs in here. But I shan't be here long, I'm clearing out.'

Me: 'A week's solitary – that's what you'll get if they pick you up. It says in the rules.'

Kurtchen: 'Makes it worth trying twice a month. Got a cigarette?'

(I give him a cigarette and a light, and we both smoke.)

'Listen to me, boy-o: we've got to get aboard the motor-launch. We'll creep aboard the launch and hide.'

Me: 'Not me.'

Kurtchen: 'You crazy or something?'

Me: 'I haven't got anywhere to go, I haven't got a place – nowhere to hole up. And I shouldn't want to spend all my time in the Central Station.'

Kurtchen: 'You can stay with me. We have an allotment in Langenhorn. Nobody'd find us in the shed out there.'

Me: 'Not me. I've had it for the present. I'd like to relax for a bit.'

Kurtchen: 'Boy, you're not normal.'

Me: 'Another time perhaps, another time I'll come along. But at the moment . . . they've been at me too much. You ought to have seen what it was like back there in Rugbüll, living with them.'

Kurtchen: 'Is your old man really a cop?'

Me: 'He did for us – all of us. He made a clean sweep from Glüserup to Rugbüll, including the family. He's not the type to need any reminding what he has to do. When he gets an assignment he sticks to it, for life.'

Kurtchen (going to the window and looking out): 'It makes me sick, just to look at it: that dump over there, the workshops, the huts. And those sandy fields. And the Elbe – I've never seen it look as mean as it does from here. How can anyone stand it?'

Me: 'Perhaps by comparing – what things were like, what they're like now.'

Kurtchen: 'You're a real comic. I've noticed that.' (Thoughtfully): 'If only I'd got the bastard—'

Me: 'You're lucky you didn't.'

(Sound of footsteps, the door opens, Governor Himpel appears.)

Himpel: 'You're both wide awake again – good! So I've nothing to reproach myself with. I was going to make a suggestion. As inmates of the New Arrivals' House, you are free to move about: you can go anywhere you like on the island. If you feel like going for a walk – I happen to have a little time to spare.'

Kurtchen: 'Thank you for nothing. The view from here is enough for me.' (To me): 'Or are *you* keen on inspecting the island?'

Me: 'Another time. Some other time perhaps.'

Himpel (sitting on the edge of the table): 'Today's Music Day, by the way – you can have the radio on as long as you like.'

Kurtchen: 'Music Day they call it.'

Himpel (breezily): 'You'll get used to it. Each day of the week has its special name here on our island. Monday is Quiet Day, for reading. Tuesday is Shiny Day, we have boots-and-clothes inspection. Today's Music Day, as I said. We call Thursday Out-of-Doors Day, because it's for sport. Friday is Organizing Day, for writing German compositions. And Saturday, ah yes, Saturday is Jolly Day, because our jolly island choir gives a concert – conducted by me, by the way. I hope I'm going to see you two in the choir. And finally, Sunday is Day of Recollection, for writing letters, darning socks, having conversation.' (He gives us a straight look as though expecting us to burst into shouts of joy.)

Kurtchen: 'So there's no Shit Day. That's something.'

Himpel (imperturbably): 'Anyone who qualifies to join the choir gets fringe benefits: he gets off work for two hours twice a week.'

Kurtchen (to me): 'Sing him something, boy-o.'

Himpel (patiently): 'Have you both decided what work you want to do? I take it, as you're sharing a room, you'd like to work in the same place too?'

Kurtchen: 'Work? What have you got to offer?'

Me: 'In my sentence there's nothing about *work*.'

Himpel (holding out bright prospects): 'Our new workshops are for all kinds of training. It's a pleasure to work in them. Anyone who chooses can learn a trade here: he can become a carpenter, a locksmith, a painter, a gardener, anything. Even a tailor. Or an electro-welder. He can get his journeyman's certificate.'

Kurtchen: 'With a lovely prison stamp on it.'

Himpel: 'No, with the master-craftsman's stamp as signature. The examination is conducted by the Guild.'

Kurtchen (to me): 'What do you think, boy-o – what trade shall we choose? If there's no getting out of it.'

Himpel: 'Of course learning a trade isn't compulsory. But work is. Everyone on the island has to work. And there are plenty of kinds of work.'

Kurtchen: 'I don't suppose you've any need of circus-artistes? Strong-man act, I mean.'

Himpel (sliding off the table and walking up and down the room, his hands clasped behind his back): 'You both have a

456

great deal to learn. There's a great deal you both don't yet understand.' (Reflectively): 'The island has all sorts of things in store for you, changes that will not come about without some struggle. You don't seem to realize yet what the connection is between working and eating. Never mind. On this island of ours you will come to understand it. You will gradually learn the need for obedience and some day, I hope, the joys of responsibility. Whatever we need on our island we make for ourselves – buildings, tools, and, yes, ideals as well. We are a community, an island community that decides for itself what it needs. Good will – that's all that's wanted.

'If you're prepared to conform to the rules of the island, you will discover new prospects for yourselves. It's *beginning* that's hard.' (Himpel stops, facing Kurtchen, scrutinizing him, then slowly puts one hand in his pocket, fumbles, and warily pulls out Kurtchen's knife, which he contemplates as it lies on the palm of his slightly outstretched hand. Kurtchen's body tenses.) 'Your knife, isn't it?' (Kurtchen reaches out for the knife, but Himpel withdraws his hand.) 'But you must know, you have read the rules: No weapons may be brought on to the island. Should any be introduced inadvertently, they must instantly be surrendered in the Administration Building, Room Four.' (A pause. They look at each other in silence. Himpel gives Kurtchen the knife and takes a step backwards.) 'You will now go over there. Immediately. You will hand in the knife in Room Four and bring the receipt to me. Off with you.' (Kurtchen hesitates, twisting the knife in his hands.) 'Do you want me to tell you how to get here?' (Kurtchen glares at Himpel, slowly walks towards him, then past him to the door, where he turns round again.)

Kurtchen: 'You won't get me down, not me. Just so you know.' He leaves the room. Himpel goes to the window and stands there, feet apart, watching Kurtchen disappear inside the Administration Building. Then, over his shoulder, Himpel: 'It's all a matter of making a start, you see. One just has to make a start. And I think I know the way for you to make a start, Siggi. How about trying the island library? It needs re-arranging and cataloguing. Books – I'm sure books would be in good hands with you.'

Me: 'Is that all?'

Himpel (in a tone that devalues the offer): 'Or of course you could go to the broom workshop. We make every conceivable type of broom here.'

Me: 'Then I'll start on brooms.'

Himpel: 'Why's that?'

Me: 'I don't know, at the moment I feel more like brooms.'

Himpel: 'You can still think it over. One can always change one's place of work here. If you like: first brooms, then books.'

(The door is flung open, a gaunt, timorous-looking man rushes in, waving a broken pair of spectacles in one hand. Herr Doktor Korbjuhn. Panting, he stands in the middle of the room, giving off a smell of hair-cream.)

Himpel: 'My dear Herr Doktor Korbjuhn, what has happened *now*?'

Korbjuhn: 'I've been looking for you, Governor. It is essential that you should know what has been going on.'

Himpel: 'During the civics lesson?'

Korbjuhn: 'No, during the German lesson. It's always the German lesson. I set a composition.'

Himpel (contemplating the spectacles): 'Are they smashed?'

Korbjuhn: 'One of the boys suddenly had a fit and fell on the floor. Ole Plötz it was. I was going to his aid, but riot developed.'

Himpel: 'Ole Plötz.'

Korbjuhn: 'They insisted that I shouldn't touch him. They threatened me. But I *had* to help him. In the skirmish – here!' (Pointing to the spectacles.) 'They were knocked off. Stamped on. And I cannot but believe: deliberately.'

Himpel: 'There will be an investigation. What was the title of the composition?'

Korbjuhn: 'The composition? Oh, very general, everyone was free to write what they liked ... "Only he who can obey is fit to command."'

Himpel: 'A useful subject.'

Korbjuhn: 'At the end of the hour two boys handed in empty copybooks. I have sent them to you.'

Himpel: 'I'll see them now.' (He holds out his hand to me.) 'Before long, Siggi, you will be writing your first German composition here. I am sure you will do better. And let me know what you have decided on.'

458

Me : 'First the broom workshop, that's settled.'

(Having shaken hands with me, he spreads out his fingers and looks at them attentively.)

Himpel : 'I hope for your sake that you will take to the island and that it will take to you.'

Me : 'We'll see.'

(Exeunt. I light a cigarette, go to the window, and watch the two of them going off. I switch on the radio. I listen to the water-level reports for the Elbe and the Weser. I switch the radio off again and shut the window. I lie down on my bed and spread out my legs and clasp my hands behind my head.)

20   Parting

First of all I have put my task away and locked it up. For the last five days the charcoal-grey copybooks have been neatly stacked on a shelf in the left side of the metal cupboard; the cupboard is locked, the key is in a flat leather pouch, and the pouch is hanging on a string round my neck, rubbing my chest when it slides to and fro. Joswig has given up asking about my work. He doesn't know whether I have finished or am just having a rest, and perhaps he doesn't even want to know, for on the morning when he saw, through the spy-hole, that I was not writing, that the table had been tidied up and the heavily notched stool pushed under the table, he came into my cell, leaning far back, using his chin to steady a pile of white shoe-boxes that he was carrying, set the load down on the bare table, and reminded me of my promise to help him sort out his collection of old bank-notes and coins.

So we sorted, glued, pasted, and arranged his old money in the boxes, writing descriptions on them in blue pencil, in bold block capitals, so making them into prisons for whole epochs, for periods in which a given currency was valid, and for the crowned heads and governors of banks portrayed on coins and notes, mostly with beards, but always with a great air of authority and a confidence-inspiring gaze by way of guarantee to the beholder. One box each sufficed to house Joswig's store dating from the Empire, the Weimar Republic, and the subsequent twelve years. But we filled two and a half boxes with his inflation-money. As a reward for my assistance, he presented me with fifty million marks.

Five days – and I still haven't handed the work in. Once I unlocked the cupboard and took out the copybooks. That was on the Jolly Day when I was first allowed visitors again, and Hilke came to see me. How short she has her hair cut now! How settled the bitterness is in the corners of her mouth! How blank and dim her gaze is – as dim as a day on the beach at Rugbüll. She came in, gave me some sweets and a limp hand-shake, and sat down on the stool with the same sigh that my mother used to produce when she sat down. Then she gazed vaguely around my cell, slowly examining the furniture, and then actually asked me if some of the things hadn't been changed, she had a sort of feeling. . . . Since I gave no answer, she looked up at me, doubtless sensing my disappointment or disapproval, and asked how I had been getting on with my task, and if I had handed it in yet and, if so, what marks I had got.

So then I unlocked the metal cupboard, took out the copy-books and piled them up before her. Hilke laid her forearm on them. She smoothed out a few dog-ears. She passed her blunt fingertips over a label and smiled. It was a long time, a suspiciously long time, before she opened one of the copybooks – and not the top one at that – and began to read, not in a relaxed attitude, but sitting tensely, perched on the stool, as if she were only going to sample it as a favour to me. Frowning, she read. Suddenly, when she came to something that she too remembered, she began commenting in a random way, con-firming what I had written, also repeating it :

'Oh yes, the gulls and the thunderstorm. Herr Doktor Busbeck's birthday party, oh yes. The Holmsens – they've died too, both of them. "The Man in the Red Cloak" – oh yes! Fancy remembering all those names! Nansen in the wind on the dyke. . . . Asmus Asmussen lives in Glüserup now. Fancy remembering Addi's fits! And that afternoon out on the flats. . . . And your hide-out in the mill. . . . The box-cart – that's gone too. Heini Bunje's emigrated. . . . What ever have you got against my legs? Poor old Okko Brodersen, with his one arm – he's retired. You certainly do tell a lot about the Rugbüll police-man. . . . Was he really like that? Didn't he tell us stories, sometimes? And what about those bright, dry summers of ours? And what about when Mother took us for rides along the beach in the milkcart? She wasn't always the way you make her out to be. And don't you remember how Nansen sometimes wouldn't utter a word for days on end? And Rugbüll in the winter, when the ditches were frozen over and there was hoar-frost on the meadows ... or in the autumn, when we lay in the orchard, listening to the apples dropping on the ground ... and remember the warm evenings on the dyke, with the June-bugs swarming ... oh well, I'll read it all, Siggi, only not today – but soon, perhaps.'

She pushed the whole pile of copybooks towards me, and while I was putting them away in the cupboard, she promised to come again, not merely soon, but quite often, there was nothing to stop her doing that now: she had left Rugbüll for ever. She was on her way now to Haus Vaterland, to apply for a job as a waitress. They had variety-turns there in the afternoons, and in the evenings there was the Alster Trio playing – that was Addi's Trio. Hilke was in a hurry.

Five days, and I still can't bring myself to part with my copybooks. Recently, during these quiet, rainy weeks, when no sound reached me from the workshops, when the motor-launch brought no psychologists over, when there were no whistles and shouts of command regulating the timetable, no sound of running footsteps, I sometimes found myself thinking they had forgotten about me. It was as if they had given up the island, abandoning it to the gulls and the crows. But then one day they reminded me that I was not alone and that they were keeping an eye on me, even if from a distance.

For instance, the last thing I was prepared for this morning was that Governor Himpel would send for me.

'Come on,' Joswig said. 'Get a move on, comb your hair, put your parade things on. The old man wants you in his office. And take your labour of love along with you.'

He accompanied me only as far as the porter's lodge, letting me then make my way alone. I was in no hurry to get to Himpel's office with my bundle of copybooks tied up with string. Far from it – I lingered to pat Senator Riebensahm's bust on the head, to peer through the barred basement window into the kitchen until I was shooed away by the cook, who always expressed her feelings about us in the grub she served up to us, and when I came on the Governor's dog lolloping down to the shore with another dog, which I hadn't seen before, in a leisurely manner, as it were engaged in philosophical discussion, I put some life into them by opening fire with some bits of broken tiles that were lying about.

Instead of crossing the rolled clay yard, I went along behind the workshops, then along the vegetable-garden with its green cabbages, red cabbages, white cabbages, and brussels sprouts, to the winding path to the Administration Building, which also led down to the ferry.

It was high water. I walked on to the ferry, which was creaking in its joints, rising and falling as though not only on some great breathing, but itself breathing. The gangway, which was loosely connected with it, shifted to and fro with a grating noise. The waves were small and choppy. The wind was flattening and beating the deserted rushes. On the big sandy field they were burning potato-tops, and the wind pressed down the smoke-streamers, grey and parsnip-green, driving them out over the Elbe. From the ferry it looked as though we were moving down-river under our own steam: the whole island was travelling, sailing past autumnal banks, driven by the potato-fires and our desire to find some other anchorage, floating off to some warmer and more hopeful clime.

Himpel's secretary had caught sight of me. She opened the window, whistled and waved, and I waved back and began to walk towards the Administration Building. Everywhere inside, on the staircase, in the corridor, in the lavatories, the painters were at work. Here the stripped walls were being washed; here layers of oil-paint were being burnt off with blow-lamps; there the wainscoting was being touched up. They were scrambling about on scaffolds, squatting at thresholds, lounging by window-sills: altogether more than forty juvenile delinquents who had been talked into becoming house-painters. Eddi Sillus was among them, almost the only one of them I knew; but even if I hardly knew any of them, they seemed to know me, they whispered, hissed, rapped out signals to each other as I came along, and the rapping accompanied me up the stairs, the handles of scrapers, brushes, and brooms hammering out a sort of salute for me – yes, it was a salute, it was their tribute to me – I could tell that from their faces.

Whom were they saluting? Their senior comrade? The

prisoner sentenced to special punishment? Or a model of un-
yielding stubbornness? 'What you've become for the rest of
them,' Joswig once said, 'is a sort of prehistoric animal, a
legend, almost a symbol. When they're down in the mouth,
they think of you and cheer up.' Anyway, the painters kept on
beating out their salute until I knocked on Himpel's door, and
at the same moment as I walked into the Governor's office, I
heard the scrapers, brushes, and brooms once more being used
for the purposes for which they were intended.

There was Himpel in shirt-sleeves and plus-fours, and both
his secretaries were cleaning his windbreaker, dabbing and
rubbing away at it with turpentine. With one hand he gestured
towards the corridor, with the other he pointed at the windbreaker, saying mournfully: 'Ah, those painters – you've seen
for yourself, Siggi, we have the painters in.'

Fastened to the lapel of his windbreaker was a badge saying
'Governor Himpel', from which I concluded that he was on his
way, either immediately or in the near future, to a congress in
Hamburg. He asked me wouldn't I like to sit down and have
a cup of tea with him and, in honour of the occasion, smoke a
cigarette. I did like. I placed the bundle of copybooks on his
desk and sat down. I watched him spurring on the secretaries,
making little fluttering movements of his hands, rapidly clicking
his tongue at them because they couldn't bring themselves to
cease work on the windbreaker, but tenderly laboured to remove
each slightest mark. He tapped one foot rhythmically to convey
his impatience. And finally he just tore the windbreaker out of
their hands and put it on again.

'Well, Siggi, you've made yourself comfortable, I see. Good.
Tea will be along in a moment. It's already made. And now
let's have a bit of a talk.'

We gazed into each other's eyes. He circled round me and
round his desk. At the piano he paused to thump a swift: tum-
tum-ta. Then, turning to me again, he asked whether I had
noted everything and whether I had realized why he had agreed
to allow me so long for my task. No? Then he would explain
to me.

He had wanted above all to provide an example of the extent
to which he appreciated and encouraged the boys' own attempts
to understand their problems and come to terms with them-

464

selves. I had been allowed to go on writing because it was clear that I wanted to do the theme justice and demonstrate its possibilities. True, he, Himpel, had also been aware of something else : he had been struck by the way that memory had become a trap which I had fallen, and he had wanted me to extricate myself unaided. And he had also come to the conclusion that the punishment he had imposed on me was a mild one compared with the punishment I had imposed on myself by insisting on completing the task. But now it was enough. It must not go any further. This was the furthest limit to which the thing must go.

Had I any comment to make? No? Then he wanted to ask me what my attitude would be to leaving the island in ten days' time, permanently. He thumped the piano again : tum-ta-ta. I had been granted a special remission; I could go any-where I liked. Although I had not learned a trade – something that he personally regretted – the work I had done, both in the broom workshop and in the island library, had been above average, and he saw no reason therefore why he should not give me a good testimonial.

I asked whether this was to be regarded as settled.

Yes, he said, definitely settled. There was to be no more delay.

Not even for a few weeks?

Not even for a few weeks.

But the task was not yet really quite finished.

That didn't matter. After all, a task of this kind could only be brought to a provisional conclusion, and that was good enough.

When was I to hand it in?

Tomorrow morning.

And that was definitely settled?

Definitely settled. I was to come to him at about eight. Tum-ta-ta, he knocked, and then asked were those all the copybooks.

Yes, but I should like to have them back till tomorrow – I hoped that was all right?

Yes, yes, of course. All right then, eight o'clock tomorrow morning. And I was to think out what I was going to say to the Board – just a few people, nothing to worry about.

465

Say?

I would be asked what I intended doing with myself after my release. And now he was afraid he had to rush away, he had to go across to town, to attend a congress (international of course).

Obviously it wouldn't have been tactful to remind him about the tea and the promised cigarette. I just took my bundle of copybooks, thanked him, and pushed off, this time passing inattentively and pretty ungratefully, I must admit, through the rank and file, the forty-odd delinquent house-painters drumming their salute to me.

So I was being released. So I had to hand over my work. What then was I left with? What was in store for me? What had I still to hope for? I hurried out of the Administration Building, but instead of going straight back to my cell, I did something that might easily have put my premature release in jeopardy, crossing the rolled clay yard, passing the locksmiths' workshop and the detention-house – where I caught a glimpse of Ole Plötz's stolid face, he was in not for the usual eight days for attempting to escape, but for twenty-one days because he had contrived to relieve a female psychologist who was doing some research on the island of the contents of her handbag – and then strolled over to the broom workshop and opened the door.

The machines were not working. It was the lunch-break. I was assailed by smells – the smell of pine-wood, the smell of glue. There was the circular saw, there was the punching-machine, there the milling-machine, there the drill. Suddenly I had an idea: I put my bundle of copybooks, meticulously patted into alignment, under the punching-machine, switched on the current, pulled the lever and punched through the whole pile, in the top left-hand corner, making a hole the diameter of a broomstick. Through this I passed a string, the ends of which I knotted together, so that the copybooks hung from it like a bag of partridge. Slipping the string over my shoulder, I left the broom workshop and strolled off, an aimless hunter, along the edge of the sandy potato-field, down to the shore. There I sat down at the foot of a weathered post at the top of which, facing out towards the water, was a No Trespassers notice, signed by the Juvenile Welfare Authority.

I sat there smoking, watching a cable-laying ship, with indented bows, approaching from the Hamburg direction. What was I to do when they released me? Where was I to go? Where should I look for a hiding-place? Klaas had left, and Hilke had left – so how could I go back to Rugbüll? But even if I stayed in Hamburg – did that mean I had really escaped from Rugbüll?

It was an English cable-laying ship. It lay low in the water, loaded to the gunwales with black cable-drums. In what seas would it sink its freight, what countries would it link together? My cable, I knew, would never extend beyond Rugbüll. Anyway, the one end of it would always lead to the brick house in which, if ever I put through the connection, a bellowing voice will be certain to answer: 'Rugbüll Police Station speaking.' Nothing that can ever happen, no tidal wave, no earthquake, will break this connection; I am linked to that place for ever. It is no use turning away, or putting one's hands over one's ears; and least of all is it any use going away. I only need to start listening, and there the humming starts, there the click, and when the voice at the other end has spoken, I can even hear the mournful cry of seagulls in the background; space widens out, expands, presences gather under the wind, and I hear the sound of the foaming waves, the North Sea washing against the breakwaters. Rugbüll is irrevocably there, the place that I have sounded out in so many directions and which nevertheless still denies me so many answers. When it's like that, how can one give up? With my ears full of the crazed crying of gulls, the long-drawn sigh of the water, and the rustling of the wind as it pokes about in our hedges, I cannot cease to seek an answer.

And I ask who it is that knocks on our doors in thunderstorms or sends puffs of smoke jerking out of the stoves; and I ask why they so belittle those who are afflicted in body and mind, and why they regard anyone who has the second sight with awe, even indeed with dread. Who is it that brings us our darkness and our murky days, who is it boiling his bubbling broth in the peat-bogs, drawing the mist around his shoulders, who groans in the rafters, whistles in the pots, hurls the crows in mid-flight down upon the fields? That is what I ask. And I ask myself why they leave the stranger there outside, scorning his help. And why they cannot turn back half-way and have a change of heart – that is what I ask myself. Who blackens the willows in the night? Who batters against the door of the shed? And I ask why it is that down our way they see farther and deeper at evening than by day, and why they are so fanatical in the performance of tasks they have taken on. Their taciturn gluttony, their smugness, their local lore, the element in which they live and move and have their being: to these as well I put my questions. And I put my questions to their way of walking and of standing, to their glances and their words. And whatever I learn from any of it does not satisfy me.

Anyway, I smoked a cigarette down there by the post, buried the stub and, before leaving, wrote the word SHIT in the wet sand with my heel. Going along the shore, by the rushes, where the migrating birds were coming to roost at nightfall, I half-circled the island without being seen or challenged. Not even the two dogs saw me. They were sitting peacefully side by side, on their haunches, gazing down-river as though waiting for their steamer.

Back then to the house ... Strolling back, I found the guard's lodge unoccupied; evidently Joswig had gone to lunch. The drawers of his desk had nothing new to offer: the curled-up cheese sandwich, by now hard as a stone, was still there, and an envelope containing obsolete paper money, apparently intended for swapping. One new thing, however, was a mackerel a good twenty years old, quietly and phosphorescently rotting away and filling the glassed-in lodge with a stench that was hard to bear even if one was fond of our favourite guard. Nor must I forget the letter, that unfinished letter which, to my astonishment, was addressed to me and which began, in typical Joswigian style:

Dear Siggi, now you will probably soon be leaving our island, and Life awaits you on the other side. Before long you will certainly have forgotten us. But it is not such an easy matter for us to let you go, not because we begrudge you your release, but because we have taken you to our hearts. But that is the way it must be, I suppose. I always say, for us on the island it is the same as for teachers: first of all you have all the trouble of getting to know someone and then, before you know where you are, you have to say goodbye to him.

That was as far as Joswig had got. Well, so he too knew that I was about to be released. So it was definitely fixed. So I had to hand over my work. Would Himpel read it? Would Korbjuhn read it and mark it? And then? Would the copybooks find a place on some shelf, where they would quietly remain, gathering dust? Or would they be thrown into the pulping-machine? Or would Korbjuhn take them home for his grandchild, who never has enough paper to use his coloured crayons on? Or would they be passed on to the Juvenile Welfare Authority? What did it matter? I had no more to say. All I had left was questions that nobody gave me an answer to, not even the painter – not even he.

This time Joswig came back softly, suddenly appearing on the other side of the glass, knocking and grinning, putting his mouth to the speaking-aperture and saying: 'Prisoner asking to be locked in, Cell Number Two.' I went out into the corridor and joined him. 'Not a bad idea, Siggi. You might think it over – being a guard here. You'd wear a uniform, have a bunch of keys, go through special training. The chaps obey your orders. Your old age is provided for. With the shortage of suitable applicants you stand a good chance. Think it over.'

'Easy as pie,' I said. I pulled the string with my copybooks on it over my shoulder and, without another word, went ahead of him to my cell.

He unlocked the door. After letting me in, he came in too. He pulled the stool to him with his foot. I went to the window and saw Himpel on the pontoon, waving to the launch that was beating up obliquely against the current.

'Time's up, eh?'

'What time?'

'Your time on the island.'

'Looks like it.'

'Glad?'

'Why should I be?'

'Getting away, crossing over to the other side, starting a new life over there.'

'New life? What would that be?'

'That's something one does all by oneself.'

'There's no such thing. Every pie – someone's got his finger in it already.'

Joswig came over to the window to me, dragging his foot, and I could sense that he wanted to say something cheerful and comforting, airborne as you might say, but he couldn't bring it off : all that occurred to him was a reminder that I was entitled to choose my last meal here and that if he were me he would choose plaice in bacon-sauce, Finkenwerder-style, that was 'the stuff'. I said I would bear his suggestion in mind. He patted me shyly, vaguely, on the shoulder, and left me alone. How gently and considerately he could lock the door when he felt like it, and with how much tact he could go away when he had a mind to.

My task has been finished for five days now. Tomorrow I must hand it in. Must? It's not the results that matter, Himpel once said; what matters is one's attitude, one's tenacity, the qualities that produce the desired results. Well, if he's 'satisfied with my tenacity, what does he still need my copybooks for? I could give them to Hilke or to Wolfgang Mackenroth or to the indifferently flowing Elbe. I could chuck them into the potato-fire or, after my release, sell them for publication. Possibilities ... there are still possibilities. But am I going to make use of them?

Hemmed in by the people I belong to, besieged by memories, drenched in all that has happened where I belong, permeated by the realization that time is not, repeat *not*, the great healer, I know what I have to do and what I shall do tomorrow morning. Is Rugbüll my undoing? Perhaps one can call it that.

Anyway, I shall get up at six, when the guards' frenzied whistles start up all along the corridors, a light goes on in all the rooms, eyes peer through all the spy-holes. Before crossing to the basin to shave and wash, I shall, as always, scrutinize the Elbe, looking for I don't know what, for a while watching navigation-lights faintly blinking in the half-light, watching their regular, almost solemn course, while I smoke my first cigarette, which makes me slightly dizzy. I shall dress for parade. Then Joswig will come in, bringing my breakfast on a tray : watery coffee and two slices of bread, with that jam made on the island from four kinds of fruit. As always, I shall eat only one slice and then lick the jam off the second. While I am eating I shall hear the song with which the juvenile delinquents down in the dining-hall greet another new day – a home-made island song, of course.

What next? I shall go to roll-call, if it happens to be a roll-call day. As hundreds of times before I shall report that I am excused duty, because I am doing a punishment-task, and shall return to my cell, from which I can see the clock on the Administration Building. I shall take my copybooks out of the metal cupboard, sit down at the table, perhaps read and smoke, or perhaps not. Perhaps I shall spend the time till Joswig comes to fetch me playing with the puzzle that Hilke brought me on her last visit, and perhaps I shall actually succeed in getting all three mice at once into the traps. I shall not make any decisions. I shall not think anything out, nor make any plans, rehearse any dramatic speech to be accompanied by any studied gestures. With my copybooks on their string I shall, when the moment comes, go over, in silence, escorted by Joswig who, I know, will pull my jacket straight and smooth my hair down on the crown of my head before taking me in to Himpel's office.

And Himpel? He will put on his jovial act, all cheery and chummy, will put one hand on my shoulder and, if he happens to have just finished composing some little song to his satisfaction, may even offer me a cup of tea. I shall lay my work on his desk. Pensively, occasionally nodding approval, he will leaf through it, without really stopping to read. He will make a gesture and we shall both sit down, shall sit facing one another without stirring, each of us thoroughly pleased with himself because he feels he has won.

New Directions Paperbooks — a partial listing

Li Po, Selected Poems
Clarice Lispector, The Hour of the Star
  The Passion According to G. H.
Federico García Lorca, Selected Poems*
  Three Tragedies
Nathaniel Mackey, Splay Anthem
Xavier de Maistre, Voyage Around My Room
Stéphane Mallarmé, Selected Poetry and Prose*
Javier Marías, Your Face Tomorrow (3 volumes)
Bernadette Mayer, The Bernadette Mayer Reader
  Midwinter Day
Carson McCullers, The Member of the Wedding
Thomas Merton, New Seeds of Contemplation
  The Way of Chuang Tzu
Henri Michaux, A Barbarian in Asia
Dunya Mikhail, The Beekeeper
Henry Miller, The Colossus of Maroussi
  Big Sur & the Oranges of Hieronymus Bosch
Yukio Mishima, Confessions of a Mask
  Death in Midsummer
  Star
Eugenio Montale, Selected Poems*
Vladimir Nabokov, Laughter in the Dark
  Nikolai Gogol
  The Real Life of Sebastian Knight
Pablo Neruda, The Captain's Verses*
  Love Poems*
Charles Olson, Selected Writings
Mary Oppen, Meaning a Life
George Oppen, New Collected Poems
Wilfred Owen, Collected Poems
Hiroko Oyamada, The Factory
Michael Palmer, The Laughter of the Sphinx
Nicanor Parra, Antipoems*
Boris Pasternak, Safe Conduct
Kenneth Patchen
  Memoirs of a Shy Pornographer
Octavio Paz, Poems of Octavio Paz
Victor Pelevin, Omon Ra
Alejandra Pizarnik
  Extracting the Stone of Madness
Ezra Pound, The Cantos
  New Selected Poems and Translations
Raymond Queneau, Exercises in Style
Qian Zhongshu, Fortress Besieged
Raja Rao, Kanthapura
Herbert Read, The Green Child
Kenneth Rexroth, Selected Poems
Keith Ridgway, Hawthorn & Child

Rainer Maria Rilke
  Poems from the Book of Hours
Arthur Rimbaud, Illuminations*
  A Season in Hell and The Drunken Boat*
Evelio Rosero, The Armies
Fran Ross, Oreo
Joseph Roth, The Emperor's Tomb
  The Hotel Years
Raymond Roussel, Locus Solus
Ihara Saikaku, The Life of an Amorous Woman
Nathalie Sarraute, Tropisms
Jean-Paul Sartre, Nausea
Delmore Schwartz
  In Dreams Begin Responsibilities
Hasan Shah, The Dancing Girl
W. G. Sebald, The Emigrants
  The Rings of Saturn
Anne Serre, The Governesses
Stevie Smith, Best Poems
Gary Snyder, Turtle Island
Dag Solstad, Professor Andersen's Night
Muriel Spark, The Driver's Seat
  Loitering with Intent
Antonio Tabucchi, Pereira Maintains
Junichiro Tanizaki, The Maids
Yoko Tawada, The Emissary
  Memoirs of a Polar Bear
Dylan Thomas, A Child's Christmas in Wales
  Collected Poems
Uwe Timm, The Invention of Curried Sausage
Tomas Tranströmer, The Great Enigma
Leonid Tsypkin, Summer in Baden-Baden
Tu Fu, Selected Poems
Paul Valéry, Selected Writings
Enrique Vila-Matas, Bartleby & Co.
Elio Vittorini, Conversations in Sicily
Rosmarie Waldrop, Gap Gardening
Robert Walser, The Assistant
  The Tanners
  The Walk
Eliot Weinberger, An Elemental Thing
  The Ghosts of Birds
Nathanael West, The Day of the Locust
  Miss Lonelyhearts
Tennessee Williams, The Glass Menagerie
  A Streetcar Named Desire
William Carlos Williams, Selected Poems
  Spring and All
Louis Zukofsky, "A"

*BILINGUAL EDITION

For a complete listing, request a free catalog from New Directions, 80 8th Avenue, New York, NY 10011
or visit us online at ndbooks.com